WHAT'S
THE FURTHEST
PLACE
F R O M
HERE?

FOR MY
FATHER.

-M.R.

VOLUME ONE:

# GETTING LOST AT THE END OF THE WORLD

TYLER BOSS & MATTHEW ROSENBERG - storytellers

HASSAN OTSMANE-ELHAOU - lettering

CLARE DeZUTTI - color assistant (issues 1-2)

SHYCHEEKS - color assistant (issues 3-6)

COURTNEY MENARD - map

"WHAT'S the FURTHEST PLACE from HERE?"
created by
TYLER BOSS & MATTHEW ROSENBERG

**IMAGE COMICS, INC.** • **Robert Kirkman**: Chief Operating Officer • **Erik Larsen**: Chief Financial Officer • **Todd McFarlane**: President • **Marc Silvestri**: Chief Executive Officer • **Jim Valentino**: Vice President • **Eric Stephenson**: Publisher / Chief Creative Officer • **Nicole Lapalme**: Controller • **Leanna Caunter**: Accounting Analyst • **Sue Korpela**: Accounting & HR Manager • **Lorelei Bunjes**: Director of Digital Services • **Dirk Wood**: Director of International Sales & Licensing • **Alex Cox**: Director of Direct Market Sales • **Chloe Ramos**: Book Market & Library Sales Manager • **Emilio Bautista**: Digital Sales Coordinator • **Jon Schlaffman**: Specialty Sales Coordinator • **Kat Salazar**: Director of PR & Marketing • **Drew Fitzgerald**: Marketing Content Associate • **Heather Doornink**: Production Director • **Drew Gill**: Art Director • **Hilary DiLoreto**: Print Manager • **Tricia Ramos**: Traffic Manager • **Melissa Gifford**: Content Manager **Erika Schnatz**: Senior Production Artist • **Ryan Brewer**: Production Artist • **Deanna Phelps**: Production Artist • **IMAGECOMICS.COM**

WHAT'S THE FURTHEST PLACE FROM HERE?, VOL. 1. First printing. June 2022. Published by Image Comics, Inc. Office of publication: PO BOX 14457, Portland, OR 97293.

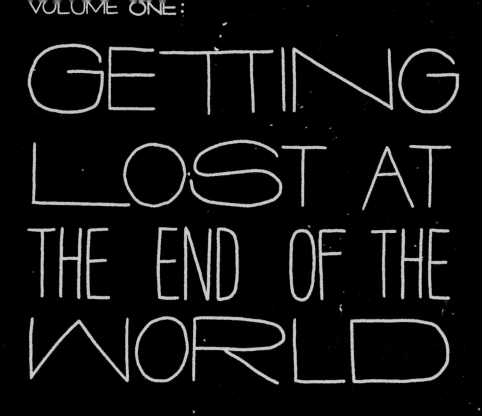

# ACT I

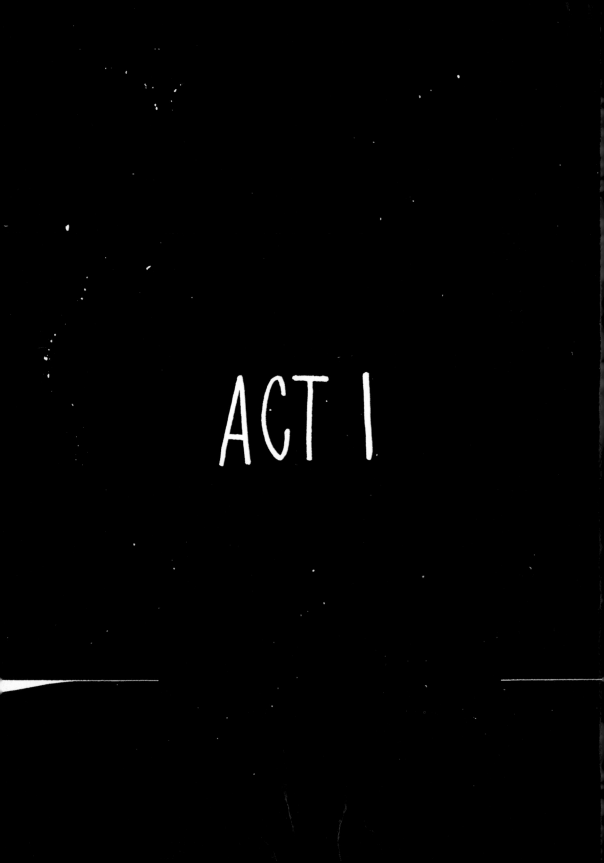

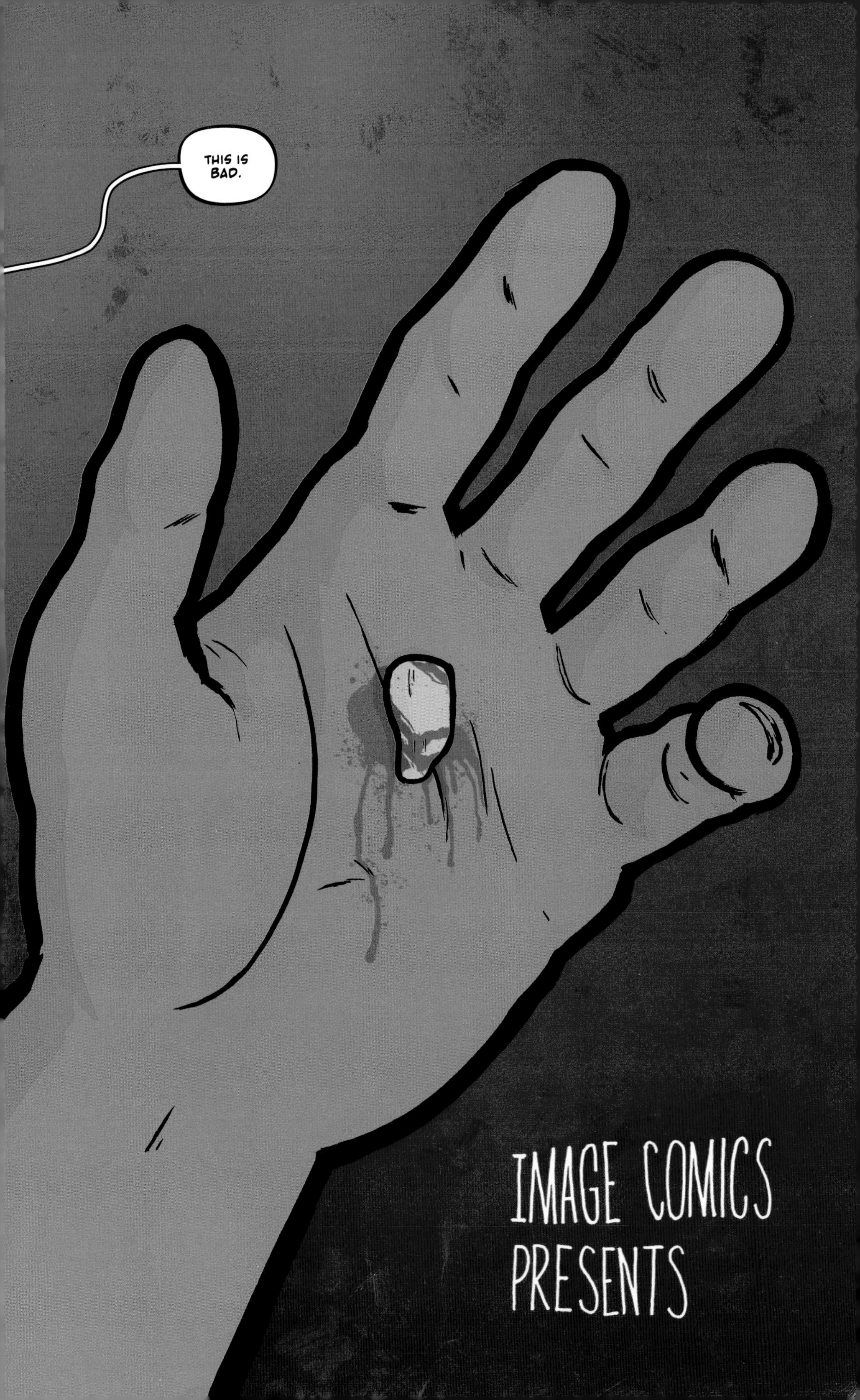
THIS IS BAD.
IMAGE COMICS PRESENTS

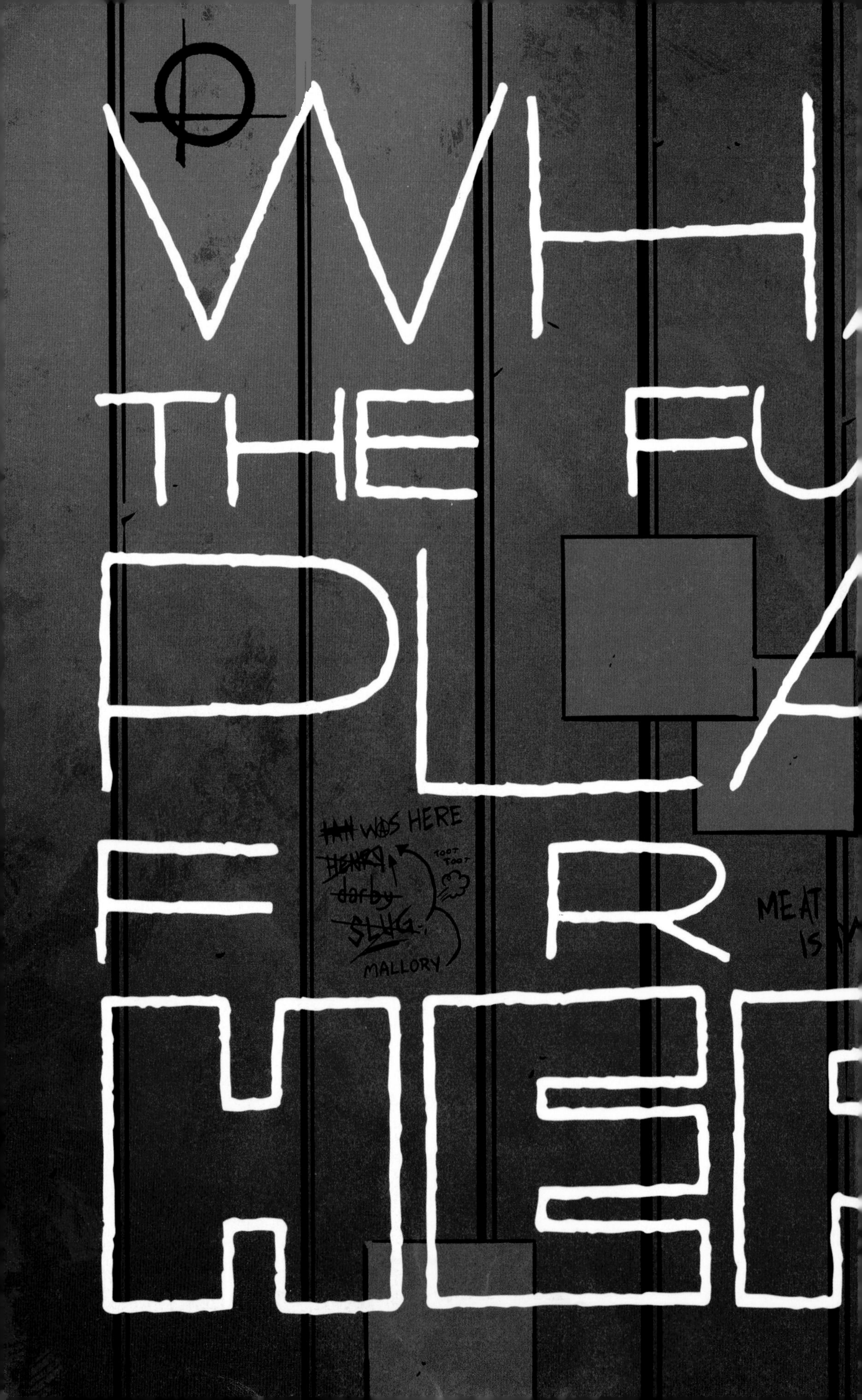

WH
THE FU
PL
F R
HE
WAS HERE
darby
SLUG
MALLORY
TOOT TOOT
MEAT
IS

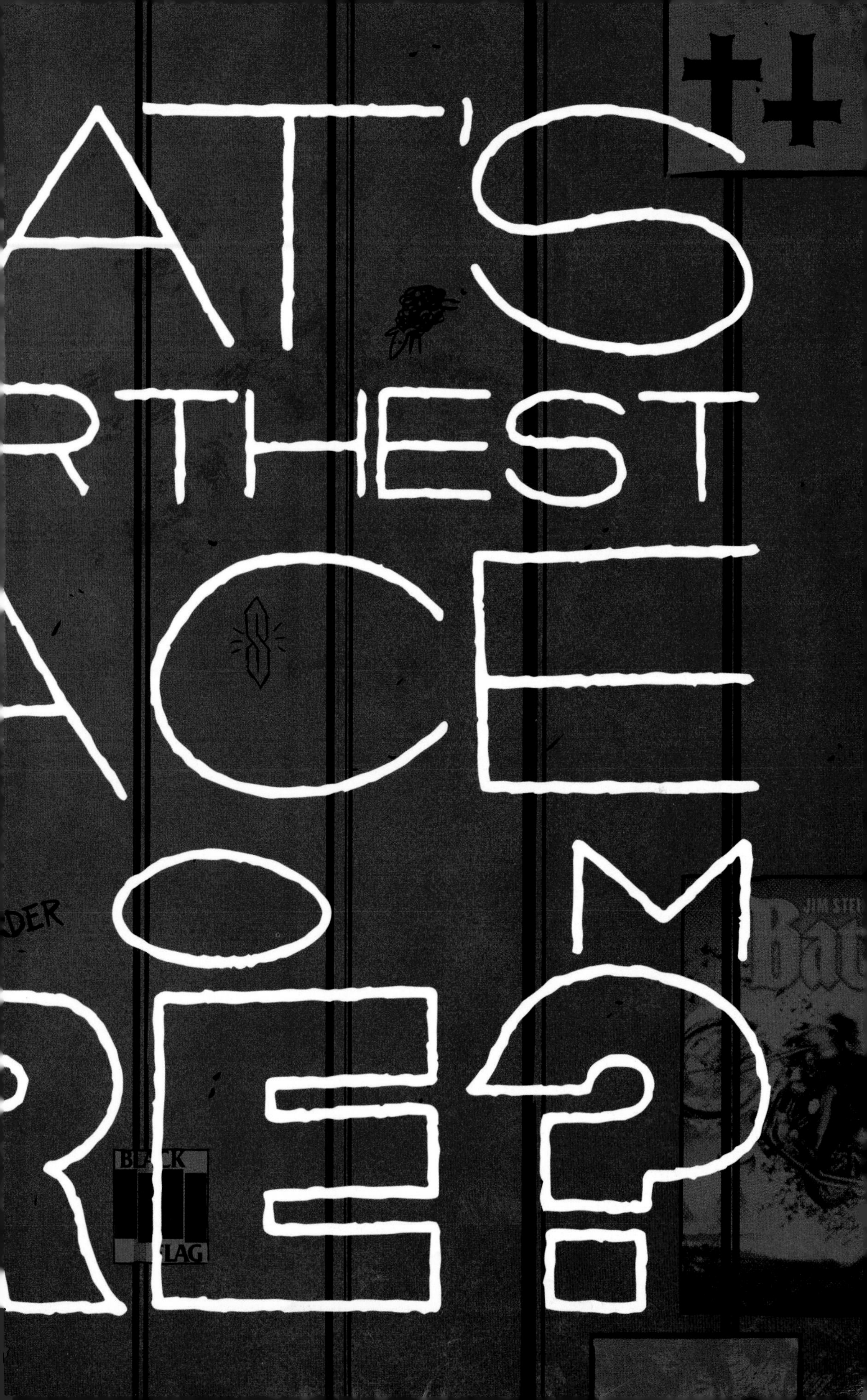

AT'S
RTHEST
ACE
O M
RE?
BLACK FLAG

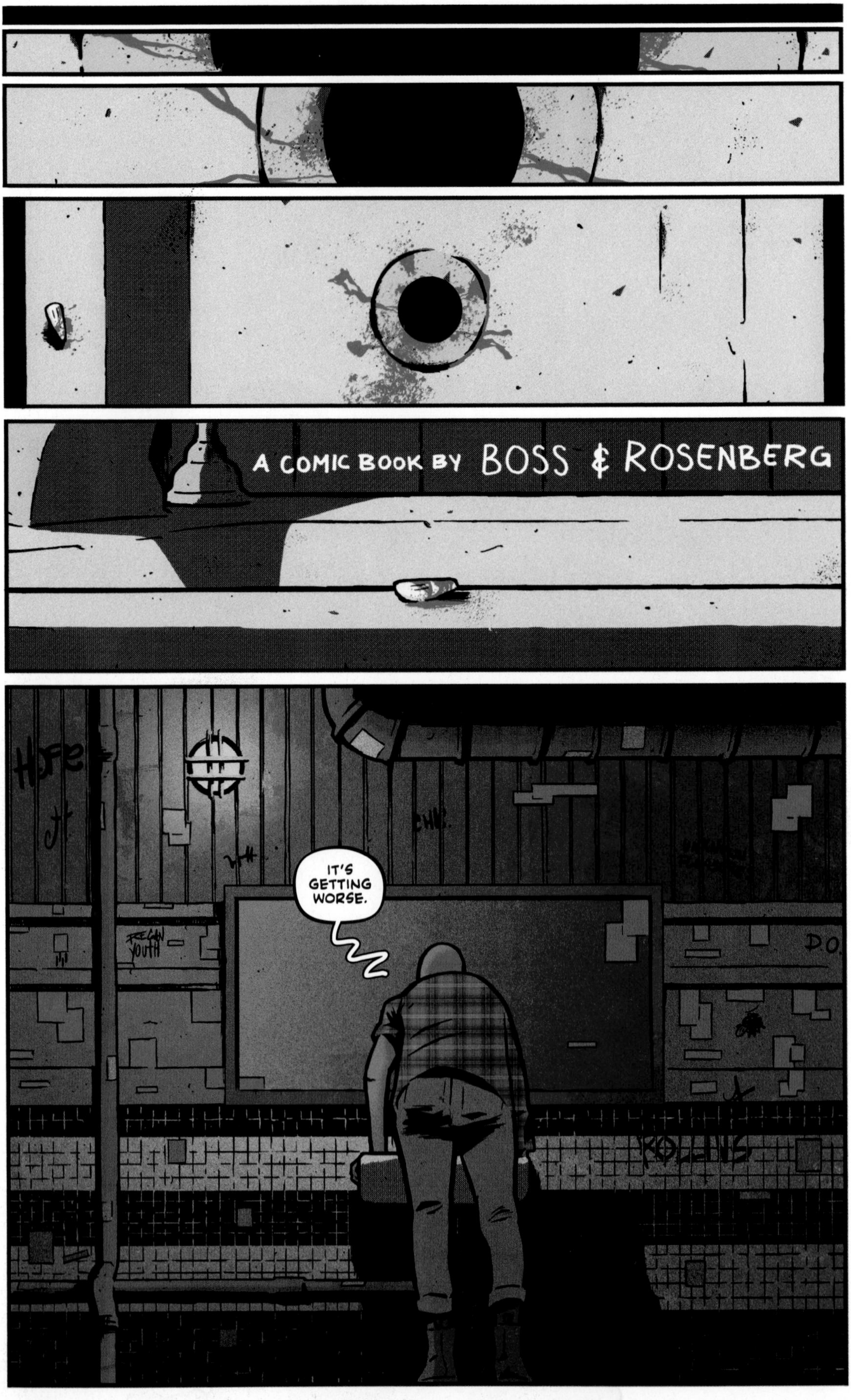
A COMIC BOOK BY BOSS & ROSENBERG
IT'S GETTING WORSE.

# CHAPTER ONE

ARE YOU SICK TOO?

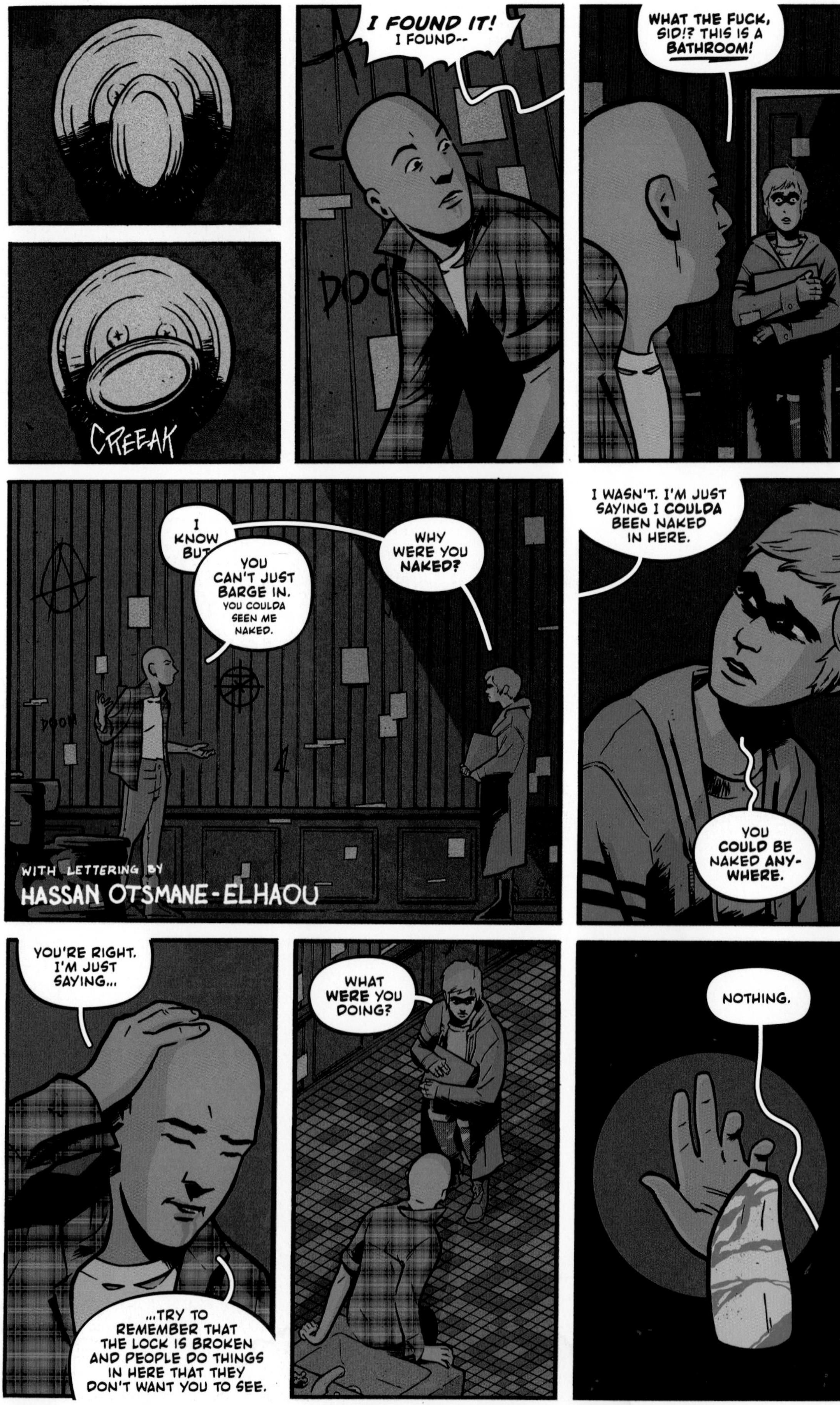
CREEAK
I FOUND IT! I FOUND--
DOO
WHAT THE FUCK, SID!? THIS IS A BATHROOM!
I KNOW BUT--
YOU CAN'T JUST BARGE IN. YOU COULDA SEEN ME NAKED.
WHY WERE YOU NAKED?
DOOM
WITH LETTERING BY
HASSAN OTSMANE-ELHAOU
I WASN'T. I'M JUST SAYING I COULDA BEEN NAKED IN HERE.
YOU COULD BE NAKED ANYWHERE.
YOU'RE RIGHT. I'M JUST SAYING...
...TRY TO REMEMBER THAT THE LOCK IS BROKEN AND PEOPLE DO THINGS IN HERE THAT THEY DON'T WANT YOU TO SEE.
WHAT WERE YOU DOING?
NOTHING.

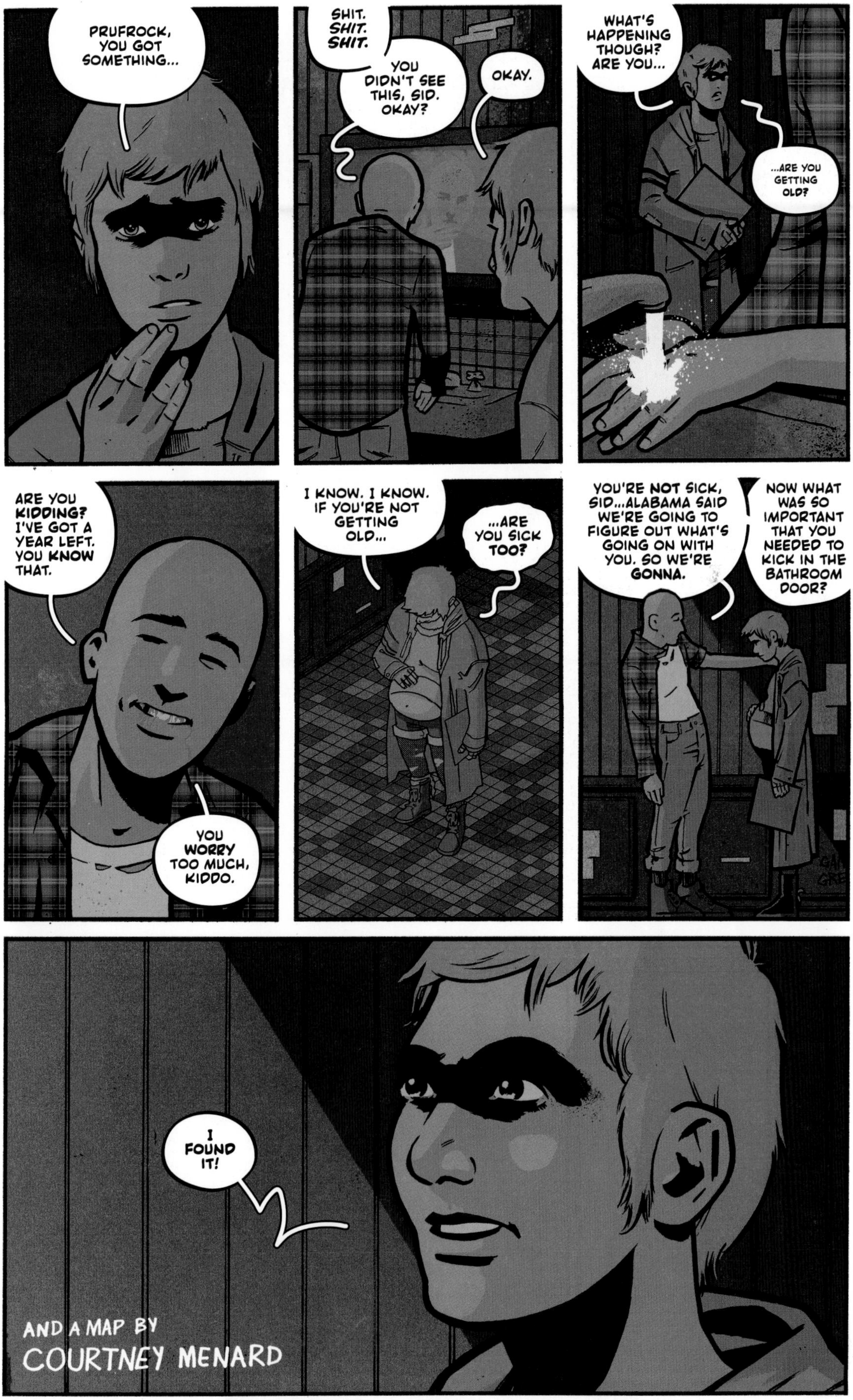
PRUFROCK, YOU GOT SOMETHING...
SHIT. SHIT. SHIT.
YOU DIDN'T SEE THIS, SID. OKAY?
OKAY.
WHAT'S HAPPENING THOUGH? ARE YOU...
...ARE YOU GETTING OLD?
ARE YOU KIDDING? I'VE GOT A YEAR LEFT. YOU KNOW THAT.
YOU WORRY TOO MUCH, KIDDO.
I KNOW. I KNOW. IF YOU'RE NOT GETTING OLD...
...ARE YOU SICK TOO?
YOU'RE NOT SICK, SID...ALABAMA SAID WE'RE GOING TO FIGURE OUT WHAT'S GOING ON WITH YOU. SO WE'RE GONNA.
NOW WHAT WAS SO IMPORTANT THAT YOU NEEDED TO KICK IN THE BATHROOM DOOR?
I FOUND IT!
AND A MAP BY
COURTNEY MENARD

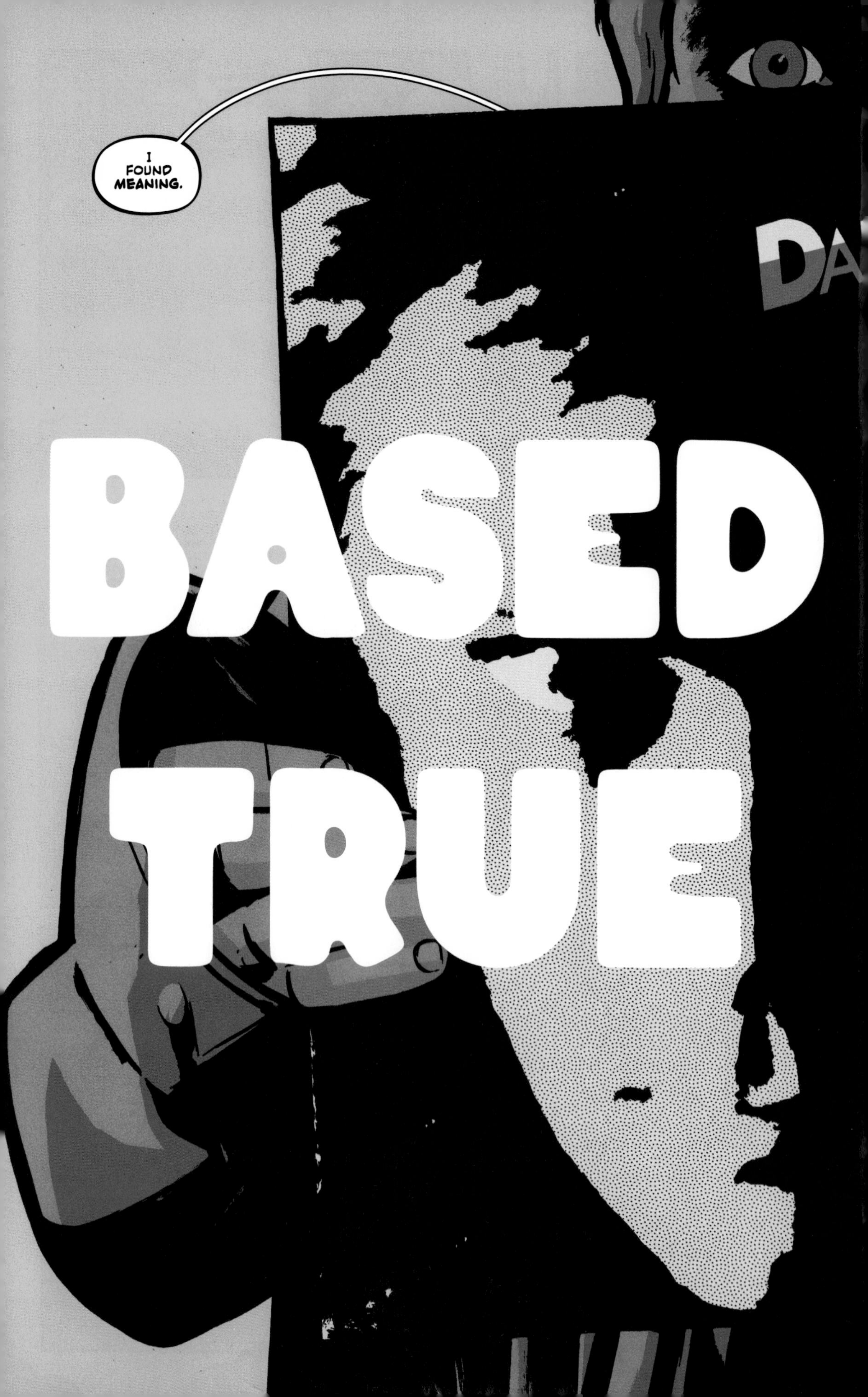
I FOUND MEANING.
DA
BASED
TRUE

# ON A STORY

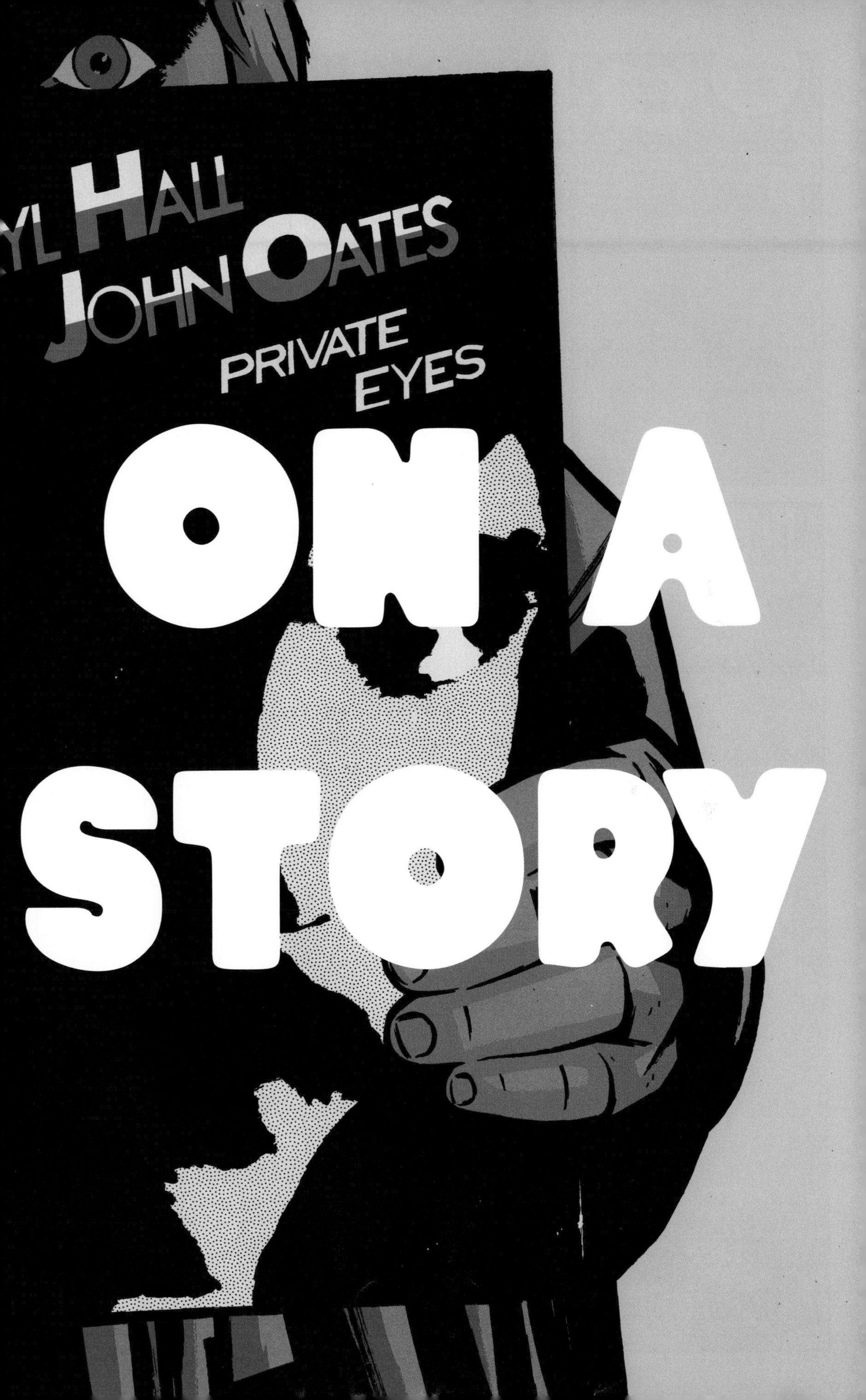
YL HALL
JOHN OATES
PRIVATE EYES

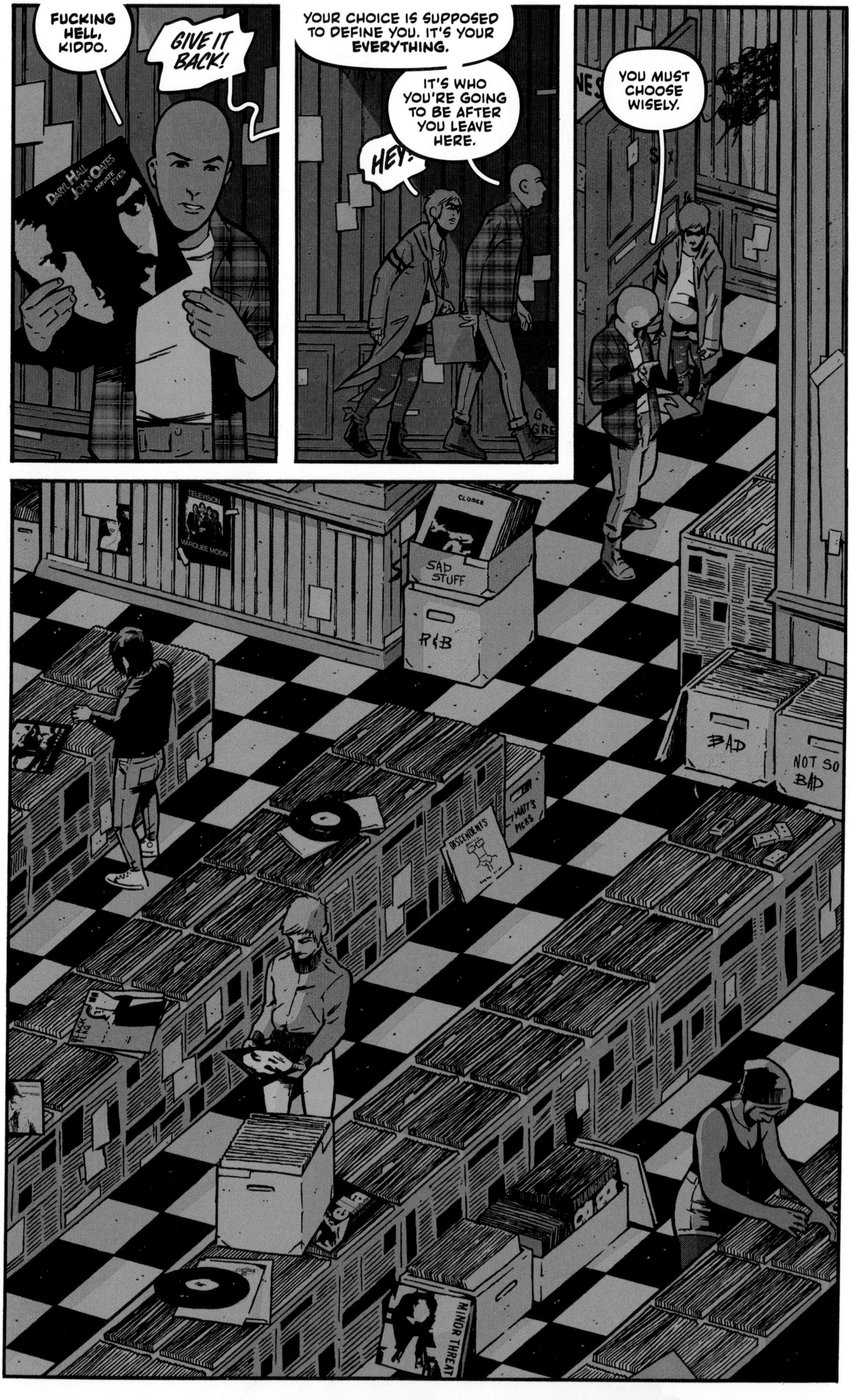
FUCKING HELL, KIDDO.
GIVE IT BACK!
DARYL HALL JOHN OATES
PRIVATE EYES
YOUR CHOICE IS SUPPOSED TO DEFINE YOU. IT'S YOUR EVERYTHING.
IT'S WHO YOU'RE GOING TO BE AFTER YOU LEAVE HERE.
HEY!
YOU MUST CHOOSE WISELY.
TELEVISION
MARQUEE MOON
CLOSER
SAD STUFF
R&B
BAD
NOT SO BAD
MATT'S PICKS
DESCENDENTS
MINOR THREAT

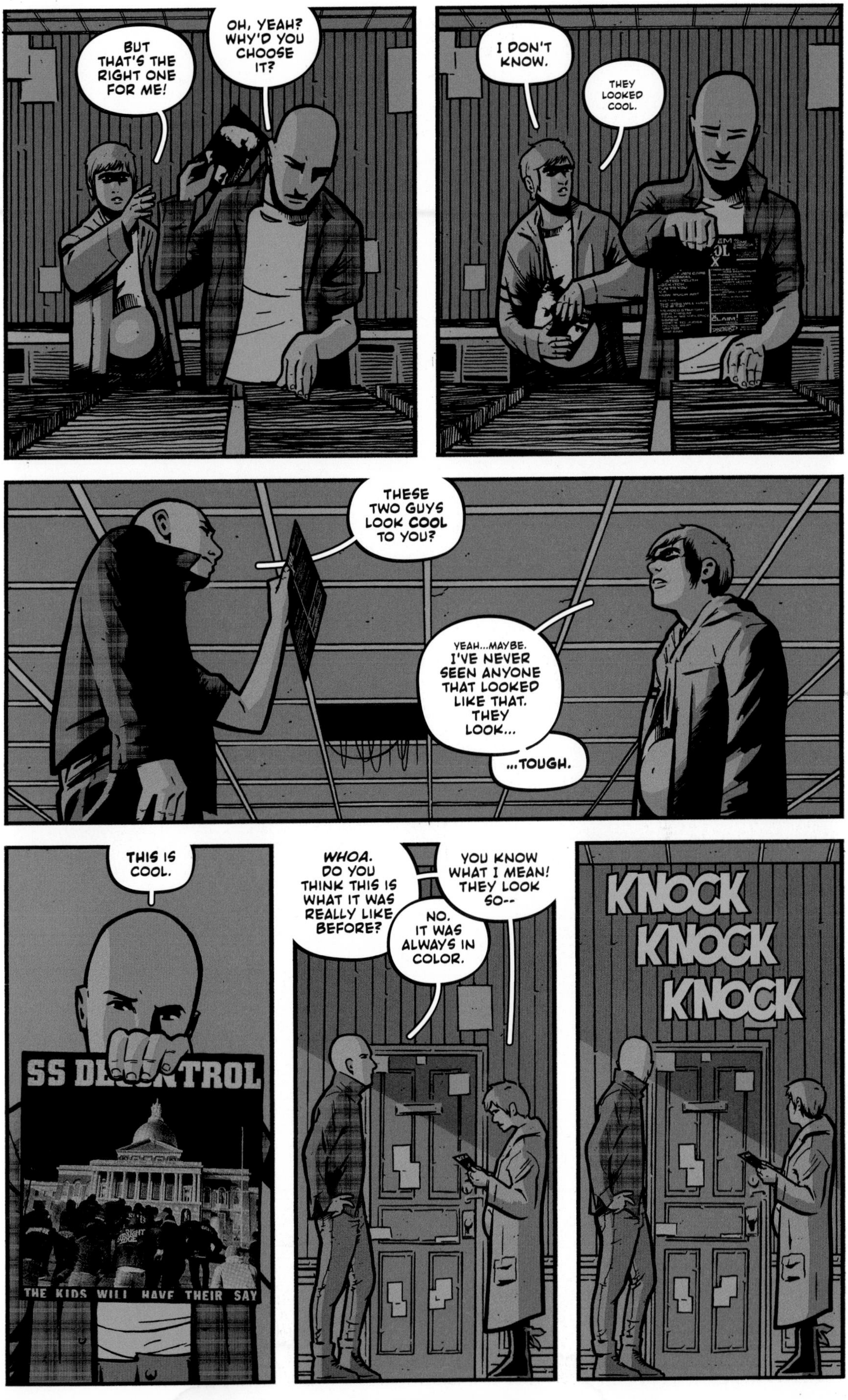
BUT THAT'S THE RIGHT ONE FOR ME!
OH, YEAH? WHY'D YOU CHOOSE IT?
I DON'T KNOW.
THEY LOOKED COOL.
THESE TWO GUYS LOOK COOL TO YOU?
YEAH...MAYBE. I'VE NEVER SEEN ANYONE THAT LOOKED LIKE THAT. THEY LOOK...
...TOUGH.
THIS IS COOL.
SS DE TROL
THE KIDS WILL HAVE THEIR SAY
WHOA. DO YOU THINK THIS IS WHAT IT WAS REALLY LIKE BEFORE?
NO. IT WAS ALWAYS IN COLOR.
YOU KNOW WHAT I MEAN! THEY LOOK SO--
KNOCK
KNOCK
KNOCK

# CHAPTER TWO

## WE'RE NOT OPEN.

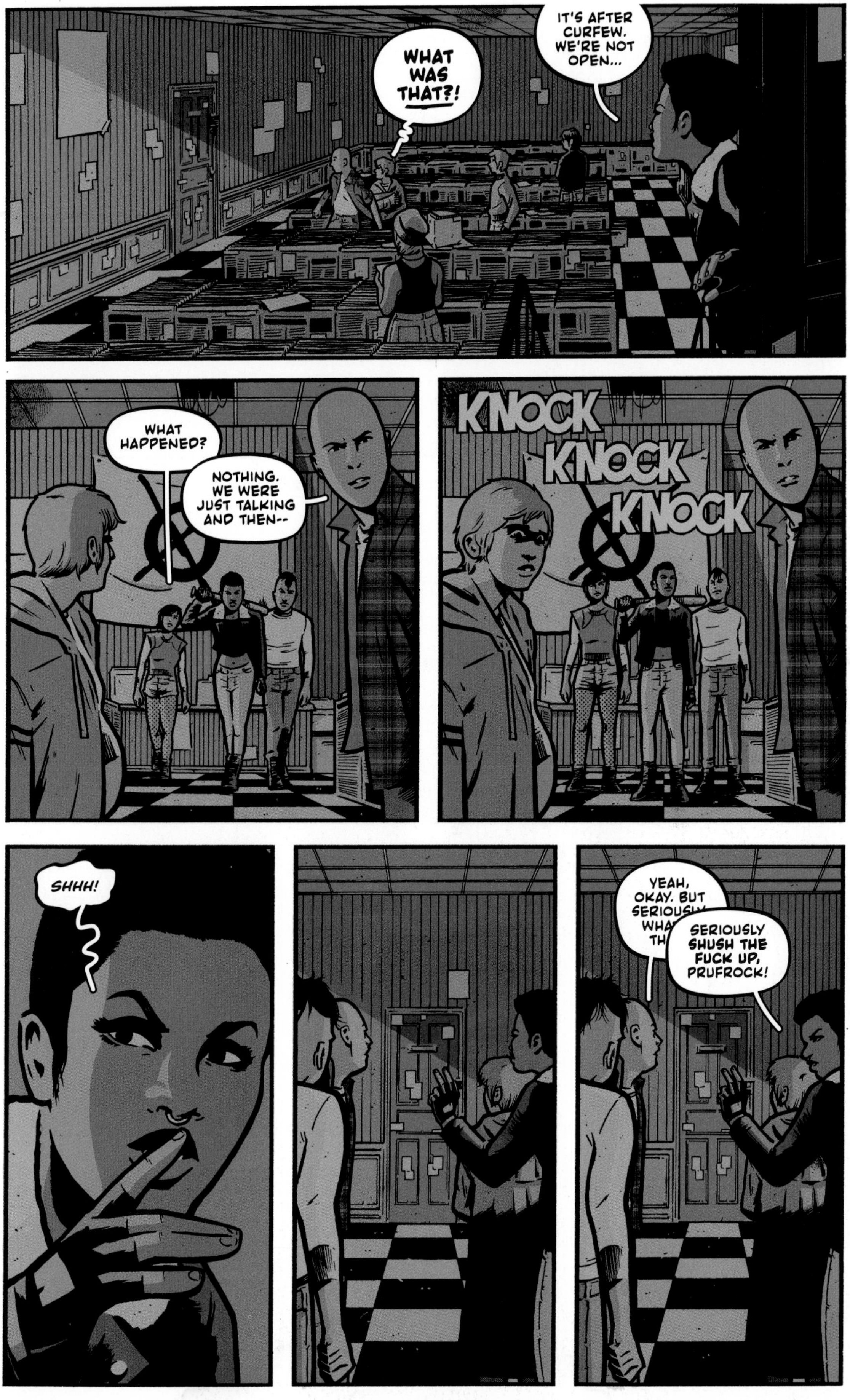
WHAT WAS THAT?!
IT'S AFTER CURFEW. WE'RE NOT OPEN...
WHAT HAPPENED?
NOTHING. WE WERE JUST TALKING AND THEN--
KNOCK
KNOCK
KNOCK
SHHH!
YEAH, OKAY. BUT
SERIOUSLY SHUSH THE FUCK UP, PRUFROCK!

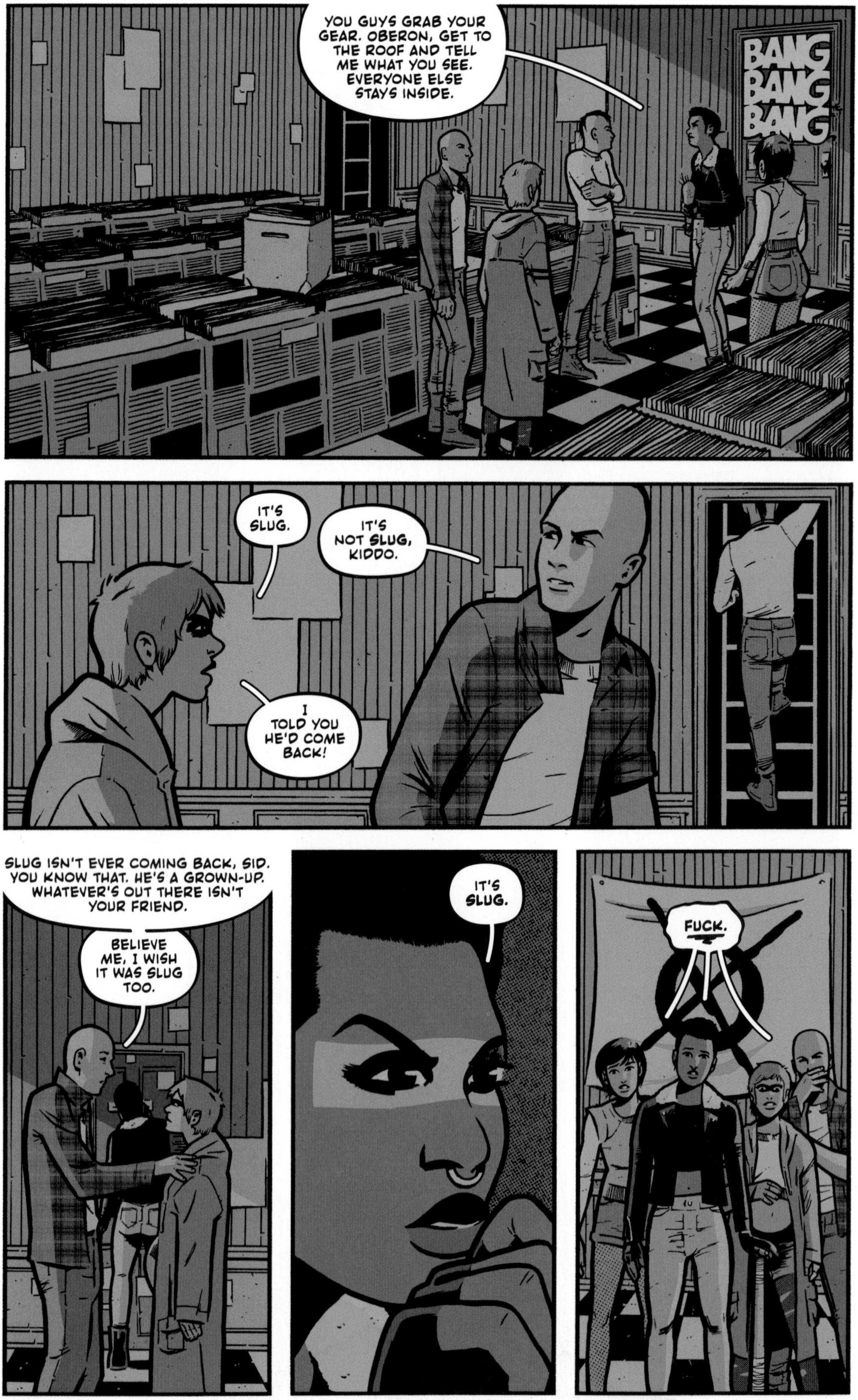
YOU GUYS GRAB YOUR GEAR. OBERON, GET TO THE ROOF AND TELL ME WHAT YOU SEE. EVERYONE ELSE STAYS INSIDE.
BANG BANG BANG
IT'S SLUG.
IT'S NOT SLUG, KIDDO.
I TOLD YOU HE'D COME BACK!
SLUG ISN'T EVER COMING BACK, SID. YOU KNOW THAT. HE'S A GROWN-UP. WHATEVER'S OUT THERE ISN'T YOUR FRIEND.
BELIEVE ME, I WISH IT WAS SLUG TOO.
IT'S SLUG.
FUCK.

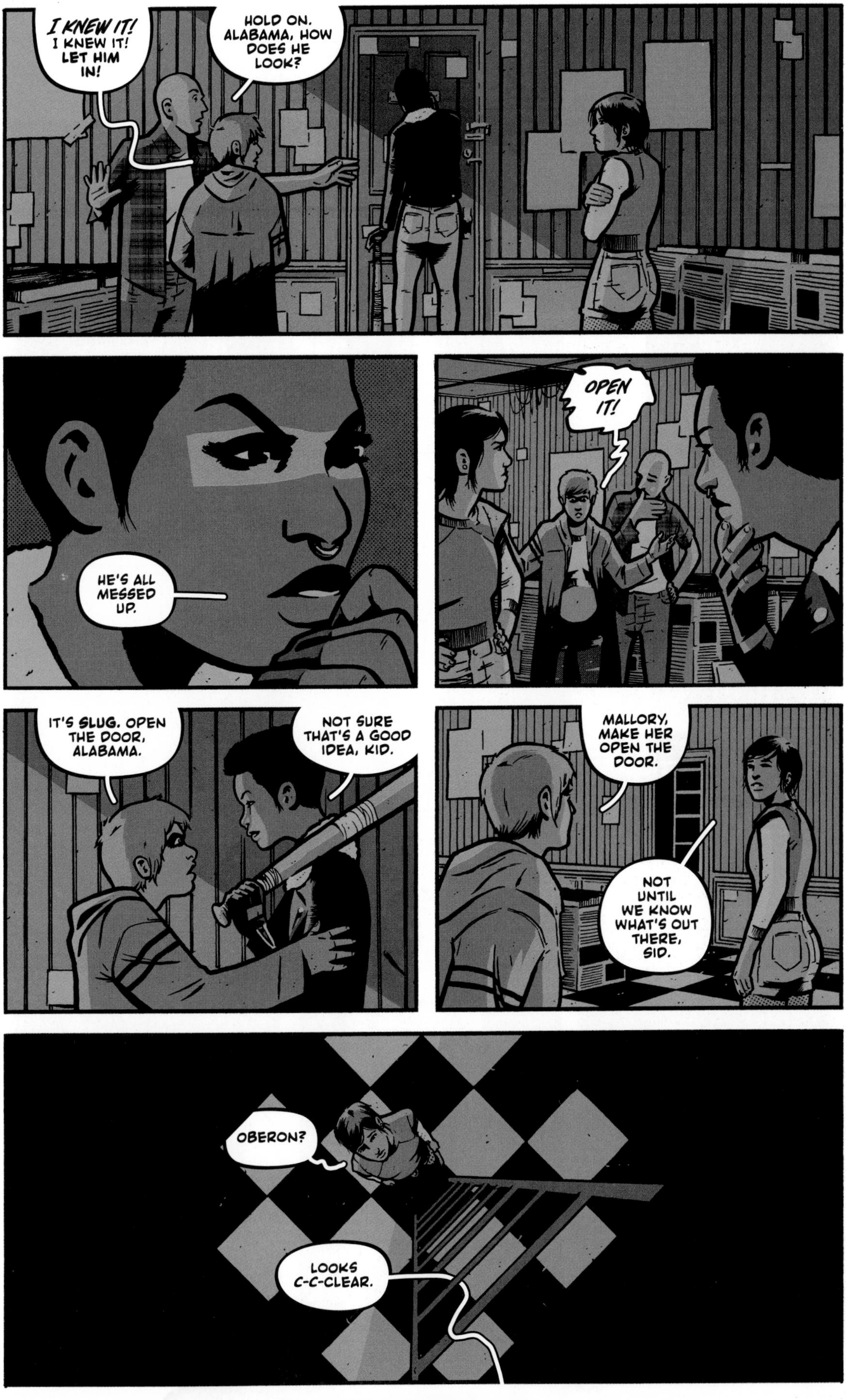
I KNEW IT! I KNEW IT! LET HIM IN!
HOLD ON. ALABAMA, HOW DOES HE LOOK?
HE'S ALL MESSED UP.
OPEN IT!
IT'S SLUG. OPEN THE DOOR, ALABAMA.
NOT SURE THAT'S A GOOD IDEA, KID.
MALLORY, MAKE HER OPEN THE DOOR.
NOT UNTIL WE KNOW WHAT'S OUT THERE, SID.
OBERON?
LOOKS C-C-CLEAR.

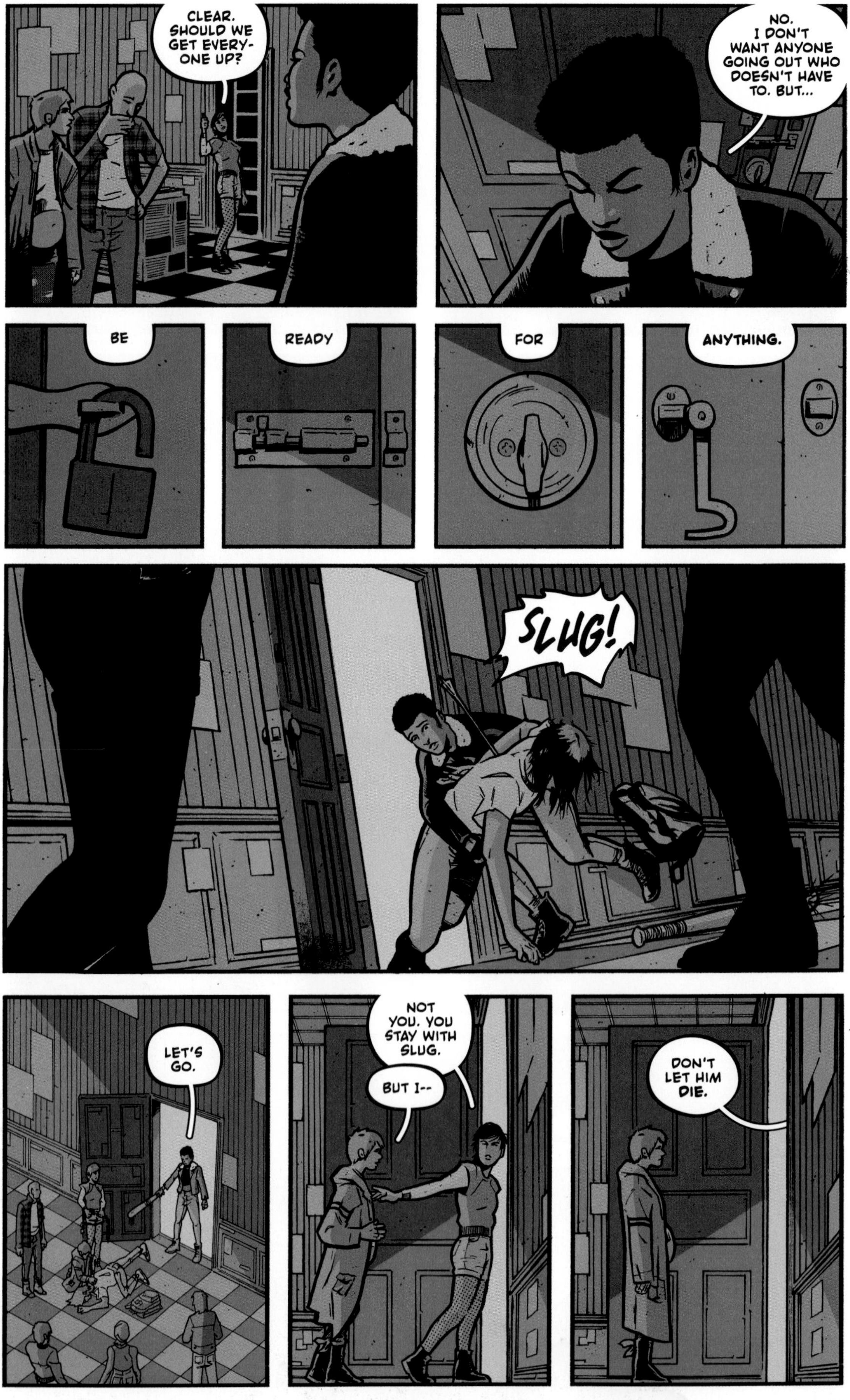
CLEAR. SHOULD WE GET EVERY-ONE UP?
NO. I DON'T WANT ANYONE GOING OUT WHO DOESN'T HAVE TO. BUT...
BE
READY
FOR
ANYTHING.
SLUG!
LET'S GO.
NOT YOU. YOU STAY WITH SLUG.
BUT I--
DON'T LET HIM DIE.

# CHAPTER THREE

## TOO LATE.

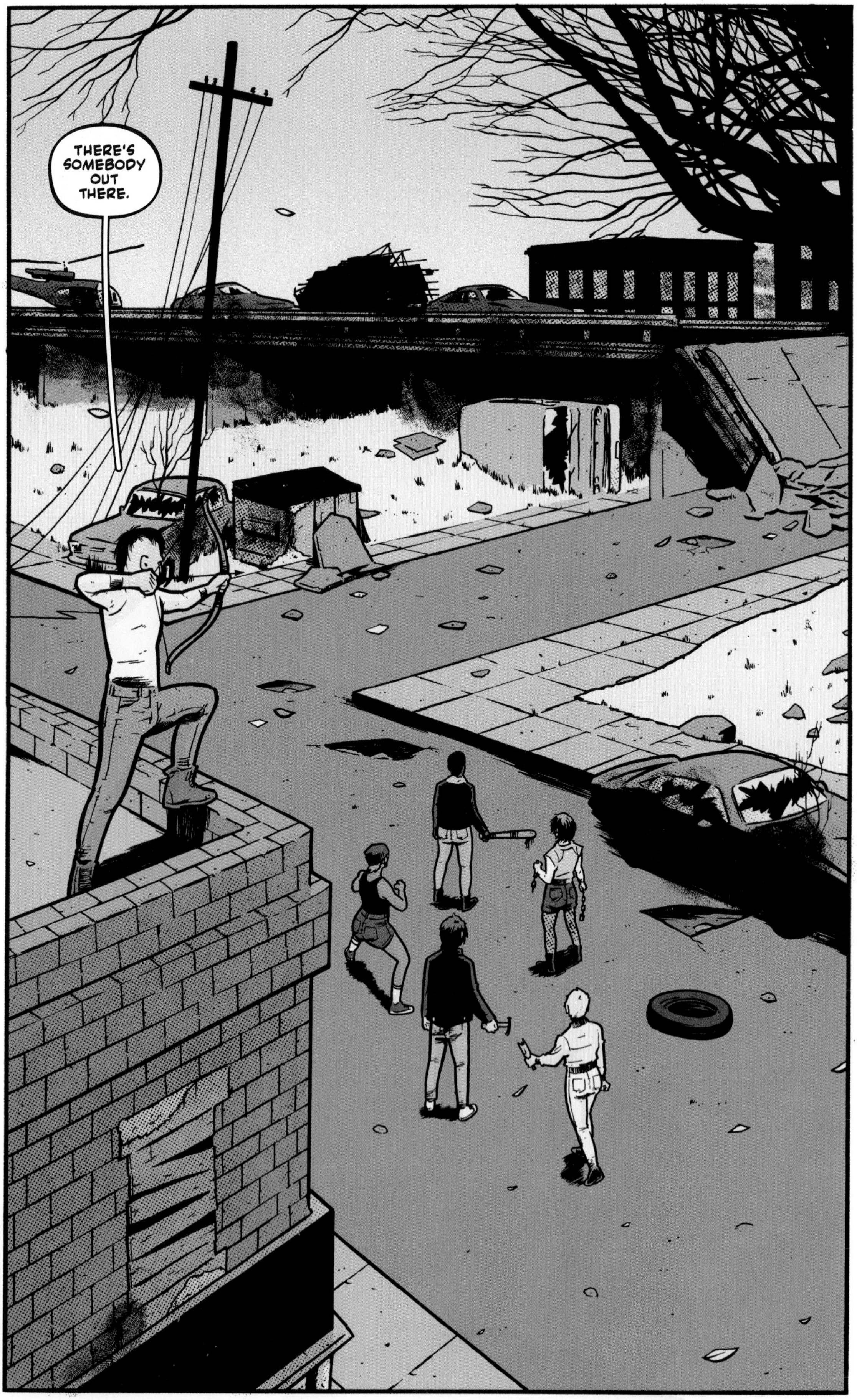
THERE'S SOMEBODY OUT THERE.

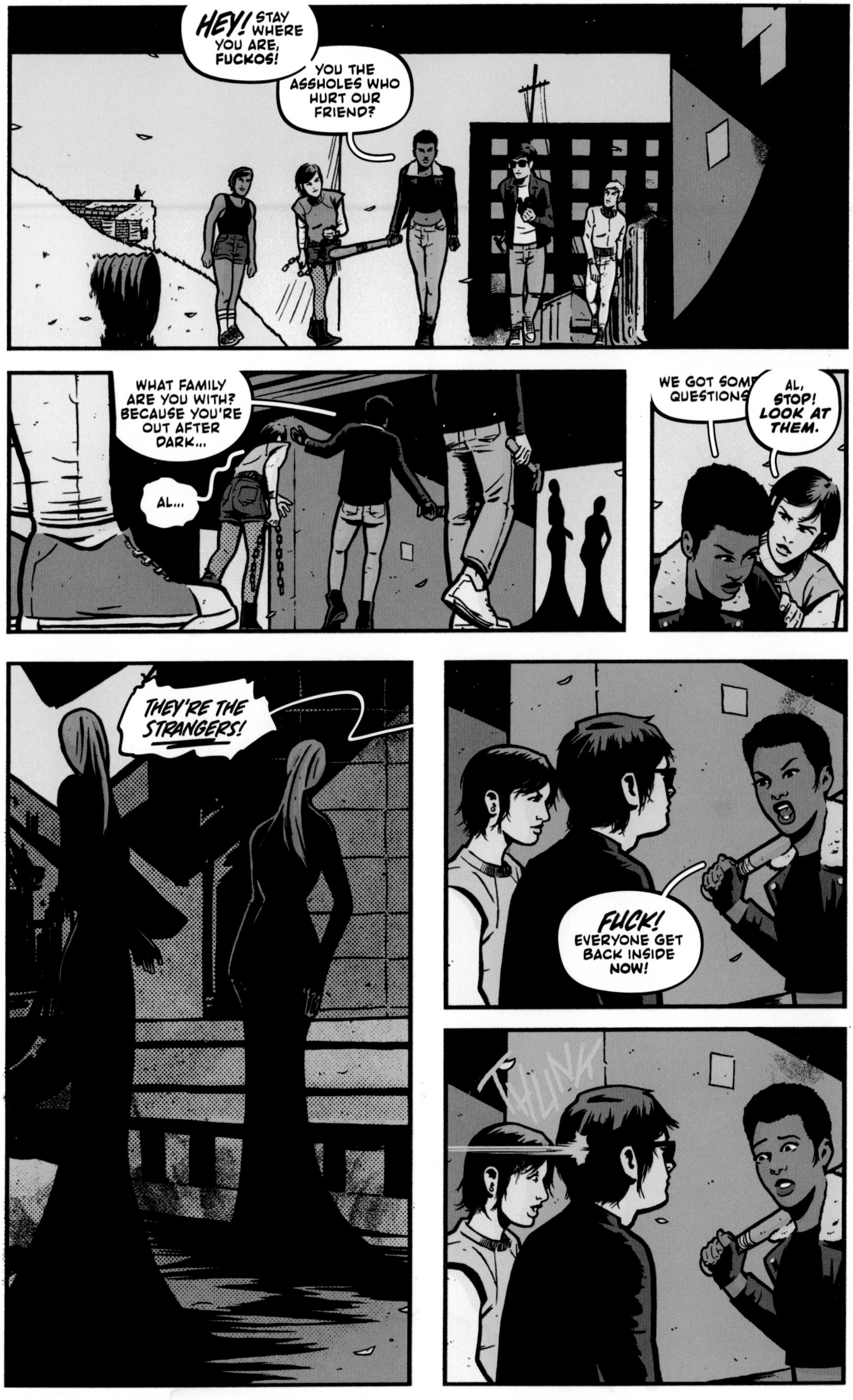
HEY! STAY WHERE YOU ARE, FUCKOS!
YOU THE ASSHOLES WHO HURT OUR FRIEND?
WHAT FAMILY ARE YOU WITH? BECAUSE YOU'RE OUT AFTER DARK...
AL...
WE GOT SOME QUESTIONS
AL, STOP! LOOK AT THEM.
THEY'RE THE STRANGERS!
FUCK! EVERYONE GET BACK INSIDE NOW!
THUNK

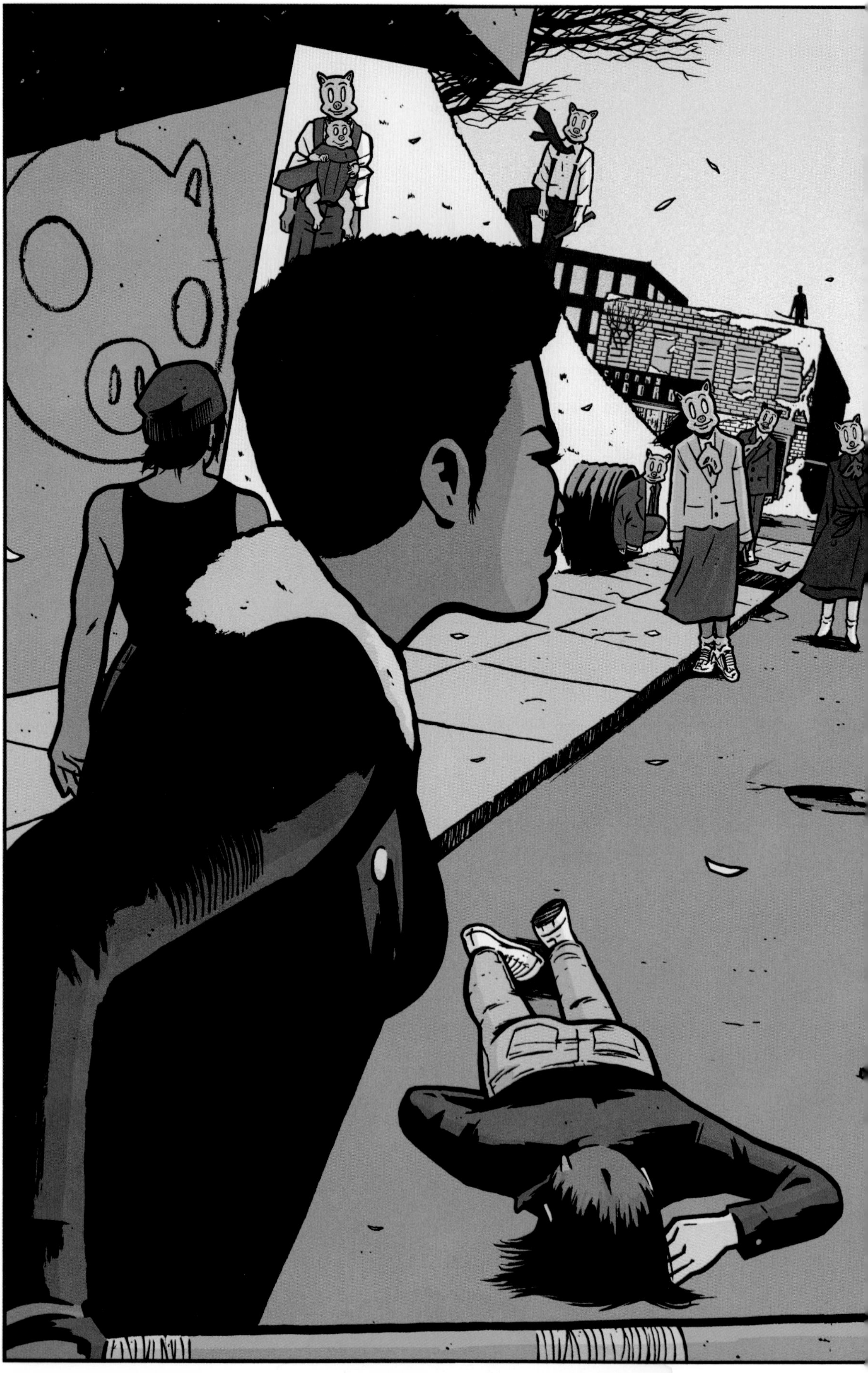

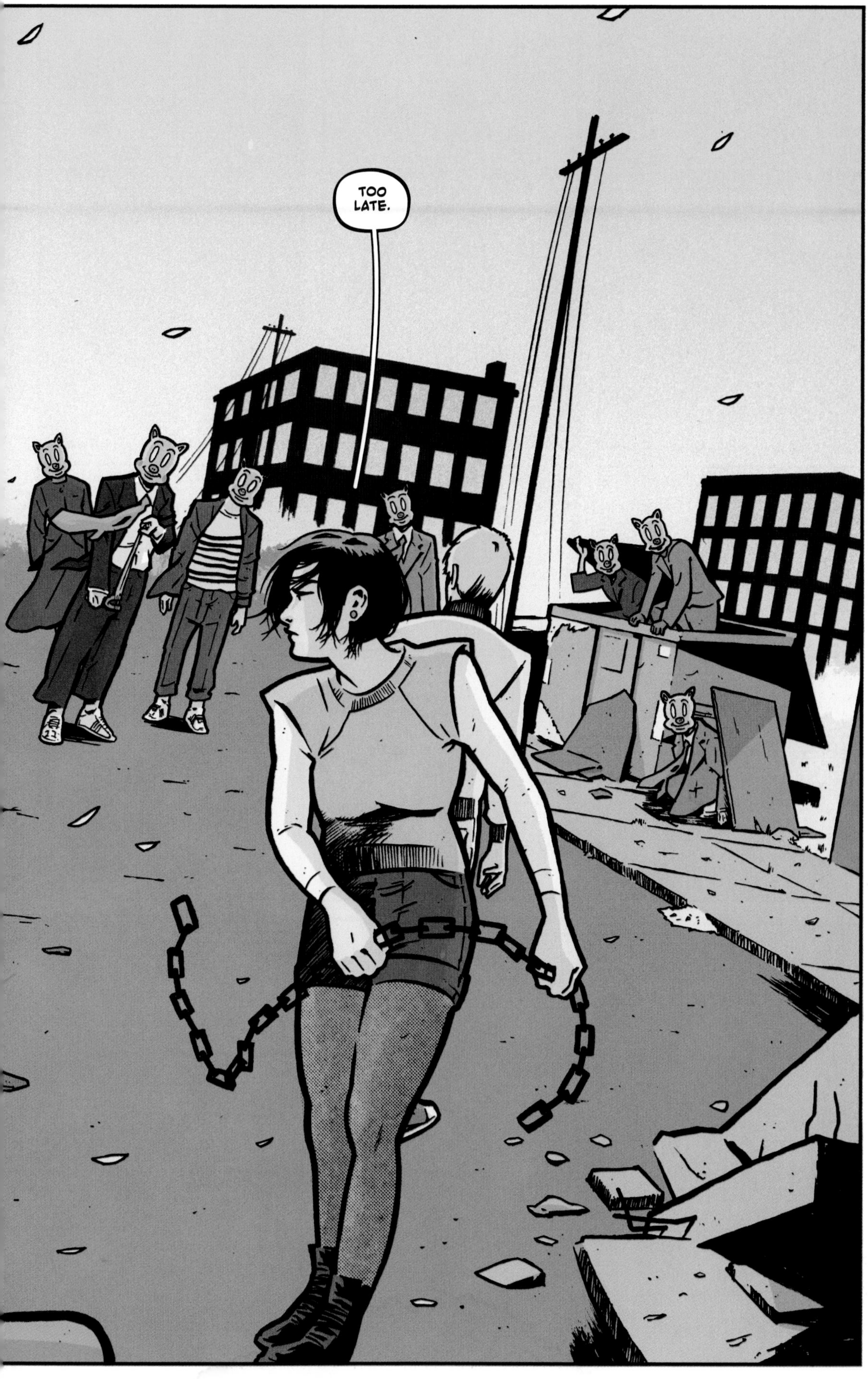
TOO LATE.

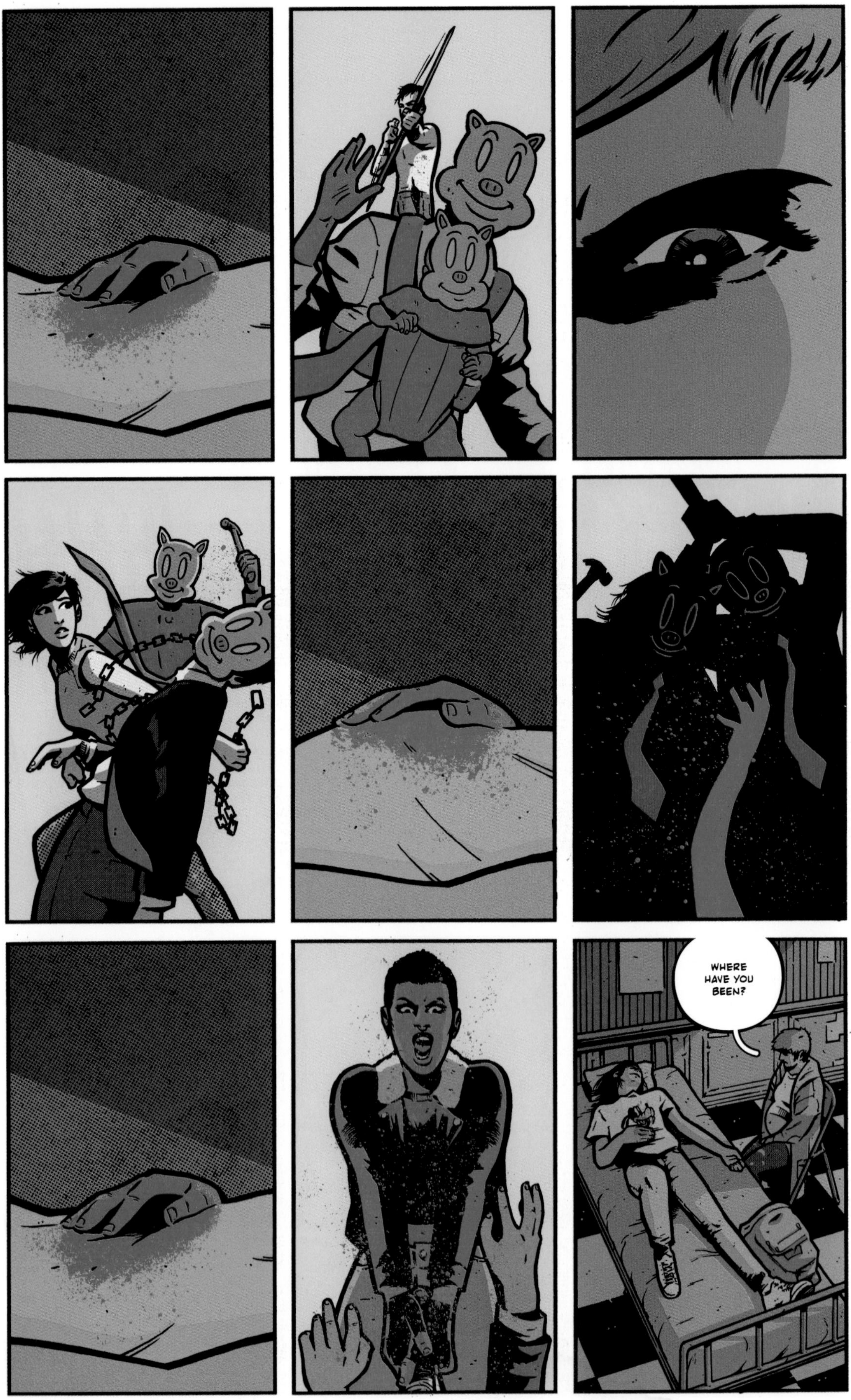
WHERE HAVE YOU BEEN?

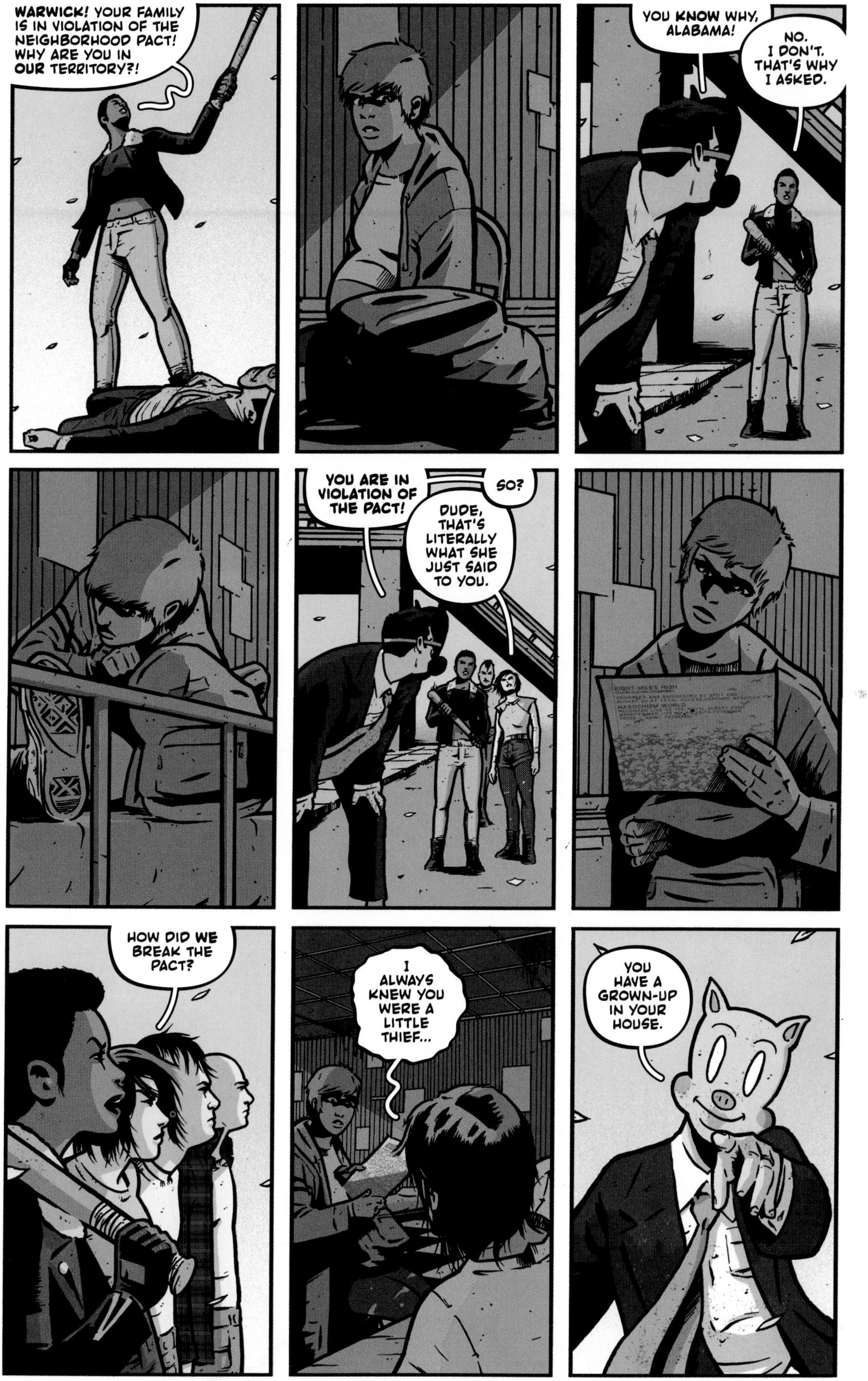
WARWICK! YOUR FAMILY IS IN VIOLATION OF THE NEIGHBORHOOD PACT! WHY ARE YOU IN OUR TERRITORY?!
YOU KNOW WHY, ALABAMA!
NO. I DON'T. THAT'S WHY I ASKED.
YOU ARE IN VIOLATION OF THE PACT!
SO?
DUDE, THAT'S LITERALLY WHAT SHE JUST SAID TO YOU.
HOW DID WE BREAK THE PACT?
I ALWAYS KNEW YOU WERE A LITTLE THIEF...
YOU HAVE A GROWN-UP IN YOUR HOUSE.

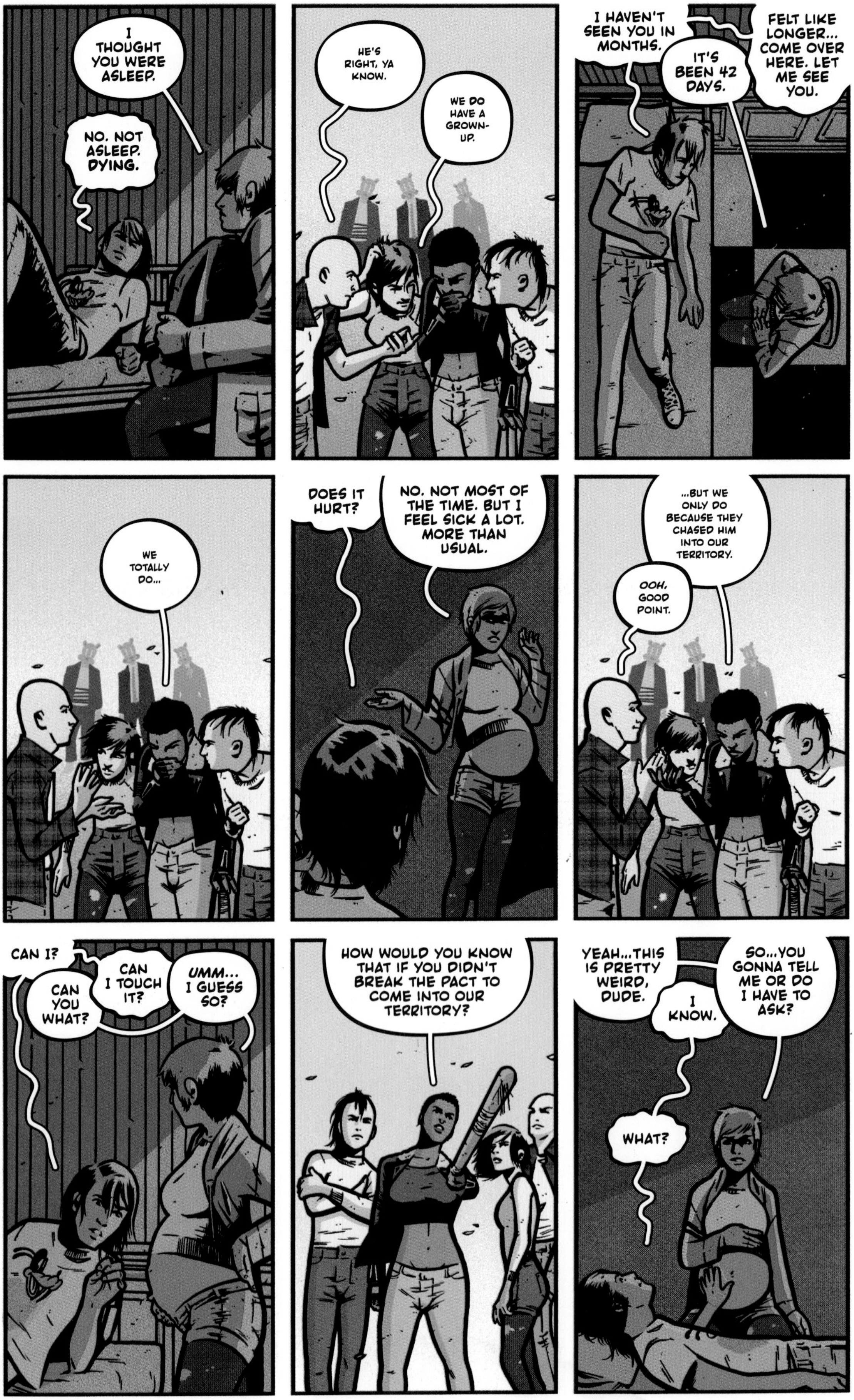
I THOUGHT YOU WERE ASLEEP.
NO. NOT ASLEEP. DYING.
HE'S RIGHT, YA KNOW.
WE DO HAVE A GROWN-UP.
I HAVEN'T SEEN YOU IN MONTHS.
IT'S BEEN 42 DAYS.
FELT LIKE LONGER... COME OVER HERE. LET ME SEE YOU.
WE TOTALLY DO...
DOES IT HURT?
NO. NOT MOST OF THE TIME. BUT I FEEL SICK A LOT. MORE THAN USUAL.
...BUT WE ONLY DO BECAUSE THEY CHASED HIM INTO OUR TERRITORY.
OOH, GOOD POINT.
CAN I?
CAN YOU WHAT?
CAN I TOUCH IT?
UMM... I GUESS SO?
HOW WOULD YOU KNOW THAT IF YOU DIDN'T BREAK THE PACT TO COME INTO OUR TERRITORY?
YEAH...THIS IS PRETTY WEIRD, DUDE.
I KNOW.
SO...YOU GONNA TELL ME OR DO I HAVE TO ASK?
WHAT?

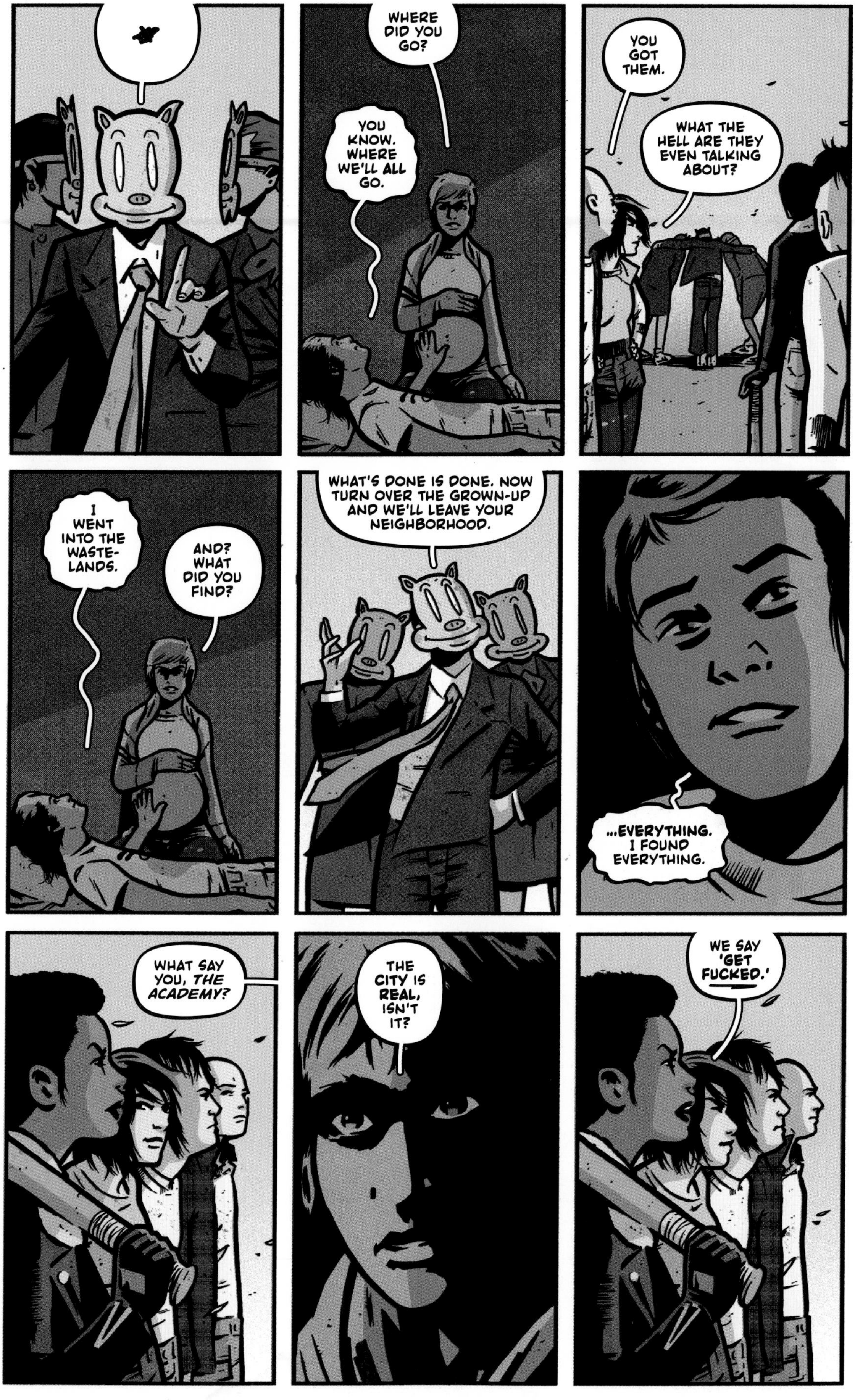
WHERE DID YOU GO?
YOU KNOW. WHERE WE'LL ALL GO.
YOU GOT THEM.
WHAT THE HELL ARE THEY EVEN TALKING ABOUT?
I WENT INTO THE WASTE-LANDS.
AND? WHAT DID YOU FIND?
WHAT'S DONE IS DONE. NOW TURN OVER THE GROWN-UP AND WE'LL LEAVE YOUR NEIGHBORHOOD.
...EVERYTHING. I FOUND EVERYTHING.
WHAT SAY YOU, *THE ACADEMY?*
THE CITY IS REAL, ISN'T IT?
WE SAY 'GET FUCKED.'

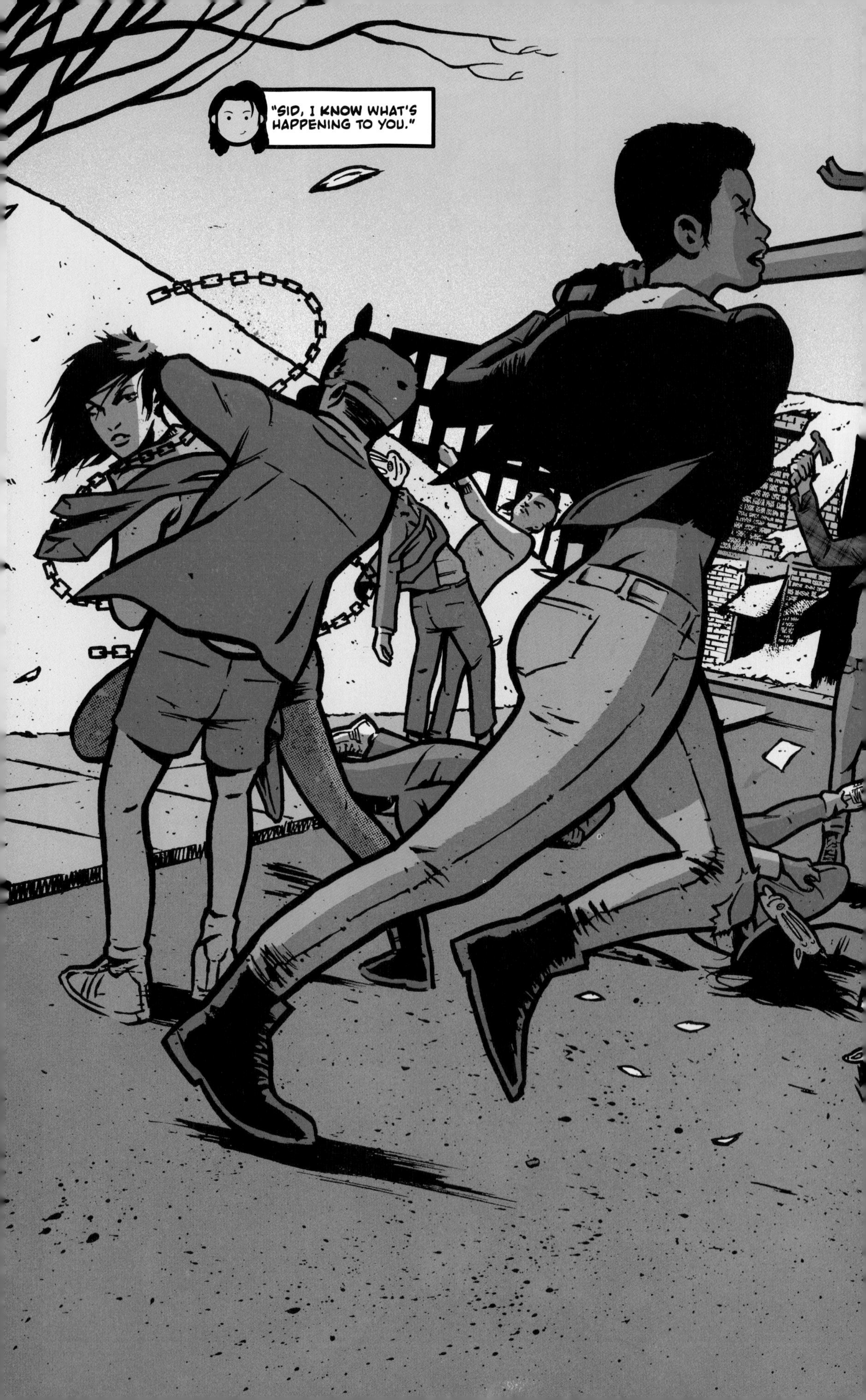
"SID, I KNOW WHAT'S HAPPENING TO YOU."

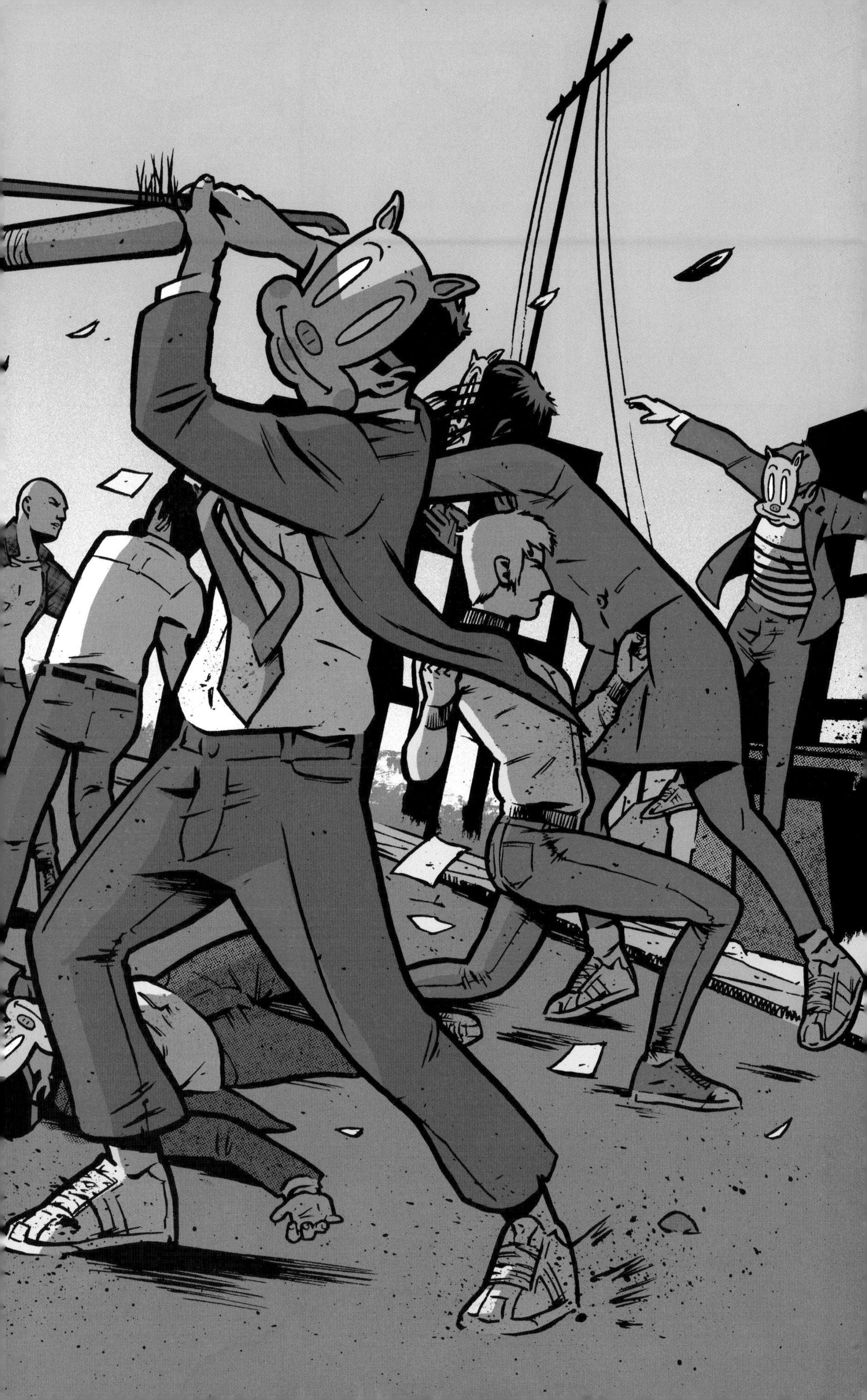

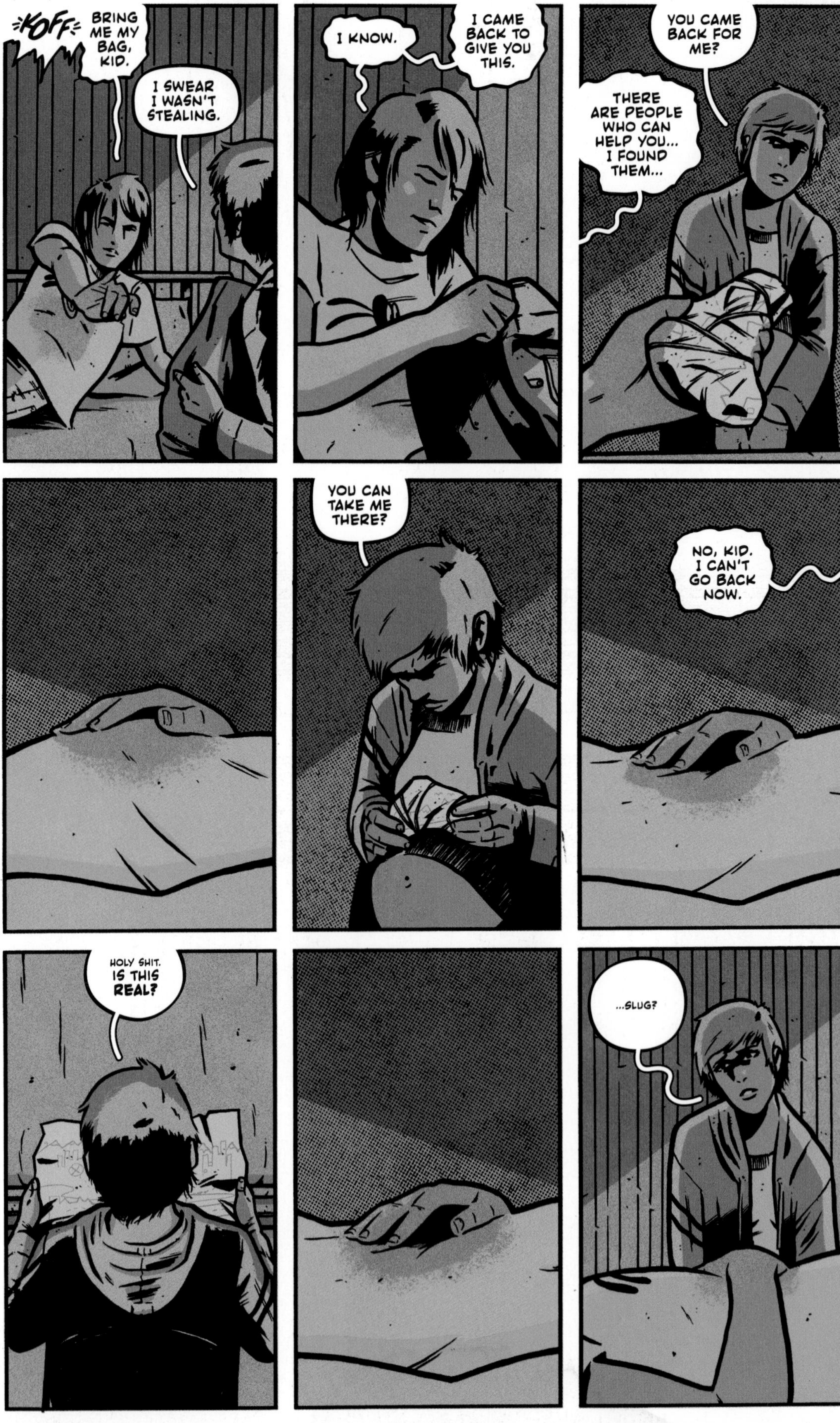
KOFF
BRING ME MY BAG, KID.
I SWEAR I WASN'T STEALING.
I KNOW.
I CAME BACK TO GIVE YOU THIS.
YOU CAME BACK FOR ME?
THERE ARE PEOPLE WHO CAN HELP YOU... I FOUND THEM...
YOU CAN TAKE ME THERE?
NO, KID. I CAN'T GO BACK NOW.
HOLY SHIT. IS THIS REAL?
...SLUG?

# CHAPTER FOUR

I DIDN'T KNOW IT WOULD DO THAT.

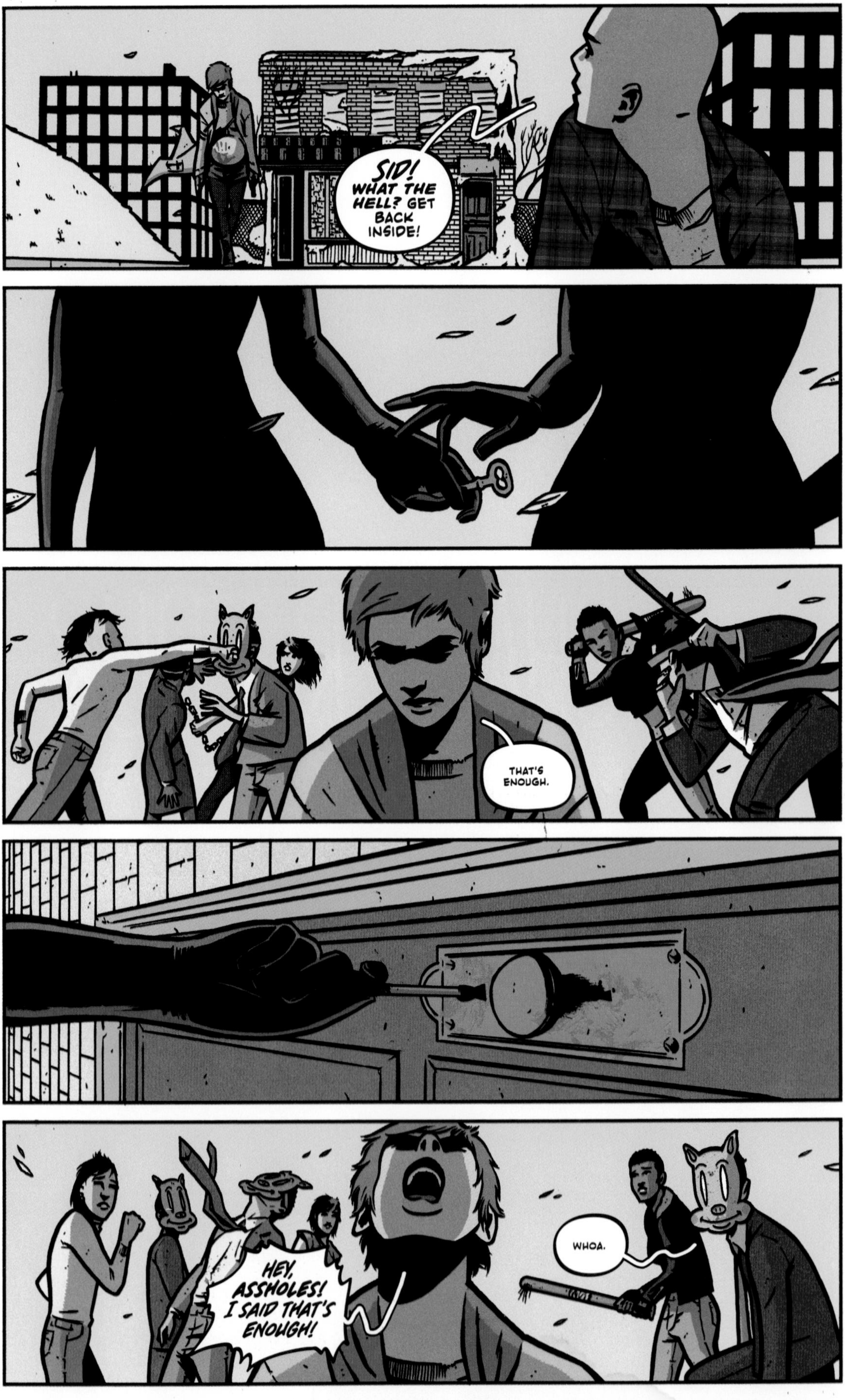
SID! WHAT THE HELL? GET BACK INSIDE!
THAT'S ENOUGH.
HEY, ASSHOLES! I SAID THAT'S ENOUGH!
WHOA.

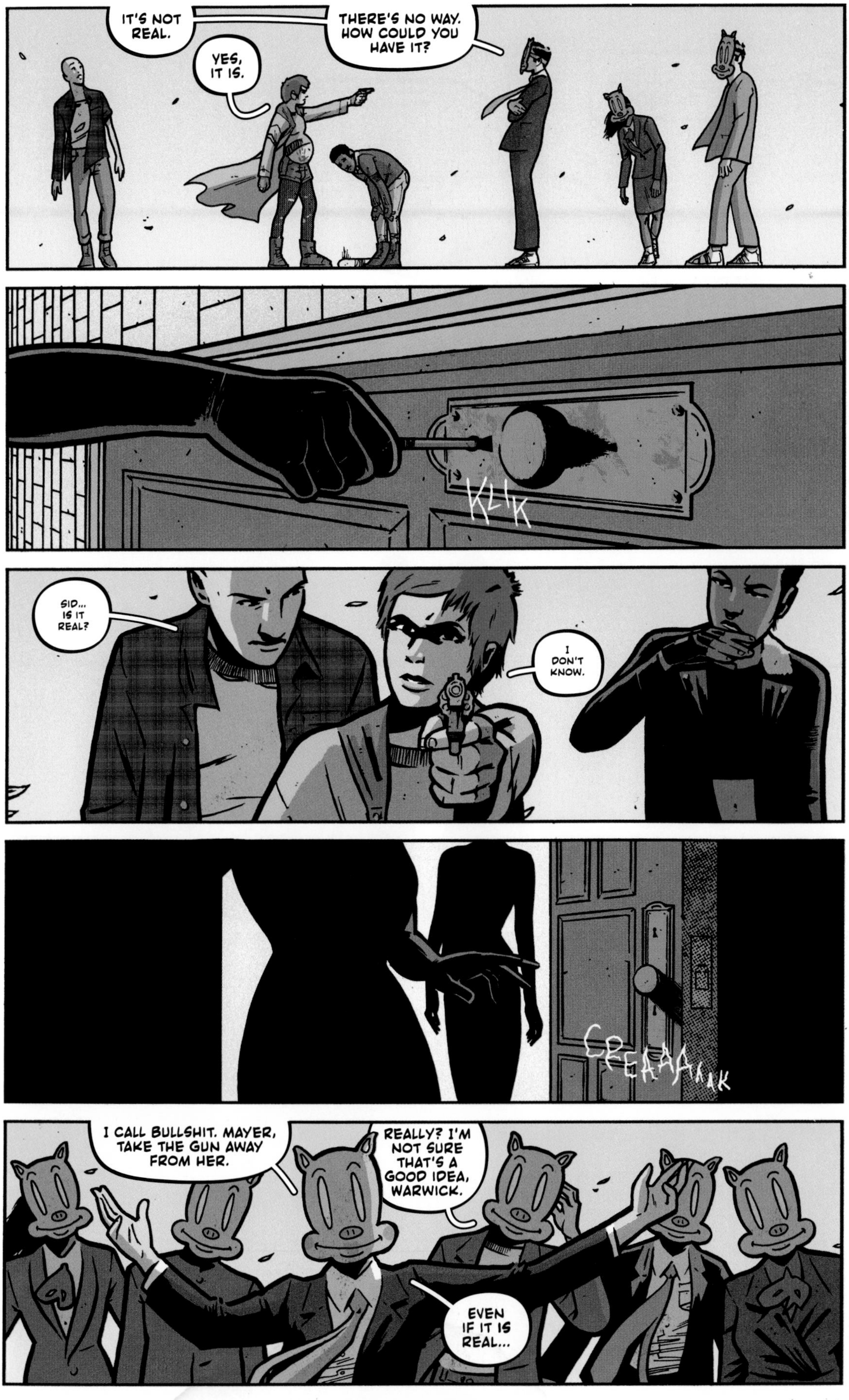
IT'S NOT REAL.
YES, IT IS.
THERE'S NO WAY. HOW COULD YOU HAVE IT?
KLIK
SID... IS IT REAL?
I DON'T KNOW.
CREAAAAAAK
I CALL BULLSHIT. MAYER, TAKE THE GUN AWAY FROM HER.
REALLY? I'M NOT SURE THAT'S A GOOD IDEA, WARWICK.
EVEN IF IT IS REAL...

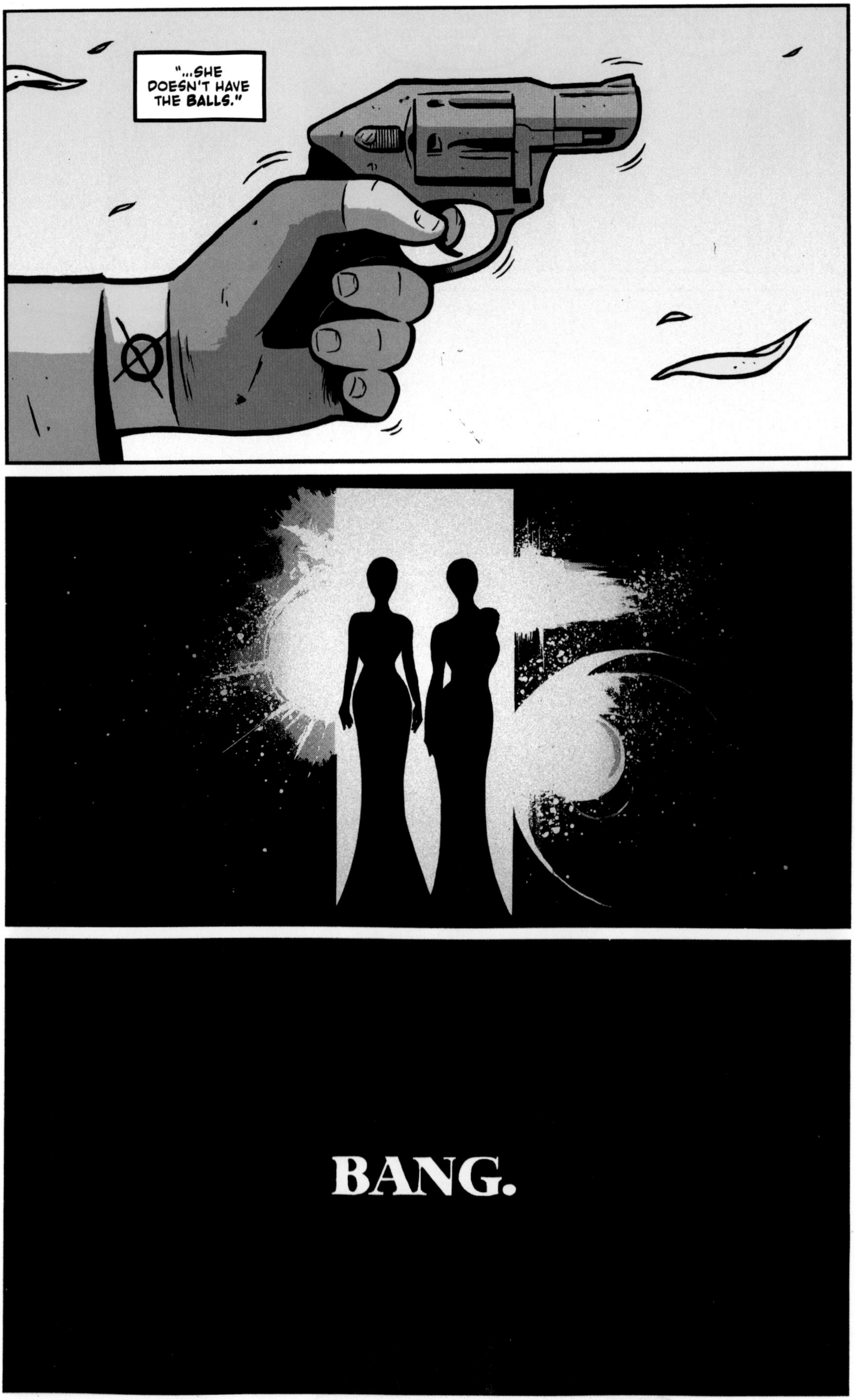
"...SHE DOESN'T HAVE THE BALLS."
BANG.

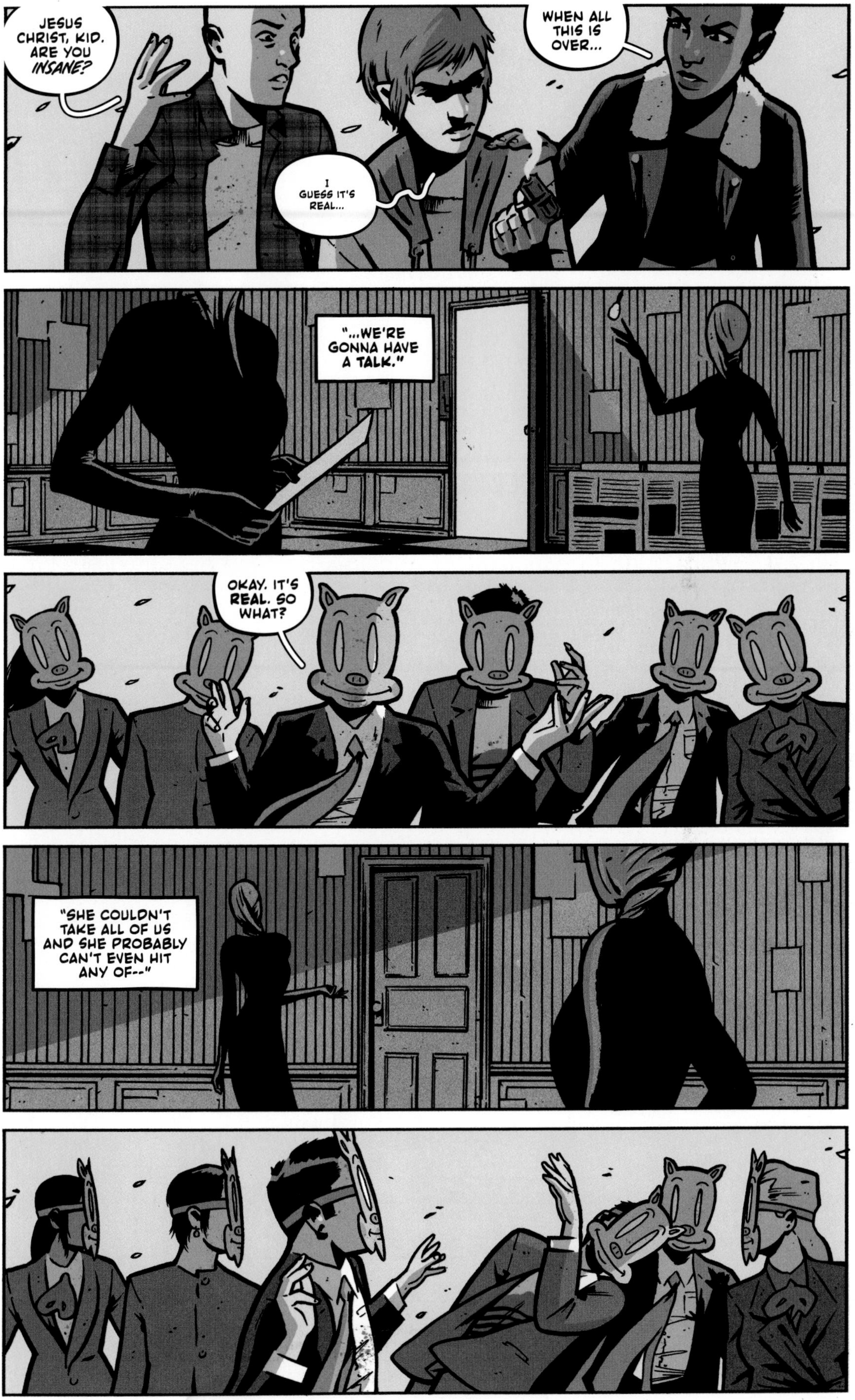
JESUS CHRIST, KID. ARE YOU *INSANE?*
I GUESS IT'S REAL...
WHEN ALL THIS IS OVER...
"...WE'RE GONNA HAVE A TALK."
OKAY. IT'S REAL. SO WHAT?
"SHE COULDN'T TAKE ALL OF US AND SHE PROBABLY CAN'T EVEN HIT ANY OF--"

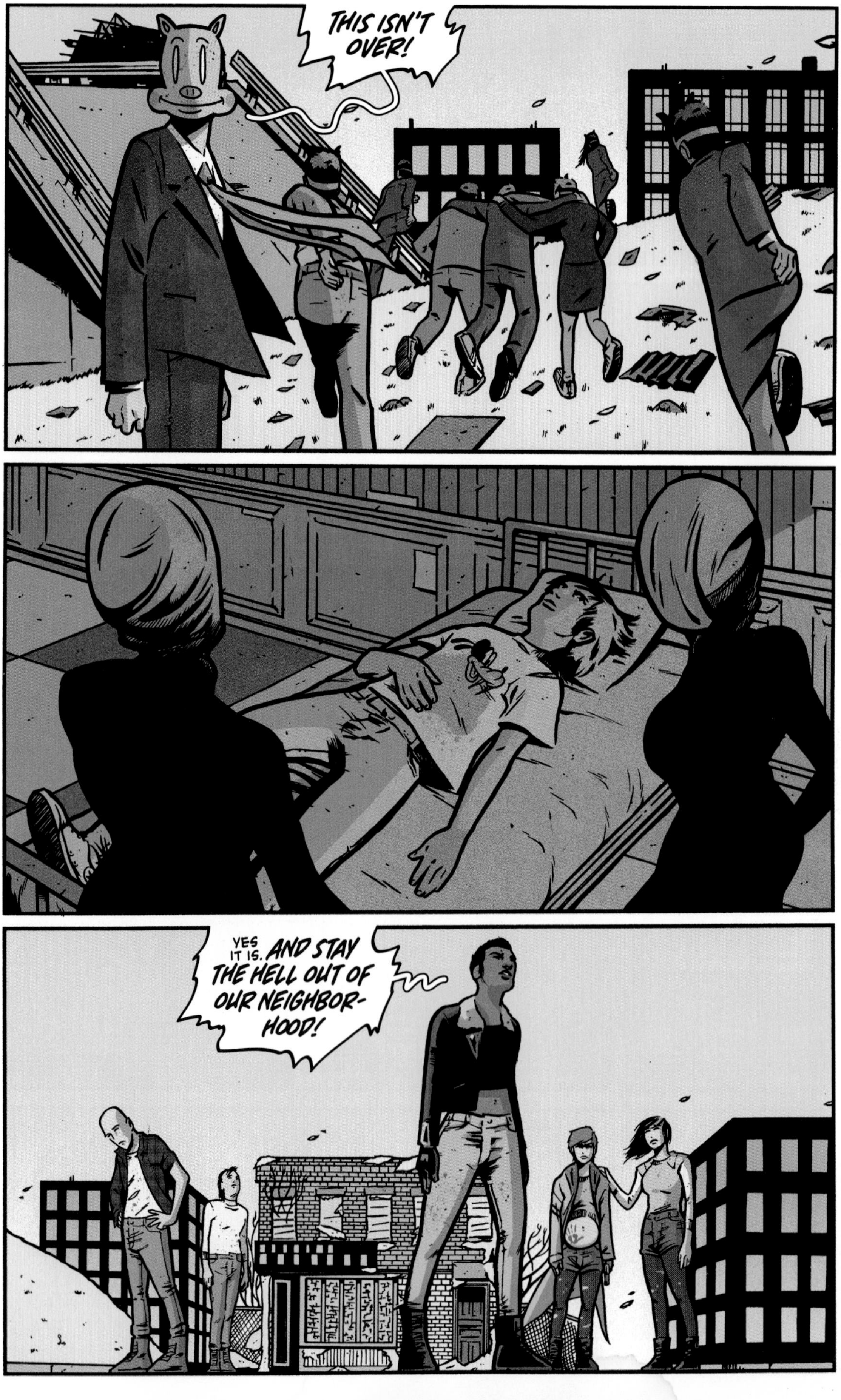
THIS ISN'T OVER!
YES IT IS. AND STAY THE HELL OUT OF OUR NEIGHBOR-HOOD!

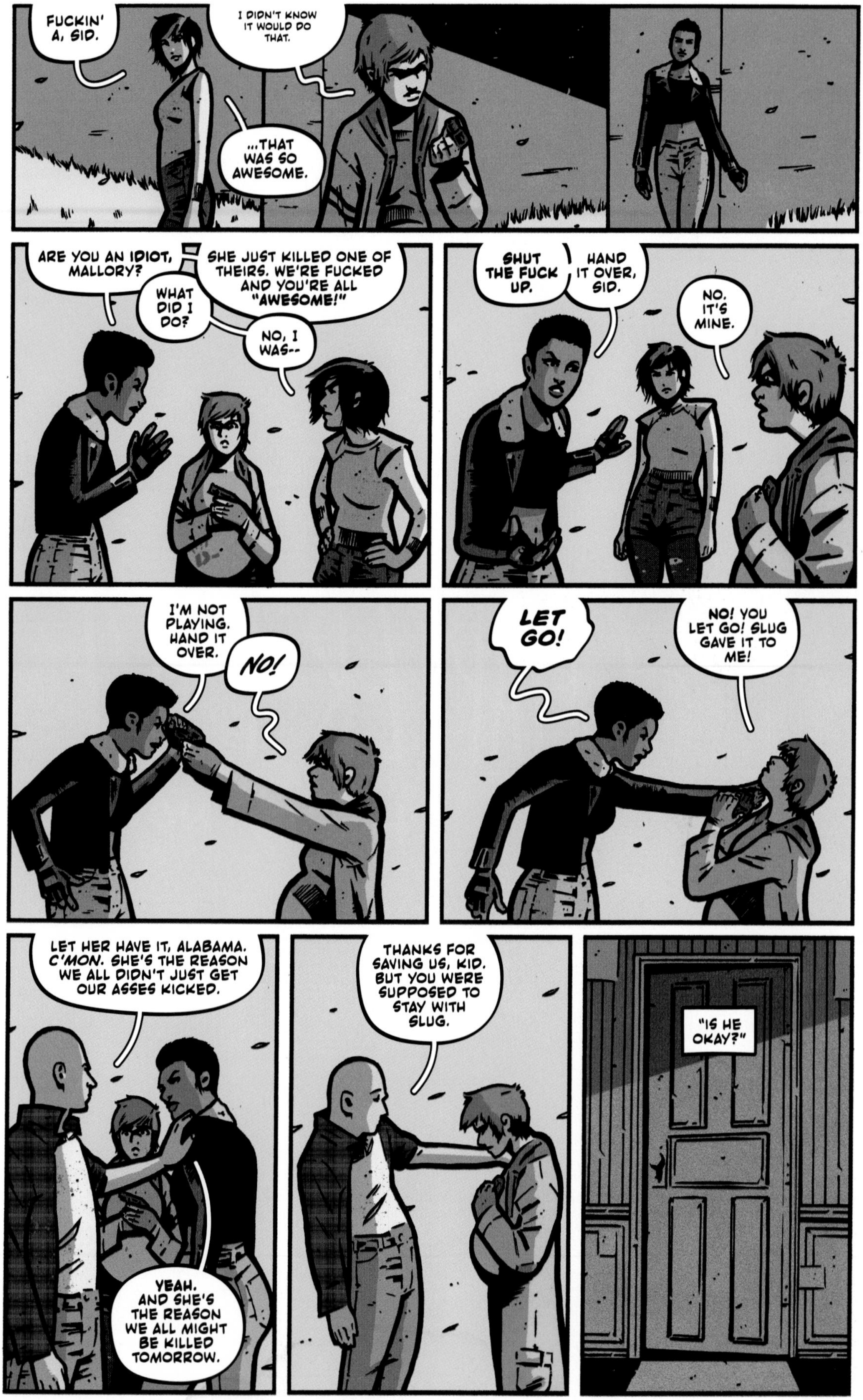
FUCKIN' A, SID.
I DIDN'T KNOW IT WOULD DO THAT.
...THAT WAS SO AWESOME.
ARE YOU AN IDIOT, MALLORY?
WHAT DID I DO?
SHE JUST KILLED ONE OF THEIRS. WE'RE FUCKED AND YOU'RE ALL "AWESOME!"
NO, I WAS--
SHUT THE FUCK UP.
HAND IT OVER, SID.
NO. IT'S MINE.
I'M NOT PLAYING. HAND IT OVER.
NO!
LET GO!
NO! YOU LET GO! SLUG GAVE IT TO ME!
LET HER HAVE IT, ALABAMA. C'MON. SHE'S THE REASON WE ALL DIDN'T JUST GET OUR ASSES KICKED.
YEAH. AND SHE'S THE REASON WE ALL MIGHT BE KILLED TOMORROW.
THANKS FOR SAVING US, KID. BUT YOU WERE SUPPOSED TO STAY WITH SLUG.
"IS HE OKAY?"

# CHAPTER FIVE

## HE IS NOW.

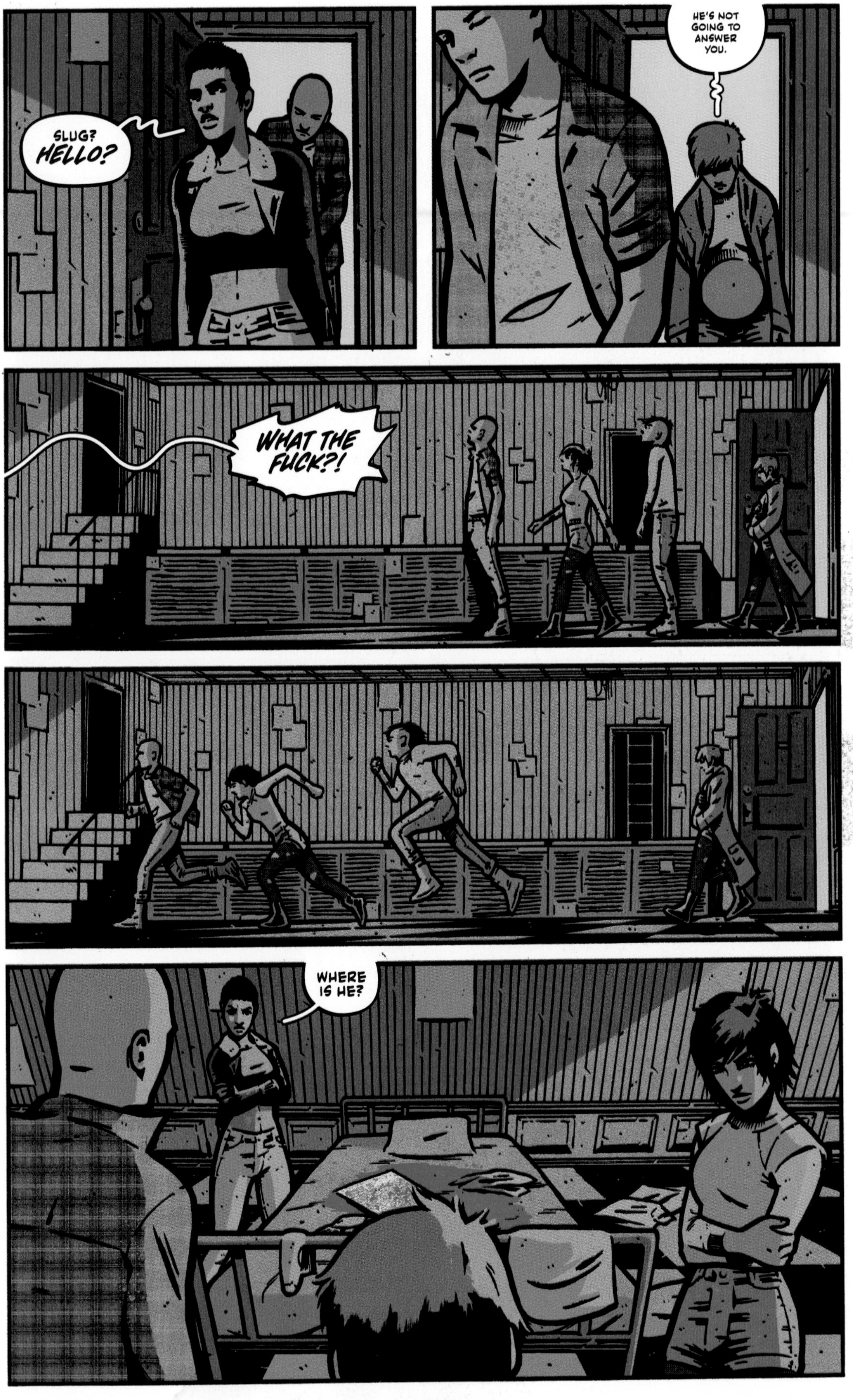
SLUG? HELLO?
HE'S NOT GOING TO ANSWER YOU.
WHAT THE FUCK?!
WHERE IS HE?

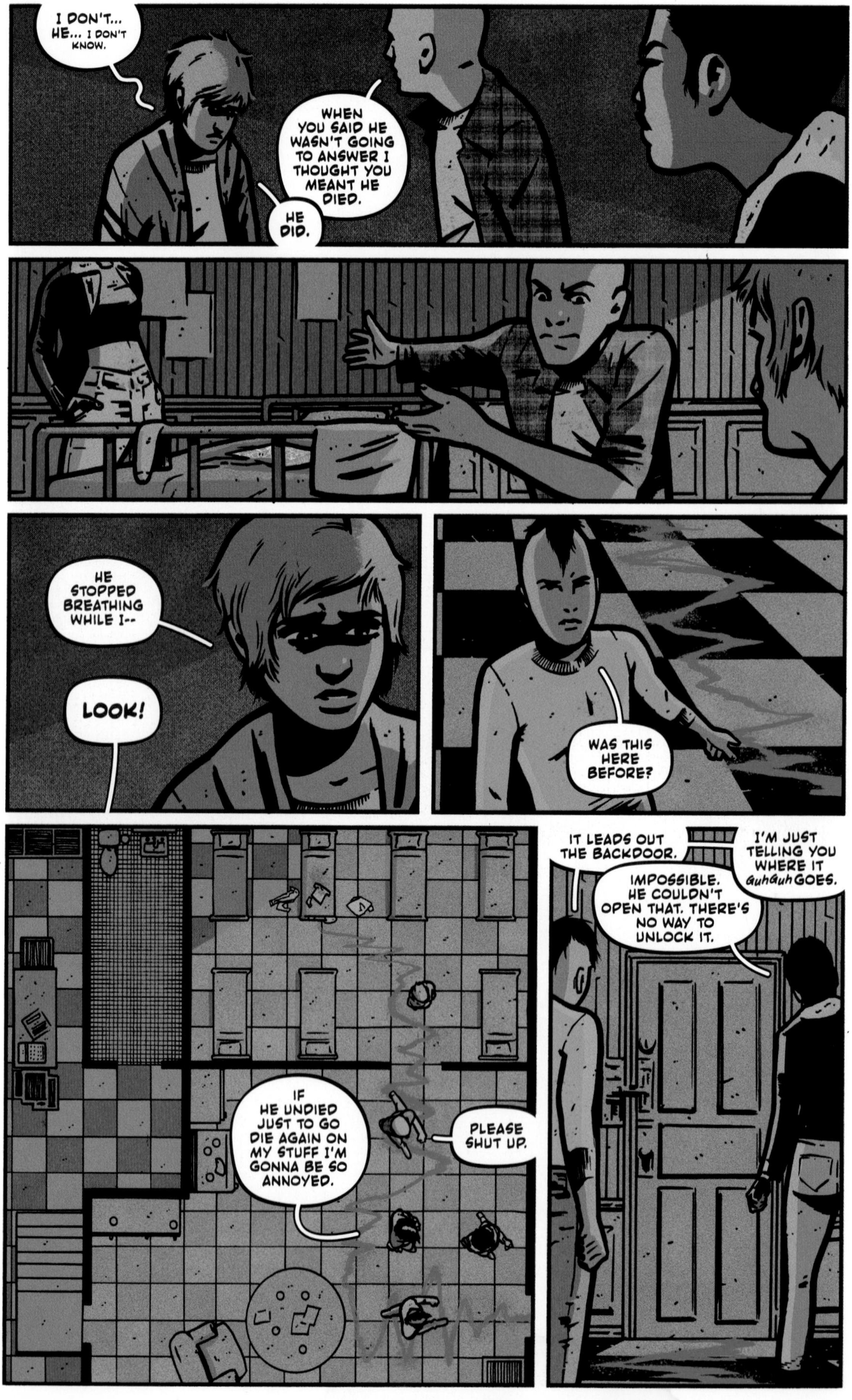
I DON'T... HE... I DON'T KNOW.
WHEN YOU SAID HE WASN'T GOING TO ANSWER I THOUGHT YOU MEANT HE DIED.
HE DID.
HE STOPPED BREATHING WHILE I--
LOOK!
WAS THIS HERE BEFORE?
IF HE UNDIED JUST TO GO DIE AGAIN ON MY STUFF I'M GONNA BE SO ANNOYED.
PLEASE SHUT UP.
IT LEADS OUT THE BACKDOOR.
I'M JUST TELLING YOU WHERE IT GuhGuh GOES.
IMPOSSIBLE. HE COULDN'T OPEN THAT. THERE'S NO WAY TO UNLOCK IT.

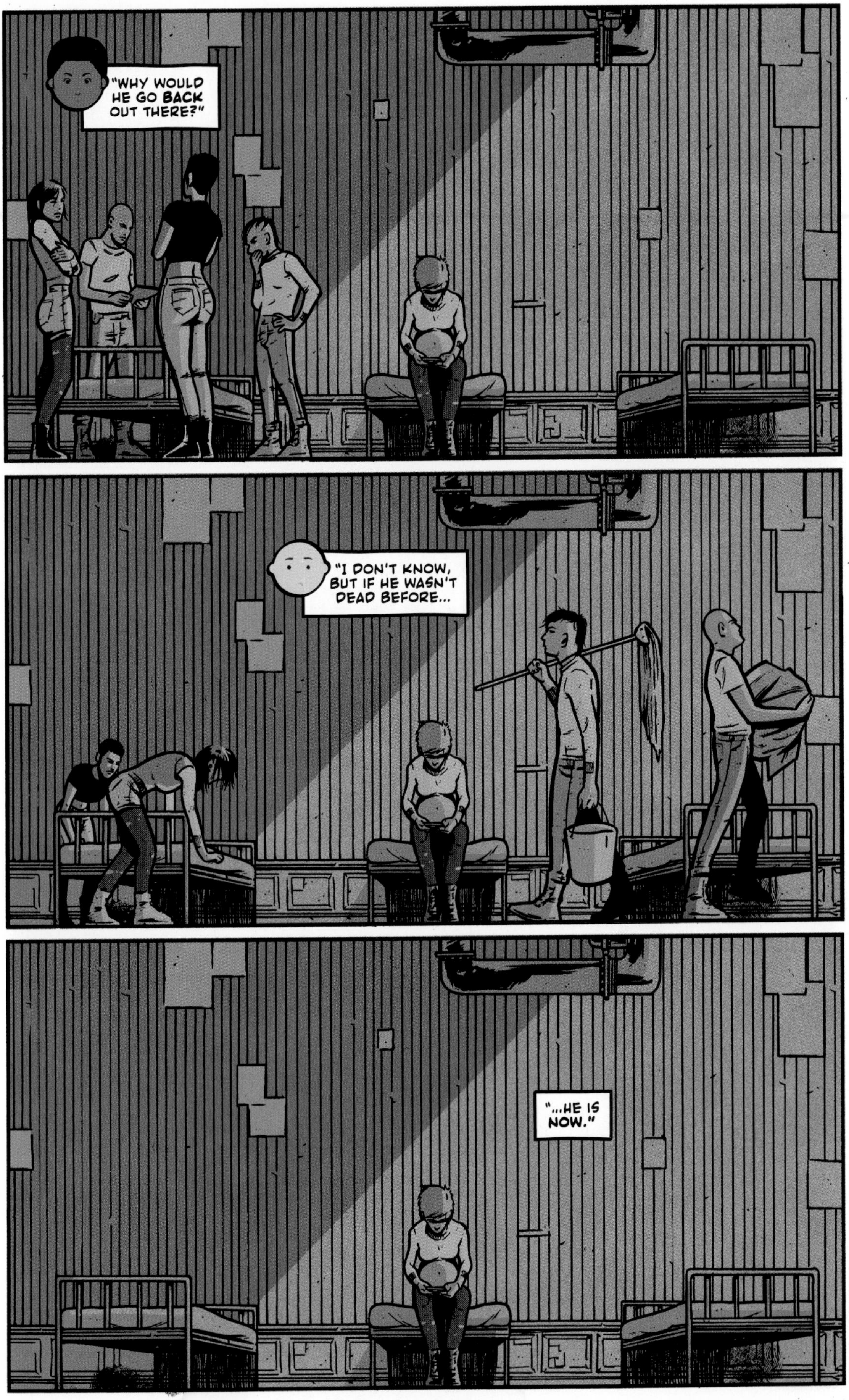
"WHY WOULD HE GO BACK OUT THERE?"
"I DON'T KNOW, BUT IF HE WASN'T DEAD BEFORE...
"...HE IS NOW."

# CHAPTER SIX

## RAISED IN THE CLUTTER.

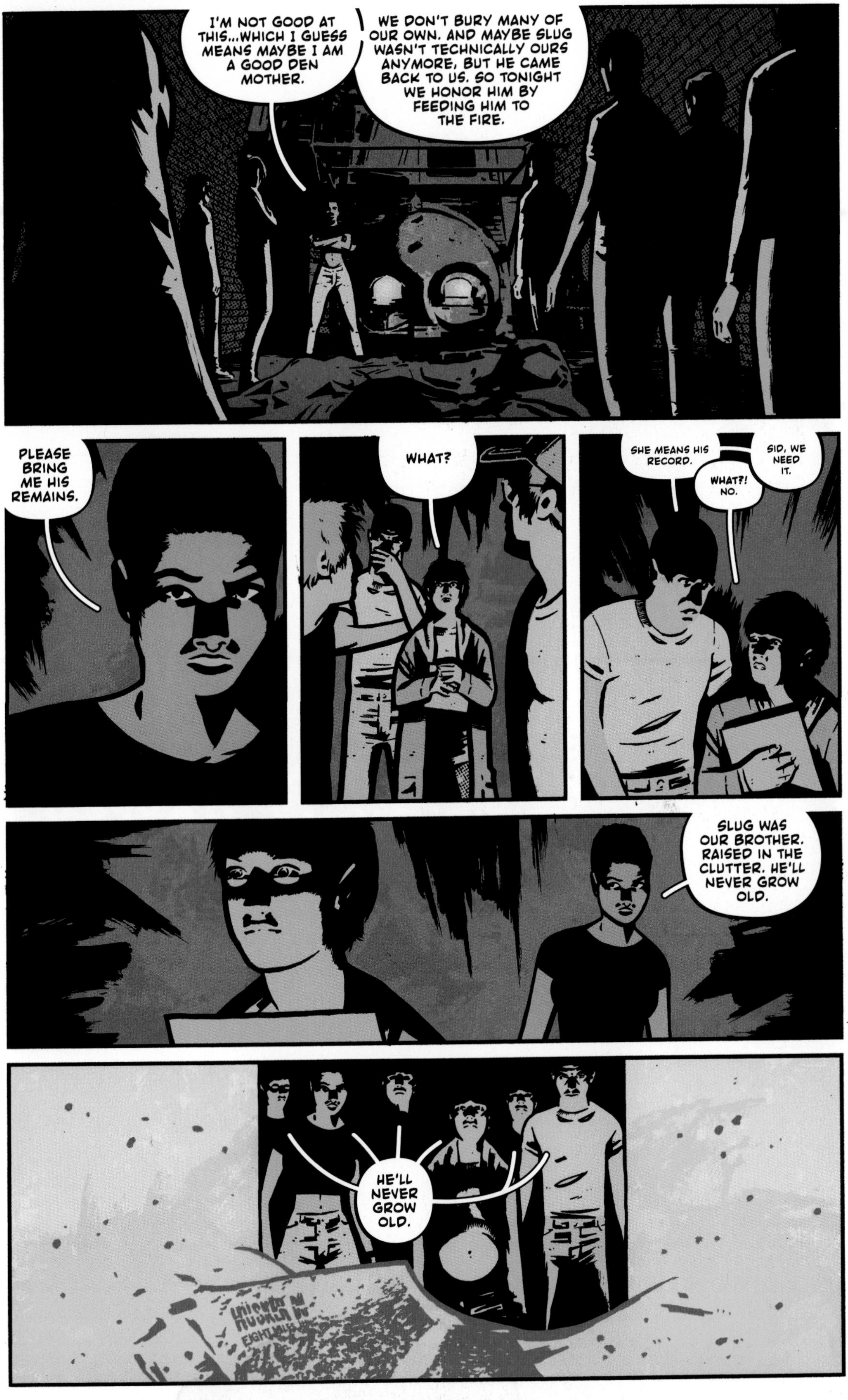
I'M NOT GOOD AT THIS...WHICH I GUESS MEANS MAYBE I AM A GOOD DEN MOTHER.
WE DON'T BURY MANY OF OUR OWN. AND MAYBE SLUG WASN'T TECHNICALLY OURS ANYMORE, BUT HE CAME BACK TO US. SO TONIGHT WE HONOR HIM BY FEEDING HIM TO THE FIRE.
PLEASE BRING ME HIS REMAINS.
WHAT?
SHE MEANS HIS RECORD.
WHAT?! NO.
SID, WE NEED IT.
SLUG WAS OUR BROTHER. RAISED IN THE CLUTTER. HE'LL NEVER GROW OLD.
HE'LL NEVER GROW OLD.

# CHAPTER SEVEN

## THINGS HAPPEN AND THEN MORE THINGS HAPPEN.

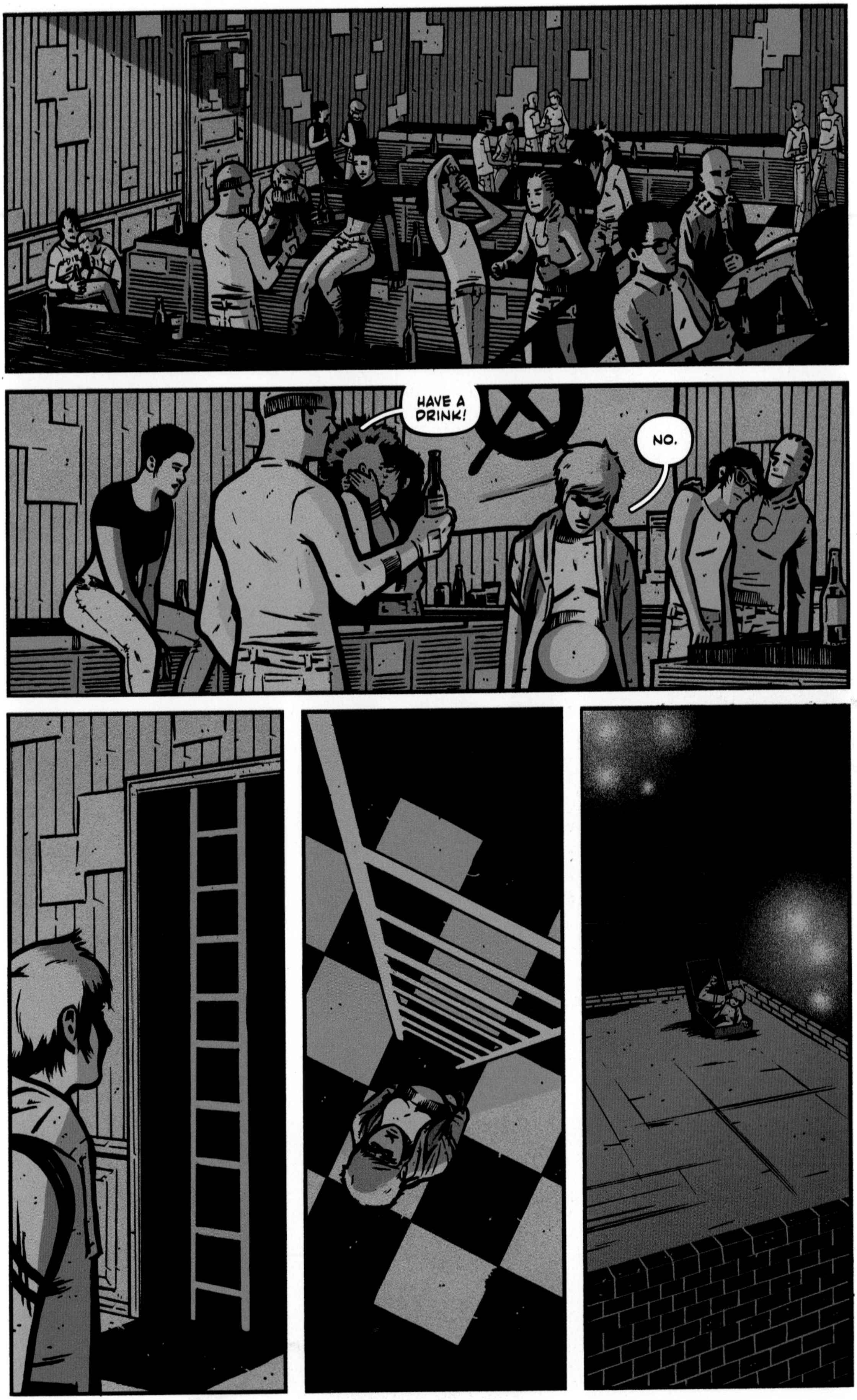
HAVE A DRINK!
NO.

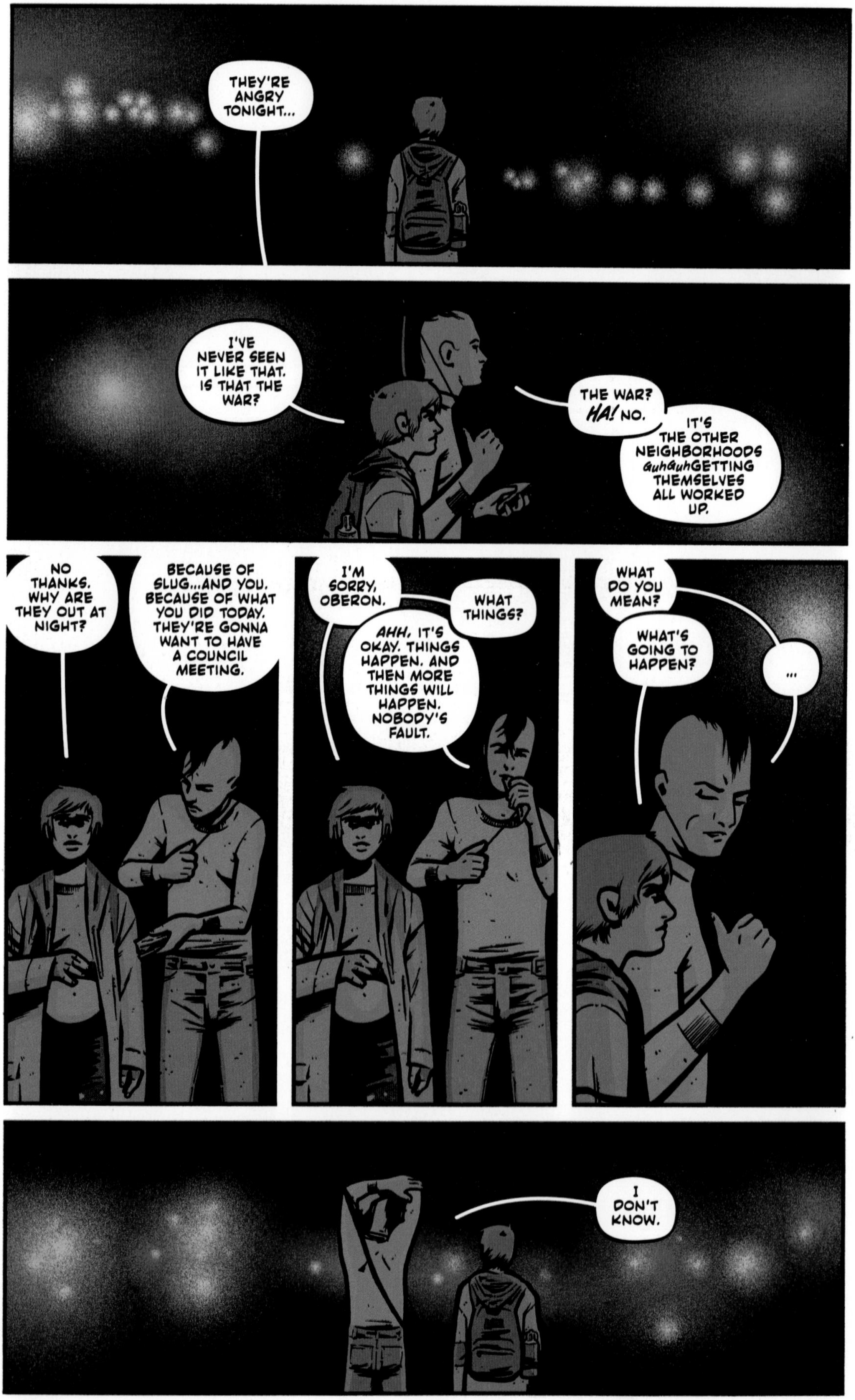
THEY'RE ANGRY TONIGHT...
I'VE NEVER SEEN IT LIKE THAT. IS THAT THE WAR?
THE WAR? HA! NO.
IT'S THE OTHER NEIGHBORHOODS GuhGuhGETTING THEMSELVES ALL WORKED UP.
NO THANKS. WHY ARE THEY OUT AT NIGHT?
BECAUSE OF SLUG...AND YOU. BECAUSE OF WHAT YOU DID TODAY. THEY'RE GONNA WANT TO HAVE A COUNCIL MEETING.
I'M SORRY, OBERON.
AHH, IT'S OKAY. THINGS HAPPEN. AND THEN MORE THINGS WILL HAPPEN. NOBODY'S FAULT.
WHAT THINGS?
WHAT DO YOU MEAN?
WHAT'S GOING TO HAPPEN?
...
I DON'T KNOW.

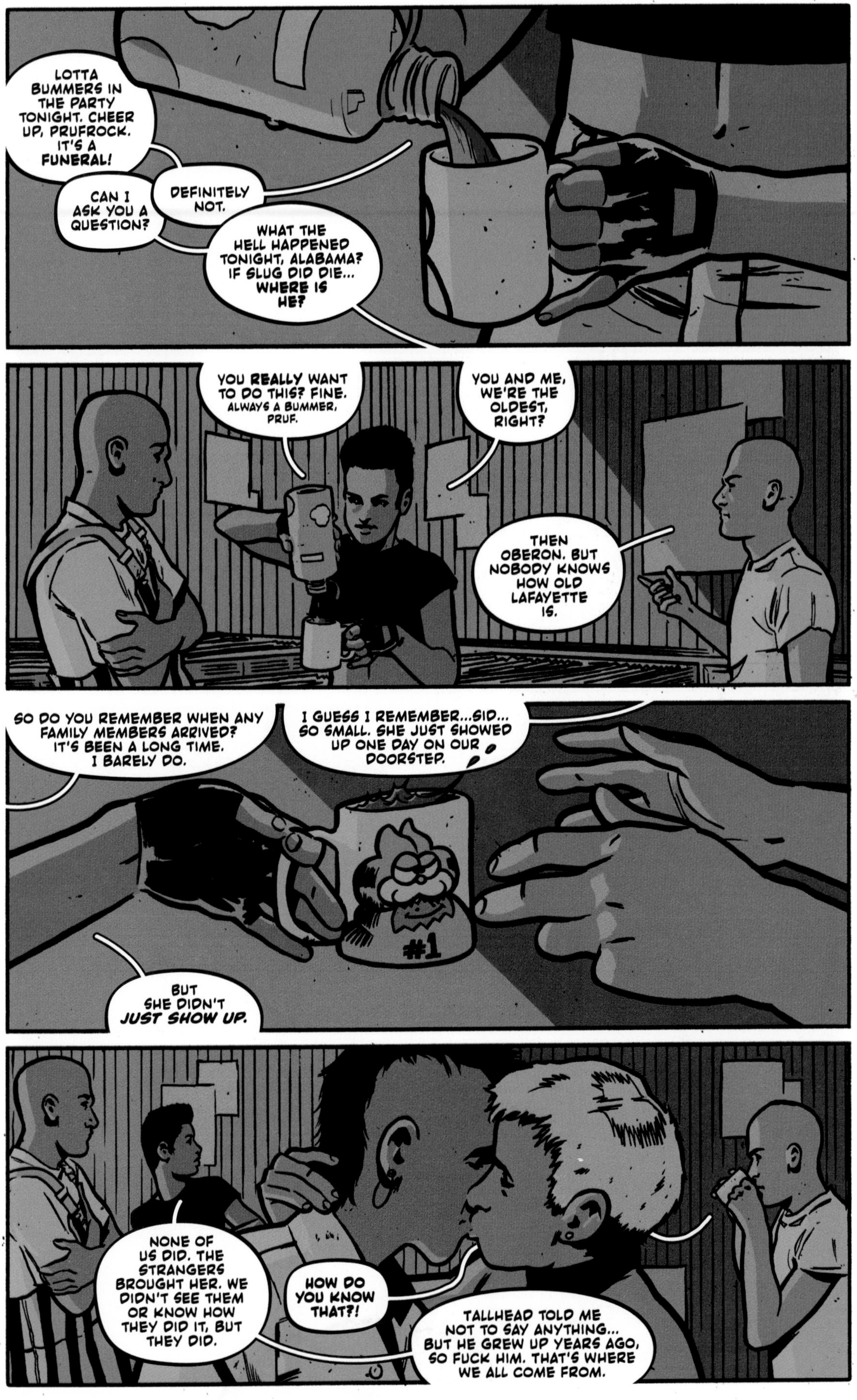

LOTTA BUMMERS IN THE PARTY TONIGHT. CHEER UP, PRUFROCK. IT'S A FUNERAL!
CAN I ASK YOU A QUESTION?
DEFINITELY NOT.
WHAT THE HELL HAPPENED TONIGHT, ALABAMA? IF SLUG DID DIE... WHERE IS HE?
YOU REALLY WANT TO DO THIS? FINE. ALWAYS A BUMMER, PRUF.
YOU AND ME, WE'RE THE OLDEST, RIGHT?
THEN OBERON. BUT NOBODY KNOWS HOW OLD LAFAYETTE IS.
SO DO YOU REMEMBER WHEN ANY FAMILY MEMBERS ARRIVED? IT'S BEEN A LONG TIME. I BARELY DO.
I GUESS I REMEMBER...SID... SO SMALL. SHE JUST SHOWED UP ONE DAY ON OUR DOORSTEP.
#1
BUT SHE DIDN'T JUST SHOW UP.
NONE OF US DID. THE STRANGERS BROUGHT HER. WE DIDN'T SEE THEM OR KNOW HOW THEY DID IT, BUT THEY DID.
HOW DO YOU KNOW THAT?!
TALLHEAD TOLD ME NOT TO SAY ANYTHING... BUT HE GREW UP YEARS AGO, SO FUCK HIM. THAT'S WHERE WE ALL COME FROM.

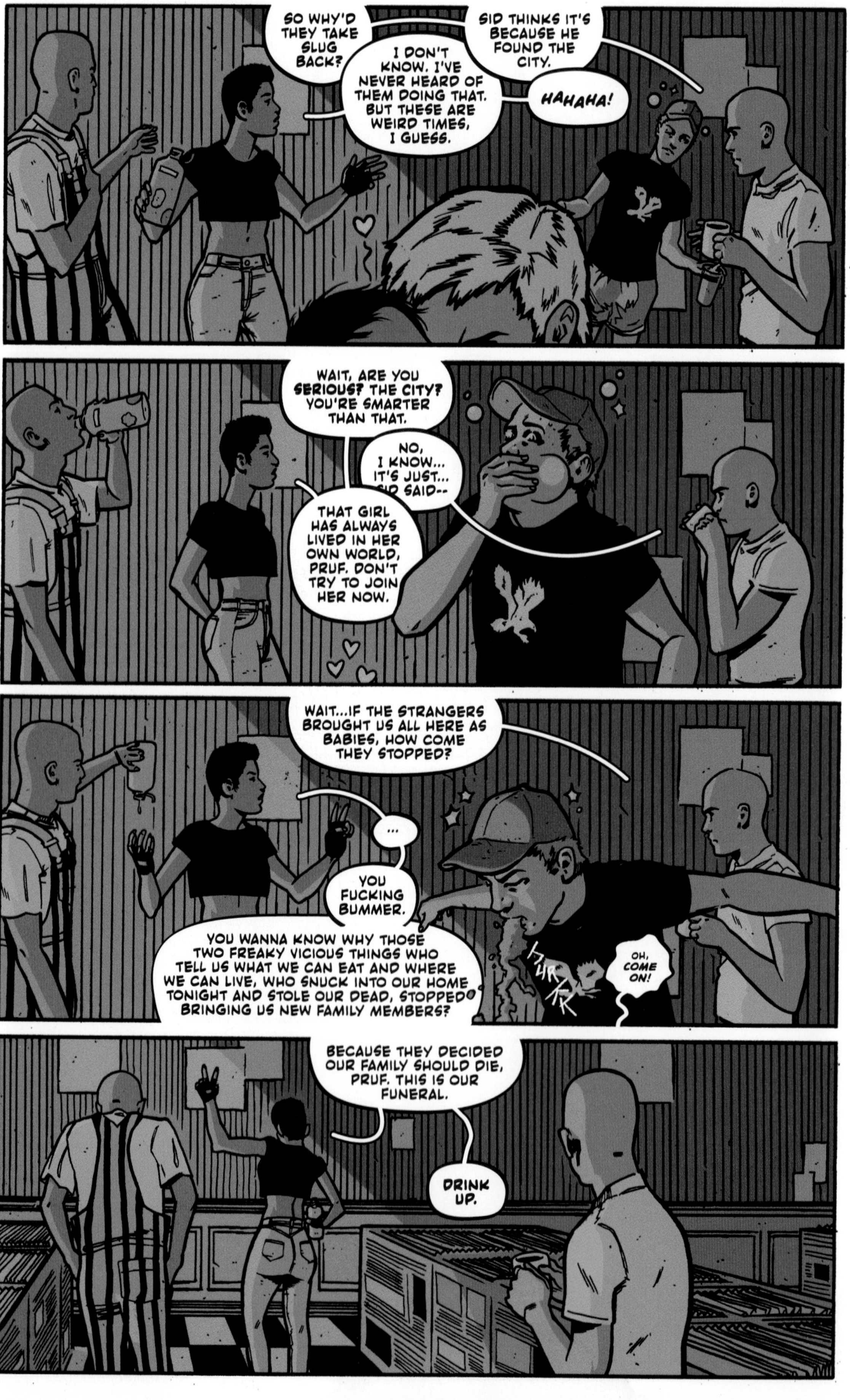
SO WHY'D THEY TAKE SLUG BACK?
SID THINKS IT'S BECAUSE HE FOUND THE CITY.
I DON'T KNOW. I'VE NEVER HEARD OF THEM DOING THAT. BUT THESE ARE WEIRD TIMES, I GUESS.
HAHAHA!
WAIT, ARE YOU SERIOUS? THE CITY? YOU'RE SMARTER THAN THAT.
NO, I KNOW... IT'S JUST... SID SAID--
THAT GIRL HAS ALWAYS LIVED IN HER OWN WORLD, PRUF. DON'T TRY TO JOIN HER NOW.
WAIT...IF THE STRANGERS BROUGHT US ALL HERE AS BABIES, HOW COME THEY STOPPED?
...
YOU FUCKING BUMMER.
YOU WANNA KNOW WHY THOSE TWO FREAKY VICIOUS THINGS WHO TELL US WHAT WE CAN EAT AND WHERE WE CAN LIVE, WHO SNUCK INTO OUR HOME TONIGHT AND STOLE OUR DEAD, STOPPED BRINGING US NEW FAMILY MEMBERS?
HURKK
OH, COME ON!
BECAUSE THEY DECIDED OUR FAMILY SHOULD DIE, PRUF. THIS IS OUR FUNERAL.
DRINK UP.

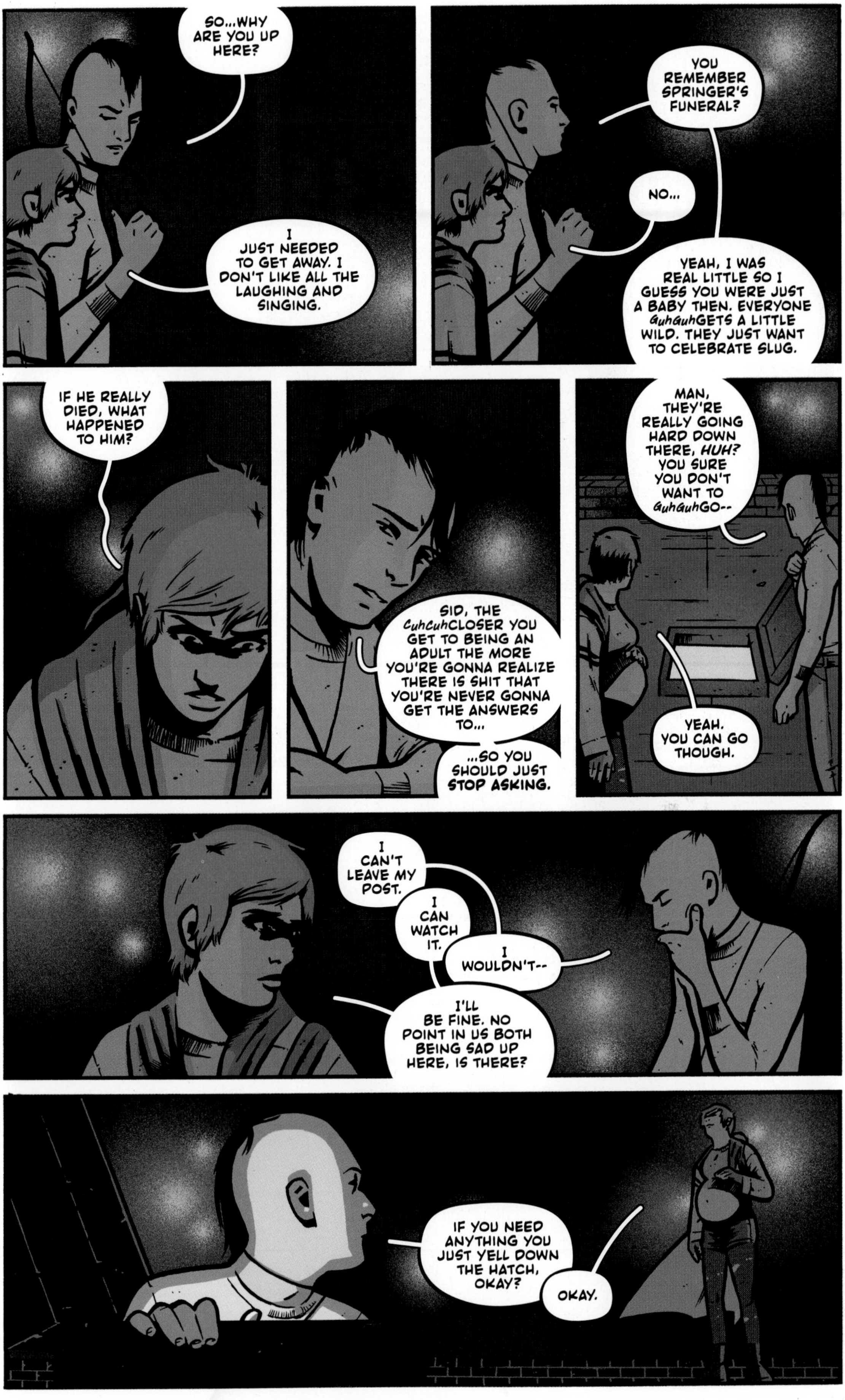
SO...WHY ARE YOU UP HERE?
I JUST NEEDED TO GET AWAY. I DON'T LIKE ALL THE LAUGHING AND SINGING.
YOU REMEMBER SPRINGER'S FUNERAL?
NO...
YEAH, I WAS REAL LITTLE SO I GUESS YOU WERE JUST A BABY THEN. EVERYONE GuhGuhGETS A LITTLE WILD. THEY JUST WANT TO CELEBRATE SLUG.
IF HE REALLY DIED, WHAT HAPPENED TO HIM?
SID, THE CuhCuhCLOSER YOU GET TO BEING AN ADULT THE MORE YOU'RE GONNA REALIZE THERE IS SHIT THAT YOU'RE NEVER GONNA GET THE ANSWERS TO...
...SO YOU SHOULD JUST STOP ASKING.
MAN, THEY'RE REALLY GOING HARD DOWN THERE, HUH? YOU SURE YOU DON'T WANT TO GuhGuhGO--
YEAH. YOU CAN GO THOUGH.
I CAN'T LEAVE MY POST.
I CAN WATCH IT.
I WOULDN'T--
I'LL BE FINE. NO POINT IN US BOTH BEING SAD UP HERE, IS THERE?
IF YOU NEED ANYTHING YOU JUST YELL DOWN THE HATCH, OKAY?
OKAY.

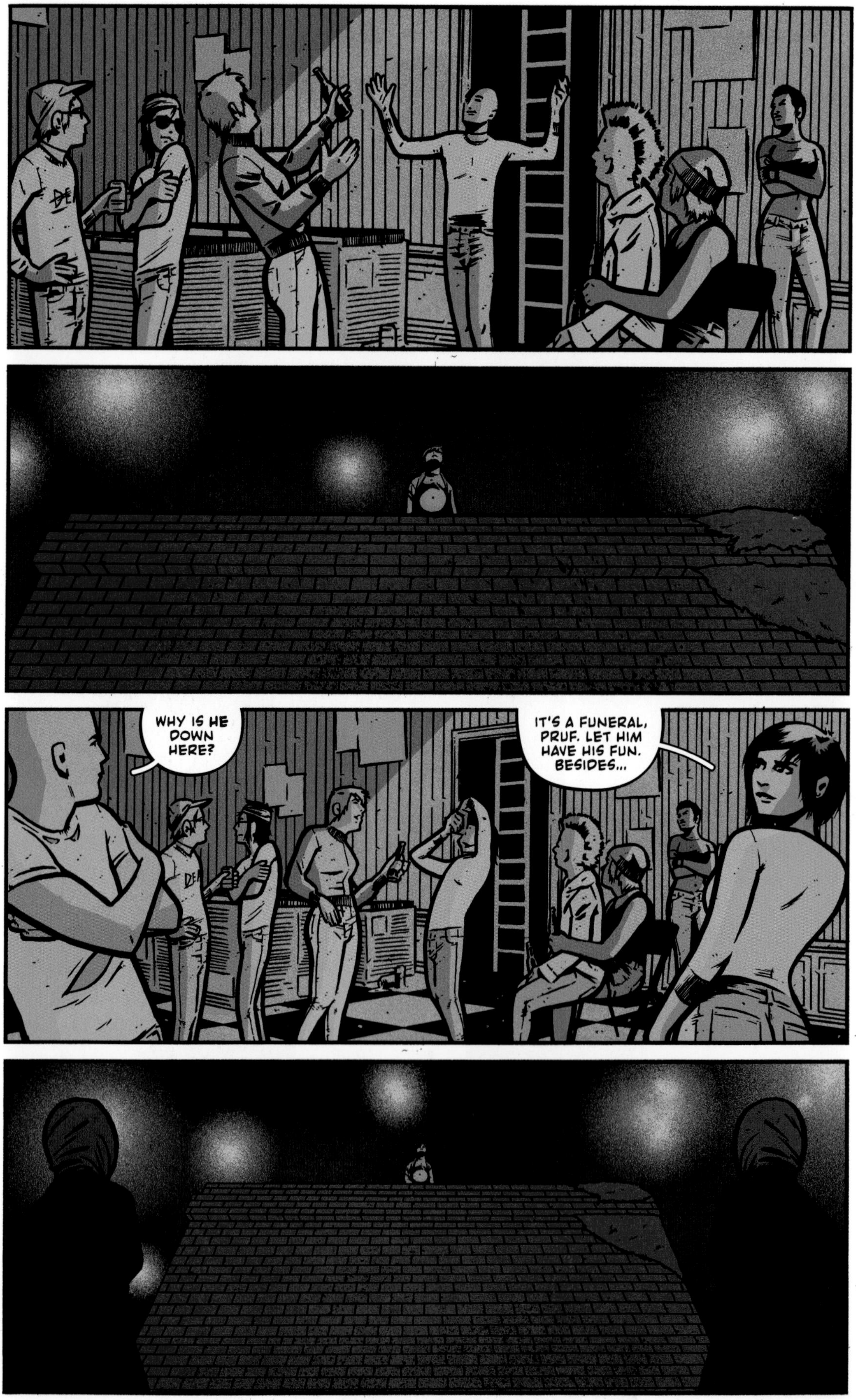
WHY IS HE DOWN HERE?
IT'S A FUNERAL, PRUF. LET HIM HAVE HIS FUN. BESIDES...

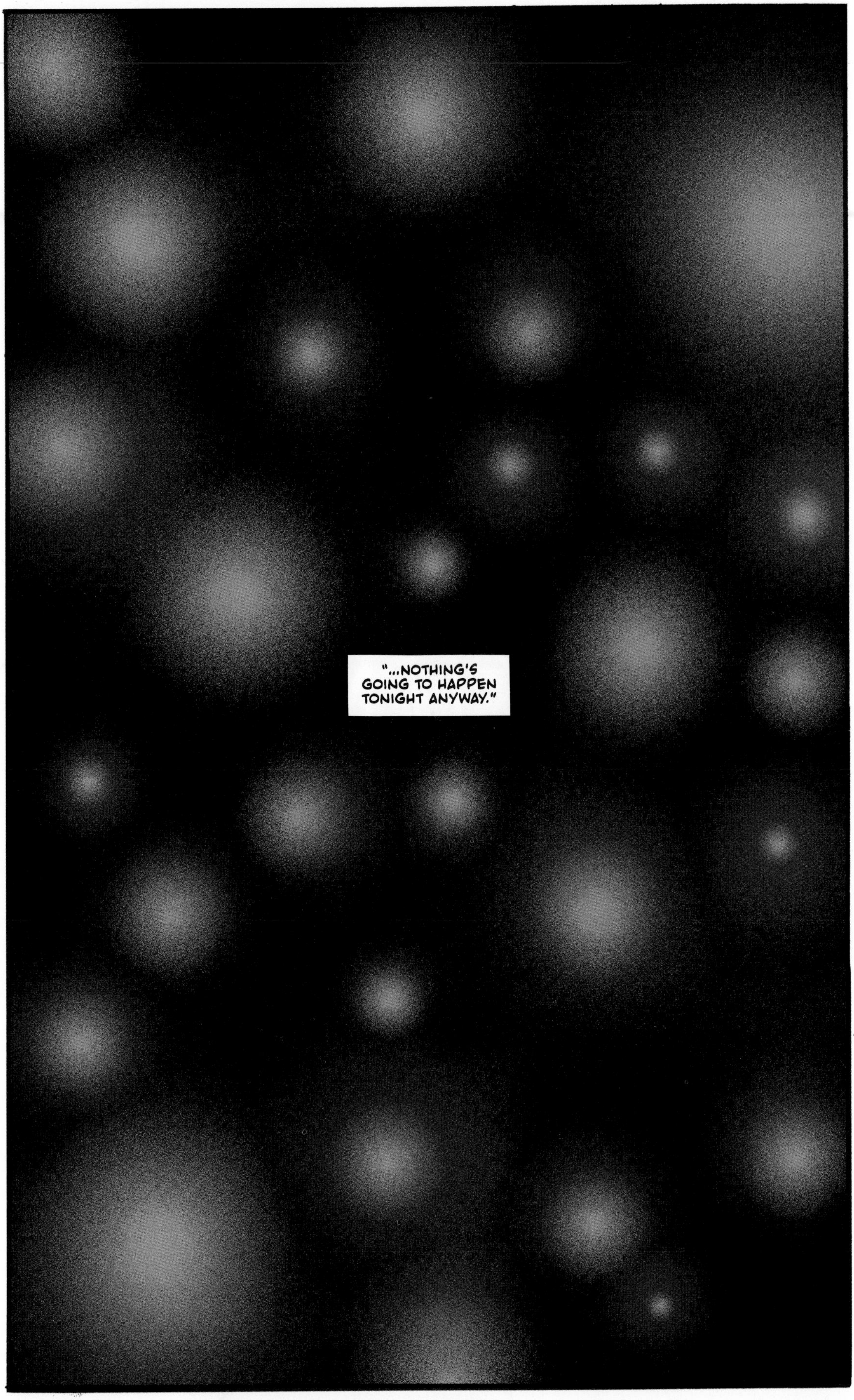
"...NOTHING'S GOING TO HAPPEN TONIGHT ANYWAY."

# CHAPTER EIGHT

## IT'S FUCKING DAYTIME.

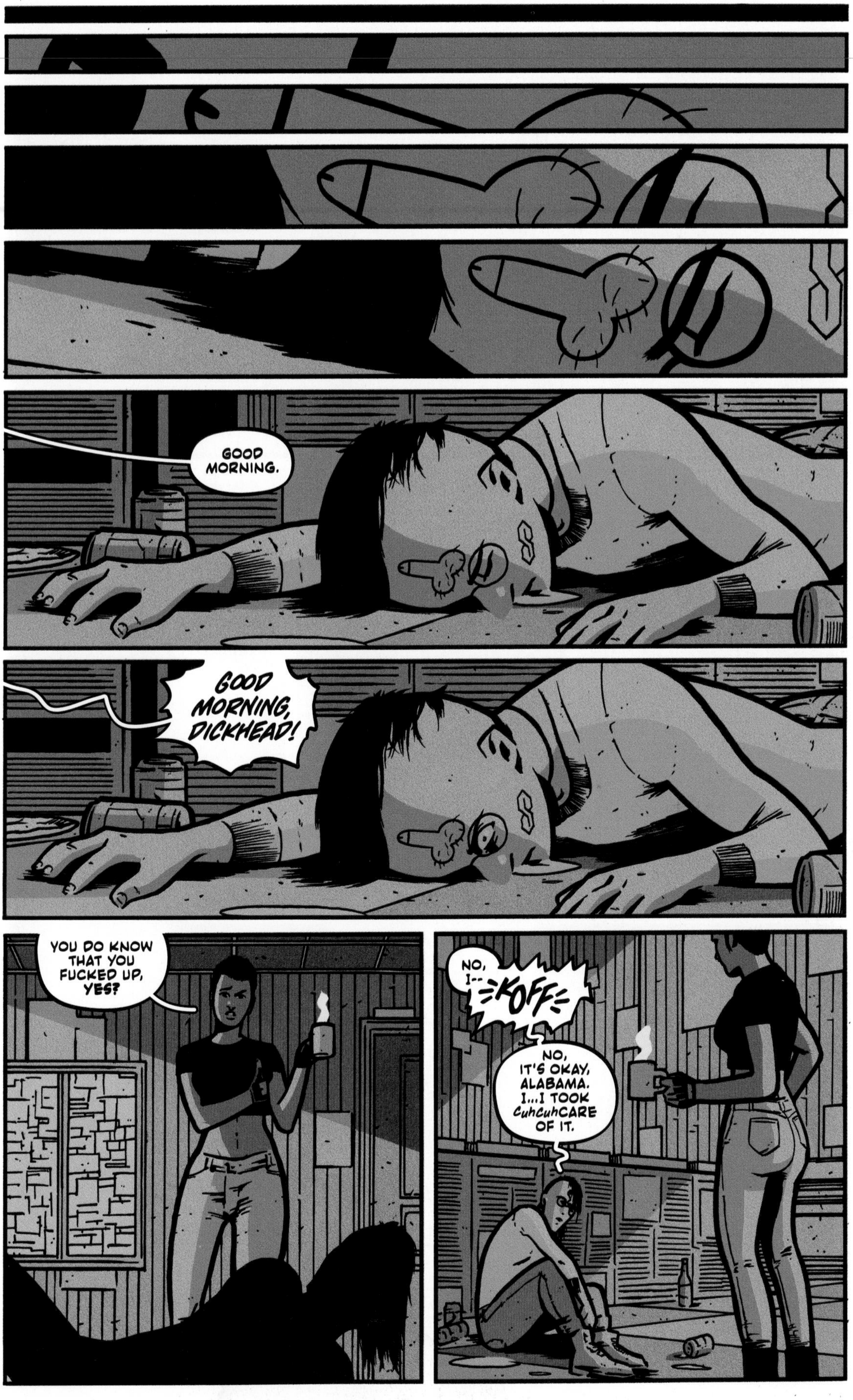
GOOD MORNING.
GOOD MORNING, DICKHEAD!
YOU DO KNOW THAT YOU FUCKED UP, YES?
NO, I--
KOFF
NO, IT'S OKAY, ALABAMA. I...I TOOK CuhCuhCARE OF IT.

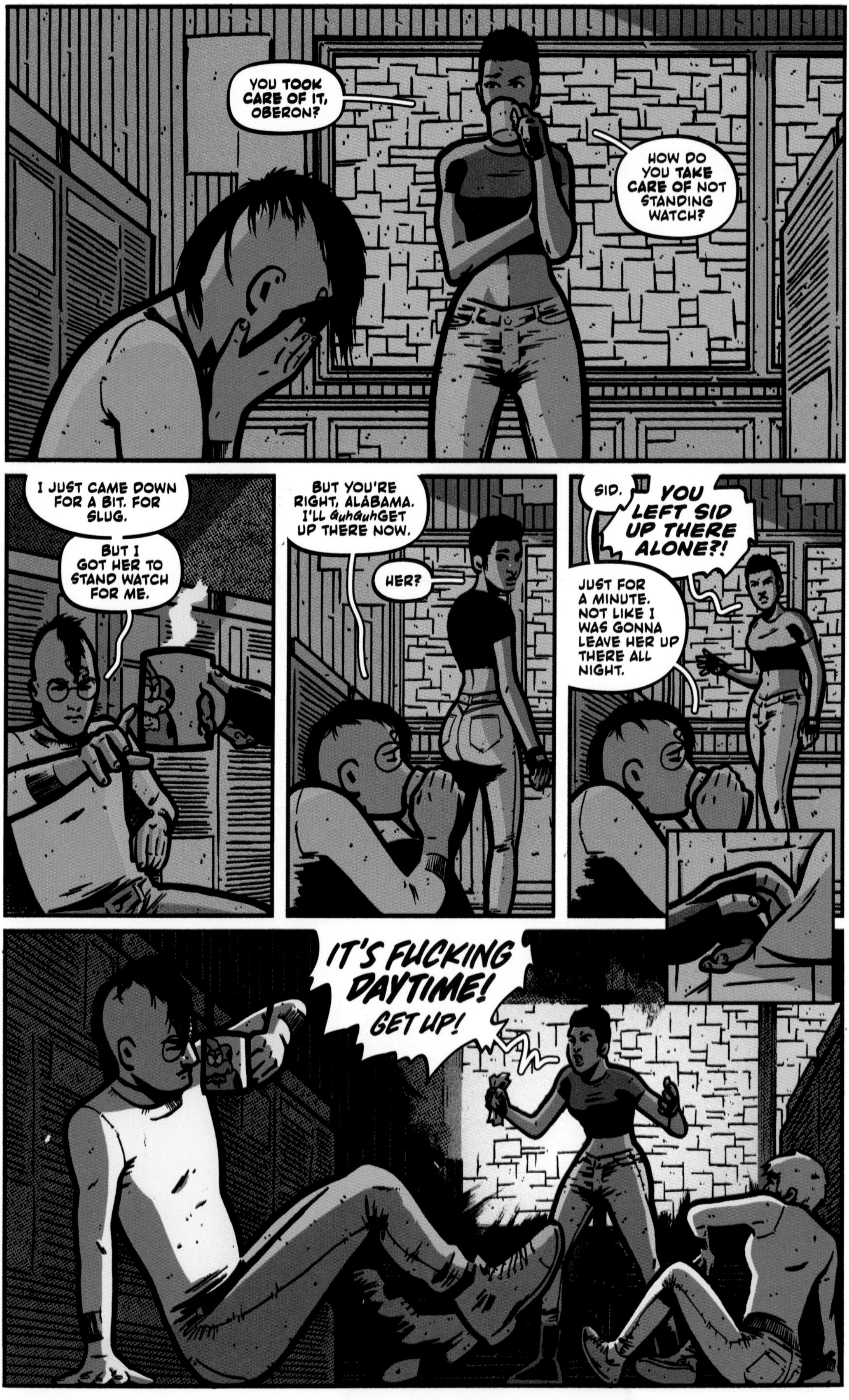
YOU TOOK CARE OF IT, OBERON?
HOW DO YOU TAKE CARE OF NOT STANDING WATCH?
I JUST CAME DOWN FOR A BIT. FOR SLUG.
BUT I GOT HER TO STAND WATCH FOR ME.
BUT YOU'RE RIGHT, ALABAMA. I'LL GuhGuhGET UP THERE NOW.
HER?
SID.
YOU LEFT SID UP THERE ALONE?!
JUST FOR A MINUTE. NOT LIKE I WAS GONNA LEAVE HER UP THERE ALL NIGHT.
IT'S FUCKING DAYTIME! GET UP!

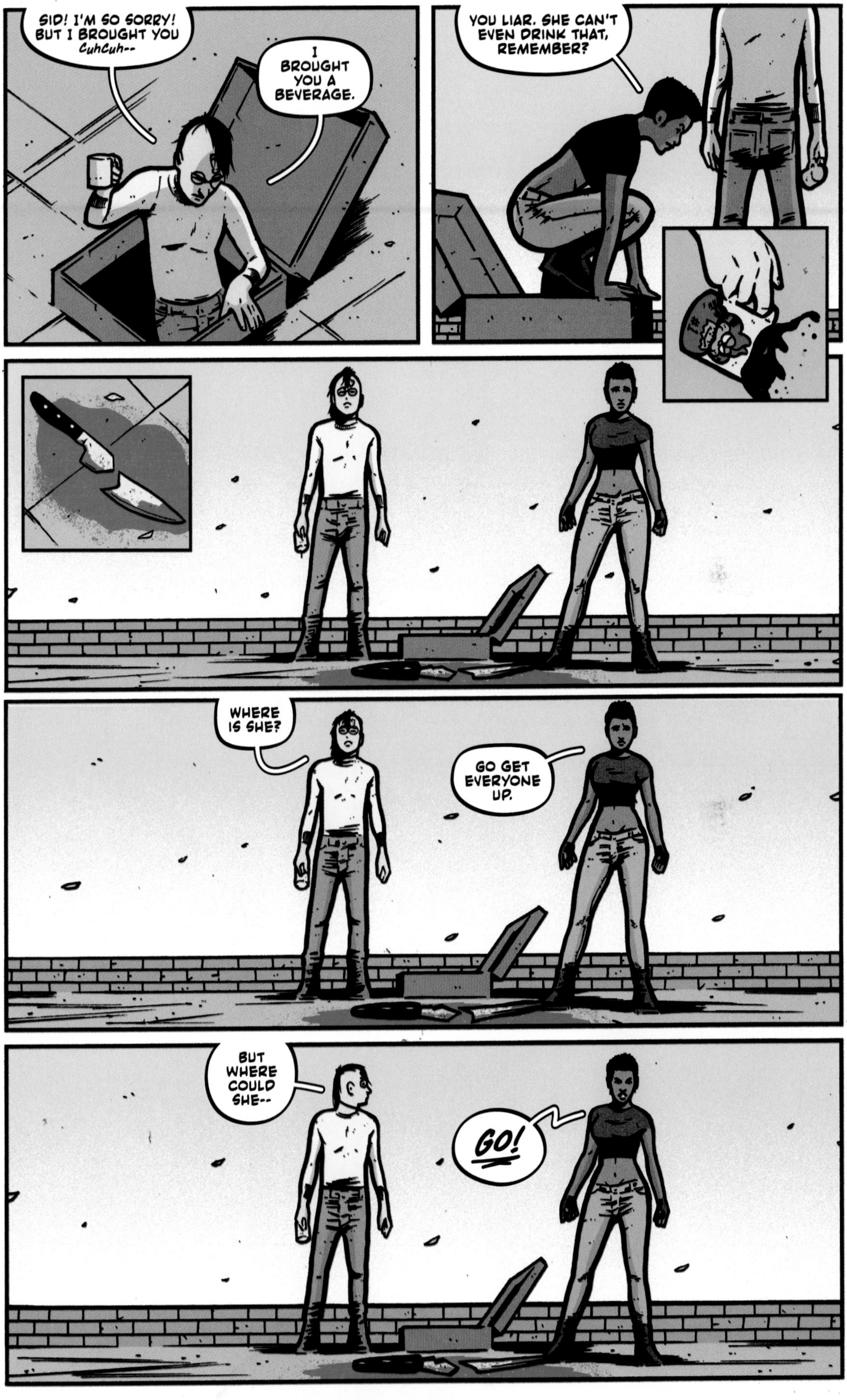
SID! I'M SO SORRY! BUT I BROUGHT YOU
CuhCuh--
I BROUGHT YOU A BEVERAGE.
YOU LIAR. SHE CAN'T EVEN DRINK THAT, REMEMBER?
WHERE IS SHE?
GO GET EVERYONE UP.
BUT WHERE COULD SHE--
GO!

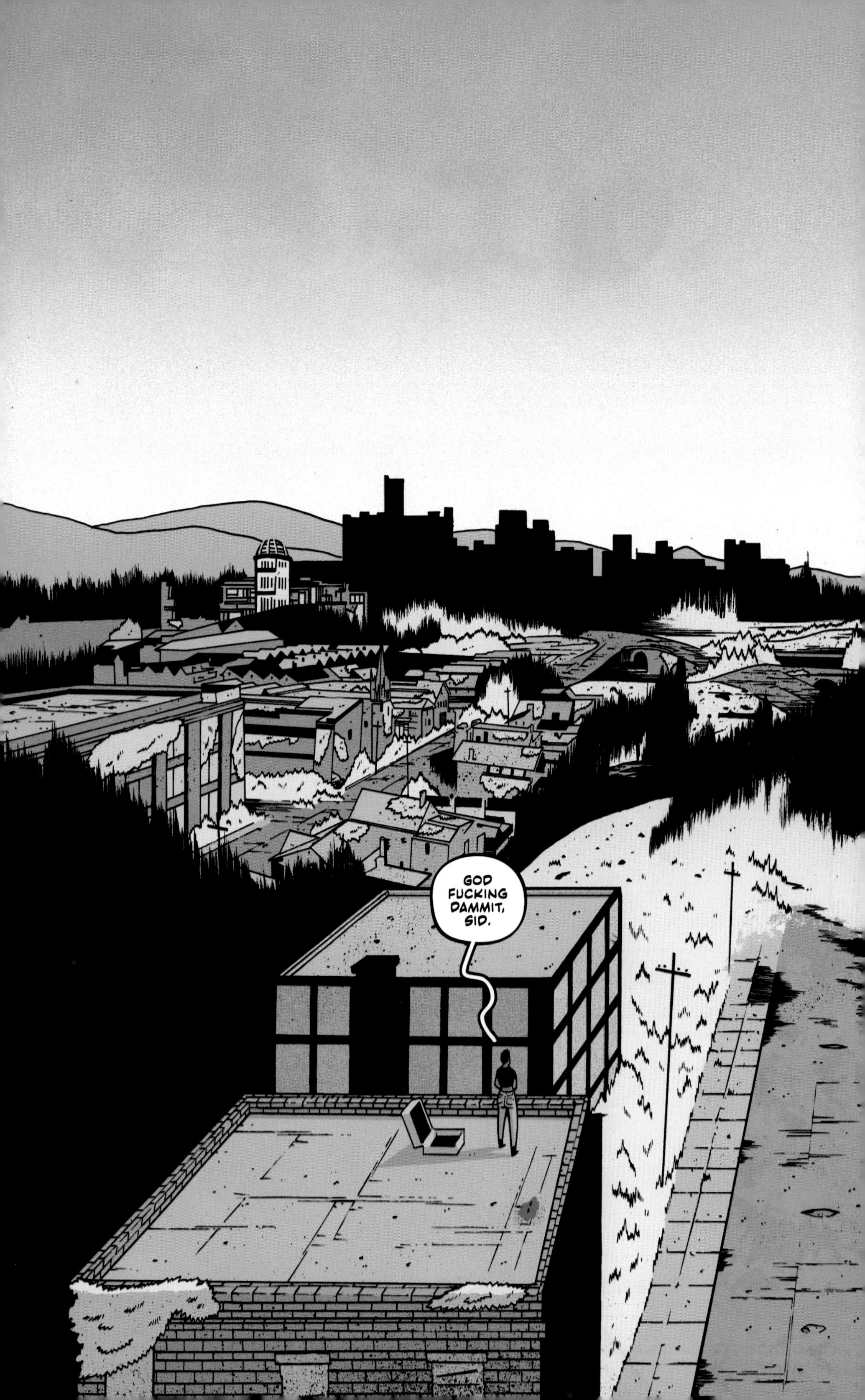
GOD FUCKING DAMMIT, SID.

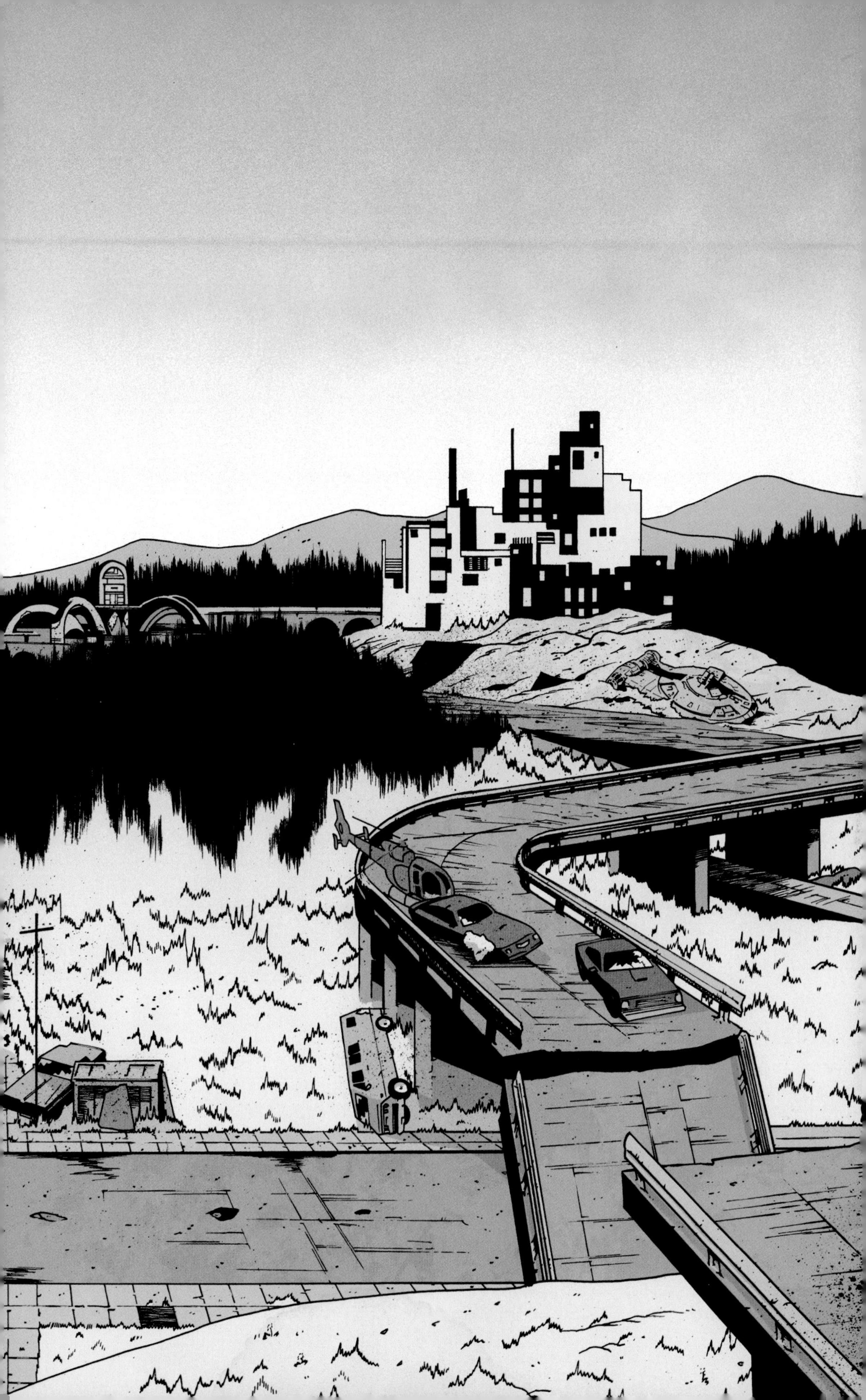

# ACT II

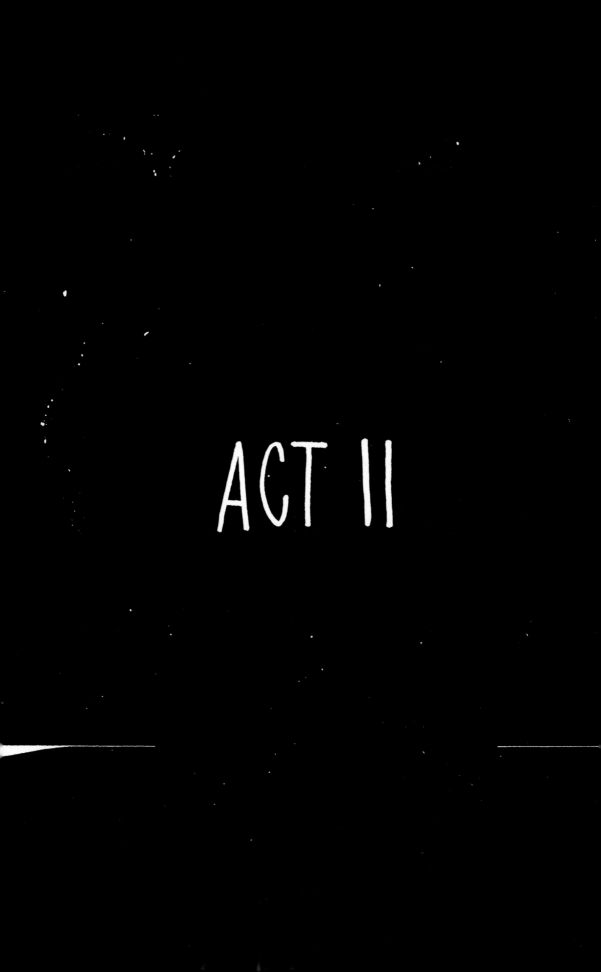

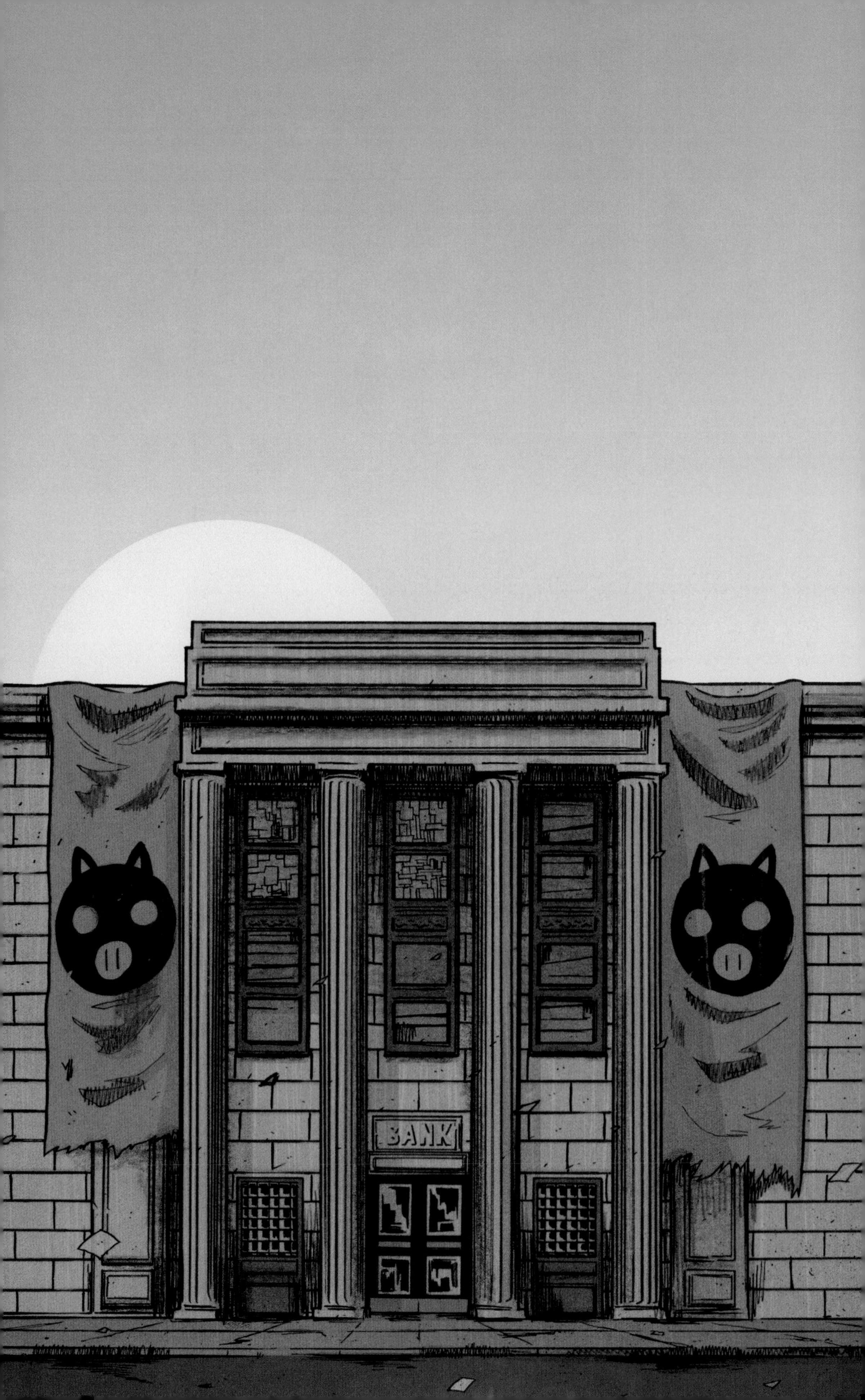
BANK

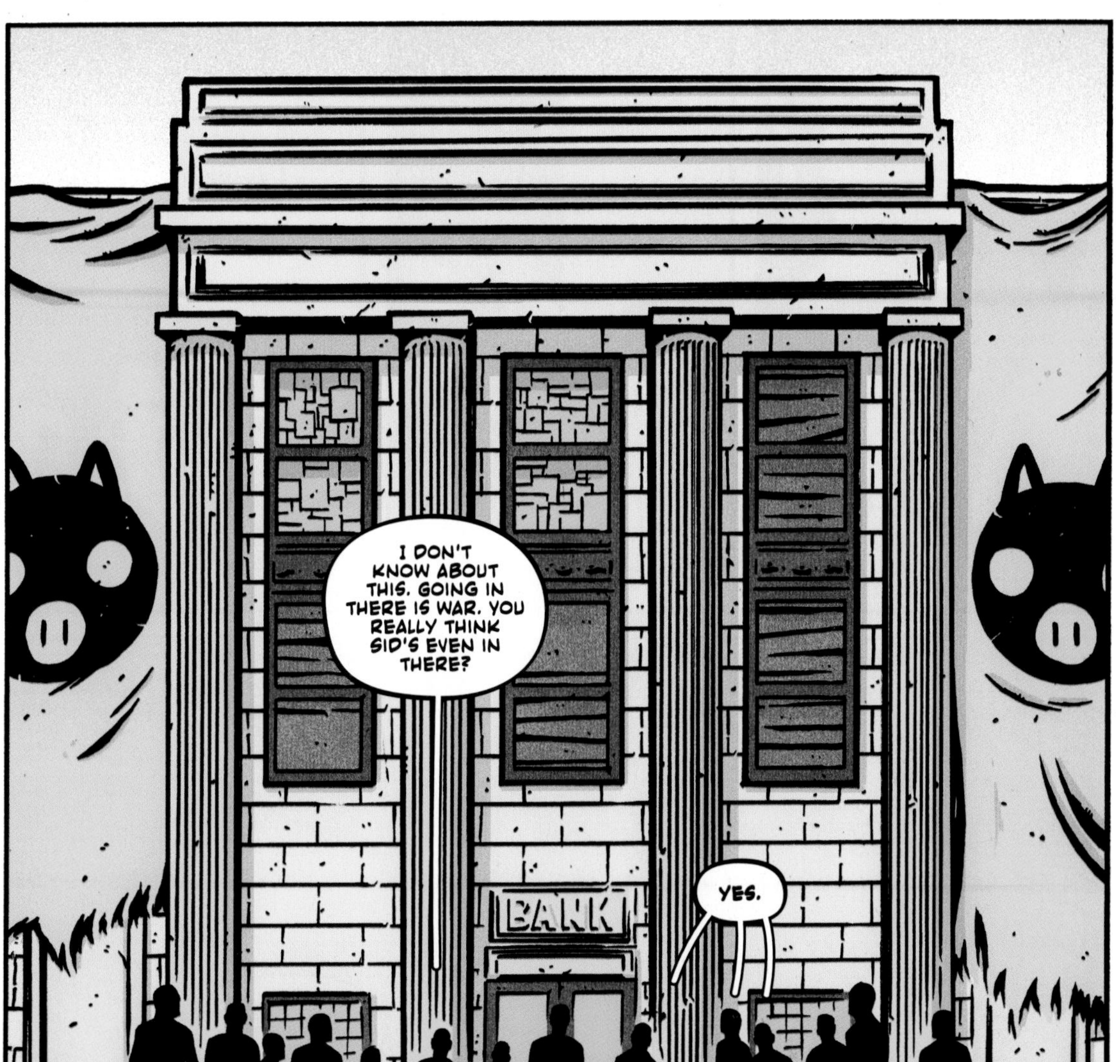
BANK
I DON'T KNOW ABOUT THIS. GOING IN THERE IS WAR. YOU REALLY THINK SID'S EVEN IN THERE?
YES.

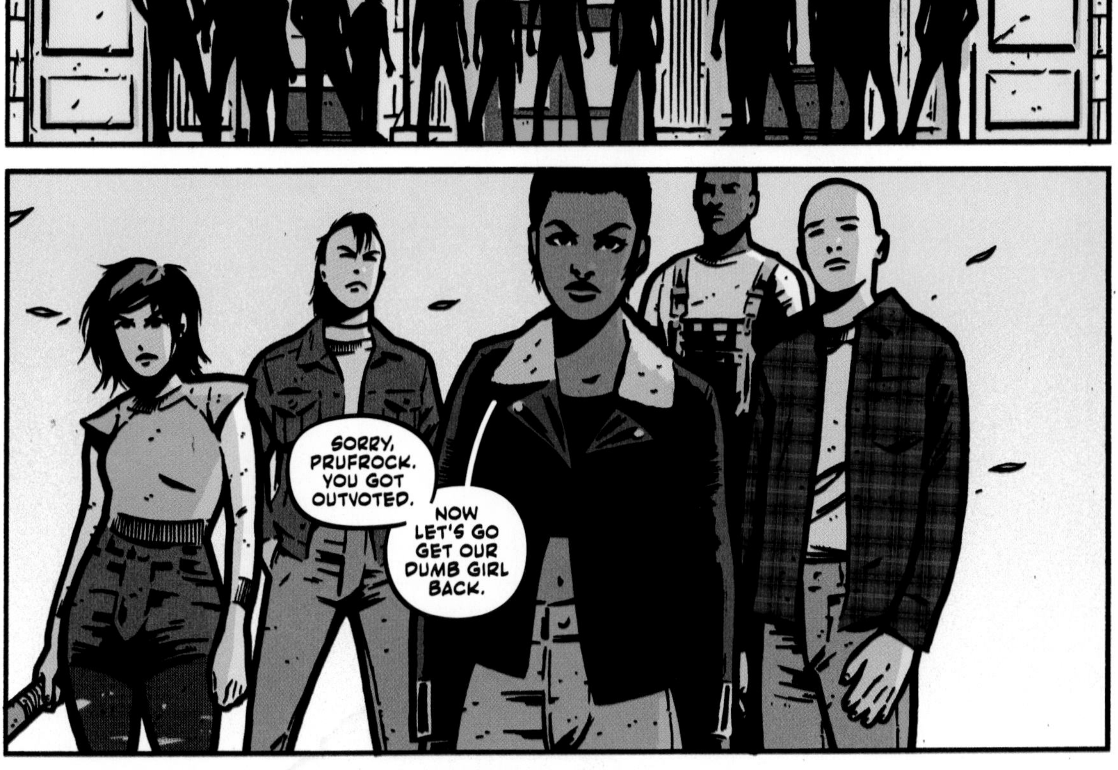
SORRY, PRUFROCK. YOU GOT OUTVOTED.
NOW LET'S GO GET OUR DUMB GIRL BACK.

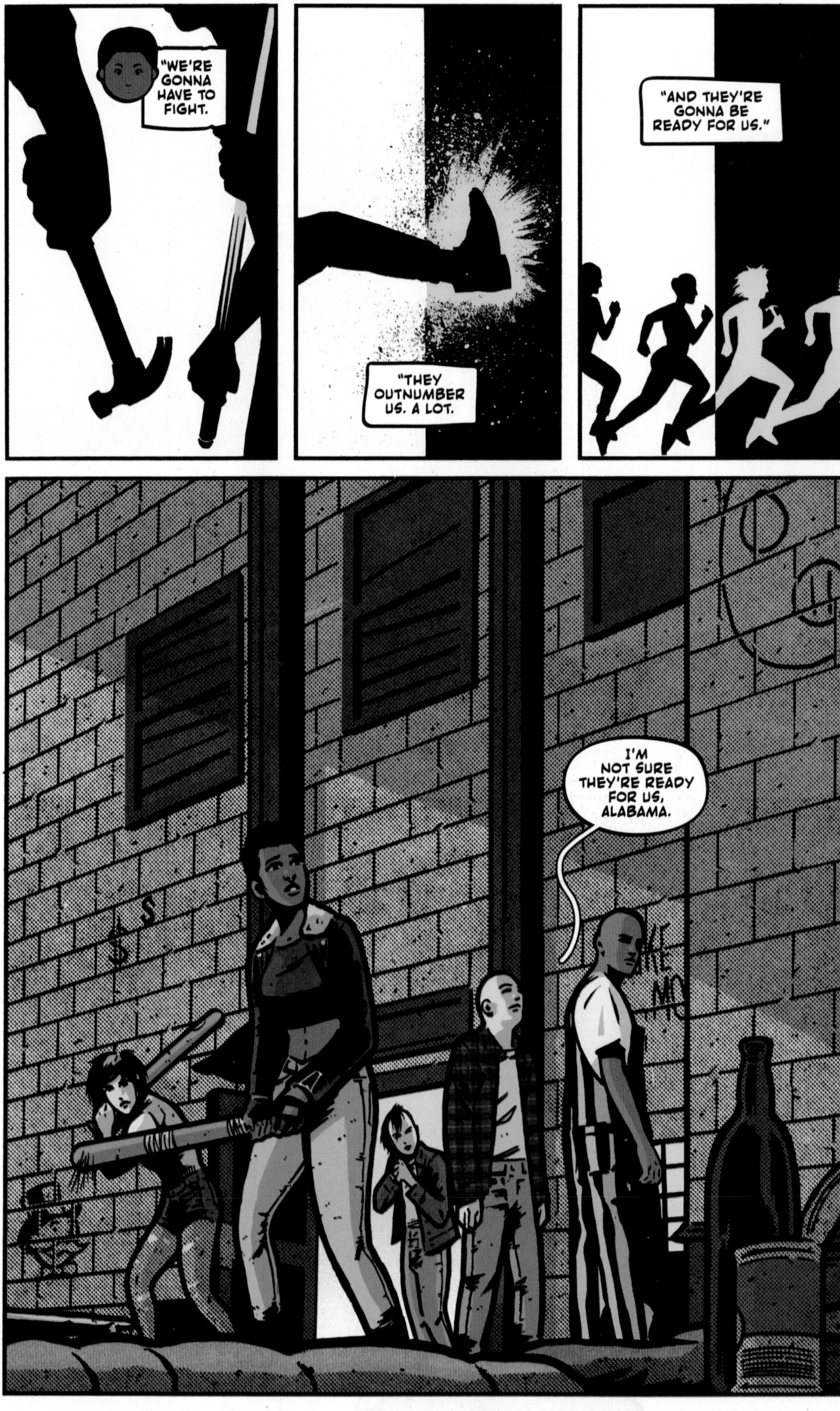
"WE'RE GONNA HAVE TO FIGHT.
"THEY OUTNUMBER US. A LOT.
"AND THEY'RE GONNA BE READY FOR US."
I'M NOT SURE THEY'RE READY FOR US, ALABAMA.

# CHAPTER NINE

## WHERE IS SID?

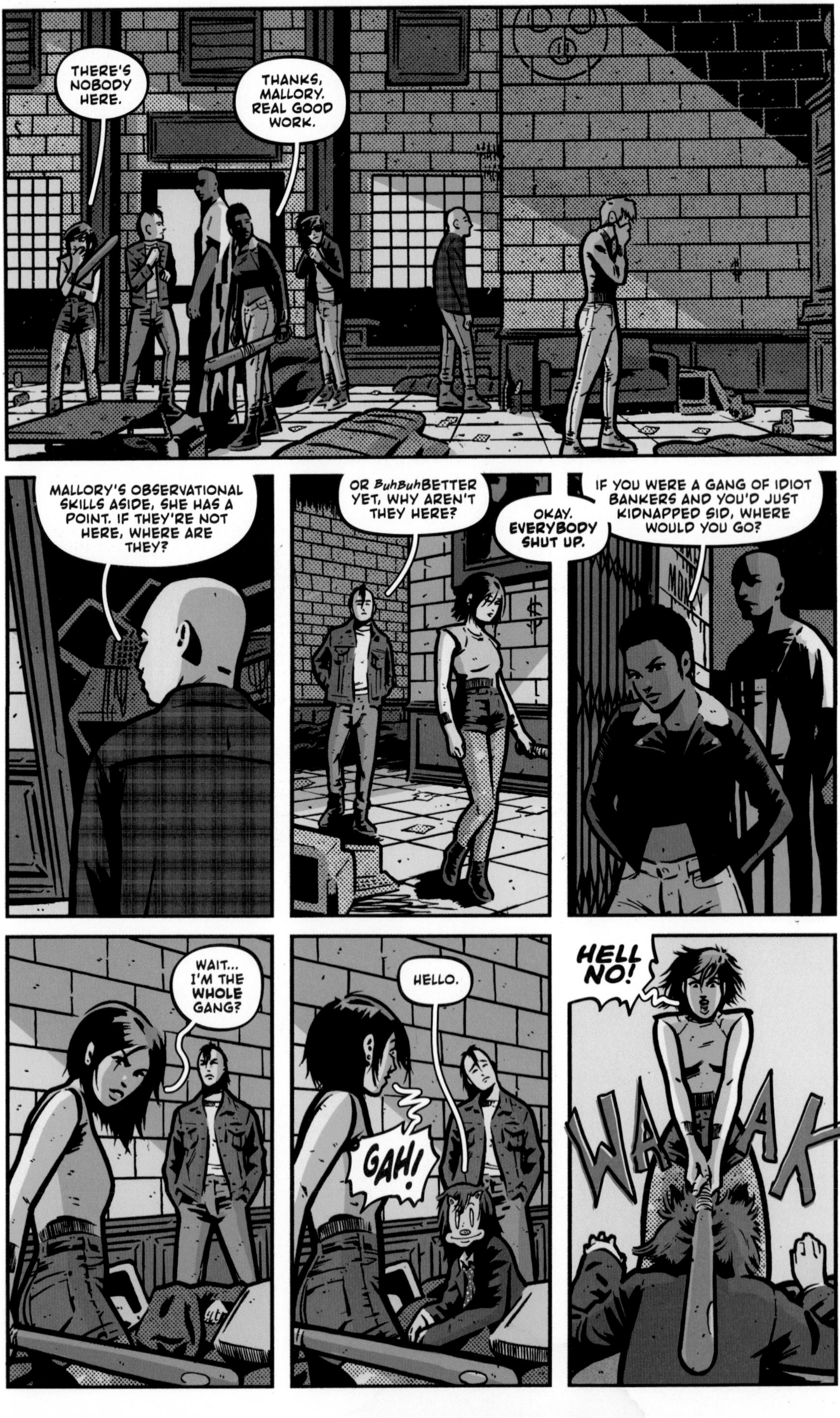
THERE'S NOBODY HERE.
THANKS, MALLORY. REAL GOOD WORK.
MALLORY'S OBSERVATIONAL SKILLS ASIDE, SHE HAS A POINT. IF THEY'RE NOT HERE, WHERE ARE THEY?
OR BuhBuhBETTER YET, WHY AREN'T THEY HERE?
OKAY. EVERYBODY SHUT UP.
IF YOU WERE A GANG OF IDIOT BANKERS AND YOU'D JUST KIDNAPPED SID, WHERE WOULD YOU GO?
WAIT... I'M THE WHOLE GANG?
HELLO.
GAH!
HELL NO!

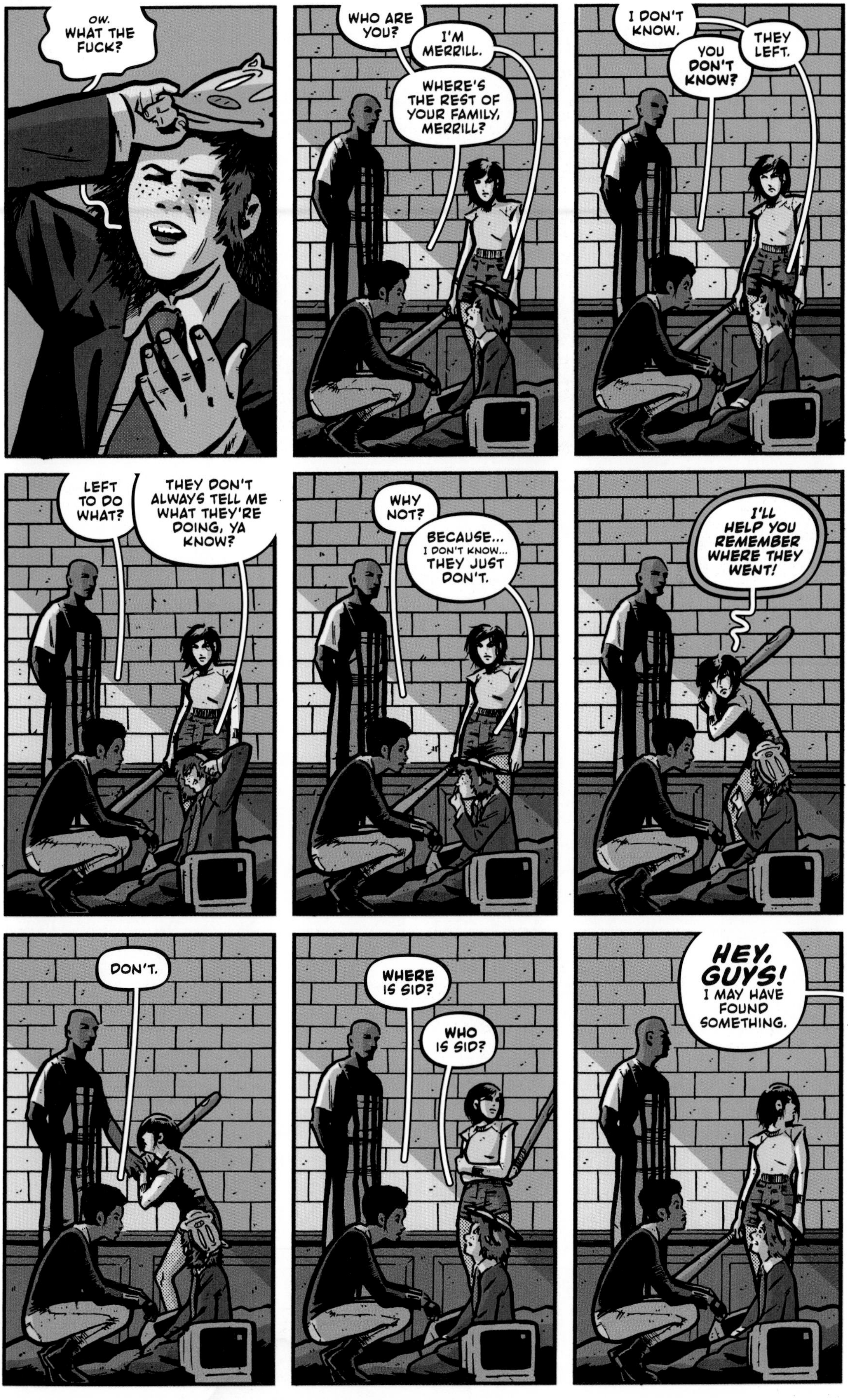
OW. WHAT THE FUCK?
WHO ARE YOU?
I'M MERRILL.
WHERE'S THE REST OF YOUR FAMILY, MERRILL?
I DON'T KNOW.
YOU DON'T KNOW?
THEY LEFT.
LEFT TO DO WHAT?
THEY DON'T ALWAYS TELL ME WHAT THEY'RE DOING, YA KNOW?
WHY NOT?
BECAUSE... I DON'T KNOW... THEY JUST DON'T.
I'LL HELP YOU REMEMBER WHERE THEY WENT!
DON'T.
WHERE IS SID?
WHO IS SID?
HEY, GUYS! I MAY HAVE FOUND SOMETHING.

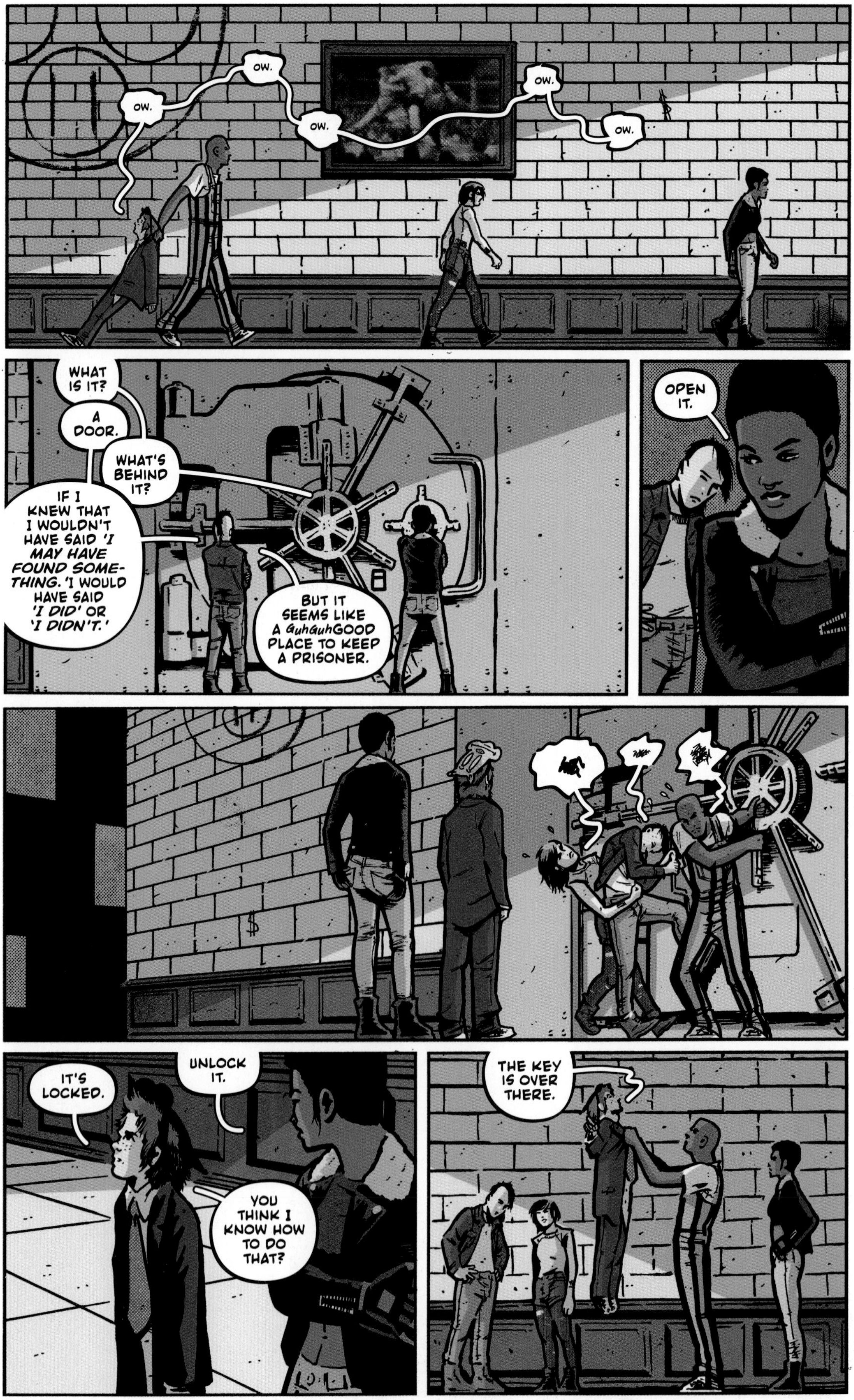
OW.
OW.
OW.
OW.
OW.
WHAT IS IT?
A DOOR.
WHAT'S BEHIND IT?
IF I KNEW THAT I WOULDN'T HAVE SAID *'I MAY HAVE FOUND SOMETHING.'* I WOULD HAVE SAID *'I DID'* OR *'I DIDN'T.'*
BUT IT SEEMS LIKE A GuhGuhGOOD PLACE TO KEEP A PRISONER.
OPEN IT.
IT'S LOCKED.
UNLOCK IT.
YOU THINK I KNOW HOW TO DO THAT?
THE KEY IS OVER THERE.

# CHAPTER TEN

OR?

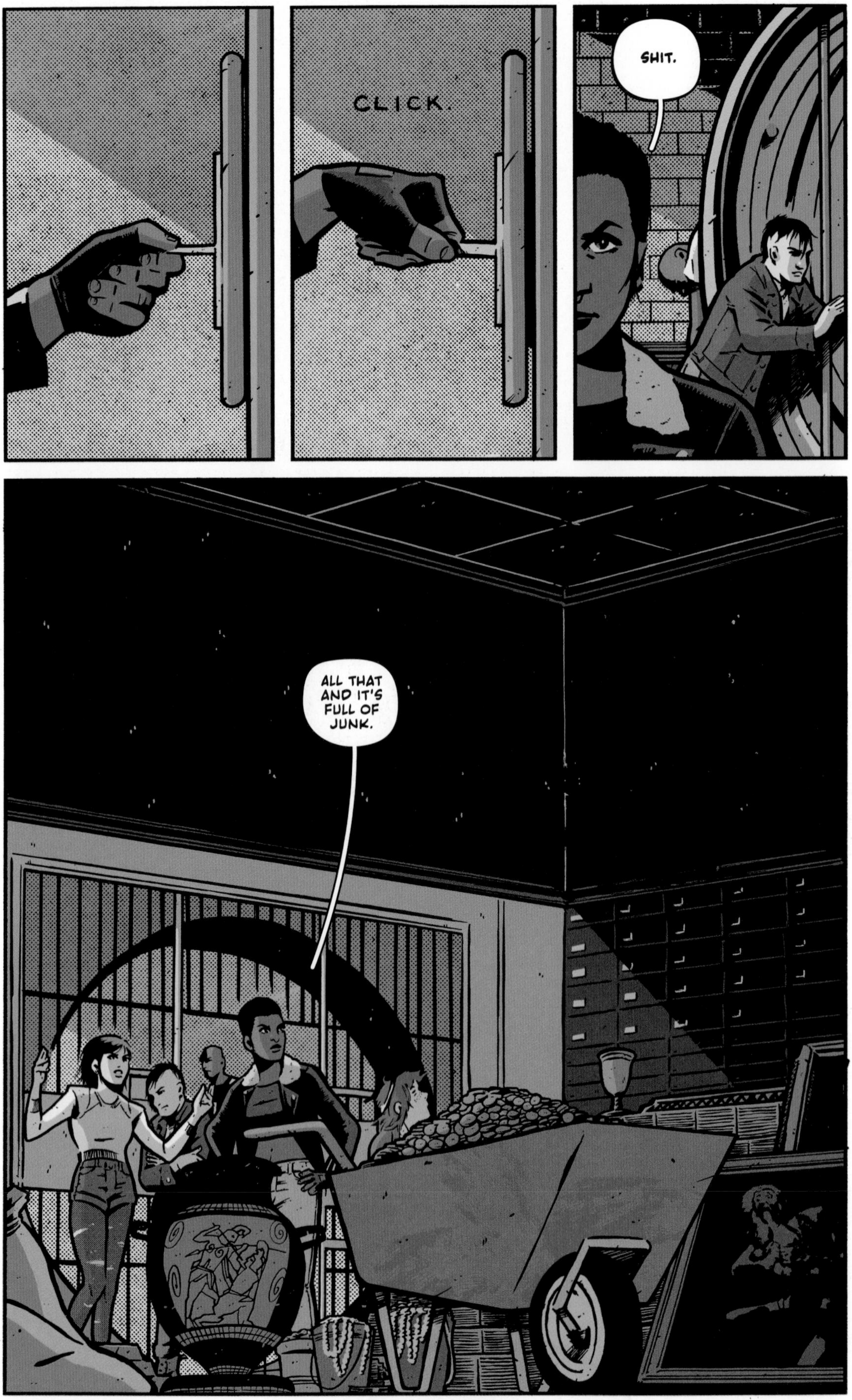
CLICK.
SHIT.
ALL THAT AND IT'S FULL OF JUNK.

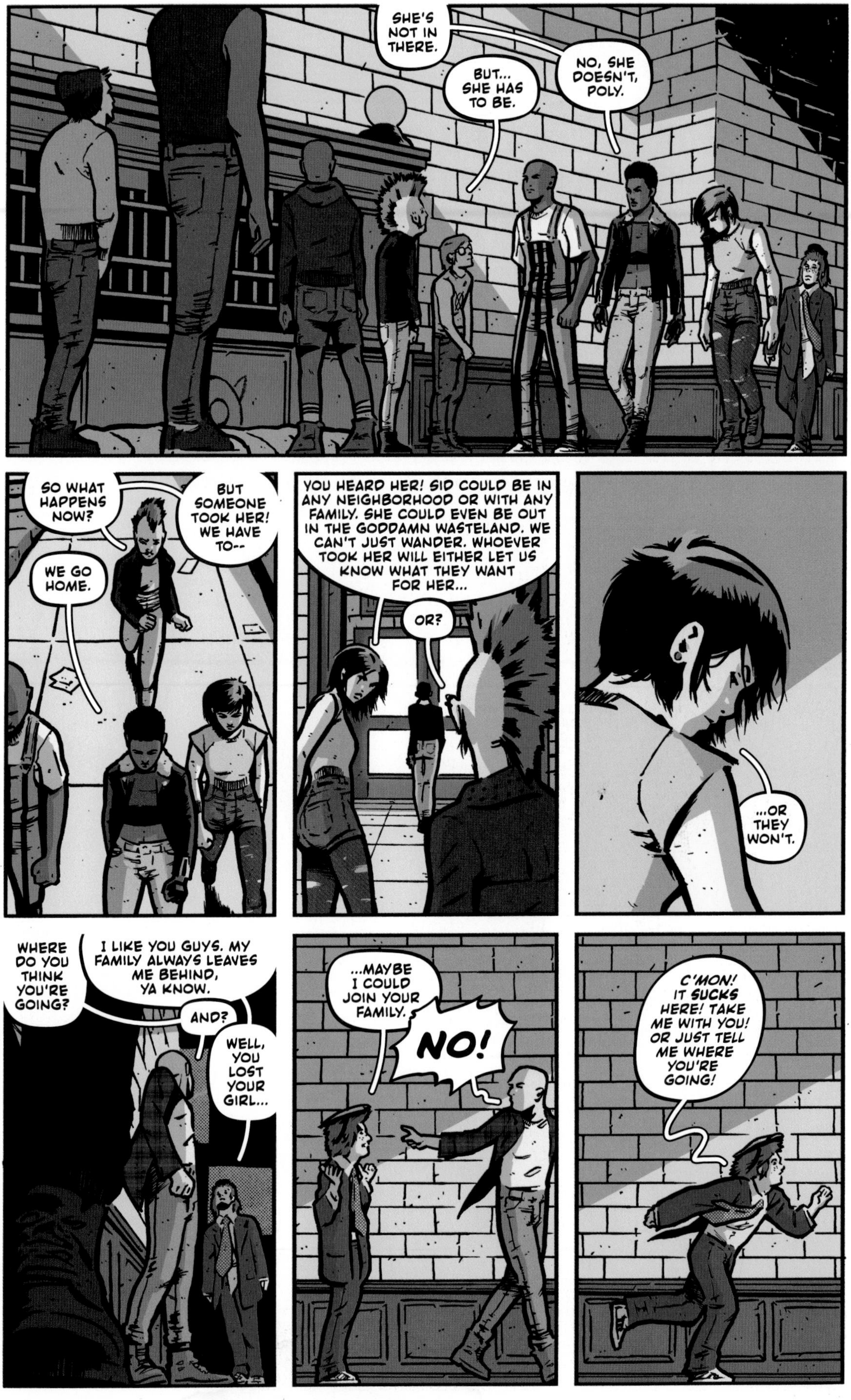
SHE'S NOT IN THERE.
BUT... SHE HAS TO BE.
NO, SHE DOESN'T, POLY.
SO WHAT HAPPENS NOW?
BUT SOMEONE TOOK HER! WE HAVE TO--
WE GO HOME.
YOU HEARD HER! SID COULD BE IN ANY NEIGHBORHOOD OR WITH ANY FAMILY. SHE COULD EVEN BE OUT IN THE GODDAMN WASTELAND. WE CAN'T JUST WANDER. WHOEVER TOOK HER WILL EITHER LET US KNOW WHAT THEY WANT FOR HER...
OR?
...OR THEY WON'T.
WHERE DO YOU THINK YOU'RE GOING?
I LIKE YOU GUYS. MY FAMILY ALWAYS LEAVES ME BEHIND, YA KNOW.
AND?
WELL, YOU LOST YOUR GIRL...
...MAYBE I COULD JOIN YOUR FAMILY.
NO!
C'MON! IT SUCKS HERE! TAKE ME WITH YOU! OR JUST TELL ME WHERE YOU'RE GOING!

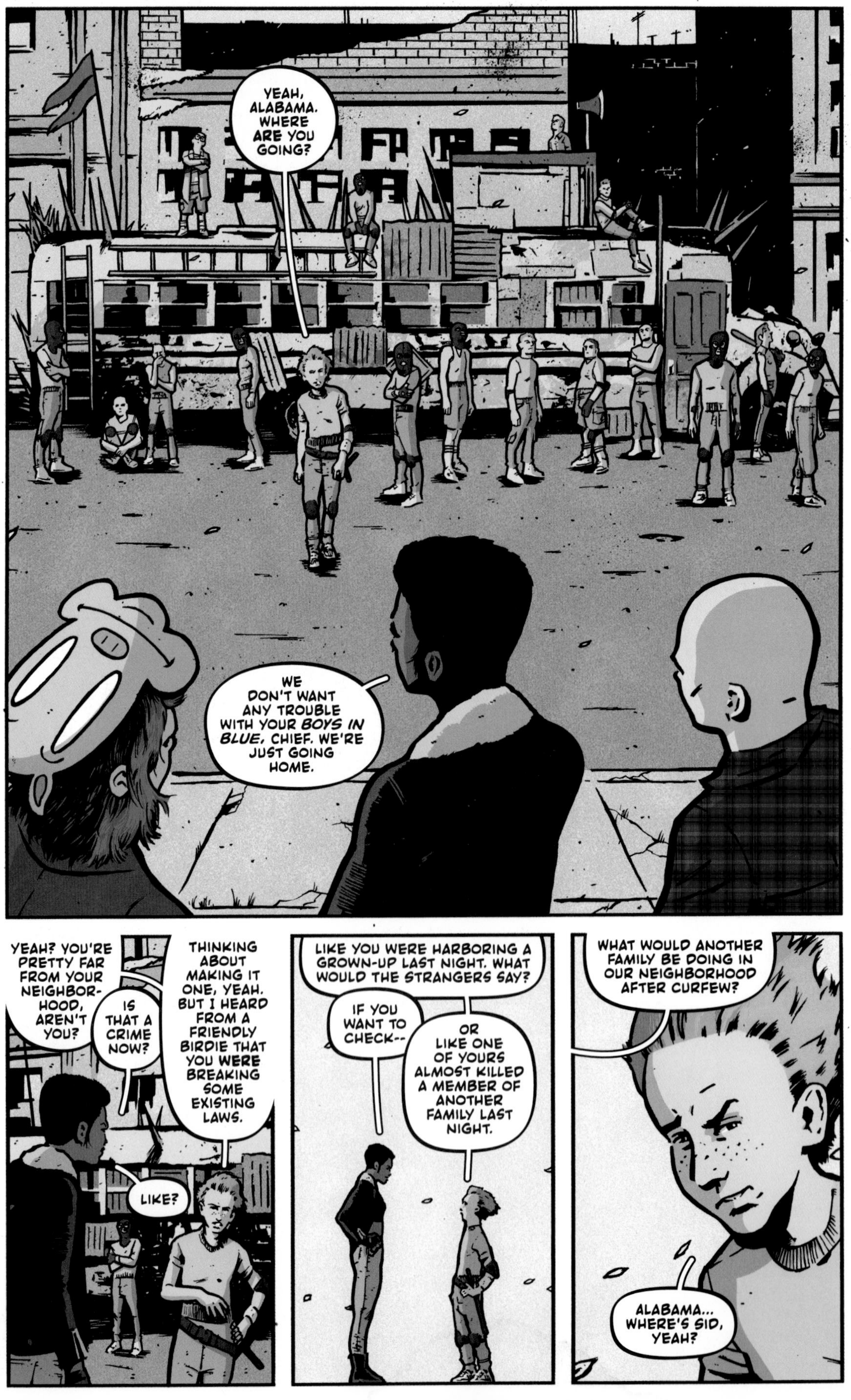
YEAH, ALABAMA. WHERE ARE YOU GOING?
WE DON'T WANT ANY TROUBLE WITH YOUR *BOYS IN BLUE*, CHIEF. WE'RE JUST GOING HOME.
YEAH? YOU'RE PRETTY FAR FROM YOUR NEIGHBOR-HOOD, AREN'T YOU?
IS THAT A CRIME NOW?
THINKING ABOUT MAKING IT ONE, YEAH. BUT I HEARD FROM A FRIENDLY BIRDIE THAT YOU WERE BREAKING SOME EXISTING LAWS.
LIKE?
LIKE YOU WERE HARBORING A GROWN-UP LAST NIGHT. WHAT WOULD THE STRANGERS SAY?
IF YOU WANT TO CHECK--
OR LIKE ONE OF YOURS ALMOST KILLED A MEMBER OF ANOTHER FAMILY LAST NIGHT.
WHAT WOULD ANOTHER FAMILY BE DOING IN OUR NEIGHBORHOOD AFTER CURFEW?
ALABAMA... WHERE'S SID, YEAH?

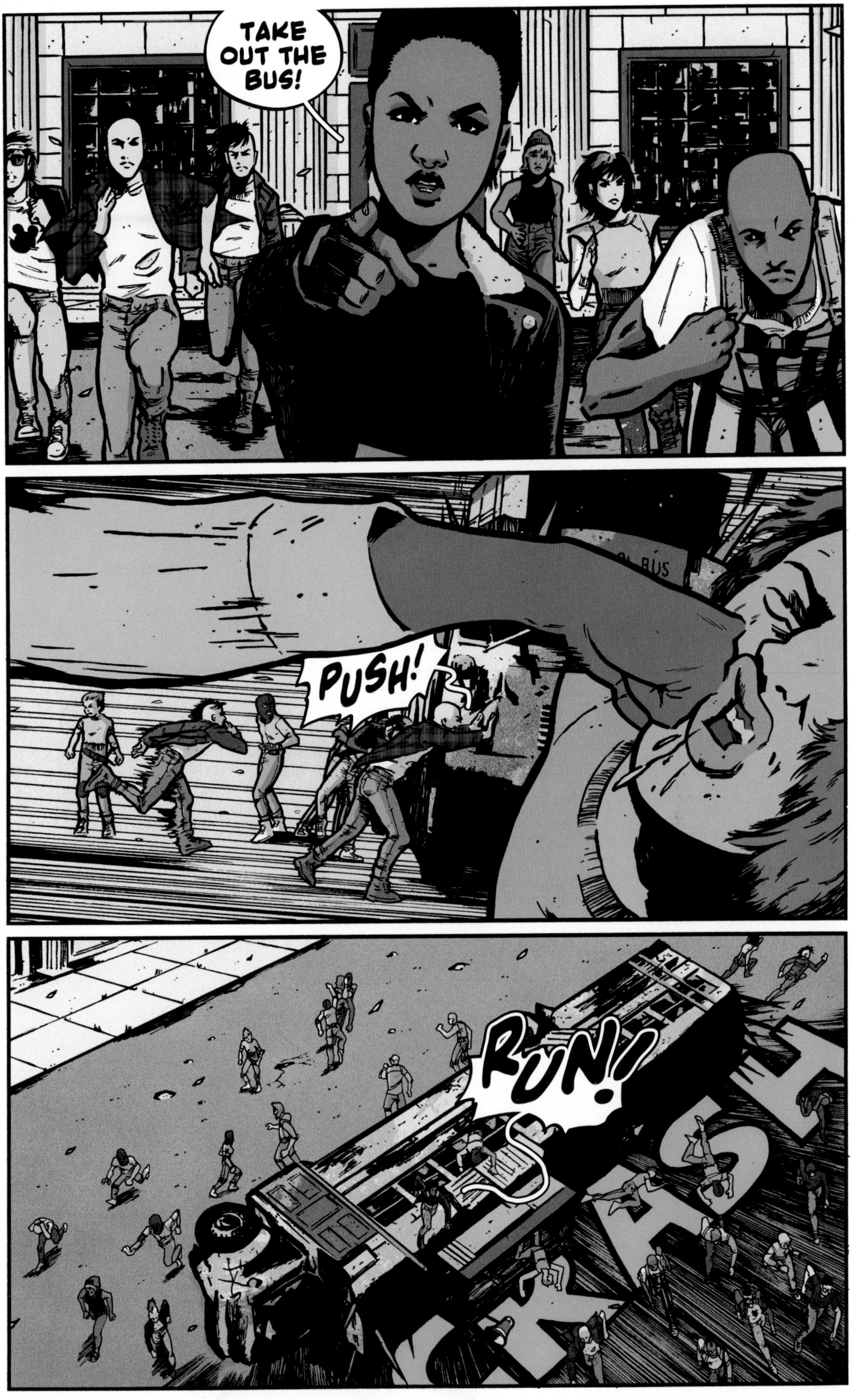
TAKE OUT THE BUS!
PUSH!
RUN!

# CHAPTER ELEVEN

WE'RE ALMOST HOME, PRUFROCK.

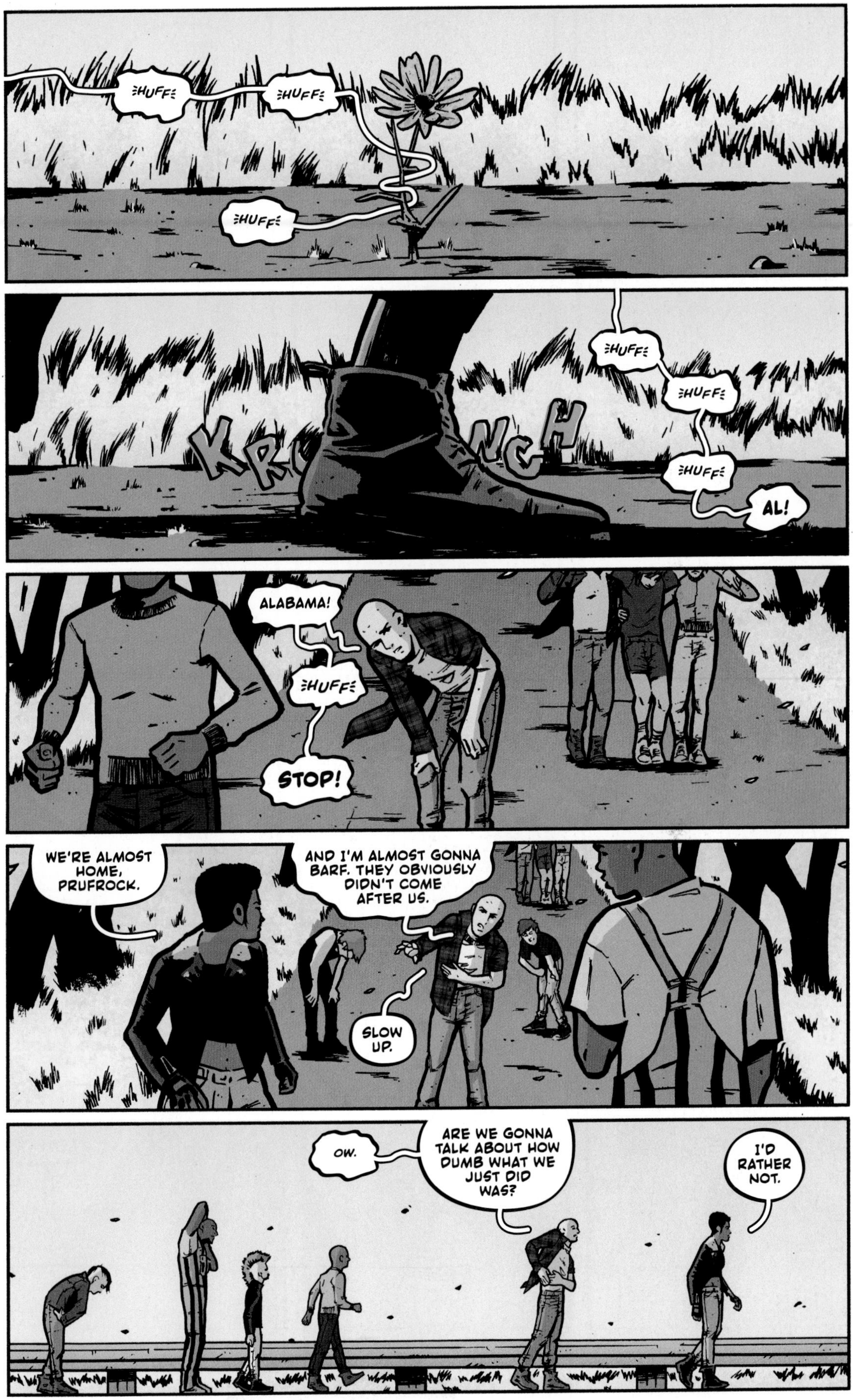
HUFF
HUFF
HUFF
KRUNCH
HUFF
HUFF
HUFF
AL!
ALABAMA!
HUFF
STOP!
WE'RE ALMOST HOME, PRUFROCK.
AND I'M ALMOST GONNA BARF. THEY OBVIOUSLY DIDN'T COME AFTER US.
SLOW UP.
OW.
ARE WE GONNA TALK ABOUT HOW DUMB WHAT WE JUST DID WAS?
I'D RATHER NOT.

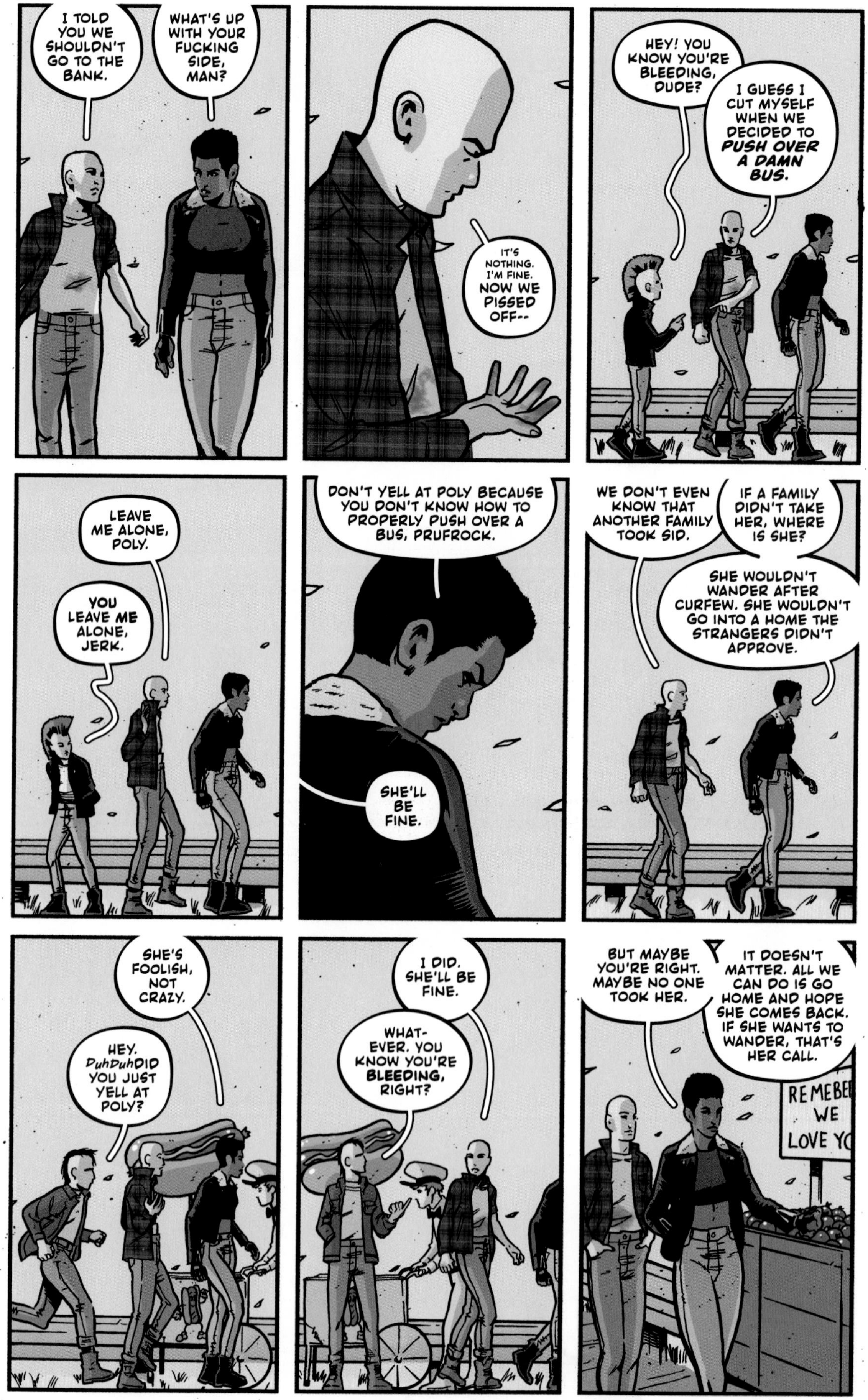
I TOLD YOU WE SHOULDN'T GO TO THE BANK.
WHAT'S UP WITH YOUR FUCKING SIDE, MAN?
IT'S NOTHING. I'M FINE. NOW WE PISSED OFF--
HEY! YOU KNOW YOU'RE BLEEDING, DUDE?
I GUESS I CUT MYSELF WHEN WE DECIDED TO PUSH OVER A DAMN BUS.
LEAVE ME ALONE, POLY.
YOU LEAVE ME ALONE, JERK.
DON'T YELL AT POLY BECAUSE YOU DON'T KNOW HOW TO PROPERLY PUSH OVER A BUS, PRUFROCK.
SHE'LL BE FINE.
WE DON'T EVEN KNOW THAT ANOTHER FAMILY TOOK SID.
IF A FAMILY DIDN'T TAKE HER, WHERE IS SHE?
SHE WOULDN'T WANDER AFTER CURFEW. SHE WOULDN'T GO INTO A HOME THE STRANGERS DIDN'T APPROVE.
SHE'S FOOLISH, NOT CRAZY.
HEY. DuhDuhDID YOU JUST YELL AT POLY?
I DID. SHE'LL BE FINE.
WHAT-EVER. YOU KNOW YOU'RE BLEEDING, RIGHT?
BUT MAYBE YOU'RE RIGHT. MAYBE NO ONE TOOK HER.
IT DOESN'T MATTER. ALL WE CAN DO IS GO HOME AND HOPE SHE COMES BACK. IF SHE WANTS TO WANDER, THAT'S HER CALL.
REMEBE
WE
LOVE YO

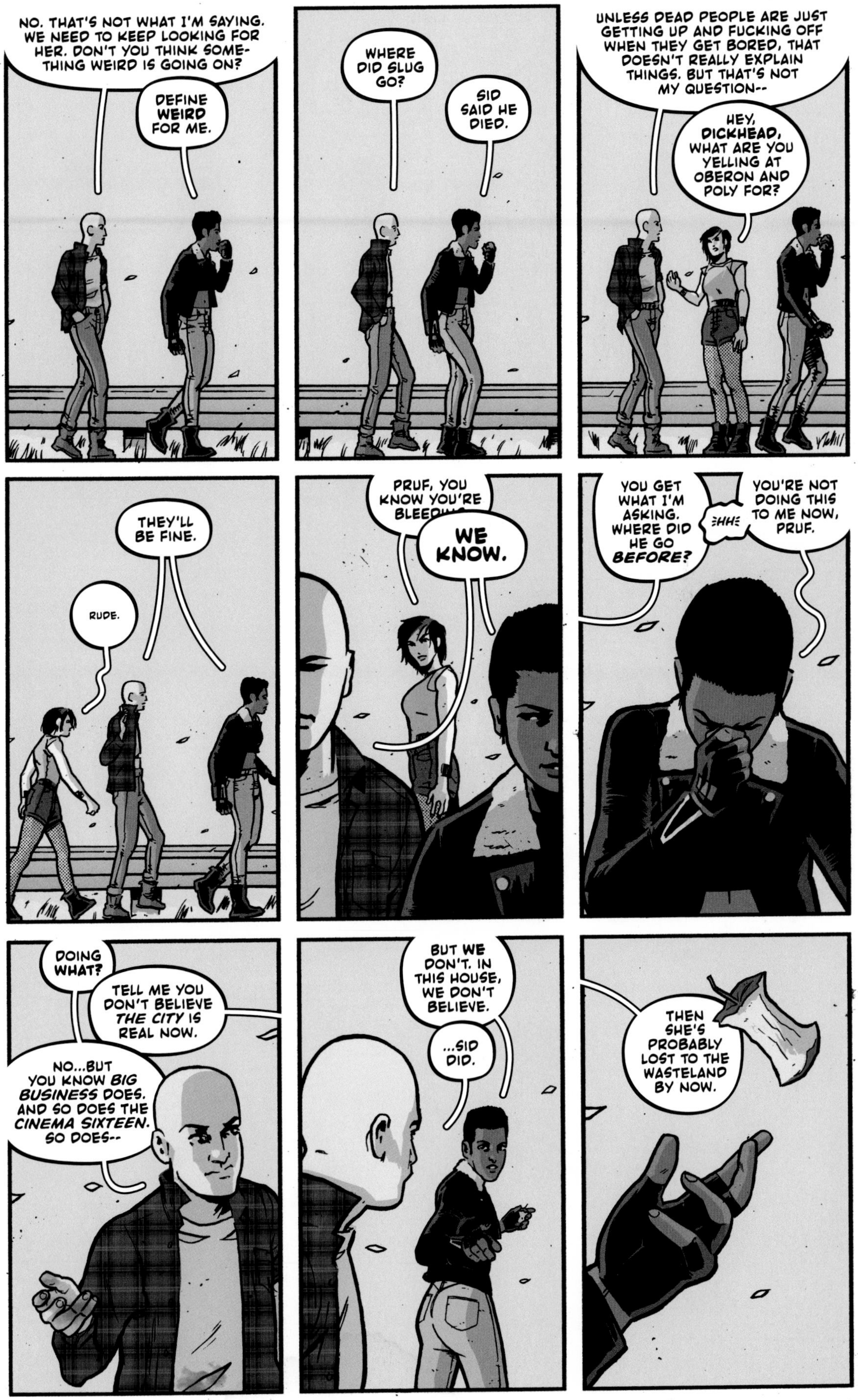

NO. THAT'S NOT WHAT I'M SAYING. WE NEED TO KEEP LOOKING FOR HER. DON'T YOU THINK SOME-THING WEIRD IS GOING ON?
DEFINE WEIRD FOR ME.
WHERE DID SLUG GO?
SID SAID HE DIED.
UNLESS DEAD PEOPLE ARE JUST GETTING UP AND FUCKING OFF WHEN THEY GET BORED, THAT DOESN'T REALLY EXPLAIN THINGS. BUT THAT'S NOT MY QUESTION--
HEY, DICKHEAD, WHAT ARE YOU YELLING AT OBERON AND POLY FOR?
THEY'LL BE FINE.
RUDE.
PRUF, YOU KNOW YOU'RE
WE KNOW.
YOU GET WHAT I'M ASKING. WHERE DID HE GO BEFORE?
YOU'RE NOT DOING THIS TO ME NOW, PRUF.
DOING WHAT?
TELL ME YOU DON'T BELIEVE THE CITY IS REAL NOW.
NO...BUT YOU KNOW BIG BUSINESS DOES. AND SO DOES THE CINEMA SIXTEEN. SO DOES--
BUT WE DON'T. IN THIS HOUSE, WE DON'T BELIEVE.
...SID DID.
THEN SHE'S PROBABLY LOST TO THE WASTELAND BY NOW.

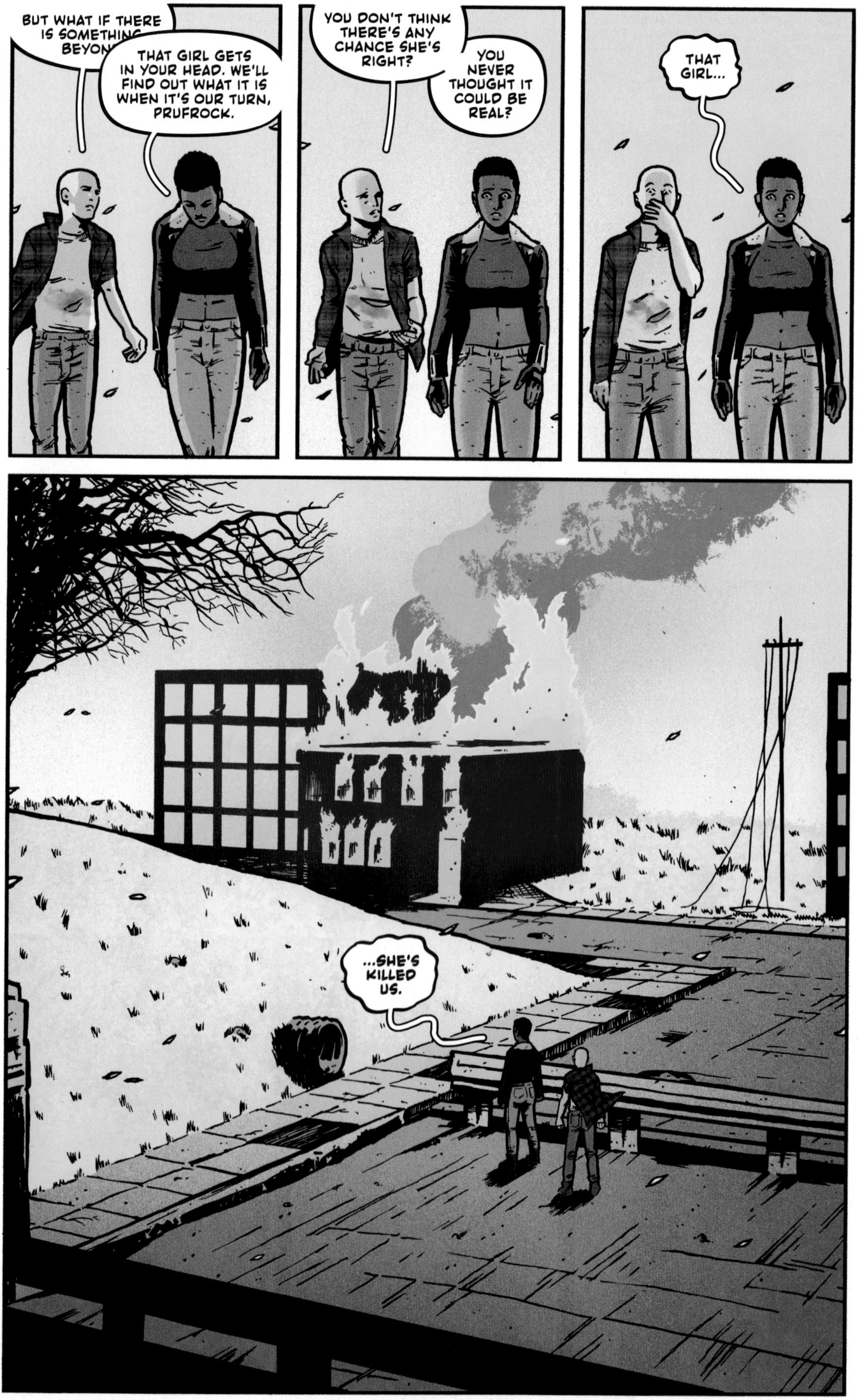
BUT WHAT IF THERE IS SOMETHING BEYON
THAT GIRL GETS IN YOUR HEAD. WE'LL FIND OUT WHAT IT IS WHEN IT'S OUR TURN, PRUFROCK.
YOU DON'T THINK THERE'S ANY CHANCE SHE'S RIGHT?
YOU NEVER THOUGHT IT COULD BE REAL?
THAT GIRL...
...SHE'S KILLED US.

# CHAPTER TWELVE

I MIGHT KNOW A PLACE.

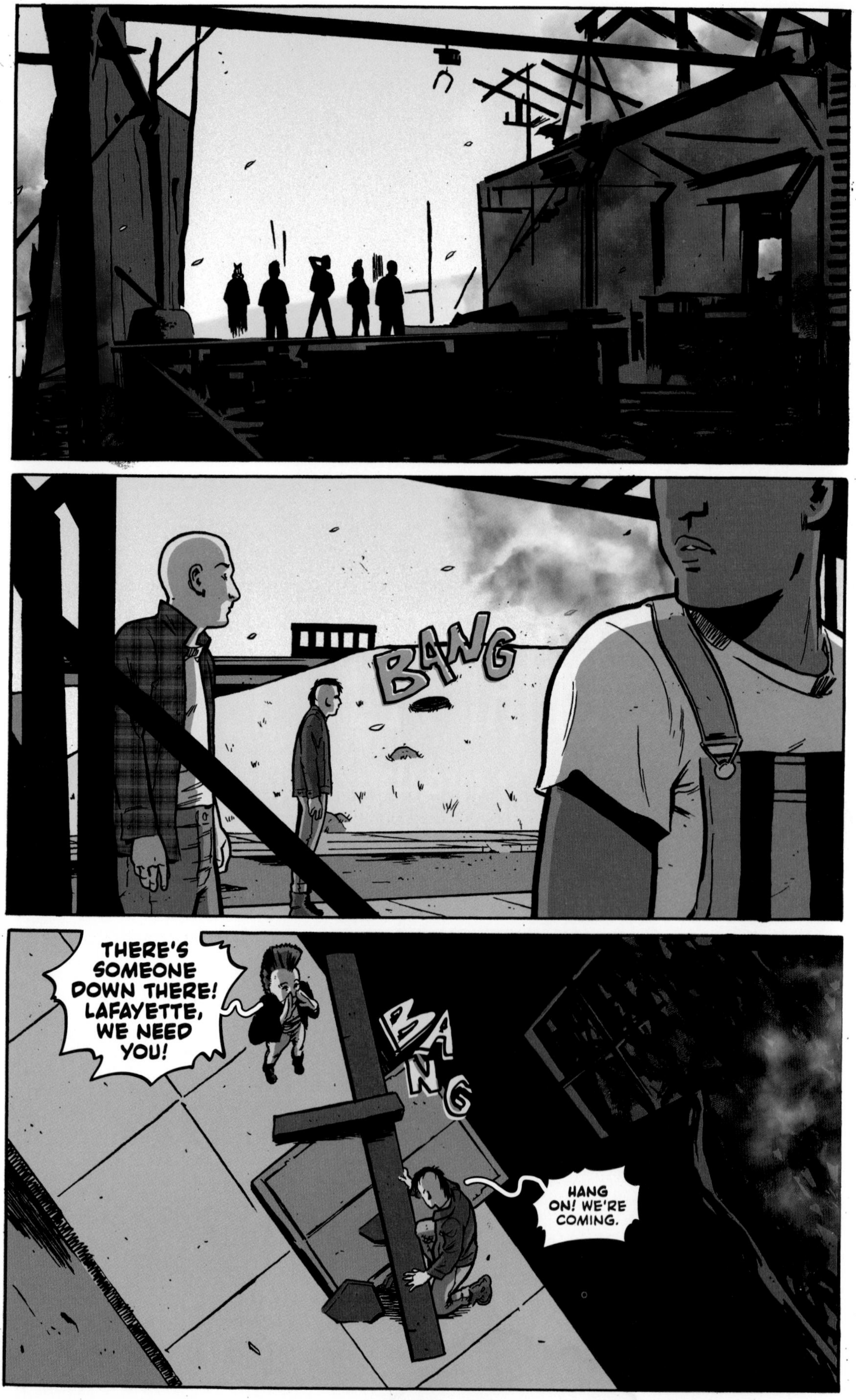
BANG
THERE'S SOMEONE DOWN THERE! LAFAYETTE, WE NEED YOU!
BANG
HANG ON! WE'RE COMING.

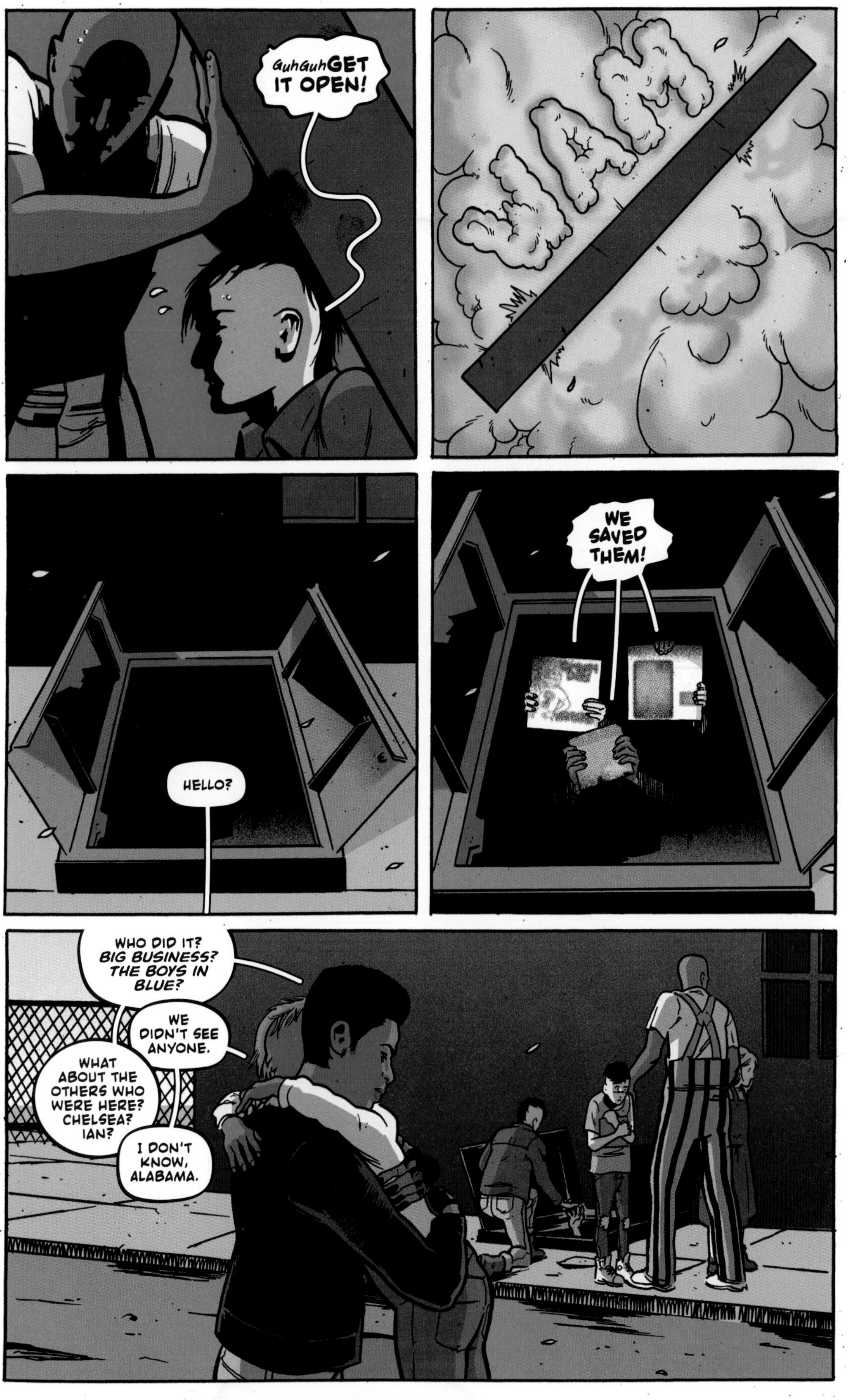
GuhGuhGET IT OPEN!
WAM
HELLO?
WE SAVED THEM!
WHO DID IT? BIG BUSINESS? THE BOYS IN BLUE?
WE DIDN'T SEE ANYONE.
WHAT ABOUT THE OTHERS WHO WERE HERE? CHELSEA? IAN?
I DON'T KNOW, ALABAMA.

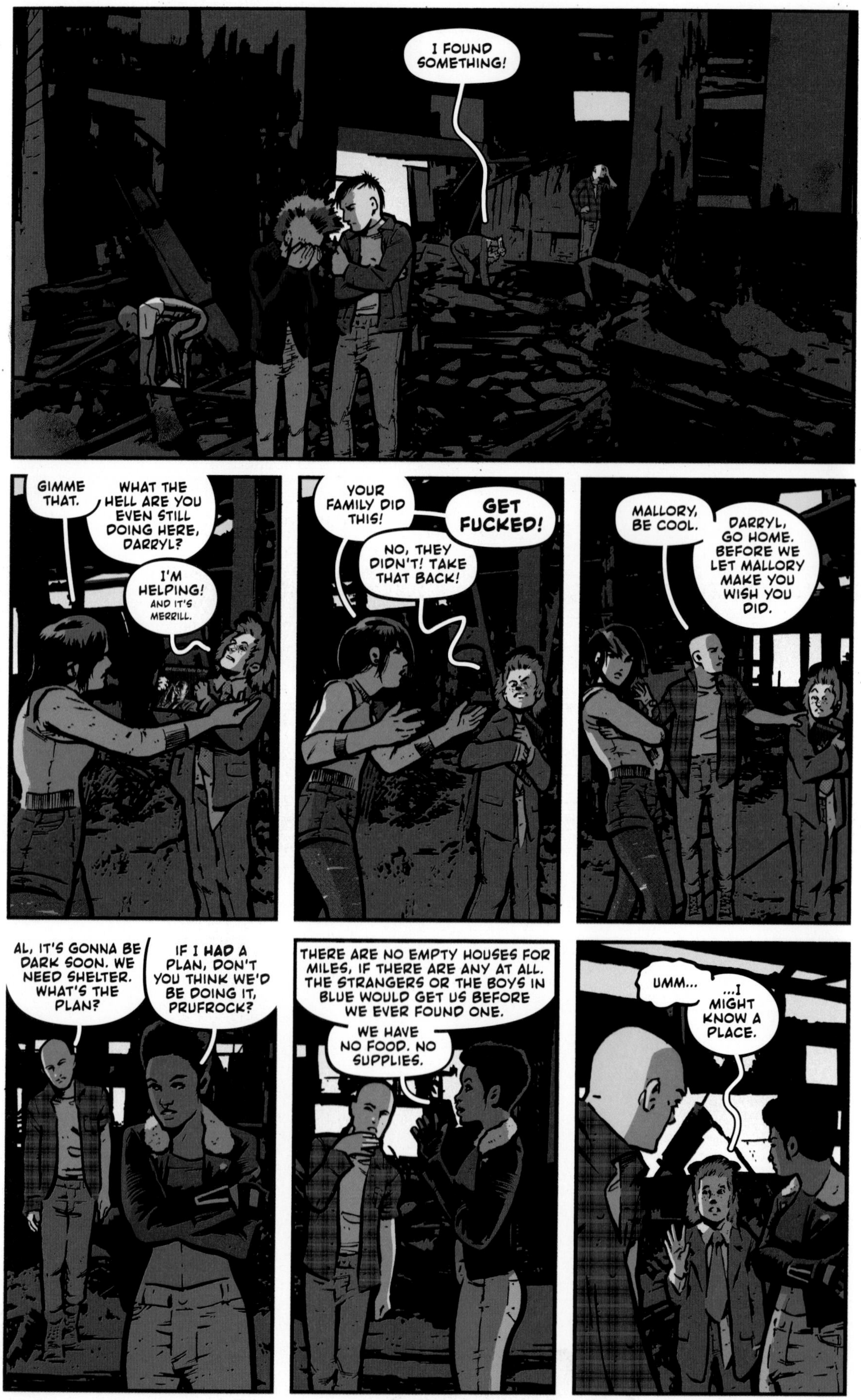
I FOUND SOMETHING!
GIMME THAT.
WHAT THE HELL ARE YOU EVEN STILL DOING HERE, DARRYL?
I'M HELPING! AND IT'S MERRILL.
YOUR FAMILY DID THIS!
GET FUCKED!
NO, THEY DIDN'T! TAKE THAT BACK!
MALLORY, BE COOL.
DARRYL, GO HOME. BEFORE WE LET MALLORY MAKE YOU WISH YOU DID.
AL, IT'S GONNA BE DARK SOON. WE NEED SHELTER. WHAT'S THE PLAN?
IF I HAD A PLAN, DON'T YOU THINK WE'D BE DOING IT, PRUFROCK?
THERE ARE NO EMPTY HOUSES FOR MILES, IF THERE ARE ANY AT ALL. THE STRANGERS OR THE BOYS IN BLUE WOULD GET US BEFORE WE EVER FOUND ONE.
WE HAVE NO FOOD. NO SUPPLIES.
UMM...
...I MIGHT KNOW A PLACE.

# CHAPTER THIRTEEN

## YEAH. DEFINITELY. TOTALLY.

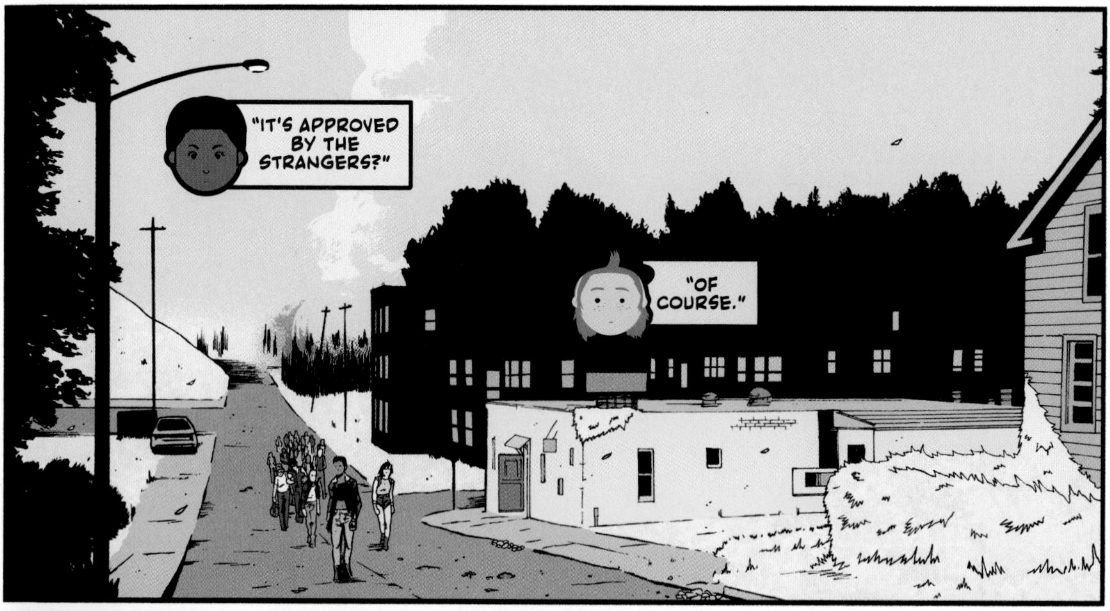
"IT'S APPROVED BY THE STRANGERS?"
"OF COURSE."

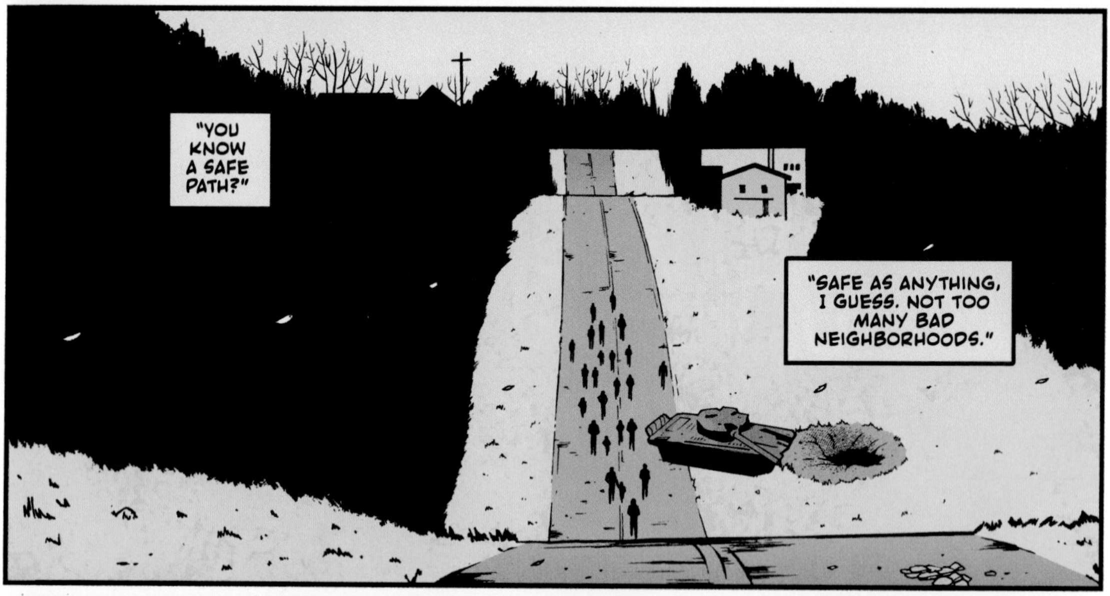
"YOU KNOW A SAFE PATH?"
"SAFE AS ANYTHING, I GUESS. NOT TOO MANY BAD NEIGHBORHOODS."

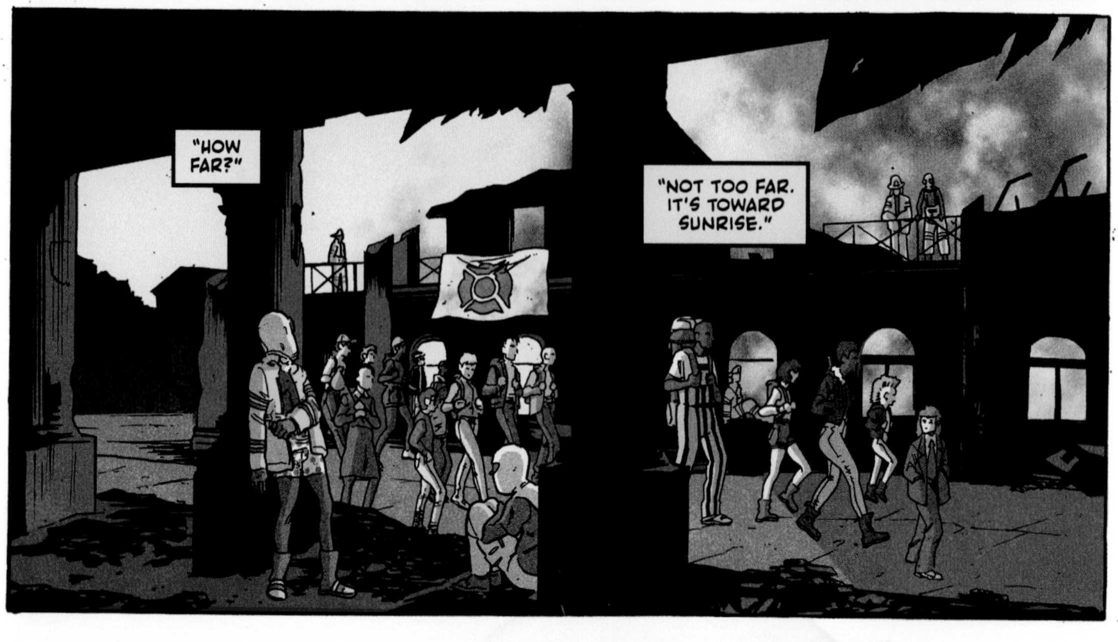
"HOW FAR?"
"NOT TOO FAR. IT'S TOWARD SUNRISE."

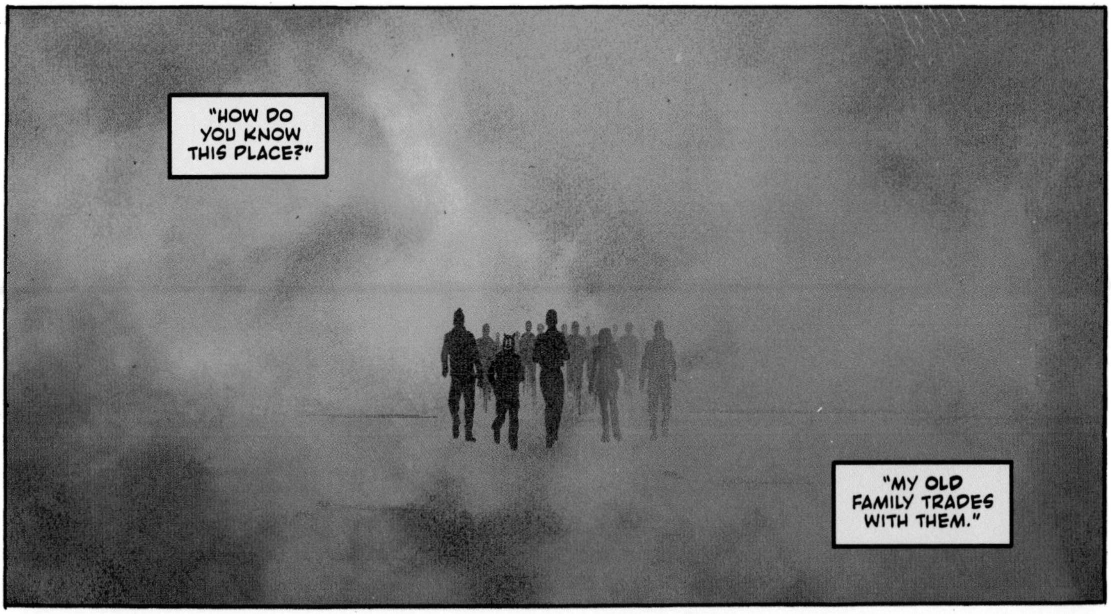
"HOW DO YOU KNOW THIS PLACE?"
"MY OLD FAMILY TRADES WITH THEM."

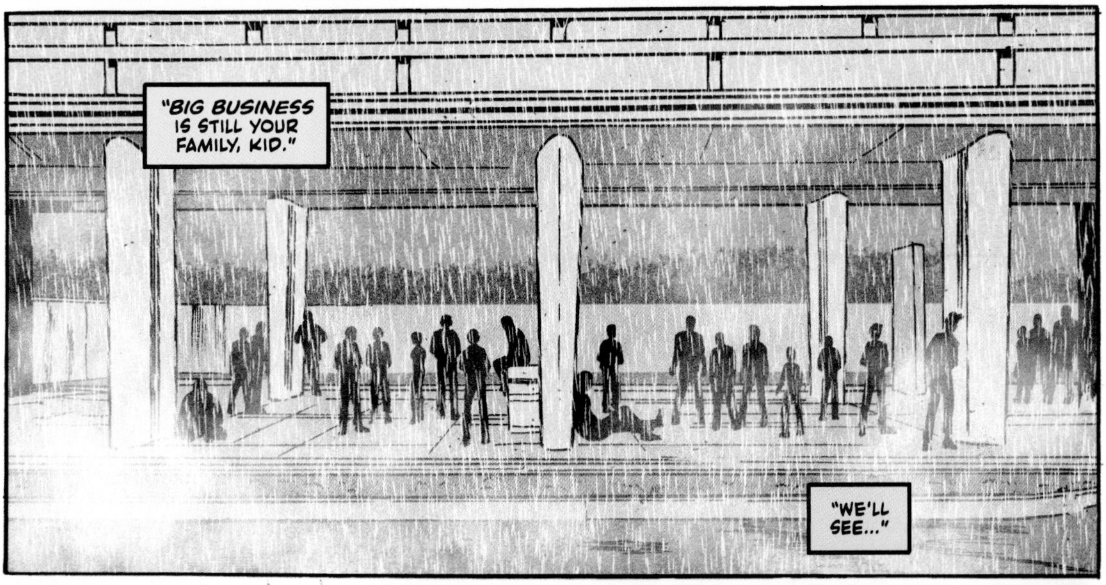
"BIG BUSINESS IS STILL YOUR FAMILY, KID."
"WE'LL SEE..."

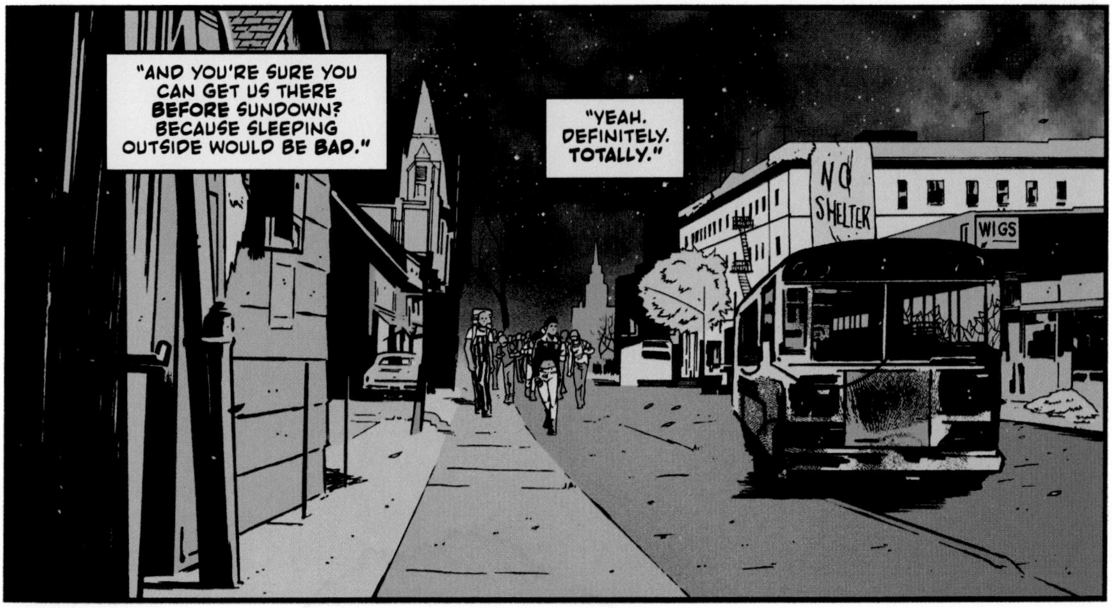
"AND YOU'RE SURE YOU CAN GET US THERE BEFORE SUNDOWN? BECAUSE SLEEPING OUTSIDE WOULD BE BAD."
"YEAH. DEFINITELY. TOTALLY."
NO SHELTER
WIGS

# CHAPTER FOURTEEN

ALL THE THINGS WE HAVE WILL
BE BURIED IN THE GROUND.

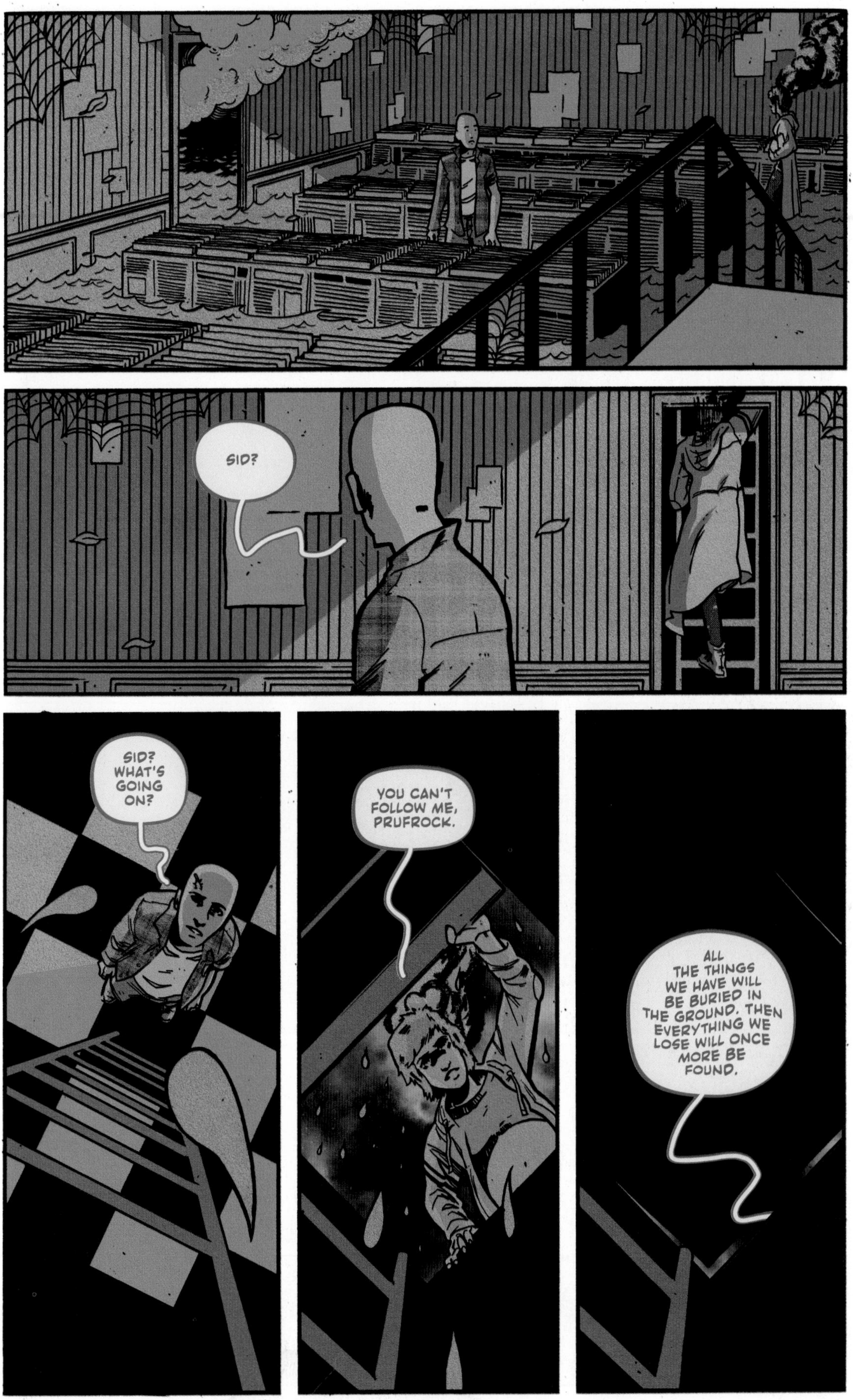
SID?
SID? WHAT'S GOING ON?
YOU CAN'T FOLLOW ME, PRUFROCK.
ALL THE THINGS WE HAVE WILL BE BURIED IN THE GROUND. THEN EVERYTHING WE LOSE WILL ONCE MORE BE FOUND.

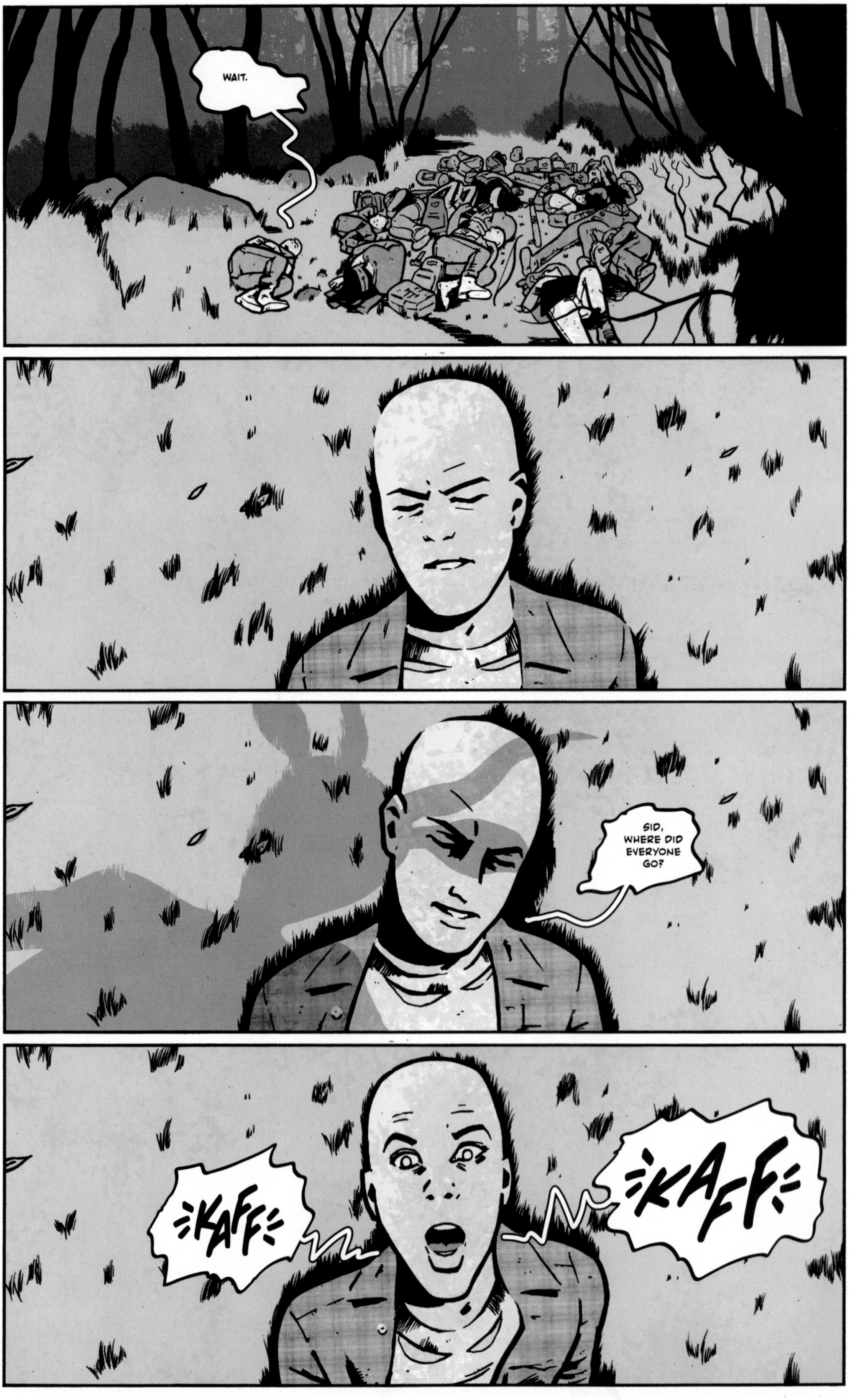
WAIT.
SID, WHERE DID EVERYONE GO?
KAFF
KAFF

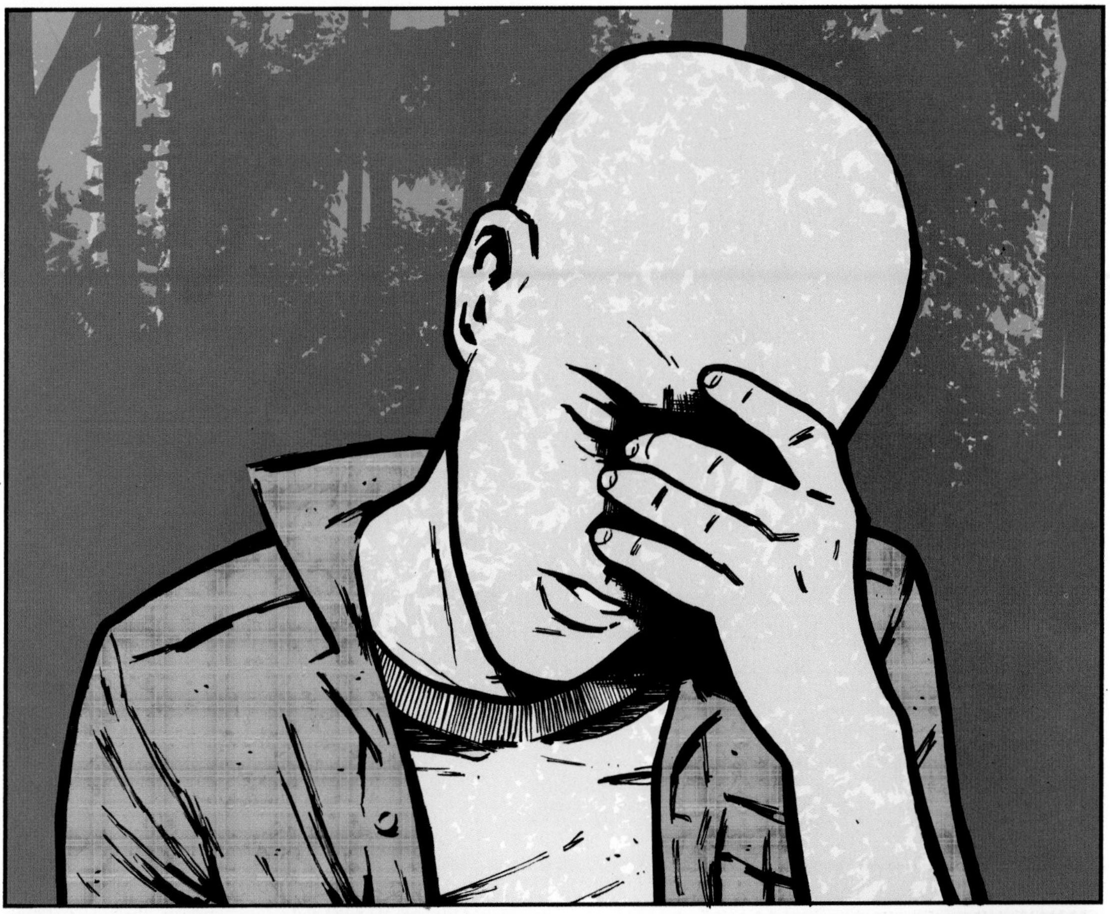

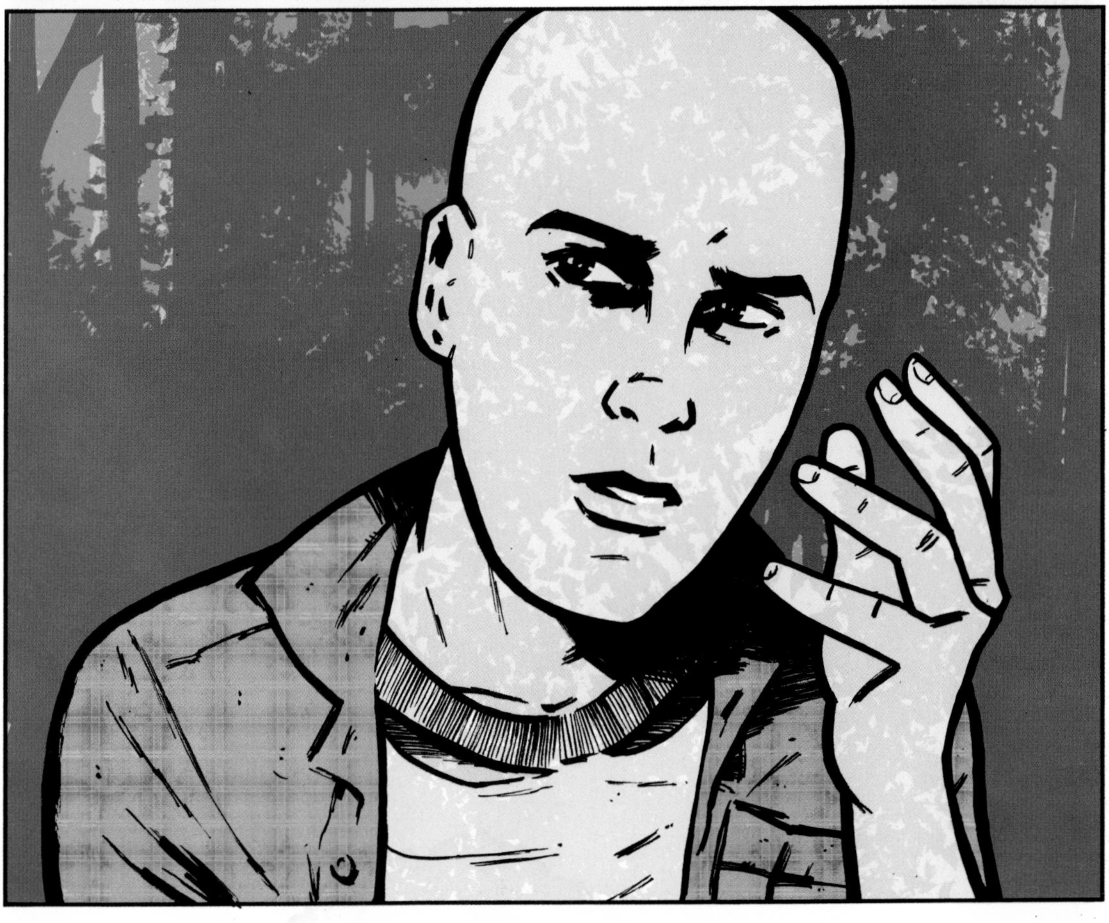

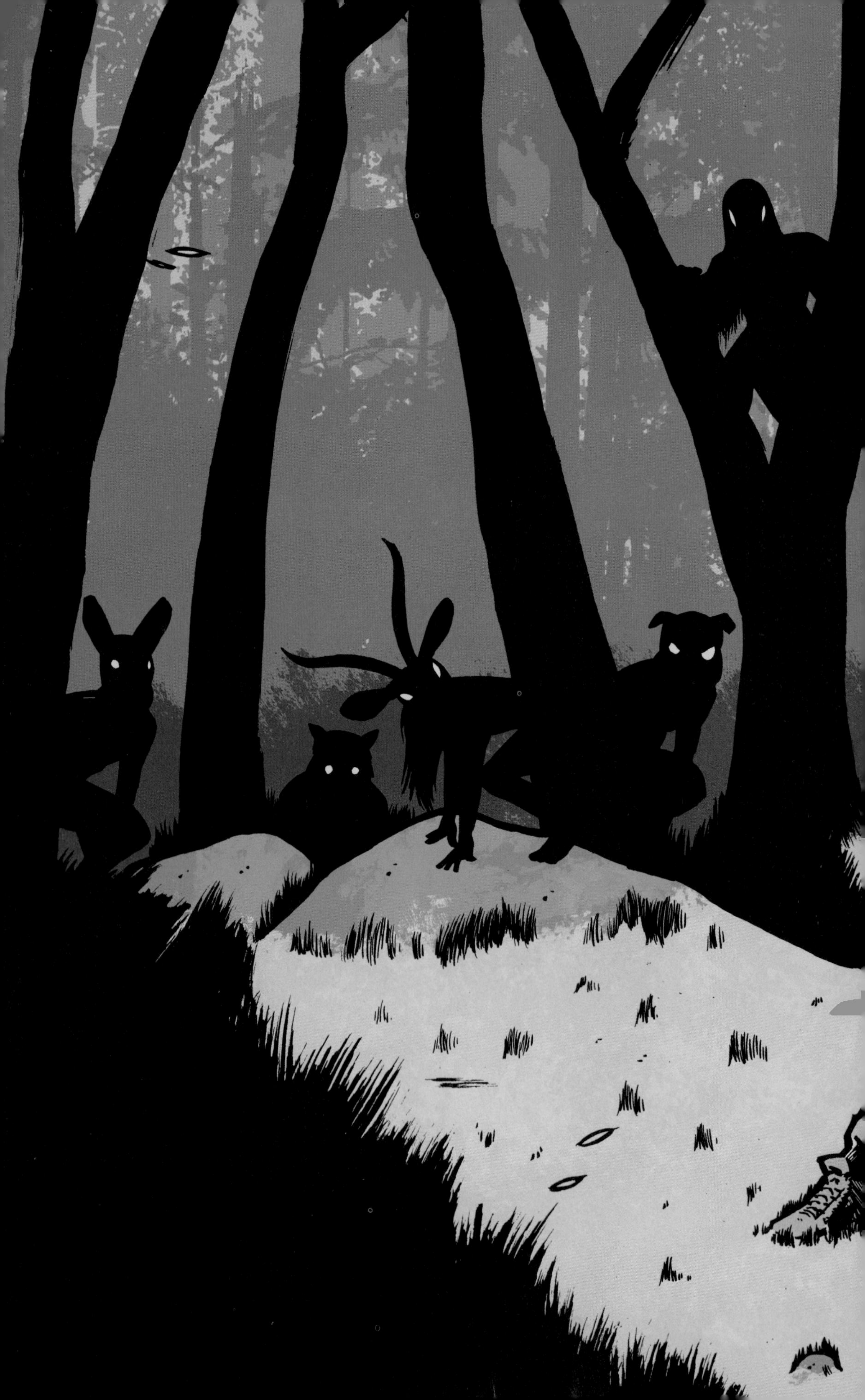

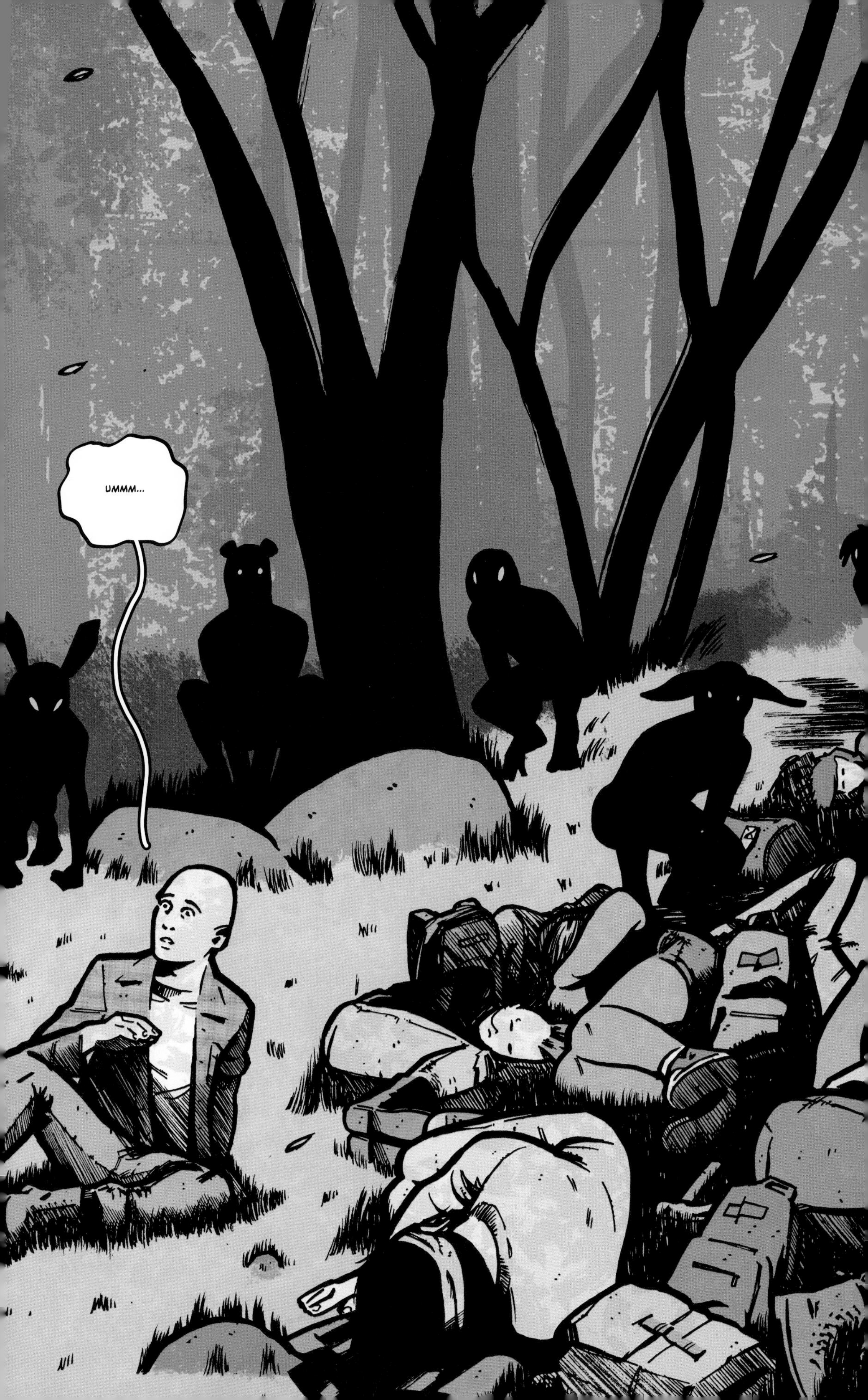
UMMM...

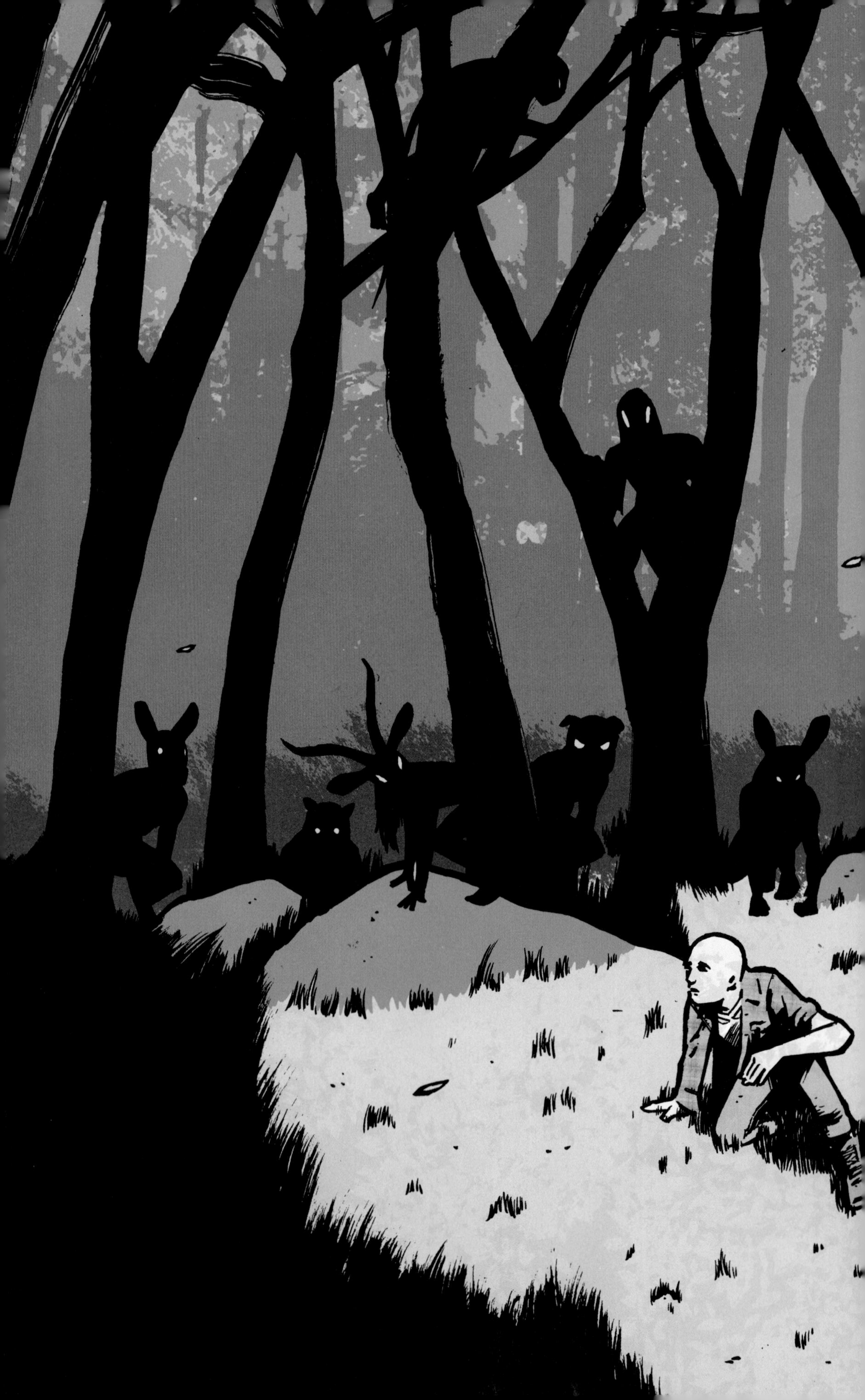

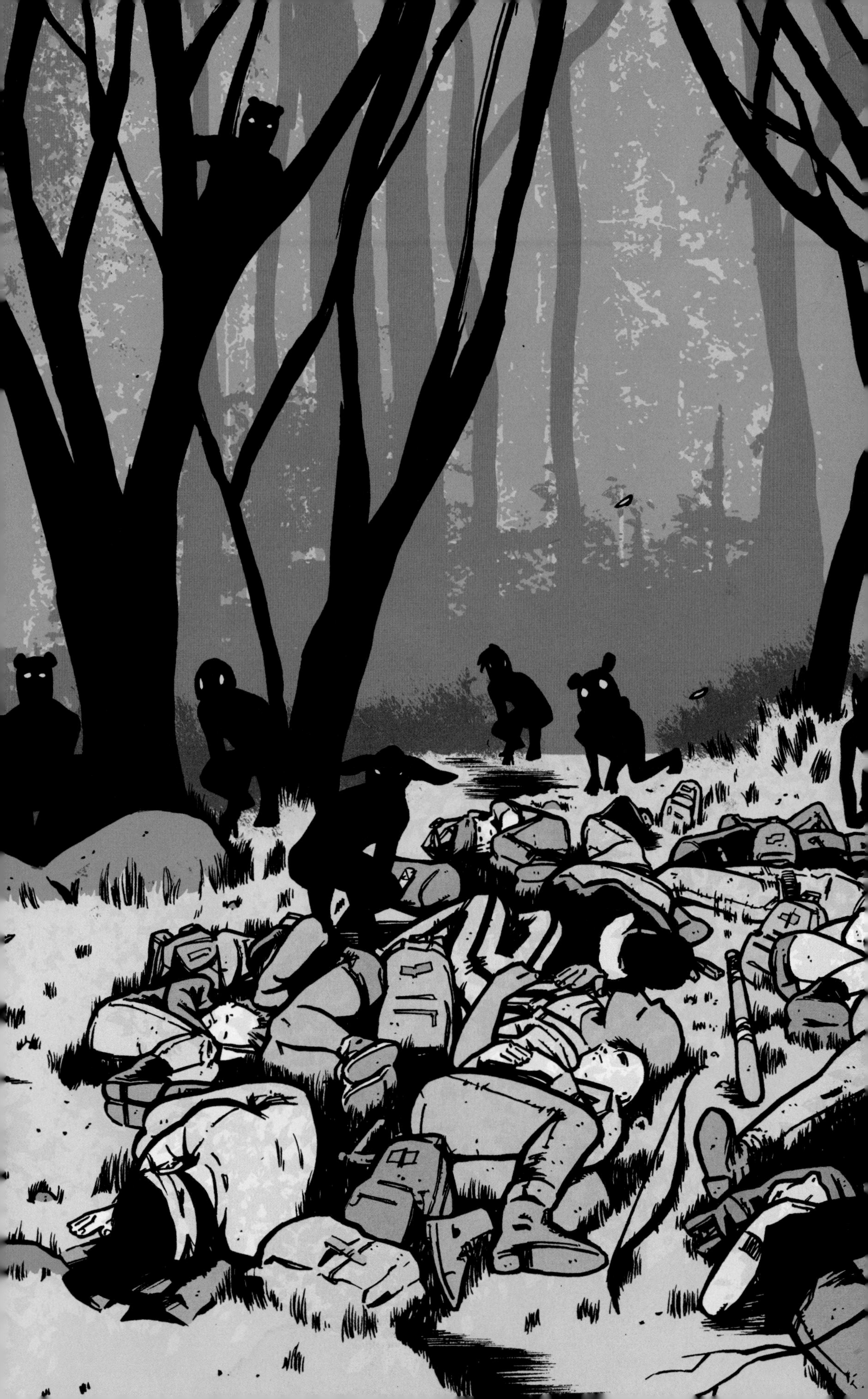

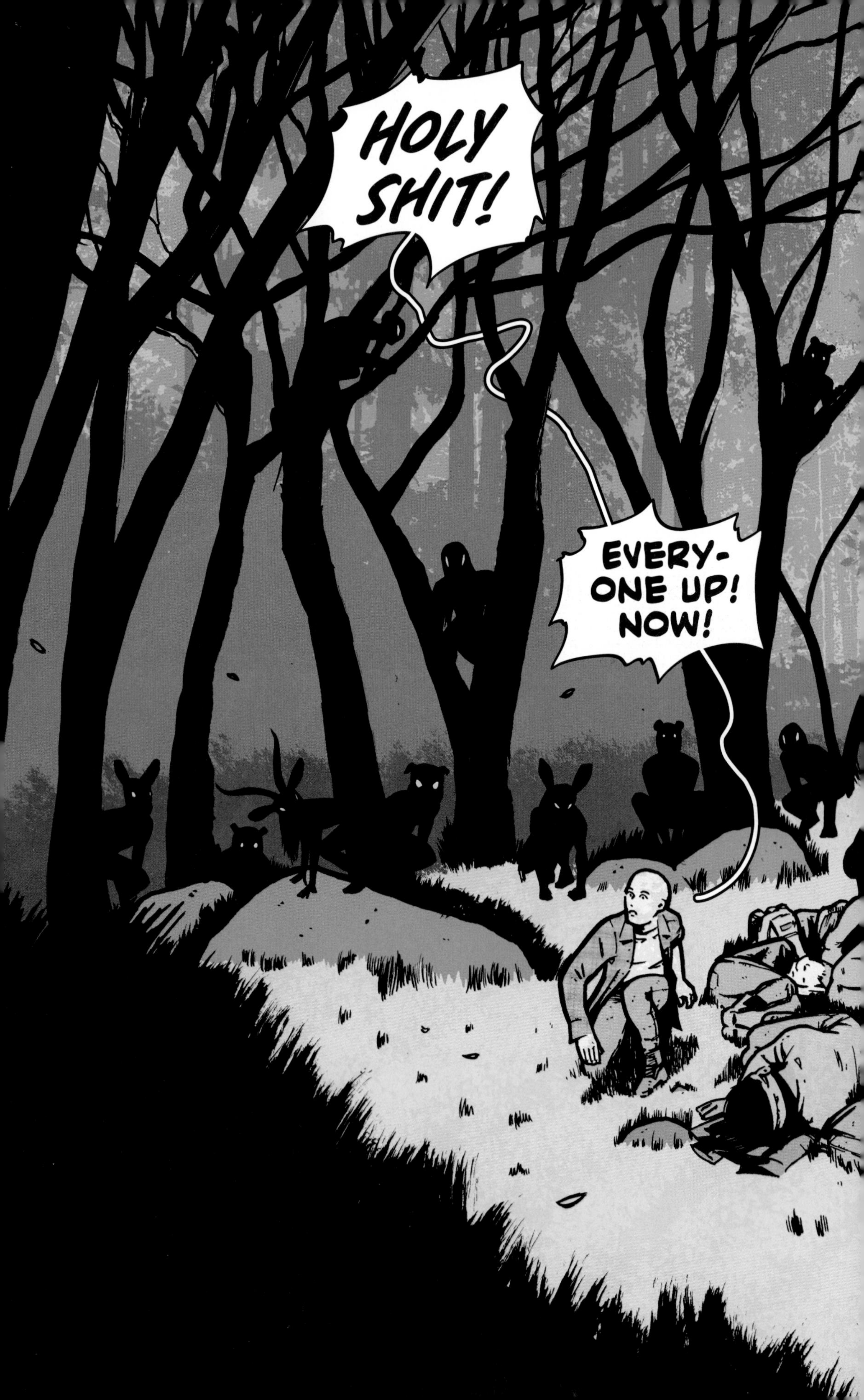
HOLY SHIT!
EVERY-ONE UP! NOW!

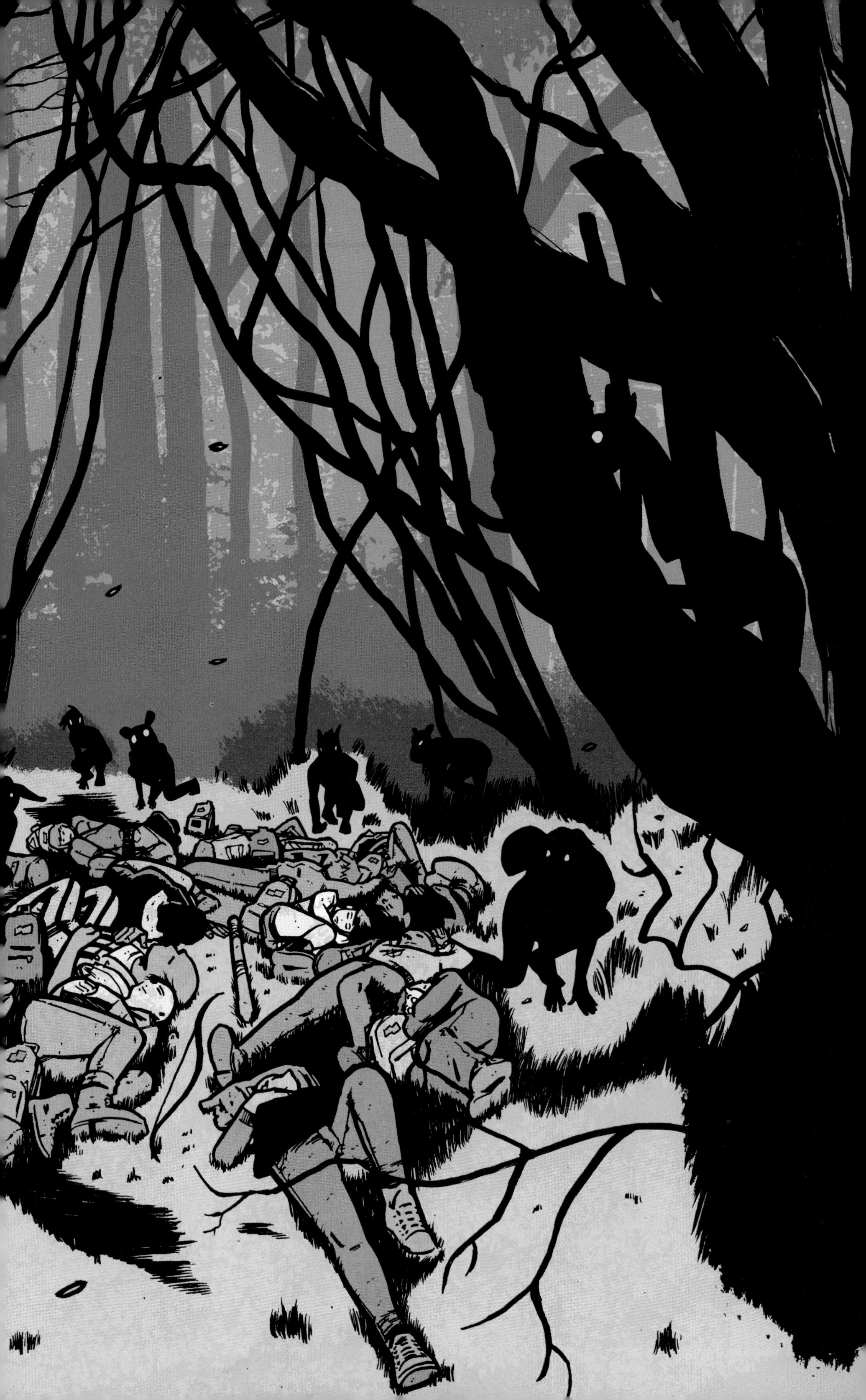

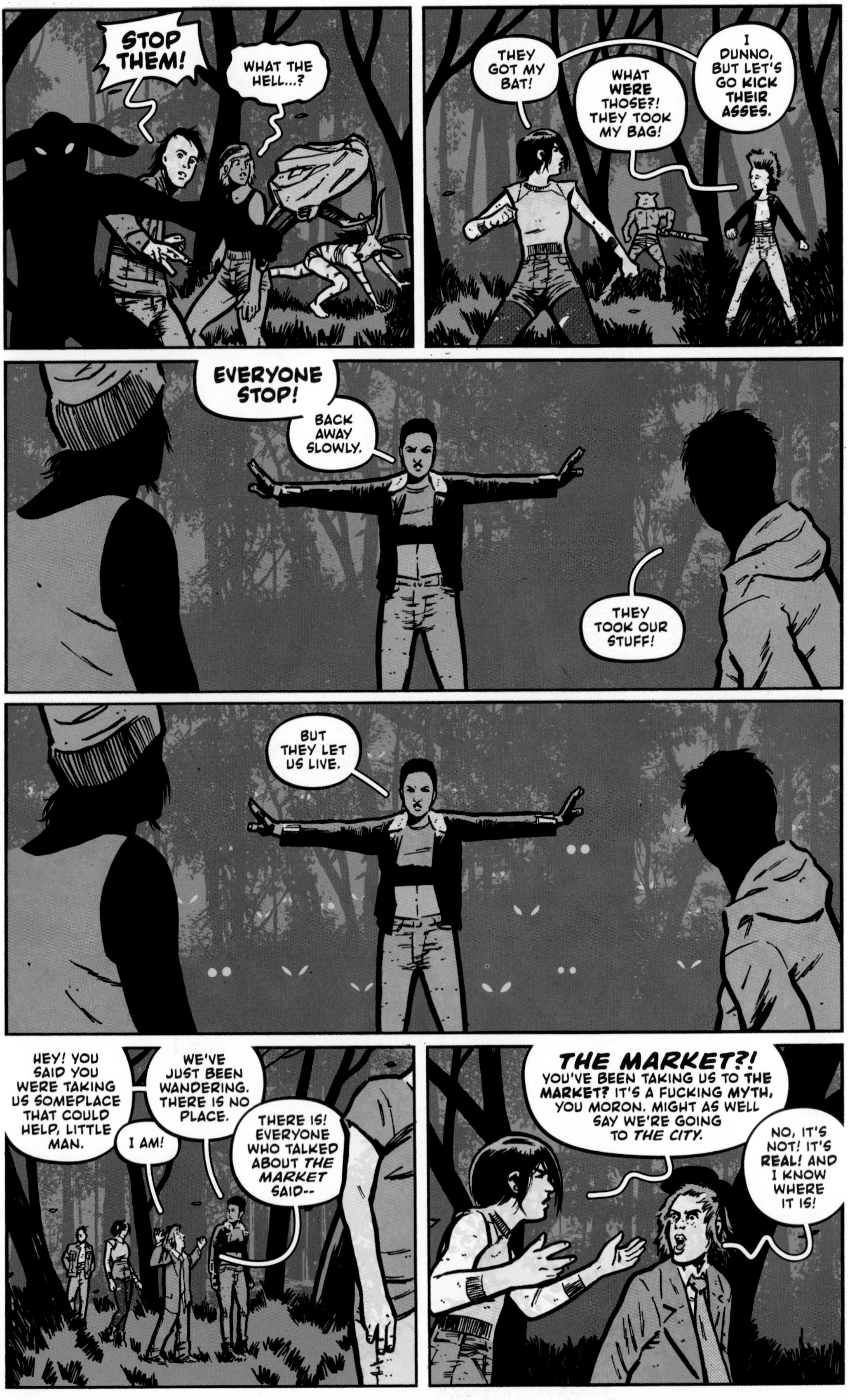

STOP THEM!
WHAT THE HELL...?
THEY GOT MY BAT!
WHAT WERE THOSE?! THEY TOOK MY BAG!
I DUNNO, BUT LET'S GO KICK THEIR ASSES.
EVERYONE STOP!
BACK AWAY SLOWLY.
THEY TOOK OUR STUFF!
BUT THEY LET US LIVE.
HEY! YOU SAID YOU WERE TAKING US SOMEPLACE THAT COULD HELP, LITTLE MAN.
I AM!
WE'VE JUST BEEN WANDERING. THERE IS NO PLACE.
THERE IS! EVERYONE WHO TALKED ABOUT THE MARKET SAID--
THE MARKET?! YOU'VE BEEN TAKING US TO THE MARKET? IT'S A FUCKING MYTH, YOU MORON. MIGHT AS WELL SAY WE'RE GOING TO THE CITY.
NO, IT'S NOT! IT'S REAL! AND I KNOW WHERE IT IS!

# CHAPTER FIFTEEN

## ...AND THAT'S TODAY!

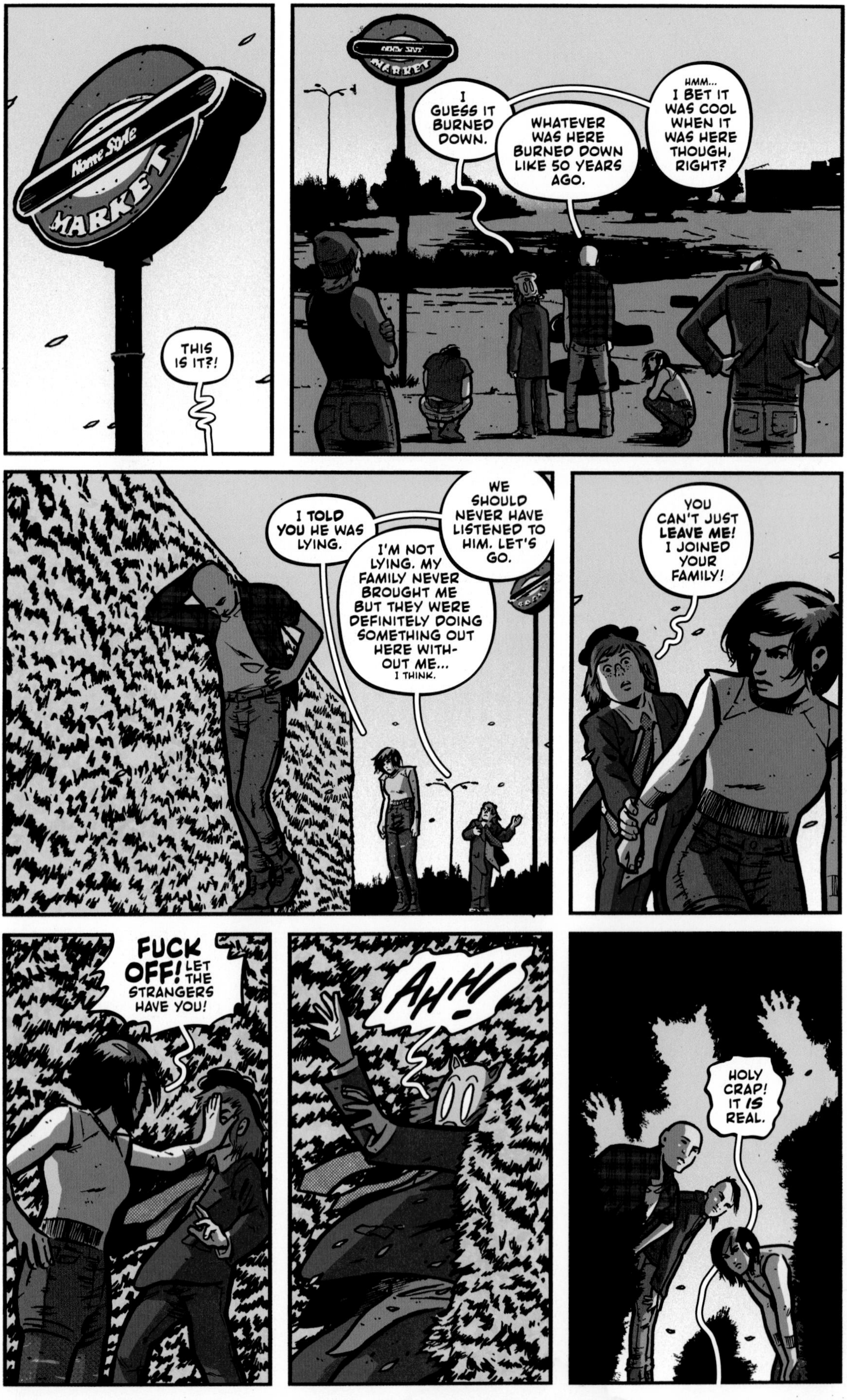
Home Style
MARKET
THIS IS IT?!
I GUESS IT BURNED DOWN.
WHATEVER WAS HERE BURNED DOWN LIKE 50 YEARS AGO.
HMM... I BET IT WAS COOL WHEN IT WAS HERE THOUGH, RIGHT?
I TOLD YOU HE WAS LYING.
WE SHOULD NEVER HAVE LISTENED TO HIM. LET'S GO.
I'M NOT LYING. MY FAMILY NEVER BROUGHT ME BUT THEY WERE DEFINITELY DOING SOMETHING OUT HERE WITH-OUT ME... I THINK.
YOU CAN'T JUST LEAVE ME! I JOINED YOUR FAMILY!
FUCK OFF! LET THE STRANGERS HAVE YOU!
AH!!
HOLY CRAP! IT IS REAL.

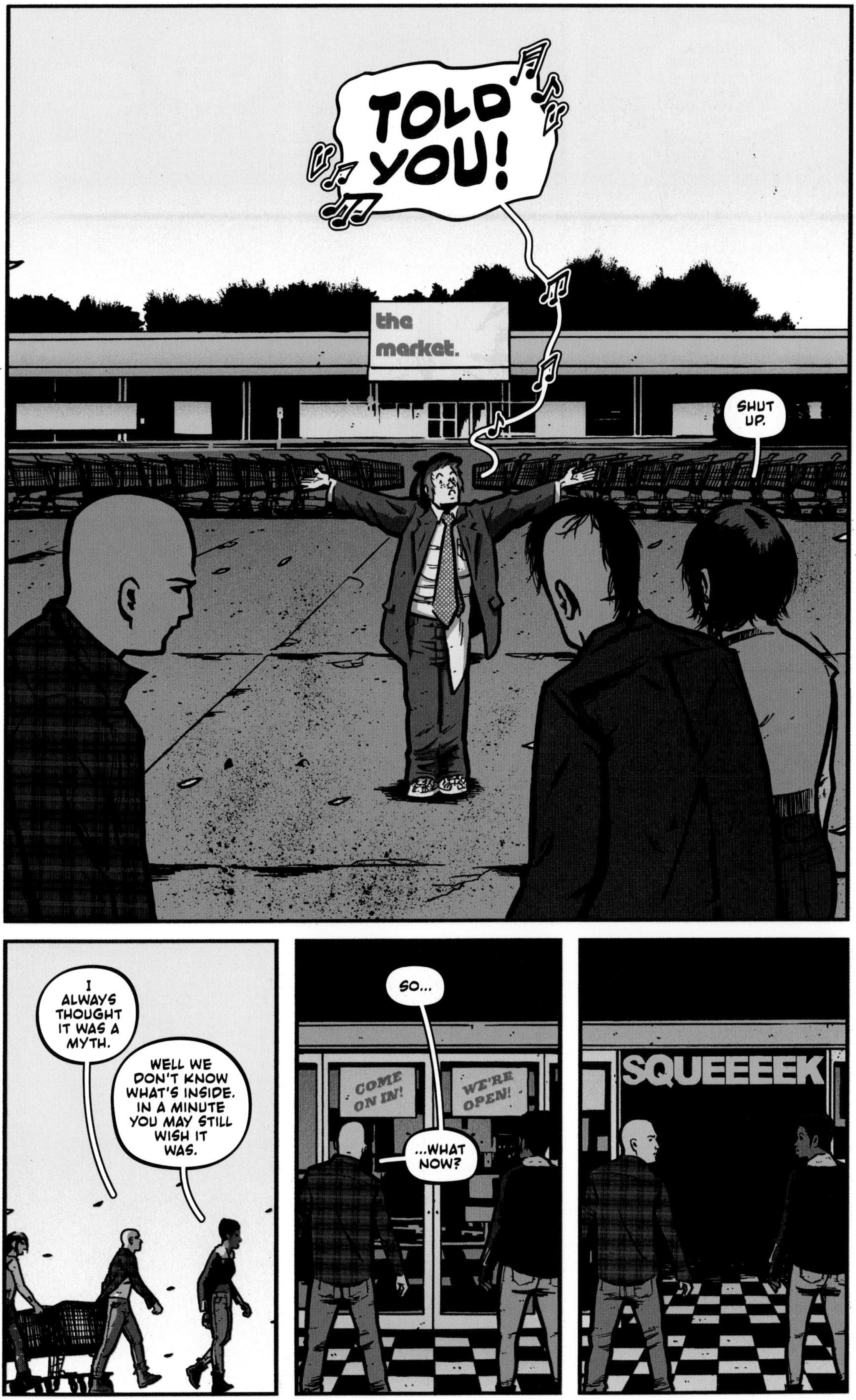
TOLD YOU!
the market.
SHUT UP.
I ALWAYS THOUGHT IT WAS A MYTH.
WELL WE DON'T KNOW WHAT'S INSIDE. IN A MINUTE YOU MAY STILL WISH IT WAS.
SO...
COME ON IN!
WE'RE OPEN!
...WHAT NOW?
SQUEEEEK

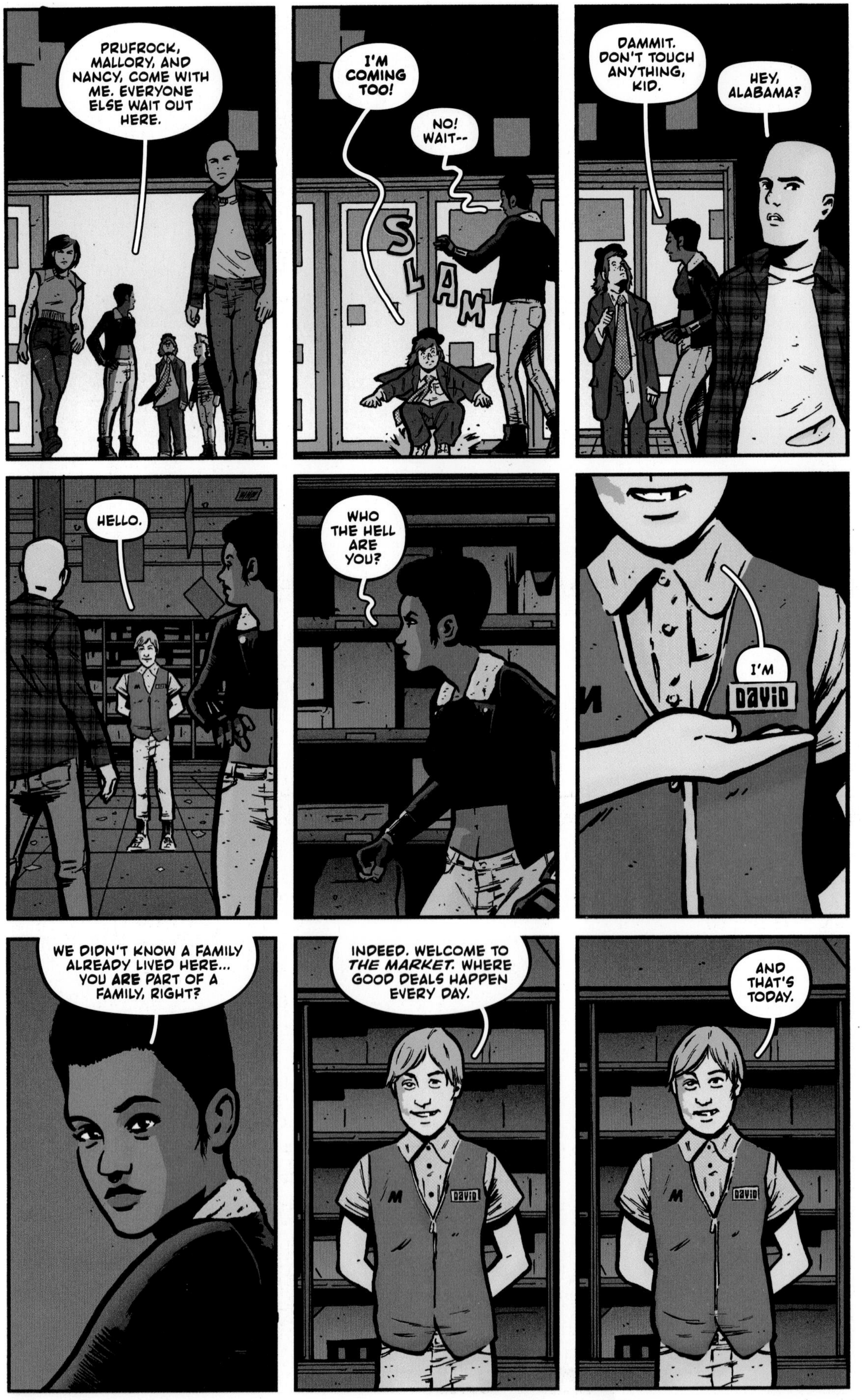
PRUFROCK, MALLORY, AND NANCY, COME WITH ME. EVERYONE ELSE WAIT OUT HERE.
I'M COMING TOO!
NO! WAIT--
SLAM
DAMMIT. DON'T TOUCH ANYTHING, KID.
HEY, ALABAMA?
HELLO.
WHO THE HELL ARE YOU?
I'M
DAVID
WE DIDN'T KNOW A FAMILY ALREADY LIVED HERE... YOU ARE PART OF A FAMILY, RIGHT?
INDEED. WELCOME TO THE MARKET. WHERE GOOD DEALS HAPPEN EVERY DAY.
AND THAT'S TODAY.

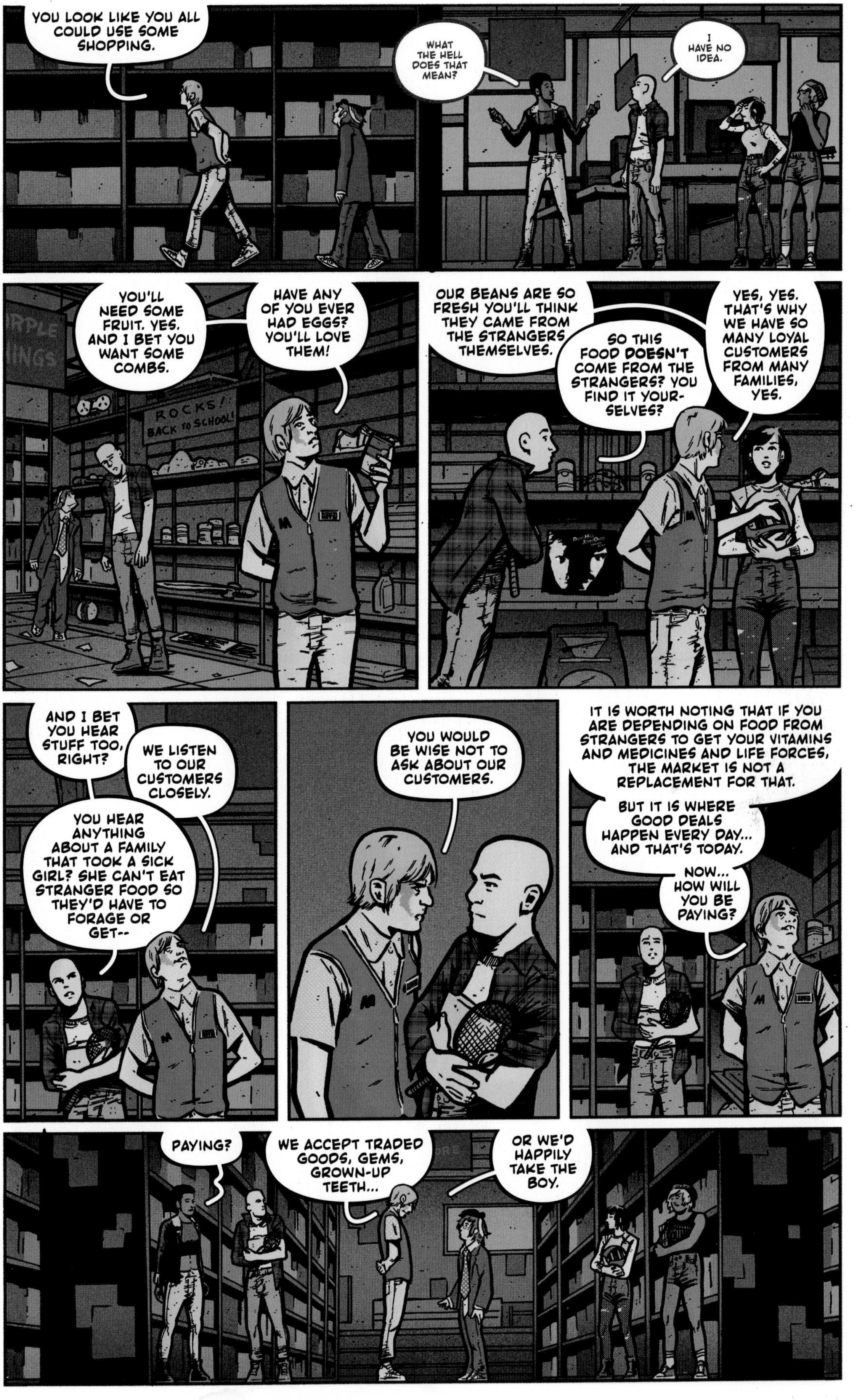
YOU LOOK LIKE YOU ALL COULD USE SOME SHOPPING.
WHAT THE HELL DOES THAT MEAN?
I HAVE NO IDEA.
YOU'LL NEED SOME FRUIT. YES. AND I BET YOU WANT SOME COMBS.
HAVE ANY OF YOU EVER HAD EGGS? YOU'LL LOVE THEM!
ROCKS!
BACK TO SCHOOL!
OUR BEANS ARE SO FRESH YOU'LL THINK THEY CAME FROM THE STRANGERS THEMSELVES.
SO THIS FOOD DOESN'T COME FROM THE STRANGERS? YOU FIND IT YOURSELVES?
YES, YES. THAT'S WHY WE HAVE SO MANY LOYAL CUSTOMERS FROM MANY FAMILIES, YES.
AND I BET YOU HEAR STUFF TOO, RIGHT?
WE LISTEN TO OUR CUSTOMERS CLOSELY.
YOU HEAR ANYTHING ABOUT A FAMILY THAT TOOK A SICK GIRL? SHE CAN'T EAT STRANGER FOOD SO THEY'D HAVE TO FORAGE OR GET--
YOU WOULD BE WISE NOT TO ASK ABOUT OUR CUSTOMERS.
IT IS WORTH NOTING THAT IF YOU ARE DEPENDING ON FOOD FROM STRANGERS TO GET YOUR VITAMINS AND MEDICINES AND LIFE FORCES, THE MARKET IS NOT A REPLACEMENT FOR THAT.
BUT IT IS WHERE GOOD DEALS HAPPEN EVERY DAY... AND THAT'S TODAY.
NOW... HOW WILL YOU BE PAYING?
PAYING?
WE ACCEPT TRADED GOODS, GEMS, GROWN-UP TEETH...
OR WE'D HAPPILY TAKE THE BOY.

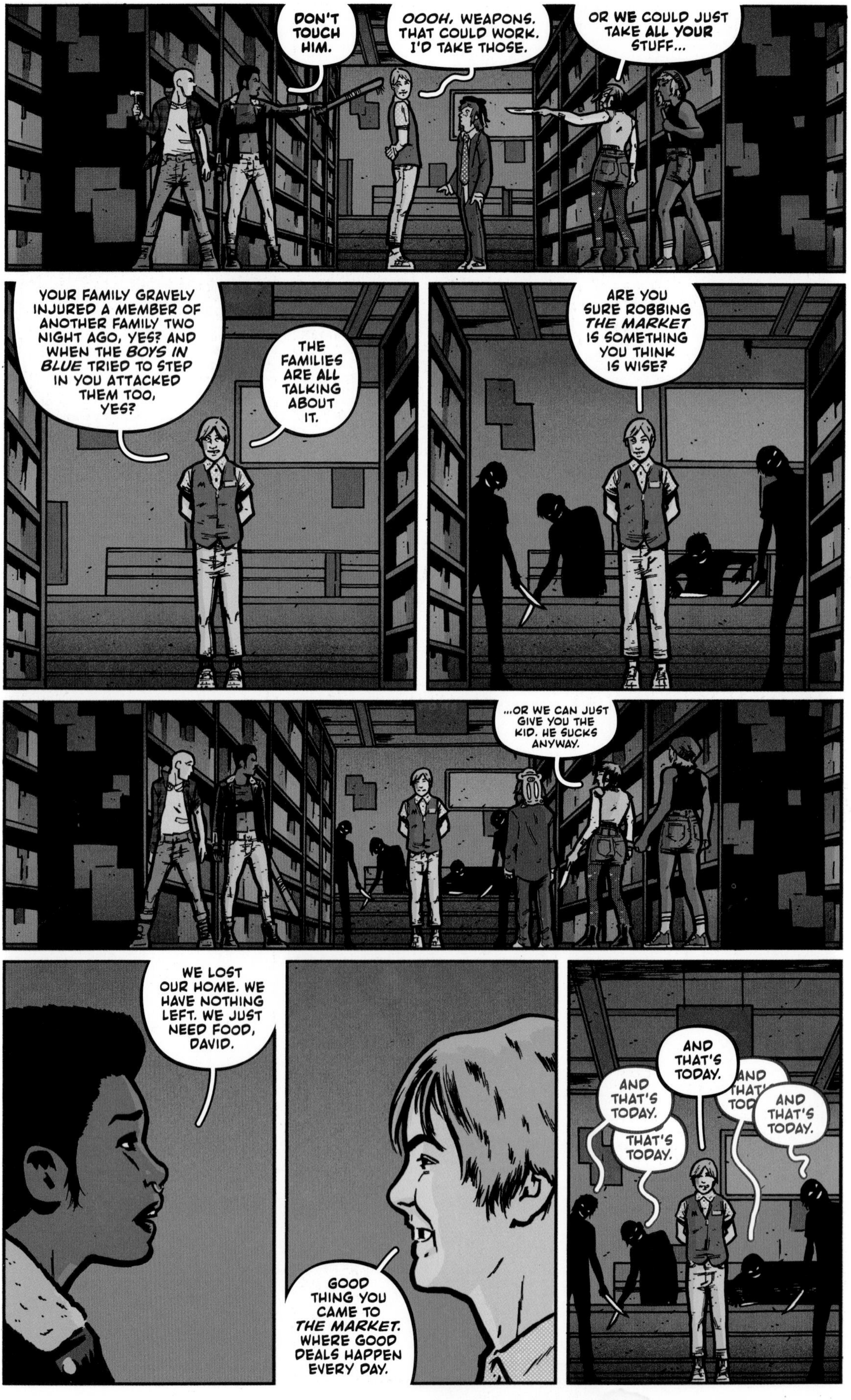
DON'T TOUCH HIM.
OOOH, WEAPONS. THAT COULD WORK. I'D TAKE THOSE.
OR WE COULD JUST TAKE ALL YOUR STUFF...
YOUR FAMILY GRAVELY INJURED A MEMBER OF ANOTHER FAMILY TWO NIGHT AGO, YES? AND WHEN THE BOYS IN BLUE TRIED TO STEP IN YOU ATTACKED THEM TOO, YES?
THE FAMILIES ARE ALL TALKING ABOUT IT.
ARE YOU SURE ROBBING THE MARKET IS SOMETHING YOU THINK IS WISE?
...OR WE CAN JUST GIVE YOU THE KID. HE SUCKS ANYWAY.
WE LOST OUR HOME. WE HAVE NOTHING LEFT. WE JUST NEED FOOD, DAVID.
GOOD THING YOU CAME TO THE MARKET. WHERE GOOD DEALS HAPPEN EVERY DAY.
AND THAT'S TODAY.
AND THAT'S TODAY.
THAT'S TODAY.
AND THAT'S TODAY.

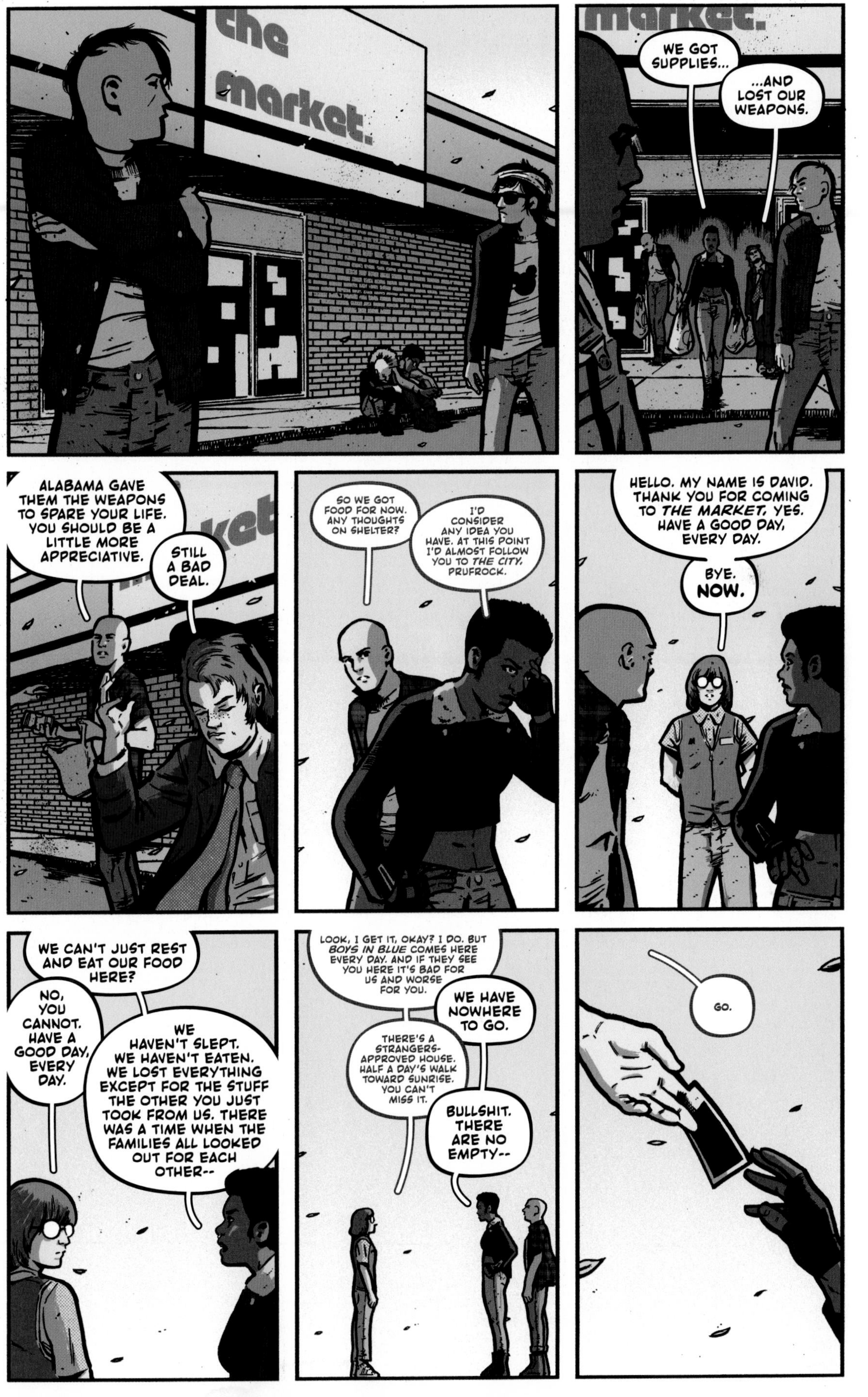
the market.
market.
WE GOT SUPPLIES...
...AND LOST OUR WEAPONS.
ALABAMA GAVE THEM THE WEAPONS TO SPARE YOUR LIFE. YOU SHOULD BE A LITTLE MORE APPRECIATIVE.
STILL A BAD DEAL.
SO WE GOT FOOD FOR NOW. ANY THOUGHTS ON SHELTER?
I'D CONSIDER ANY IDEA YOU HAVE. AT THIS POINT I'D ALMOST FOLLOW YOU TO THE CITY, PRUFROCK.
HELLO. MY NAME IS DAVID. THANK YOU FOR COMING TO THE MARKET, YES. HAVE A GOOD DAY, EVERY DAY.
BYE. NOW.
WE CAN'T JUST REST AND EAT OUR FOOD HERE?
NO, YOU CANNOT. HAVE A GOOD DAY, EVERY DAY.
WE HAVEN'T SLEPT. WE HAVEN'T EATEN. WE LOST EVERYTHING EXCEPT FOR THE STUFF THE OTHER YOU JUST TOOK FROM US. THERE WAS A TIME WHEN THE FAMILIES ALL LOOKED OUT FOR EACH OTHER--
LOOK, I GET IT, OKAY? I DO. BUT BOYS IN BLUE COMES HERE EVERY DAY. AND IF THEY SEE YOU HERE IT'S BAD FOR US AND WORSE FOR YOU.
WE HAVE NOWHERE TO GO.
THERE'S A STRANGERS-APPROVED HOUSE. HALF A DAY'S WALK TOWARD SUNRISE. YOU CAN'T MISS IT.
BULLSHIT. THERE ARE NO EMPTY--
GO.

# CHAPTER SIXTEEN

## IT'S EMPTY NOW.

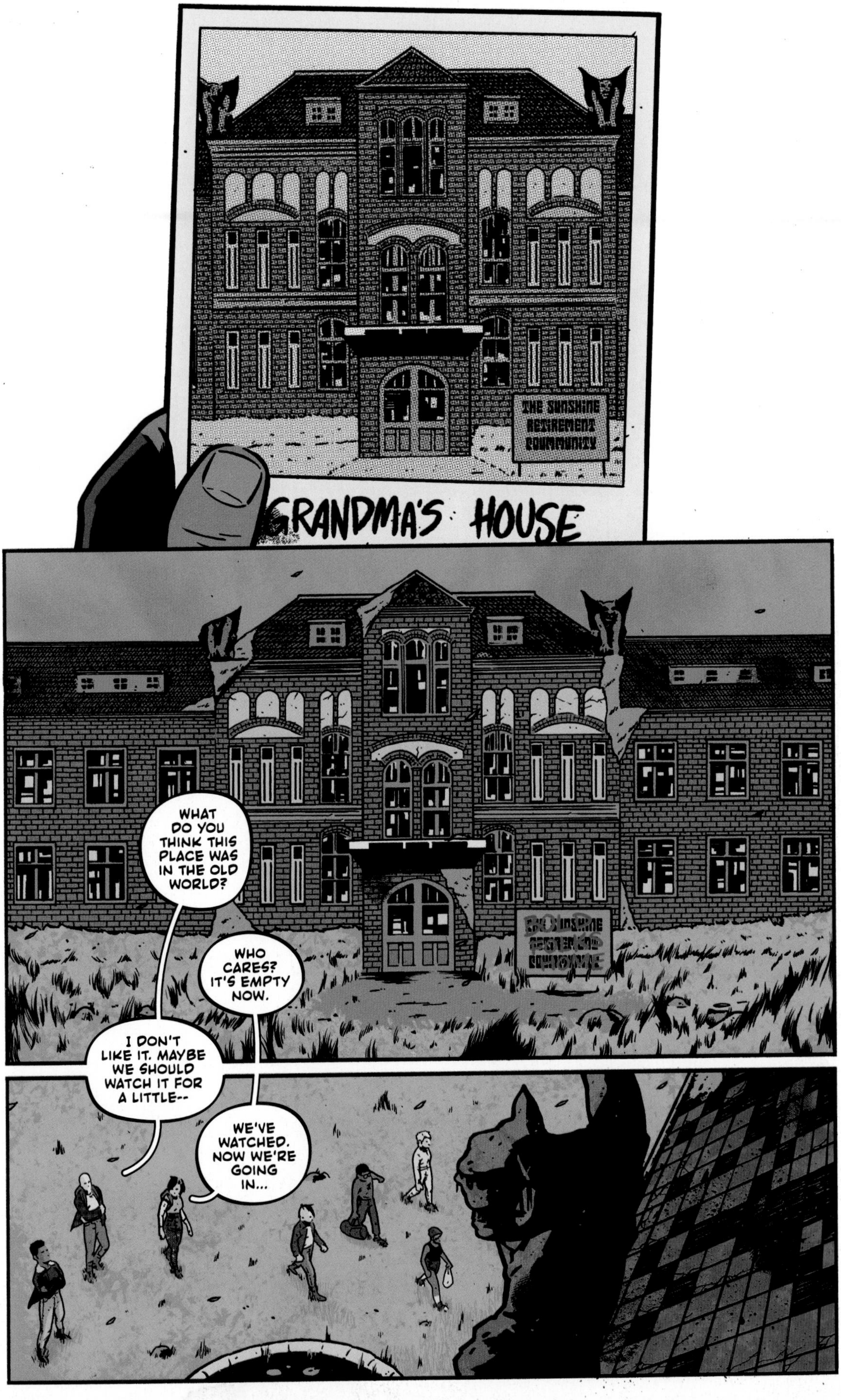
THE SUNSHINE RETIREMENT COMMUNITY
GRANDMA'S HOUSE
WHAT DO YOU THINK THIS PLACE WAS IN THE OLD WORLD?
WHO CARES? IT'S EMPTY NOW.
I DON'T LIKE IT. MAYBE WE SHOULD WATCH IT FOR A LITTLE--
WE'VE WATCHED. NOW WE'RE GOING IN...

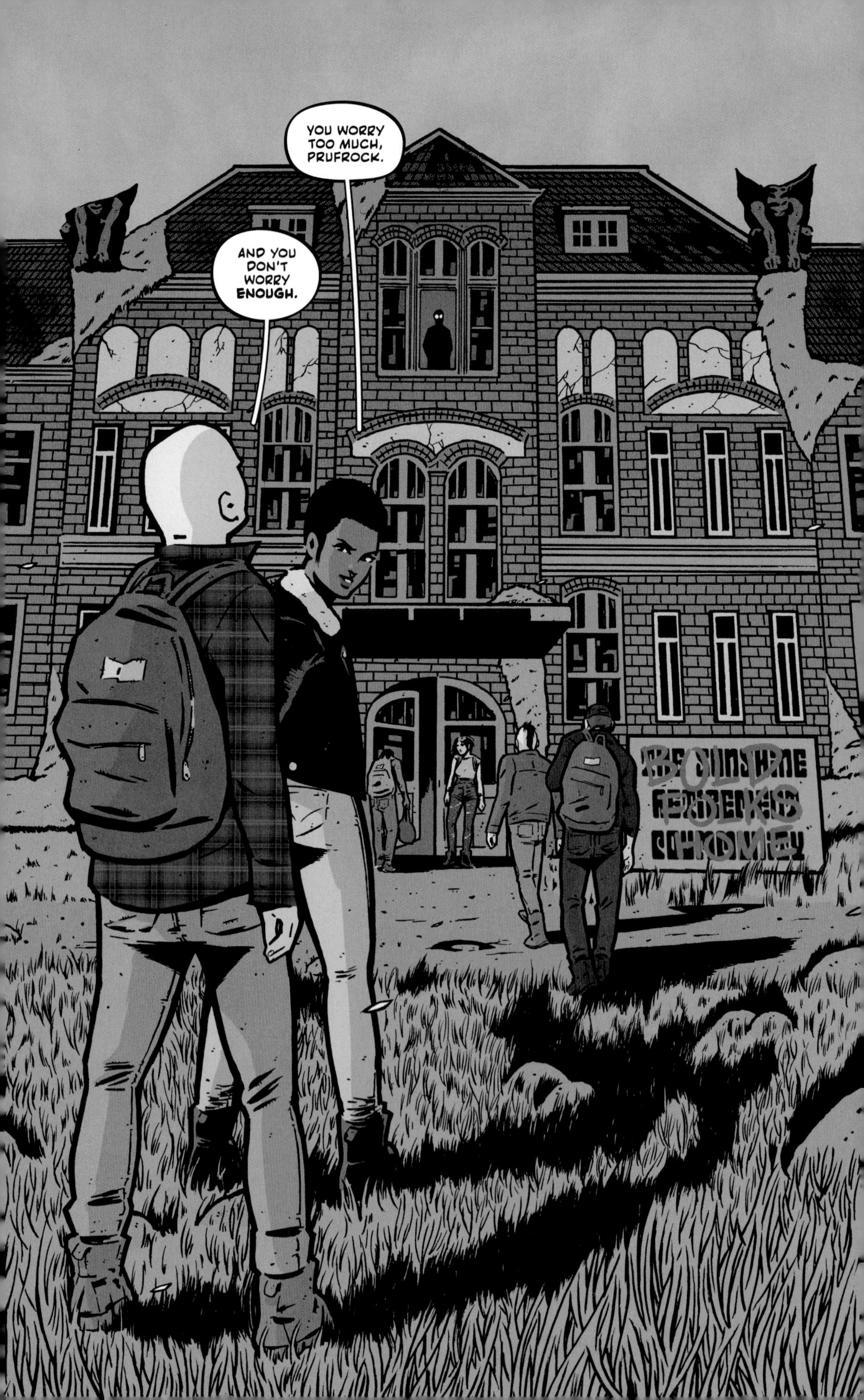
YOU WORRY TOO MUCH, PRUFROCK.
AND YOU DON'T WORRY **ENOUGH.**
BOLD FOLKS HOME

# ACT III

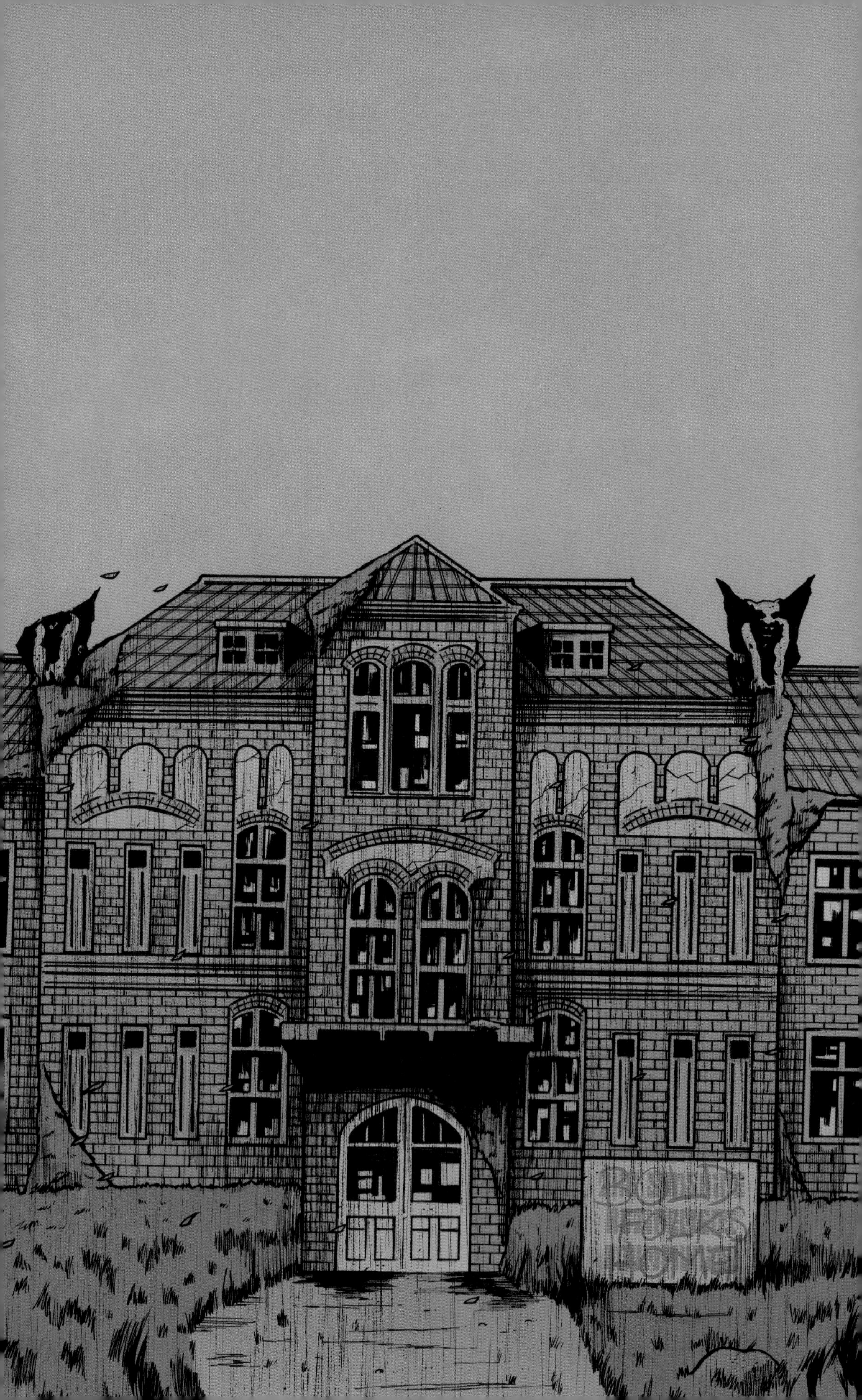

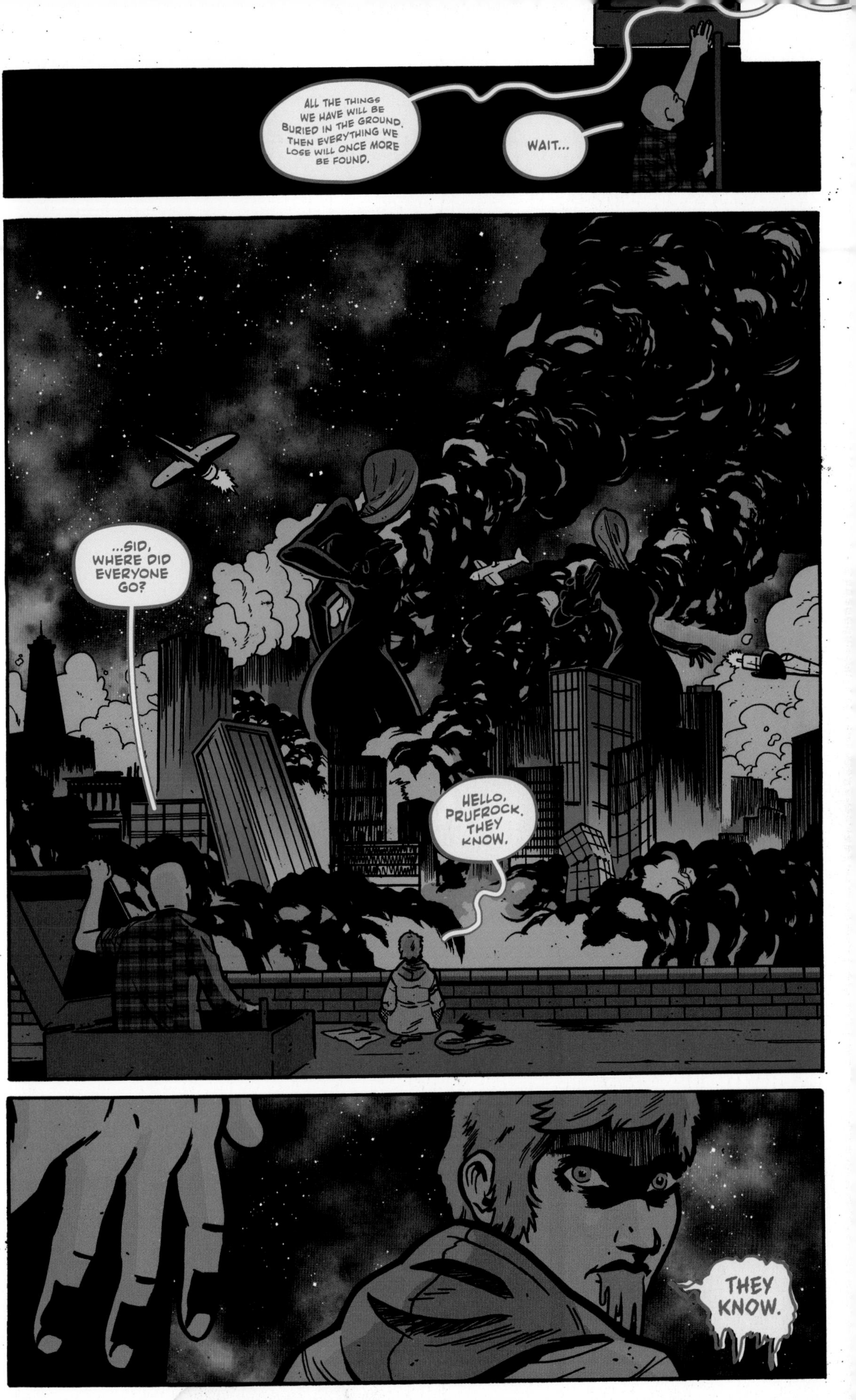
ALL THE THINGS WE HAVE WILL BE BURIED IN THE GROUND. THEN EVERYTHING WE LOSE WILL ONCE MORE BE FOUND.
WAIT...
...SID, WHERE DID EVERYONE GO?
HELLO, PRUFROCK. THEY KNOW.
THEY KNOW.

# CHAPTER SEVENTEEN

## WHAT WAS THIS PLACE?

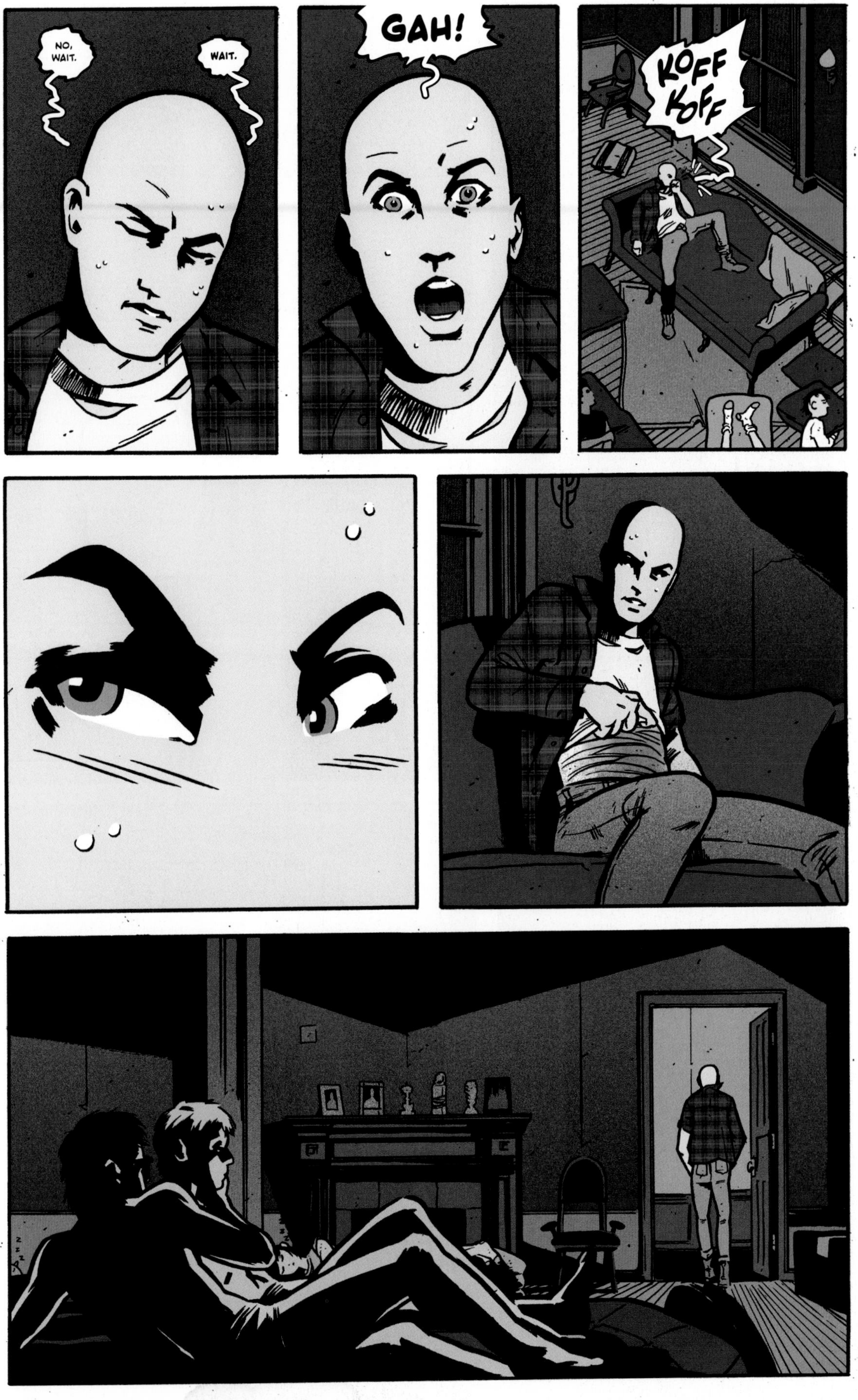
NO, WAIT.
WAIT.
GAH!
KOFF KOFF

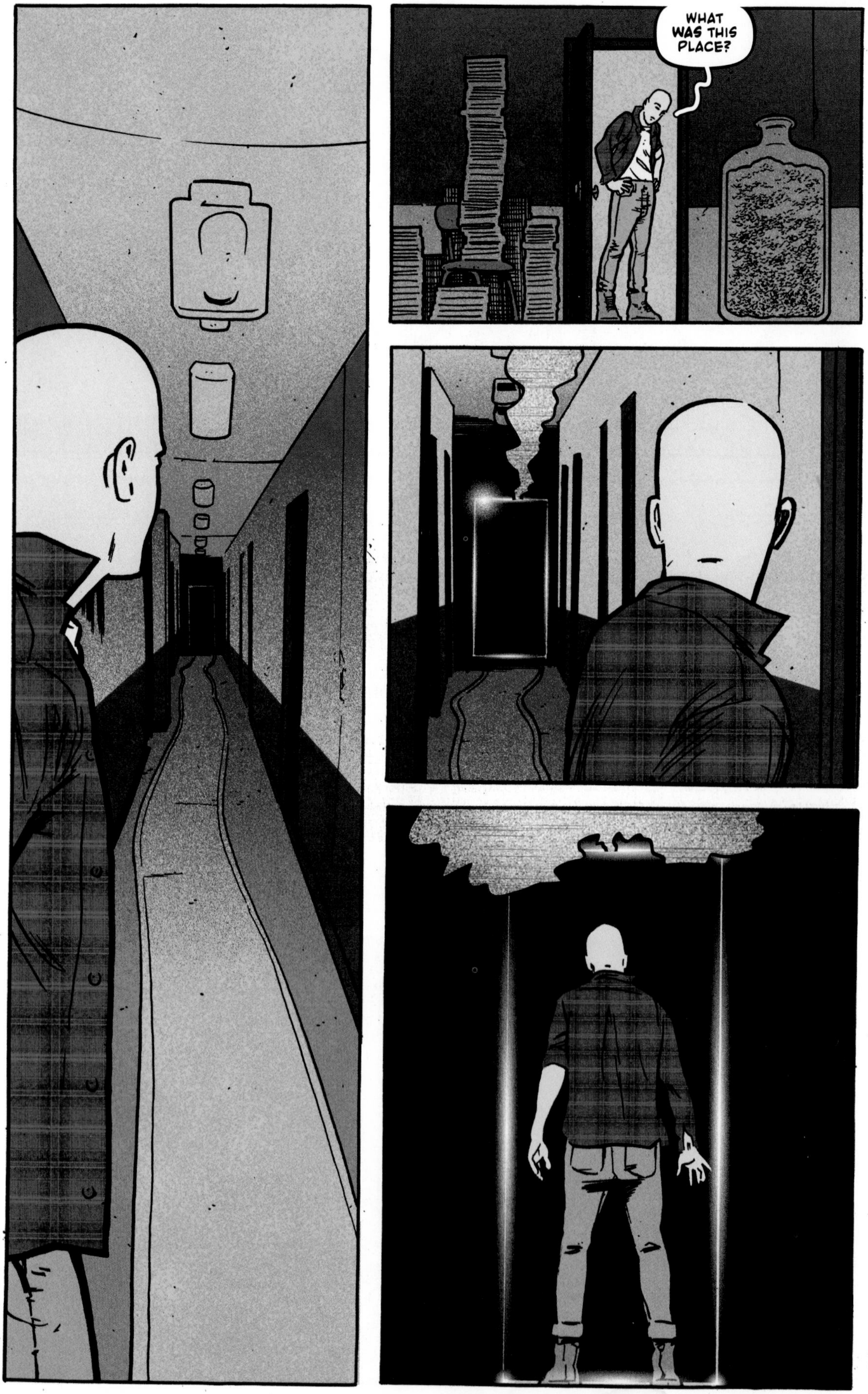
WHAT WAS THIS PLACE?

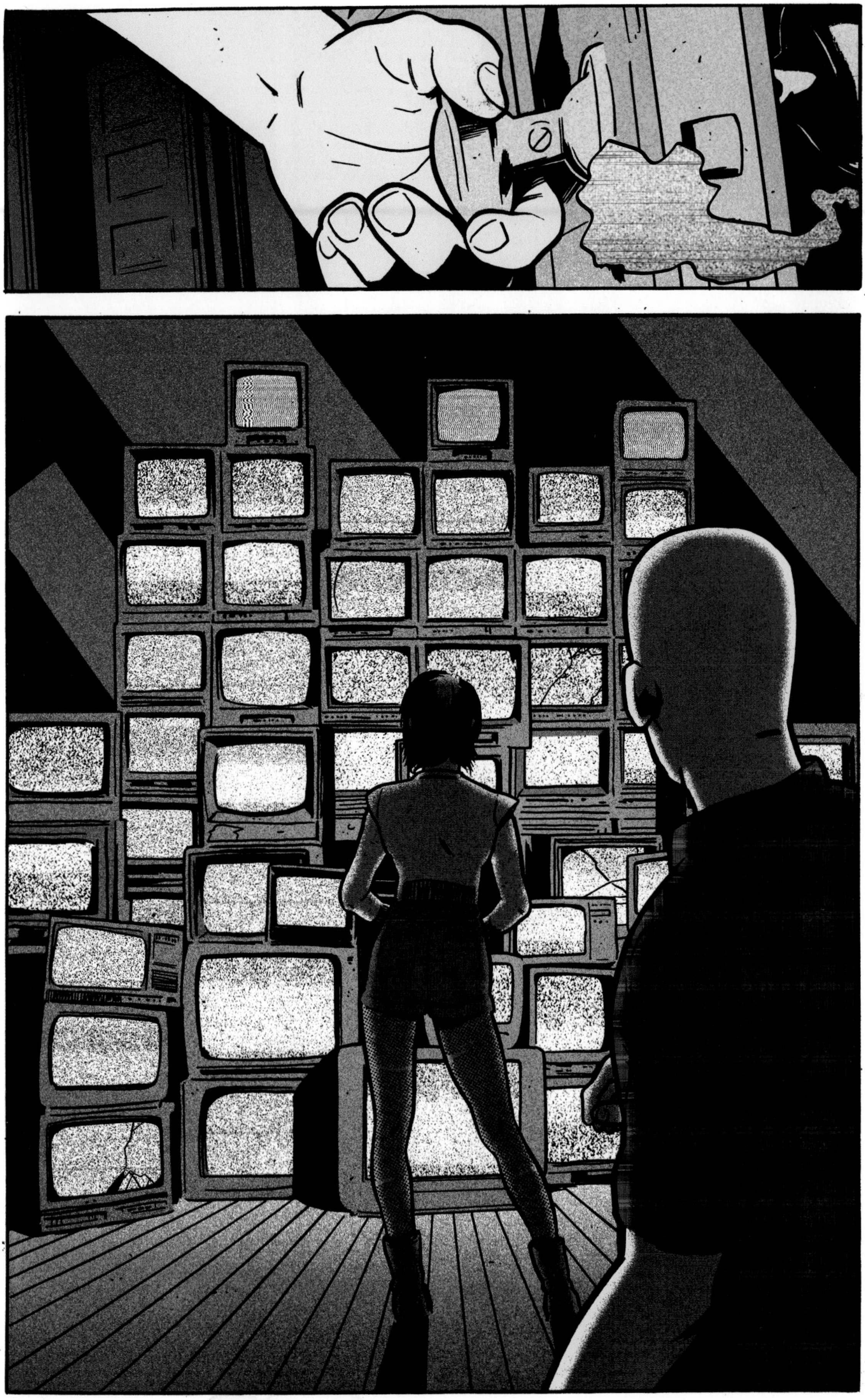

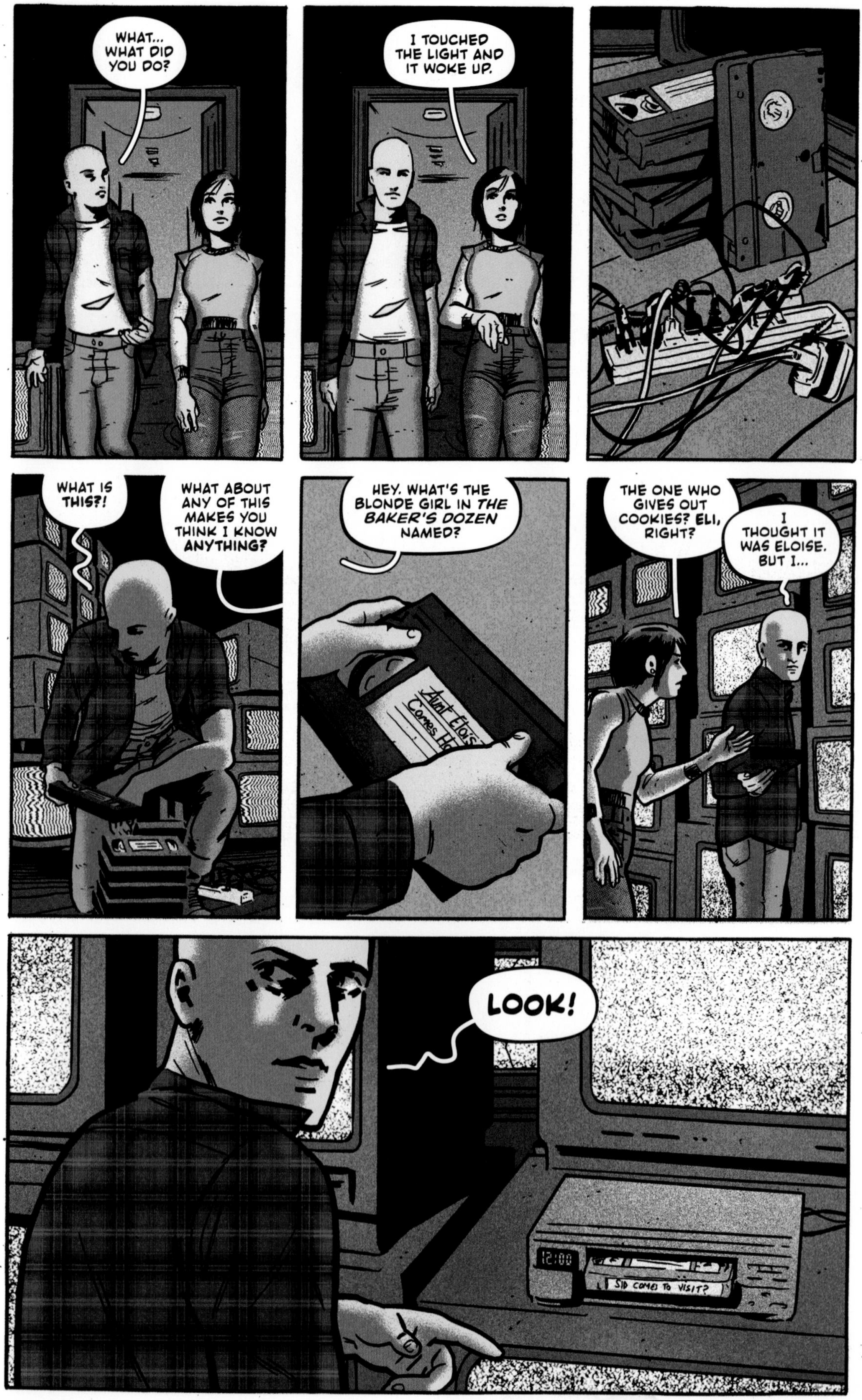
WHAT... WHAT DID YOU DO?
I TOUCHED THE LIGHT AND IT WOKE UP.
WHAT IS THIS?!
WHAT ABOUT ANY OF THIS MAKES YOU THINK I KNOW ANYTHING?
HEY. WHAT'S THE BLONDE GIRL IN *THE BAKER'S DOZEN* NAMED?
THE ONE WHO GIVES OUT COOKIES? ELI, RIGHT?
I THOUGHT IT WAS ELOISE. BUT I...
LOOK!
12:00
SID COMES TO VISIT?

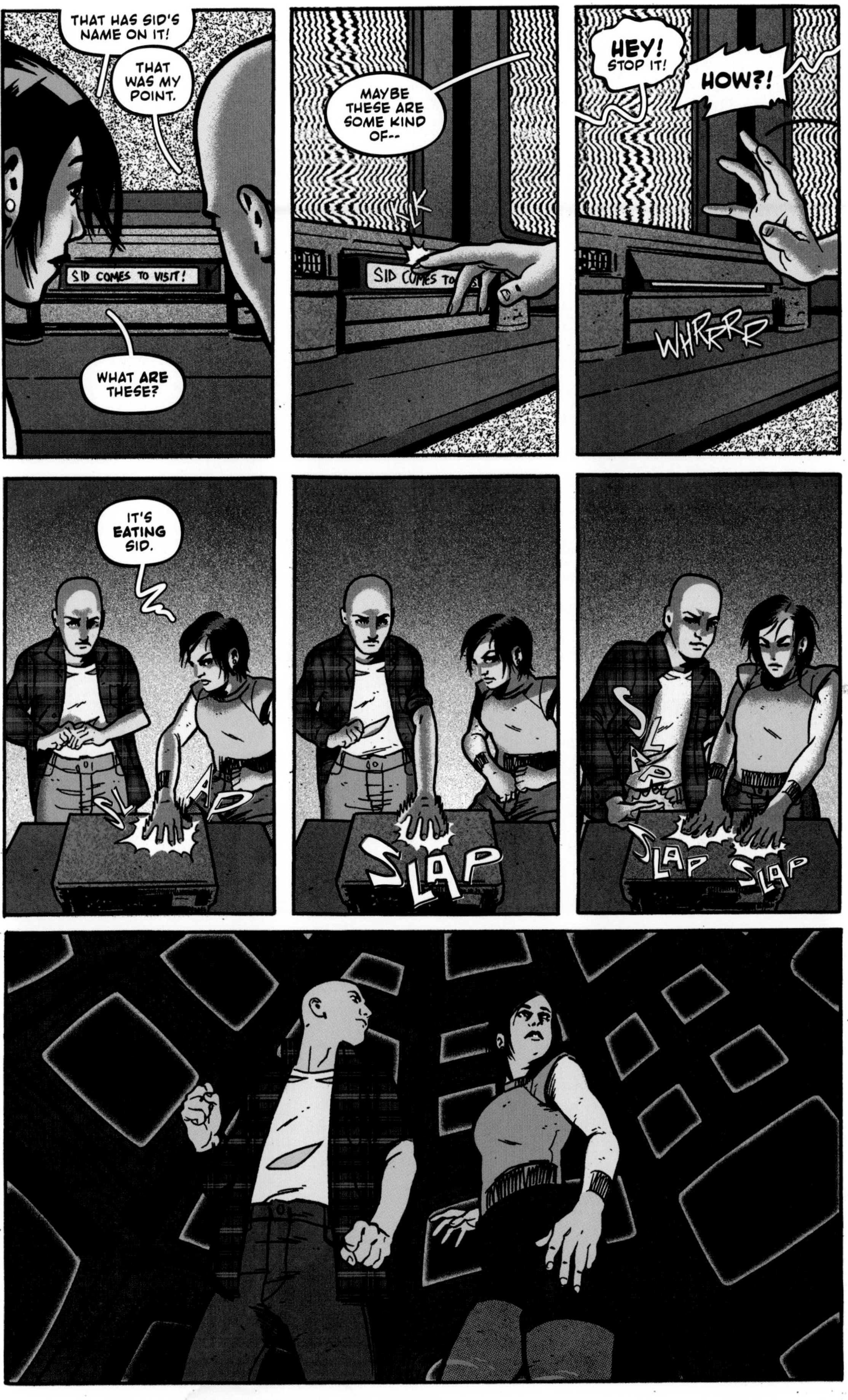
THAT HAS SID'S NAME ON IT!
THAT WAS MY POINT.
SID COMES TO VISIT!
WHAT ARE THESE?
MAYBE THESE ARE SOME KIND OF--
KLIK
SID COMES TO
HEY! STOP IT!
HOW?!
WHRRRR
IT'S EATING SID.
SLAP
SLAP
SLAP
SLAP
SLAP

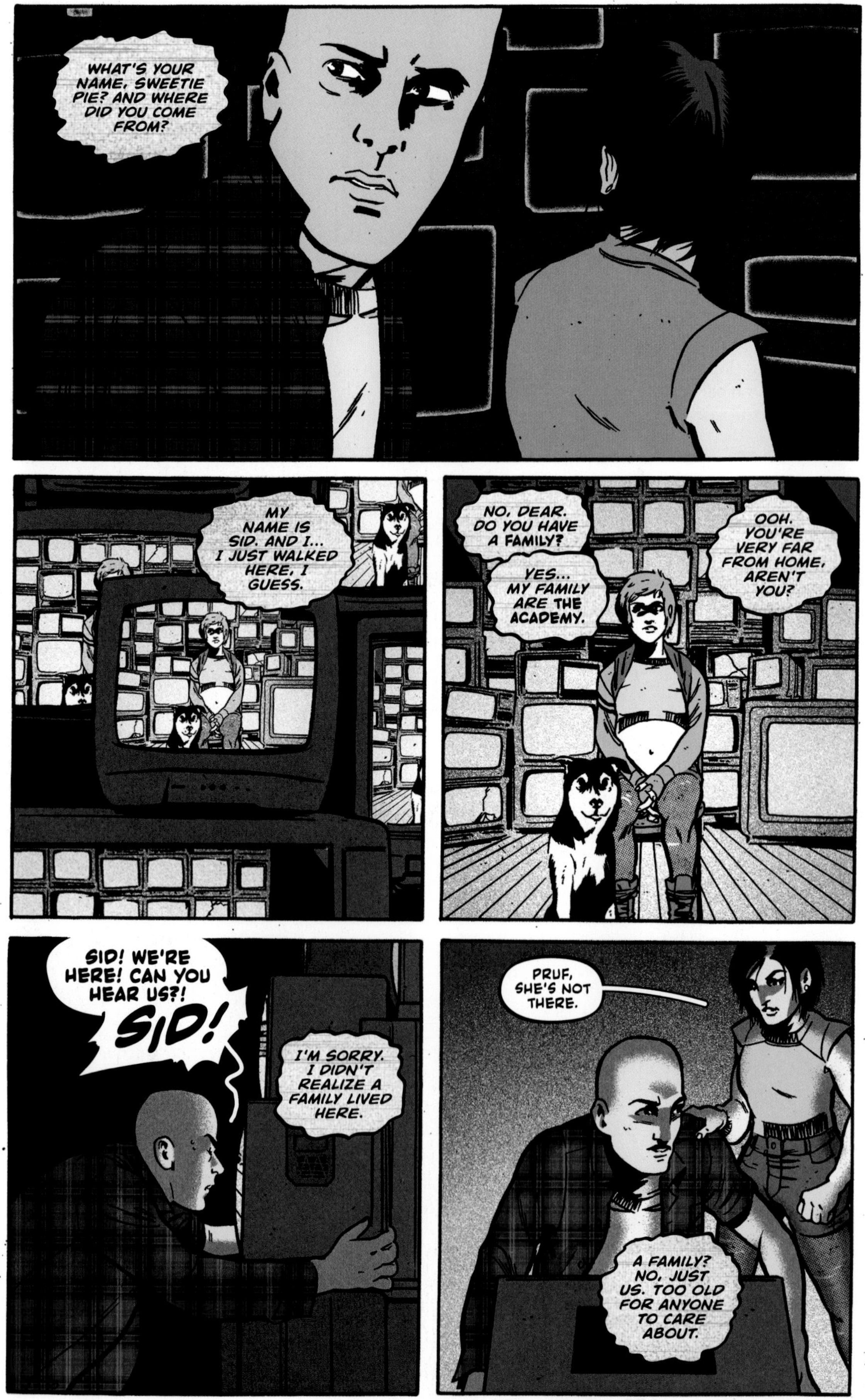
WHAT'S YOUR NAME, SWEETIE PIE? AND WHERE DID YOU COME FROM?
MY NAME IS SID. AND I... I JUST WALKED HERE, I GUESS.
NO, DEAR. DO YOU HAVE A FAMILY?
YES... MY FAMILY ARE THE ACADEMY.
OOH. YOU'RE VERY FAR FROM HOME, AREN'T YOU?
SID! WE'RE HERE! CAN YOU HEAR US?!
SID!
I'M SORRY. I DIDN'T REALIZE A FAMILY LIVED HERE.
PRUF, SHE'S NOT THERE.
A FAMILY? NO, JUST US. TOO OLD FOR ANYONE TO CARE ABOUT.

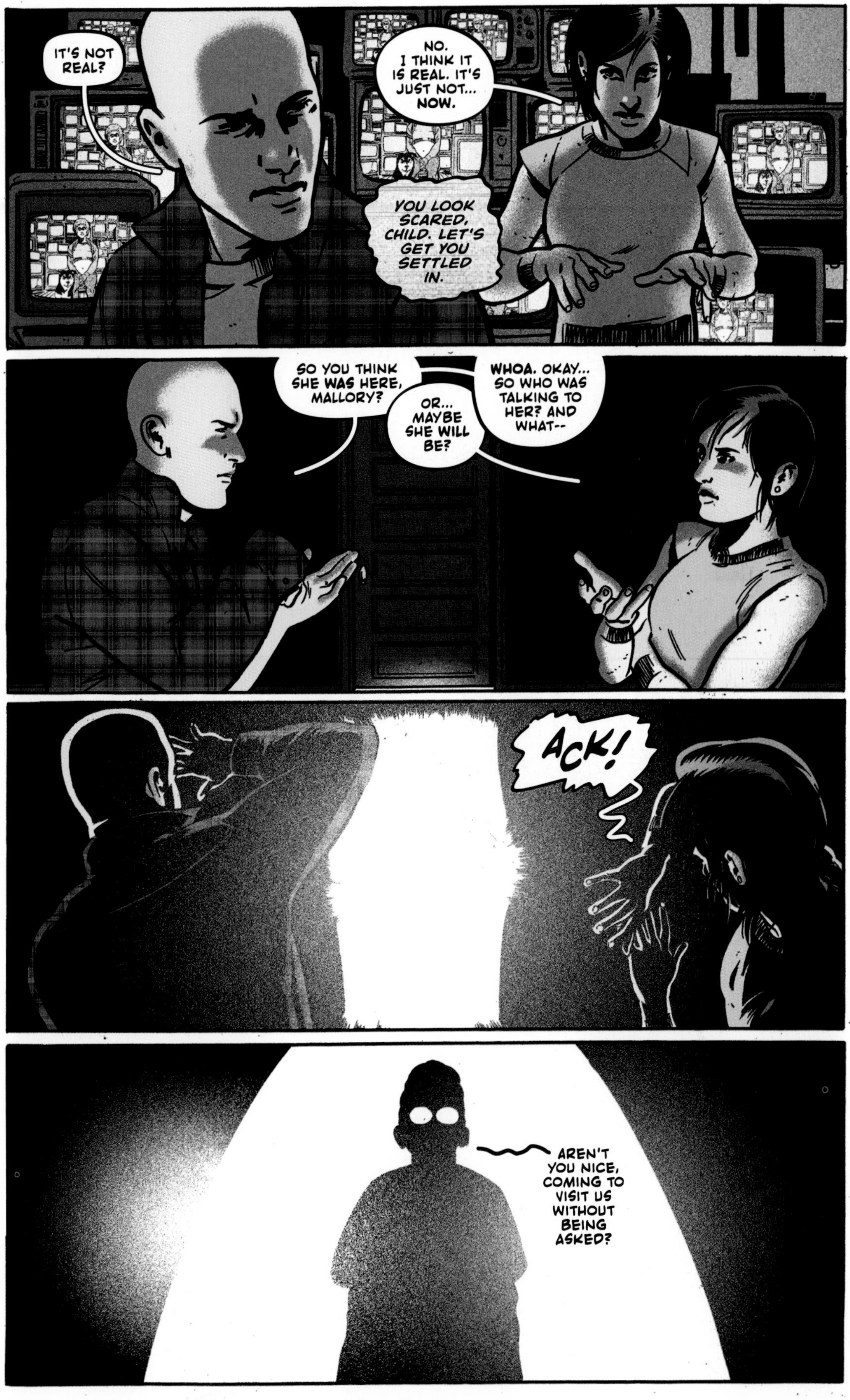
IT'S NOT REAL?
NO. I THINK IT IS REAL. IT'S JUST NOT... NOW.
YOU LOOK SCARED, CHILD. LET'S GET YOU SETTLED IN.
SO YOU THINK SHE WAS HERE, MALLORY?
OR... MAYBE SHE WILL BE?
WHOA. OKAY... SO WHO WAS TALKING TO HER? AND WHAT--
ACK!
AREN'T YOU NICE, COMING TO VISIT US WITHOUT BEING ASKED?

# CHAPTER EIGHTEEN

## WHAT THE H- E- DOUBLE HOCKEY STICKS, MAN?!

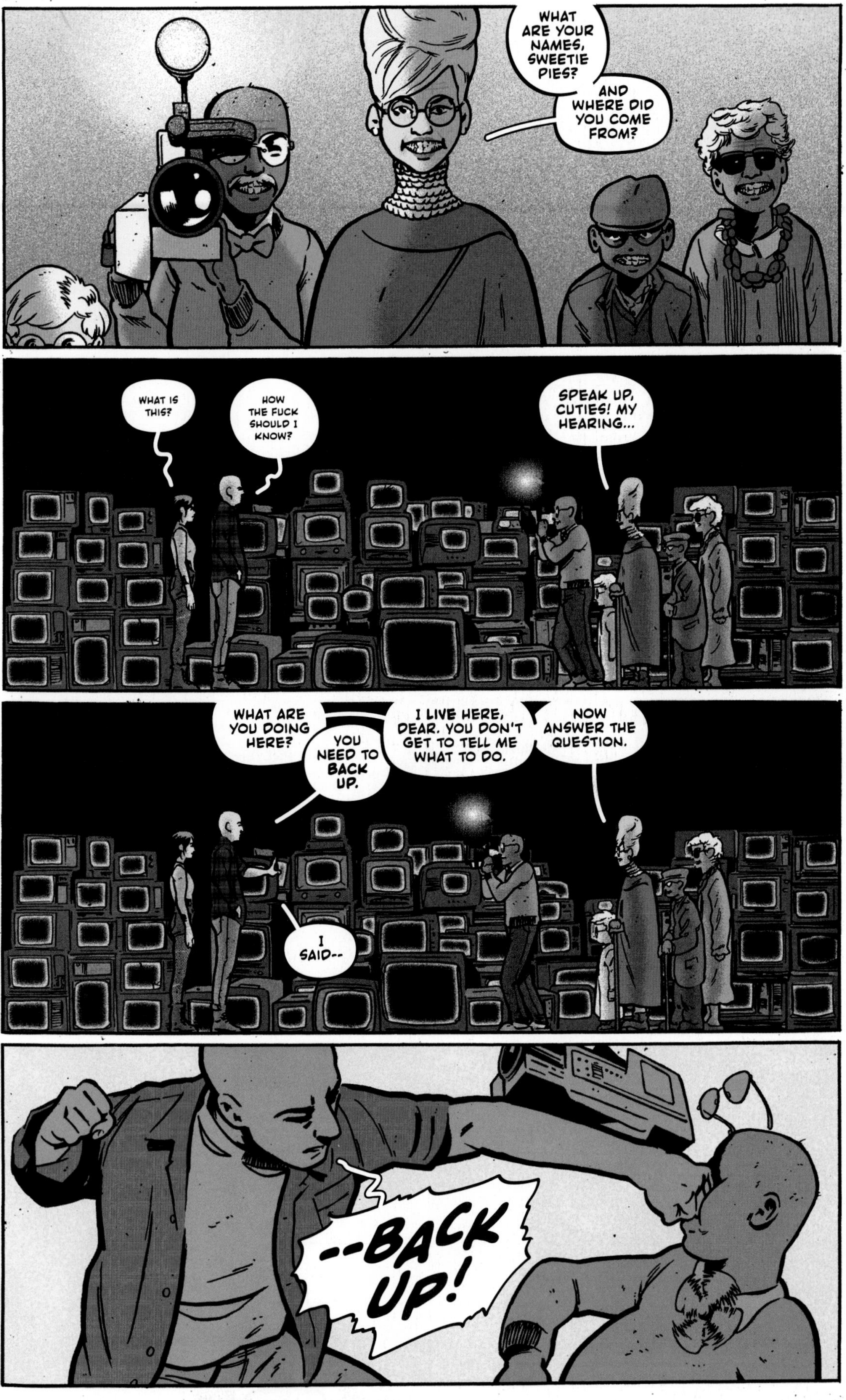
WHAT ARE YOUR NAMES, SWEETIE PIES?
AND WHERE DID YOU COME FROM?
WHAT IS THIS?
HOW THE FUCK SHOULD I KNOW?
SPEAK UP, CUTIES! MY HEARING...
WHAT ARE YOU DOING HERE?
YOU NEED TO BACK UP.
I LIVE HERE, DEAR. YOU DON'T GET TO TELL ME WHAT TO DO.
NOW ANSWER THE QUESTION.
I SAID--
--BACK UP!

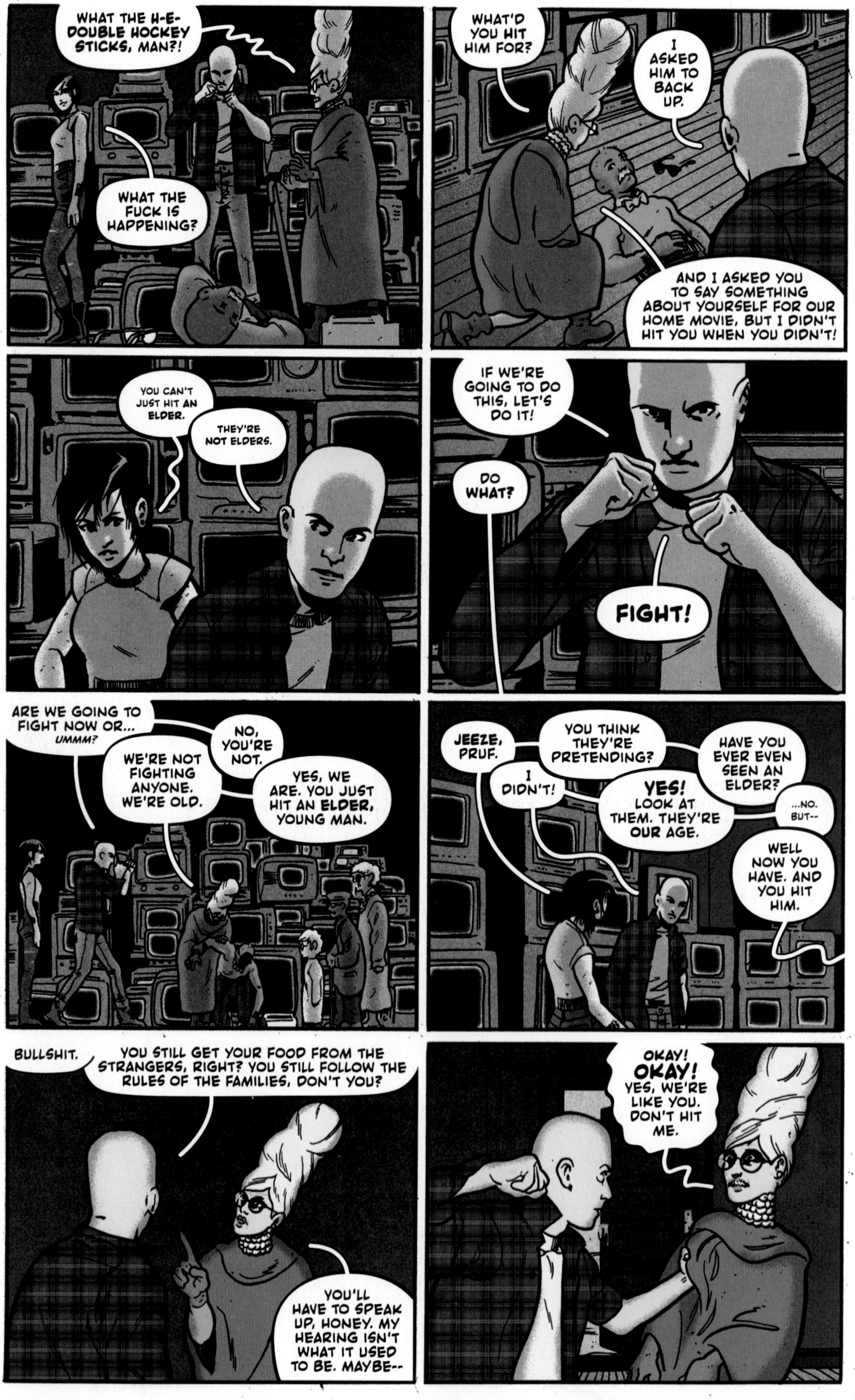
WHAT THE H-E-DOUBLE HOCKEY STICKS, MAN?!
WHAT THE FUCK IS HAPPENING?
WHAT'D YOU HIT HIM FOR?
I ASKED HIM TO BACK UP.
AND I ASKED YOU TO SAY SOMETHING ABOUT YOURSELF FOR OUR HOME MOVIE, BUT I DIDN'T HIT YOU WHEN YOU DIDN'T!
YOU CAN'T JUST HIT AN ELDER.
THEY'RE NOT ELDERS.
IF WE'RE GOING TO DO THIS, LET'S DO IT!
DO WHAT?
FIGHT!
ARE WE GOING TO FIGHT NOW OR... UMMM?
NO, YOU'RE NOT.
WE'RE NOT FIGHTING ANYONE. WE'RE OLD.
YES, WE ARE. YOU JUST HIT AN ELDER, YOUNG MAN.
JEEZE, PRUF.
YOU THINK THEY'RE PRETENDING?
I DIDN'T!
YES! LOOK AT THEM. THEY'RE OUR AGE.
HAVE YOU EVER EVEN SEEN AN ELDER?
...NO. BUT--
WELL NOW YOU HAVE. AND YOU HIT HIM.
BULLSHIT.
YOU STILL GET YOUR FOOD FROM THE STRANGERS, RIGHT? YOU STILL FOLLOW THE RULES OF THE FAMILIES, DON'T YOU?
YOU'LL HAVE TO SPEAK UP, HONEY. MY HEARING ISN'T WHAT IT USED TO BE. MAYBE--
OKAY! OKAY! YES, WE'RE LIKE YOU. DON'T HIT ME.

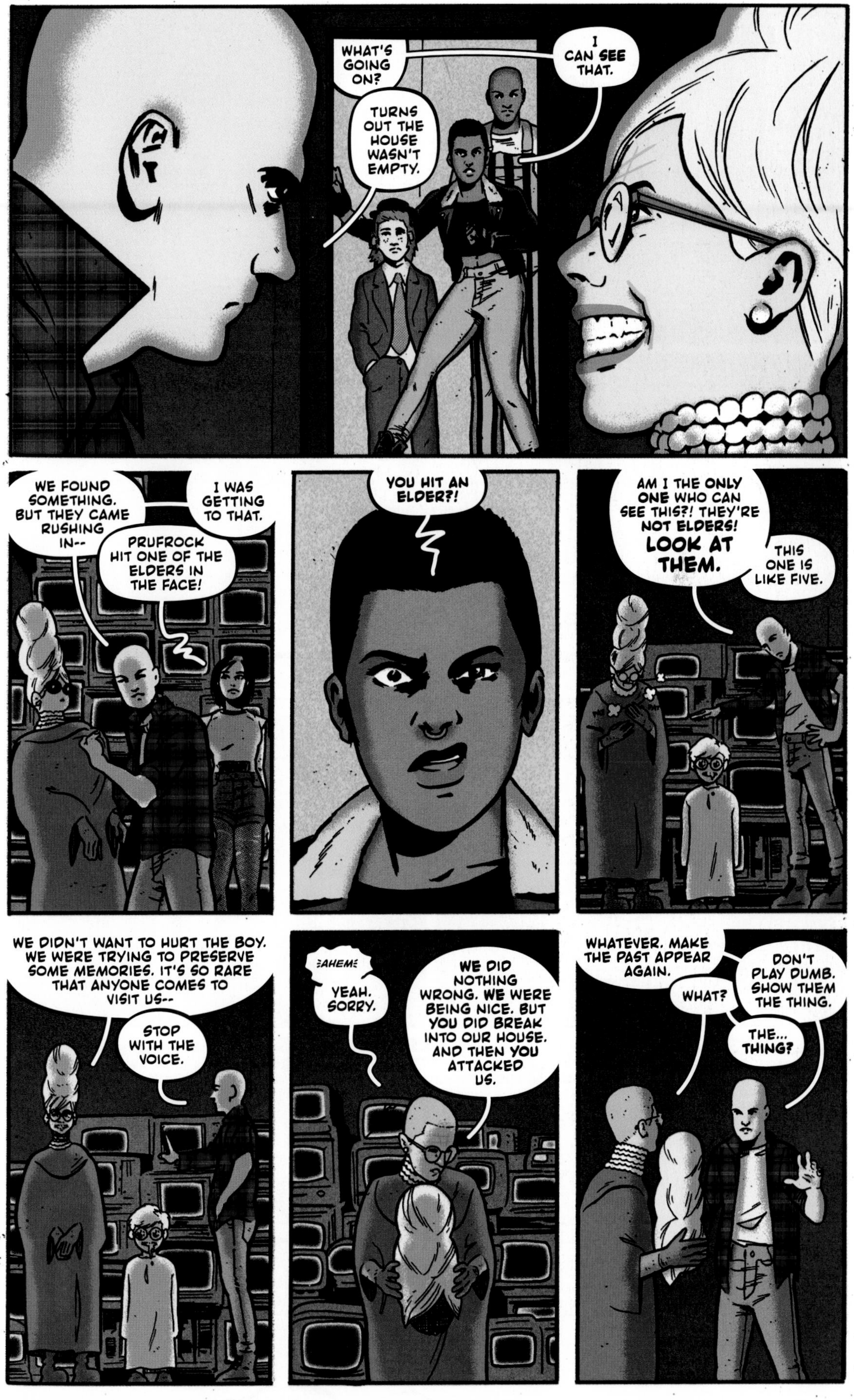
WHAT'S GOING ON?
I CAN SEE THAT.
TURNS OUT THE HOUSE WASN'T EMPTY.
WE FOUND SOMETHING. BUT THEY CAME RUSHING IN--
I WAS GETTING TO THAT.
PRUFROCK HIT ONE OF THE ELDERS IN THE FACE!
YOU HIT AN ELDER?!
AM I THE ONLY ONE WHO CAN SEE THIS?! THEY'RE NOT ELDERS! LOOK AT THEM.
THIS ONE IS LIKE FIVE.
WE DIDN'T WANT TO HURT THE BOY. WE WERE TRYING TO PRESERVE SOME MEMORIES. IT'S SO RARE THAT ANYONE COMES TO VISIT US--
STOP WITH THE VOICE.
AHEM
YEAH. SORRY.
WE DID NOTHING WRONG. WE WERE BEING NICE. BUT YOU DID BREAK INTO OUR HOUSE. AND THEN YOU ATTACKED US.
WHATEVER. MAKE THE PAST APPEAR AGAIN.
DON'T PLAY DUMB. SHOW THEM THE THING.
WHAT?
THE... THING?

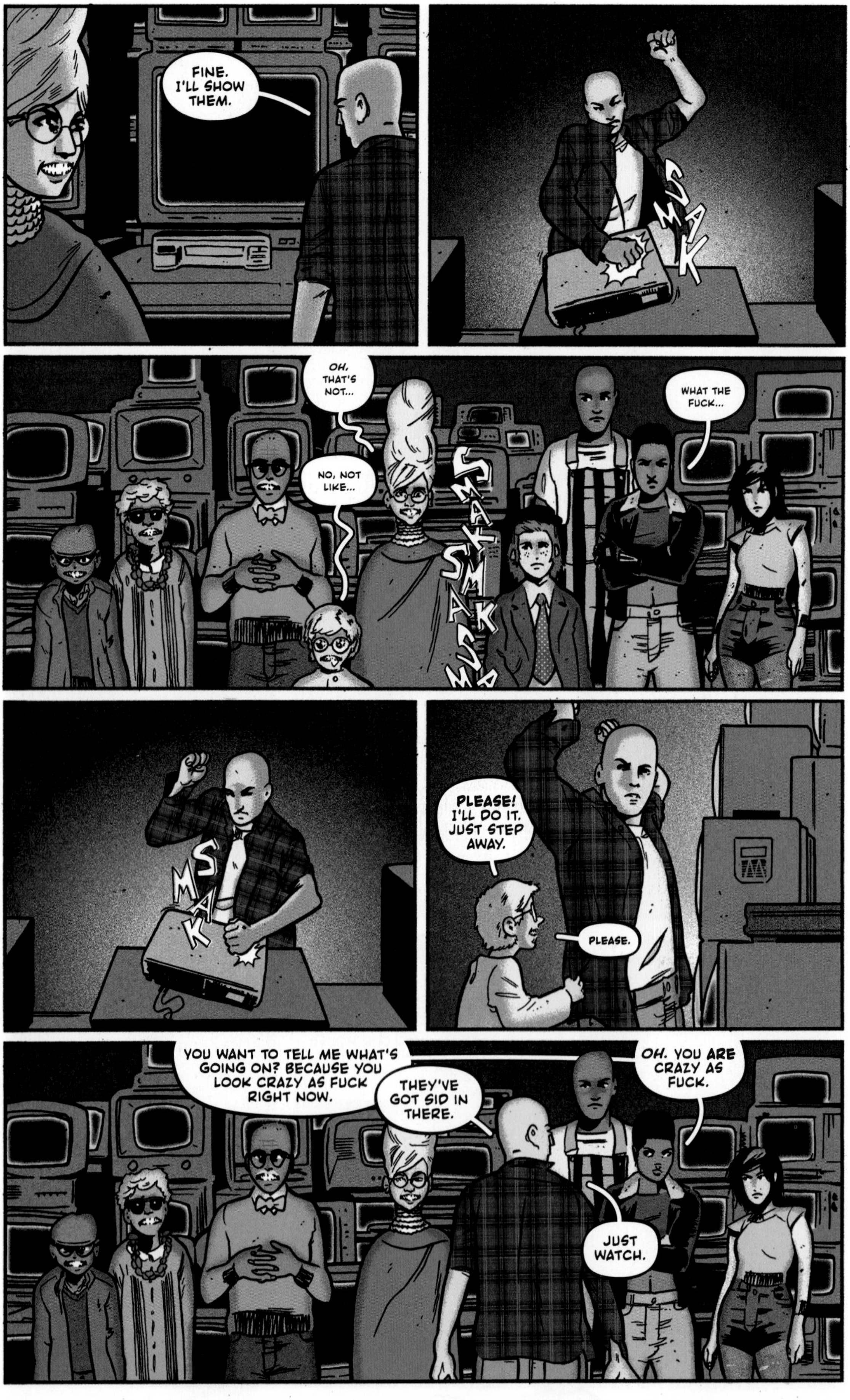
FINE. I'LL SHOW THEM.
SMAK
OH, THAT'S NOT...
NO, NOT LIKE...
SMAK SMAK SMAK
WHAT THE FUCK...
SMAK
PLEASE! I'LL DO IT. JUST STEP AWAY.
PLEASE.
YOU WANT TO TELL ME WHAT'S GOING ON? BECAUSE YOU LOOK CRAZY AS FUCK RIGHT NOW.
THEY'VE GOT SID IN THERE.
OH. YOU ARE CRAZY AS FUCK.
JUST WATCH.

WHAT'S YOUR NAME, SWEETIE PIE? AND WHERE DID YOU COME FROM?

MY NAME IS SID.

AM I SUPPOSED TO KNOW WHO THAT IS?

TOLD YOU.

THIS IS SOMETHING THAT HAPPENED ALREADY?

YES.

SO SID WAS HERE?

SID?

HER! THE GIRL THAT'S TALKING!

OH, RIGHT. WE CALL HER HONEY BABY. SHE WAS HERE.

AND?

THEY TOOK HER.

WHO?

YOU KNOW WHO. THEY.

THE STRANGERS TOOK HER.

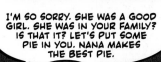

I'M SO SORRY. SHE WAS A GOOD GIRL. SHE WAS IN YOUR FAMILY? IS THAT IT? LET'S PUT SOME PIE IN YOU. NANA MAKES THE BEST PIE.

WHAT THE FUCK IS NANA?

I'M YOUR NANA.

HE DOESN'T LIKE PIE?

SLAM

# CHAPTER NINETEEN

## SHOW US YOUR GODS.

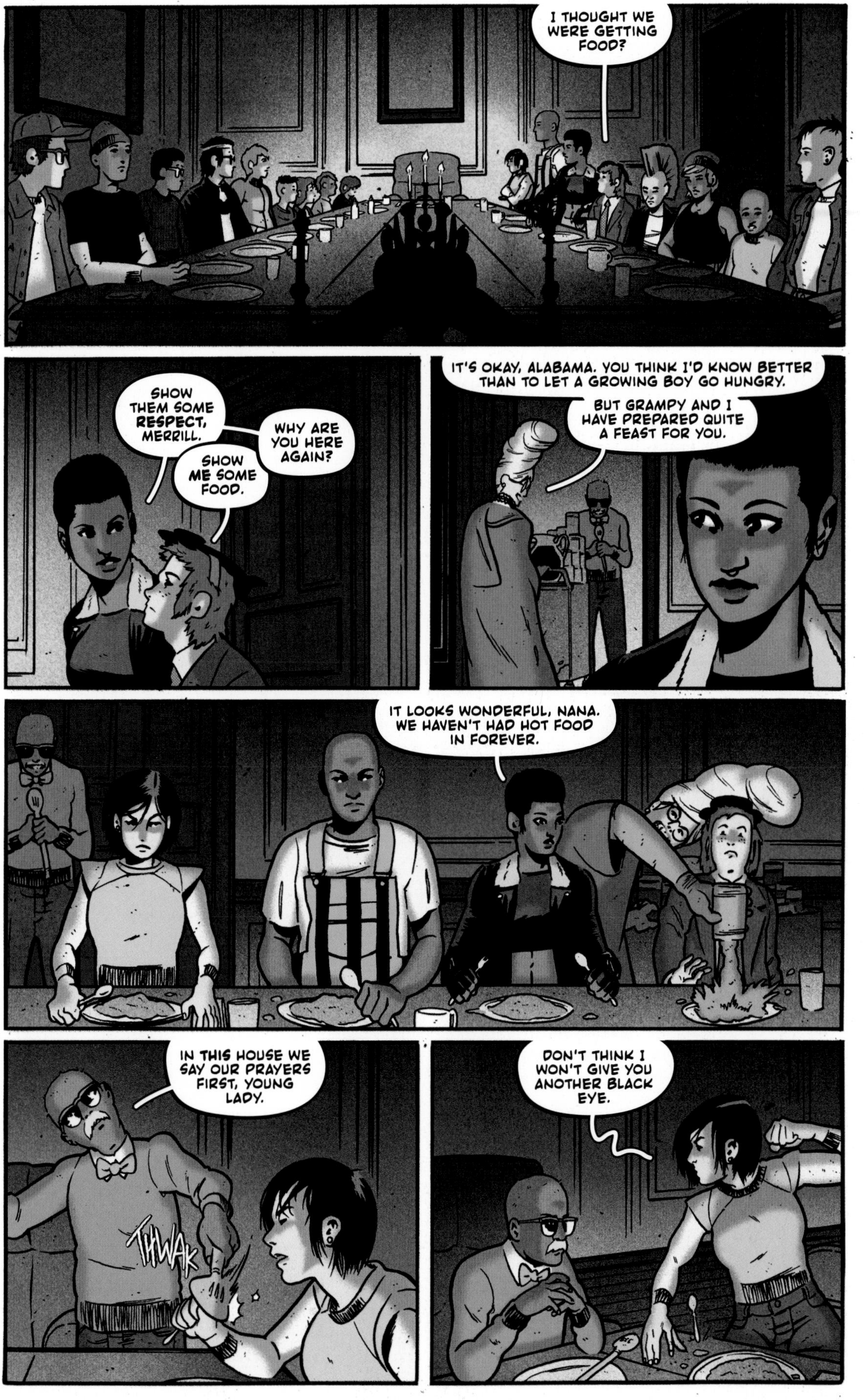
I THOUGHT WE WERE GETTING FOOD?
SHOW THEM SOME RESPECT, MERRILL.
WHY ARE YOU HERE AGAIN?
SHOW ME SOME FOOD.
IT'S OKAY, ALABAMA. YOU THINK I'D KNOW BETTER THAN TO LET A GROWING BOY GO HUNGRY.
BUT GRAMPY AND I HAVE PREPARED QUITE A FEAST FOR YOU.
IT LOOKS WONDERFUL, NANA. WE HAVEN'T HAD HOT FOOD IN FOREVER.
IN THIS HOUSE WE SAY OUR PRAYERS FIRST, YOUNG LADY.
THWAK
DON'T THINK I WON'T GIVE YOU ANOTHER BLACK EYE.

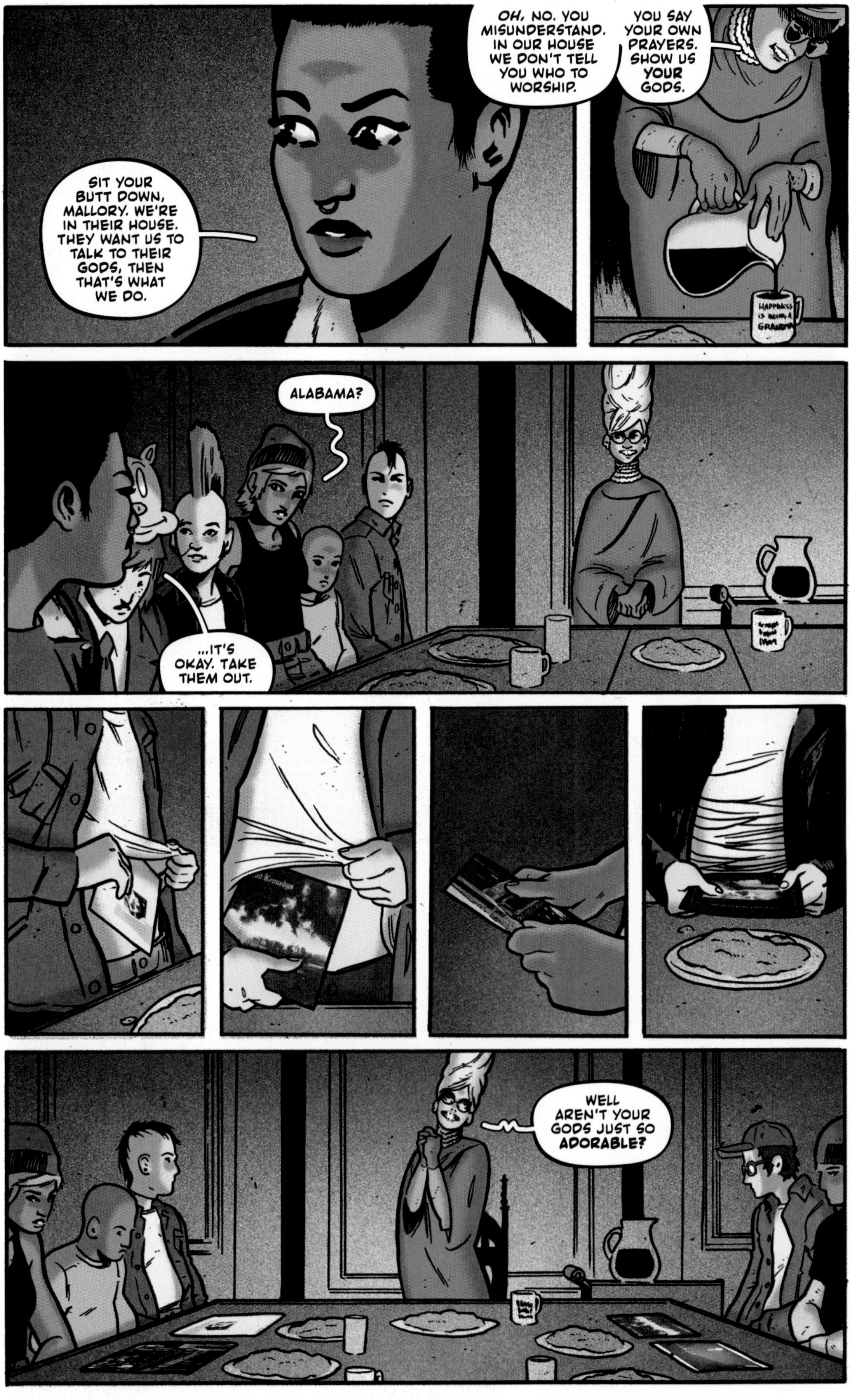
SIT YOUR BUTT DOWN, MALLORY. WE'RE IN THEIR HOUSE. THEY WANT US TO TALK TO THEIR GODS, THEN THAT'S WHAT WE DO.
OH, NO. YOU MISUNDERSTAND. IN OUR HOUSE WE DON'T TELL YOU WHO TO WORSHIP.
YOU SAY YOUR OWN PRAYERS. SHOW US YOUR GODS.
ALABAMA?
...IT'S OKAY. TAKE THEM OUT.
WELL AREN'T YOUR GODS JUST SO ADORABLE?

# CHAPTER TWENTY

## I MUST BE LOSING MY MIND.

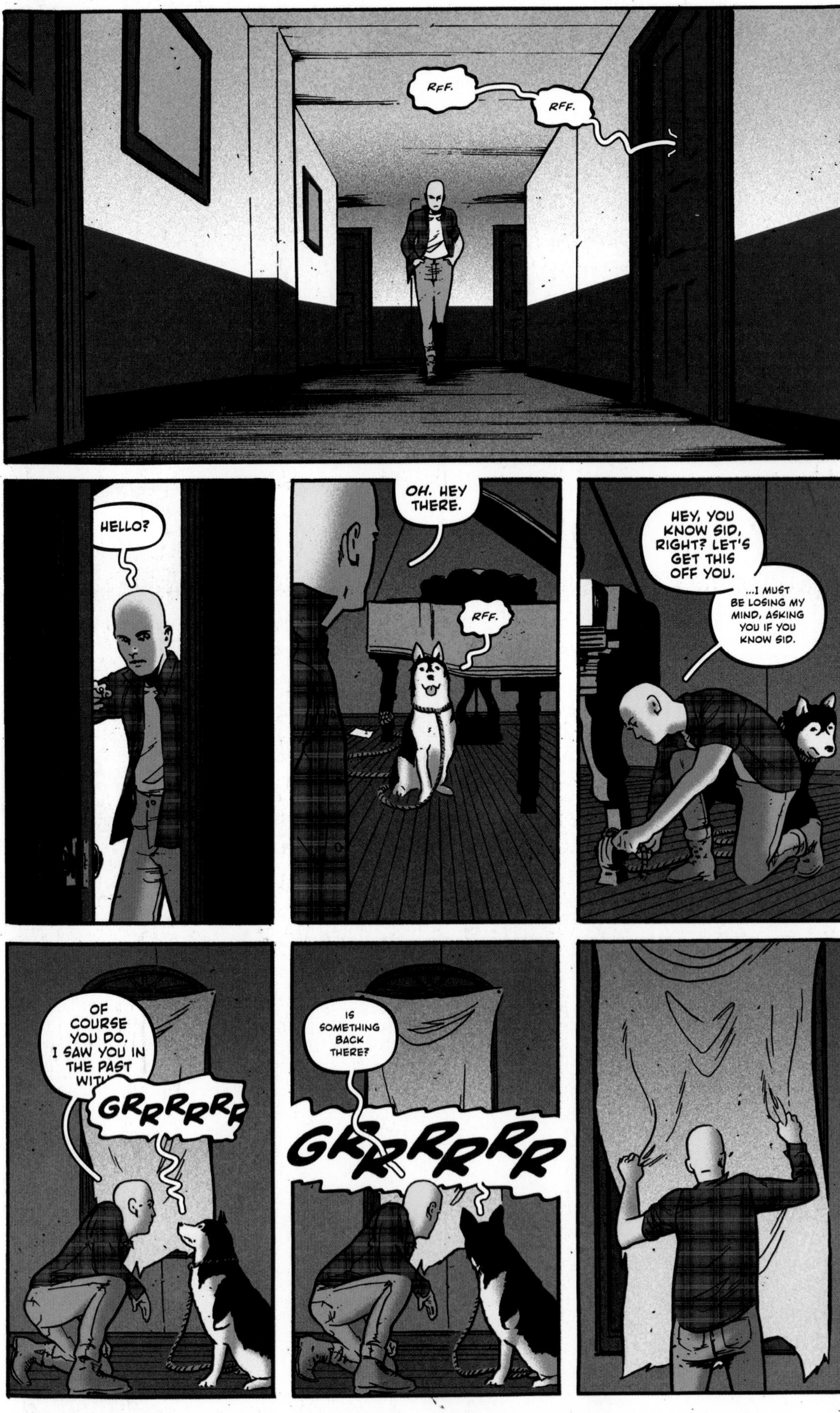
RFF.
RFF.
HELLO?
OH. HEY THERE.
RFF.
HEY, YOU KNOW SID, RIGHT? LET'S GET THIS OFF YOU.
...I MUST BE LOSING MY MIND, ASKING YOU IF YOU KNOW SID.
OF COURSE YOU DO. I SAW YOU IN THE PAST WITH
GRRRRRR
IS SOMETHING BACK THERE?
GRRRRRRR

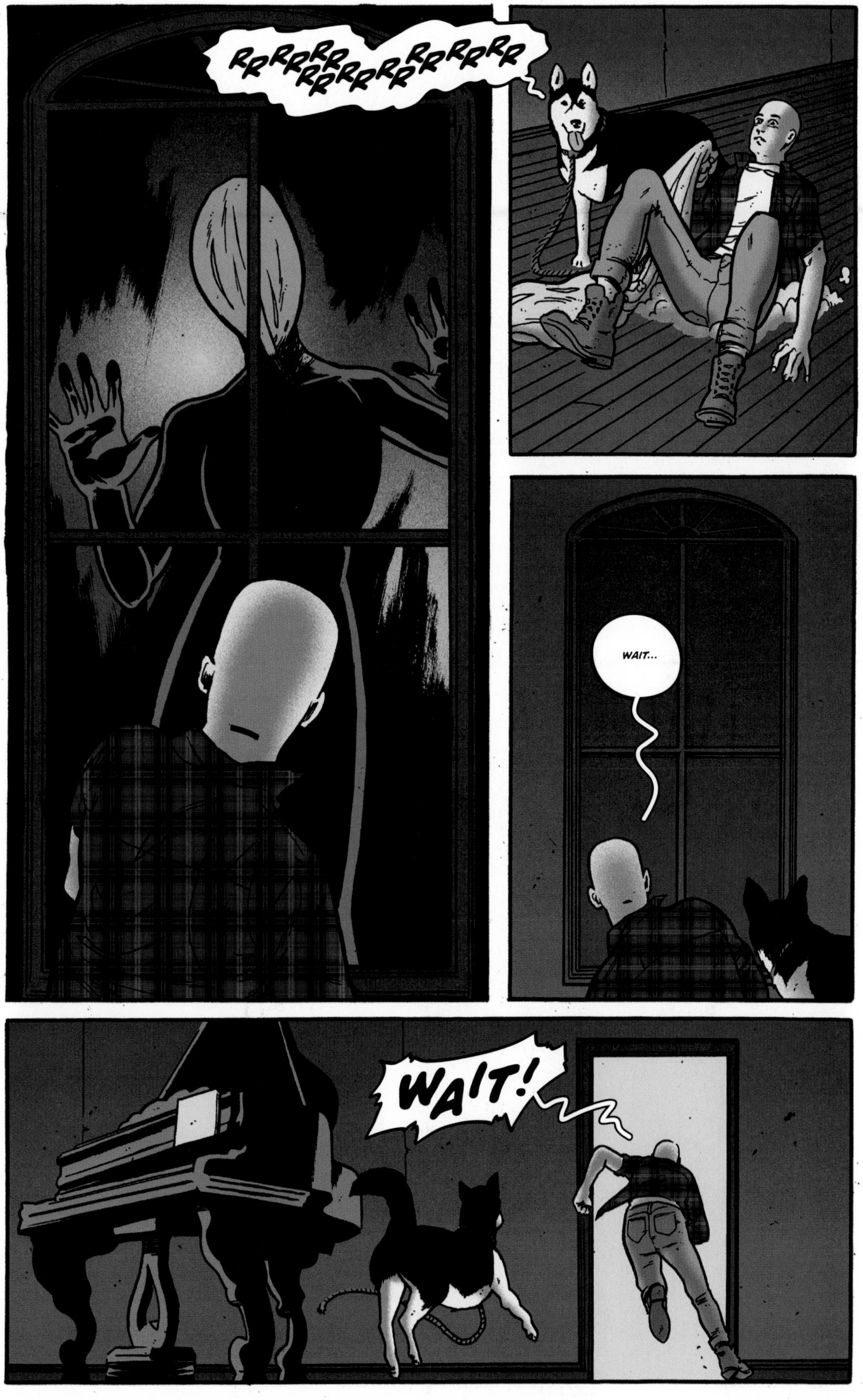
RRRRRRRRRRRRRRRRRR
WAIT...
WAIT!

# CHAPTER TWENTY-ONE

A STRANGER IN OUR HUMBLE HOME.

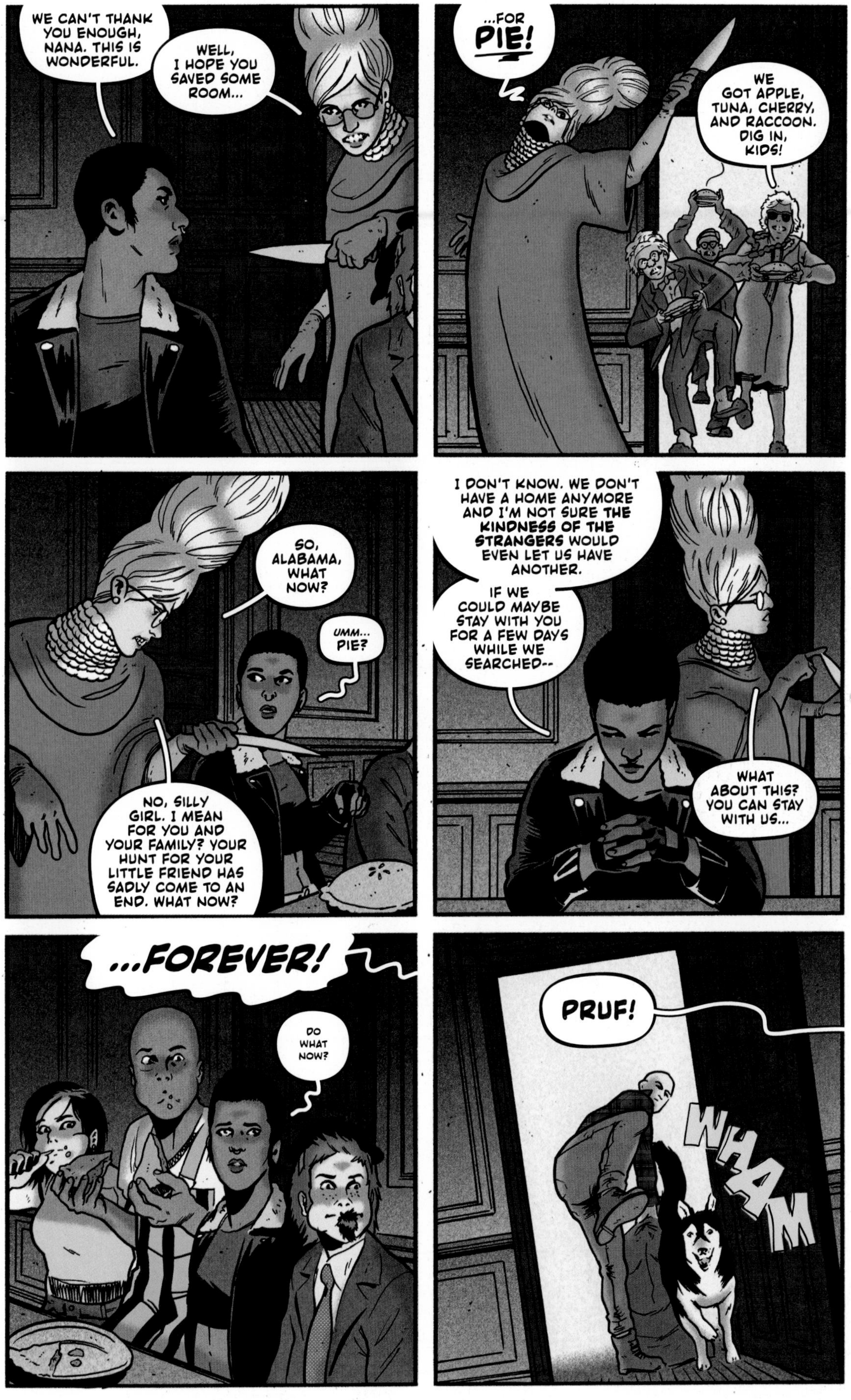
WE CAN'T THANK YOU ENOUGH, NANA. THIS IS WONDERFUL.
WELL, I HOPE YOU SAVED SOME ROOM...
...FOR PIE!
WE GOT APPLE, TUNA, CHERRY, AND RACCOON. DIG IN, KIDS!
SO, ALABAMA, WHAT NOW?
UMM... PIE?
NO, SILLY GIRL. I MEAN FOR YOU AND YOUR FAMILY? YOUR HUNT FOR YOUR LITTLE FRIEND HAS SADLY COME TO AN END. WHAT NOW?
I DON'T KNOW. WE DON'T HAVE A HOME ANYMORE AND I'M NOT SURE THE KINDNESS OF THE STRANGERS WOULD EVEN LET US HAVE ANOTHER.
IF WE COULD MAYBE STAY WITH YOU FOR A FEW DAYS WHILE WE SEARCHED--
WHAT ABOUT THIS? YOU CAN STAY WITH US...
...FOREVER!
DO WHAT NOW?
PRUF!
WHAM

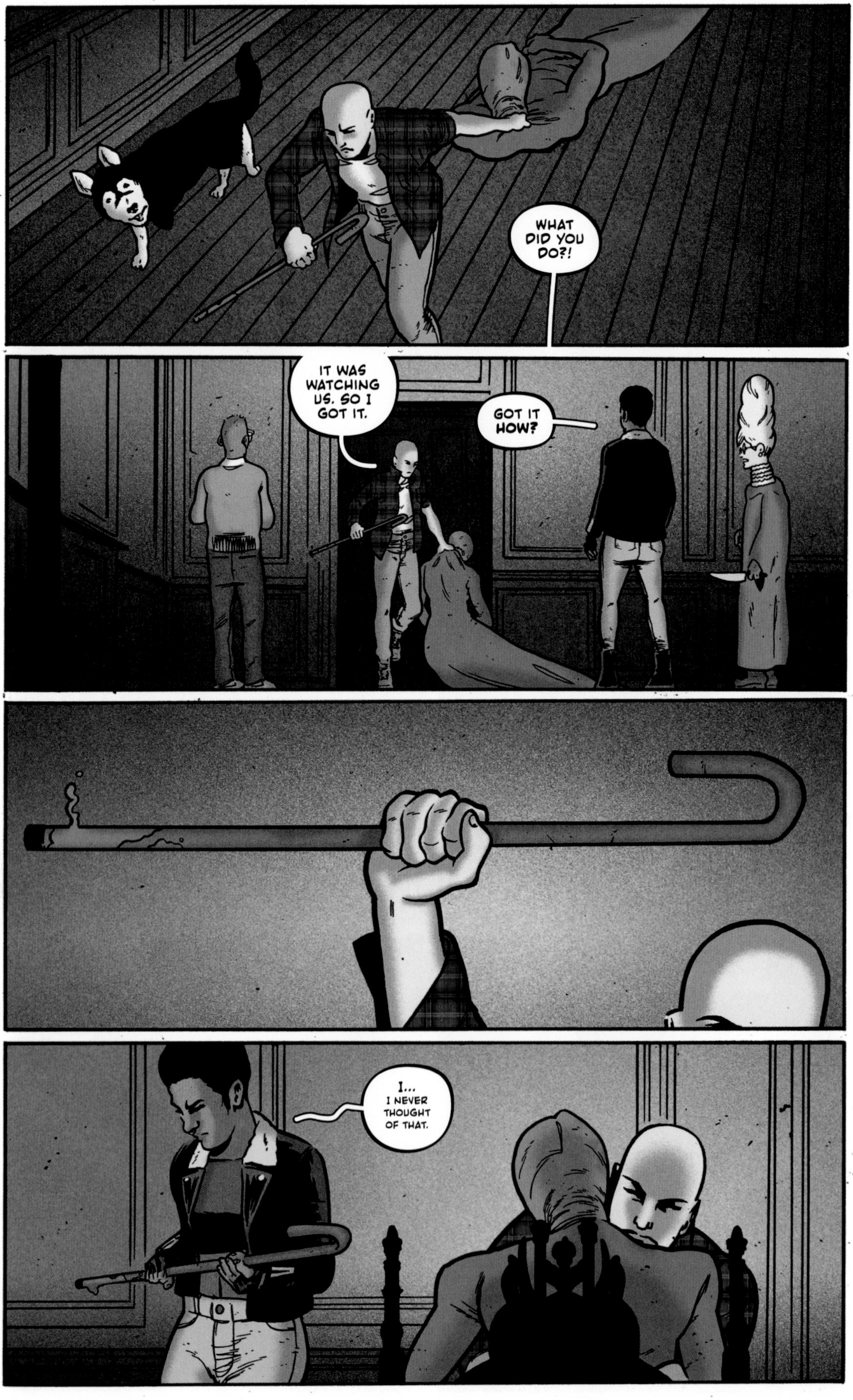
WHAT DID YOU DO?!
IT WAS WATCHING US. SO I GOT IT.
GOT IT HOW?
I... I NEVER THOUGHT OF THAT.

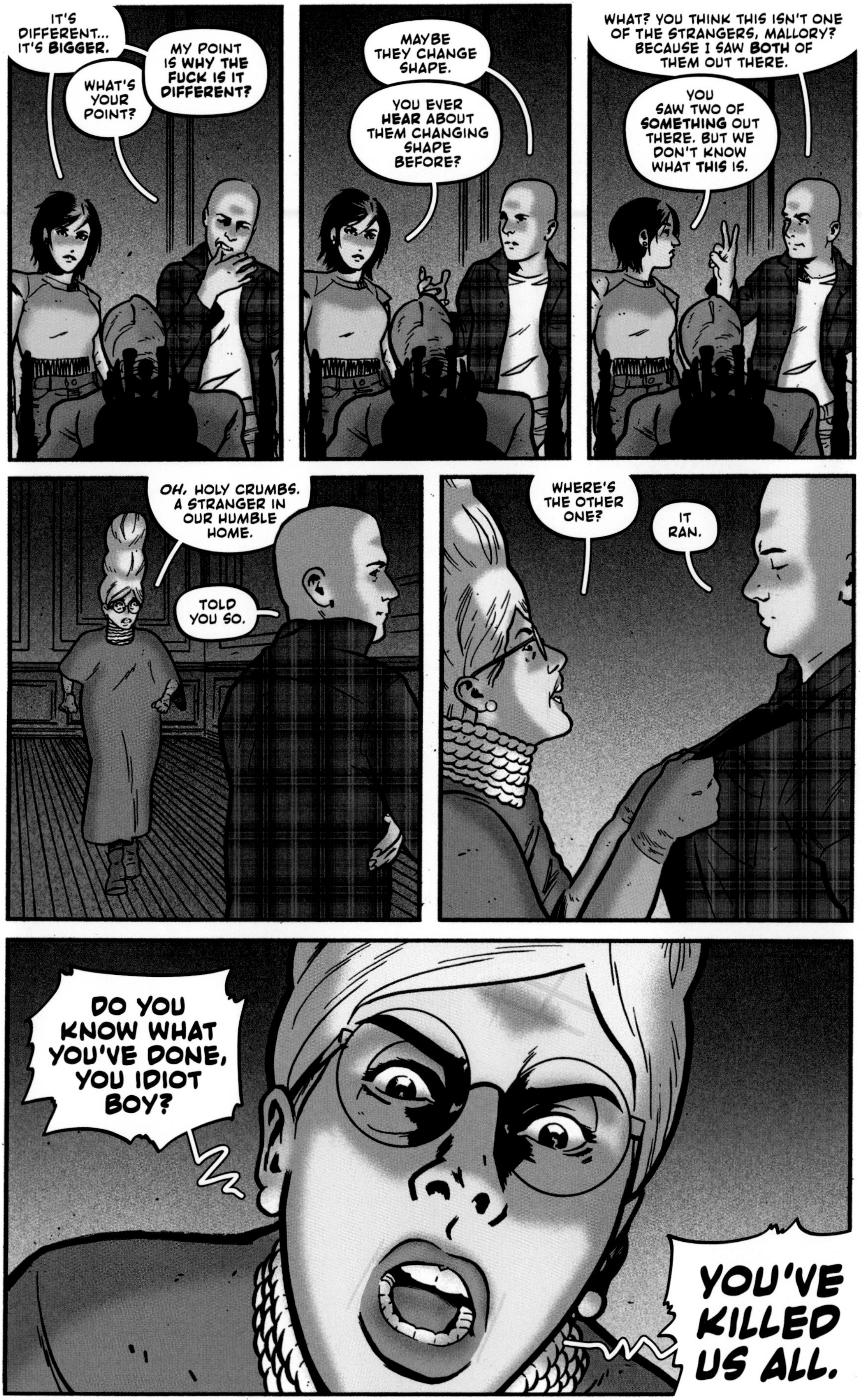

IT'S DIFFERENT... IT'S BIGGER.
WHAT'S YOUR POINT?
MY POINT IS WHY THE FUCK IS IT DIFFERENT?
MAYBE THEY CHANGE SHAPE.
YOU EVER HEAR ABOUT THEM CHANGING SHAPE BEFORE?
WHAT? YOU THINK THIS ISN'T ONE OF THE STRANGERS, MALLORY? BECAUSE I SAW BOTH OF THEM OUT THERE.
YOU SAW TWO OF SOMETHING OUT THERE. BUT WE DON'T KNOW WHAT THIS IS.
OH, HOLY CRUMBS. A STRANGER IN OUR HUMBLE HOME.
TOLD YOU SO.
WHERE'S THE OTHER ONE?
IT RAN.
DO YOU KNOW WHAT YOU'VE DONE, YOU IDIOT BOY?
YOU'VE KILLED US ALL.

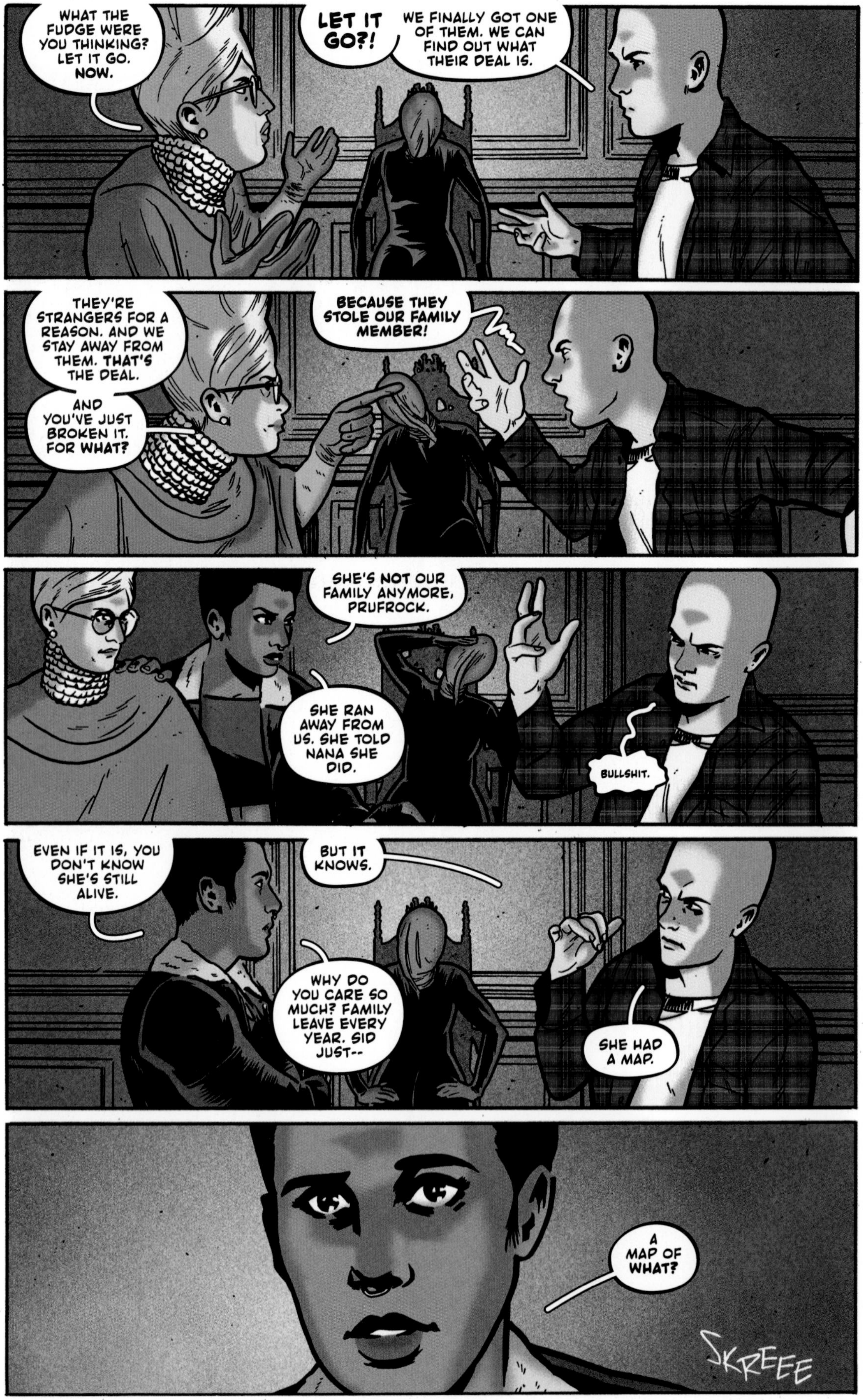
WHAT THE FUDGE WERE YOU THINKING? LET IT GO. NOW.
LET IT GO?!
WE FINALLY GOT ONE OF THEM. WE CAN FIND OUT WHAT THEIR DEAL IS.
THEY'RE STRANGERS FOR A REASON. AND WE STAY AWAY FROM THEM. THAT'S THE DEAL.
AND YOU'VE JUST BROKEN IT. FOR WHAT?
BECAUSE THEY STOLE OUR FAMILY MEMBER!
SHE'S NOT OUR FAMILY ANYMORE, PRUFROCK.
SHE RAN AWAY FROM US. SHE TOLD NANA SHE DID.
BULLSHIT.
EVEN IF IT IS, YOU DON'T KNOW SHE'S STILL ALIVE.
BUT IT KNOWS.
WHY DO YOU CARE SO MUCH? FAMILY LEAVE EVERY YEAR. SID JUST--
SHE HAD A MAP.
A MAP OF WHAT?
SKREEE

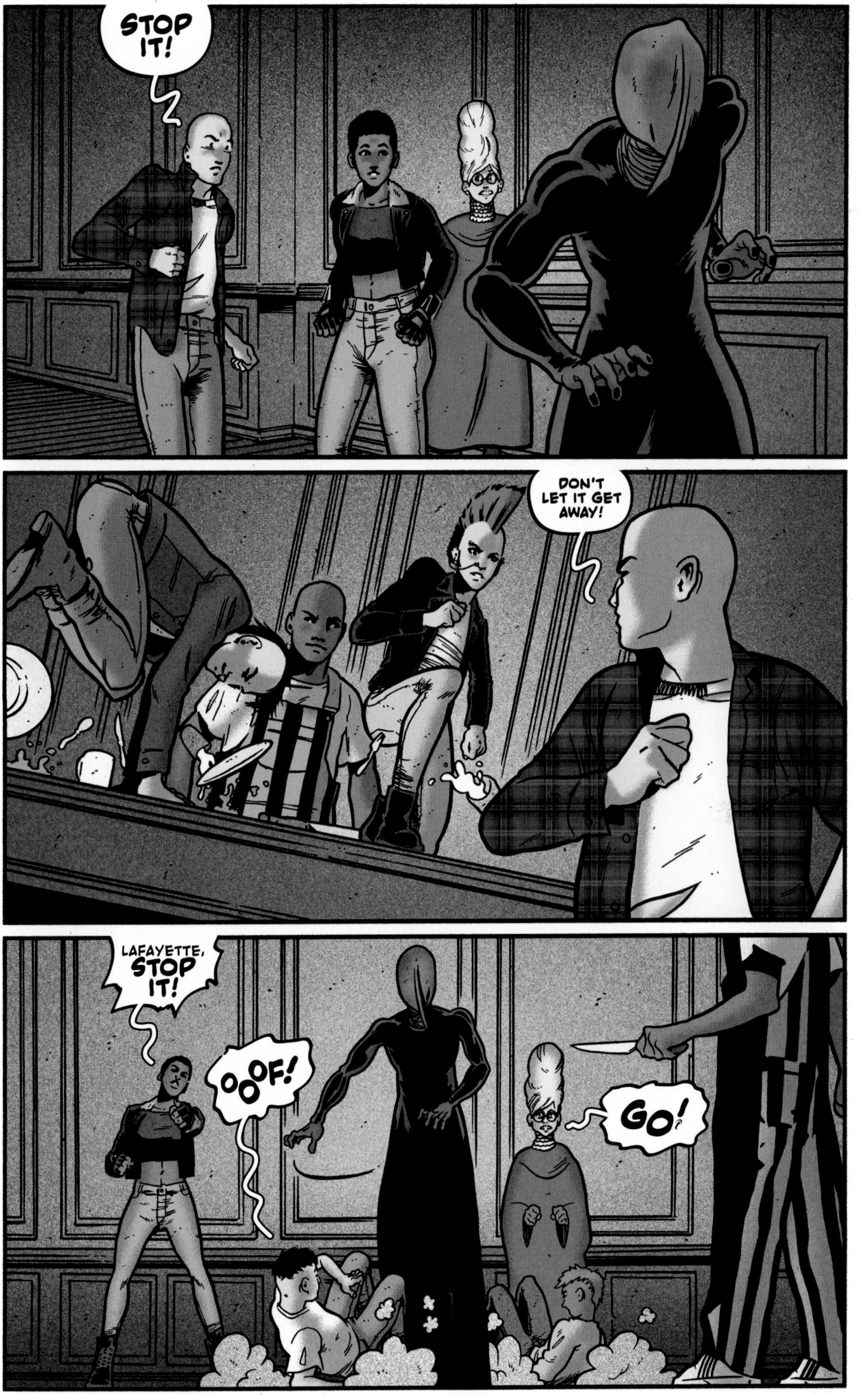
STOP IT!
DON'T LET IT GET AWAY!
LAFAYETTE, STOP IT!
OOOF!
GO!

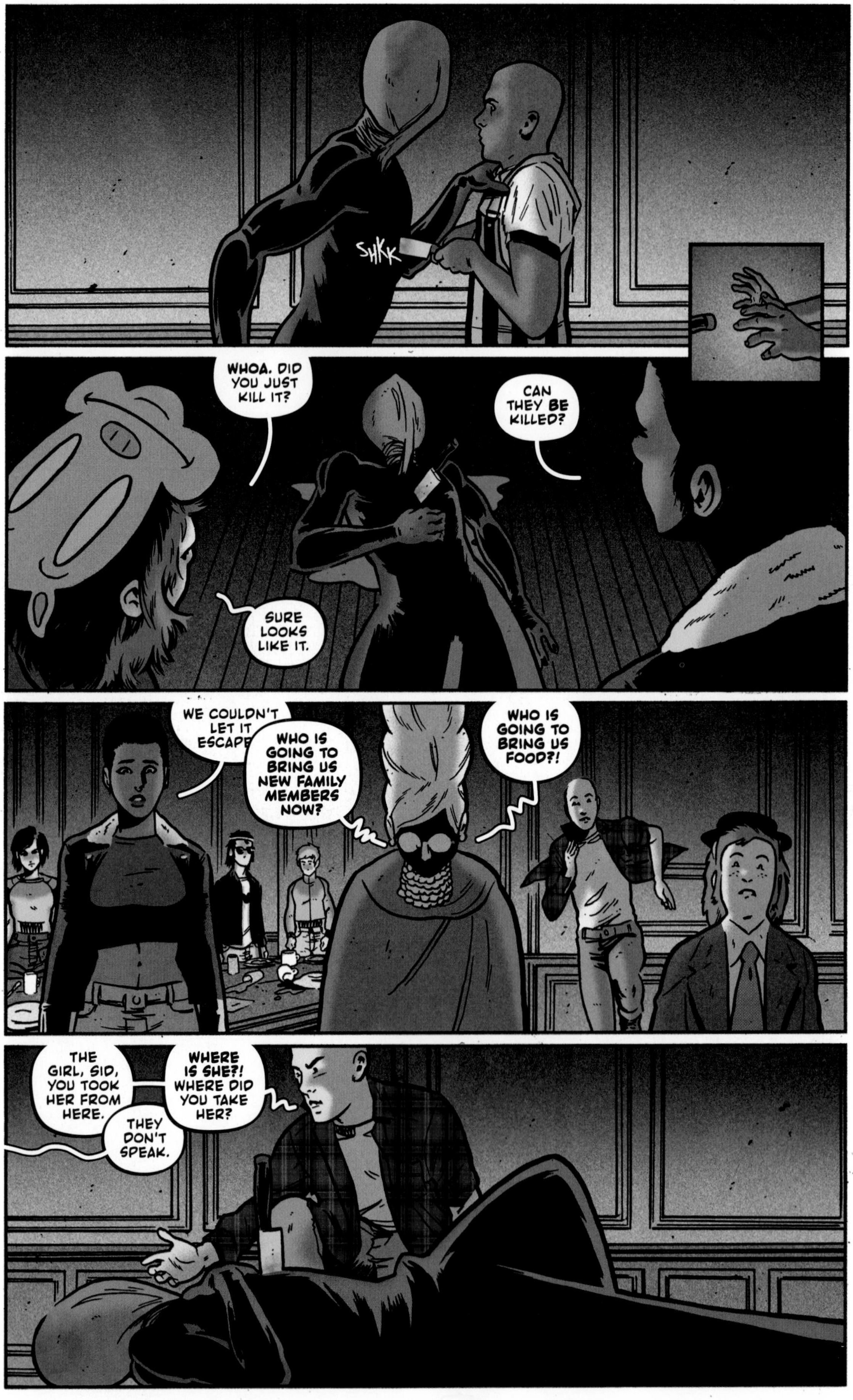
SHKK
WHOA. DID YOU JUST KILL IT?
CAN THEY BE KILLED?
SURE LOOKS LIKE IT.
WE COULDN'T LET IT ESCAPE
WHO IS GOING TO BRING US NEW FAMILY MEMBERS NOW?
WHO IS GOING TO BRING US FOOD?!
THE GIRL, SID, YOU TOOK HER FROM HERE.
WHERE IS SHE?! WHERE DID YOU TAKE HER?
THEY DON'T SPEAK.

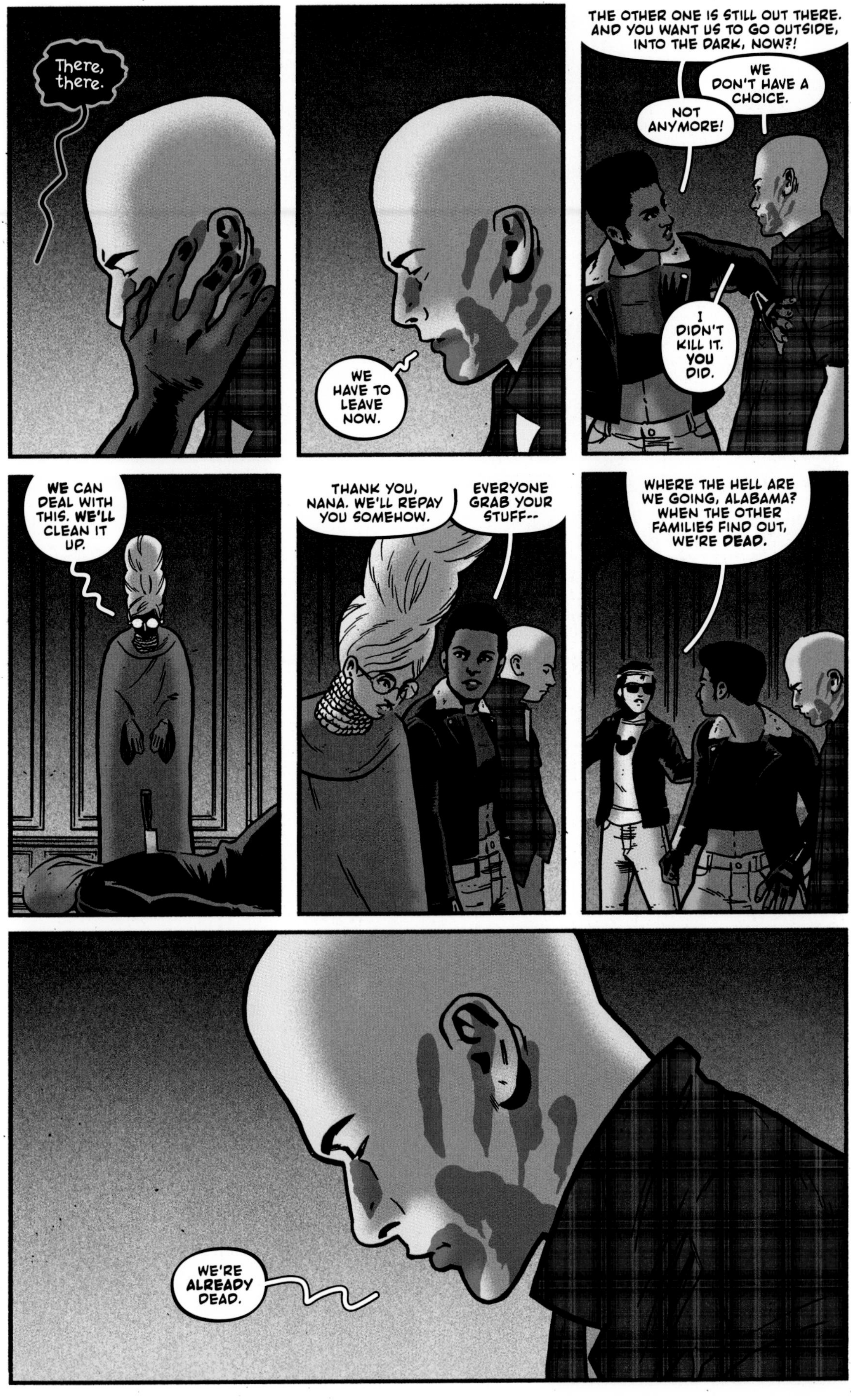
There, there.
WE HAVE TO LEAVE NOW.
THE OTHER ONE IS STILL OUT THERE. AND YOU WANT US TO GO OUTSIDE, INTO THE DARK, NOW?!
WE DON'T HAVE A CHOICE.
NOT ANYMORE!
I DIDN'T KILL IT. YOU DID.
WE CAN DEAL WITH THIS. WE'LL CLEAN IT UP.
THANK YOU, NANA. WE'LL REPAY YOU SOMEHOW.
EVERYONE GRAB YOUR STUFF--
WHERE THE HELL ARE WE GOING, ALABAMA? WHEN THE OTHER FAMILIES FIND OUT, WE'RE DEAD.
WE'RE ALREADY DEAD.

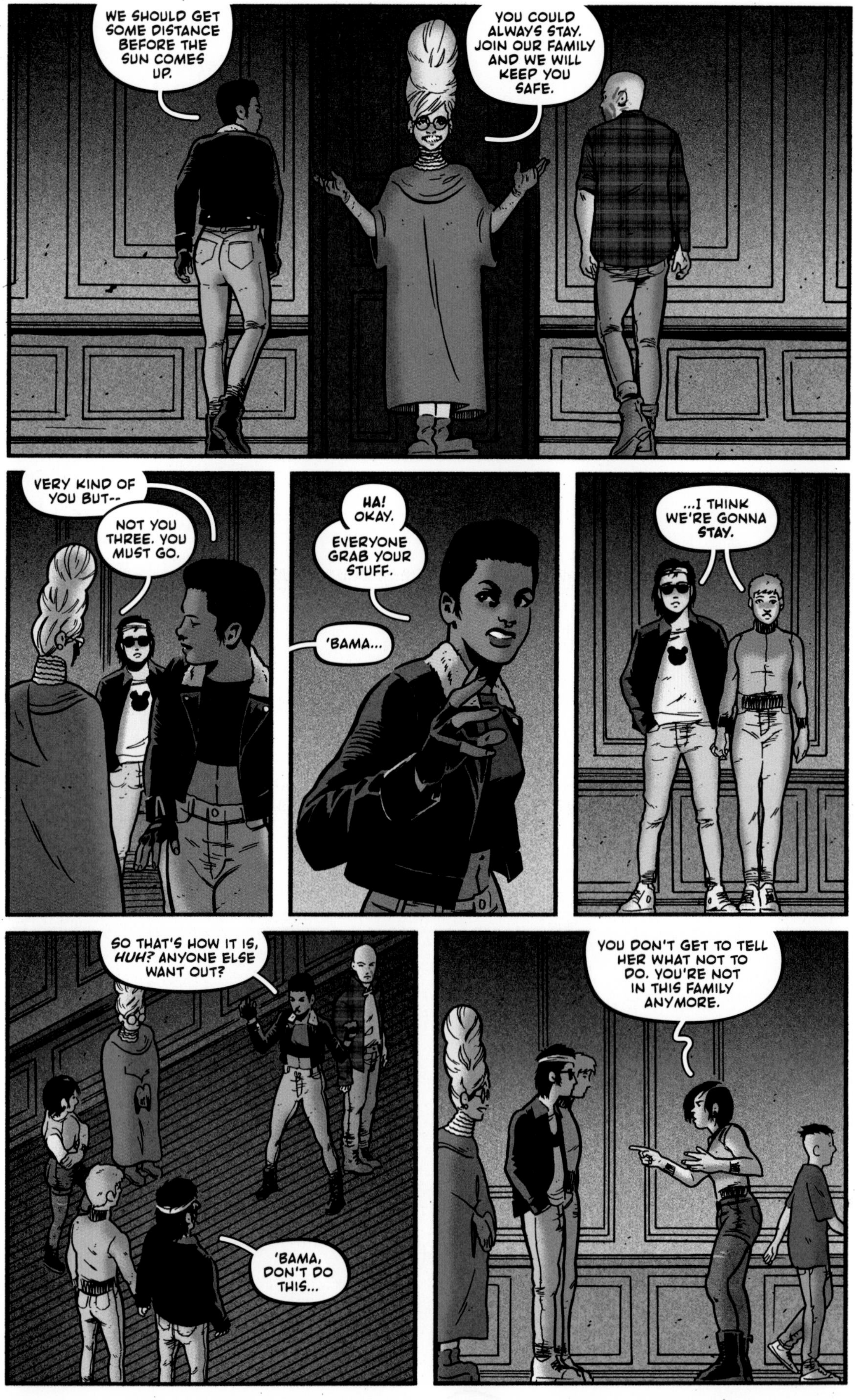
WE SHOULD GET SOME DISTANCE BEFORE THE SUN COMES UP.
YOU COULD ALWAYS STAY. JOIN OUR FAMILY AND WE WILL KEEP YOU SAFE.
VERY KIND OF YOU BUT--
NOT YOU THREE. YOU MUST GO.
HA! OKAY.
EVERYONE GRAB YOUR STUFF.
'BAMA...
...I THINK WE'RE GONNA STAY.
SO THAT'S HOW IT IS, *HUH?* ANYONE ELSE WANT OUT?
'BAMA, DON'T DO THIS...
YOU DON'T GET TO TELL HER WHAT NOT TO DO. YOU'RE NOT IN THIS FAMILY ANYMORE.

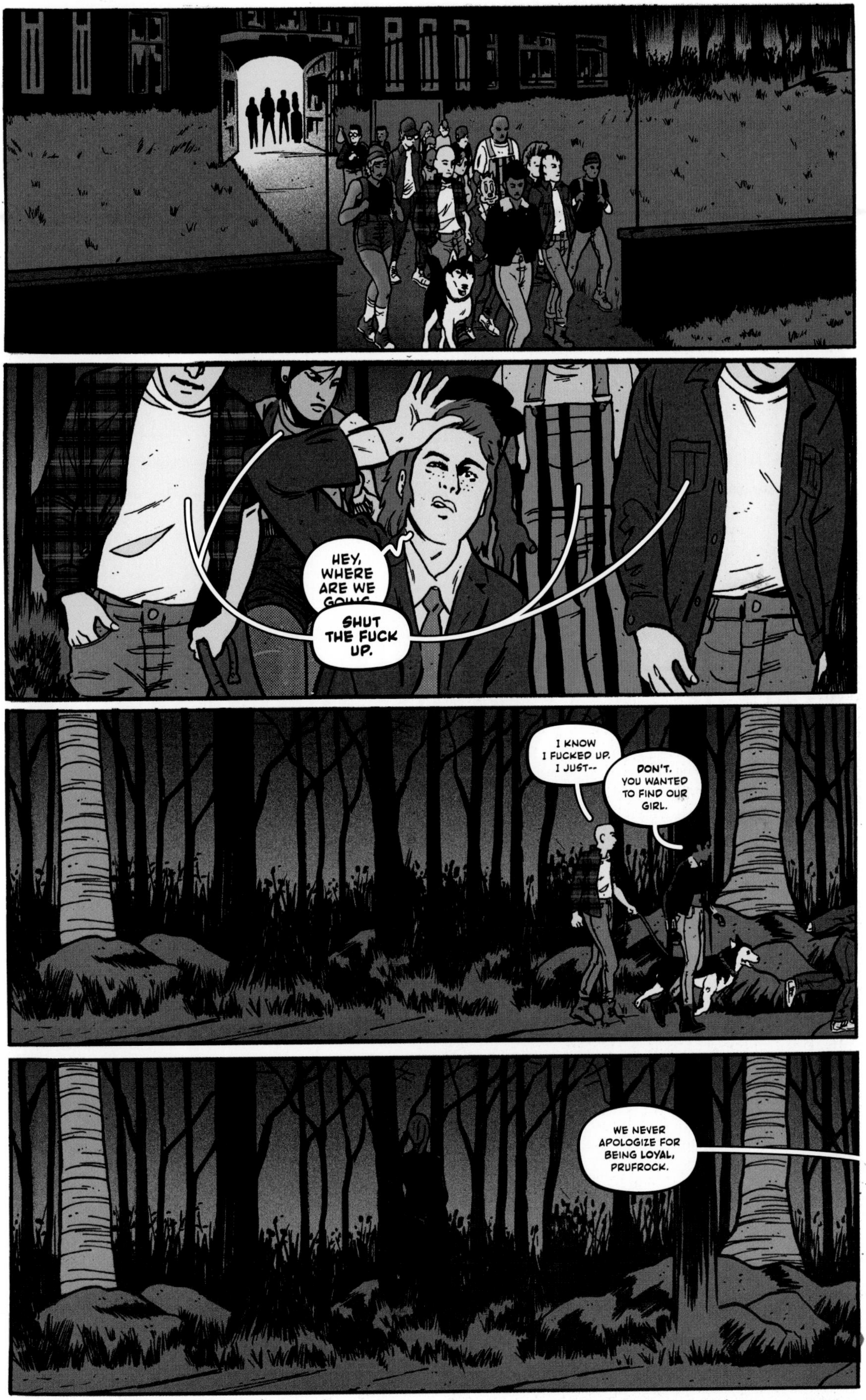
HEY, WHERE ARE WE GOING
SHUT THE FUCK UP.
I KNOW I FUCKED UP. I JUST--
DON'T. YOU WANTED TO FIND OUR GIRL.
WE NEVER APOLOGIZE FOR BEING LOYAL, PRUFROCK.

# CHAPTER TWENTY-TWO

## DRINK YOUR COCOA WHEN WE MAKE IT FOR YOU!

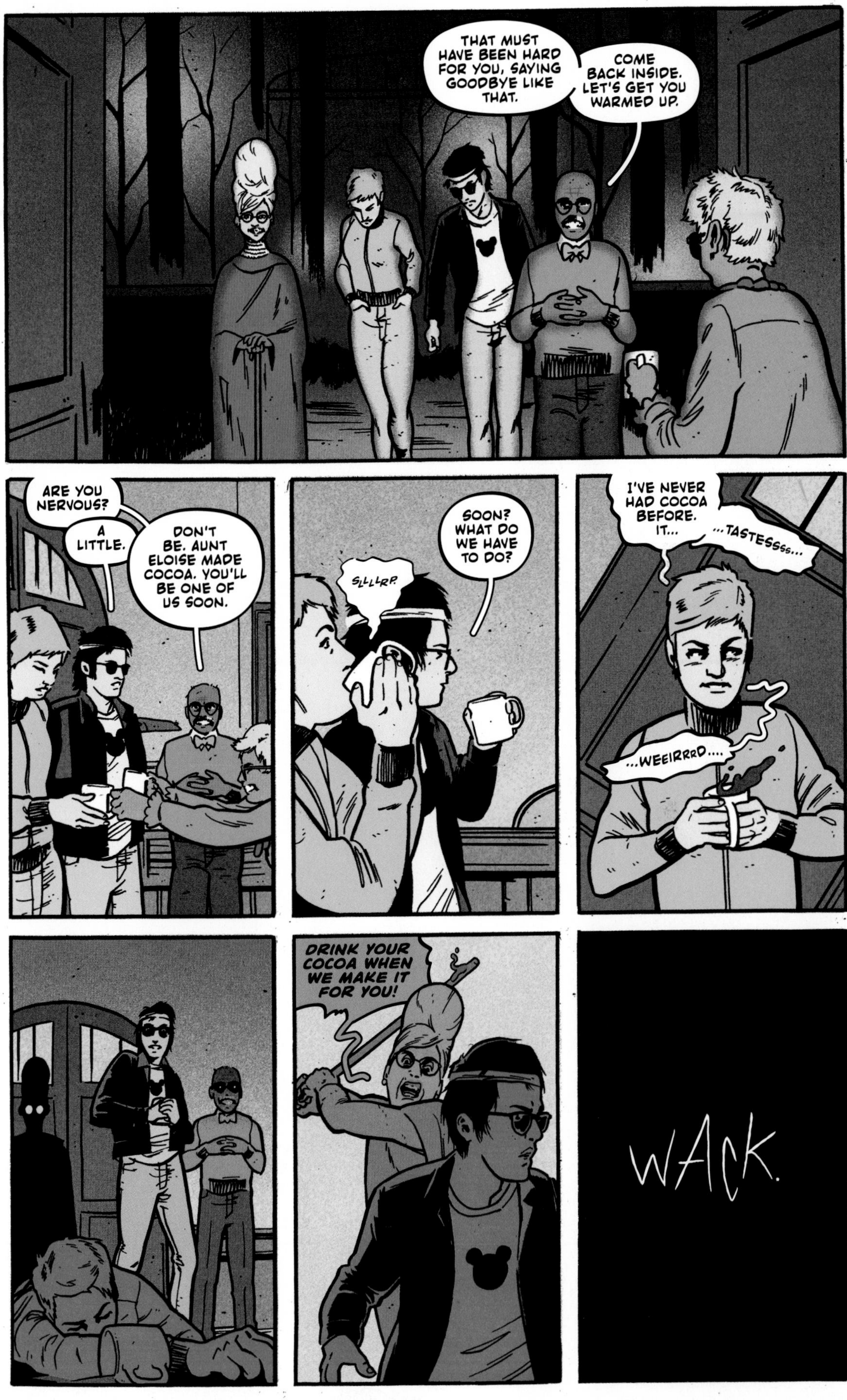
THAT MUST HAVE BEEN HARD FOR YOU, SAYING GOODBYE LIKE THAT.
COME BACK INSIDE. LET'S GET YOU WARMED UP.
ARE YOU NERVOUS?
A LITTLE.
DON'T BE. AUNT ELOISE MADE COCOA. YOU'LL BE ONE OF US SOON.
SLLLLRP.
SOON? WHAT DO WE HAVE TO DO?
I'VE NEVER HAD COCOA BEFORE. IT...
...TASTESSSSS...
...WEEIRRRD....
DRINK YOUR COCOA WHEN WE MAKE IT FOR YOU!
WACK.

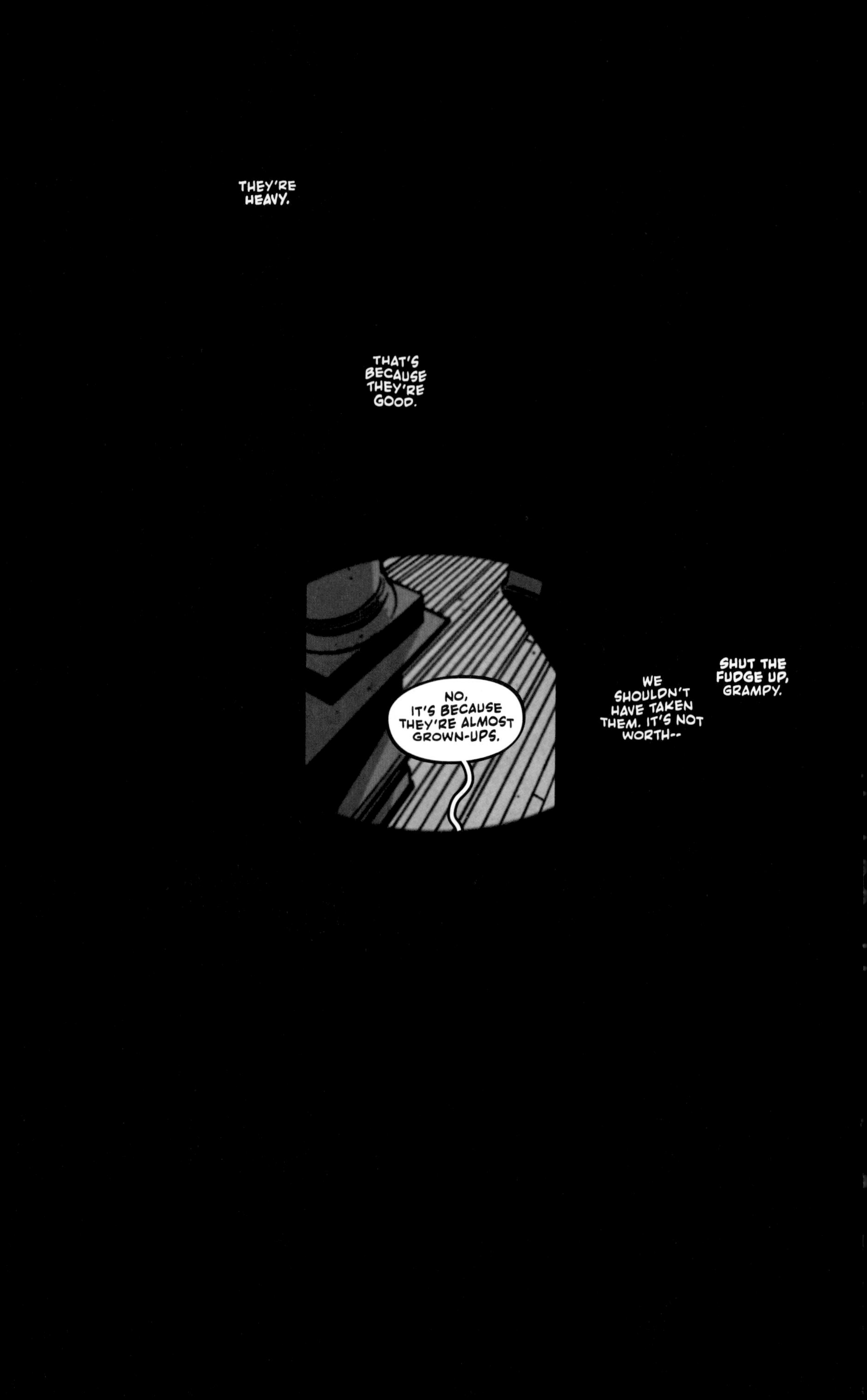
THEY'RE HEAVY.
THAT'S BECAUSE THEY'RE GOOD.
NO, IT'S BECAUSE THEY'RE ALMOST GROWN-UPS.
WE SHOULDN'T HAVE TAKEN THEM. IT'S NOT WORTH--
SHUT THE FUDGE UP, GRAMPY.

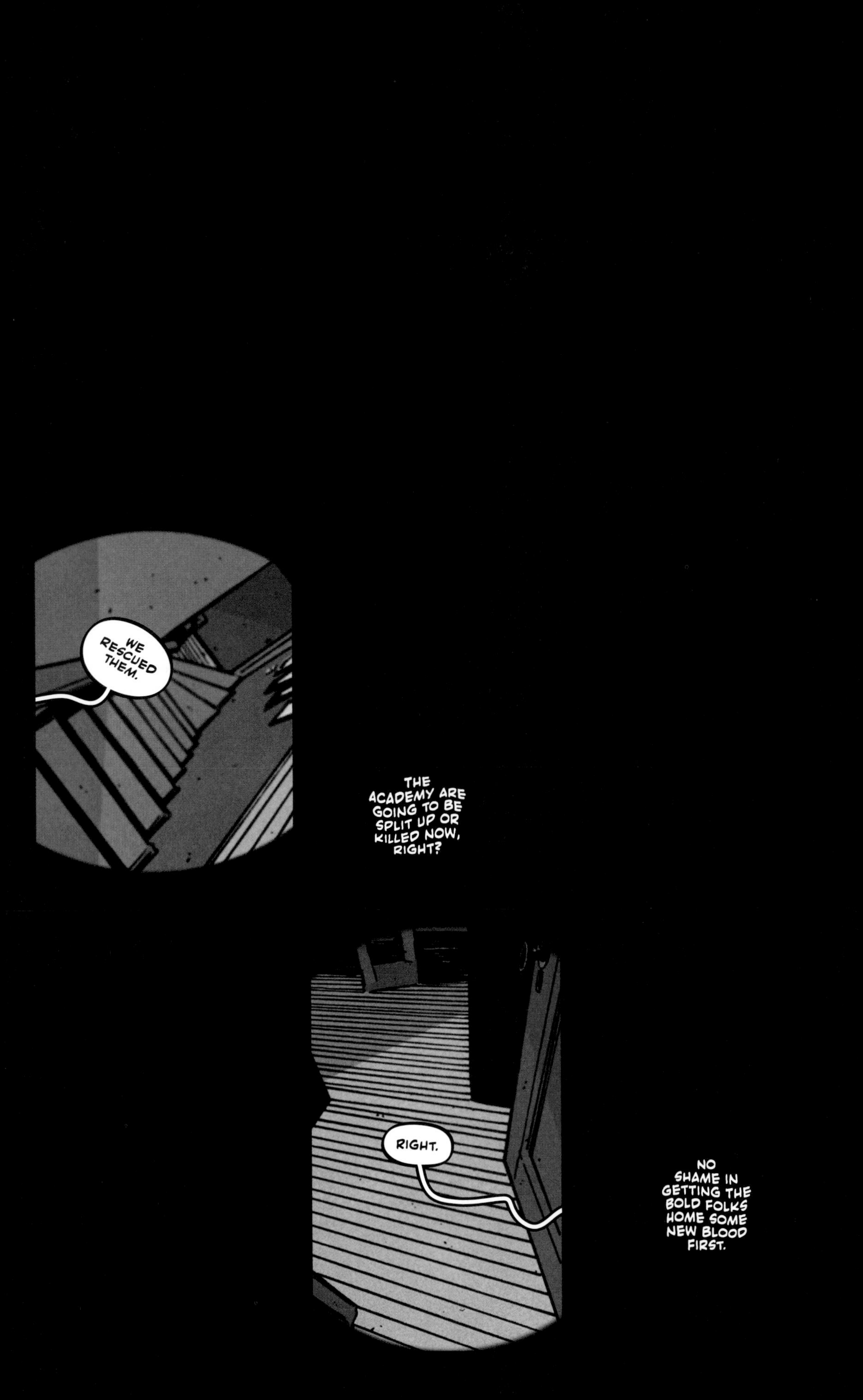
WE RESCUED THEM.
THE ACADEMY ARE GOING TO BE SPLIT UP OR KILLED NOW, RIGHT?
RIGHT.
NO SHAME IN GETTING THE BOLD FOLKS HOME SOME NEW BLOOD FIRST.

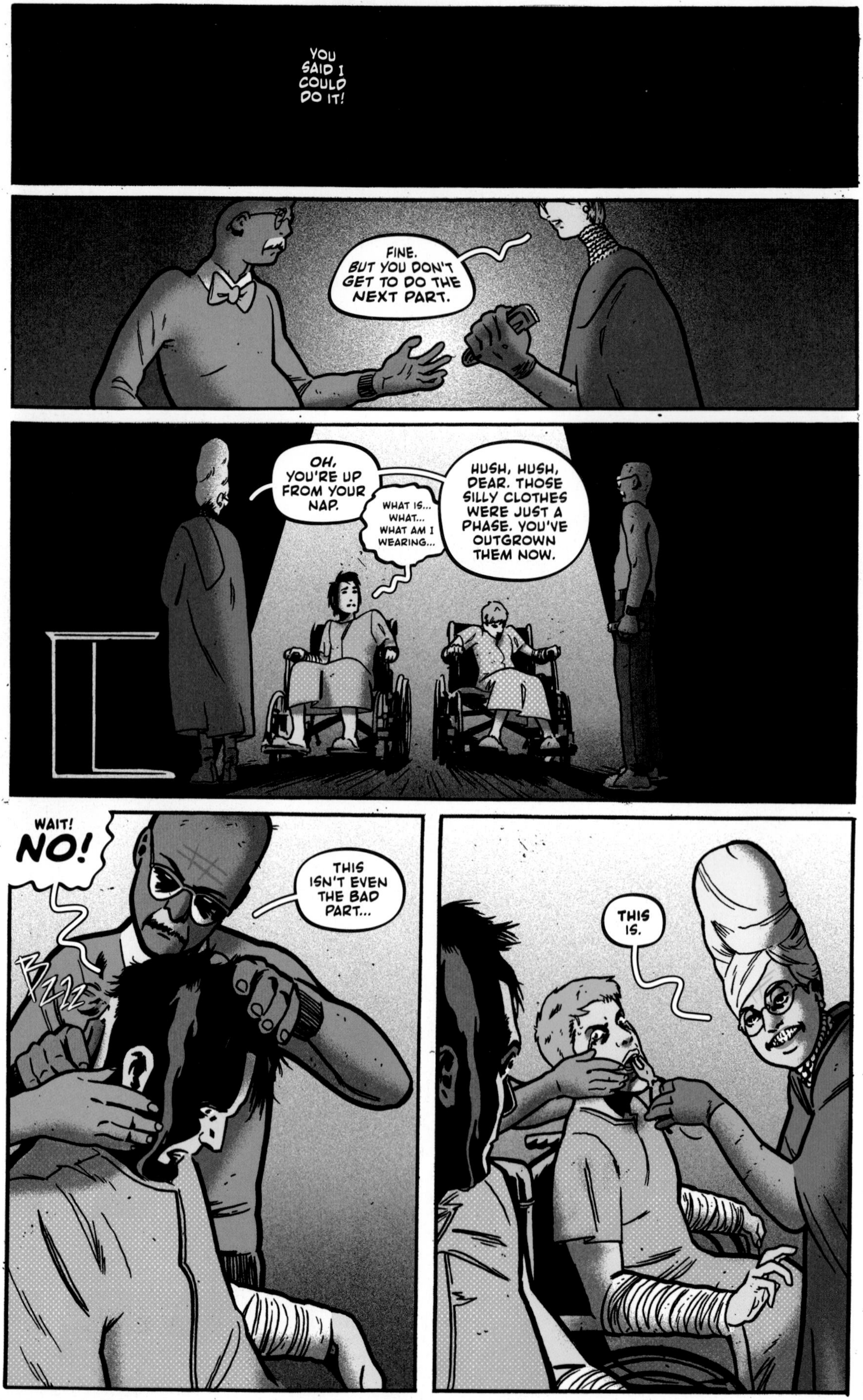

YOU SAID I COULD DO IT!
FINE. BUT YOU DON'T GET TO DO THE NEXT PART.
OH, YOU'RE UP FROM YOUR NAP.
WHAT IS... WHAT... WHAT AM I WEARING...
HUSH, HUSH, DEAR. THOSE SILLY CLOTHES WERE JUST A PHASE. YOU'VE OUTGROWN THEM NOW.
WAIT! NO!
BZZZ
THIS ISN'T EVEN THE BAD PART...
THIS IS.

# CHAPTER TWENTY-THREE

SOMETHING'S COMING.

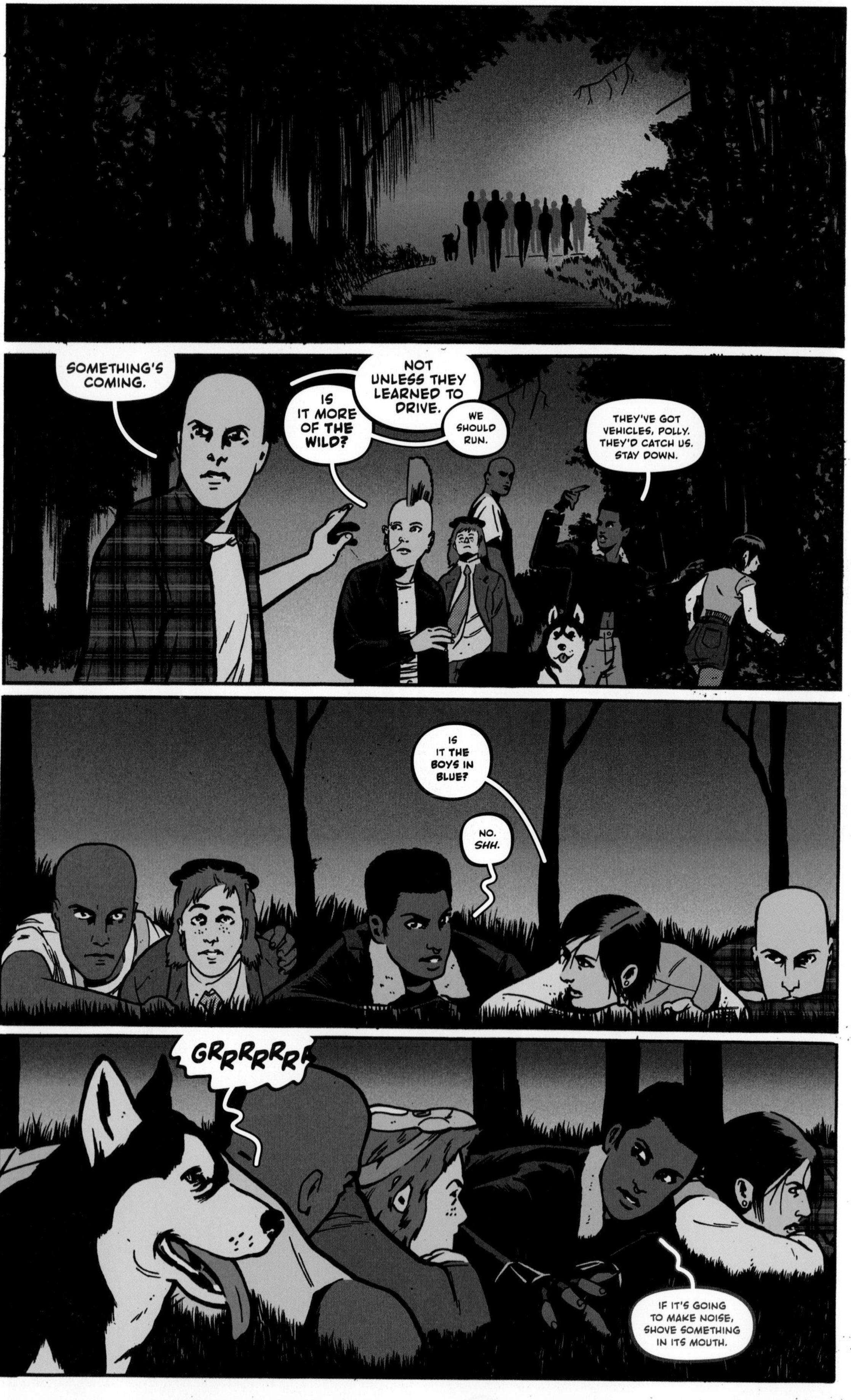
SOMETHING'S COMING.
IS IT MORE OF THE WILD?
NOT UNLESS THEY LEARNED TO DRIVE.
WE SHOULD RUN.
THEY'VE GOT VEHICLES, POLLY. THEY'D CATCH US. STAY DOWN.
IS IT THE BOYS IN BLUE?
NO. SHH.
GRRRRRR
IF IT'S GOING TO MAKE NOISE, SHOVE SOMETHING IN ITS MOUTH.

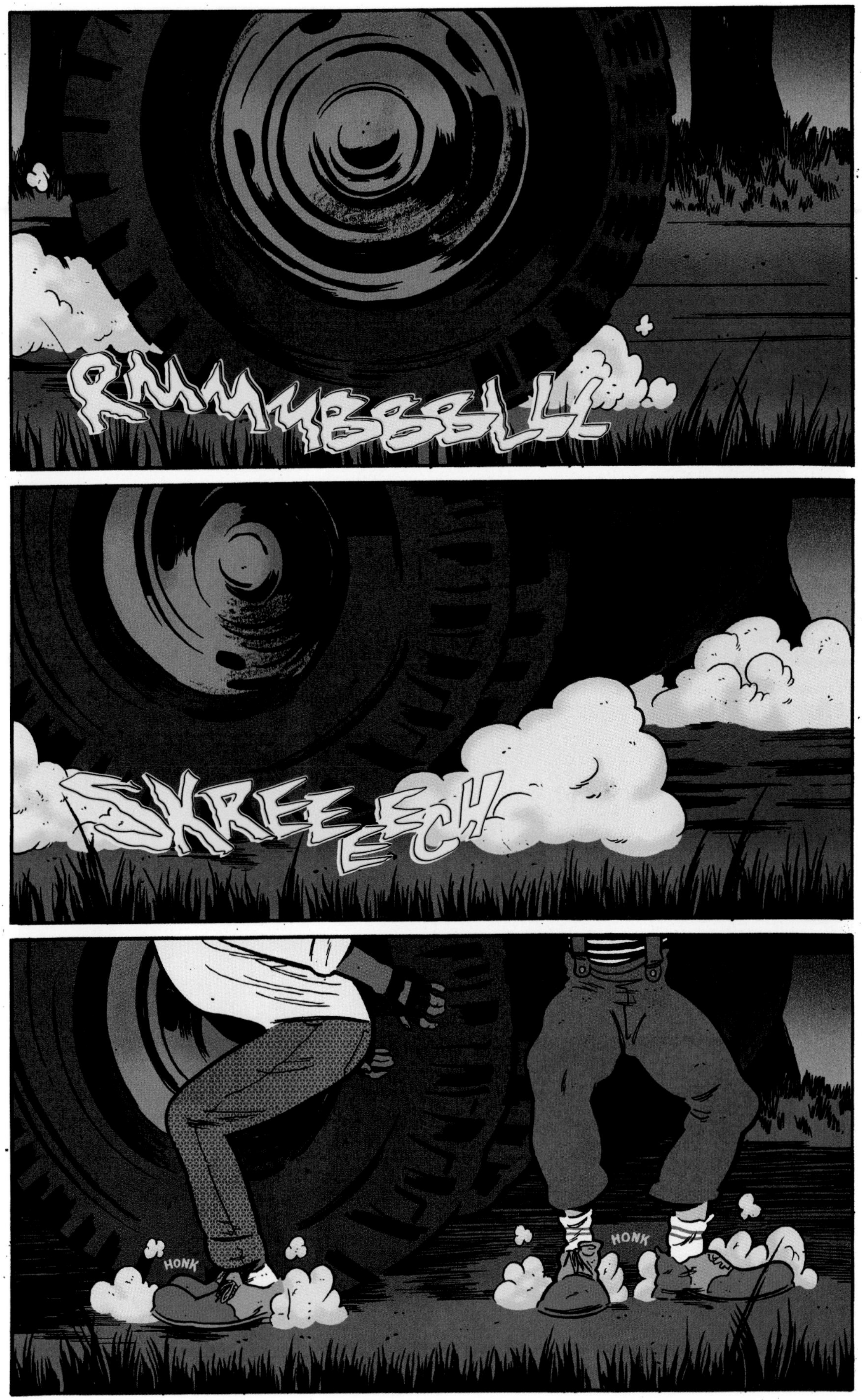
RMMMBBBLLL
SKREEEECH
HONK
HONK

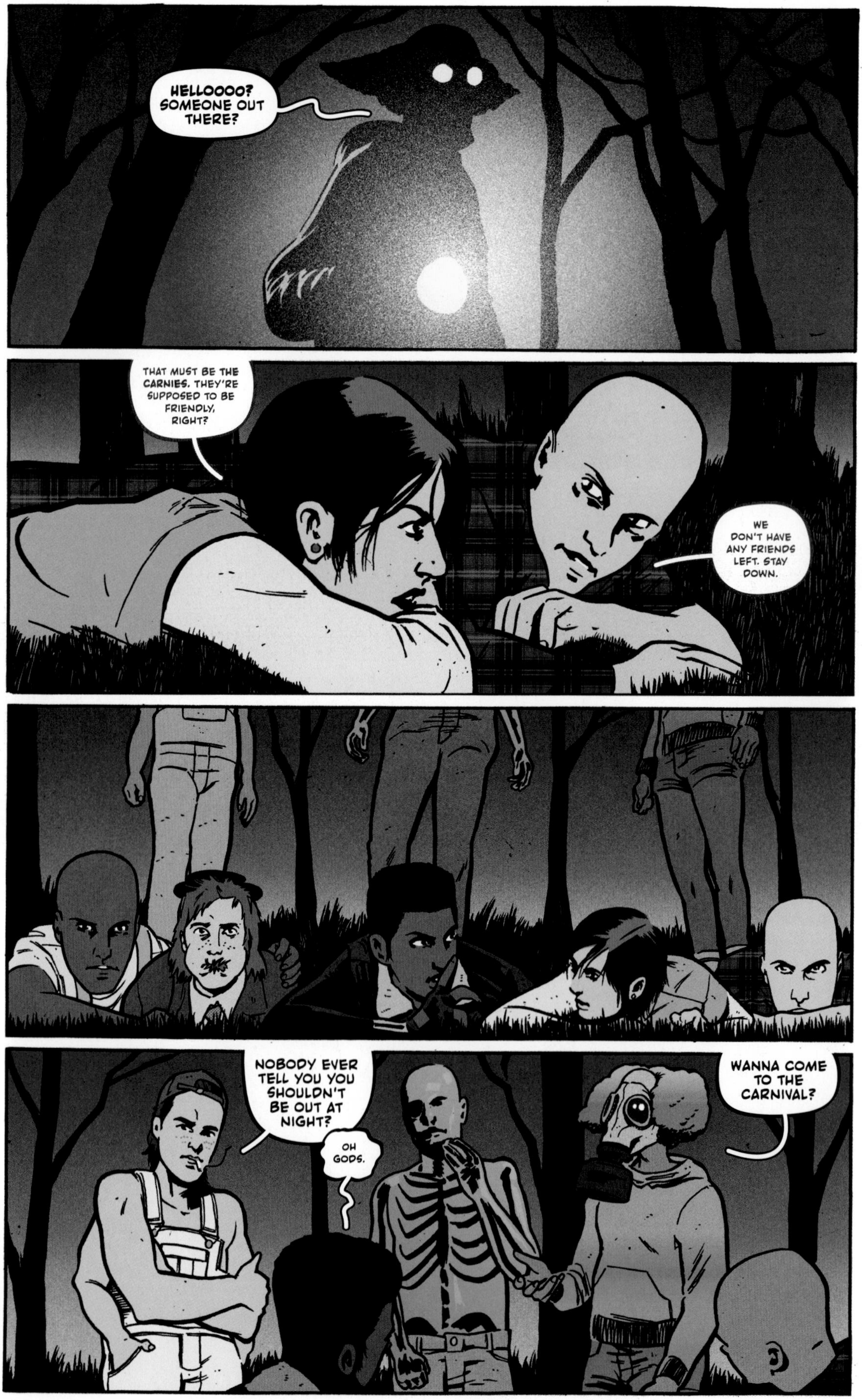
HELLOOOO? SOMEONE OUT THERE?
THAT MUST BE THE CARNIES. THEY'RE SUPPOSED TO BE FRIENDLY, RIGHT?
WE DON'T HAVE ANY FRIENDS LEFT. STAY DOWN.
NOBODY EVER TELL YOU YOU SHOULDN'T BE OUT AT NIGHT?
OH GODS.
WANNA COME TO THE CARNIVAL?

# CHAPTER TWENTY-FOUR

## YOU GOT OUR MESSAGE?

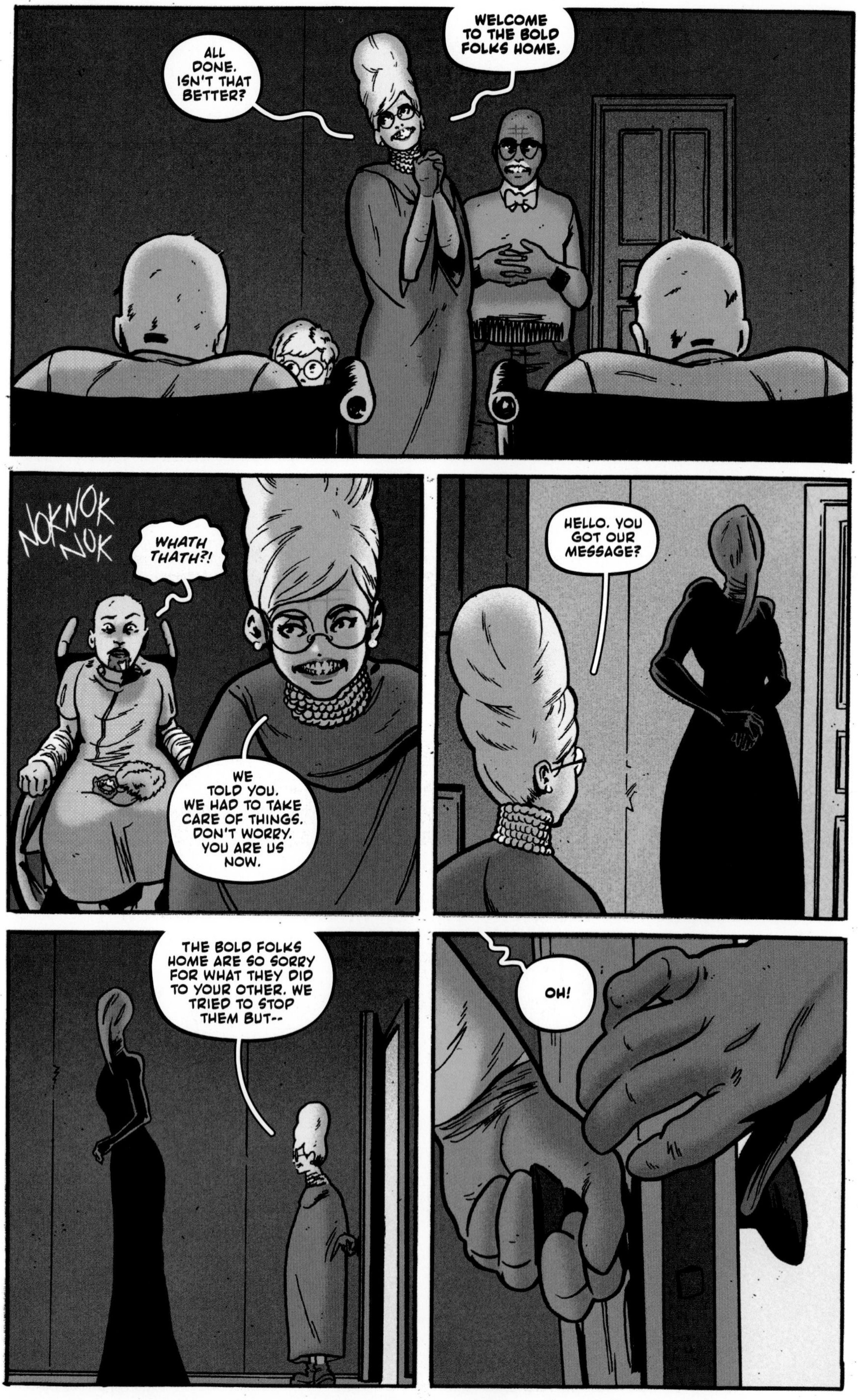
ALL DONE. ISN'T THAT BETTER?
WELCOME TO THE BOLD FOLKS HOME.
NOKNOK NOK
WHATH THATH?!
WE TOLD YOU. WE HAD TO TAKE CARE OF THINGS. DON'T WORRY. YOU ARE US NOW.
HELLO. YOU GOT OUR MESSAGE?
THE BOLD FOLKS HOME ARE SO SORRY FOR WHAT THEY DID TO YOUR OTHER. WE TRIED TO STOP THEM BUT--
OH!

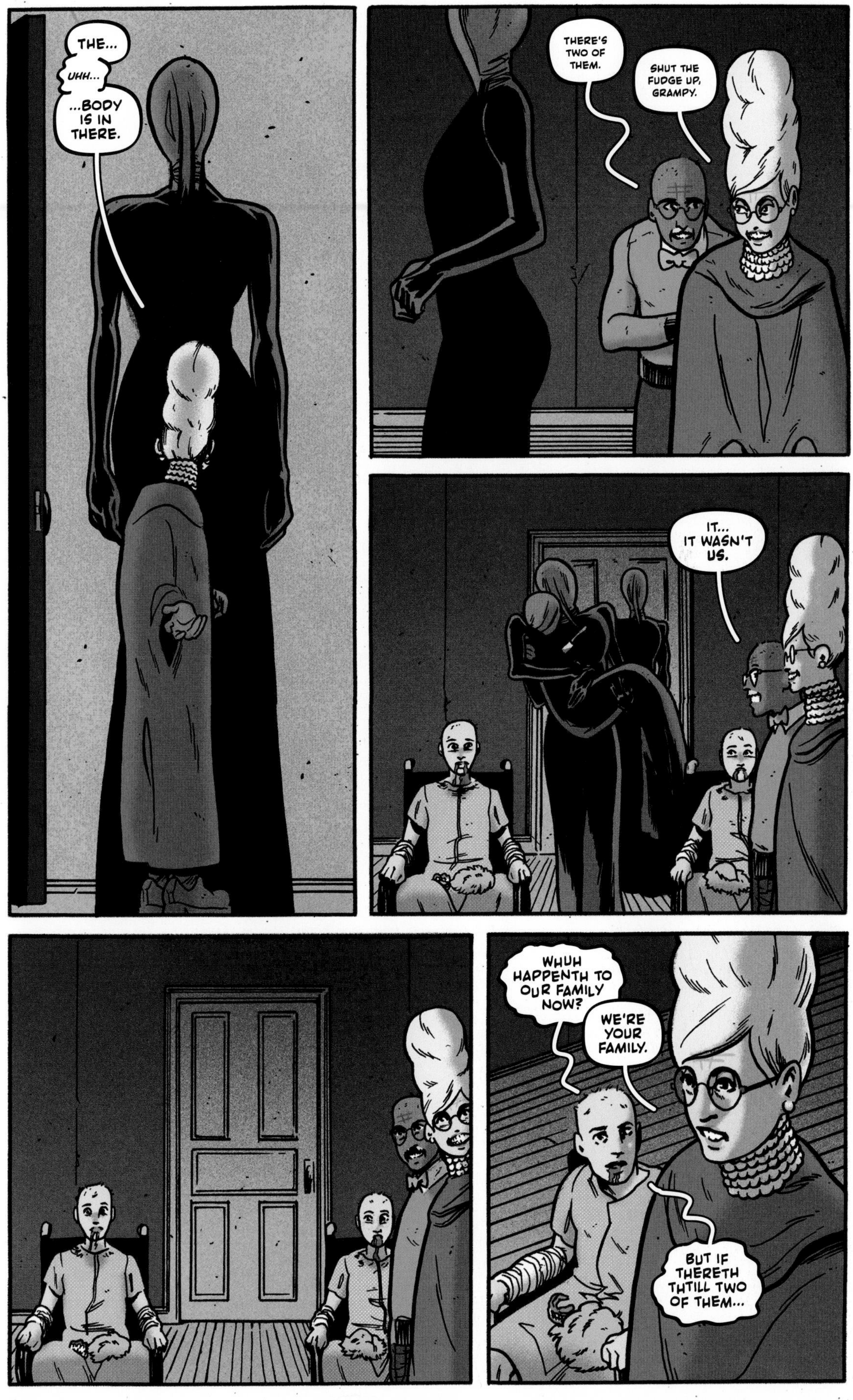
THE...
UHH...
...BODY IS IN THERE.
THERE'S TWO OF THEM.
SHUT THE FUDGE UP, GRAMPY.
IT... IT WASN'T US.
WHUH HAPPENTH TO OUR FAMILY NOW?
WE'RE YOUR FAMILY.
BUT IF THERETH THTILL TWO OF THEM...

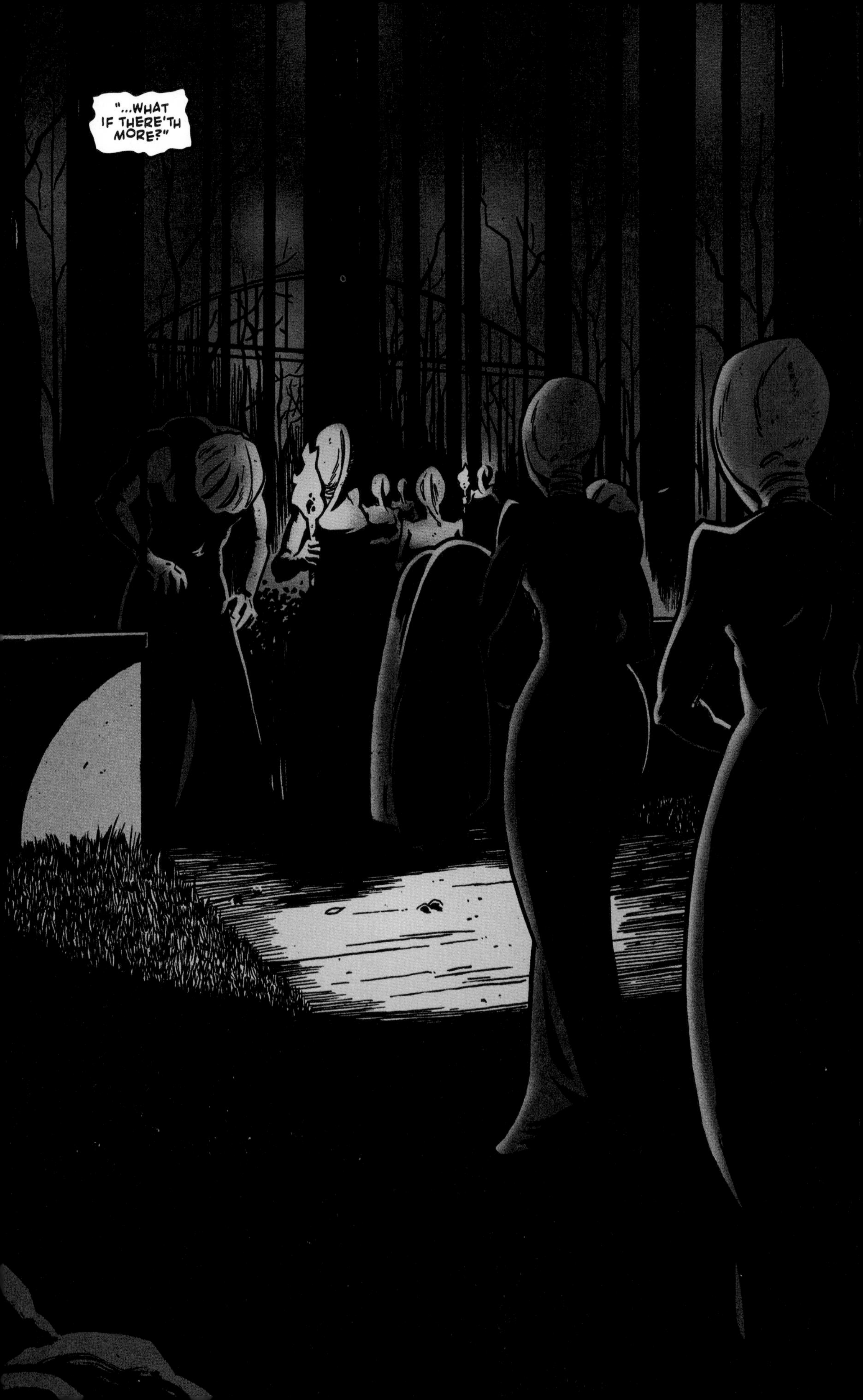
"...WHAT IF THERE'TH MORE?"

# ACT IV

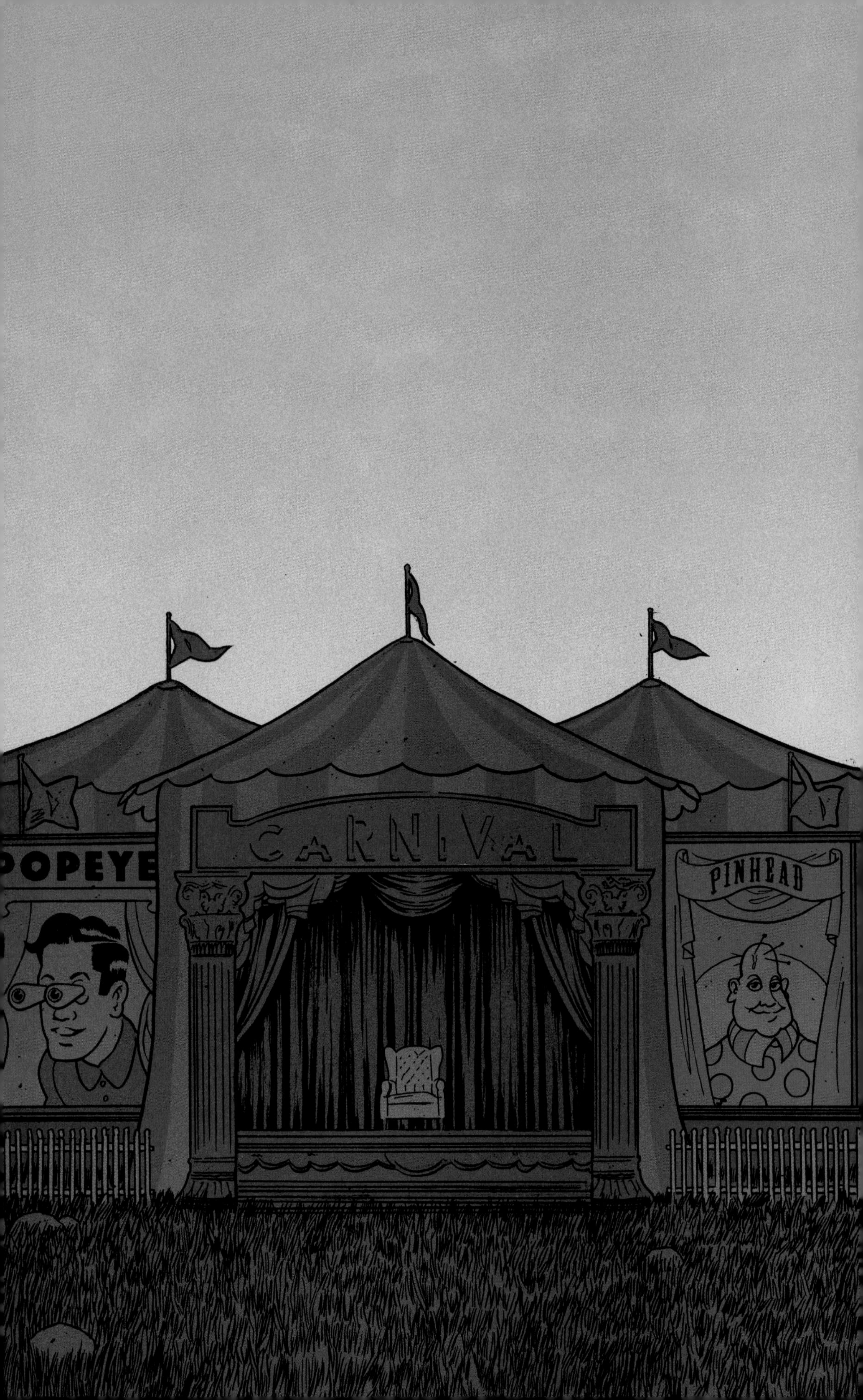

POPEYE
CARNIVAL
PINHEAD

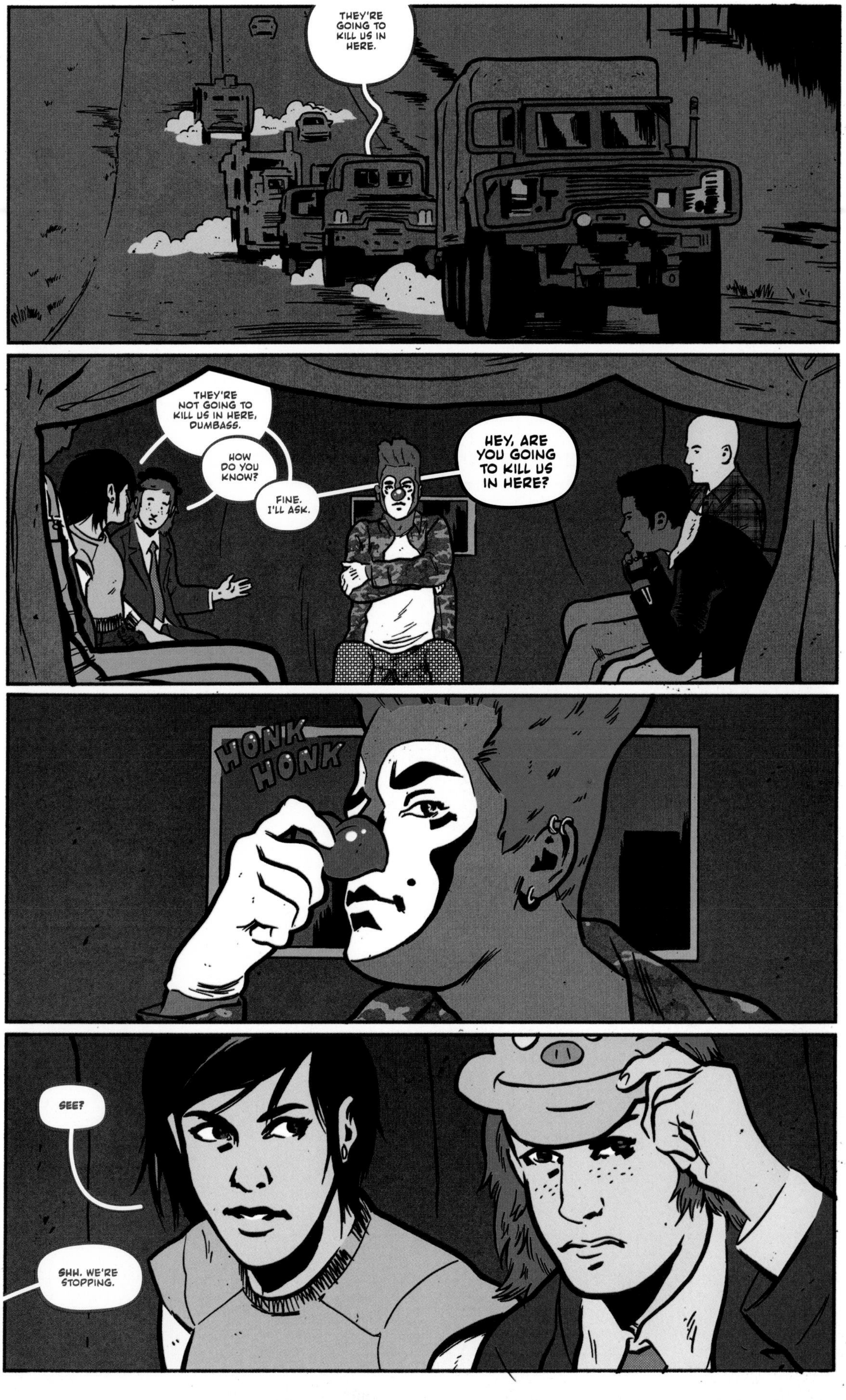
THEY'RE GOING TO KILL US IN HERE.
THEY'RE NOT GOING TO KILL US IN HERE, DUMBASS.
HOW DO YOU KNOW?
FINE. I'LL ASK.
HEY, ARE YOU GOING TO KILL US IN HERE?
HONK HONK
SEE?
SHH. WE'RE STOPPING.

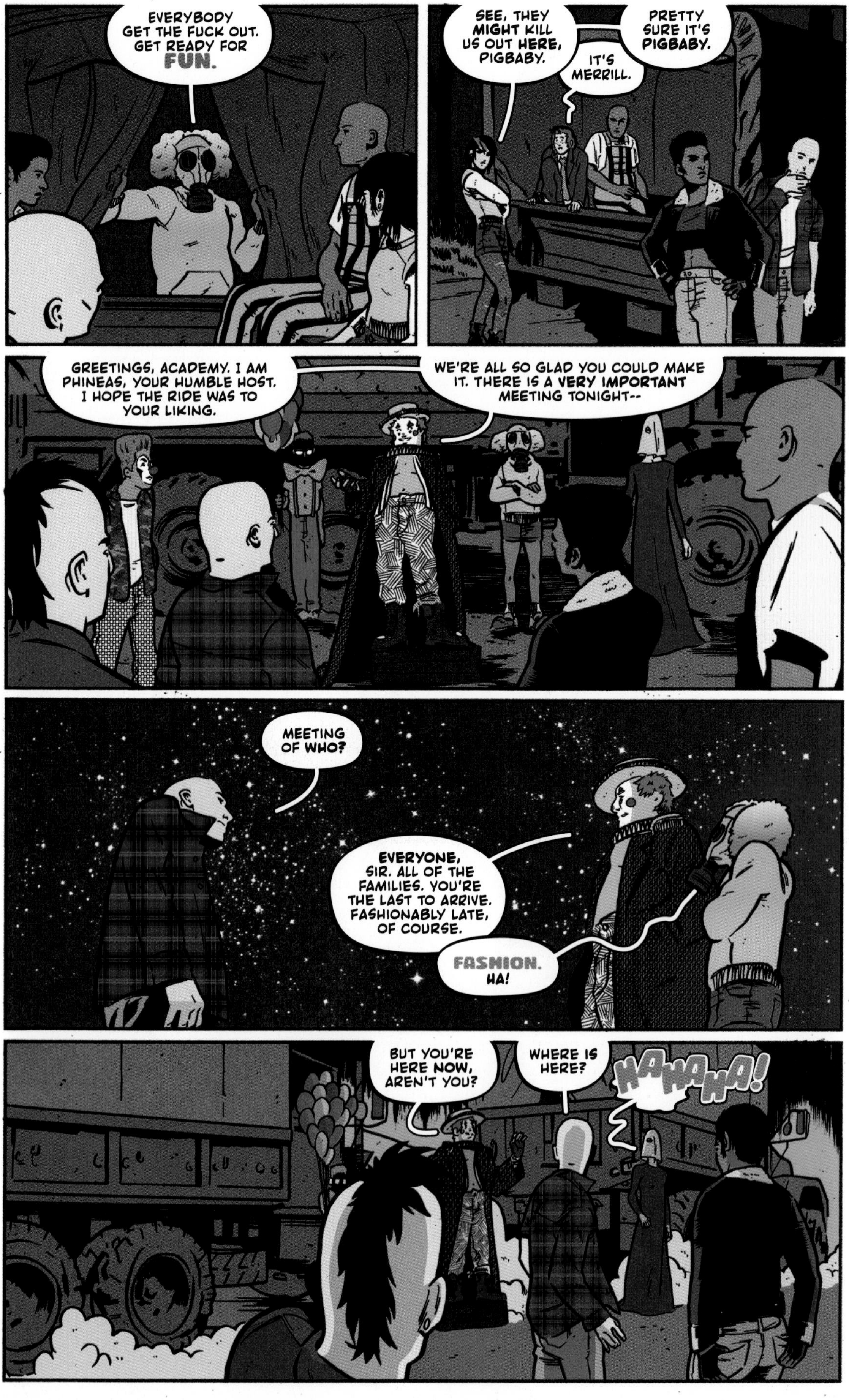
EVERYBODY GET THE FUCK OUT. GET READY FOR FUN.
SEE, THEY MIGHT KILL US OUT HERE, PIGBABY.
PRETTY SURE IT'S PIGBABY.
IT'S MERRILL.
GREETINGS, ACADEMY. I AM PHINEAS, YOUR HUMBLE HOST. I HOPE THE RIDE WAS TO YOUR LIKING.
WE'RE ALL SO GLAD YOU COULD MAKE IT. THERE IS A VERY IMPORTANT MEETING TONIGHT--
MEETING OF WHO?
EVERYONE, SIR. ALL OF THE FAMILIES. YOU'RE THE LAST TO ARRIVE. FASHIONABLY LATE, OF COURSE.
FASHION. HA!
BUT YOU'RE HERE NOW, AREN'T YOU?
WHERE IS HERE?
HAHAHA!

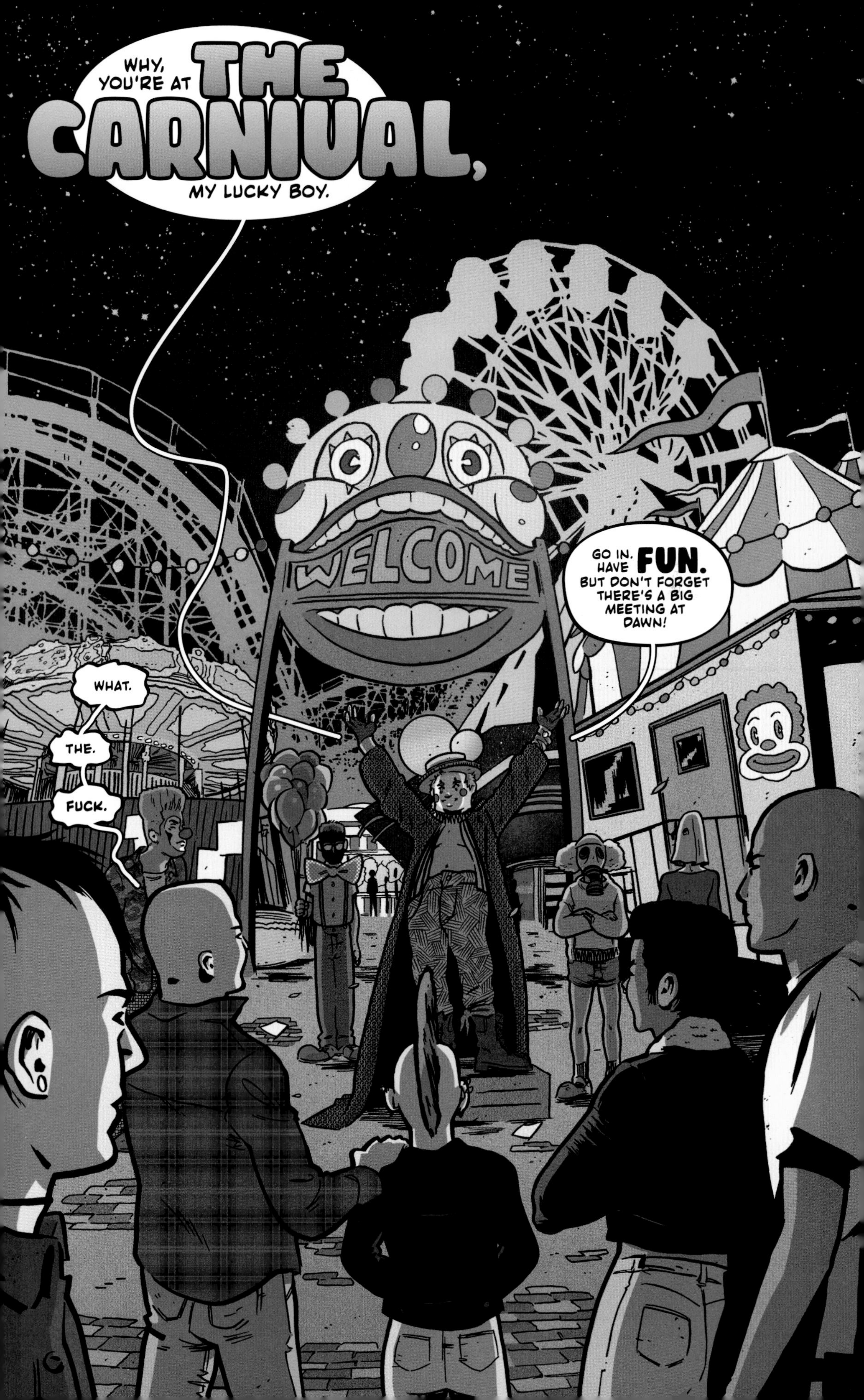
WHY, YOU'RE AT THE CARNIVAL, MY LUCKY BOY.
GO IN. HAVE FUN. BUT DON'T FORGET THERE'S A BIG MEETING AT DAWN!
WHAT.
THE.
FUCK.
WELCOME

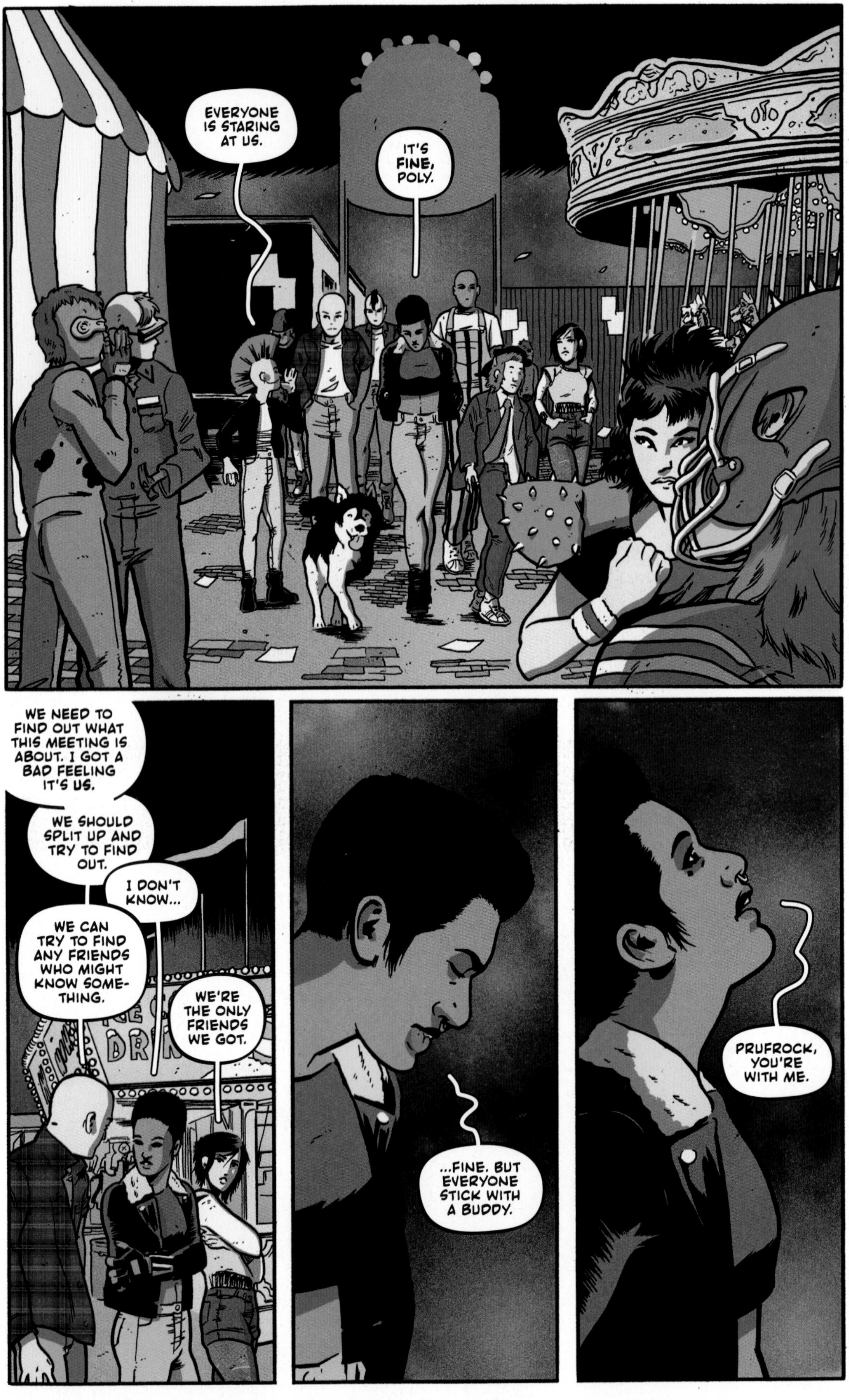
EVERYONE IS STARING AT US.
IT'S FINE, POLY.
WE NEED TO FIND OUT WHAT THIS MEETING IS ABOUT. I GOT A BAD FEELING IT'S US.
WE SHOULD SPLIT UP AND TRY TO FIND OUT.
I DON'T KNOW...
WE CAN TRY TO FIND ANY FRIENDS WHO MIGHT KNOW SOME-THING.
WE'RE THE ONLY FRIENDS WE GOT.
...FINE. BUT EVERYONE STICK WITH A BUDDY.
PRUFROCK, YOU'RE WITH ME.

# CHAPTER TWENTY-FIVE

SURE I AM. YOU KNOW MY NAME!

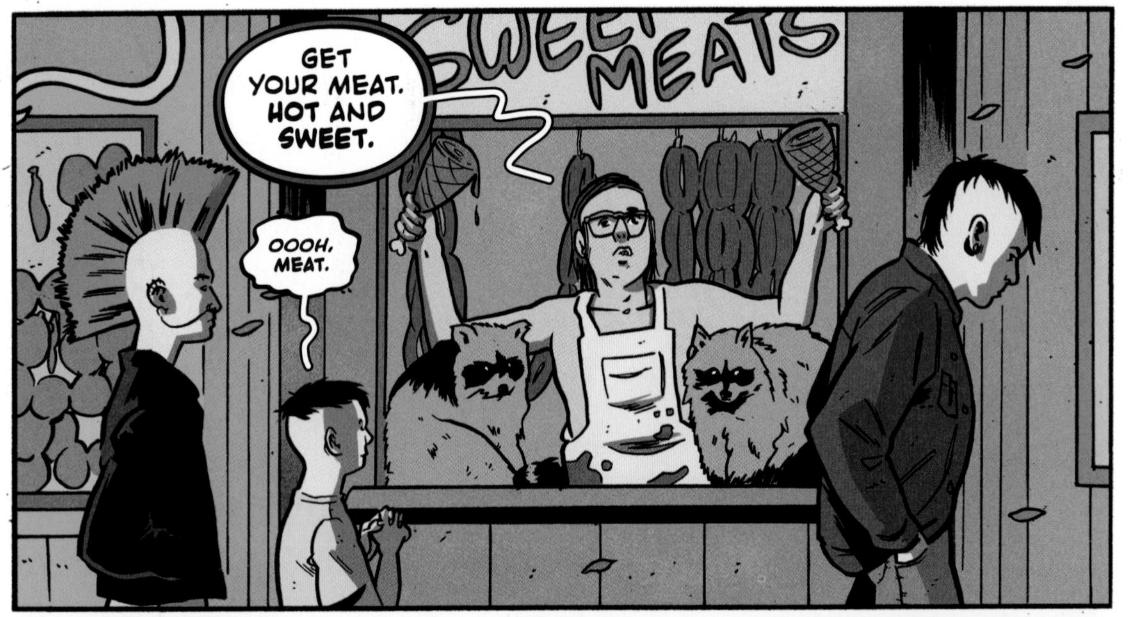
SWEET MEATS
GET YOUR MEAT. HOT AND SWEET.
OOOH, MEAT.

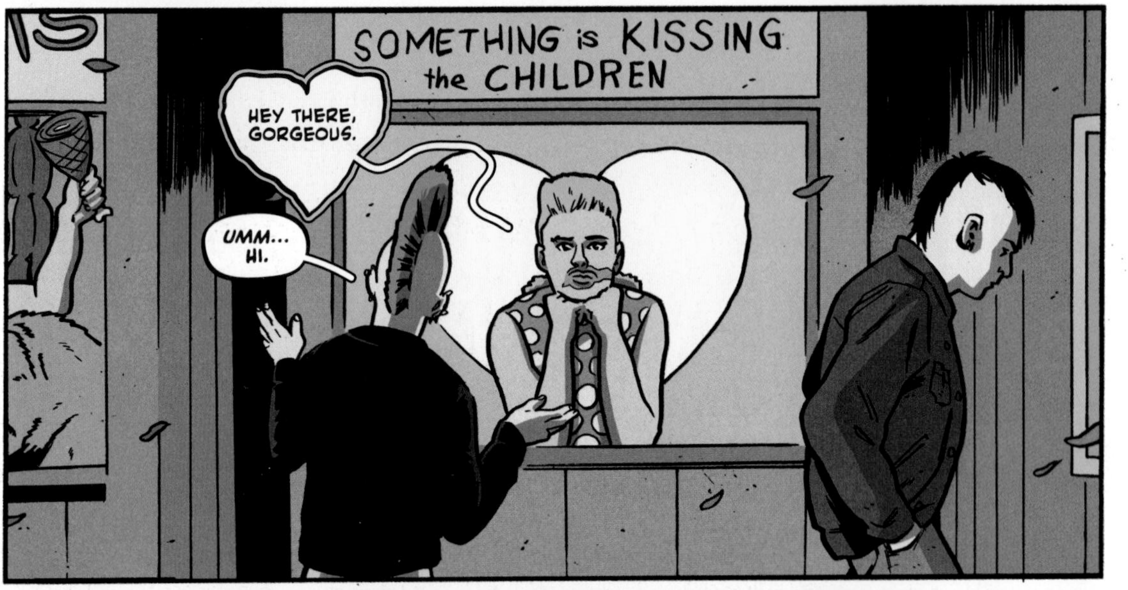
SOMETHING is KISSING the CHILDREN
HEY THERE, GORGEOUS.
UMM... HI.

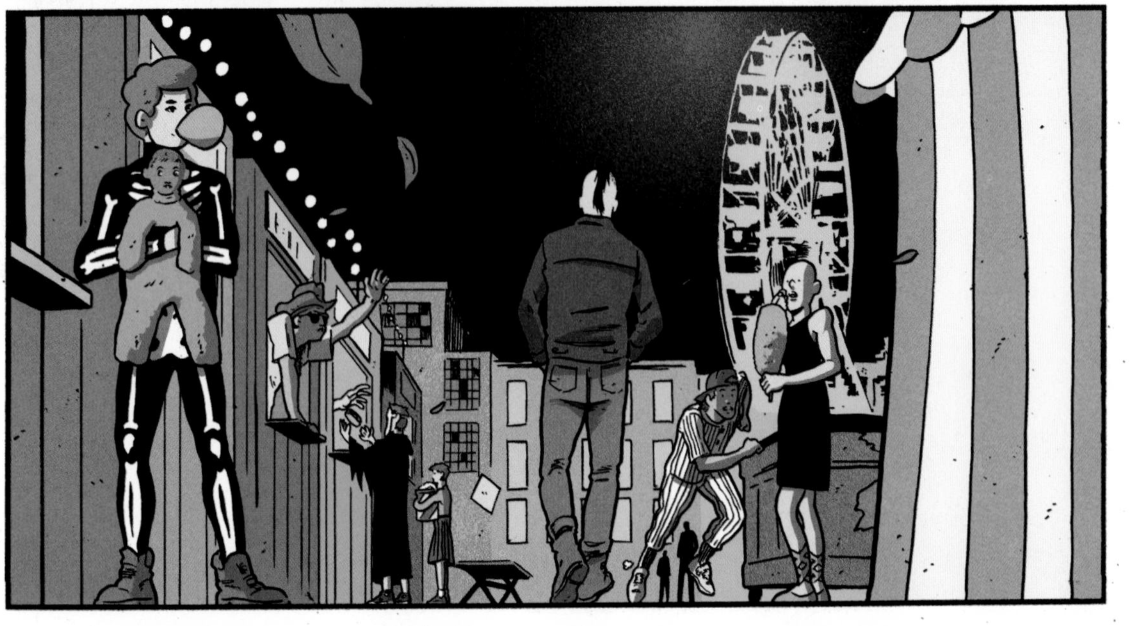

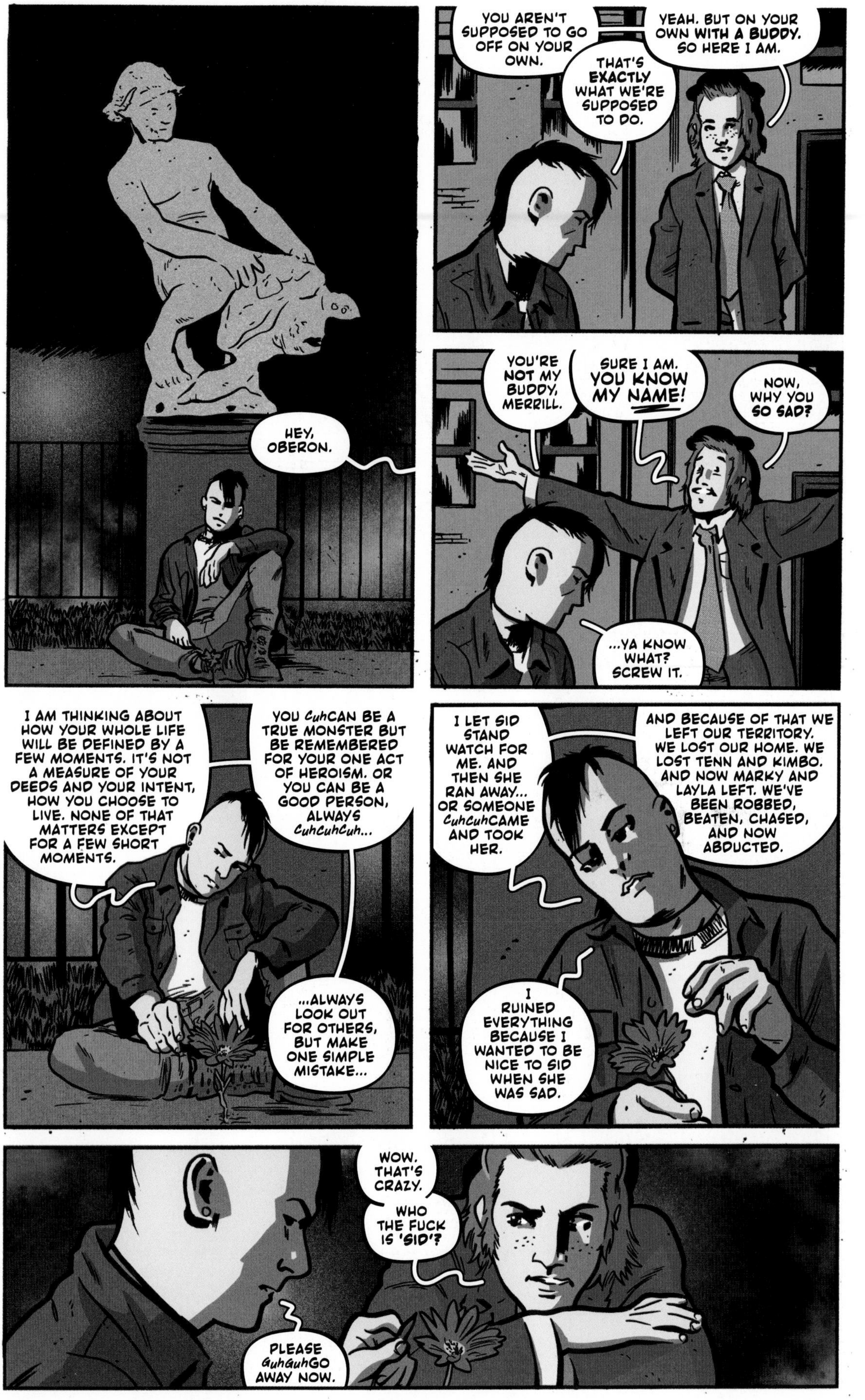
HEY, OBERON.
YOU AREN'T SUPPOSED TO GO OFF ON YOUR OWN.
THAT'S EXACTLY WHAT WE'RE SUPPOSED TO DO.
YEAH. BUT ON YOUR OWN WITH A BUDDY. SO HERE I AM.
YOU'RE NOT MY BUDDY, MERRILL.
SURE I AM. YOU KNOW MY NAME!
NOW, WHY YOU SO SAD?
...YA KNOW WHAT? SCREW IT.
I AM THINKING ABOUT HOW YOUR WHOLE LIFE WILL BE DEFINED BY A FEW MOMENTS. IT'S NOT A MEASURE OF YOUR DEEDS AND YOUR INTENT, HOW YOU CHOOSE TO LIVE. NONE OF THAT MATTERS EXCEPT FOR A FEW SHORT MOMENTS.
YOU CuhCAN BE A TRUE MONSTER BUT BE REMEMBERED FOR YOUR ONE ACT OF HEROISM. OR YOU CAN BE A GOOD PERSON, ALWAYS CuhCuhCuh...
...ALWAYS LOOK OUT FOR OTHERS, BUT MAKE ONE SIMPLE MISTAKE...
I LET SID STAND WATCH FOR ME. AND THEN SHE RAN AWAY... OR SOMEONE CuhCuhCAME AND TOOK HER.
AND BECAUSE OF THAT WE LEFT OUR TERRITORY. WE LOST OUR HOME. WE LOST TENN AND KIMBO. AND NOW MARKY AND LAYLA LEFT. WE'VE BEEN ROBBED, BEATEN, CHASED, AND NOW ABDUCTED.
I RUINED EVERYTHING BECAUSE I WANTED TO BE NICE TO SID WHEN SHE WAS SAD.
WOW. THAT'S CRAZY.
WHO THE FUCK IS 'SID'?
PLEASE GuhGuhGO AWAY NOW.

# CHAPTER TWENTY-SIX

WHAT ARE YOU LOOKING AT?

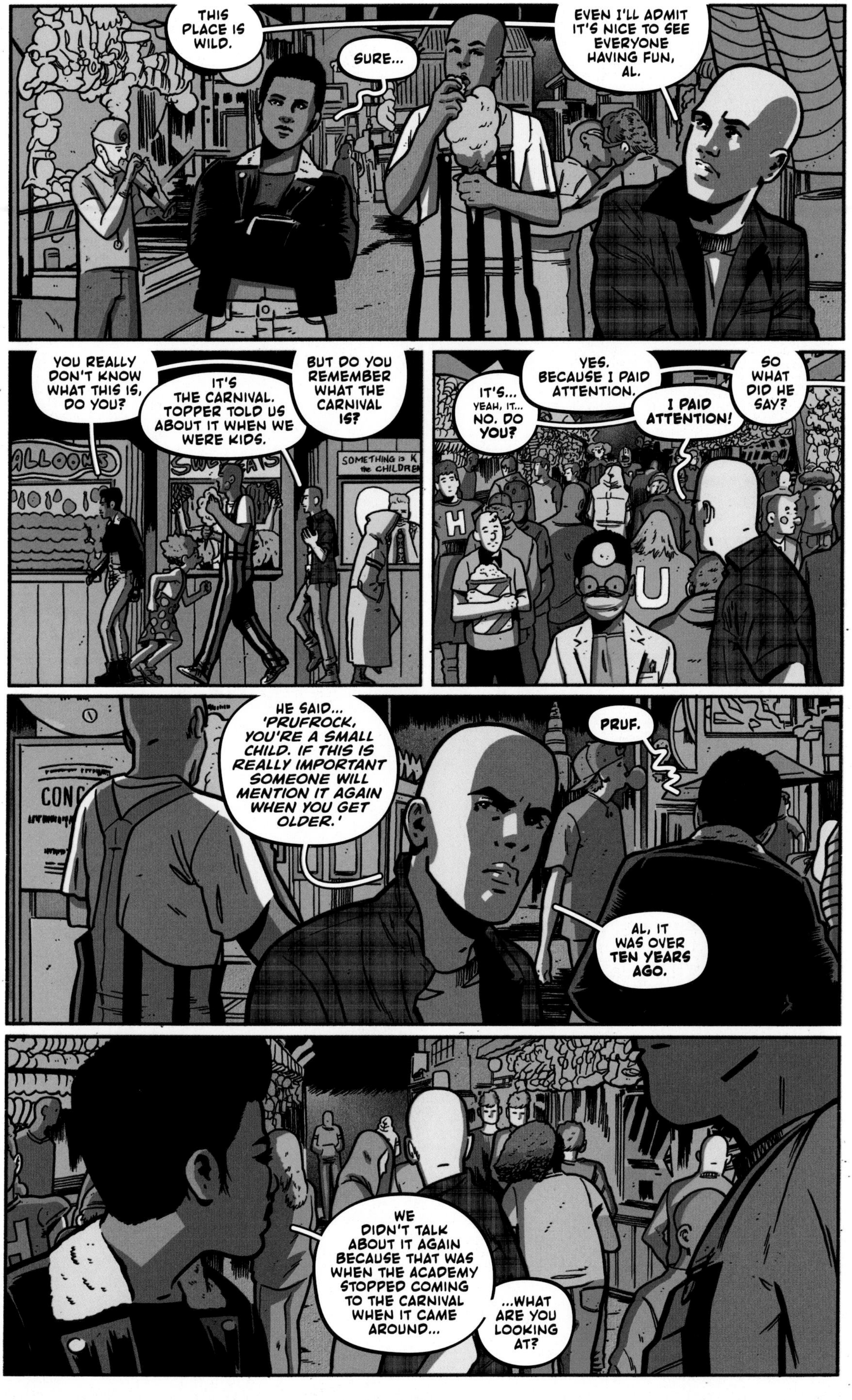
THIS PLACE IS WILD.
SURE...
EVEN I'LL ADMIT IT'S NICE TO SEE EVERYONE HAVING FUN, AL.
YOU REALLY DON'T KNOW WHAT THIS IS, DO YOU?
IT'S THE CARNIVAL. TOPPER TOLD US ABOUT IT WHEN WE WERE KIDS.
BUT DO YOU REMEMBER WHAT THE CARNIVAL IS?
ALLOONS
SWEETS
SOMETHING IS K the CHILDREN
IT'S... YEAH, IT... NO. DO YOU?
YES. BECAUSE I PAID ATTENTION.
I PAID ATTENTION!
SO WHAT DID HE SAY?
HE SAID... 'PRUFROCK, YOU'RE A SMALL CHILD. IF THIS IS REALLY IMPORTANT SOMEONE WILL MENTION IT AGAIN WHEN YOU GET OLDER.'
PRUF.
AL, IT WAS OVER TEN YEARS AGO.
WE DIDN'T TALK ABOUT IT AGAIN BECAUSE THAT WAS WHEN THE ACADEMY STOPPED COMING TO THE CARNIVAL WHEN IT CAME AROUND...
...WHAT ARE YOU LOOKING AT?

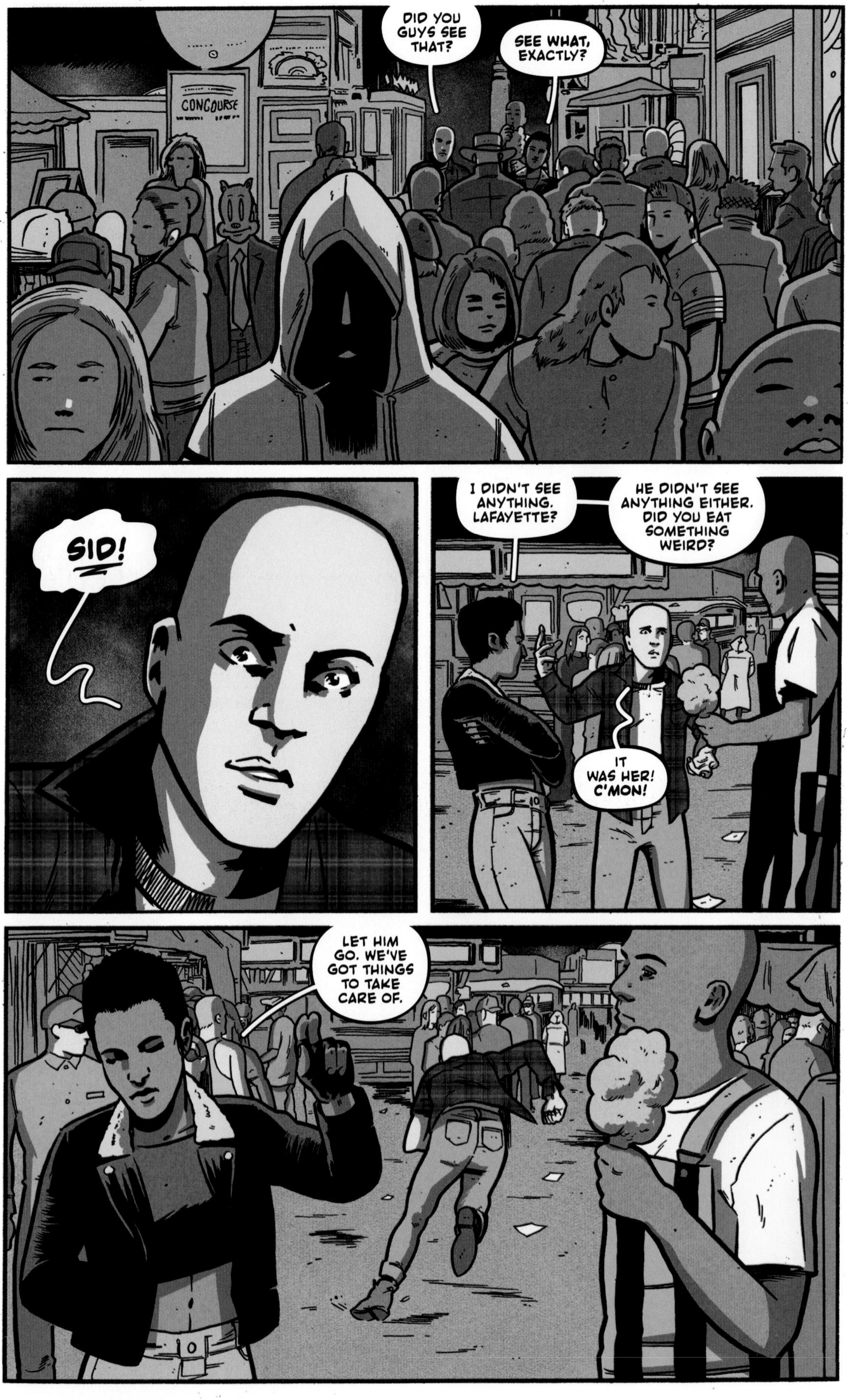
CONCOURSE
DID YOU GUYS SEE THAT?
SEE WHAT, EXACTLY?
SID!
I DIDN'T SEE ANYTHING. LAFAYETTE?
HE DIDN'T SEE ANYTHING EITHER. DID YOU EAT SOMETHING WEIRD?
IT WAS HER! C'MON!
LET HIM GO. WE'VE GOT THINGS TO TAKE CARE OF.

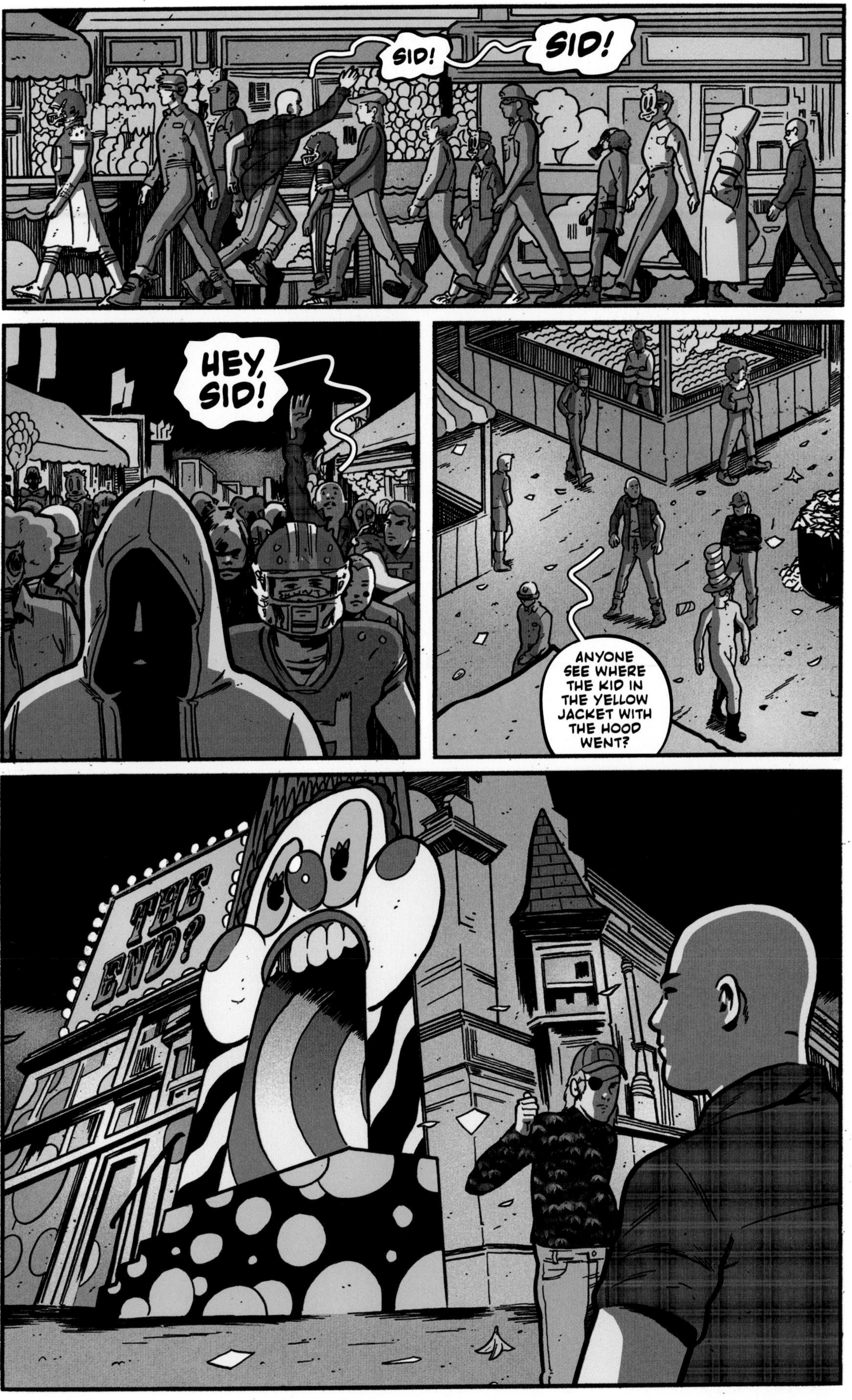
SID!
SID!
HEY, SID!
ANYONE SEE WHERE THE KID IN THE YELLOW JACKET WITH THE HOOD WENT?
THE END?

# CHAPTER TWENTY-SEVEN

BUT I LEFT...

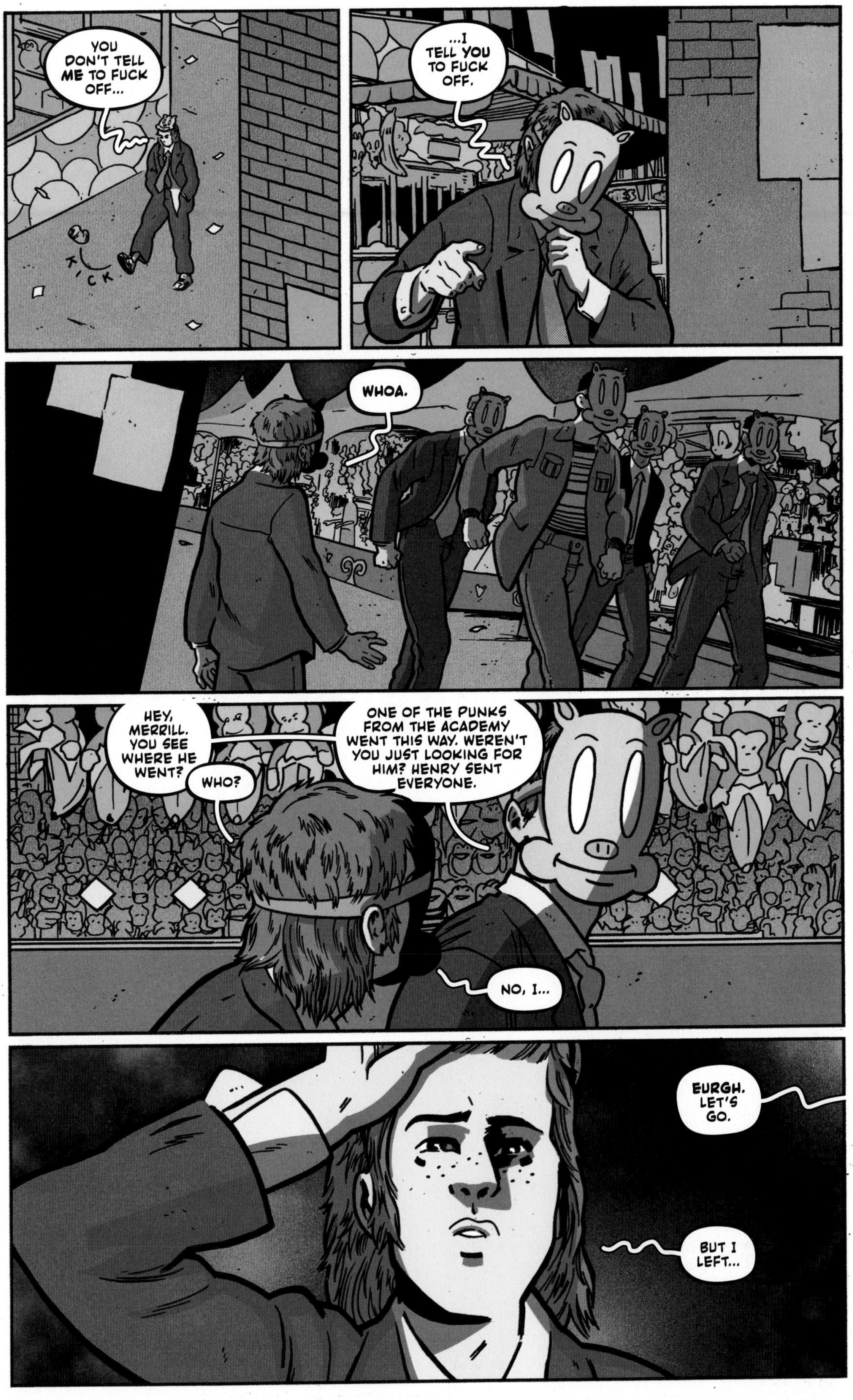
YOU DON'T TELL ME TO FUCK OFF...
KICK
...I TELL YOU TO FUCK OFF.
WHOA.
HEY, MERRILL. YOU SEE WHERE HE WENT?
WHO?
ONE OF THE PUNKS FROM THE ACADEMY WENT THIS WAY. WEREN'T YOU JUST LOOKING FOR HIM? HENRY SENT EVERYONE.
NO, I...
EURGH. LET'S GO.
BUT I LEFT...

# CHAPTER TWENTY-EIGHT

## THAT'S WHY I'VE COME TO YOU.

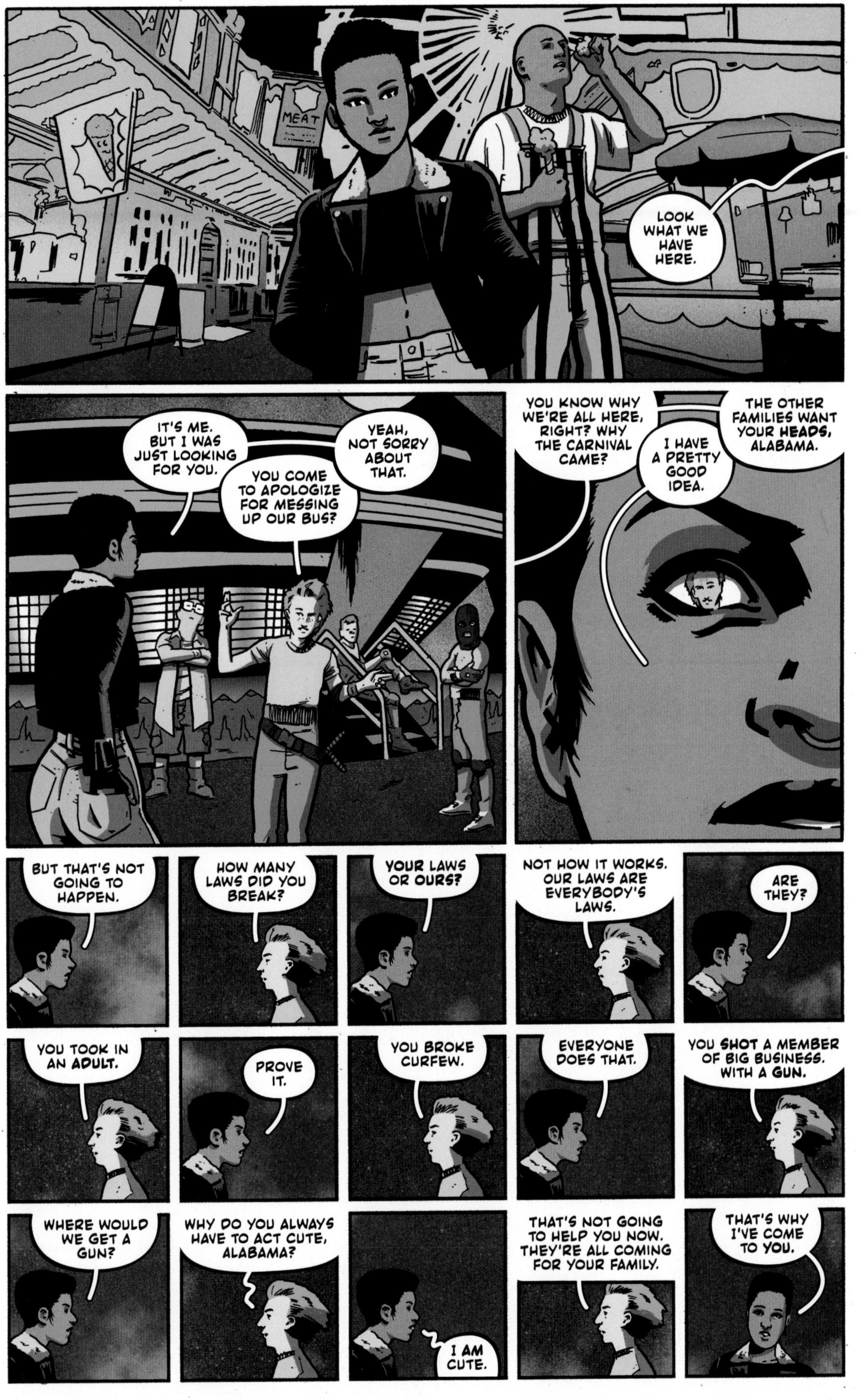
MEAT
LOOK WHAT WE HAVE HERE.
IT'S ME. BUT I WAS JUST LOOKING FOR YOU.
YEAH, NOT SORRY ABOUT THAT.
YOU COME TO APOLOGIZE FOR MESSING UP OUR BUS?
YOU KNOW WHY WE'RE ALL HERE, RIGHT? WHY THE CARNIVAL CAME?
I HAVE A PRETTY GOOD IDEA.
THE OTHER FAMILIES WANT YOUR HEADS, ALABAMA.
BUT THAT'S NOT GOING TO HAPPEN.
HOW MANY LAWS DID YOU BREAK?
YOUR LAWS OR OURS?
NOT HOW IT WORKS. OUR LAWS ARE EVERYBODY'S LAWS.
ARE THEY?
YOU TOOK IN AN ADULT.
PROVE IT.
YOU BROKE CURFEW.
EVERYONE DOES THAT.
YOU SHOT A MEMBER OF BIG BUSINESS. WITH A GUN.
WHERE WOULD WE GET A GUN?
WHY DO YOU ALWAYS HAVE TO ACT CUTE, ALABAMA?
I AM CUTE.
THAT'S NOT GOING TO HELP YOU NOW. THEY'RE ALL COMING FOR YOUR FAMILY.
THAT'S WHY I'VE COME TO YOU.

# CHAPTER TWENTY-NINE

## HOLD HIM DOWN!

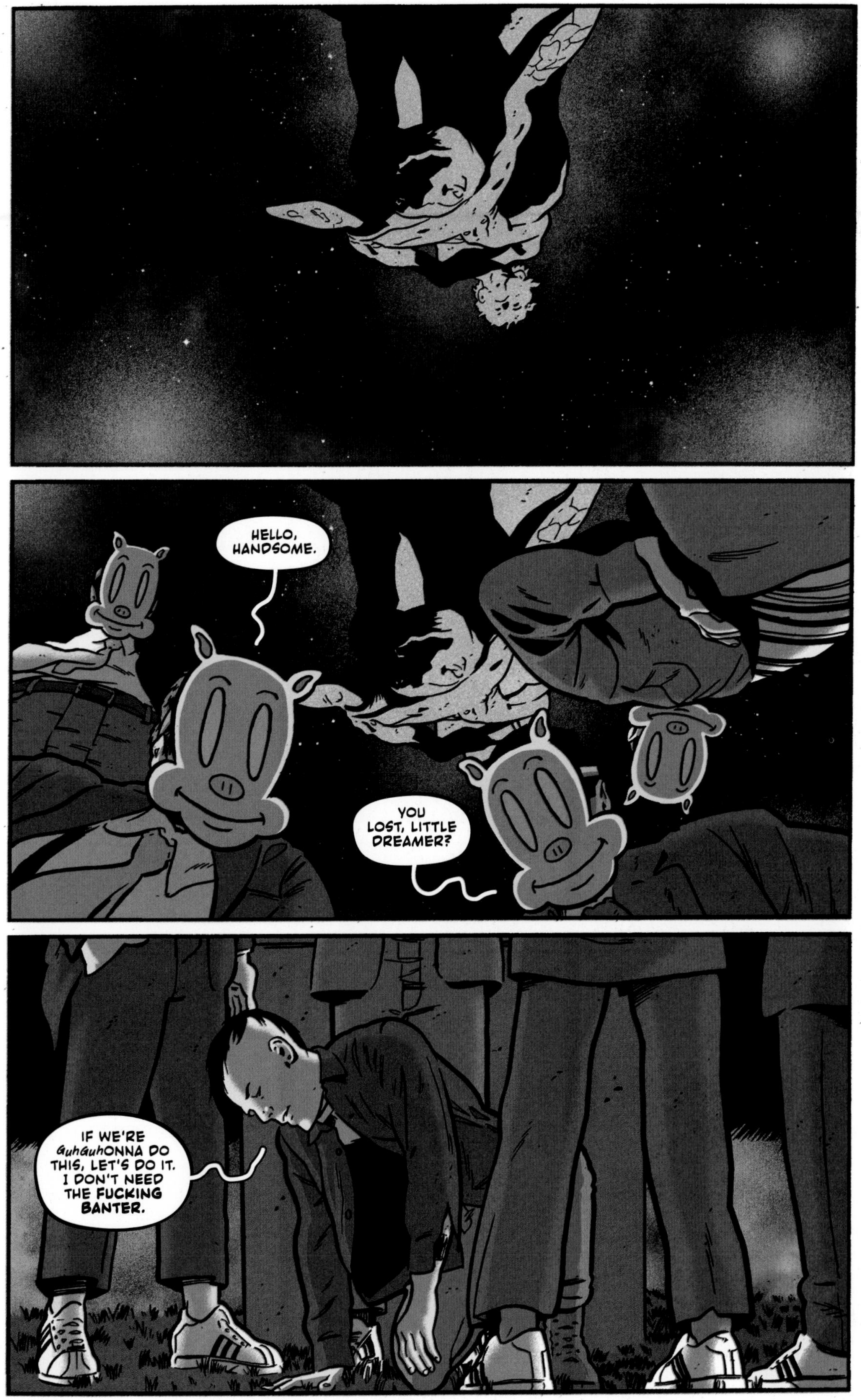
HELLO, HANDSOME.
YOU LOST, LITTLE DREAMER?
IF WE'RE GuhGuhONNA DO THIS, LET'S DO IT. I DON'T NEED THE FUCKING BANTER.

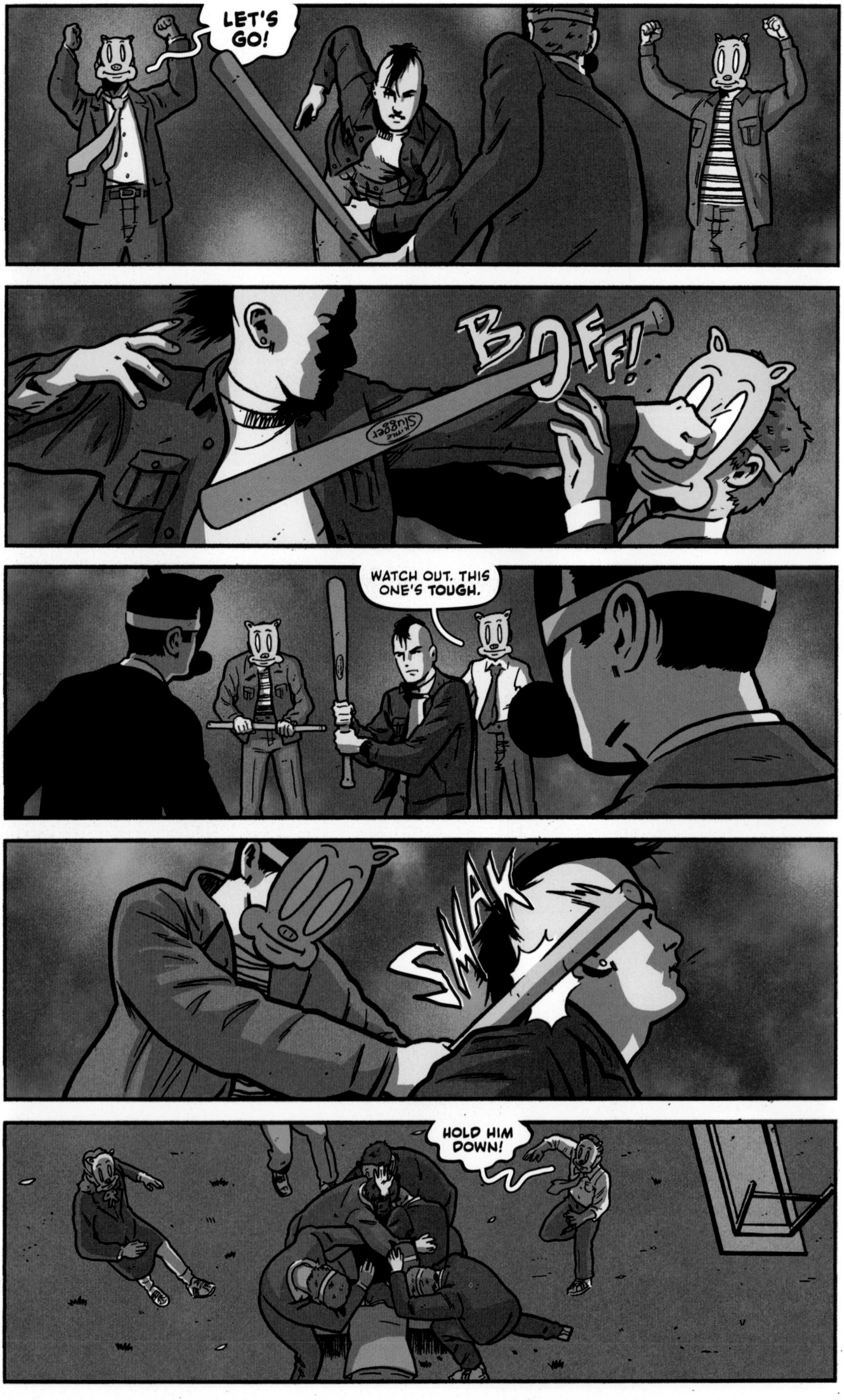
LET'S GO!
BOFF!
Little Slugger
WATCH OUT. THIS ONE'S TOUGH.
SMAK
HOLD HIM DOWN!

# CHAPTER THIRTY

WHAT DID THAT LITTLE
FUCKER JUST SAY?

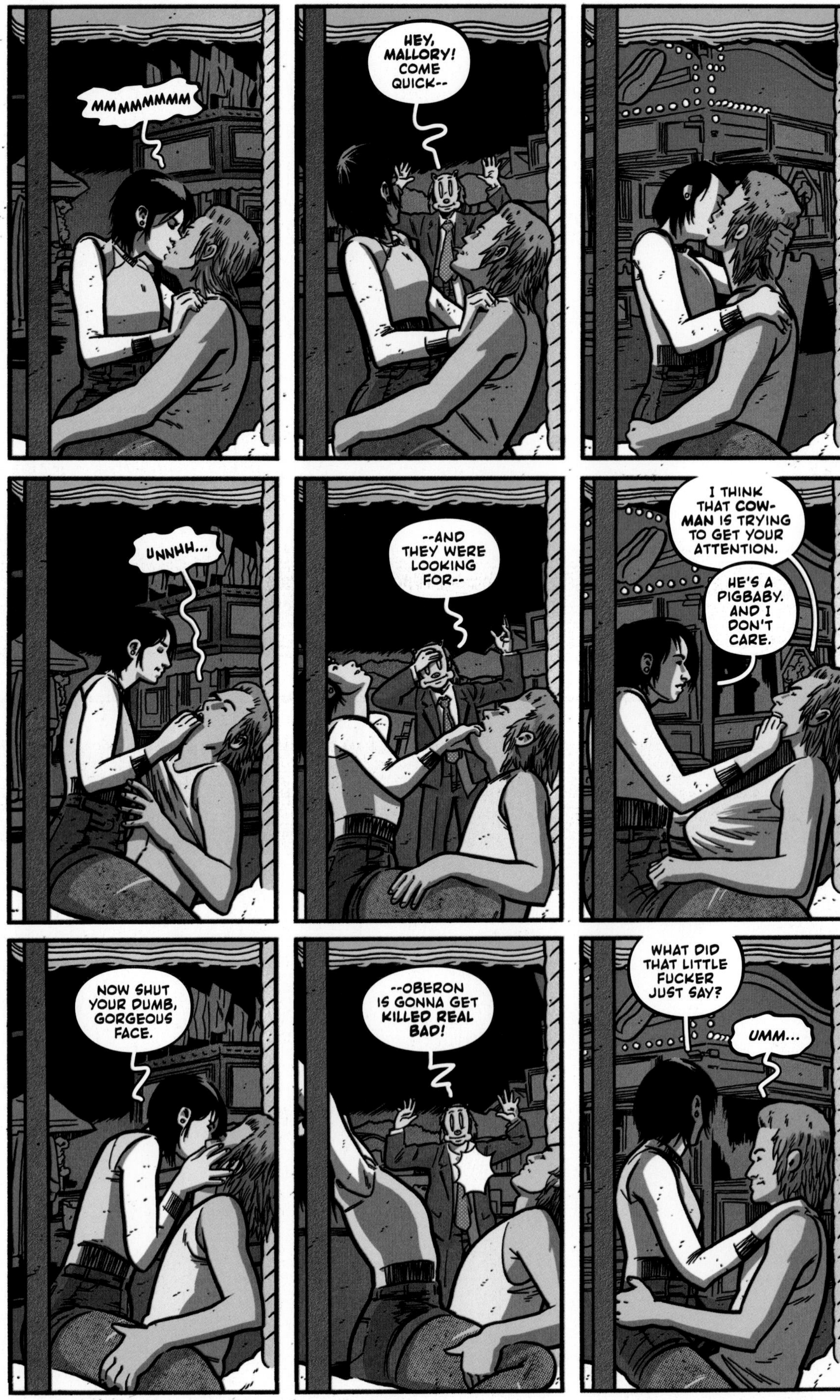
MMMMMMMM
HEY, MALLORY! COME QUICK--
UNNHH...
--AND THEY WERE LOOKING FOR--
I THINK THAT COW-MAN IS TRYING TO GET YOUR ATTENTION.
HE'S A PIGBABY. AND I DON'T CARE.
NOW SHUT YOUR DUMB, GORGEOUS FACE.
--OBERON IS GONNA GET KILLED REAL BAD!
WHAT DID THAT LITTLE FUCKER JUST SAY?
UMM...

# CHAPTER THIRTY-ONE

## HELLO? ANYBODY THERE?

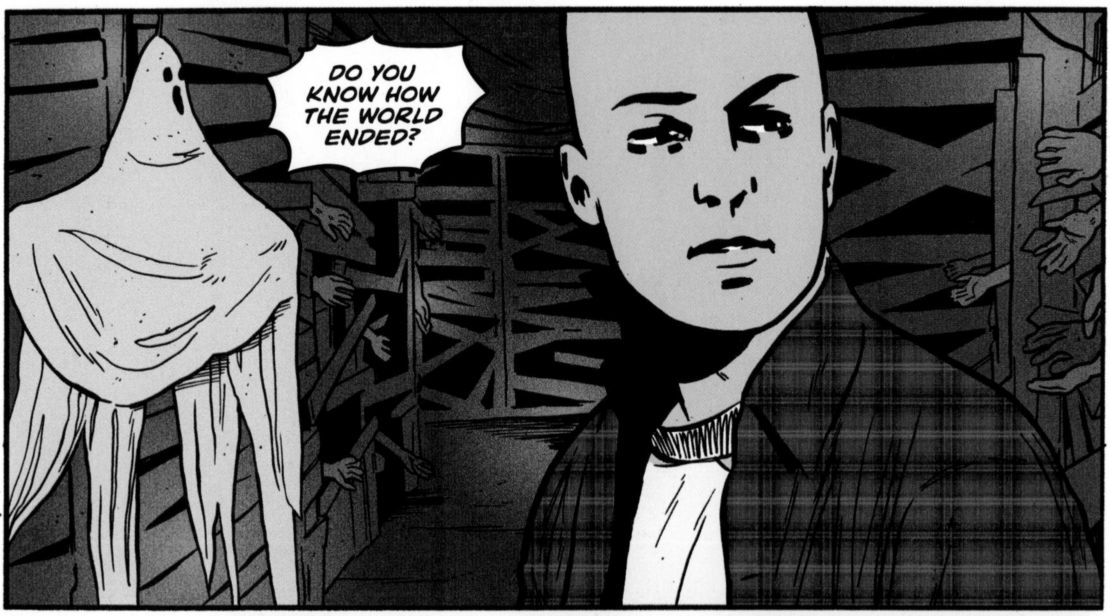
DO YOU KNOW HOW THE WORLD ENDED?

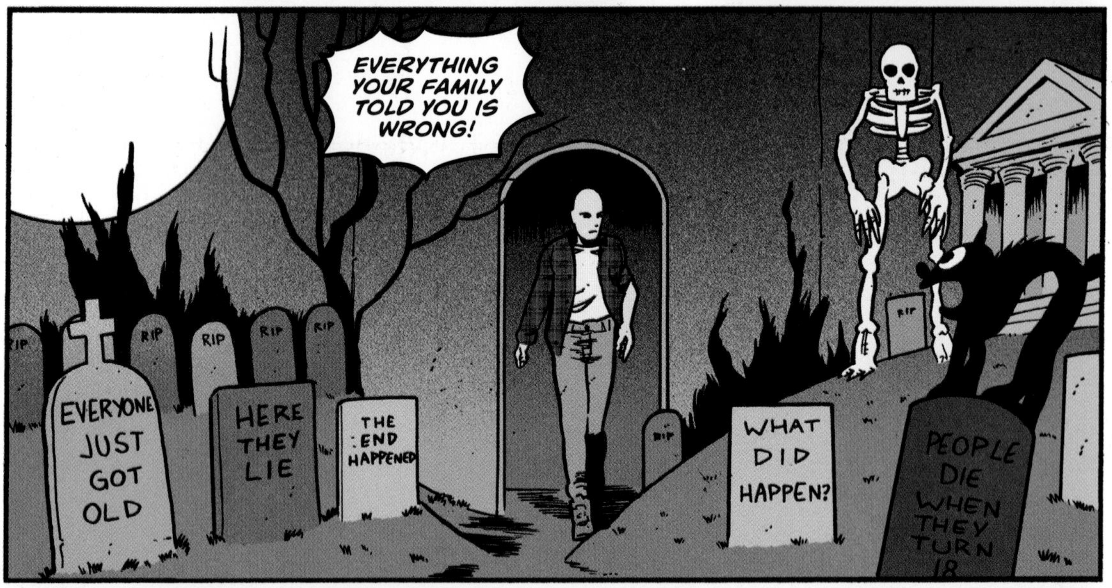
EVERYTHING YOUR FAMILY TOLD YOU IS WRONG!
RIP
RIP
RIP
RIP
RIP
EVERYONE JUST GOT OLD
HERE THEY LIE
THE END HAPPENED
RIP
WHAT DID HAPPEN?
PEOPLE DIE WHEN THEY TURN 18

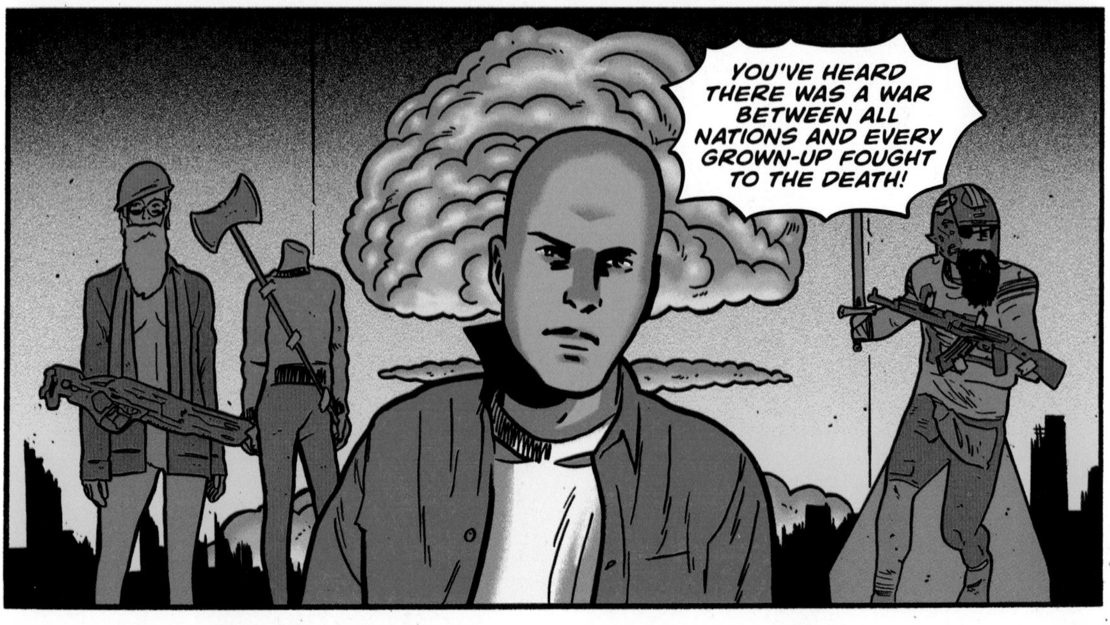
YOU'VE HEARD THERE WAS A WAR BETWEEN ALL NATIONS AND EVERY GROWN-UP FOUGHT TO THE DEATH!

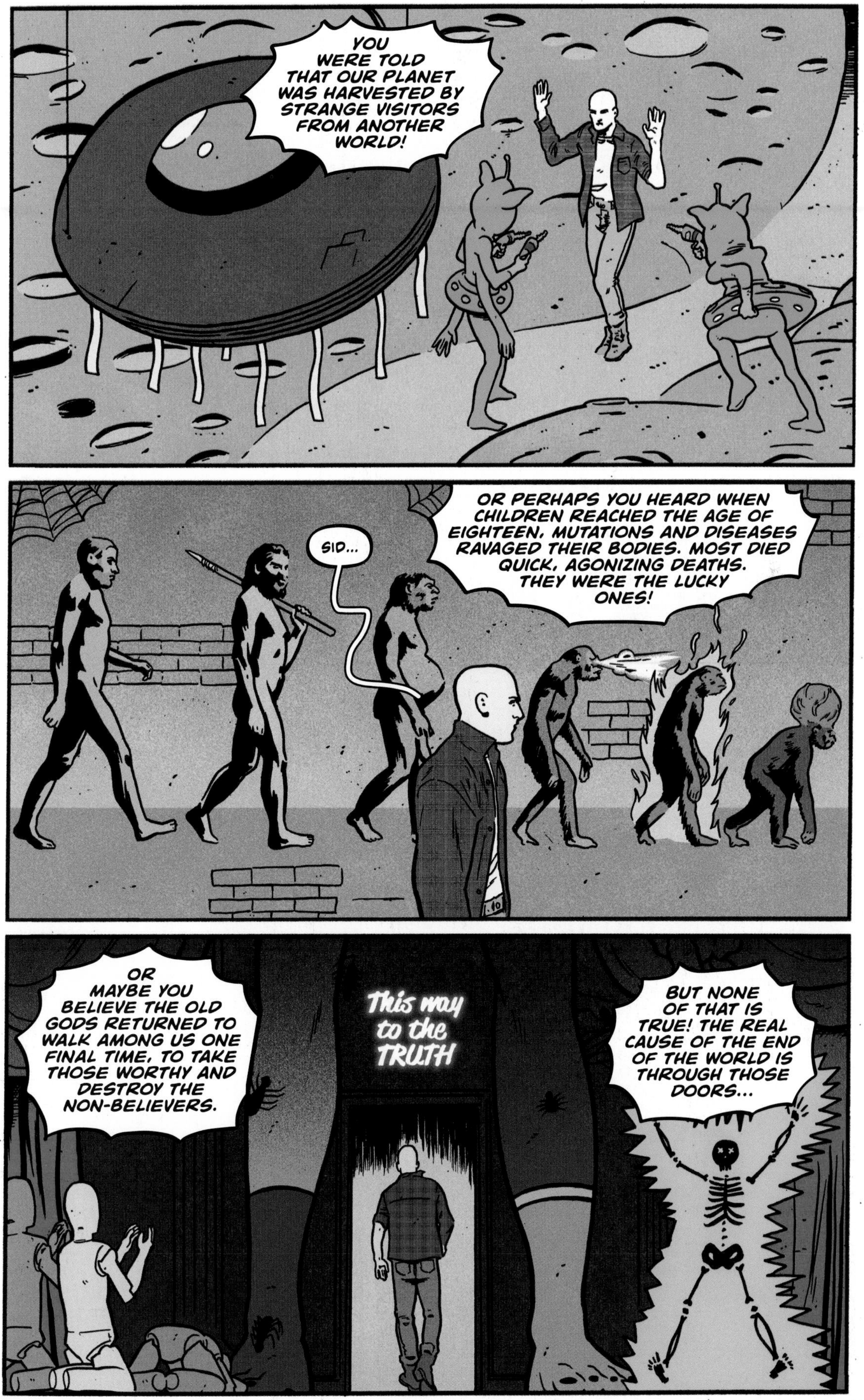

YOU WERE TOLD THAT OUR PLANET WAS HARVESTED BY STRANGE VISITORS FROM ANOTHER WORLD!
SID...
OR PERHAPS YOU HEARD WHEN CHILDREN REACHED THE AGE OF EIGHTEEN, MUTATIONS AND DISEASES RAVAGED THEIR BODIES. MOST DIED QUICK, AGONIZING DEATHS. THEY WERE THE LUCKY ONES!
OR MAYBE YOU BELIEVE THE OLD GODS RETURNED TO WALK AMONG US ONE FINAL TIME, TO TAKE THOSE WORTHY AND DESTROY THE NON-BELIEVERS.
This way to the TRUTH
BUT NONE OF THAT IS TRUE! THE REAL CAUSE OF THE END OF THE WORLD IS THROUGH THOSE DOORS...

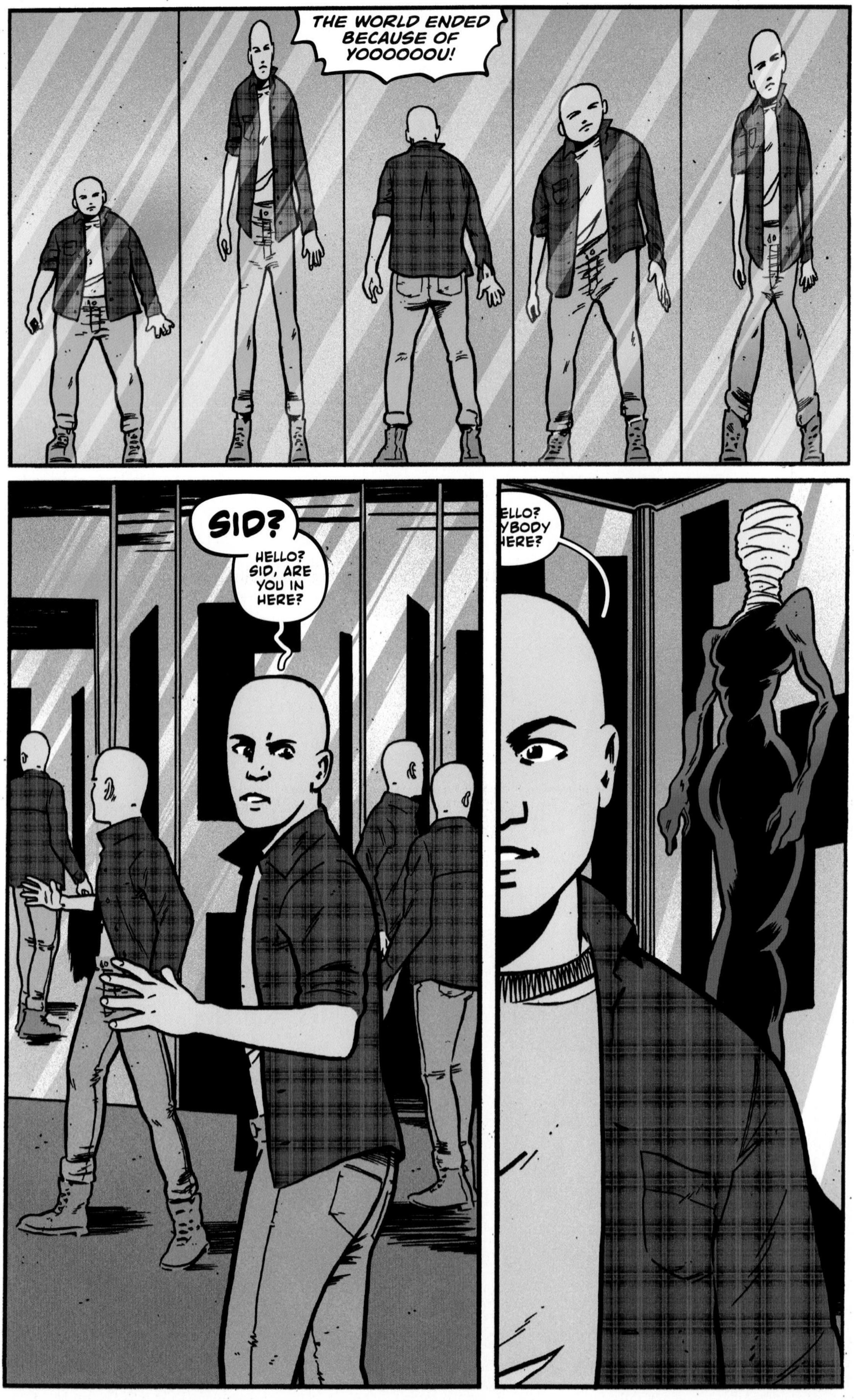
THE WORLD ENDED BECAUSE OF YOOOOOOU!
SID?
HELLO? SID, ARE YOU IN HERE?
HELLO? YBODY HERE?

# CHAPTER THIRTY-TWO

## DO WE HAVE A DEAL?

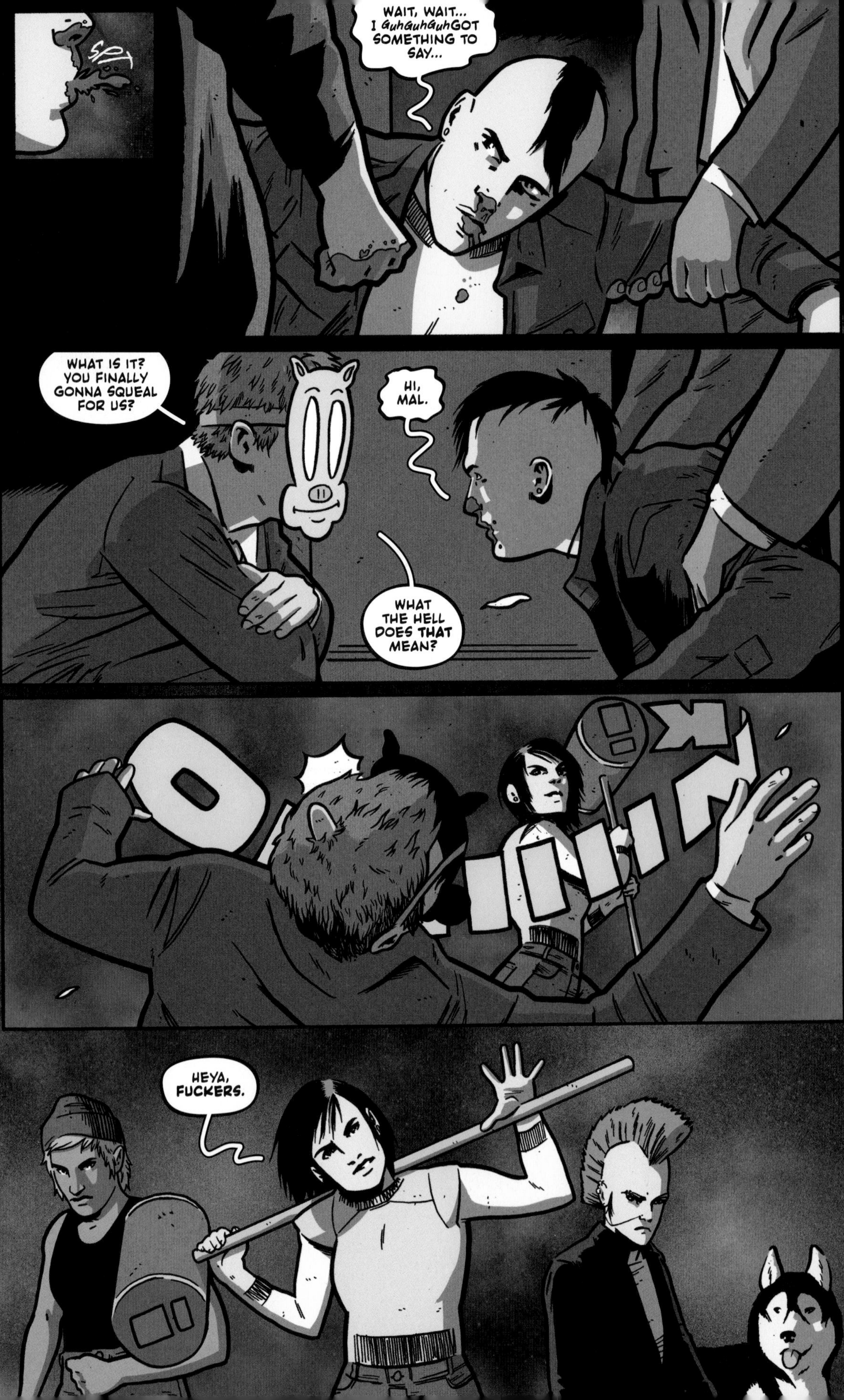
SPIT
WAIT, WAIT... I GuhGuhGuhGOT SOMETHING TO SAY...
WHAT IS IT? YOU FINALLY GONNA SQUEAL FOR US?
HI, MAL.
WHAT THE HELL DOES THAT MEAN?
HEYA, FUCKERS.

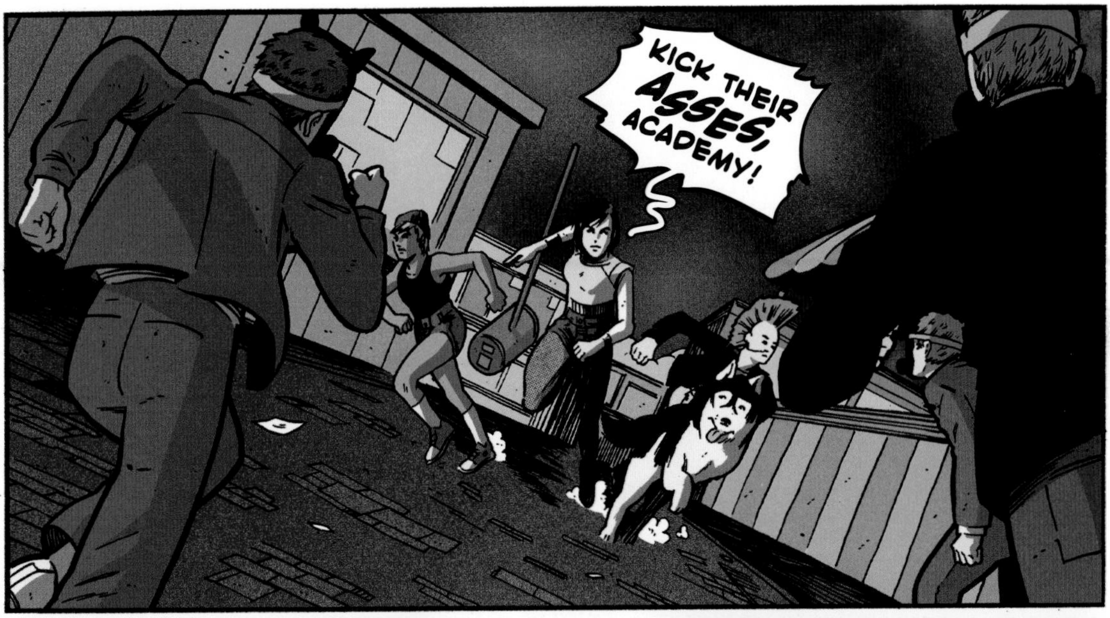
KICK THEIR ASSES, ACADEMY!

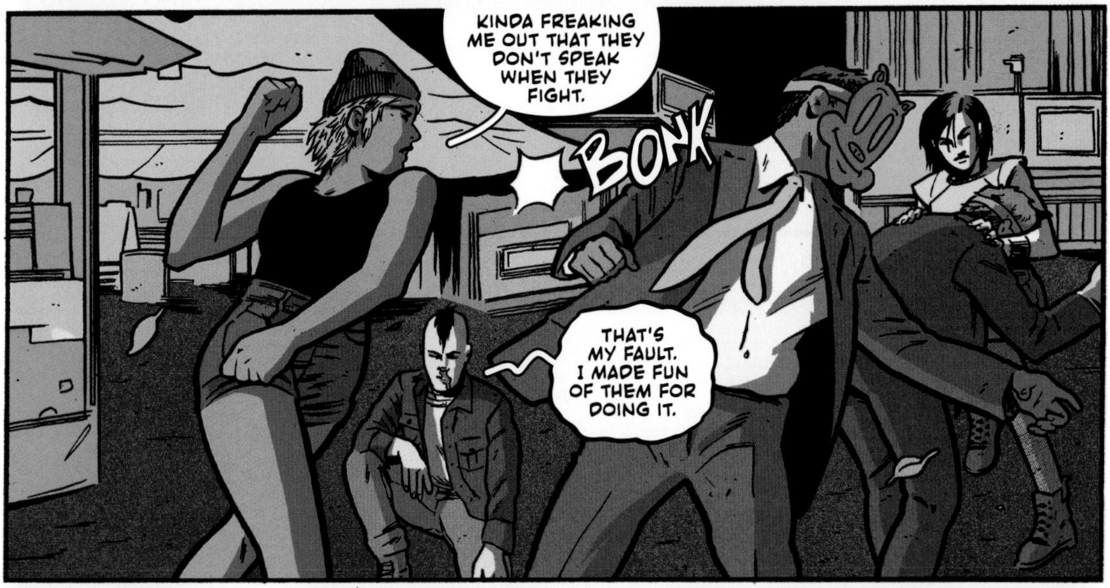
KINDA FREAKING ME OUT THAT THEY DON'T SPEAK WHEN THEY FIGHT.
BONK
THAT'S MY FAULT. I MADE FUN OF THEM FOR DOING IT.

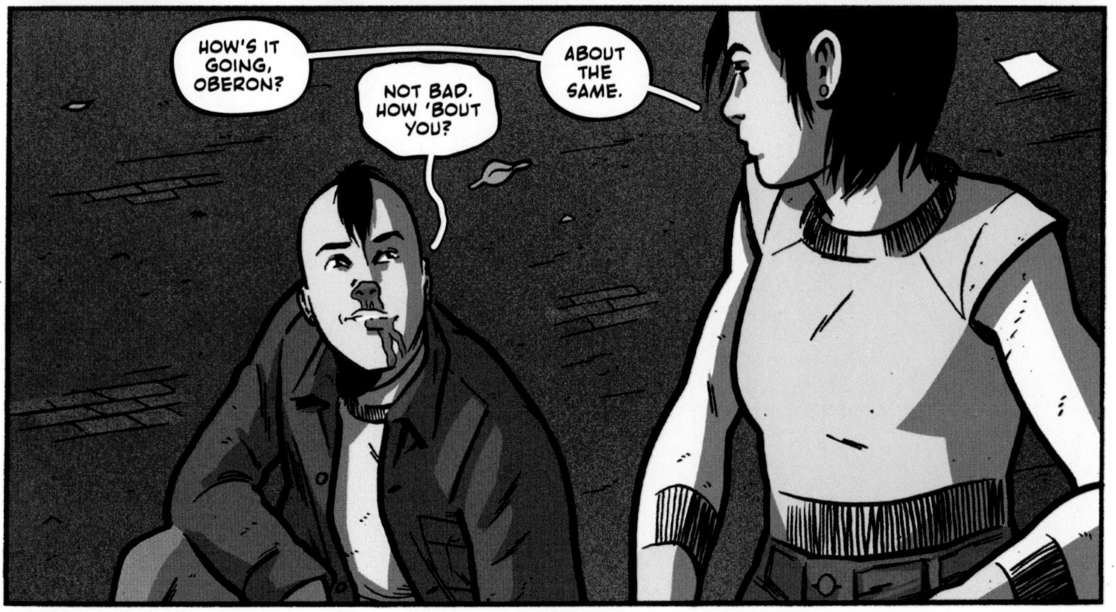
HOW'S IT GOING, OBERON?
ABOUT THE SAME.
NOT BAD. HOW 'BOUT YOU?

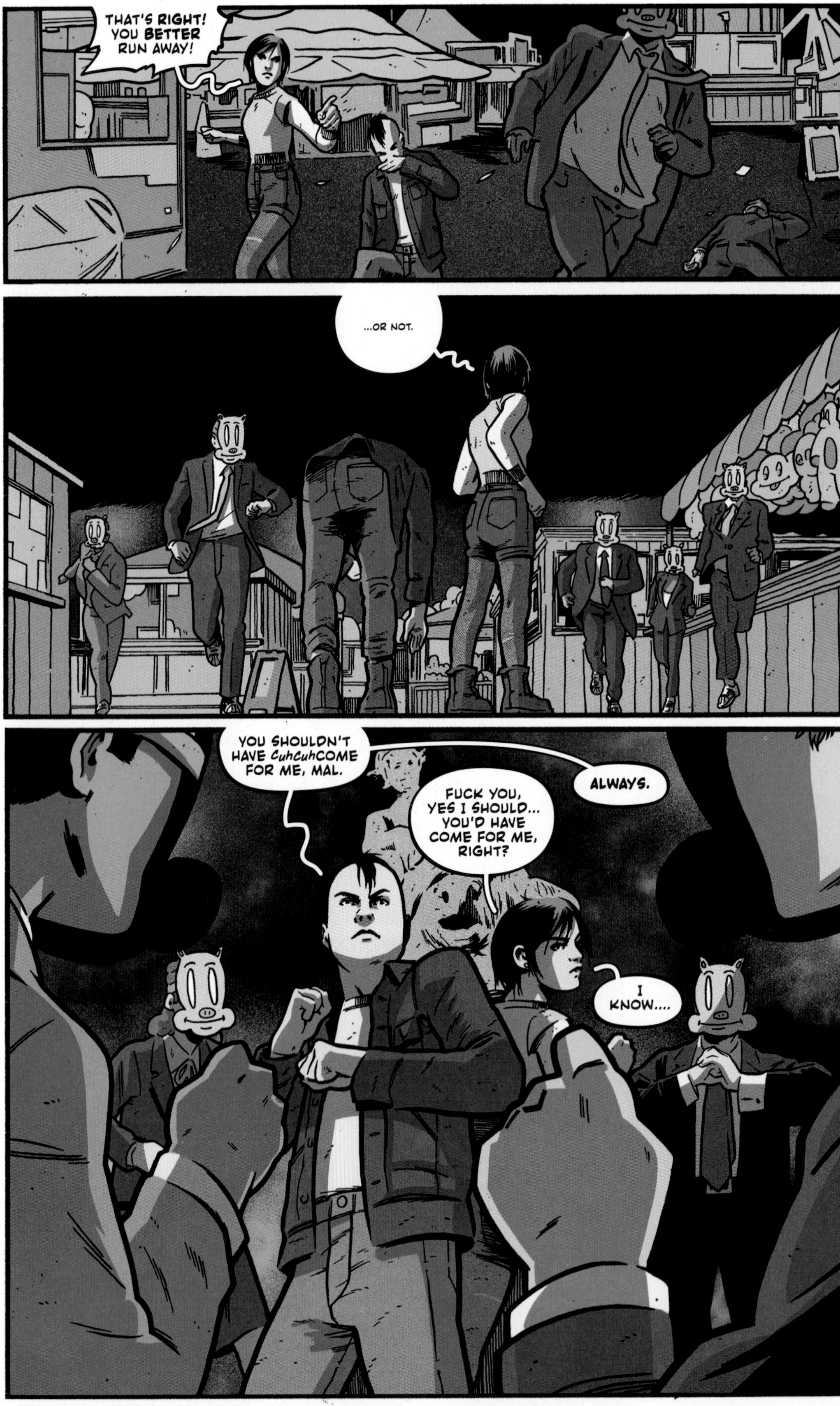

THAT'S RIGHT! YOU BETTER RUN AWAY!
...OR NOT.
YOU SHOULDN'T HAVE CuhCuhCOME FOR ME, MAL.
FUCK YOU, YES I SHOULD... YOU'D HAVE COME FOR ME, RIGHT?
ALWAYS.
I KNOW....

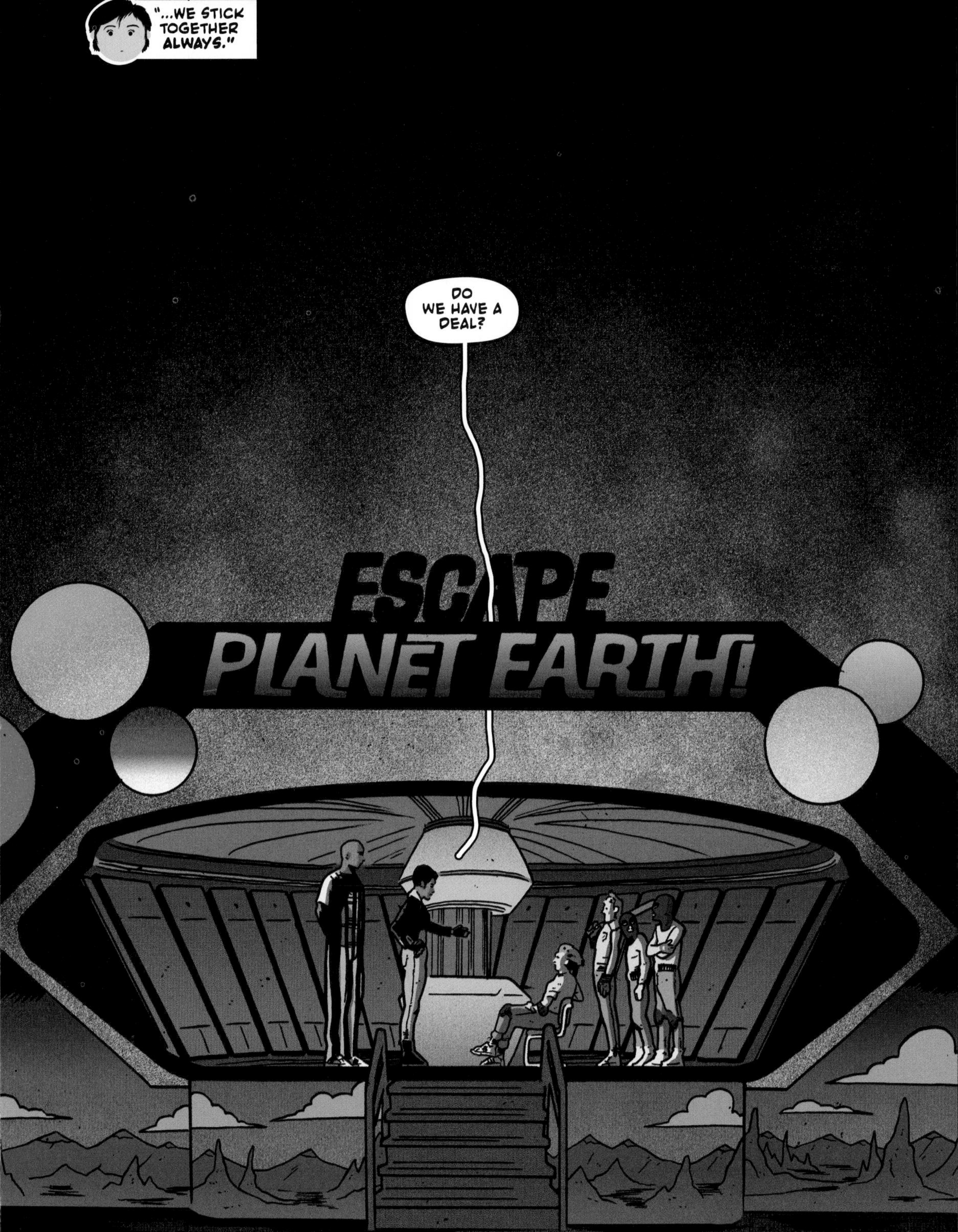
"...WE STICK TOGETHER ALWAYS."
ESCAPE PLANET EARTH!
DO WE HAVE A DEAL?

# ACT V

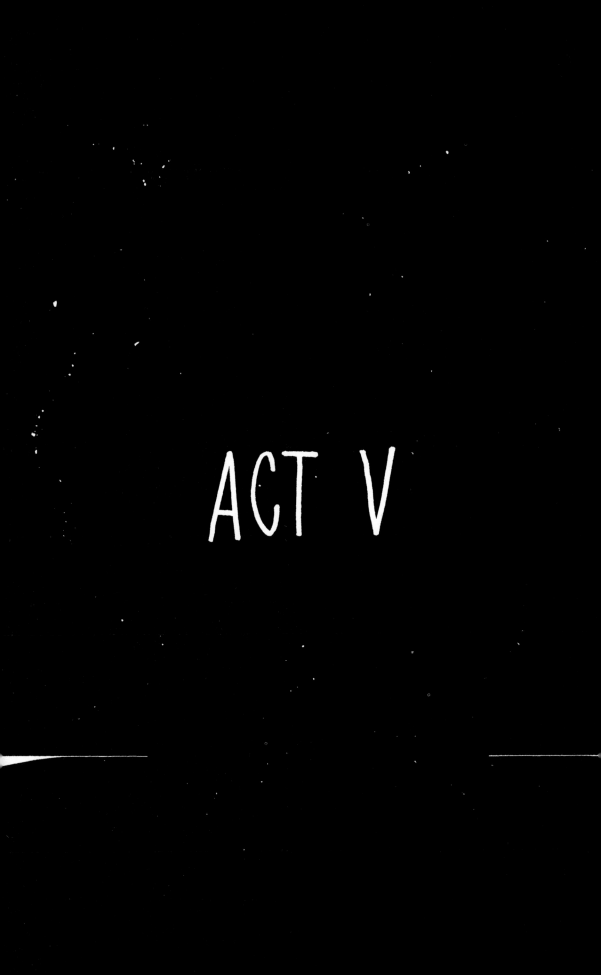

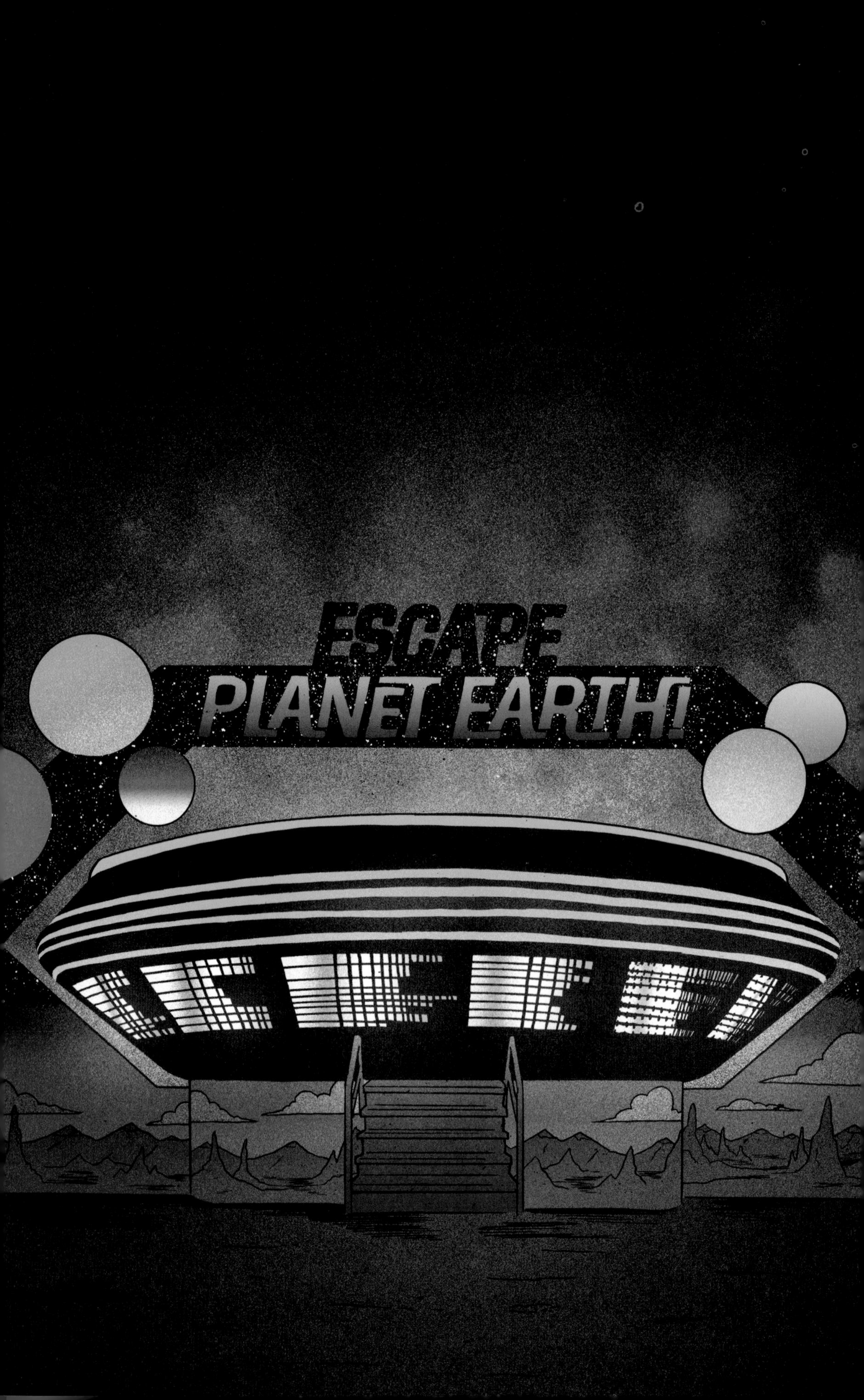
ESCAPE
PLANET EARTH!

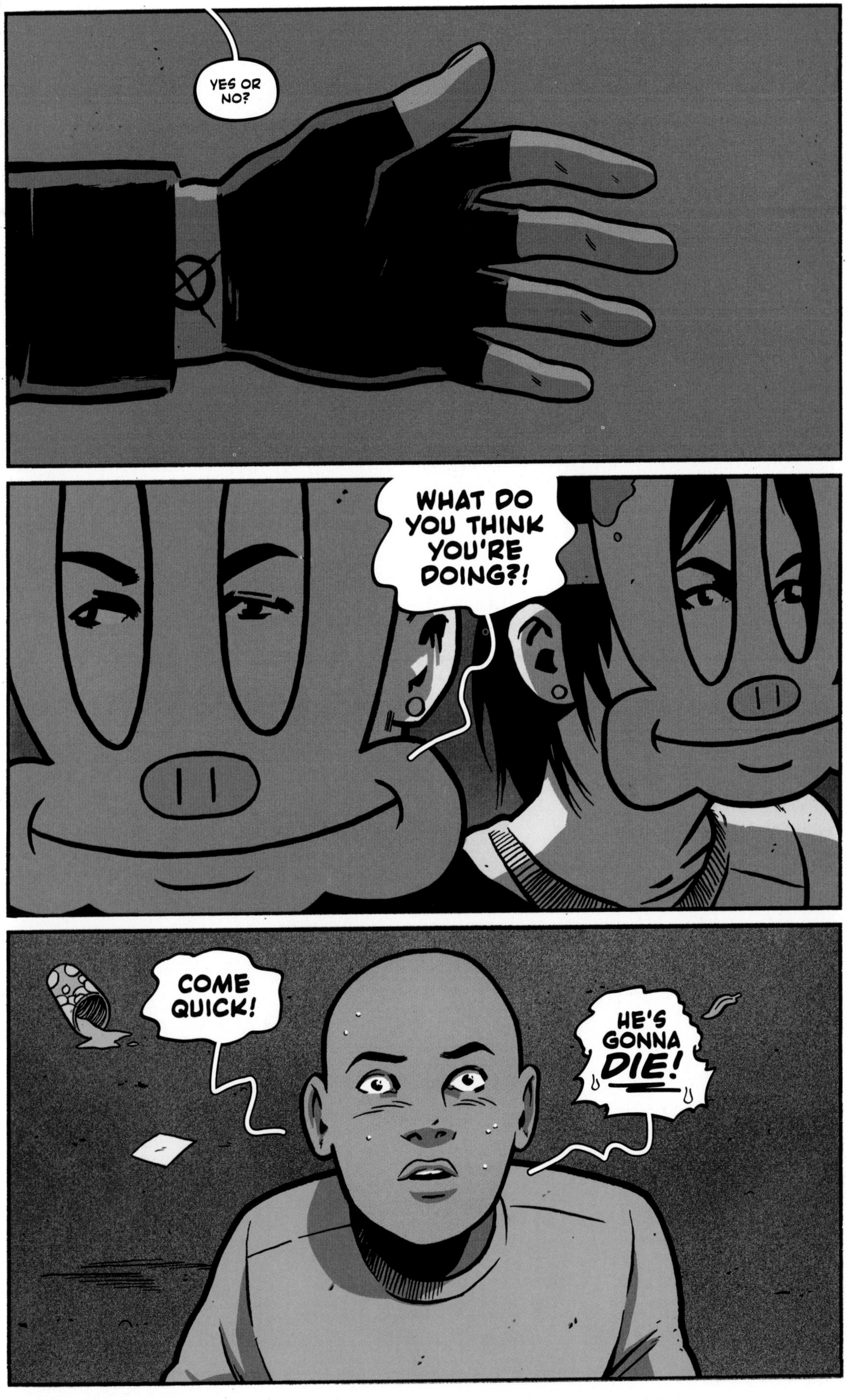
YES OR NO?
WHAT DO YOU THINK YOU'RE DOING?!
COME QUICK!
HE'S GONNA DIE!

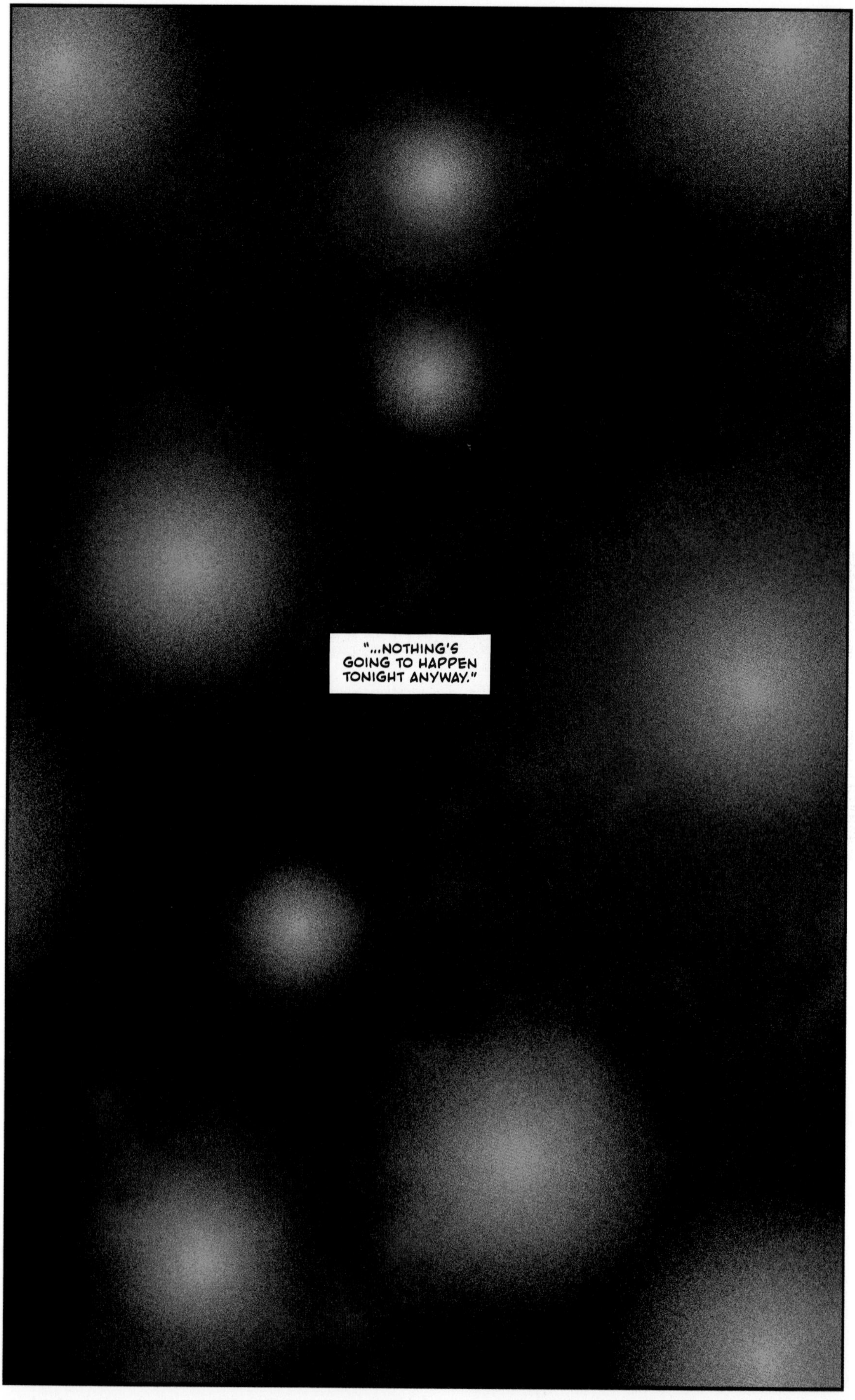
"...NOTHING'S GOING TO HAPPEN TONIGHT ANYWAY."

# CHAPTER THIRTY-THREE

PTOO!

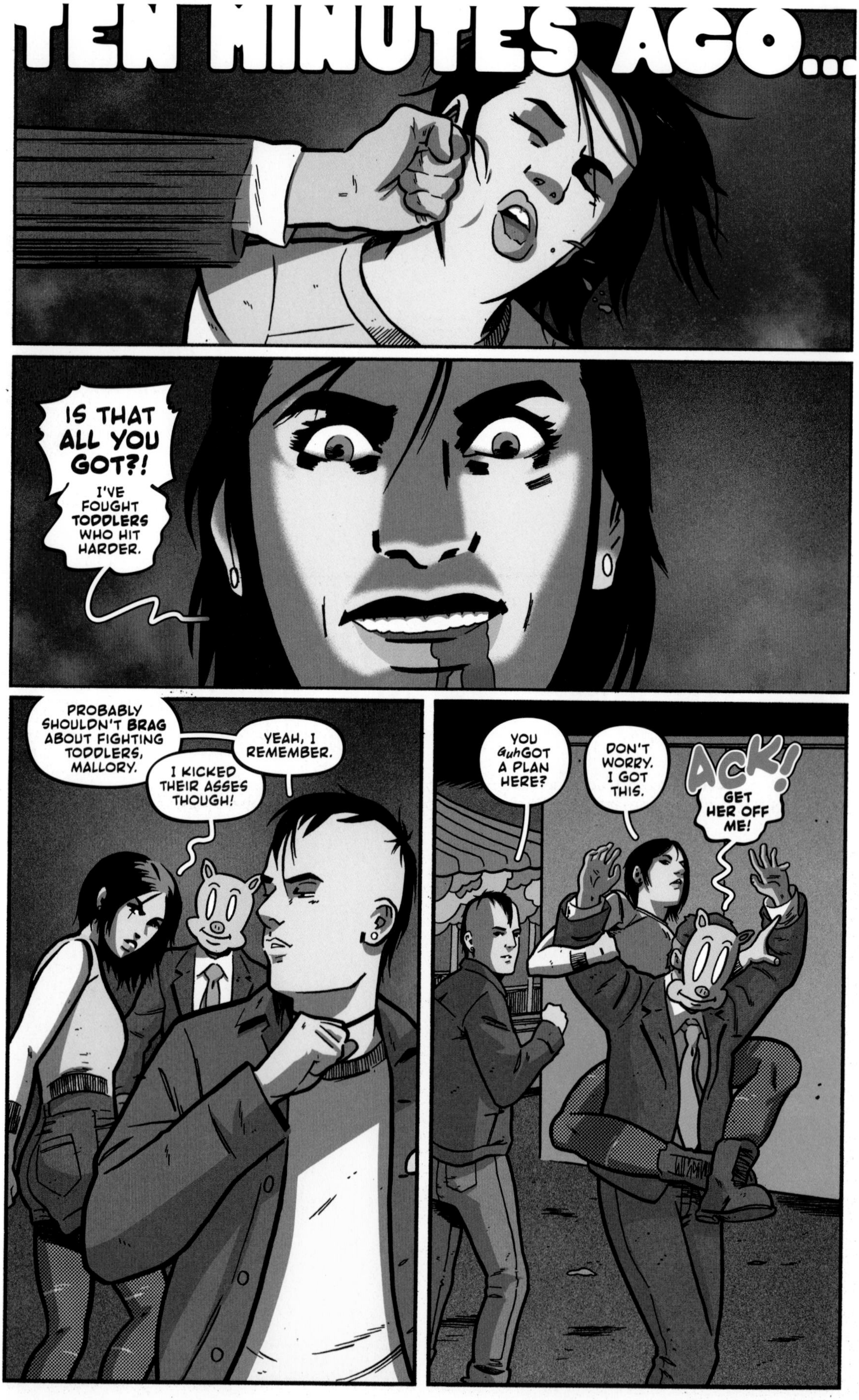
TEN MINUTES AGO...
IS THAT ALL YOU GOT?!
I'VE FOUGHT TODDLERS WHO HIT HARDER.
PROBABLY SHOULDN'T BRAG ABOUT FIGHTING TODDLERS, MALLORY.
YEAH, I REMEMBER.
I KICKED THEIR ASSES THOUGH!
YOU GuhGOT A PLAN HERE?
DON'T WORRY. I GOT THIS.
ACK!
GET HER OFF ME!

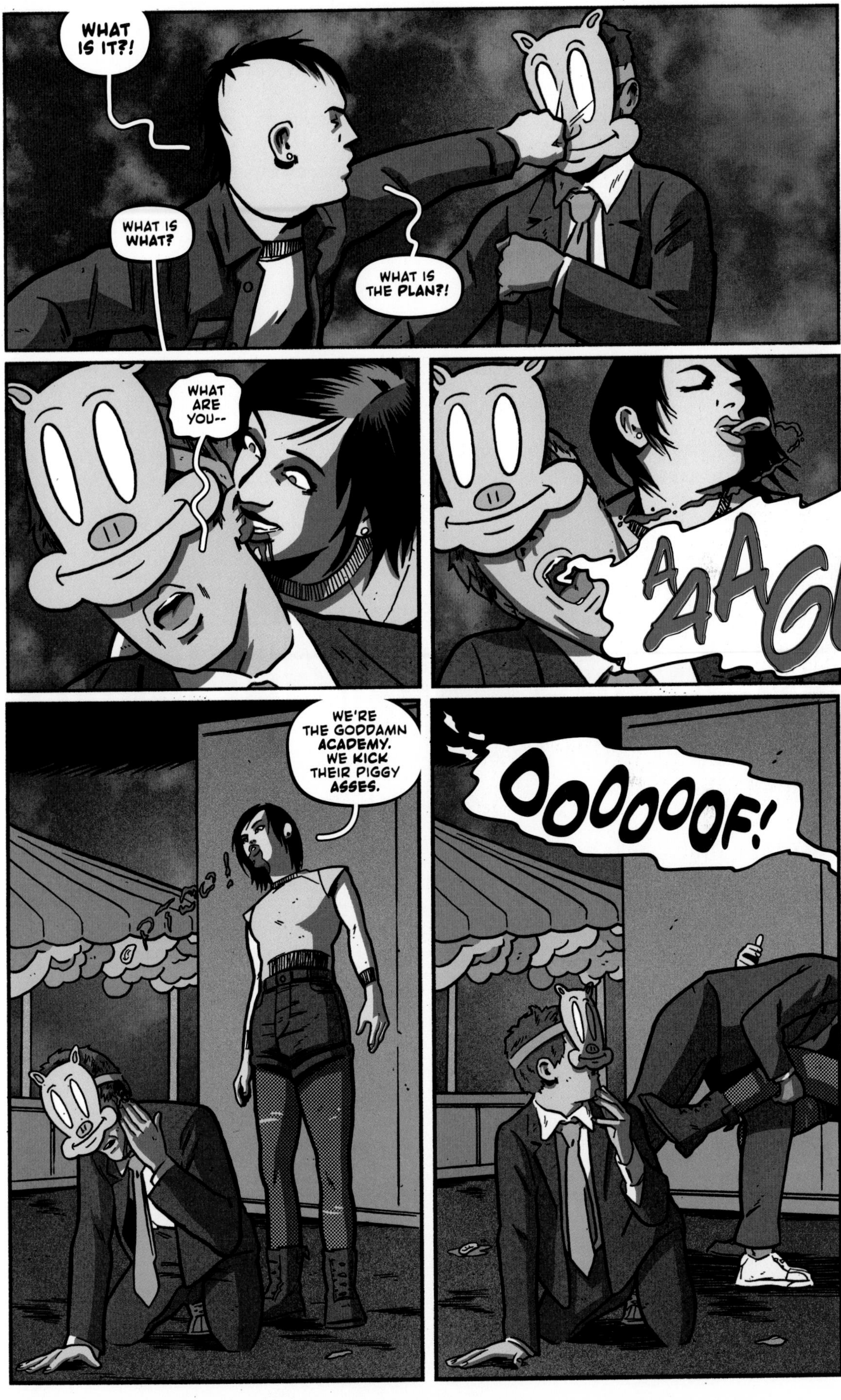
WHAT IS IT?!
WHAT IS WHAT?
WHAT IS THE PLAN?!
WHAT ARE YOU--
AAAGH
WE'RE THE GODDAMN ACADEMY. WE KICK THEIR PIGGY ASSES.
OOOOOOF!

# CHAPTER THIRTY-FOUR

OH MY GODS.

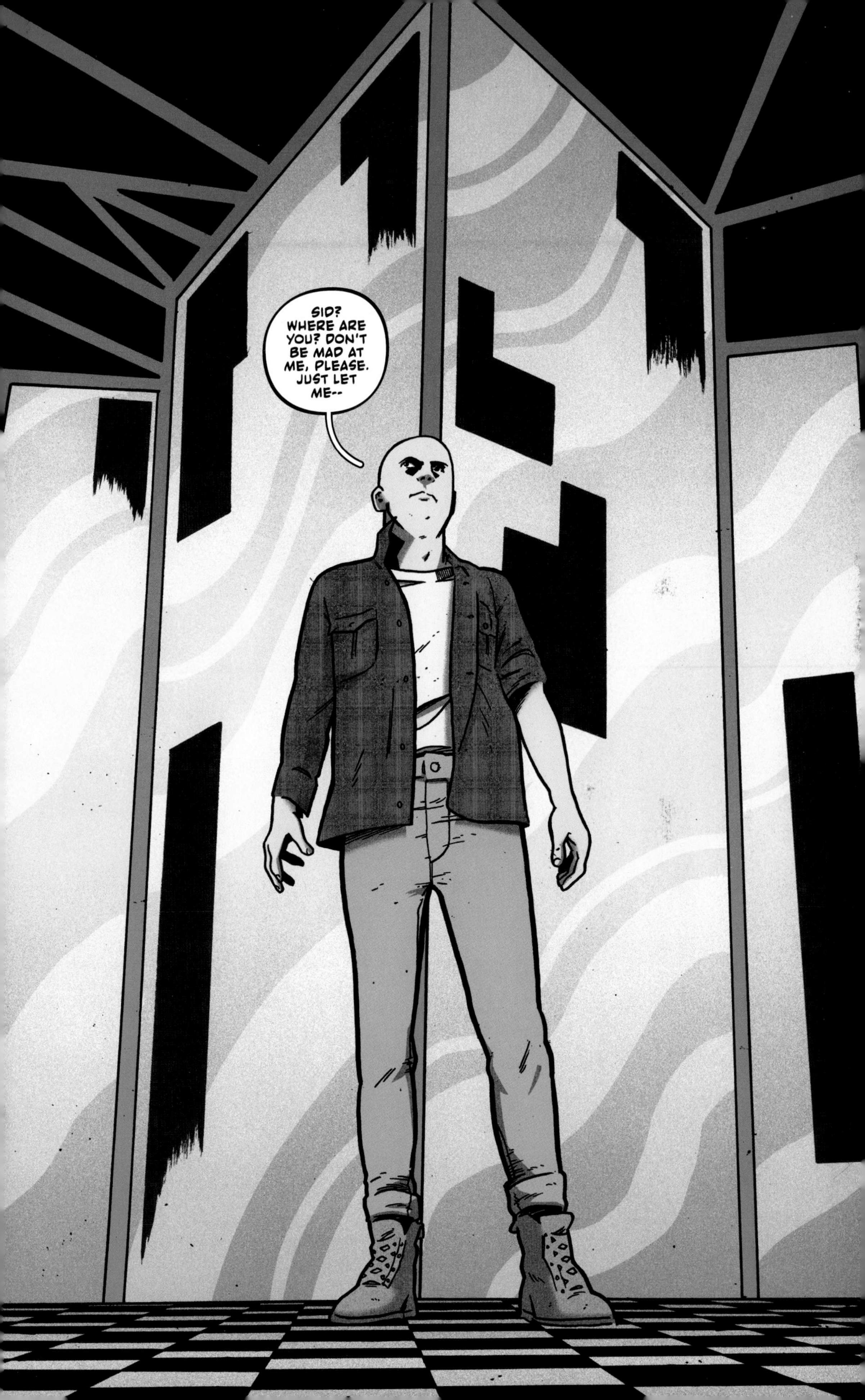
SID? WHERE ARE YOU? DON'T BE MAD AT ME, PLEASE. JUST LET ME--

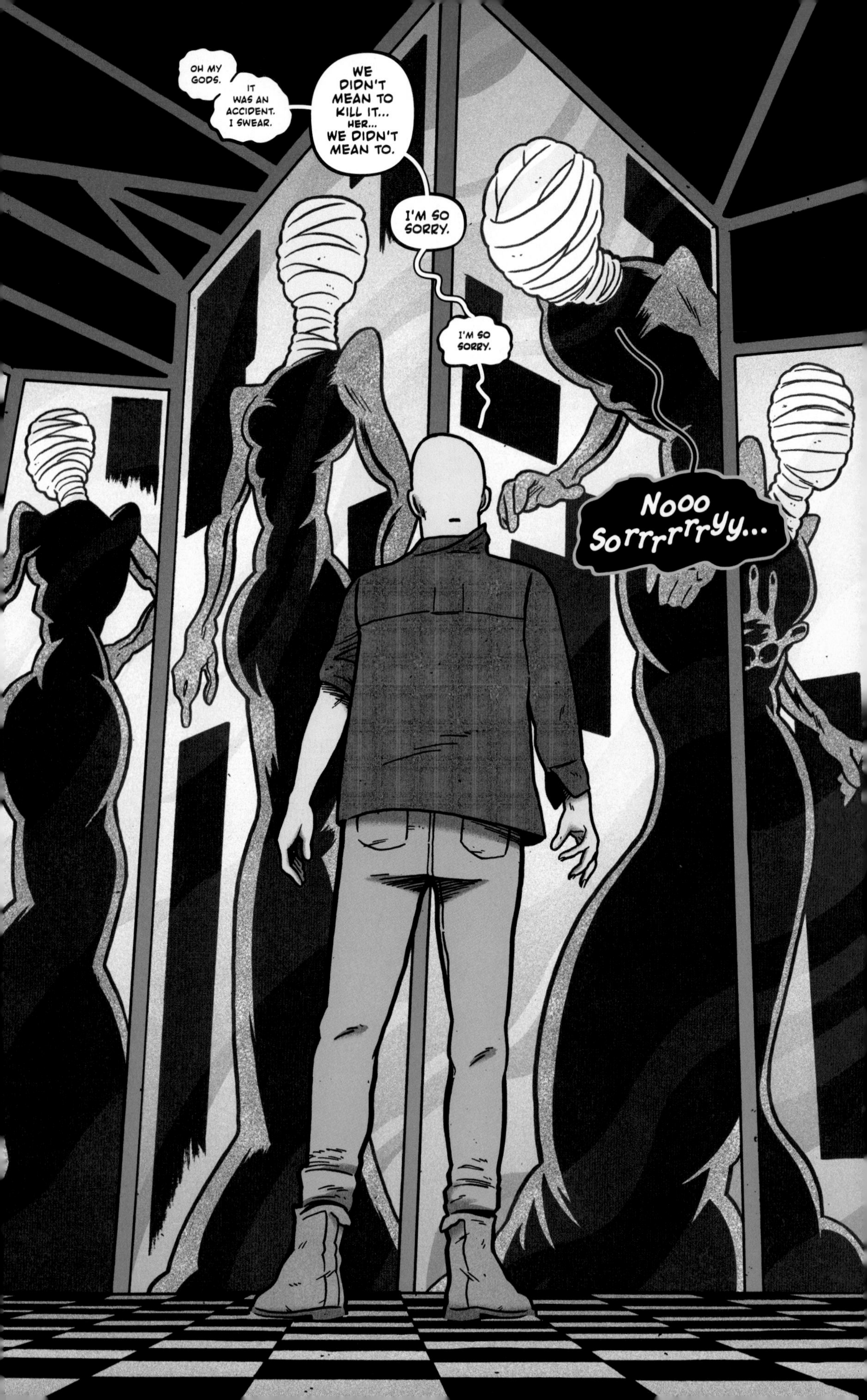
OH MY GODS.
IT WAS AN ACCIDENT. I SWEAR.
WE DIDN'T MEAN TO KILL IT... HER... WE DIDN'T MEAN TO.
I'M SO SORRY.
I'M SO SORRY.
Nooo Sorrrrrrryy...

# CHAPTER THIRTY-FIVE

## KICK THEIR ASSES, KEITH!

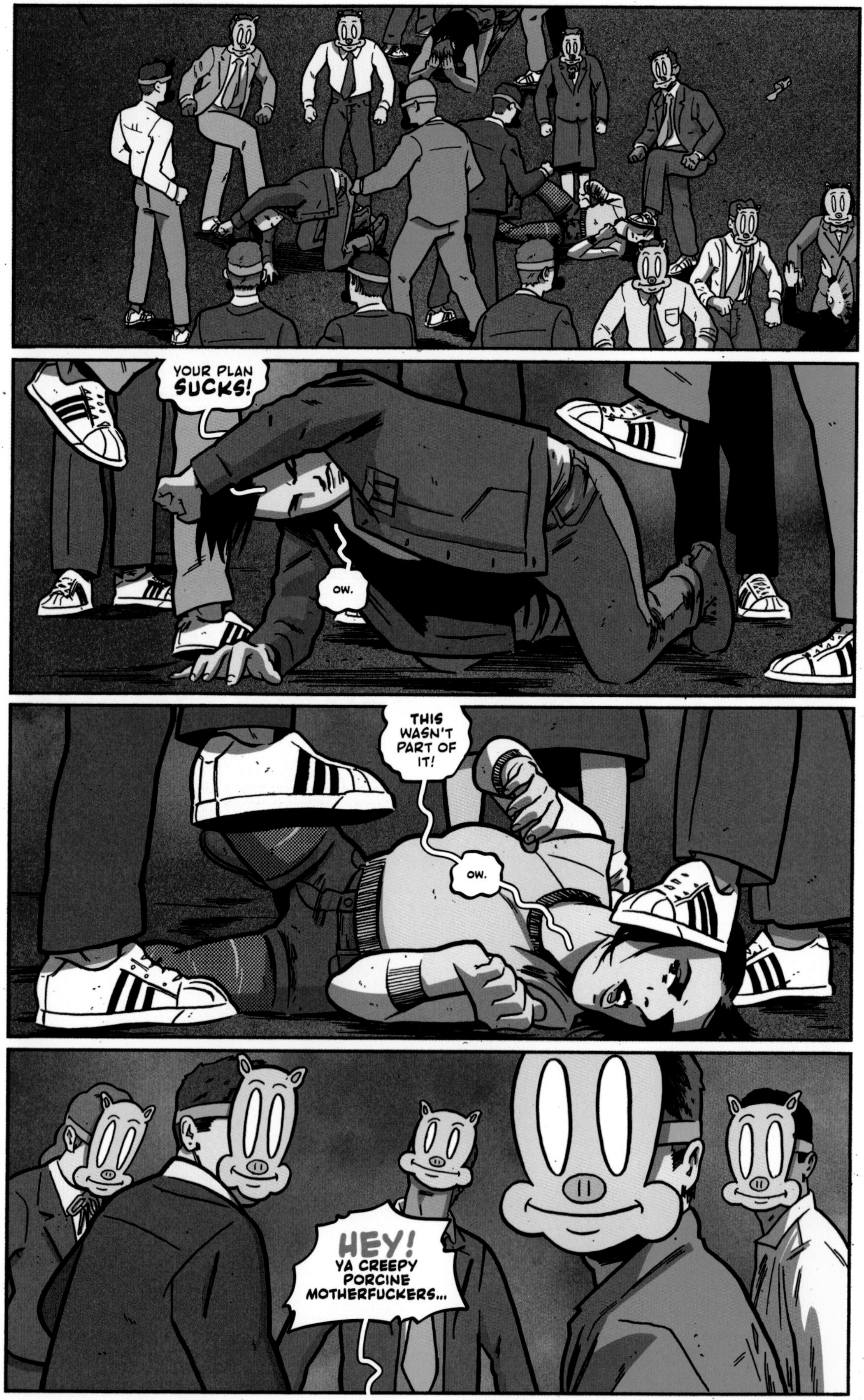
YOUR PLAN SUCKS!
OW.
THIS WASN'T PART OF IT!
OW.
HEY! YA CREEPY PORCINE MOTHERFUCKERS...

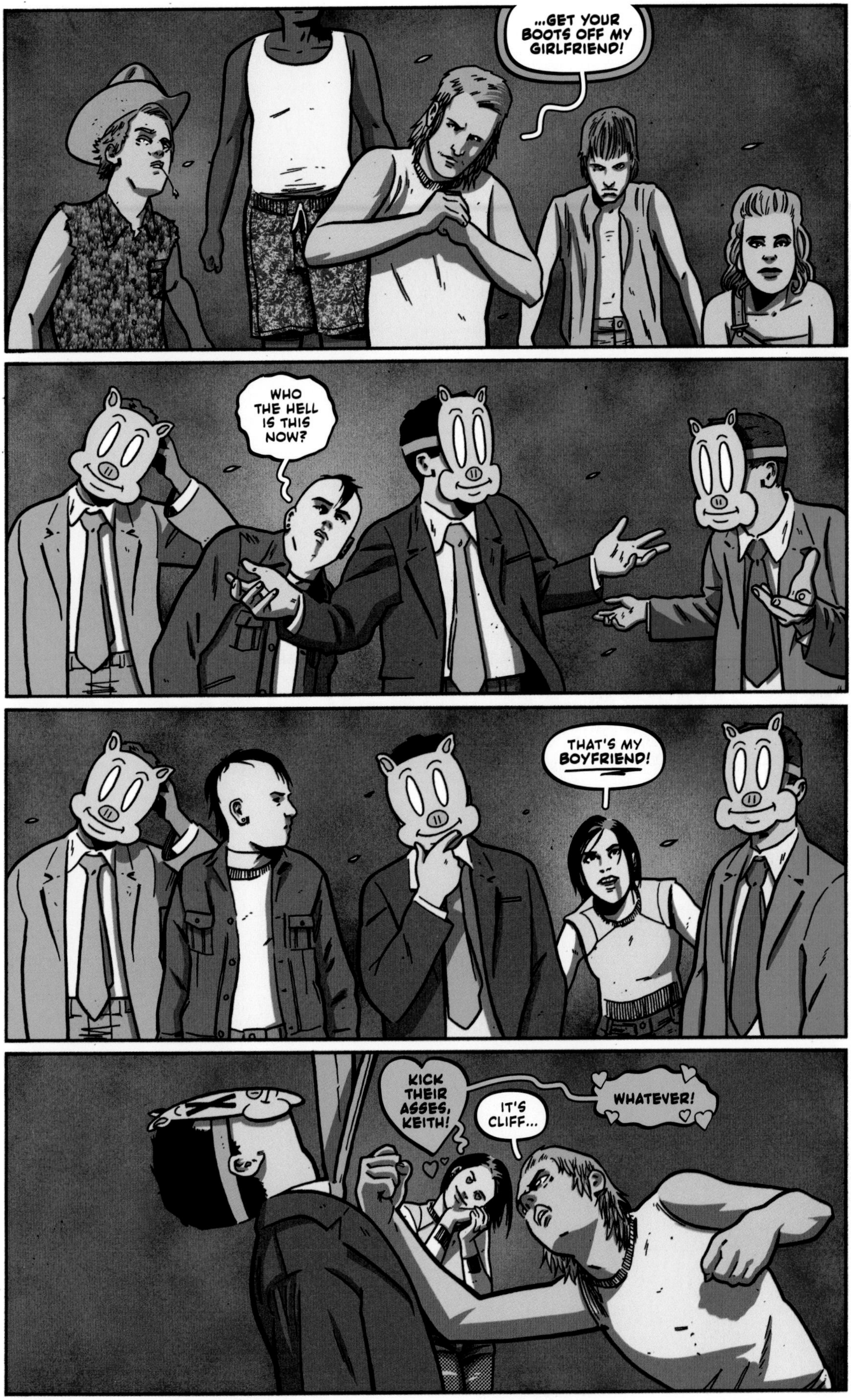
...GET YOUR BOOTS OFF MY GIRLFRIEND!
WHO THE HELL IS THIS NOW?
THAT'S MY BOYFRIEND!
KICK THEIR ASSES, KEITH!
IT'S CLIFF...
WHATEVER!

# CHAPTER THIRTY-SIX

NO. I'M GOOD. BYE.

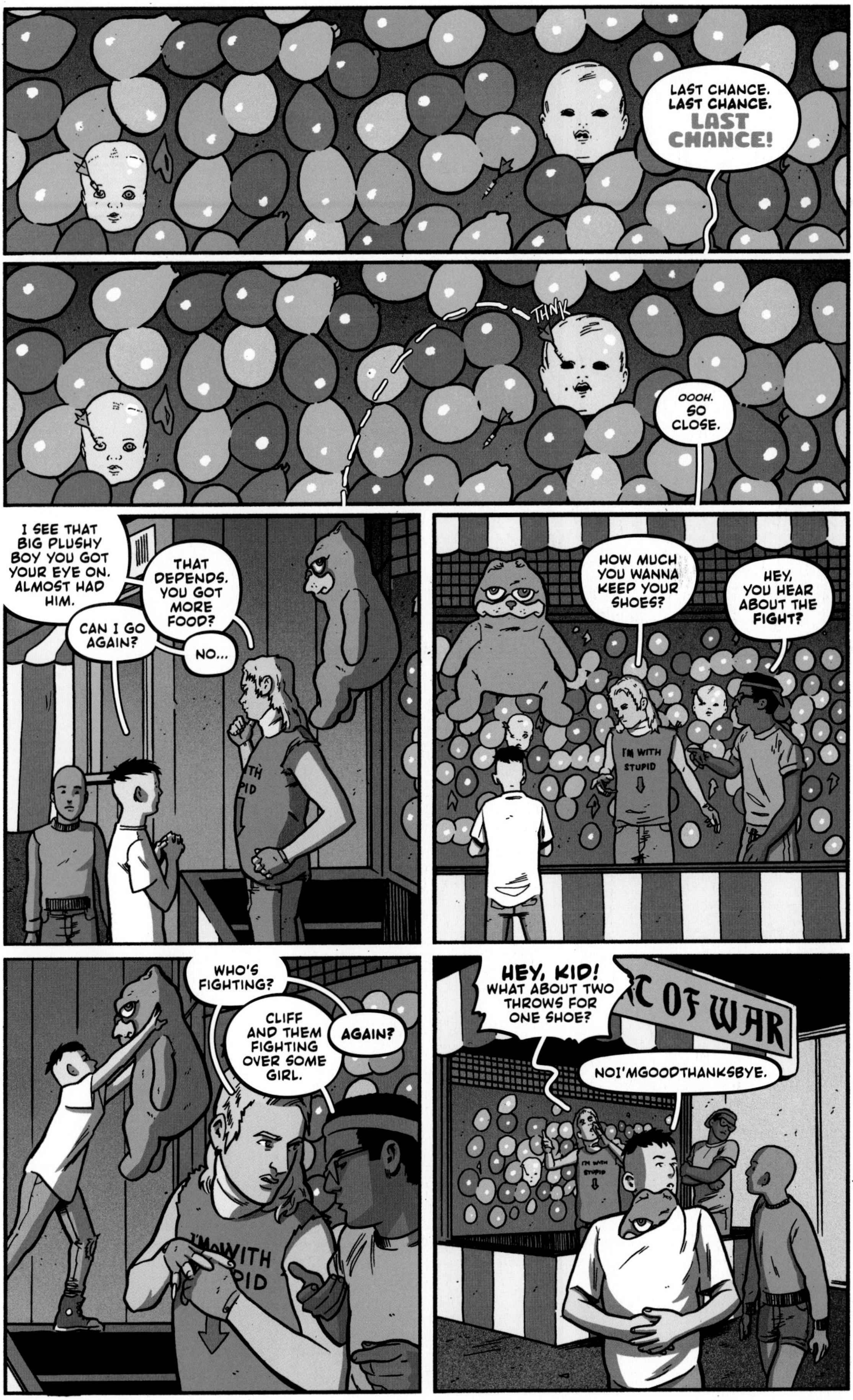

LAST CHANCE.
LAST CHANCE.
LAST CHANCE!
THNK
OOOH. SO CLOSE.
I SEE THAT BIG PLUSHY BOY YOU GOT YOUR EYE ON. ALMOST HAD HIM.
THAT DEPENDS. YOU GOT MORE FOOD?
CAN I GO AGAIN?
NO...
HOW MUCH YOU WANNA KEEP YOUR SHOES?
HEY, YOU HEAR ABOUT THE FIGHT?
I'M WITH STUPID
WHO'S FIGHTING?
CLIFF AND THEM FIGHTING OVER SOME GIRL.
AGAIN?
HEY, KID! WHAT ABOUT TWO THROWS FOR ONE SHOE?
OF WAR
NOI'MGOODTHANKSBYE.

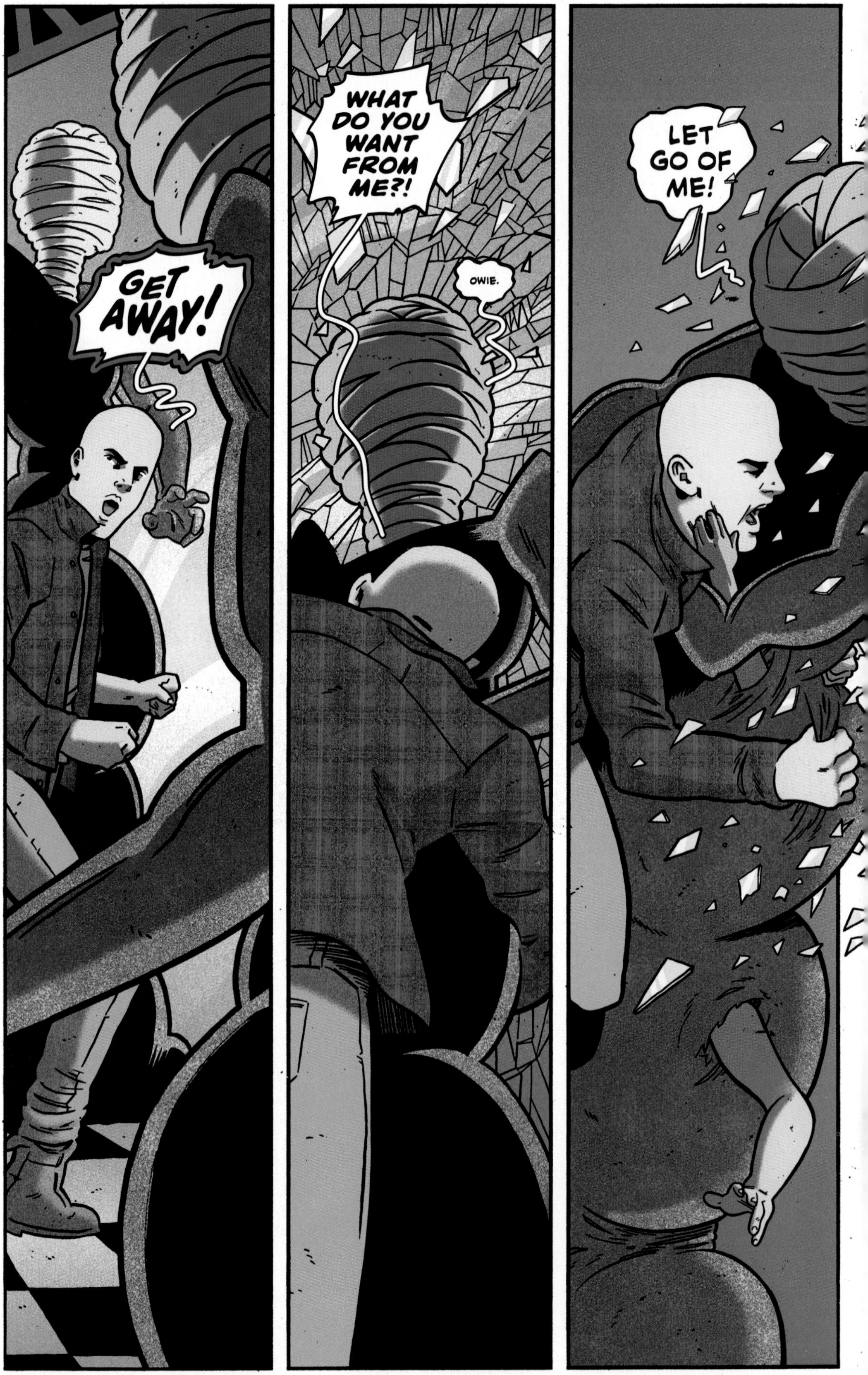
GET AWAY!
WHAT DO YOU WANT FROM ME?!
OWIE.
LET GO OF ME!

# CHAPTER THIRTY-SEVEN

## WACK!

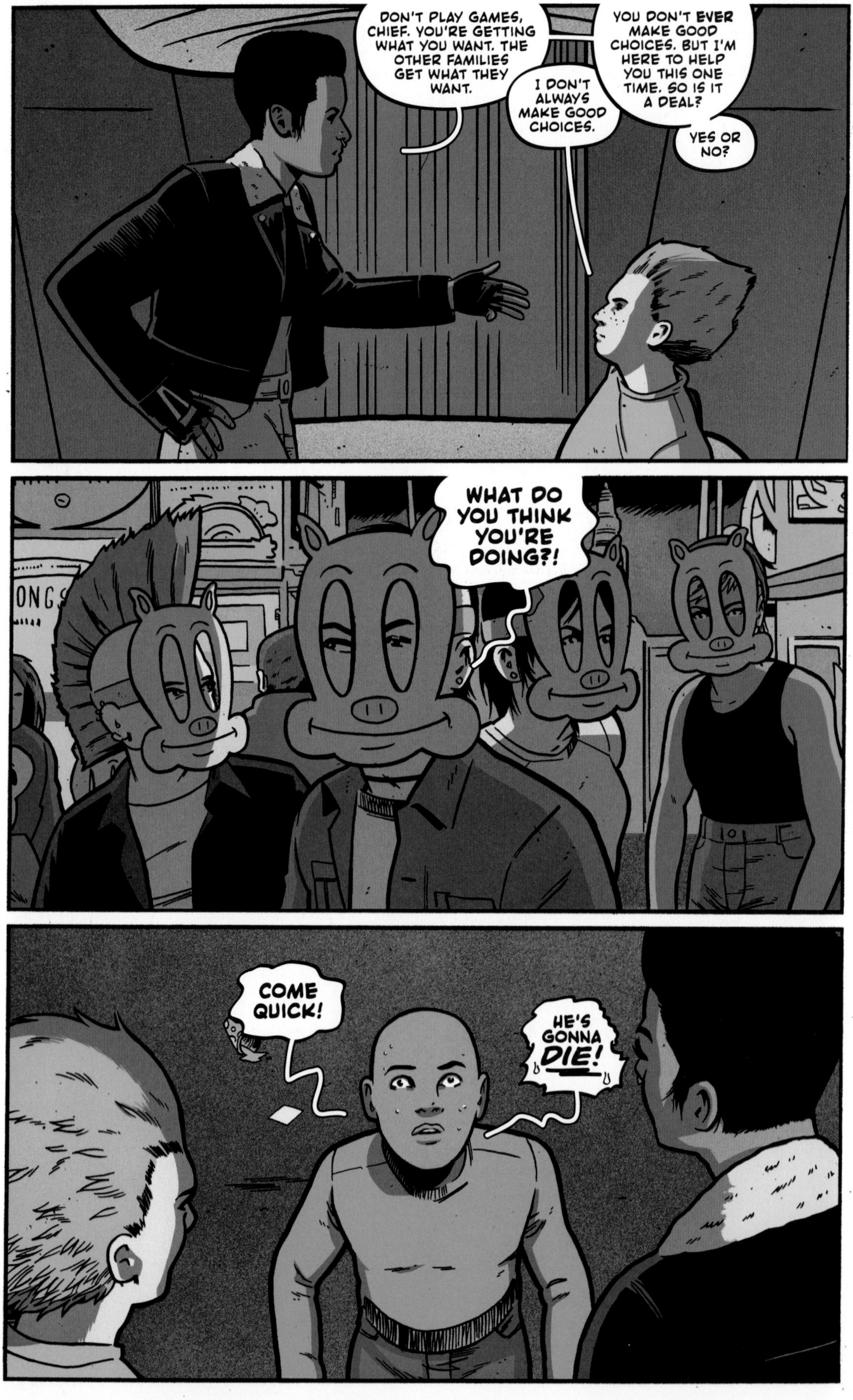
DON'T PLAY GAMES, CHIEF. YOU'RE GETTING WHAT YOU WANT. THE OTHER FAMILIES GET WHAT THEY WANT.
I DON'T ALWAYS MAKE GOOD CHOICES.
YOU DON'T EVER MAKE GOOD CHOICES. BUT I'M HERE TO HELP YOU THIS ONE TIME. SO IS IT A DEAL?
YES OR NO?
ONGS
WHAT DO YOU THINK YOU'RE DOING?!
COME QUICK!
HE'S GONNA DIE!

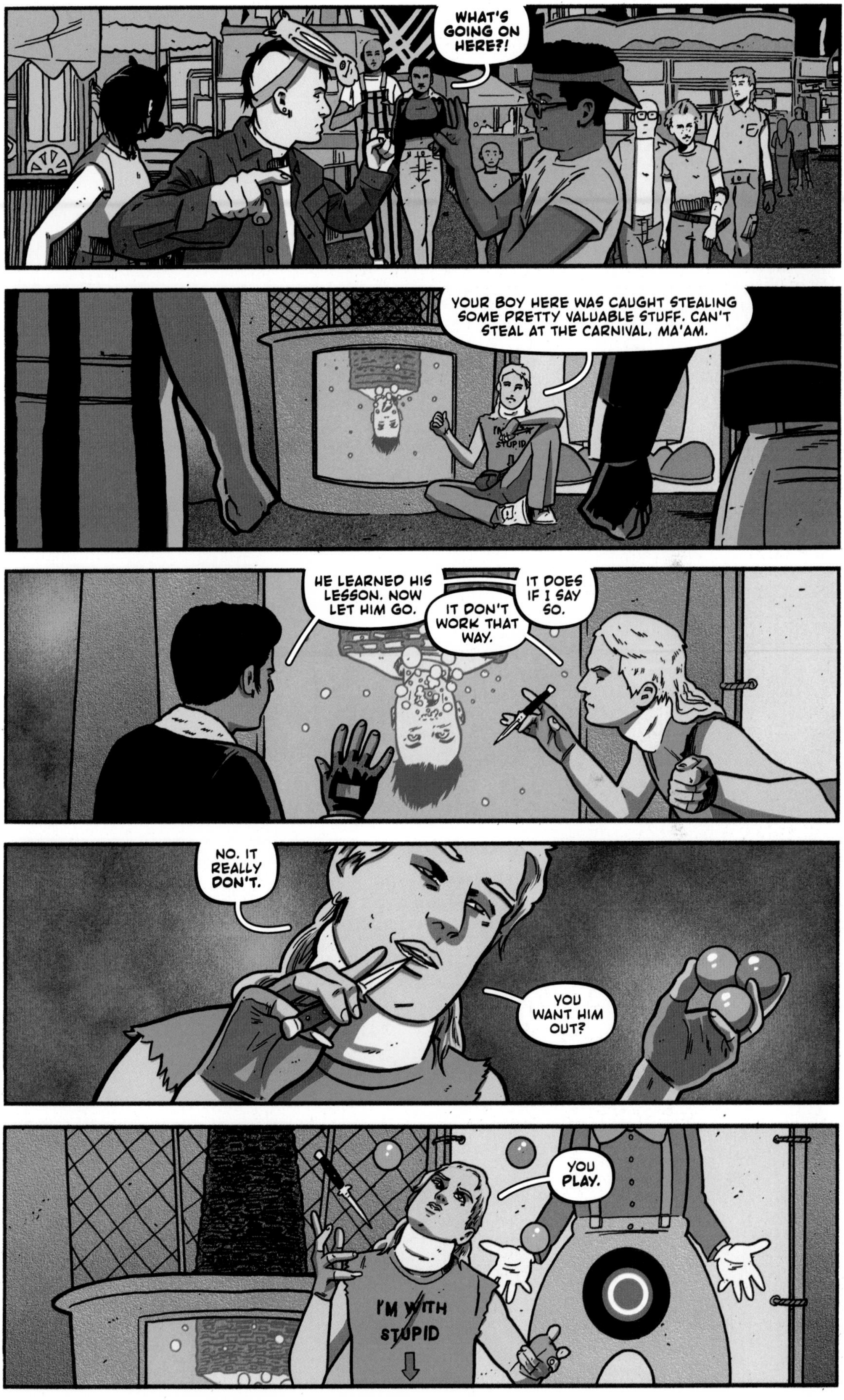
WHAT'S GOING ON HERE?!
YOUR BOY HERE WAS CAUGHT STEALING SOME PRETTY VALUABLE STUFF. CAN'T STEAL AT THE CARNIVAL, MA'AM.
HE LEARNED HIS LESSON. NOW LET HIM GO.
IT DON'T WORK THAT WAY.
IT DOES IF I SAY SO.
NO. IT REALLY DON'T.
YOU WANT HIM OUT?
YOU PLAY.
I'M WITH STUPID

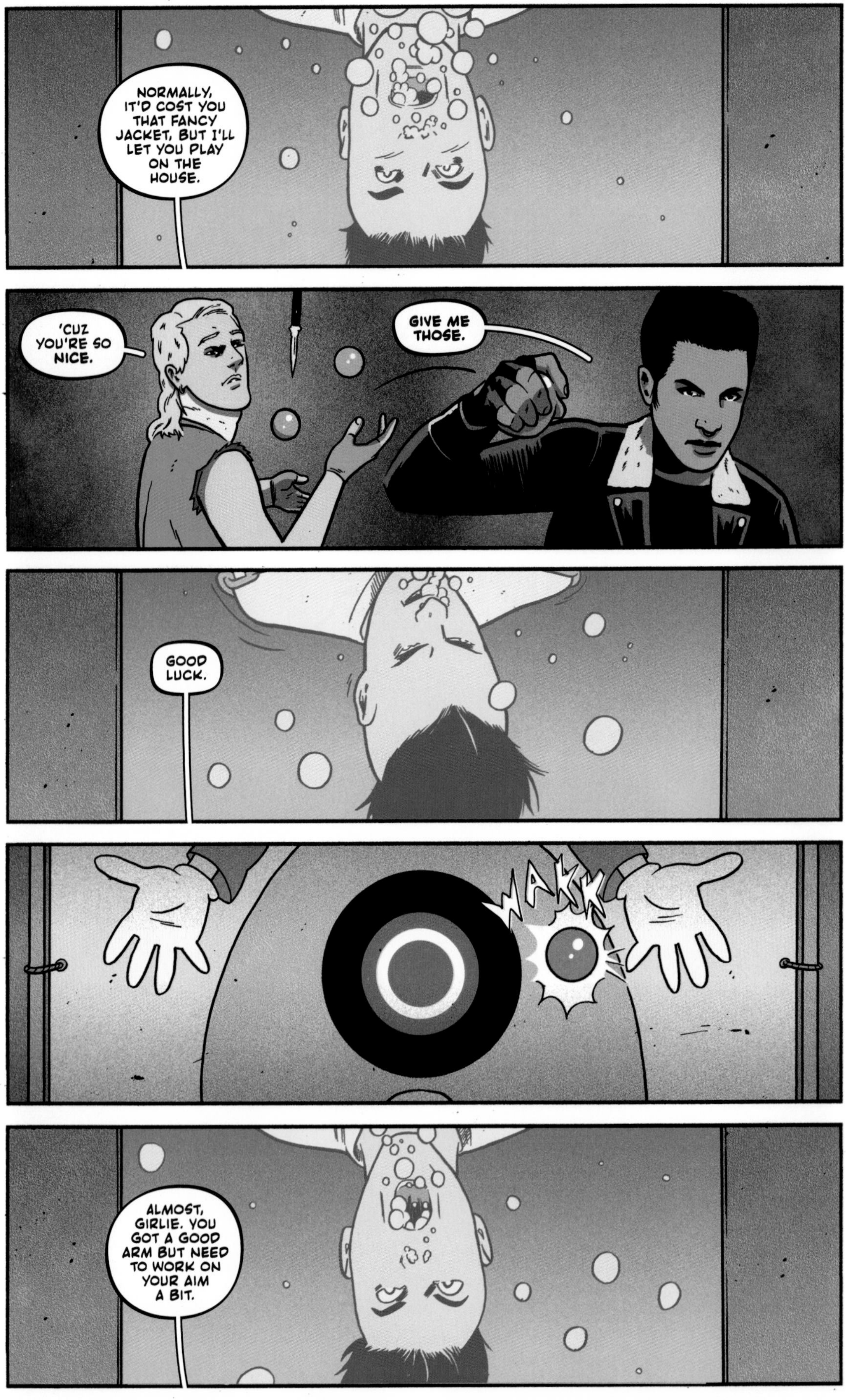
NORMALLY, IT'D COST YOU THAT FANCY JACKET, BUT I'LL LET YOU PLAY ON THE HOUSE.
'CUZ YOU'RE SO NICE.
GIVE ME THOSE.
GOOD LUCK.
WAKK
ALMOST, GIRLIE. YOU GOT A GOOD ARM BUT NEED TO WORK ON YOUR AIM A BIT.

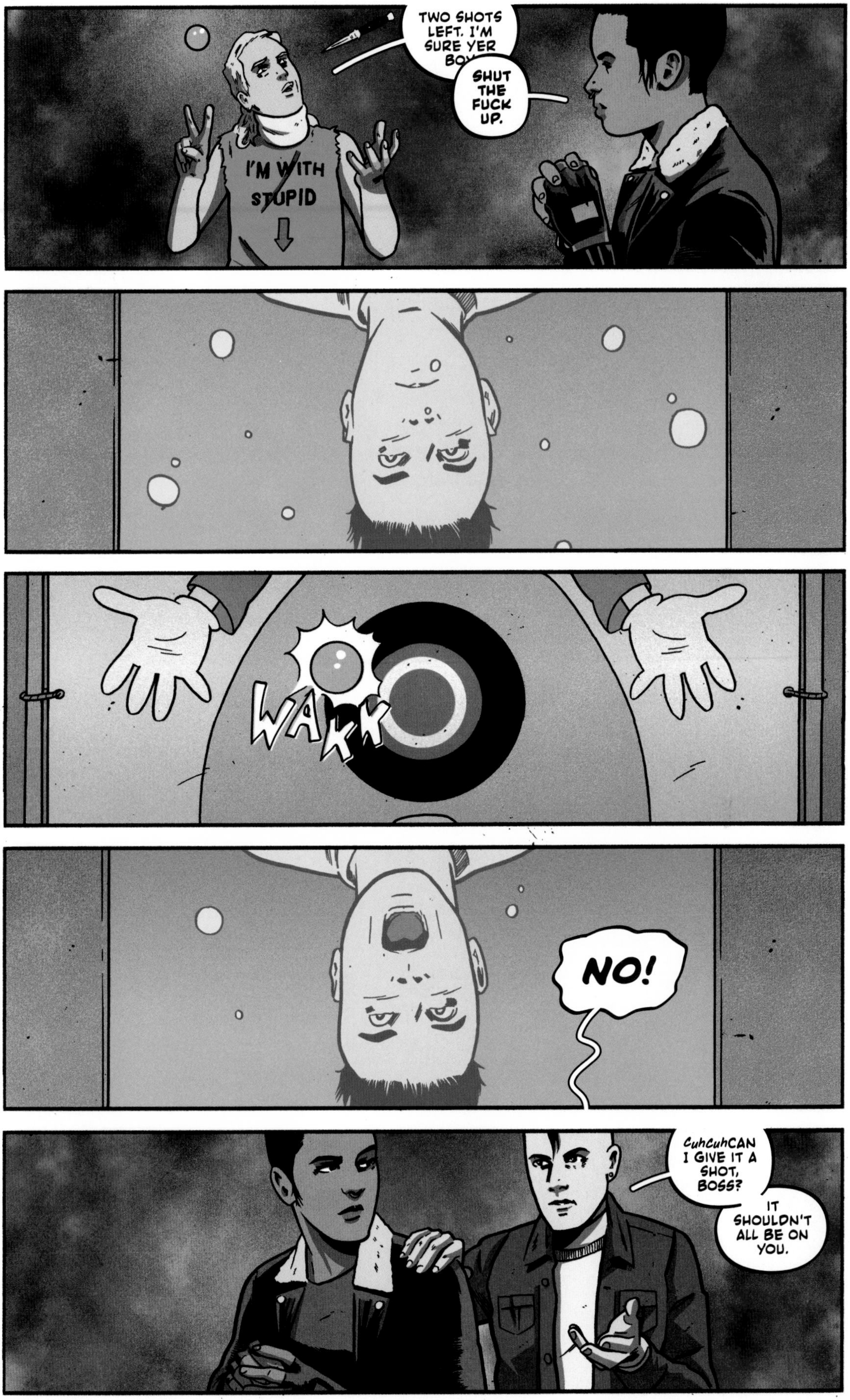

TWO SHOTS LEFT. I'M SURE YER BOY
SHUT THE FUCK UP.
I'M WITH STUPID
WAKK
NO!
CuhCuhCAN I GIVE IT A SHOT, BOSS?
IT SHOULDN'T ALL BE ON YOU.

WAP
WHAT'S HAPPENING?!
I HIT IT!
DOESN'T SEEM LIKE IT. IF YOU HIT IT, HE'D BE OUT.

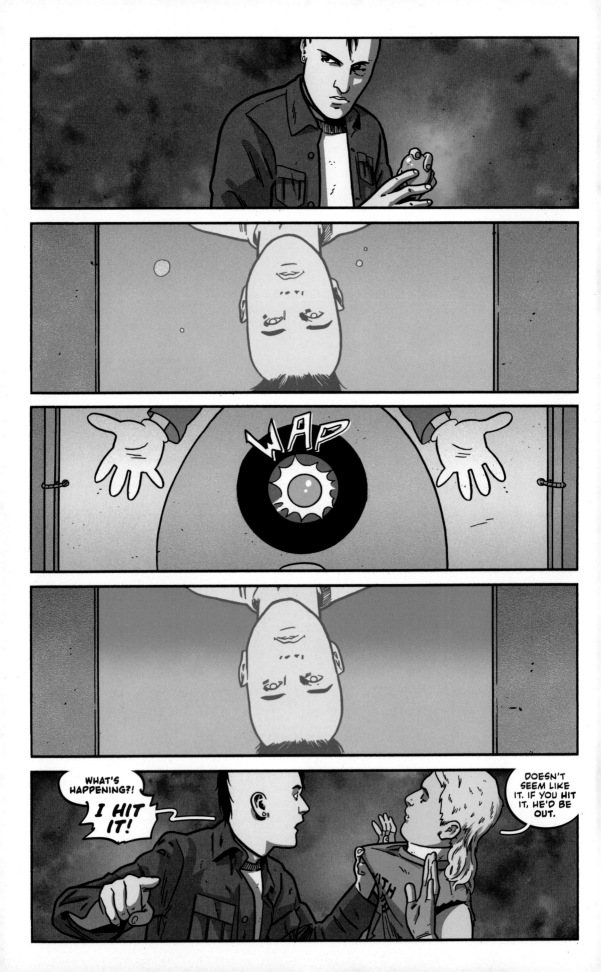

# CHAPTER THIRTY-EIGHT

## SAVE YOUR PEOPLE, ALABAMA.

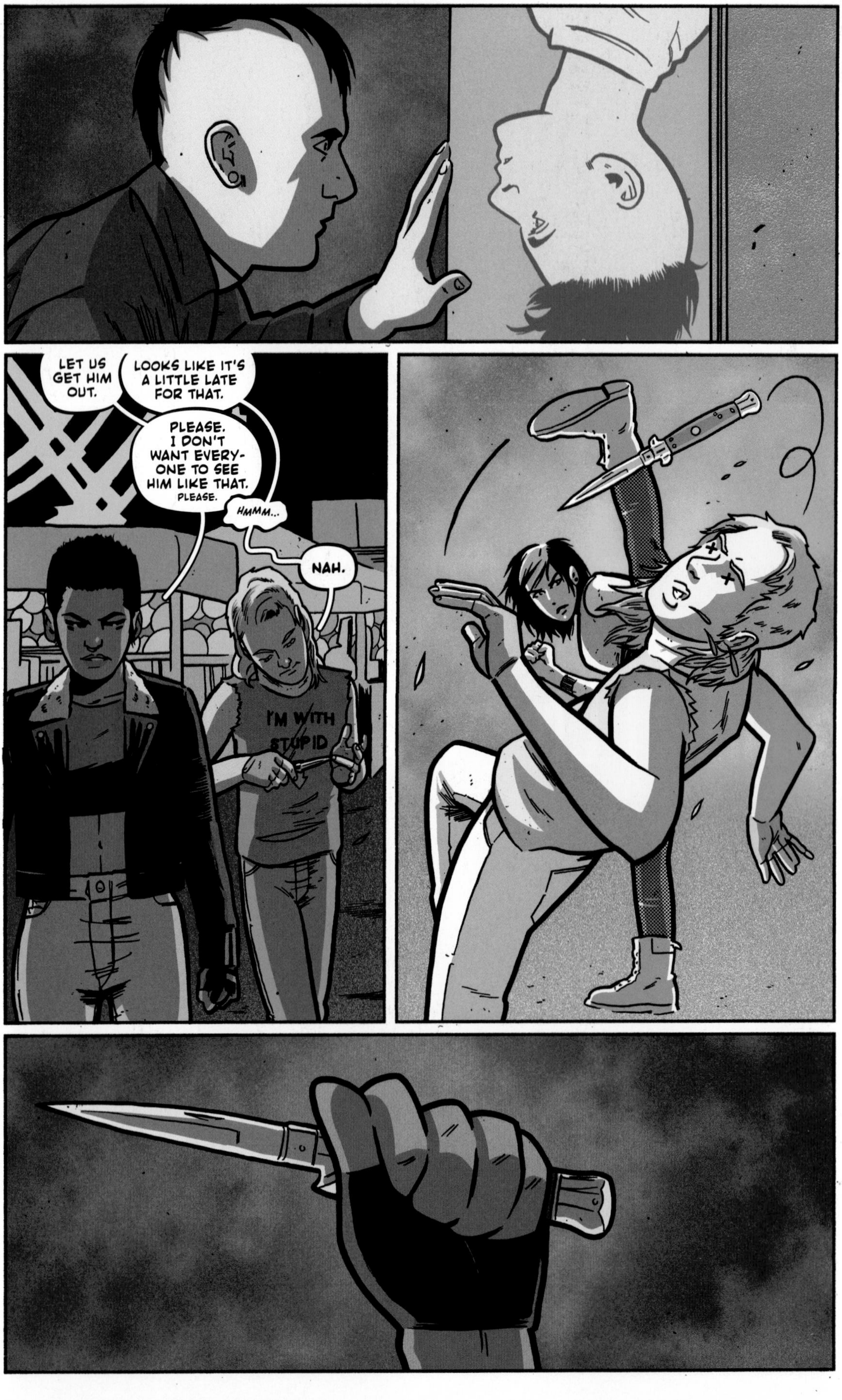
LET US GET HIM OUT.
LOOKS LIKE IT'S A LITTLE LATE FOR THAT.
PLEASE. I DON'T WANT EVERY-ONE TO SEE HIM LIKE THAT. PLEASE.
HMMM...
NAH.
I'M WITH STUPID

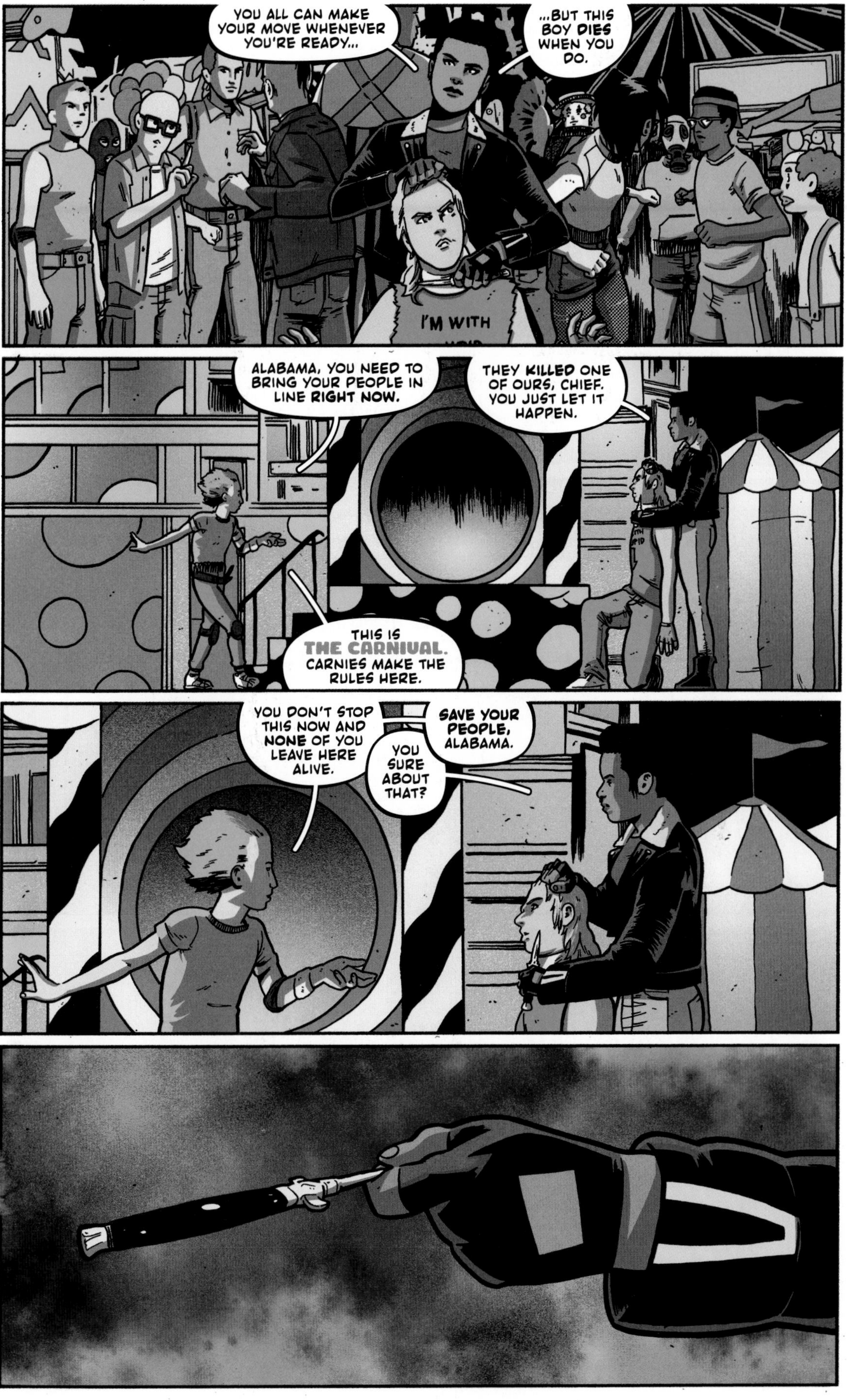
YOU ALL CAN MAKE YOUR MOVE WHENEVER YOU'RE READY...
...BUT THIS BOY DIES WHEN YOU DO.
I'M WITH
ALABAMA, YOU NEED TO BRING YOUR PEOPLE IN LINE RIGHT NOW.
THEY KILLED ONE OF OURS, CHIEF. YOU JUST LET IT HAPPEN.
THIS IS THE CARNIVAL. CARNIES MAKE THE RULES HERE.
YOU DON'T STOP THIS NOW AND NONE OF YOU LEAVE HERE ALIVE.
SAVE YOUR PEOPLE, ALABAMA.
YOU SURE ABOUT THAT?

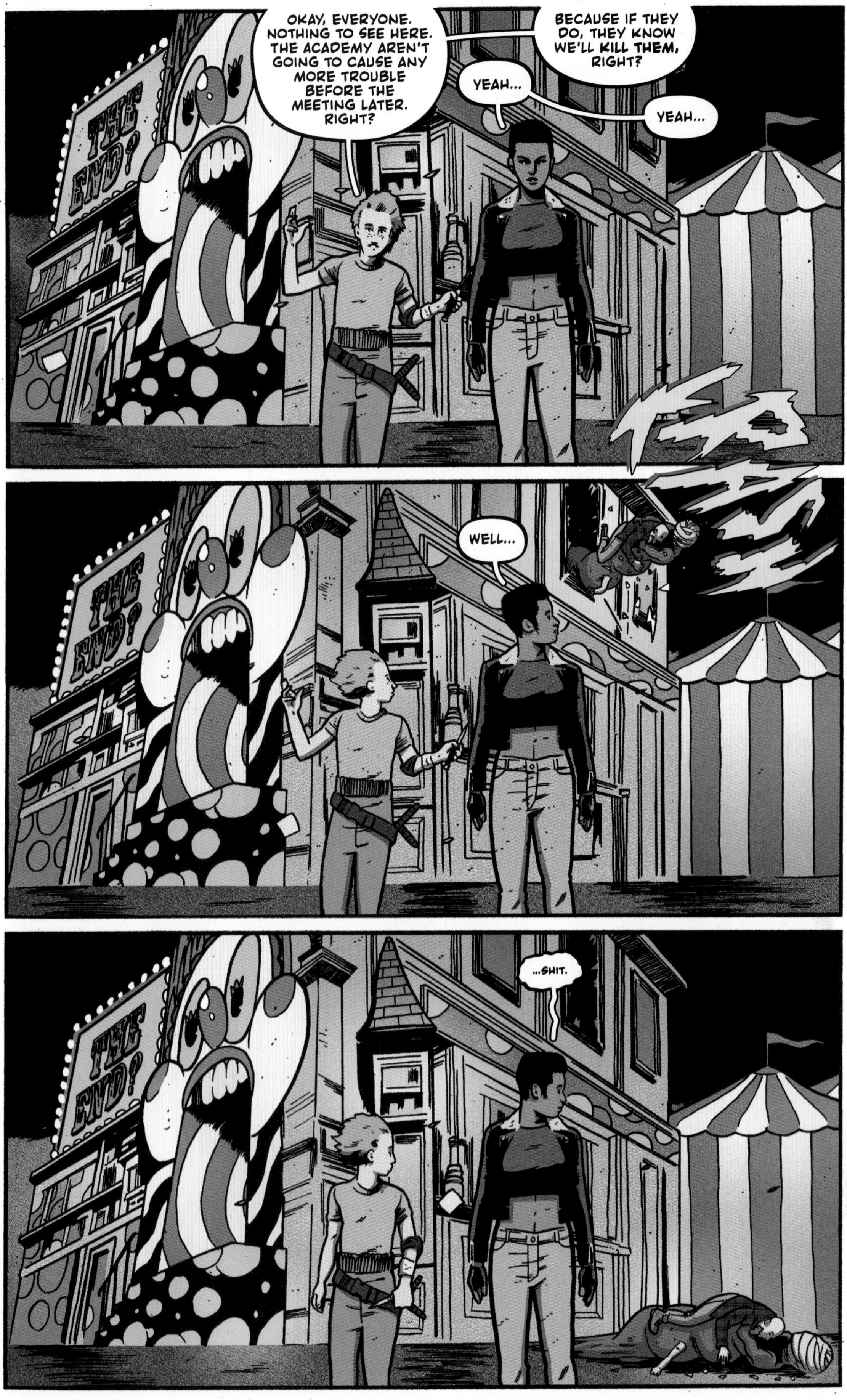
OKAY, EVERYONE. NOTHING TO SEE HERE. THE ACADEMY AREN'T GOING TO CAUSE ANY MORE TROUBLE BEFORE THE MEETING LATER. RIGHT?
BECAUSE IF THEY DO, THEY KNOW WE'LL KILL THEM, RIGHT?
YEAH...
YEAH...
WELL...
...SHIT.

# CHAPTER THIRTY-NINE

GAH!

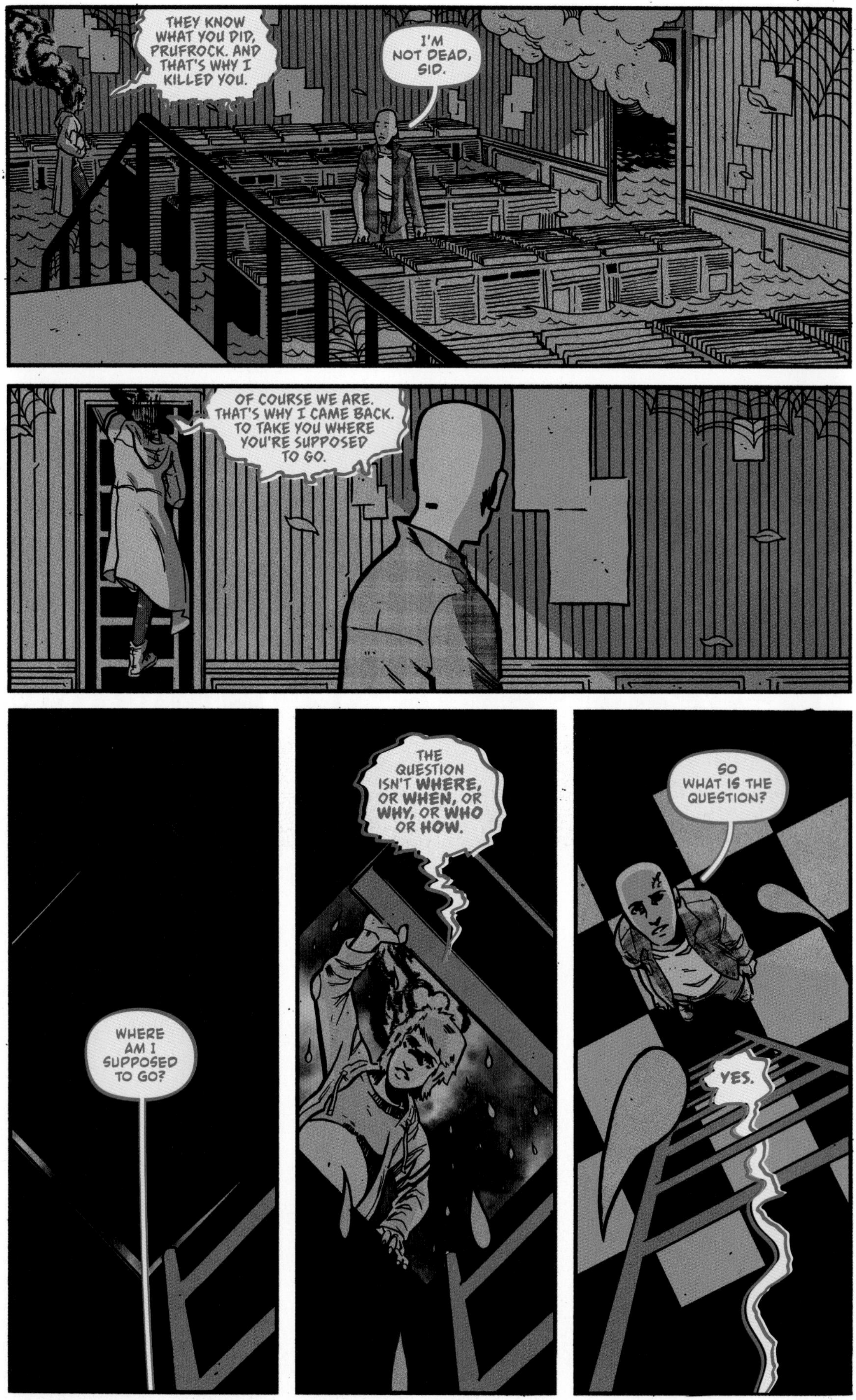
THEY KNOW WHAT YOU DID, PRUFROCK. AND THAT'S WHY I KILLED YOU.
I'M NOT DEAD, SID.
OF COURSE WE ARE. THAT'S WHY I CAME BACK. TO TAKE YOU WHERE YOU'RE SUPPOSED TO GO.
WHERE AM I SUPPOSED TO GO?
THE QUESTION ISN'T WHERE, OR WHEN, OR WHY, OR WHO OR HOW.
SO WHAT IS THE QUESTION?
YES.

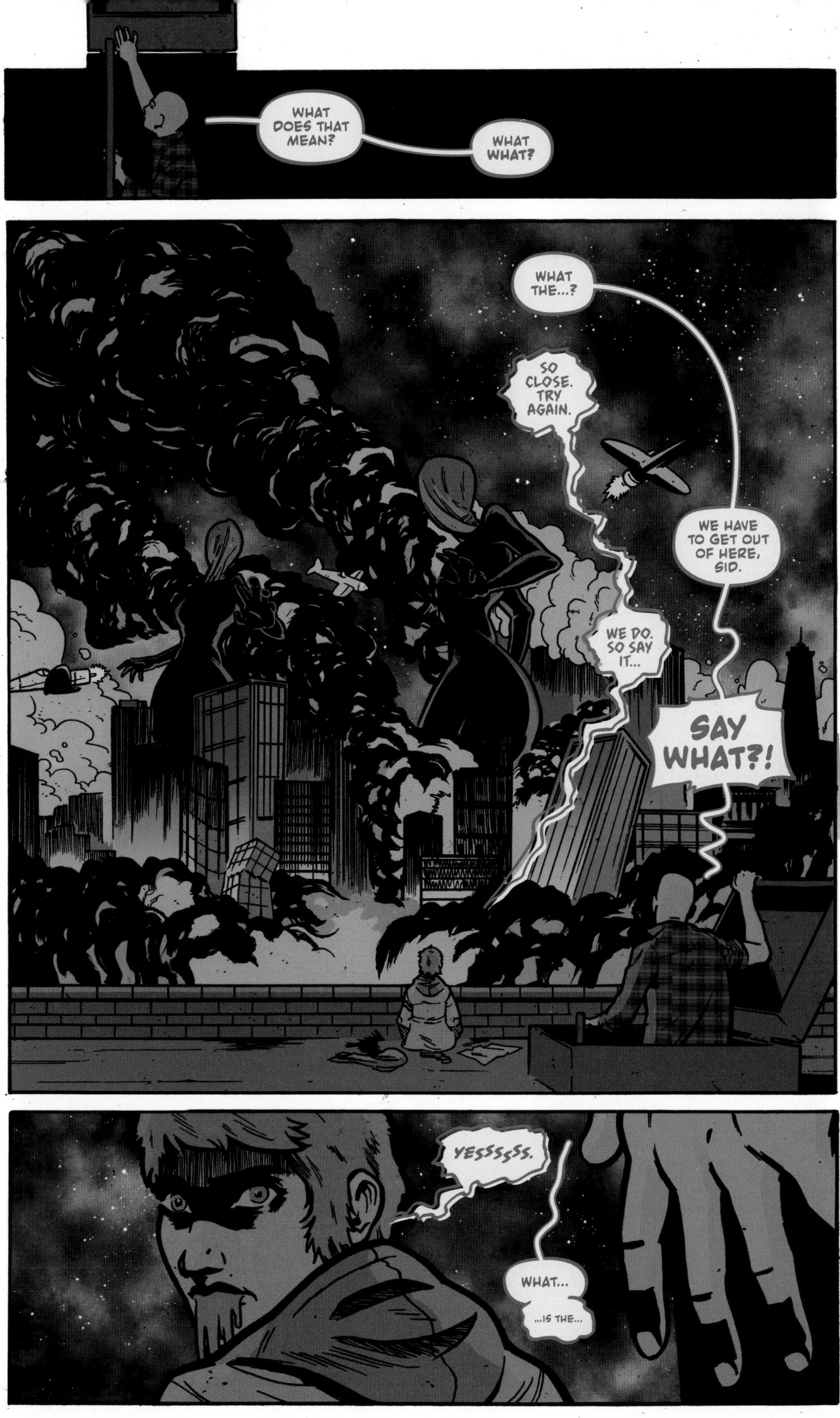
WHAT DOES THAT MEAN?
WHAT WHAT?
WHAT THE...?
SO CLOSE. TRY AGAIN.
WE HAVE TO GET OUT OF HERE, SID.
WE DO. SO SAY IT...
SAY WHAT?!
YESSSSSS.
WHAT...
...IS THE...

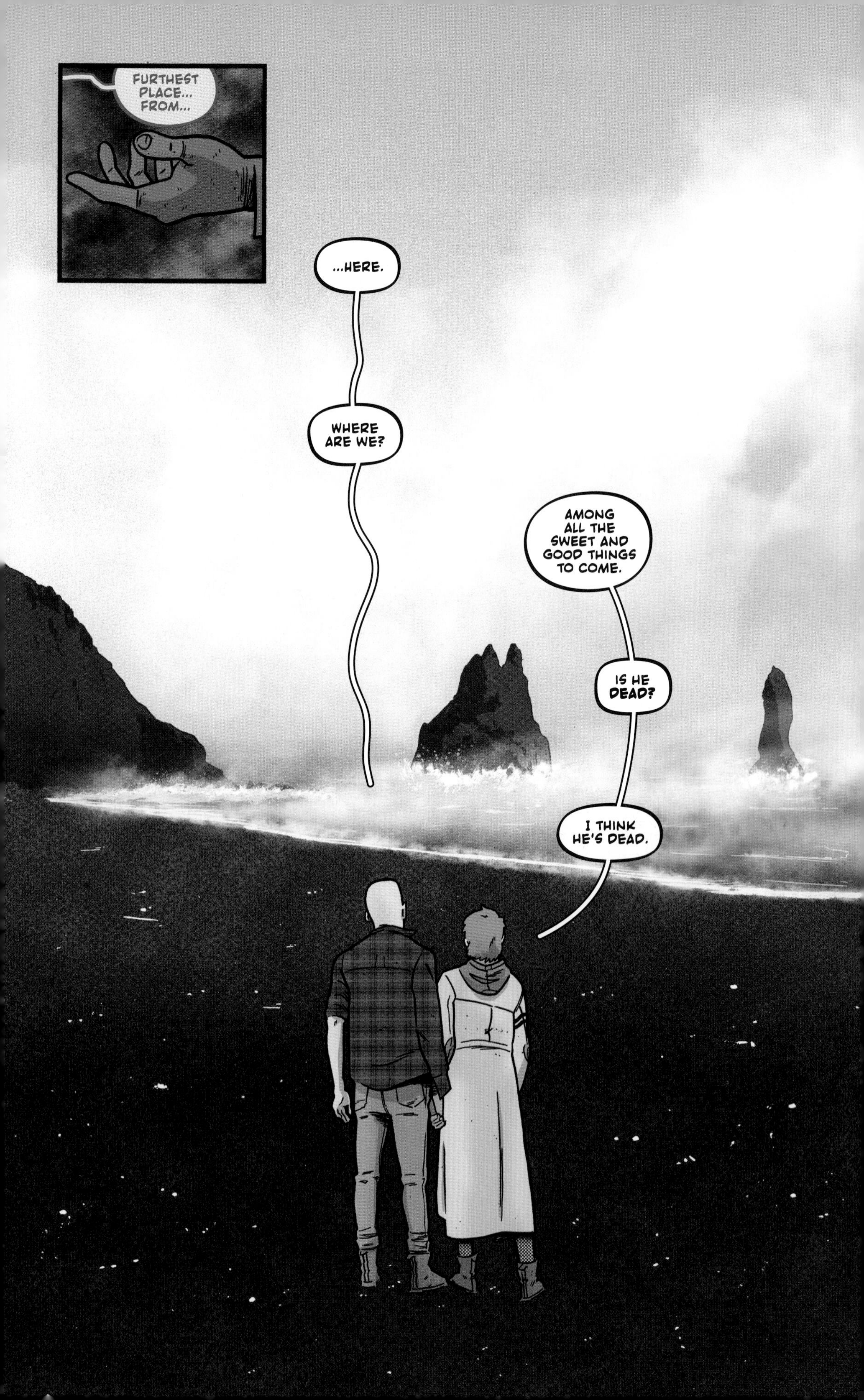
FURTHEST PLACE... FROM...
...HERE.
WHERE ARE WE?
AMONG ALL THE SWEET AND GOOD THINGS TO COME.
IS HE DEAD?
I THINK HE'S DEAD.

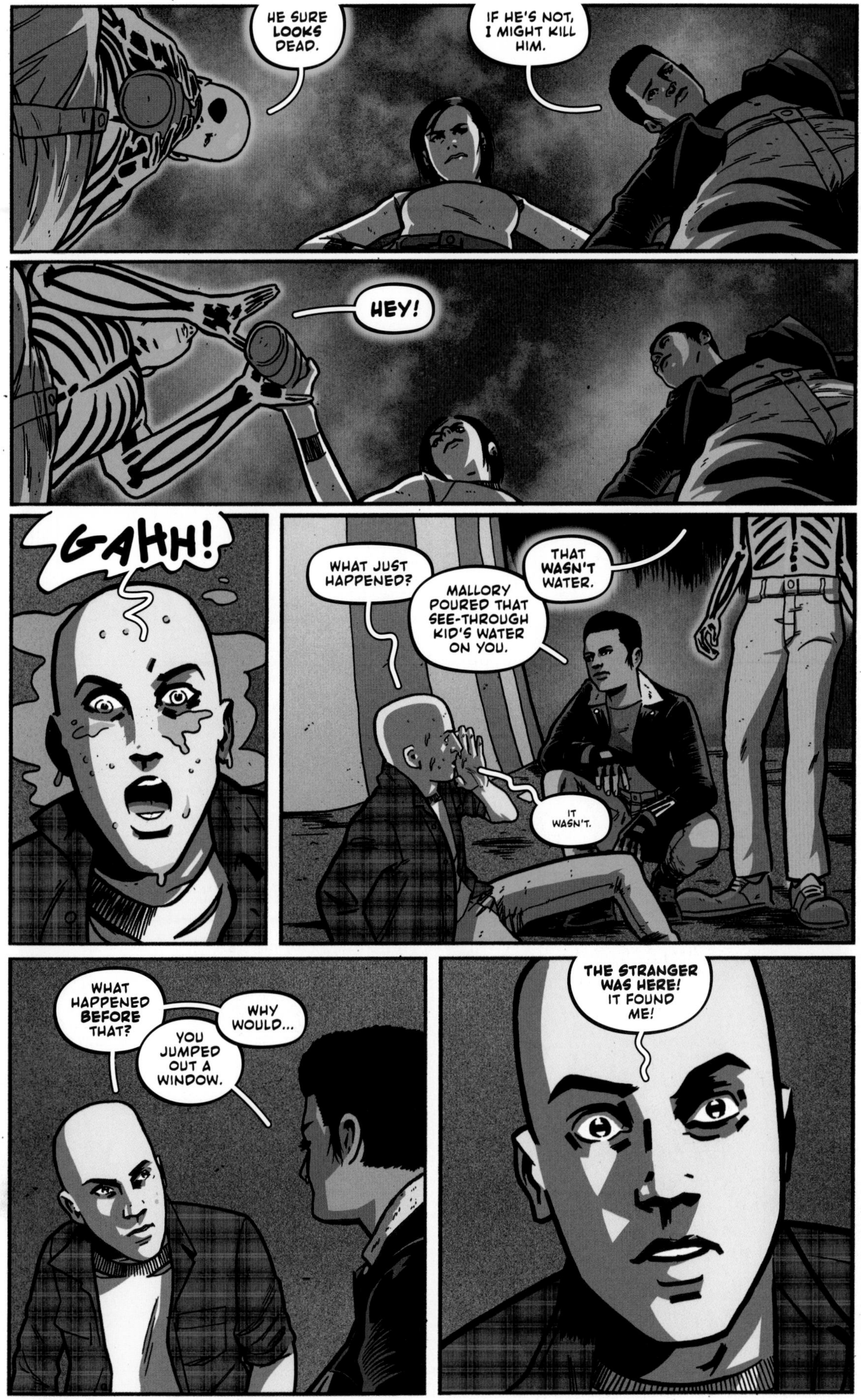
HE SURE LOOKS DEAD.
IF HE'S NOT, I MIGHT KILL HIM.
HEY!
GAHH!
WHAT JUST HAPPENED?
THAT WASN'T WATER.
MALLORY POURED THAT SEE-THROUGH KID'S WATER ON YOU.
IT WASN'T.
WHAT HAPPENED BEFORE THAT?
WHY WOULD...
YOU JUMPED OUT A WINDOW.
THE STRANGER WAS HERE! IT FOUND ME!

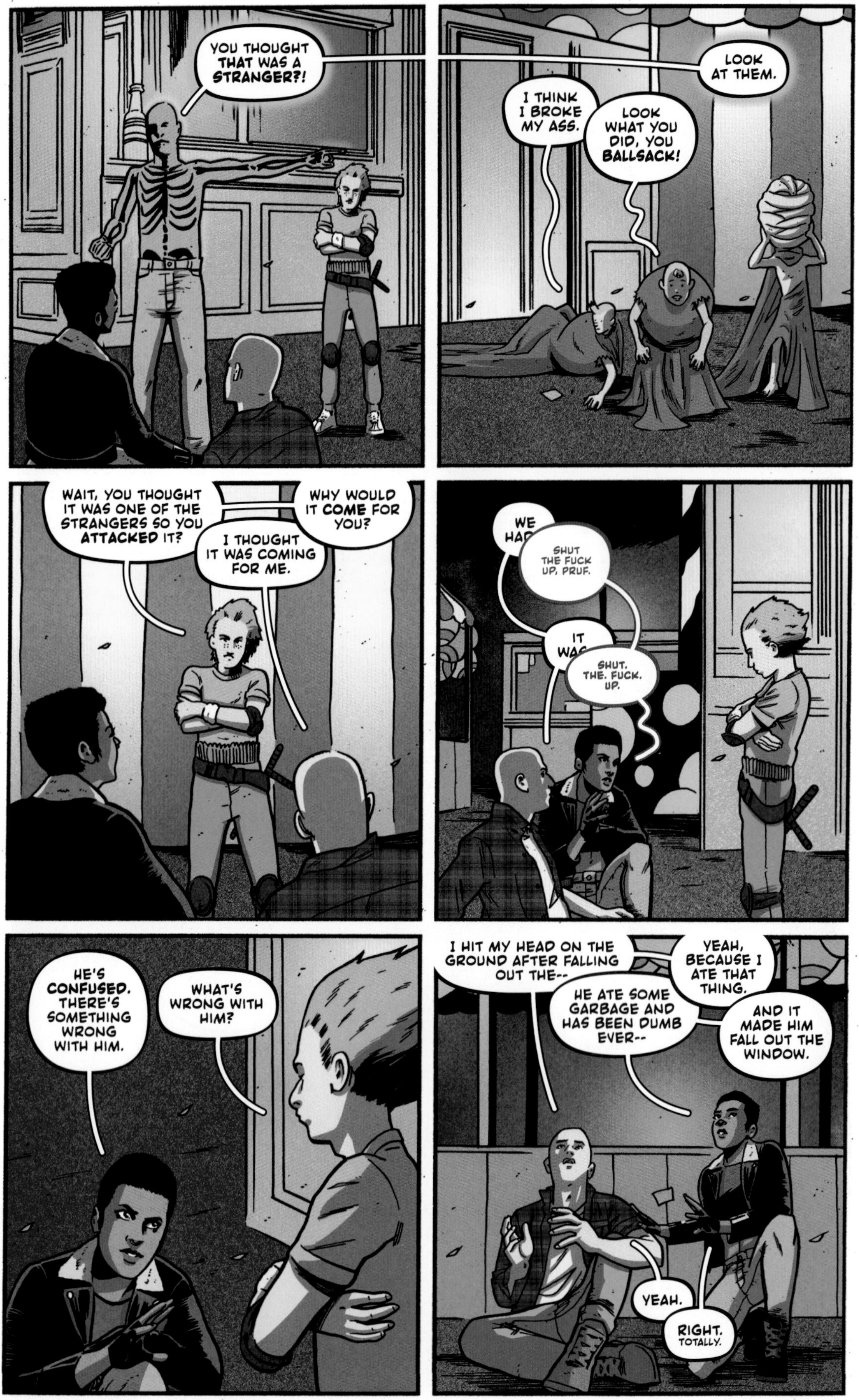
YOU THOUGHT THAT WAS A STRANGER?!
LOOK AT THEM.
I THINK I BROKE MY ASS.
LOOK WHAT YOU DID, YOU BALLSACK!
WAIT, YOU THOUGHT IT WAS ONE OF THE STRANGERS SO YOU ATTACKED IT?
WHY WOULD IT COME FOR YOU?
I THOUGHT IT WAS COMING FOR ME.
WE HA
SHUT THE FUCK UP, PRUF.
IT WA
SHUT. THE. FUCK. UP.
HE'S CONFUSED. THERE'S SOMETHING WRONG WITH HIM.
WHAT'S WRONG WITH HIM?
I HIT MY HEAD ON THE GROUND AFTER FALLING OUT THE--
YEAH, BECAUSE I ATE THAT THING.
HE ATE SOME GARBAGE AND HAS BEEN DUMB EVER--
AND IT MADE HIM FALL OUT THE WINDOW.
YEAH.
RIGHT. TOTALLY.

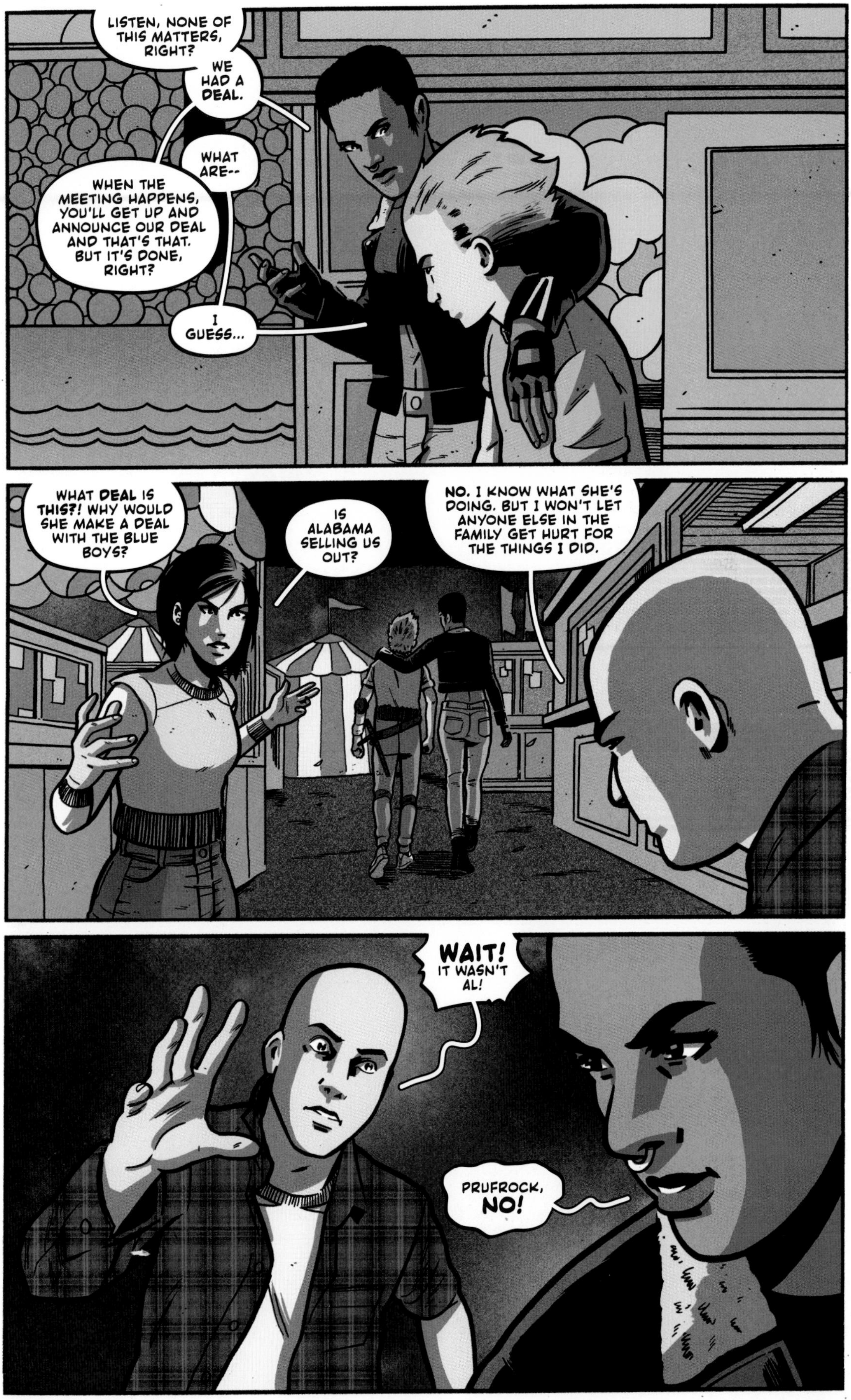
LISTEN, NONE OF THIS MATTERS, RIGHT?
WE HAD A DEAL.
WHAT ARE--
WHEN THE MEETING HAPPENS, YOU'LL GET UP AND ANNOUNCE OUR DEAL AND THAT'S THAT. BUT IT'S DONE, RIGHT?
I GUESS...
WHAT DEAL IS THIS?! WHY WOULD SHE MAKE A DEAL WITH THE BLUE BOYS?
IS ALABAMA SELLING US OUT?
NO. I KNOW WHAT SHE'S DOING. BUT I WON'T LET ANYONE ELSE IN THE FAMILY GET HURT FOR THE THINGS I DID.
WAIT! IT WASN'T AL!
PRUFROCK, NO!

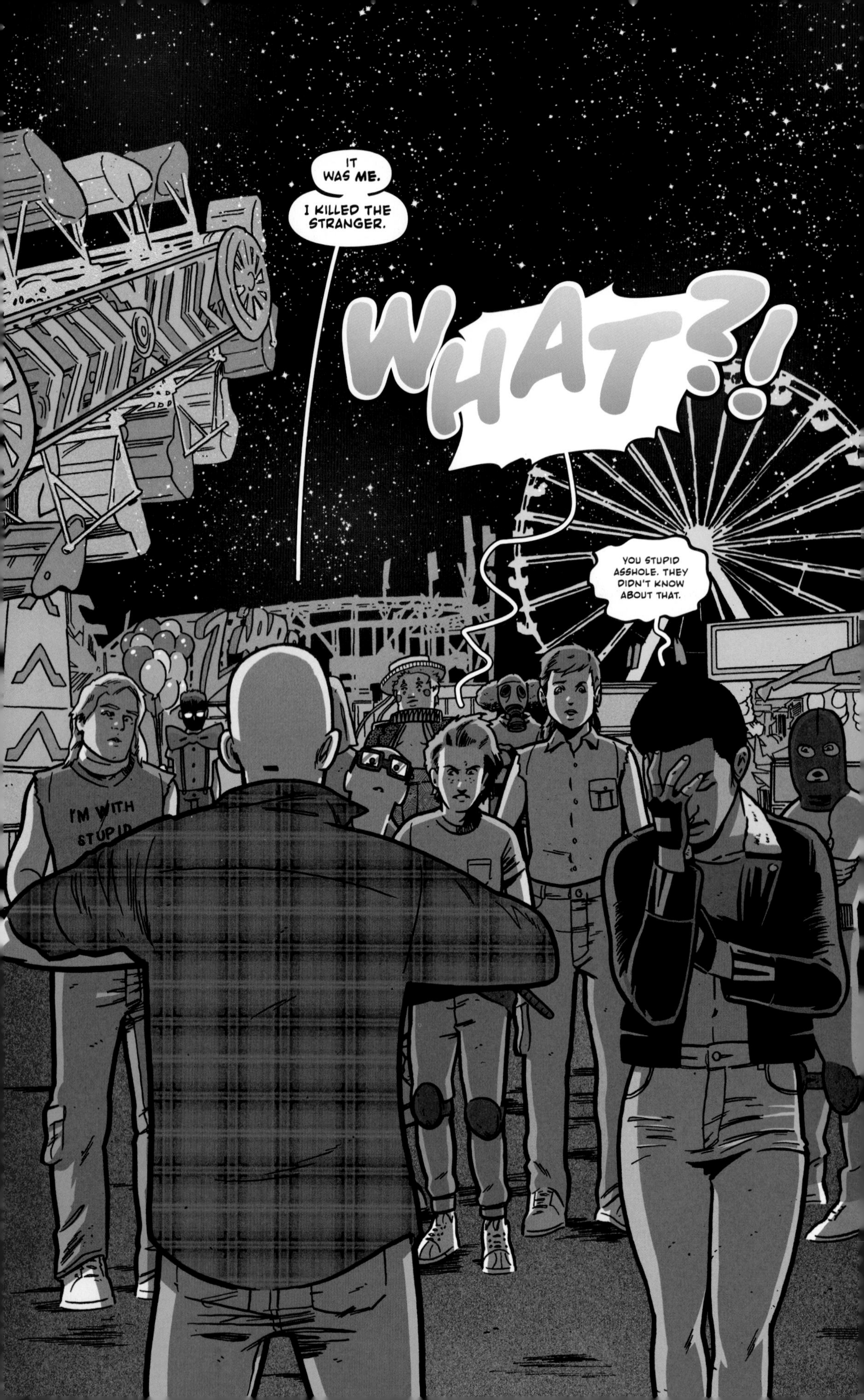
IT WAS ME.
I KILLED THE STRANGER.
WHAT?!
YOU STUPID ASSHOLE. THEY DIDN'T KNOW ABOUT THAT.
I'M WITH STUPID

# ACT VI

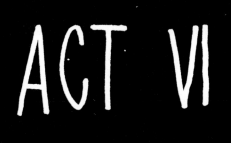

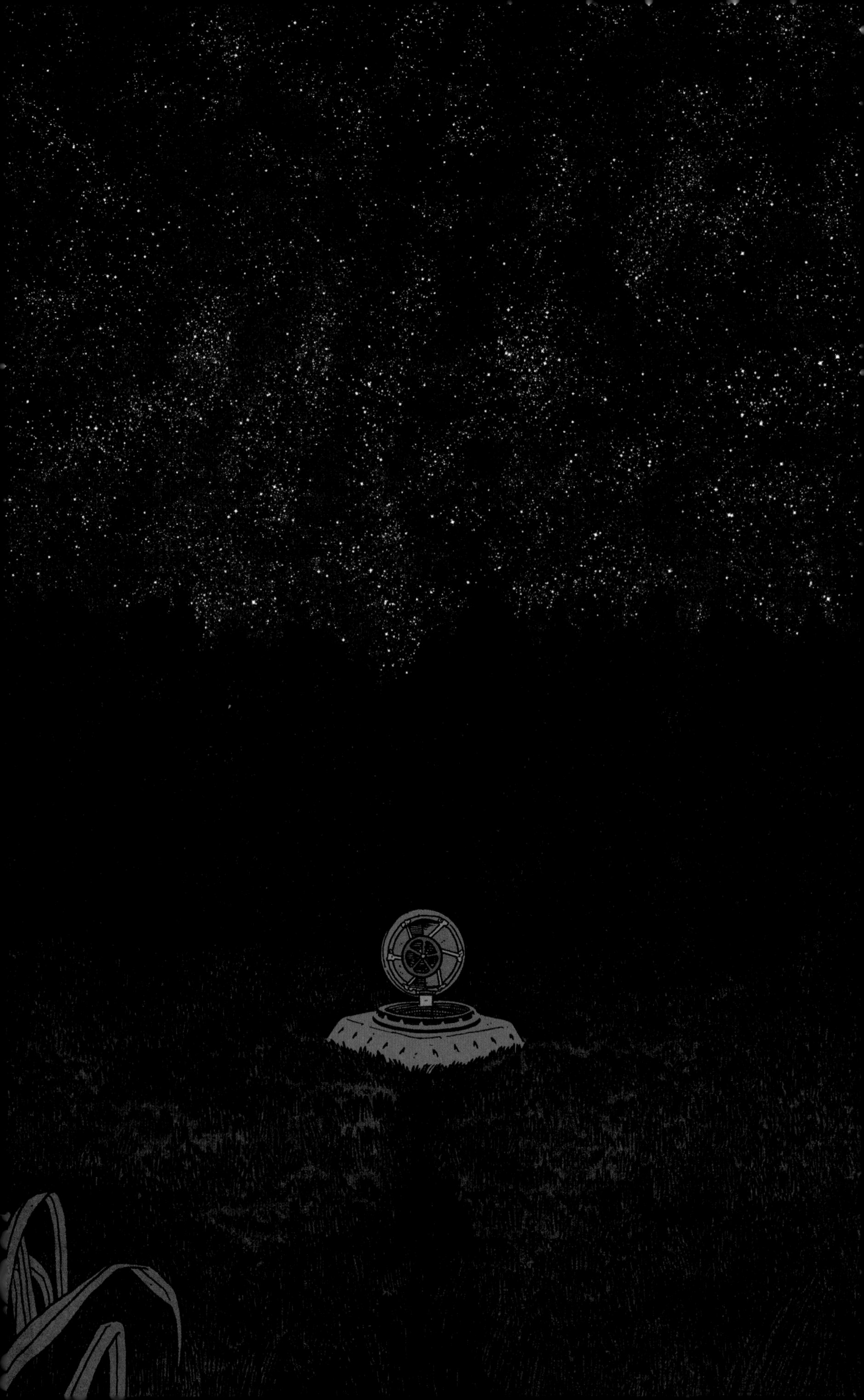

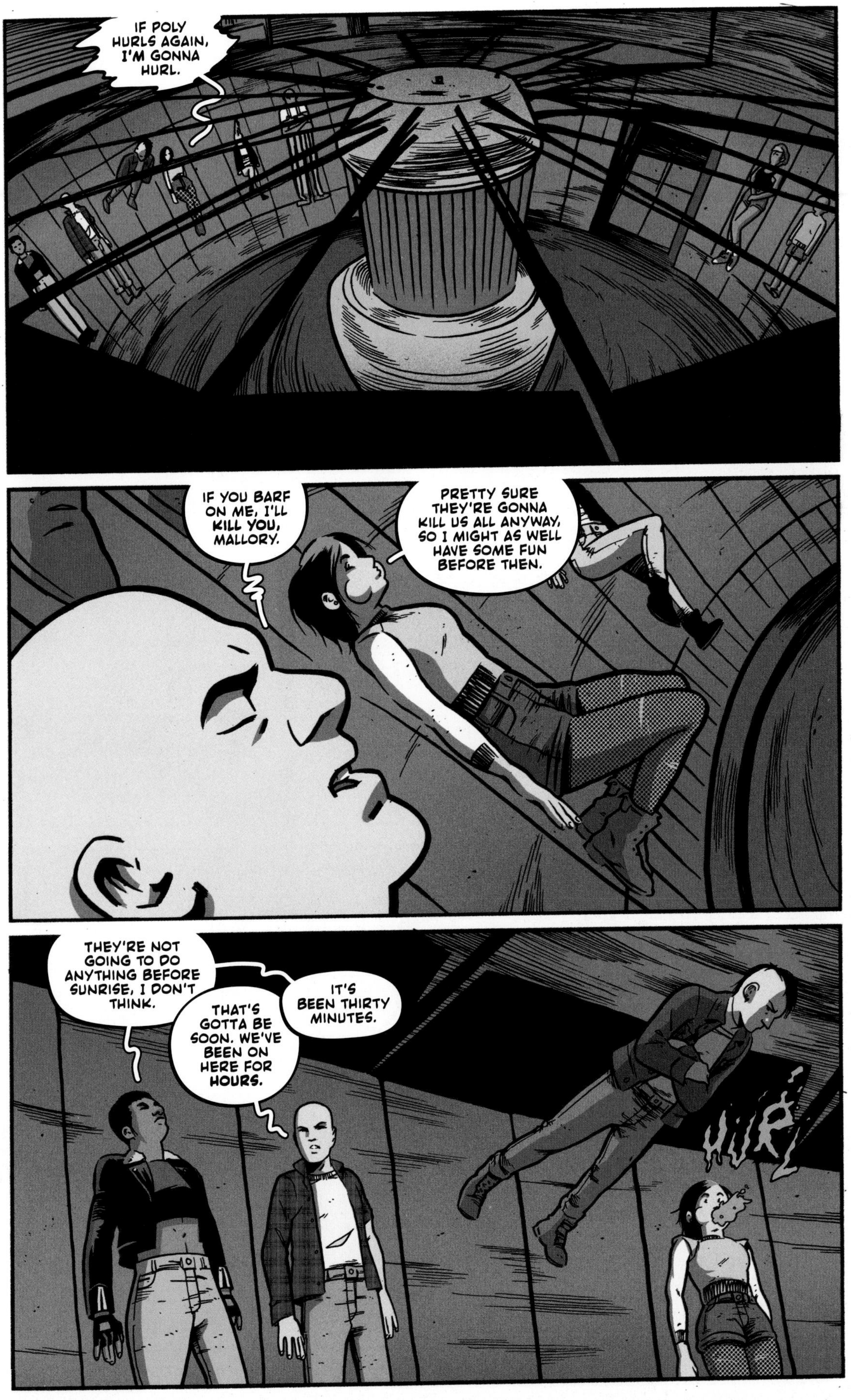
IF POLY HURLS AGAIN, I'M GONNA HURL.
IF YOU BARF ON ME, I'LL KILL YOU, MALLORY.
PRETTY SURE THEY'RE GONNA KILL US ALL ANYWAY, SO I MIGHT AS WELL HAVE SOME FUN BEFORE THEN.
THEY'RE NOT GOING TO DO ANYTHING BEFORE SUNRISE, I DON'T THINK.
THAT'S GOTTA BE SOON. WE'VE BEEN ON HERE FOR HOURS.
IT'S BEEN THIRTY MINUTES.
HURL

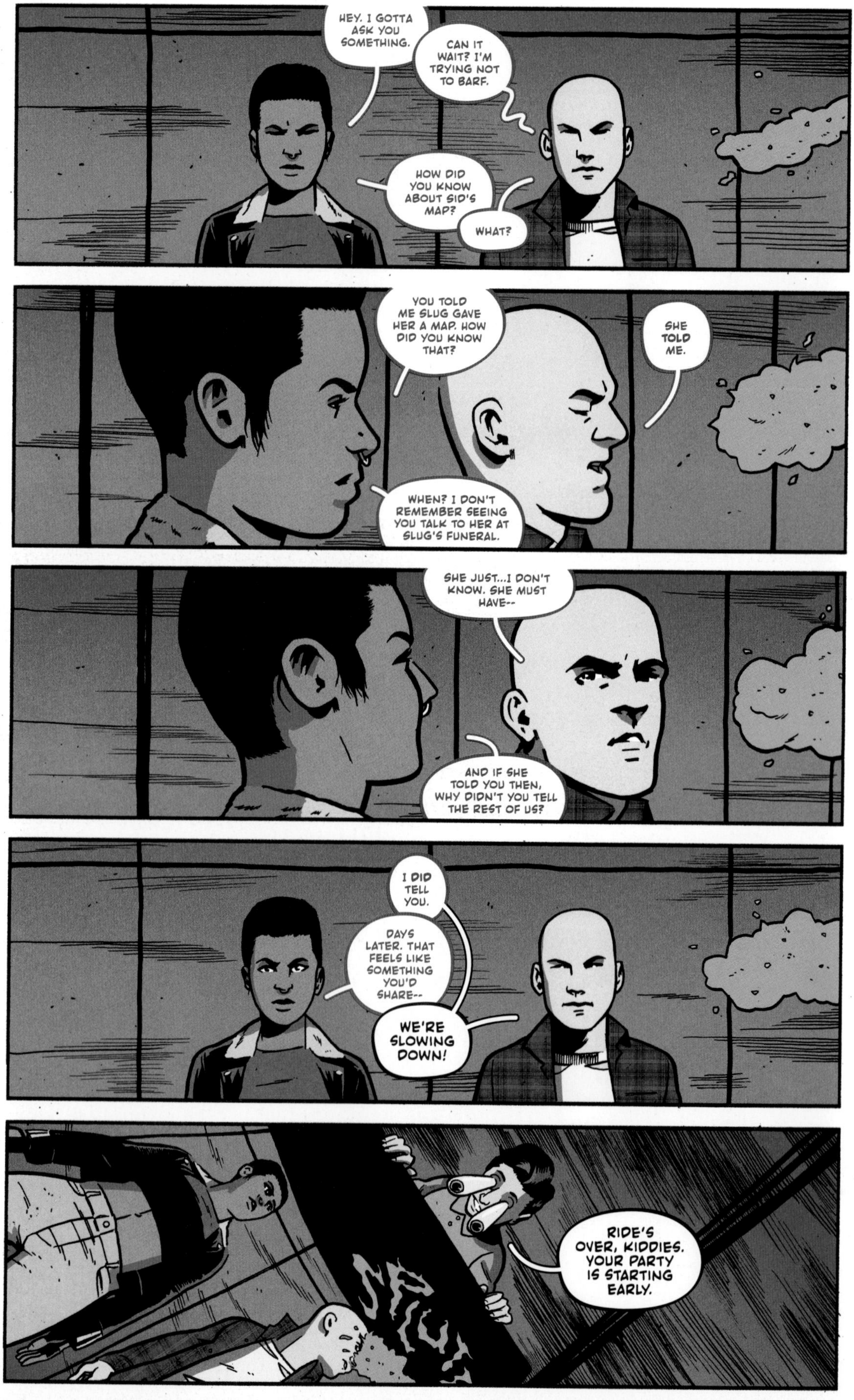
HEY. I GOTTA ASK YOU SOMETHING.
CAN IT WAIT? I'M TRYING NOT TO BARF.
HOW DID YOU KNOW ABOUT SID'S MAP?
WHAT?
YOU TOLD ME SLUG GAVE HER A MAP. HOW DID YOU KNOW THAT?
SHE TOLD ME.
WHEN? I DON'T REMEMBER SEEING YOU TALK TO HER AT SLUG'S FUNERAL.
SHE JUST...I DON'T KNOW. SHE MUST HAVE--
AND IF SHE TOLD YOU THEN, WHY DIDN'T YOU TELL THE REST OF US?
I DID TELL YOU.
DAYS LATER. THAT FEELS LIKE SOMETHING YOU'D SHARE--
WE'RE SLOWING DOWN!
RIDE'S OVER, KIDDIES. YOUR PARTY IS STARTING EARLY.

# CHAPTER FORTY

## JUDGMENT NIGHT!

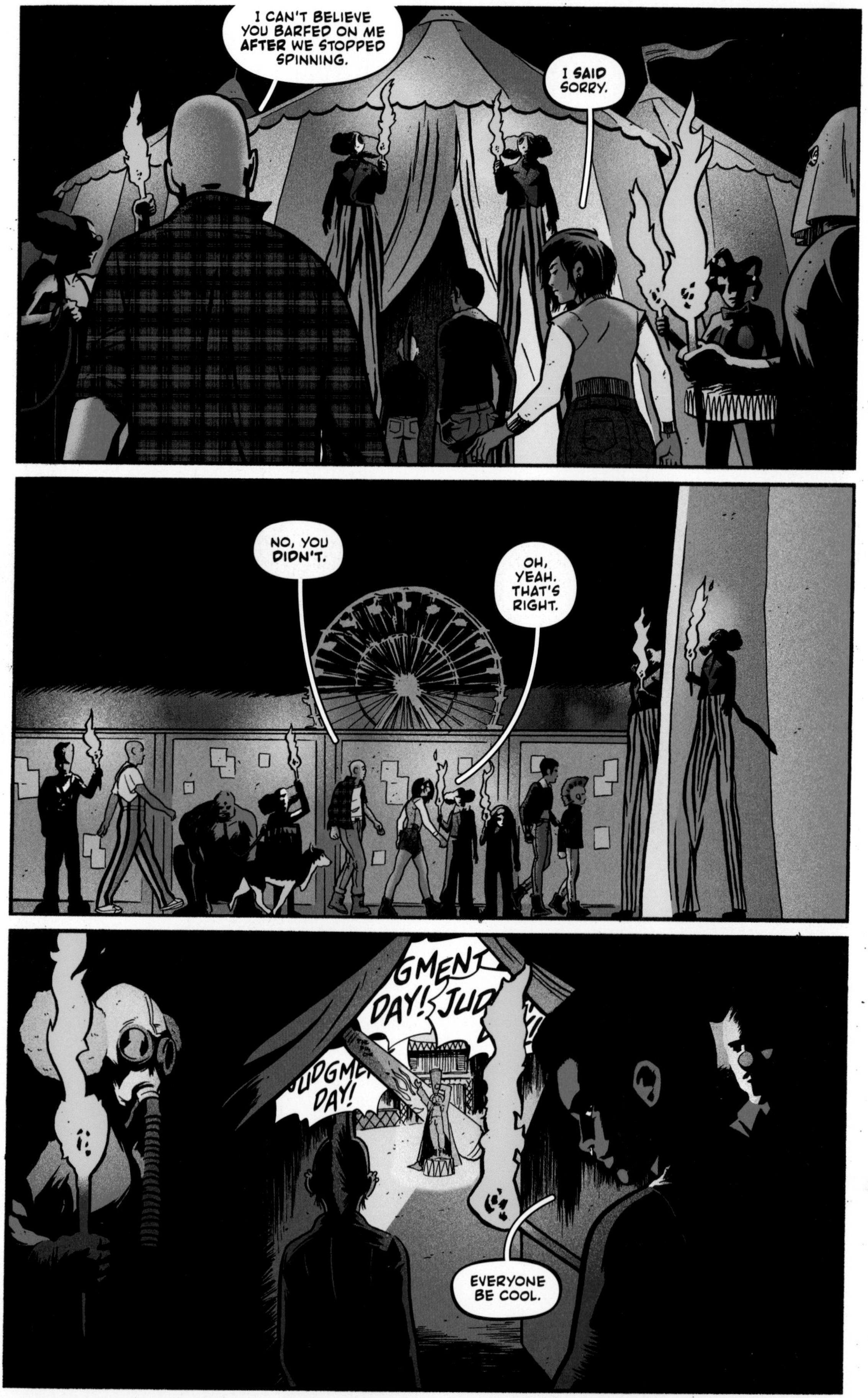
I CAN'T BELIEVE YOU BARFED ON ME AFTER WE STOPPED SPINNING.
I SAID SORRY.
NO, YOU DIDN'T.
OH, YEAH. THAT'S RIGHT.
GMENT DAY! JUD
JUDGME DAY!
EVERYONE BE COOL.

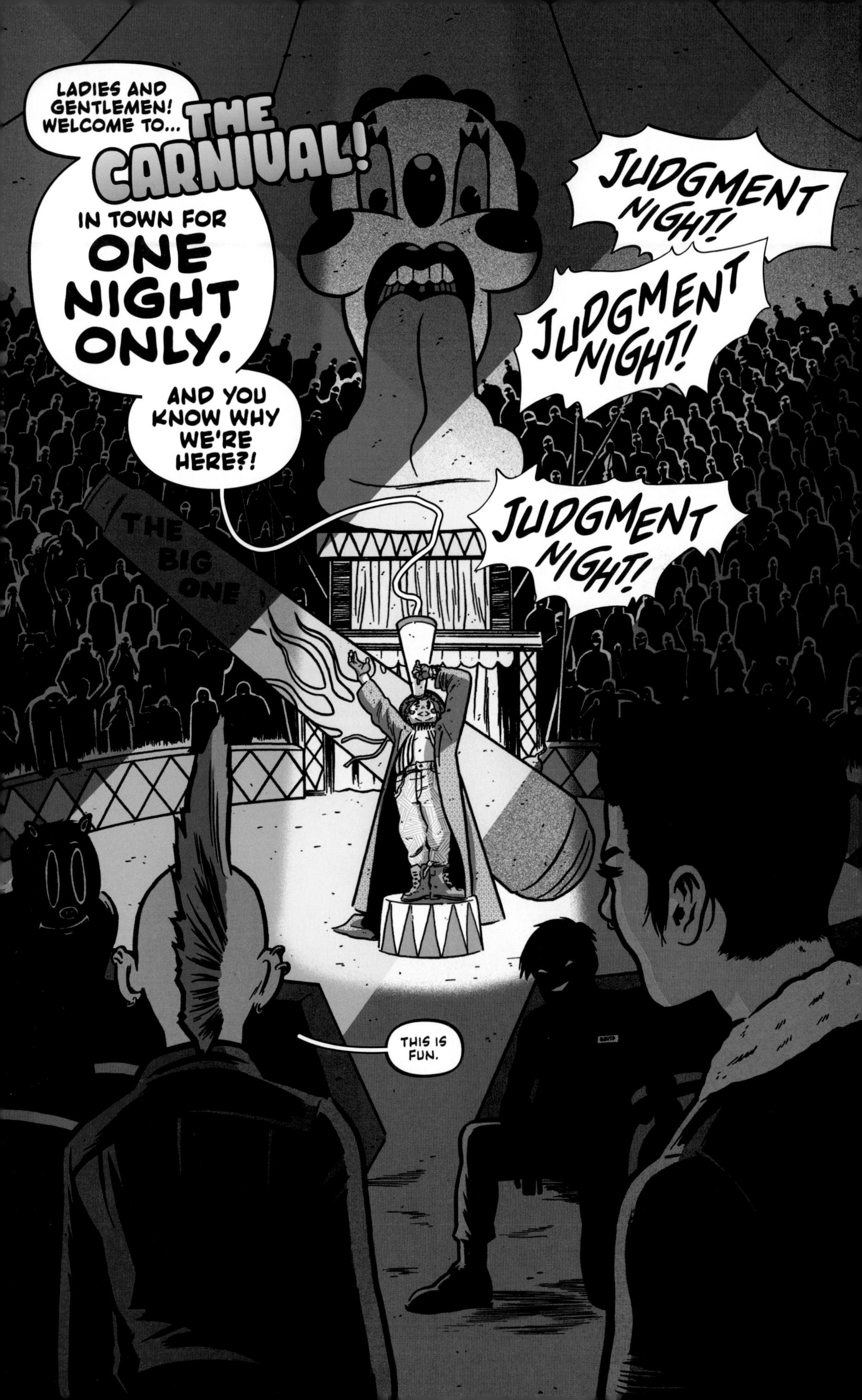
LADIES AND GENTLEMEN! WELCOME TO... THE CARNIVAL!
IN TOWN FOR ONE NIGHT ONLY.
AND YOU KNOW WHY WE'RE HERE?!
JUDGMENT NIGHT!
JUDGMENT NIGHT!
JUDGMENT NIGHT!
THE BIG ONE
THIS IS FUN.

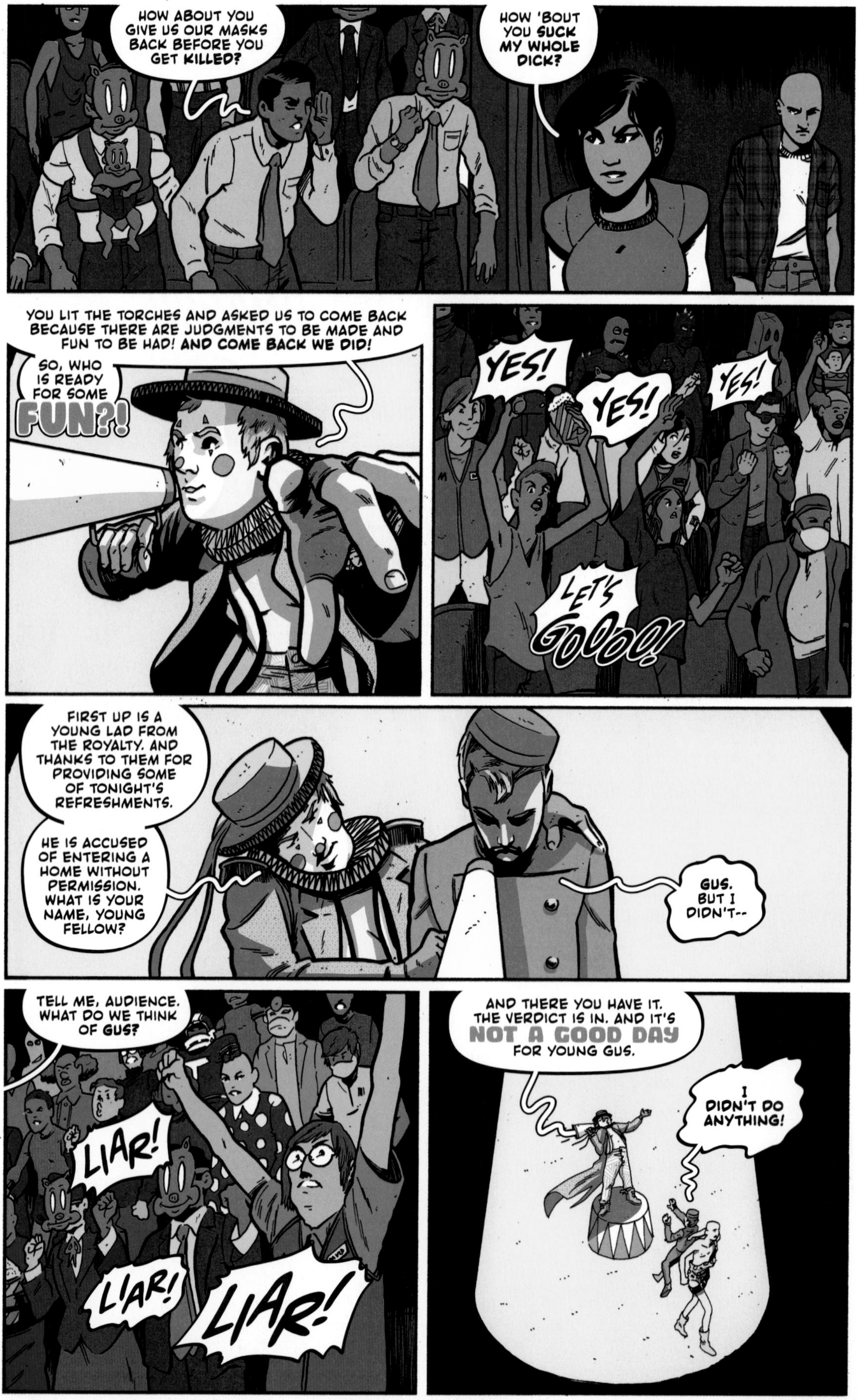
HOW ABOUT YOU GIVE US OUR MASKS BACK BEFORE YOU GET KILLED?
HOW 'BOUT YOU SUCK MY WHOLE DICK?
YOU LIT THE TORCHES AND ASKED US TO COME BACK BECAUSE THERE ARE JUDGMENTS TO BE MADE AND FUN TO BE HAD! AND COME BACK WE DID!
SO, WHO IS READY FOR SOME FUN?!
YES!
YES!
YES!
LET'S GOOOO!
FIRST UP IS A YOUNG LAD FROM THE ROYALTY. AND THANKS TO THEM FOR PROVIDING SOME OF TONIGHT'S REFRESHMENTS.
HE IS ACCUSED OF ENTERING A HOME WITHOUT PERMISSION. WHAT IS YOUR NAME, YOUNG FELLOW?
GUS. BUT I DIDN'T--
TELL ME, AUDIENCE. WHAT DO WE THINK OF GUS?
LIAR!
LIAR!
LIAR!
AND THERE YOU HAVE IT. THE VERDICT IS IN. AND IT'S NOT A GOOD DAY FOR YOUNG GUS.
I DIDN'T DO ANYTHING!

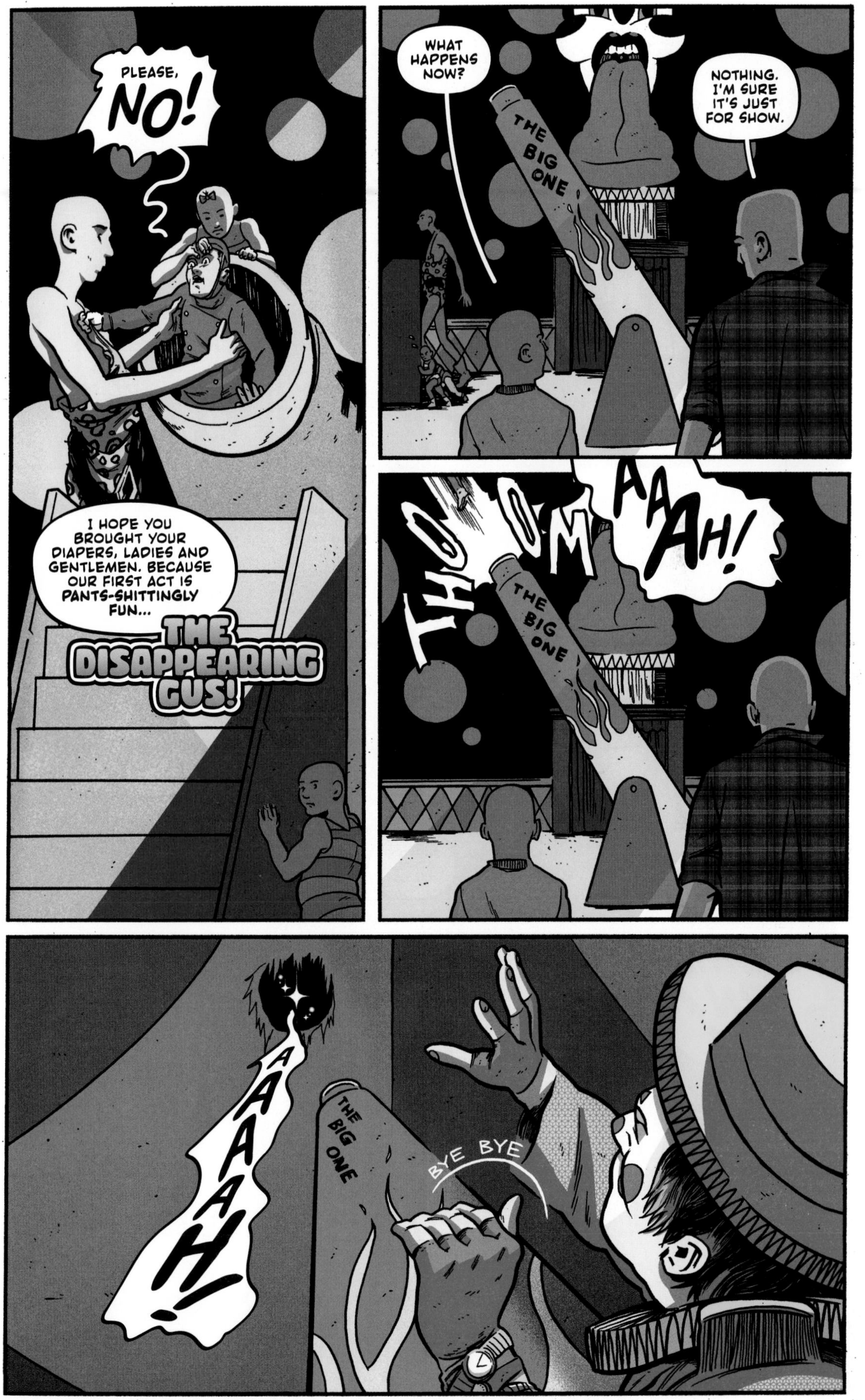
PLEASE, NO!
I HOPE YOU BROUGHT YOUR DIAPERS, LADIES AND GENTLEMEN. BECAUSE OUR FIRST ACT IS PANTS-SHITTINGLY FUN...
THE DISAPPEARING GUS!
WHAT HAPPENS NOW?
THE BIG ONE
NOTHING. I'M SURE IT'S JUST FOR SHOW.
THOOOM
AAAAH!
THE BIG ONE
AAAAAH!
THE BIG ONE
BYE BYE

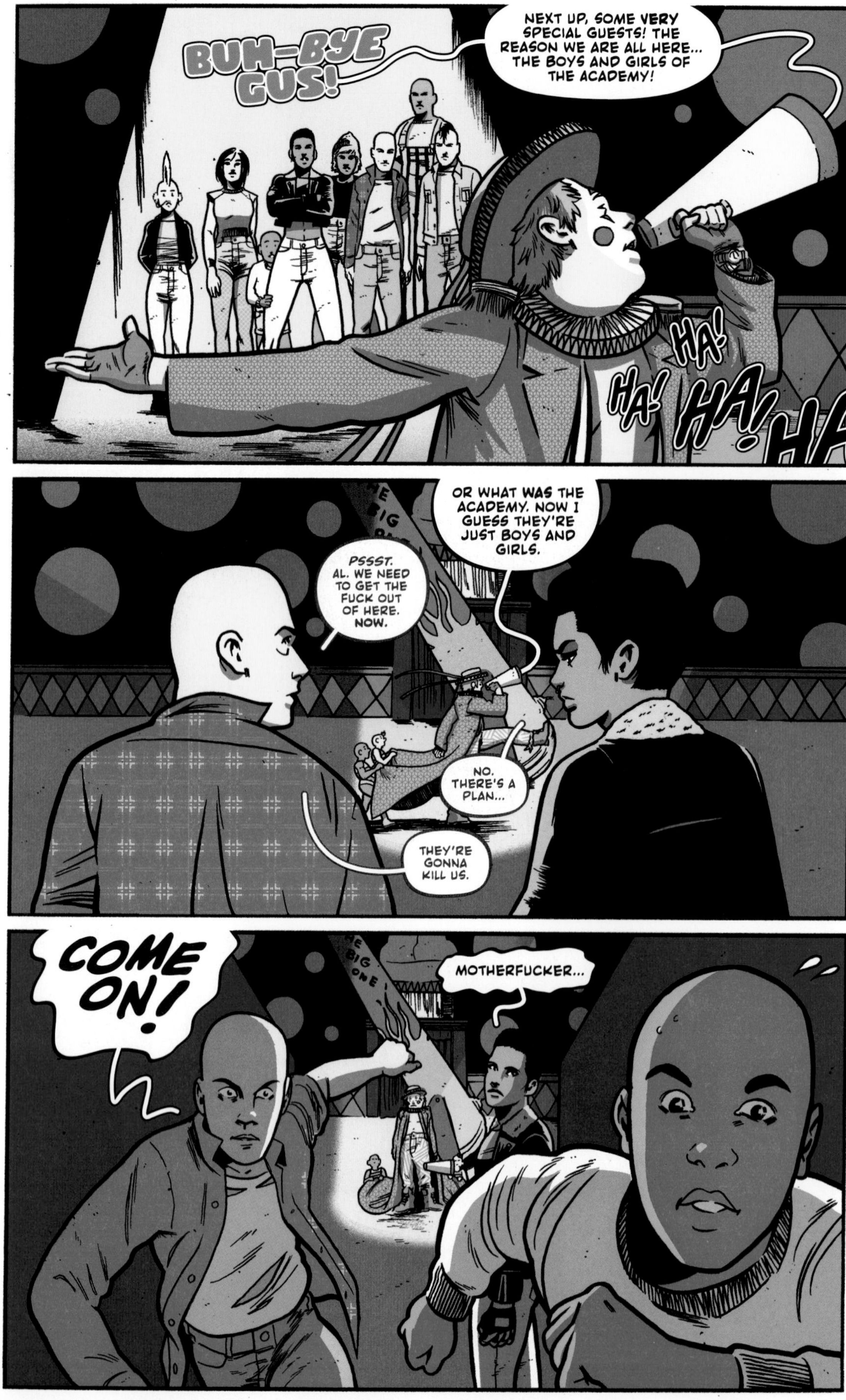

BUH-BYE GUS!
NEXT UP, SOME VERY SPECIAL GUESTS! THE REASON WE ARE ALL HERE... THE BOYS AND GIRLS OF THE ACADEMY!
HA! HA! HA! HA!
OR WHAT WAS THE ACADEMY. NOW I GUESS THEY'RE JUST BOYS AND GIRLS.
PSSST. AL. WE NEED TO GET THE FUCK OUT OF HERE. NOW.
NO. THERE'S A PLAN...
THEY'RE GONNA KILL US.
COME ON!
MOTHERFUCKER...

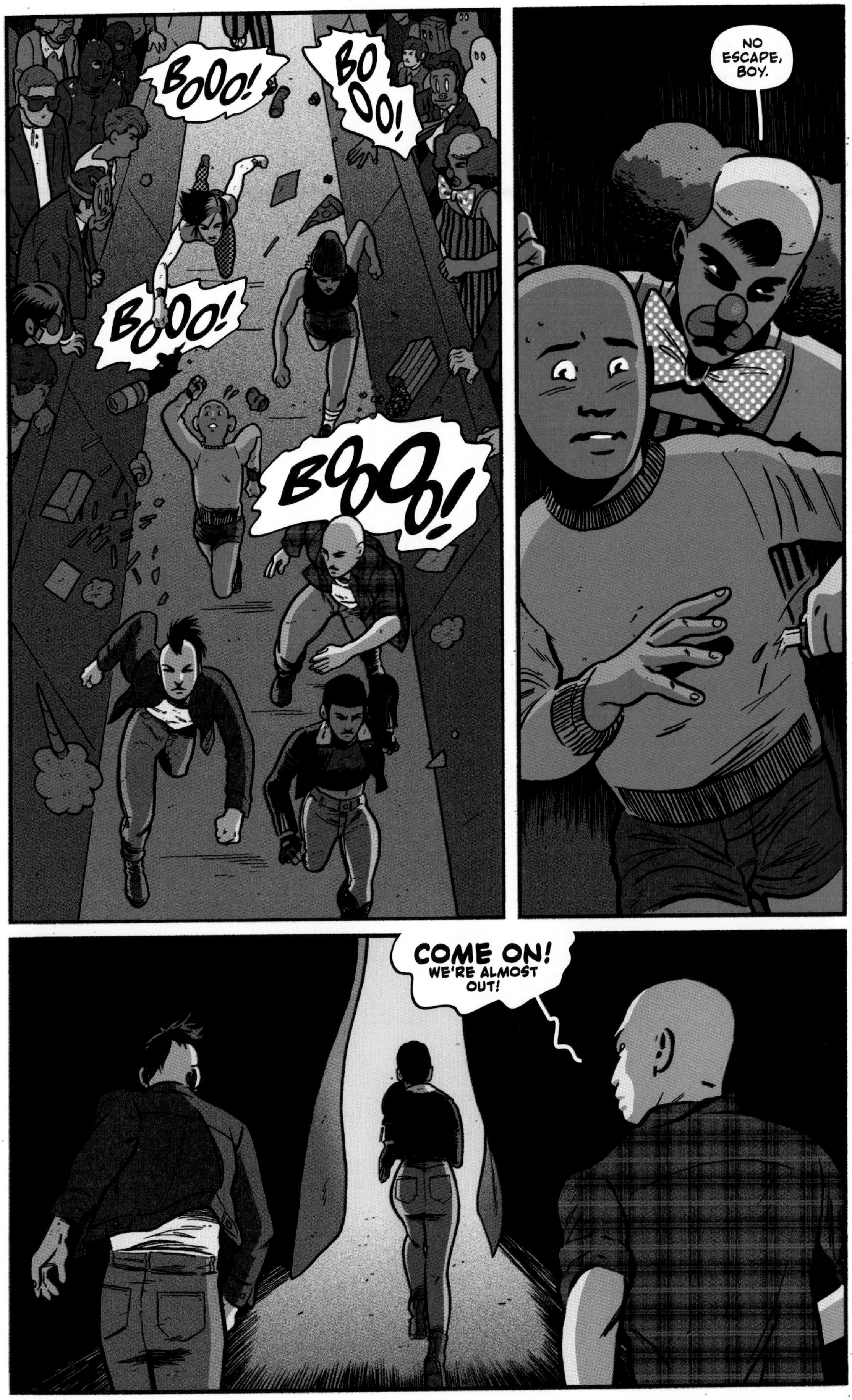
BOOO!
BOOO!
BOOO!
BOOOO!
NO ESCAPE, BOY.
COME ON! WE'RE ALMOST OUT!

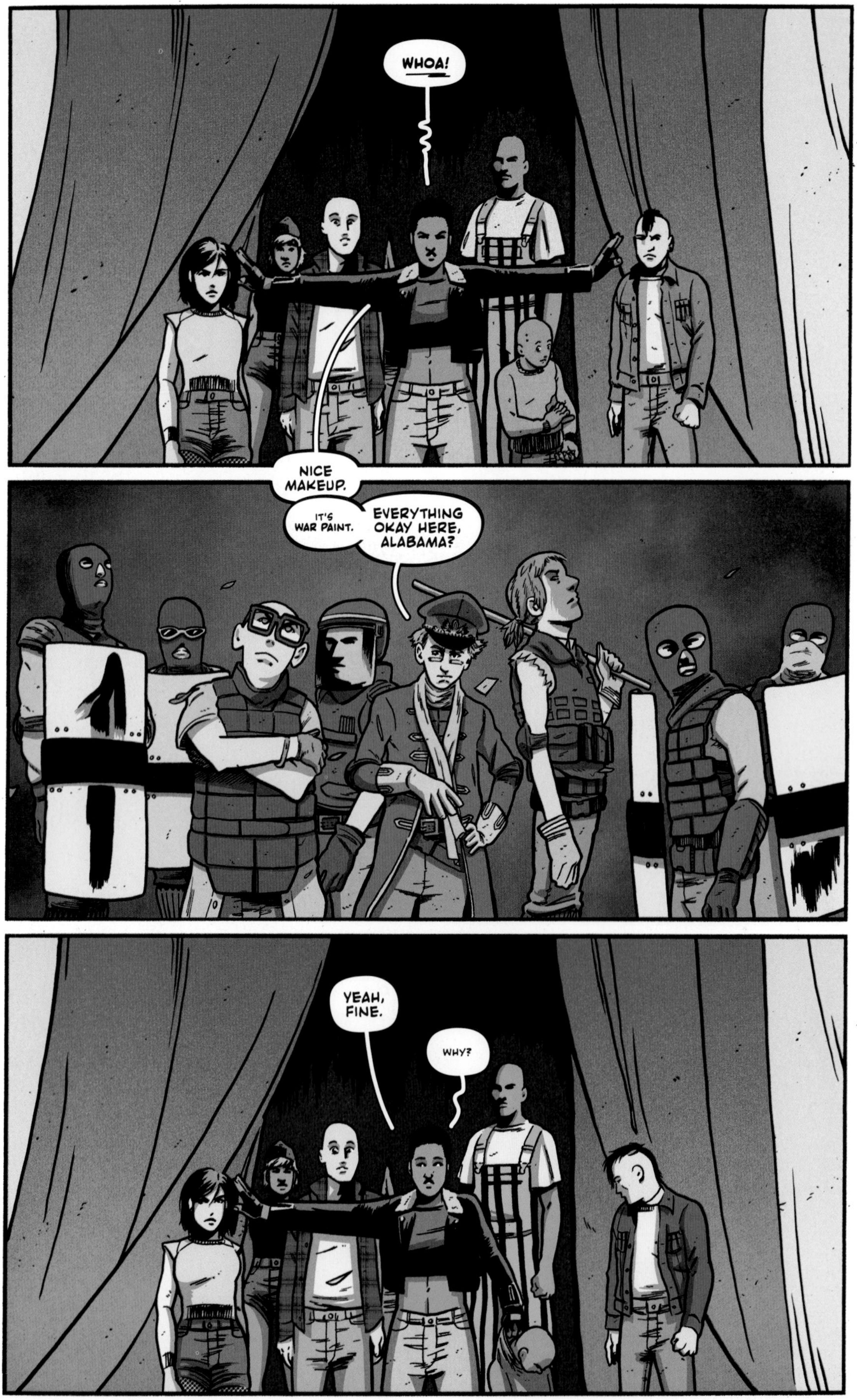
WHOA!
NICE MAKEUP.
IT'S WAR PAINT.
EVERYTHING OKAY HERE, ALABAMA?
YEAH, FINE.
WHY?

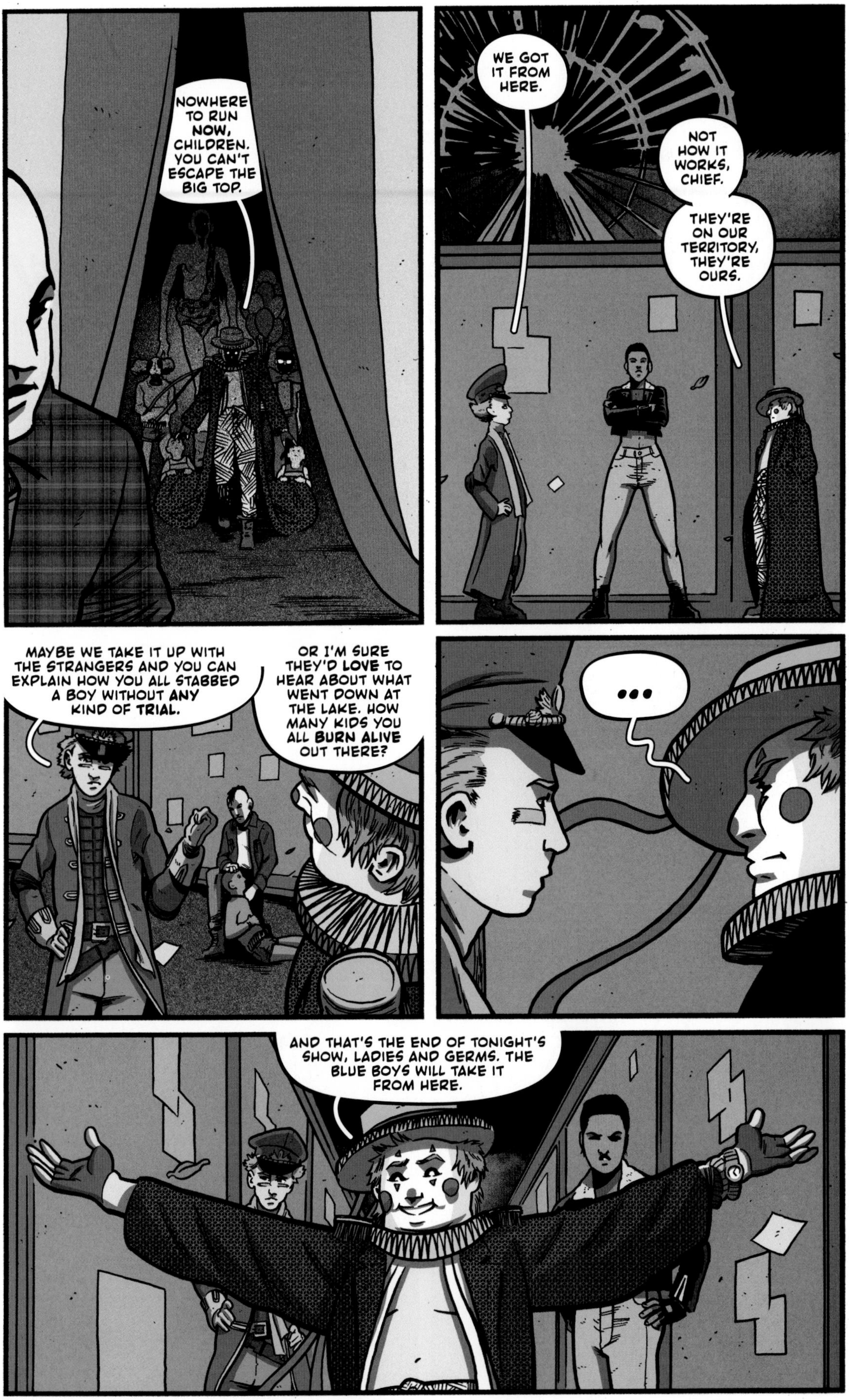
NOWHERE TO RUN NOW, CHILDREN. YOU CAN'T ESCAPE THE BIG TOP.
WE GOT IT FROM HERE.
NOT HOW IT WORKS, CHIEF.
THEY'RE ON OUR TERRITORY, THEY'RE OURS.
MAYBE WE TAKE IT UP WITH THE STRANGERS AND YOU CAN EXPLAIN HOW YOU ALL STABBED A BOY WITHOUT ANY KIND OF TRIAL.
OR I'M SURE THEY'D LOVE TO HEAR ABOUT WHAT WENT DOWN AT THE LAKE. HOW MANY KIDS YOU ALL BURN ALIVE OUT THERE?
...
AND THAT'S THE END OF TONIGHT'S SHOW, LADIES AND GERMS. THE BLUE BOYS WILL TAKE IT FROM HERE.

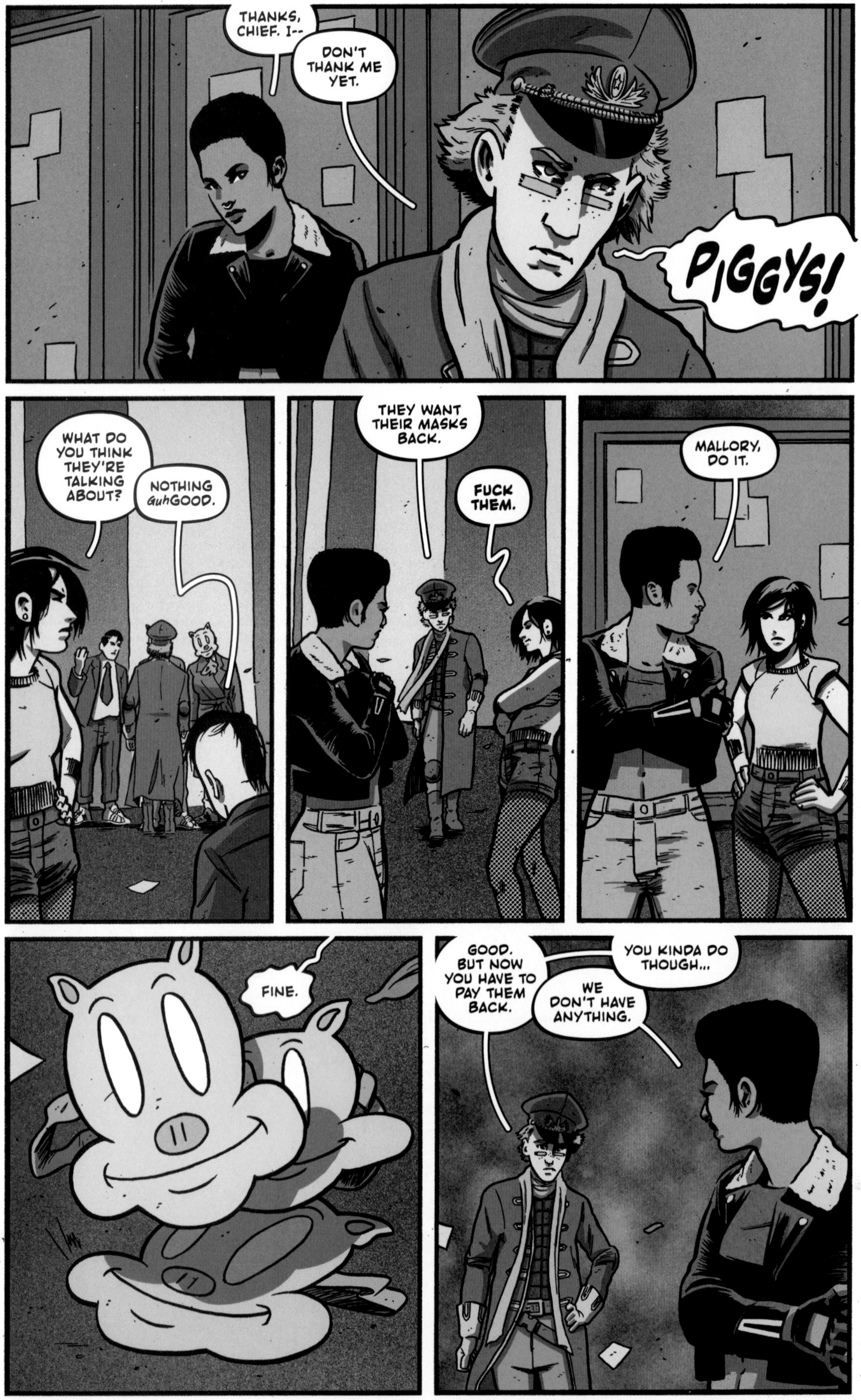
THANKS, CHIEF. I--
DON'T THANK ME YET.
PIGGYS!
WHAT DO YOU THINK THEY'RE TALKING ABOUT?
NOTHING GuhGOOD.
THEY WANT THEIR MASKS BACK.
FUCK THEM.
MALLORY, DO IT.
FINE.
GOOD. BUT NOW YOU HAVE TO PAY THEM BACK.
YOU KINDA DO THOUGH...
WE DON'T HAVE ANYTHING.

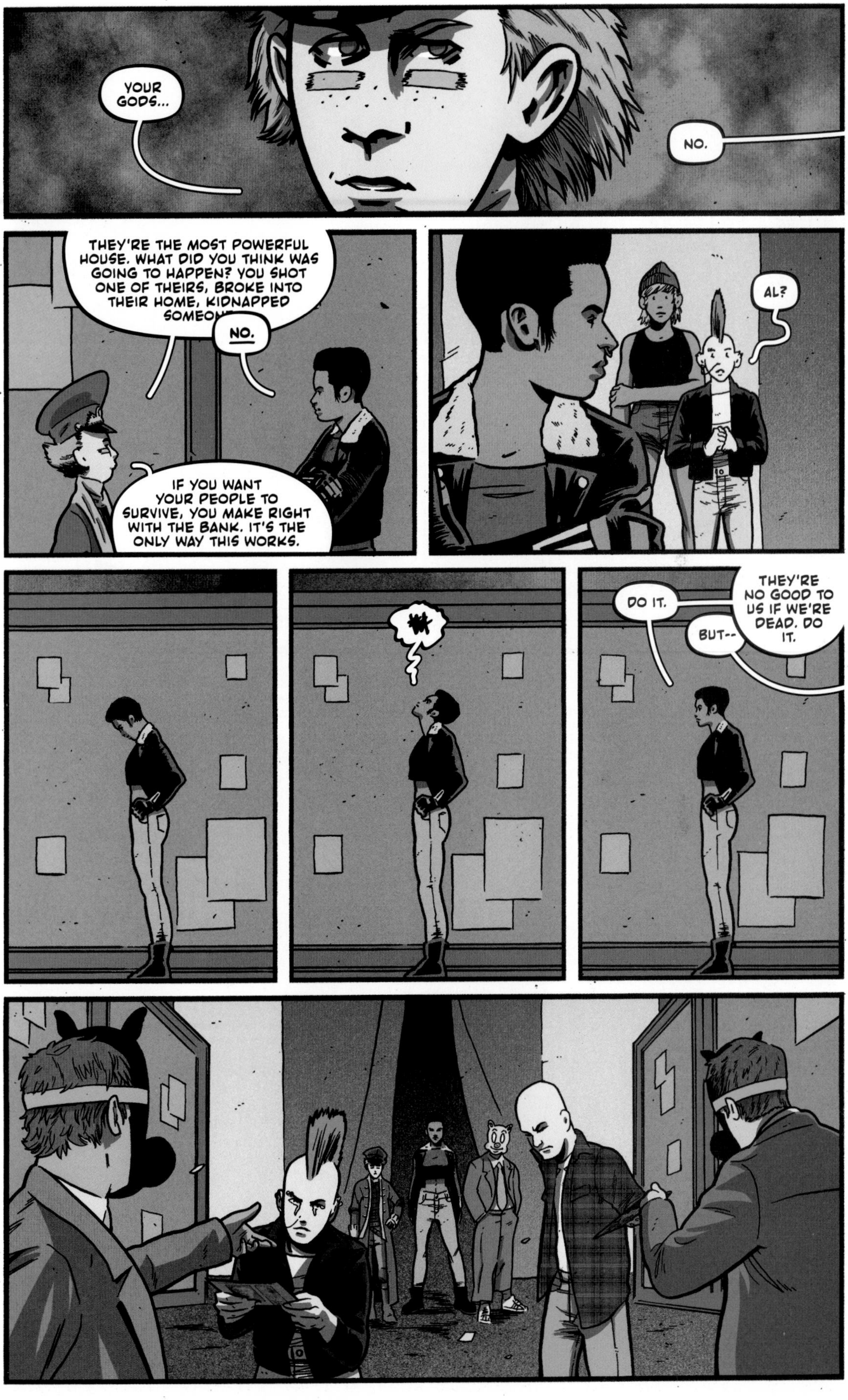
YOUR GODS...
NO.
THEY'RE THE MOST POWERFUL HOUSE. WHAT DID YOU THINK WAS GOING TO HAPPEN? YOU SHOT ONE OF THEIRS, BROKE INTO THEIR HOME, KIDNAPPED SOMEON--
NO.
IF YOU WANT YOUR PEOPLE TO SURVIVE, YOU MAKE RIGHT WITH THE BANK. IT'S THE ONLY WAY THIS WORKS.
AL?
DO IT.
BUT--
THEY'RE NO GOOD TO US IF WE'RE DEAD. DO IT.

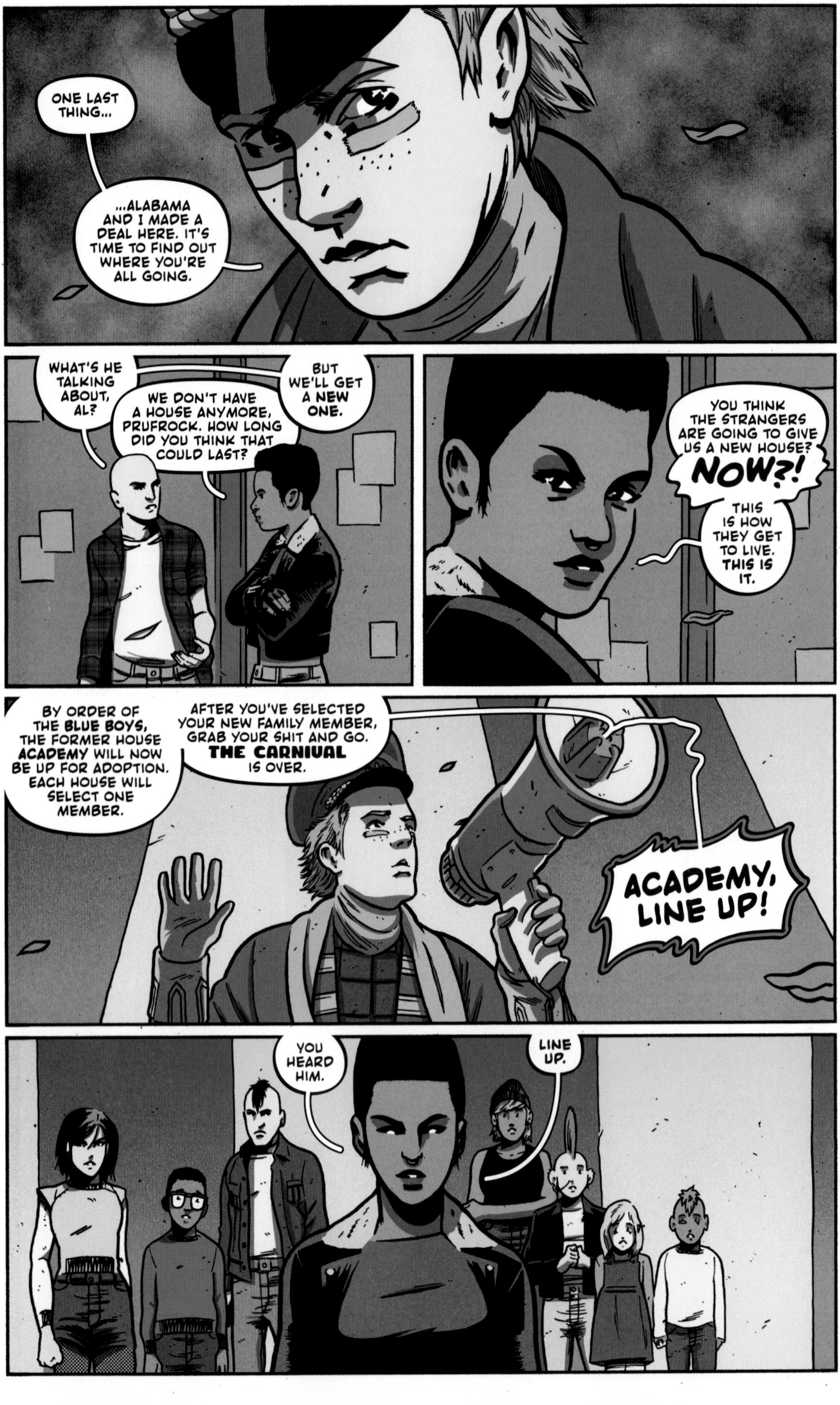
ONE LAST THING...
...ALABAMA AND I MADE A DEAL HERE. IT'S TIME TO FIND OUT WHERE YOU'RE ALL GOING.
WHAT'S HE TALKING ABOUT, AL?
BUT WE'LL GET A NEW ONE.
WE DON'T HAVE A HOUSE ANYMORE, PRUFROCK. HOW LONG DID YOU THINK THAT COULD LAST?
YOU THINK THE STRANGERS ARE GOING TO GIVE US A NEW HOUSE? NOW?!
THIS IS HOW THEY GET TO LIVE. THIS IS IT.
BY ORDER OF THE BLUE BOYS, THE FORMER HOUSE ACADEMY WILL NOW BE UP FOR ADOPTION. EACH HOUSE WILL SELECT ONE MEMBER.
AFTER YOU'VE SELECTED YOUR NEW FAMILY MEMBER, GRAB YOUR SHIT AND GO. THE CARNIVAL IS OVER.
ACADEMY, LINE UP!
YOU HEARD HIM.
LINE UP.

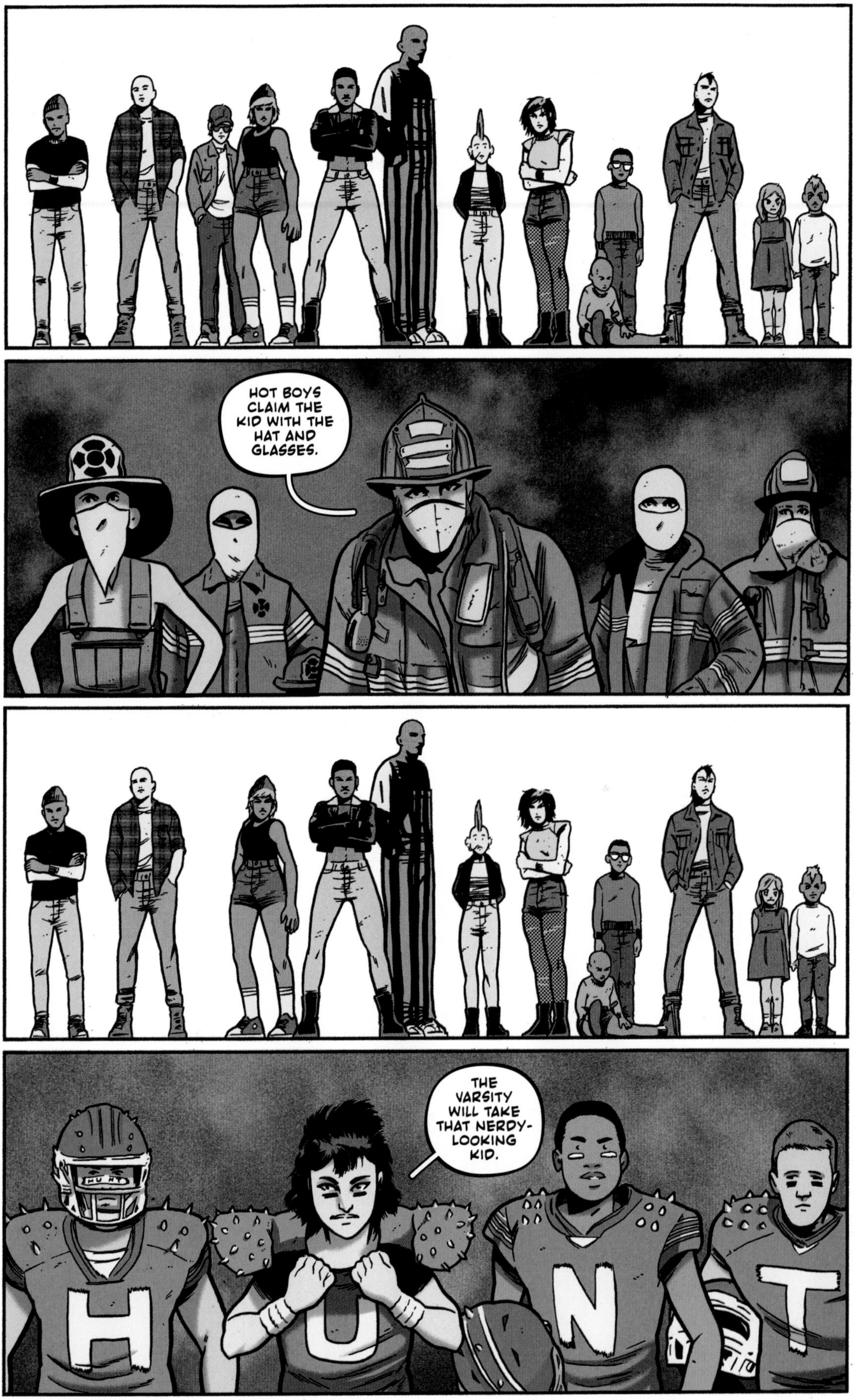
HOT BOYS CLAIM THE KID WITH THE HAT AND GLASSES.
THE VARSITY WILL TAKE THAT NERDY-LOOKING KID.

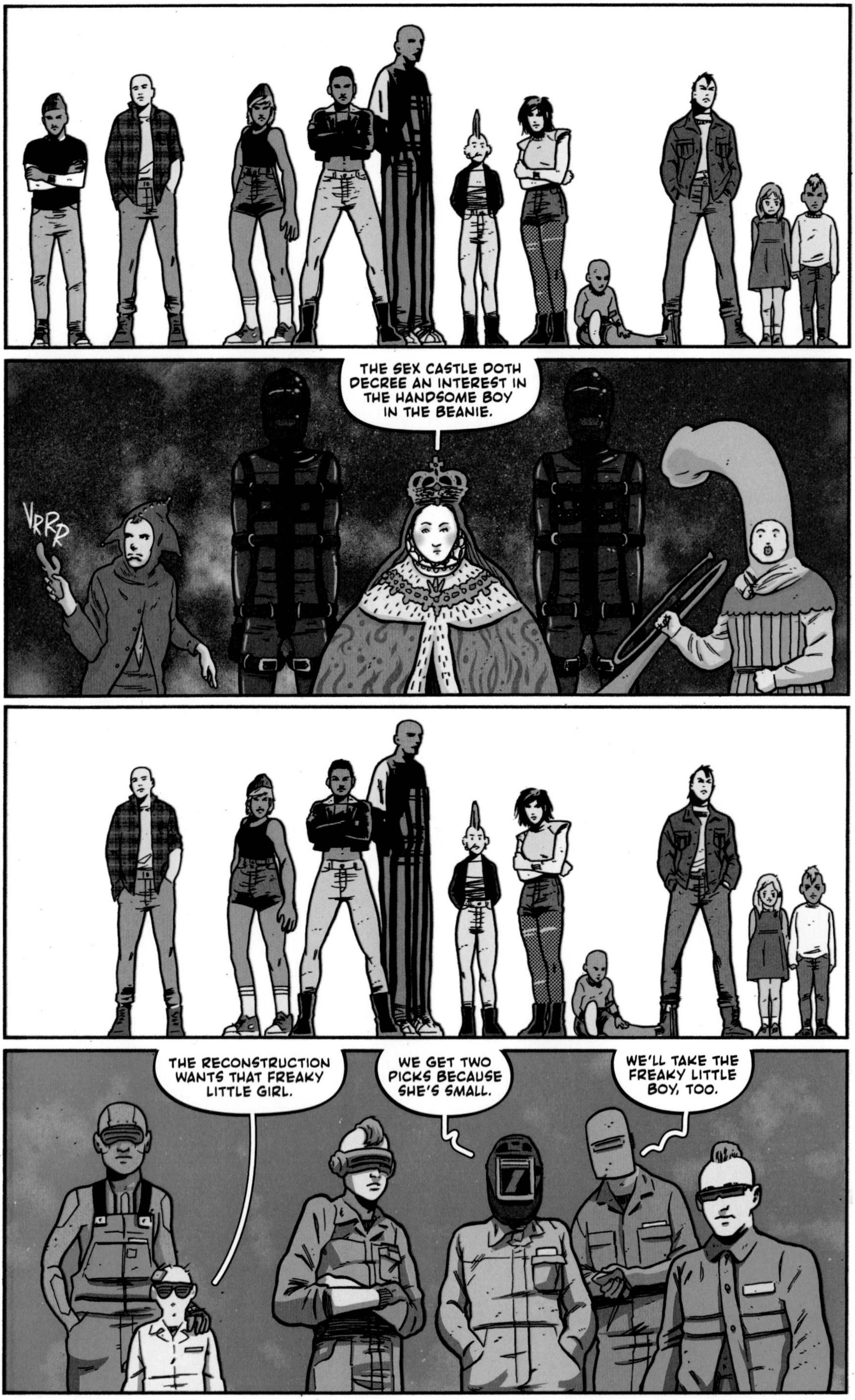
THE SEX CASTLE DOTH DECREE AN INTEREST IN THE HANDSOME BOY IN THE BEANIE.
VRRR
THE RECONSTRUCTION WANTS THAT FREAKY LITTLE GIRL.
WE GET TWO PICKS BECAUSE SHE'S SMALL.
WE'LL TAKE THE FREAKY LITTLE BOY, TOO.

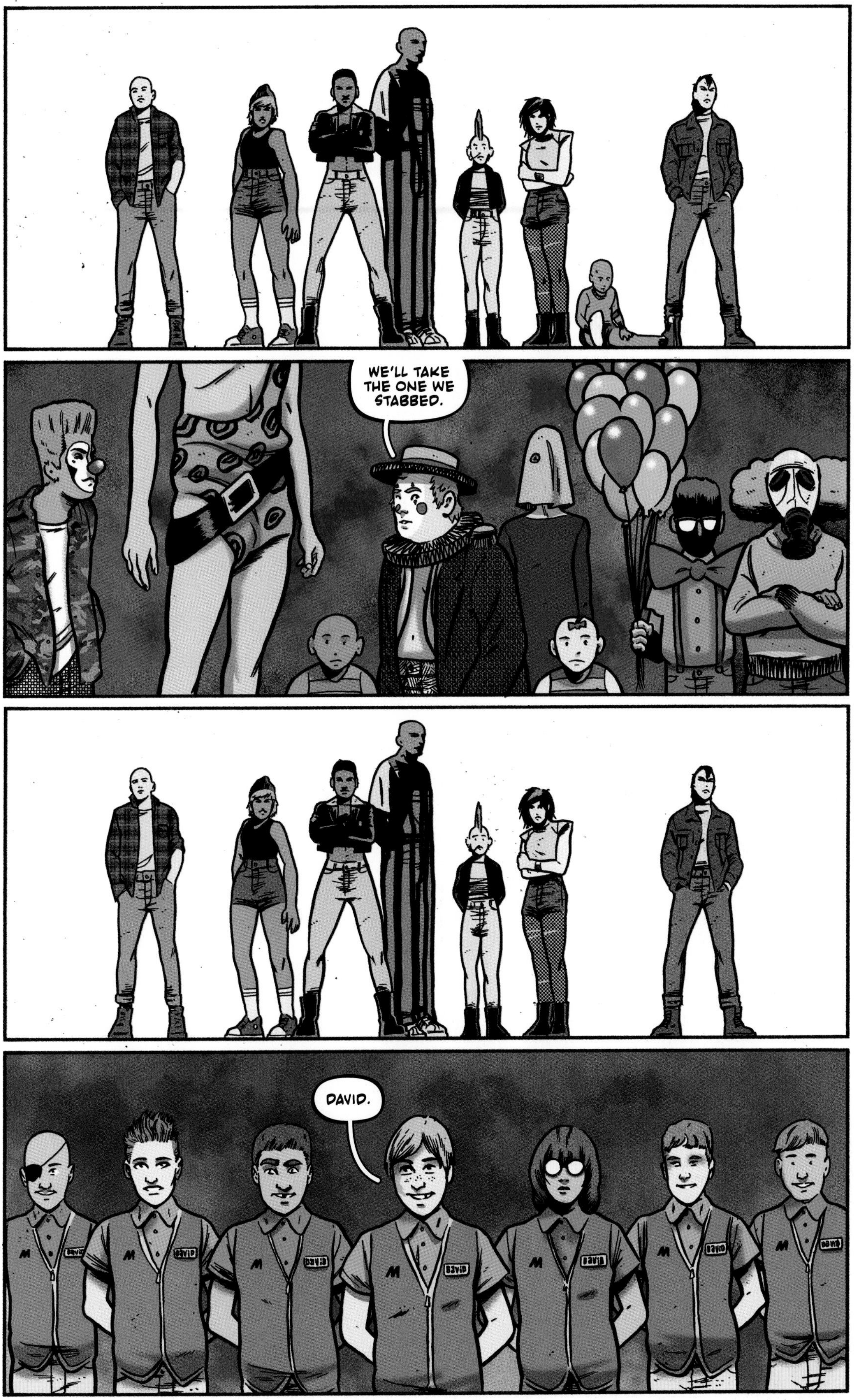
WE'LL TAKE THE ONE WE STABBED.
DAVID.

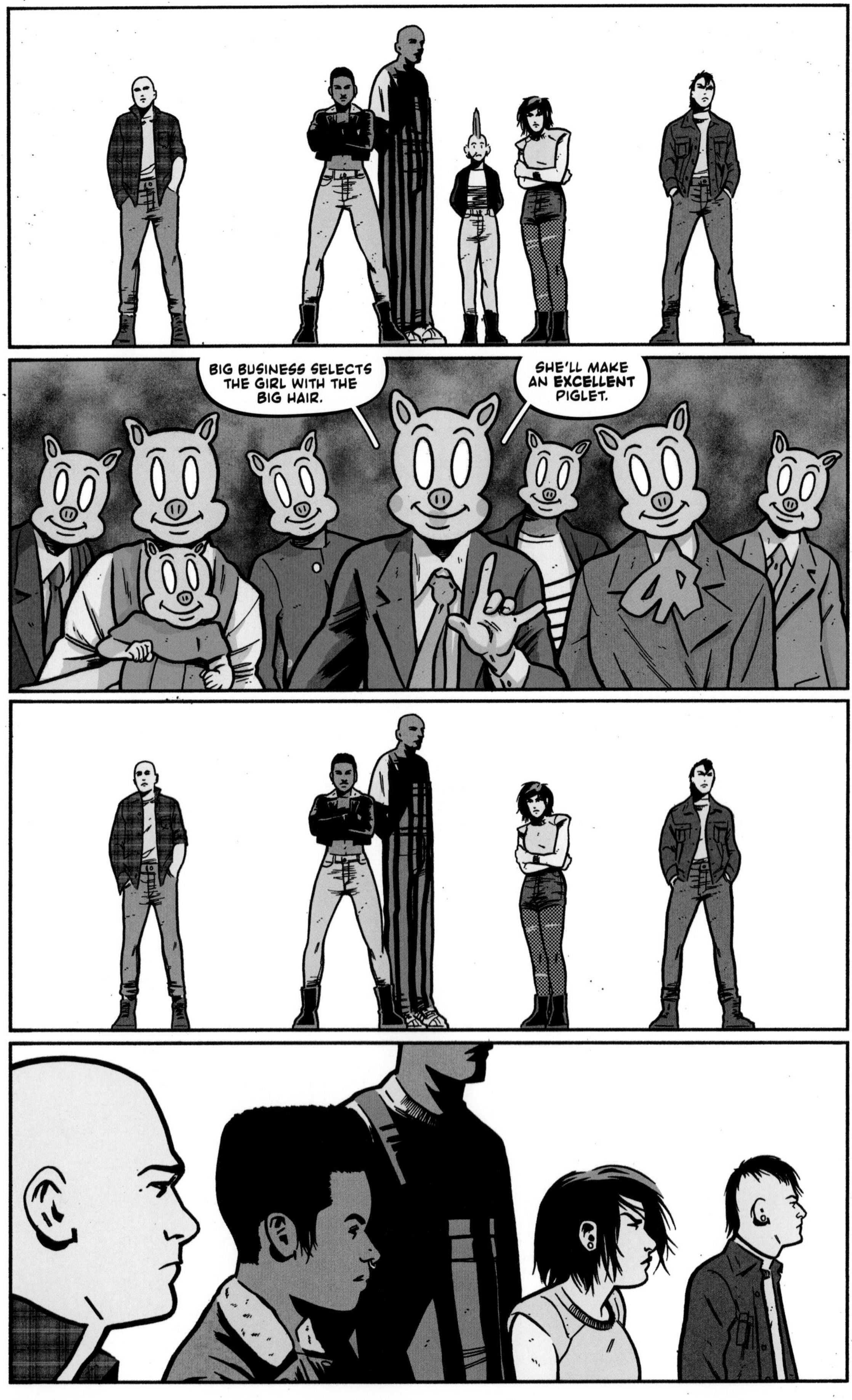
BIG BUSINESS SELECTS THE GIRL WITH THE BIG HAIR.
SHE'LL MAKE AN EXCELLENT PIGLET.

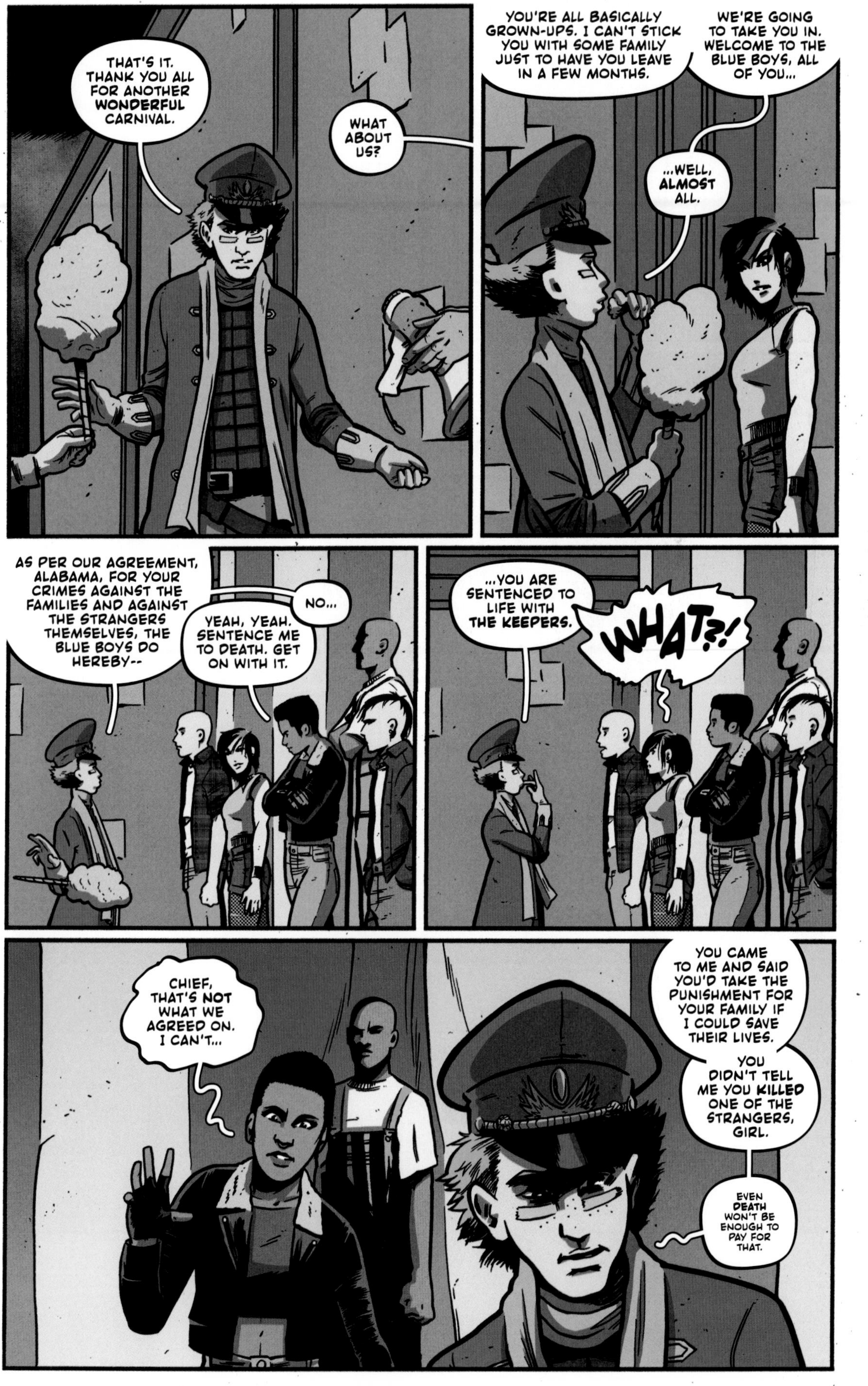

THAT'S IT. THANK YOU ALL FOR ANOTHER **WONDERFUL** CARNIVAL.
WHAT ABOUT US?
YOU'RE ALL BASICALLY GROWN-UPS. I CAN'T STICK YOU WITH SOME FAMILY JUST TO HAVE YOU LEAVE IN A FEW MONTHS.
WE'RE GOING TO TAKE YOU IN. WELCOME TO THE BLUE BOYS, ALL OF YOU...
...WELL, **ALMOST** ALL.
AS PER OUR AGREEMENT, ALABAMA, FOR YOUR CRIMES AGAINST THE FAMILIES AND AGAINST THE STRANGERS THEMSELVES, THE BLUE BOYS DO HEREBY--
NO...
YEAH, YEAH. SENTENCE ME TO DEATH. GET ON WITH IT.
...YOU ARE SENTENCED TO LIFE WITH **THE KEEPERS.**
WHAT?!
CHIEF, THAT'S **NOT** WHAT WE AGREED ON. I CAN'T...
YOU CAME TO ME AND SAID YOU'D TAKE THE PUNISHMENT FOR YOUR FAMILY IF I COULD SAVE THEIR LIVES.
YOU DIDN'T TELL ME YOU **KILLED** ONE OF THE STRANGERS, GIRL.
EVEN **DEATH** WON'T BE ENOUGH TO PAY FOR THAT.

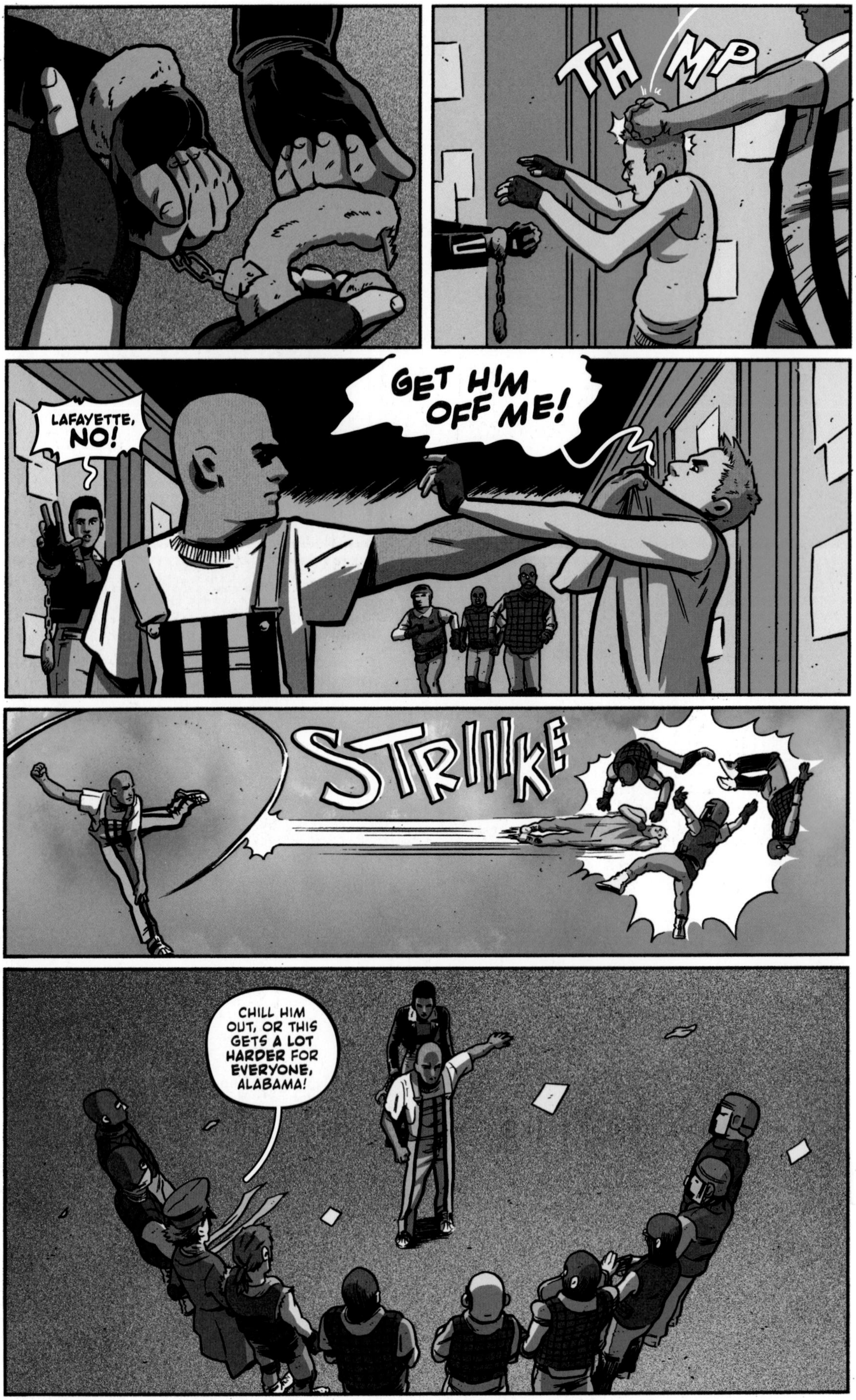
TH MP
GET HIM OFF ME!
LAFAYETTE, NO!
STRIIIKE
CHILL HIM OUT, OR THIS GETS A LOT HARDER FOR EVERYONE, ALABAMA!

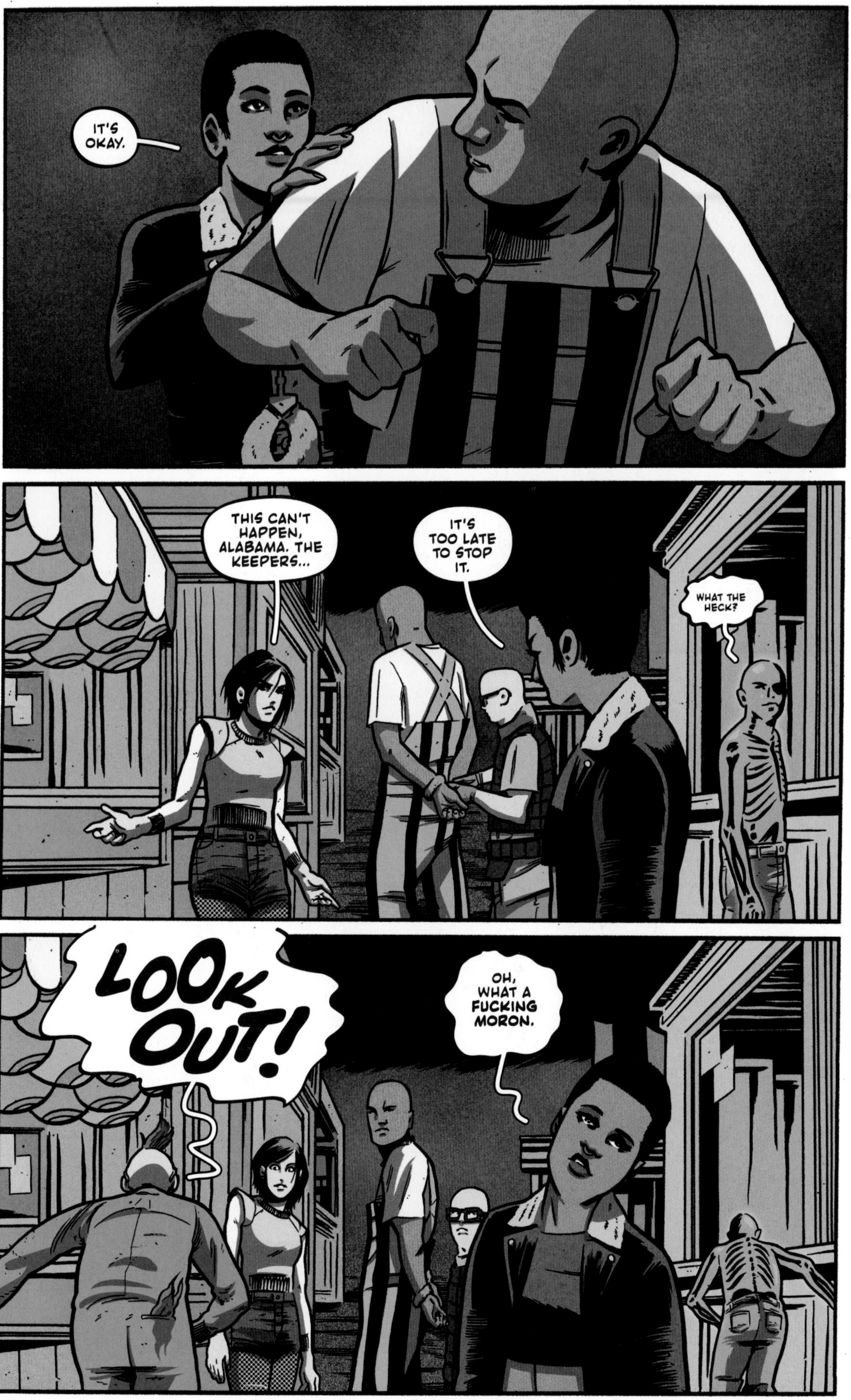
IT'S OKAY.
THIS CAN'T HAPPEN, ALABAMA. THE KEEPERS...
IT'S TOO LATE TO STOP IT.
WHAT THE HECK?
LOOK OUT!
OH, WHAT A FUCKING MORON.

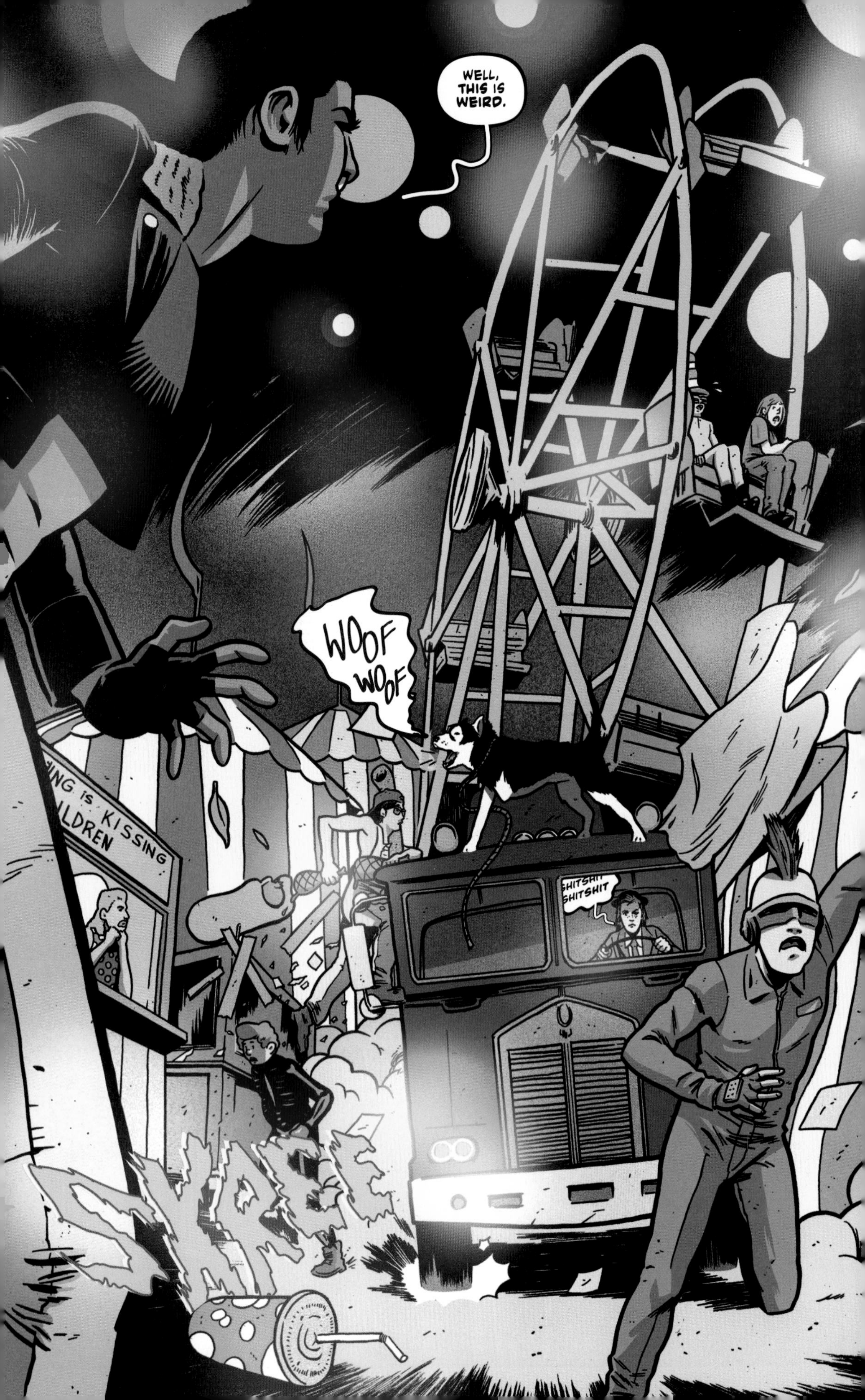
WELL, THIS IS WEIRD.
WOOF WOOF
ING is KISSING
ILDREN
SHITSHIT SHITSHIT

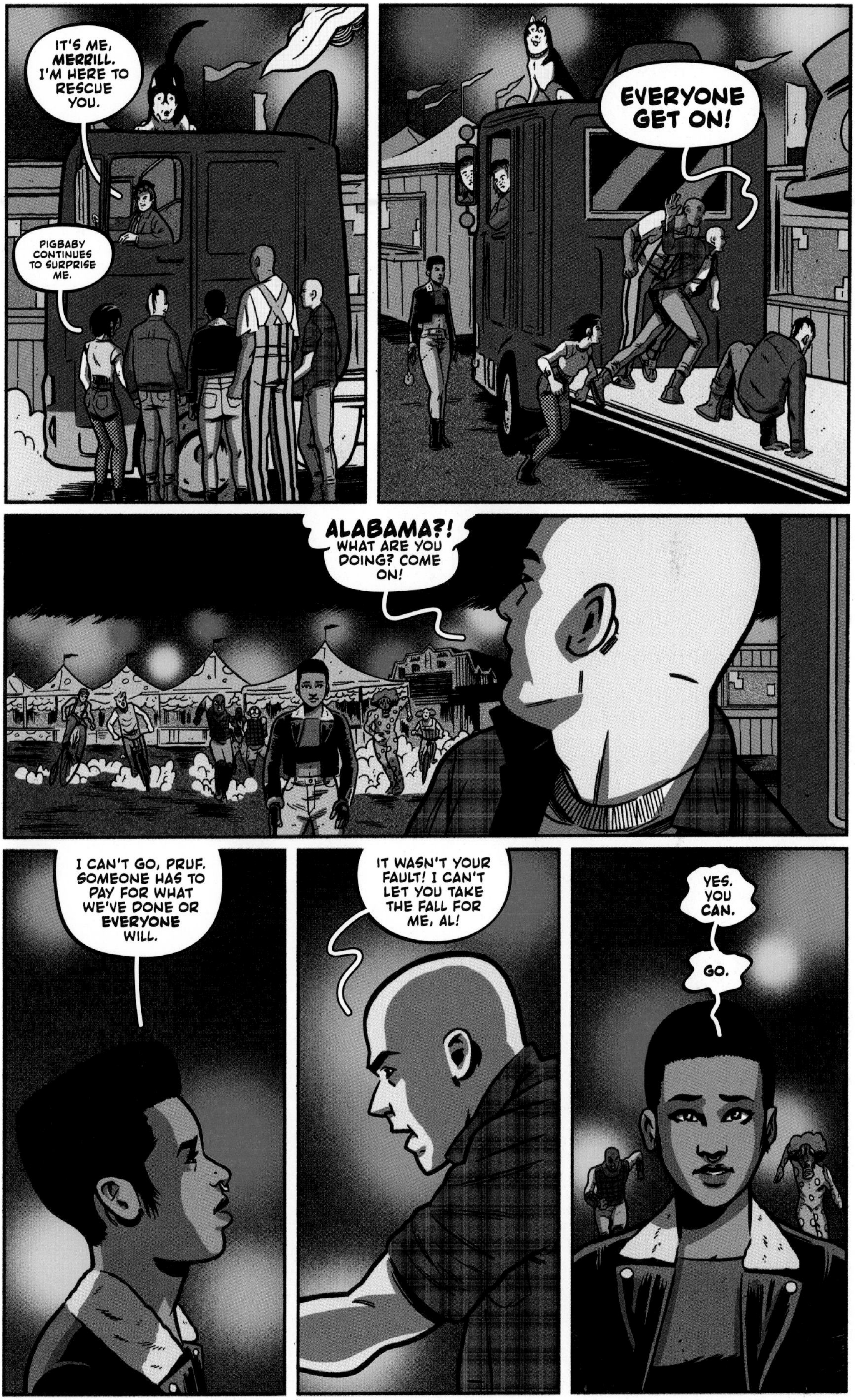
IT'S ME, MERRILL. I'M HERE TO RESCUE YOU.
PIGBABY CONTINUES TO SURPRISE ME.
EVERYONE GET ON!
ALABAMA?! WHAT ARE YOU DOING? COME ON!
I CAN'T GO, PRUF. SOMEONE HAS TO PAY FOR WHAT WE'VE DONE OR EVERYONE WILL.
IT WASN'T YOUR FAULT! I CAN'T LET YOU TAKE THE FALL FOR ME, AL!
YES. YOU CAN.
GO.

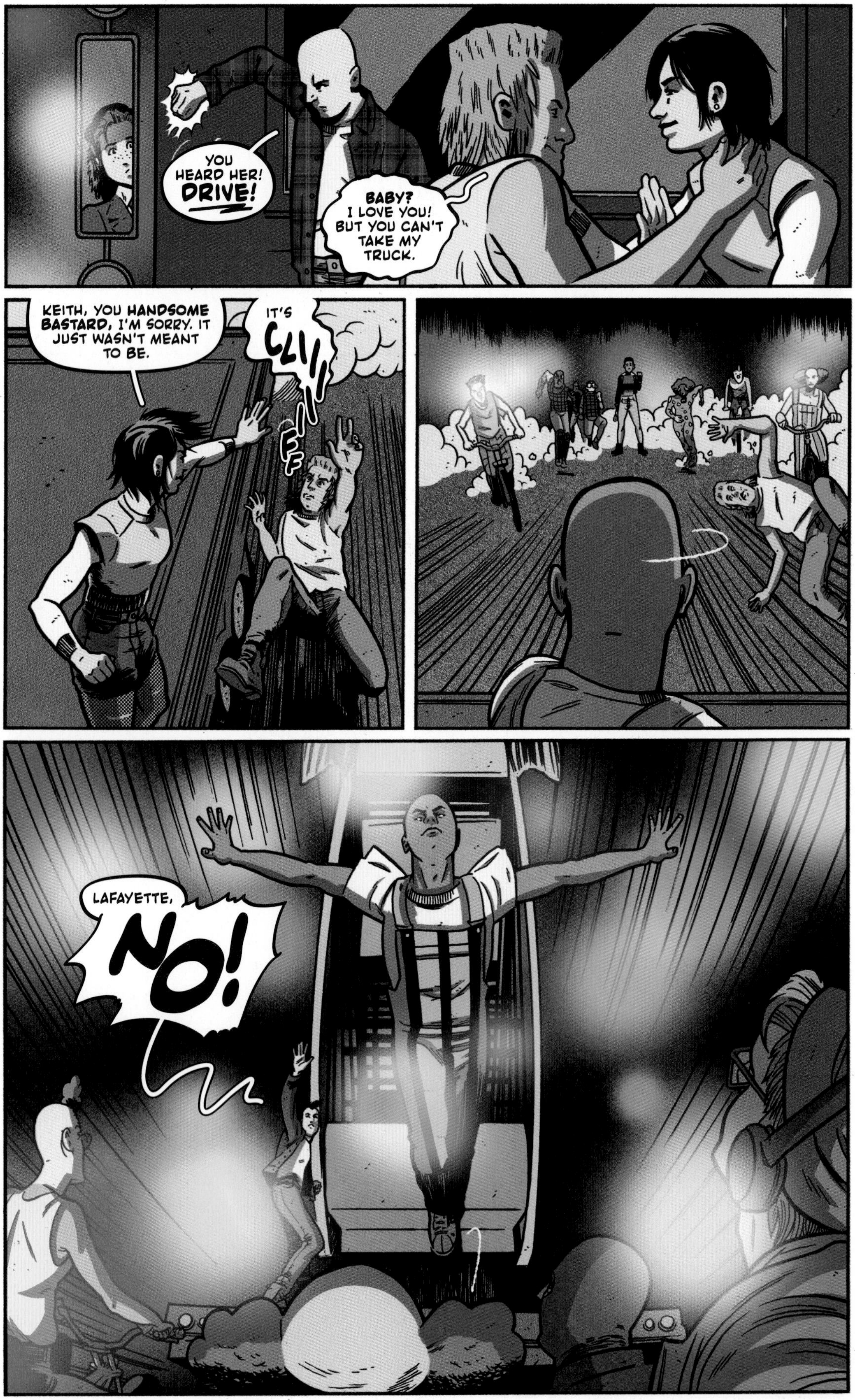
YOU HEARD HER! DRIVE!
BABY? I LOVE YOU! BUT YOU CAN'T TAKE MY TRUCK.
KEITH, YOU HANDSOME BASTARD, I'M SORRY. IT JUST WASN'T MEANT TO BE.
IT'S CLIIIIIFF
LAFAYETTE,
NO!

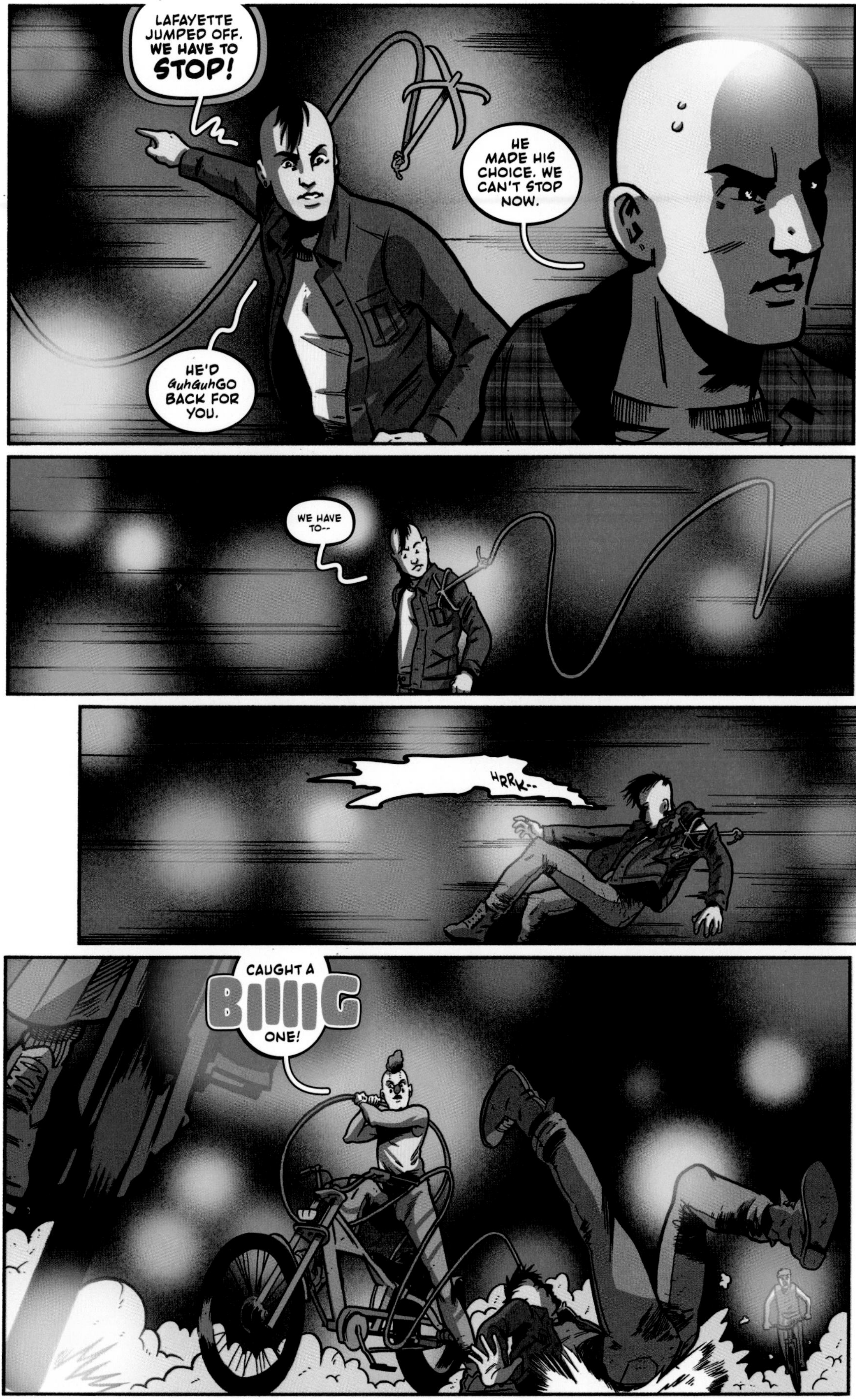
LAFAYETTE JUMPED OFF. WE HAVE TO STOP!
HE MADE HIS CHOICE. WE CAN'T STOP NOW.
HE'D GuhGuhGO BACK FOR YOU.
WE HAVE TO--
HRRK--
CAUGHT A BIIIIG ONE!

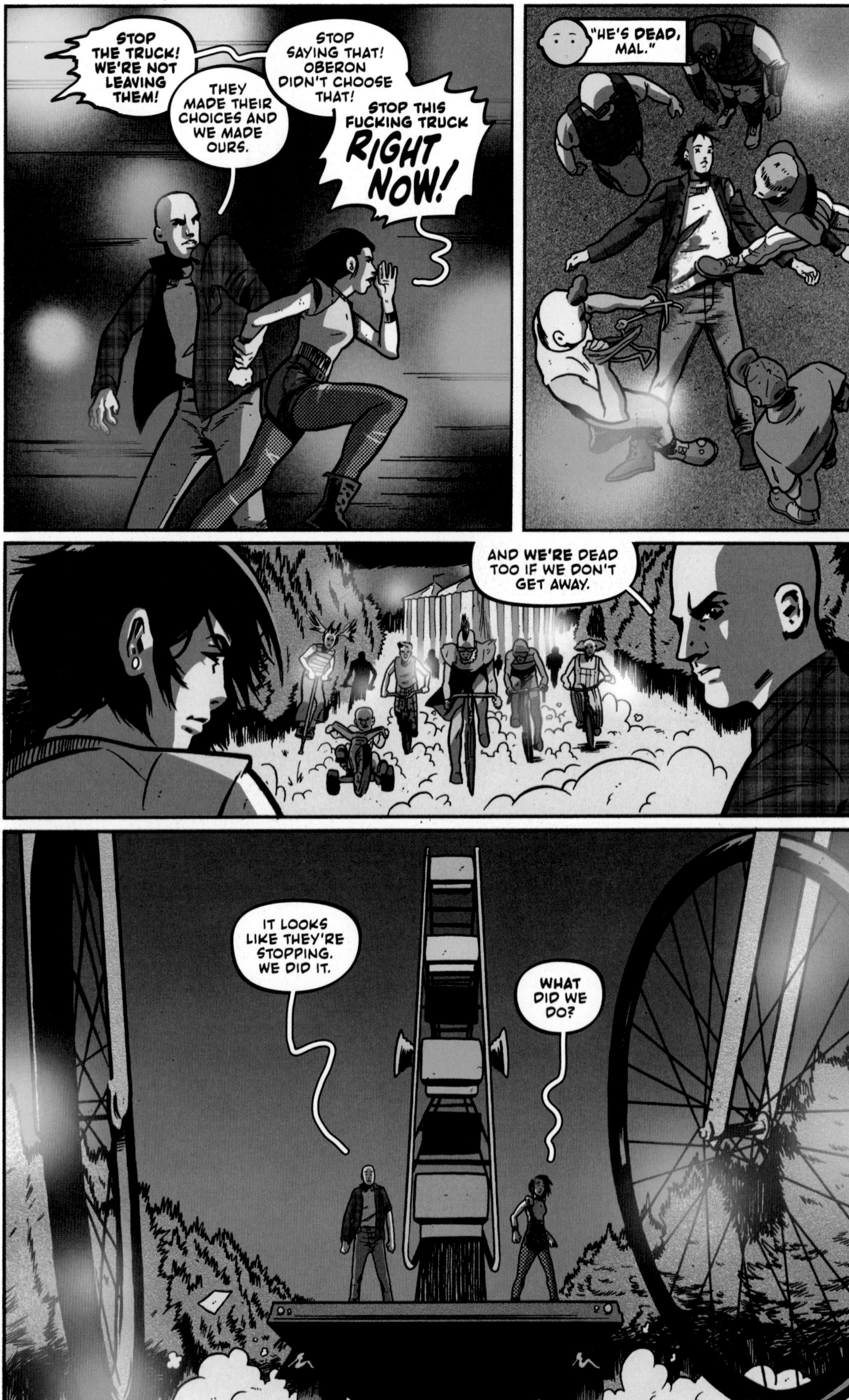
STOP THE TRUCK! WE'RE NOT LEAVING THEM!
THEY MADE THEIR CHOICES AND WE MADE OURS.
STOP SAYING THAT! OBERON DIDN'T CHOOSE THAT!
STOP THIS FUCKING TRUCK RIGHT NOW!
"HE'S DEAD, MAL."
AND WE'RE DEAD TOO IF WE DON'T GET AWAY.
IT LOOKS LIKE THEY'RE STOPPING. WE DID IT.
WHAT DID WE DO?

# CHAPTER FORTY-ONE

## CRAZY WORLD.

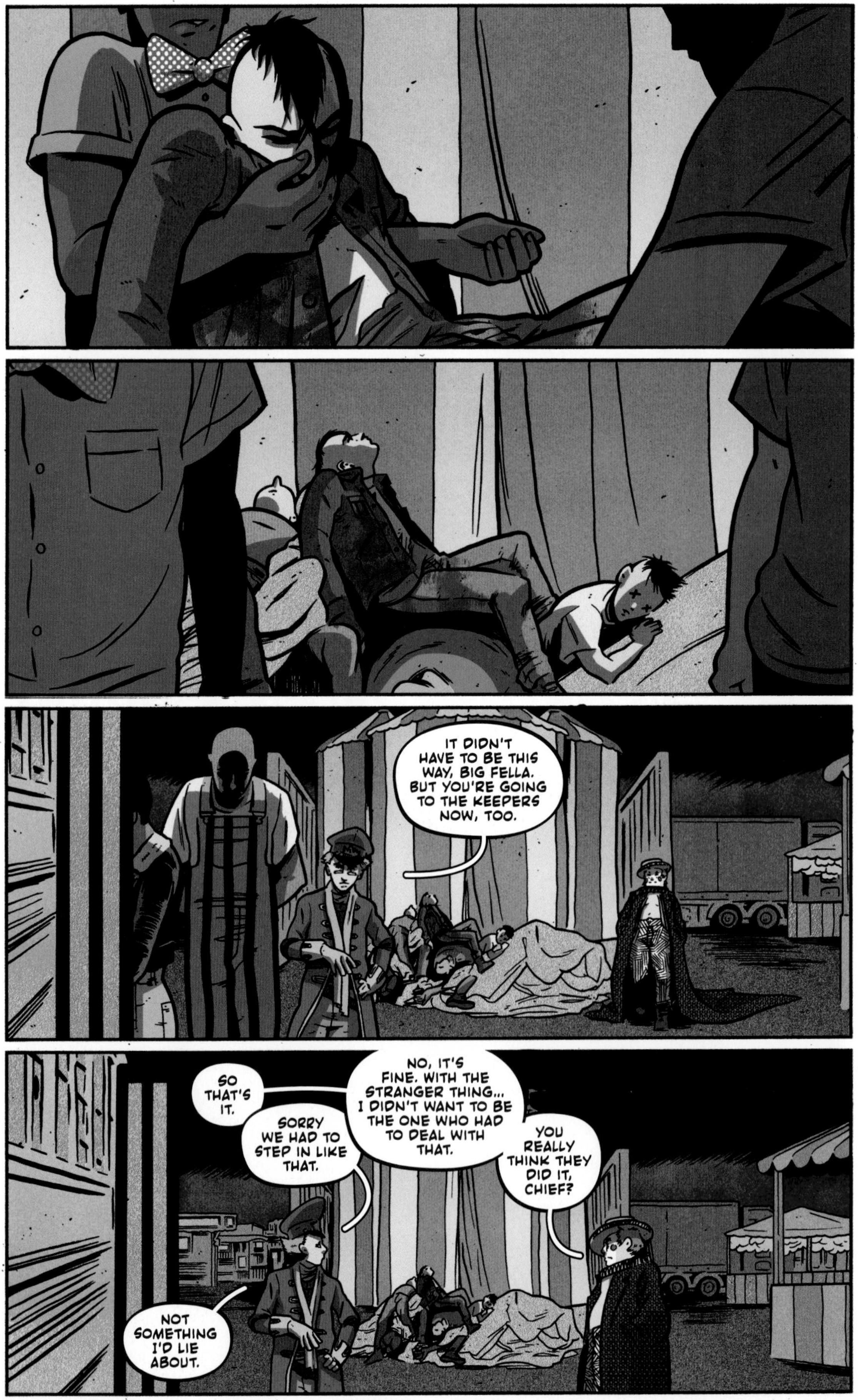
IT DIDN'T HAVE TO BE THIS WAY, BIG FELLA. BUT YOU'RE GOING TO THE KEEPERS NOW, TOO.
SO THAT'S IT.
SORRY WE HAD TO STEP IN LIKE THAT.
NO, IT'S FINE. WITH THE STRANGER THING... I DIDN'T WANT TO BE THE ONE WHO HAD TO DEAL WITH THAT.
YOU REALLY THINK THEY DID IT, CHIEF?
NOT SOMETHING I'D LIE ABOUT.

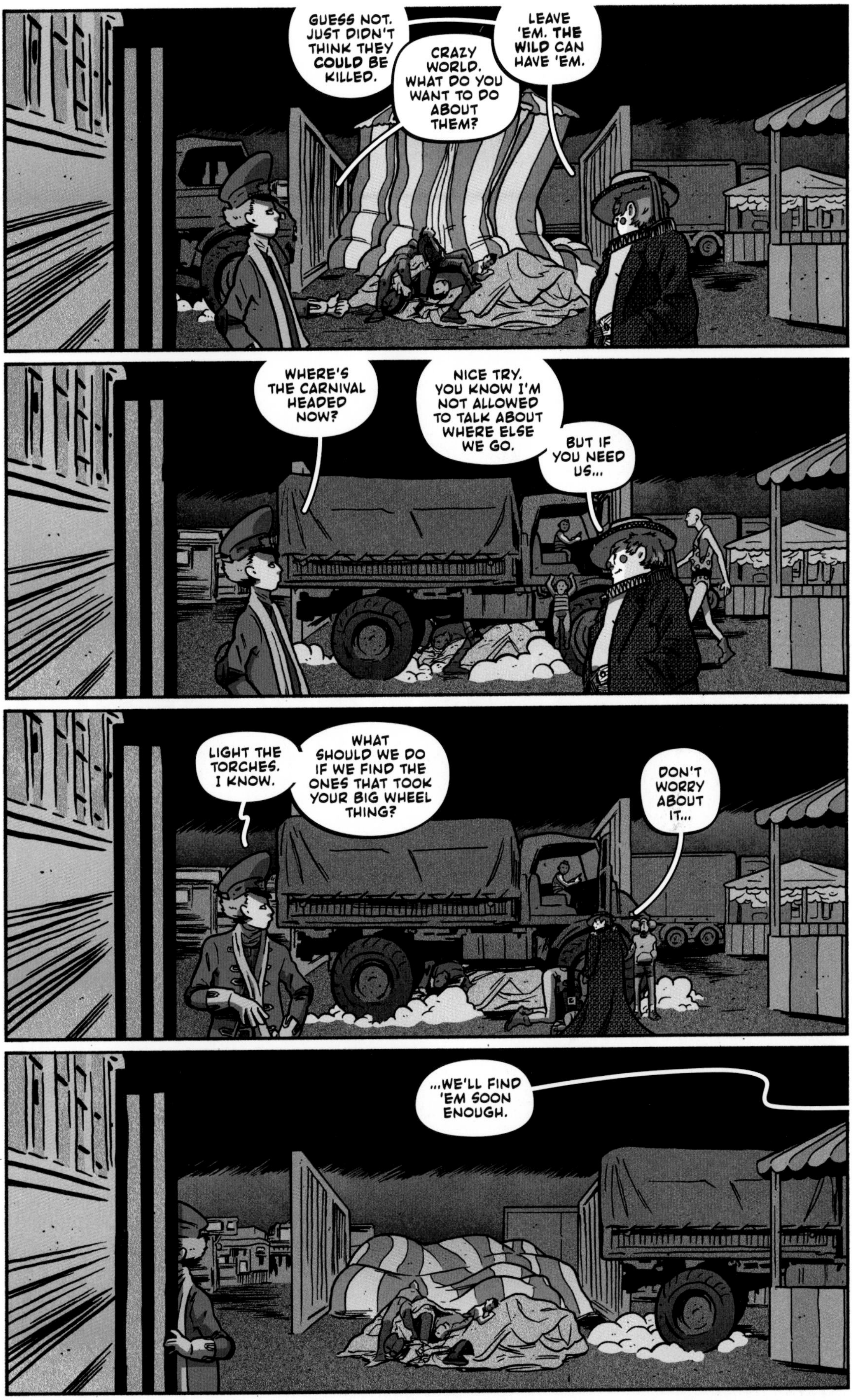
GUESS NOT. JUST DIDN'T THINK THEY COULD BE KILLED.
CRAZY WORLD. WHAT DO YOU WANT TO DO ABOUT THEM?
LEAVE 'EM. THE WILD CAN HAVE 'EM.
WHERE'S THE CARNIVAL HEADED NOW?
NICE TRY. YOU KNOW I'M NOT ALLOWED TO TALK ABOUT WHERE ELSE WE GO.
BUT IF YOU NEED US...
LIGHT THE TORCHES. I KNOW.
WHAT SHOULD WE DO IF WE FIND THE ONES THAT TOOK YOUR BIG WHEEL THING?
DON'T WORRY ABOUT IT...
...WE'LL FIND 'EM SOON ENOUGH.

# CHAPTER FORTY-TWO

## WHAT FAMILY?

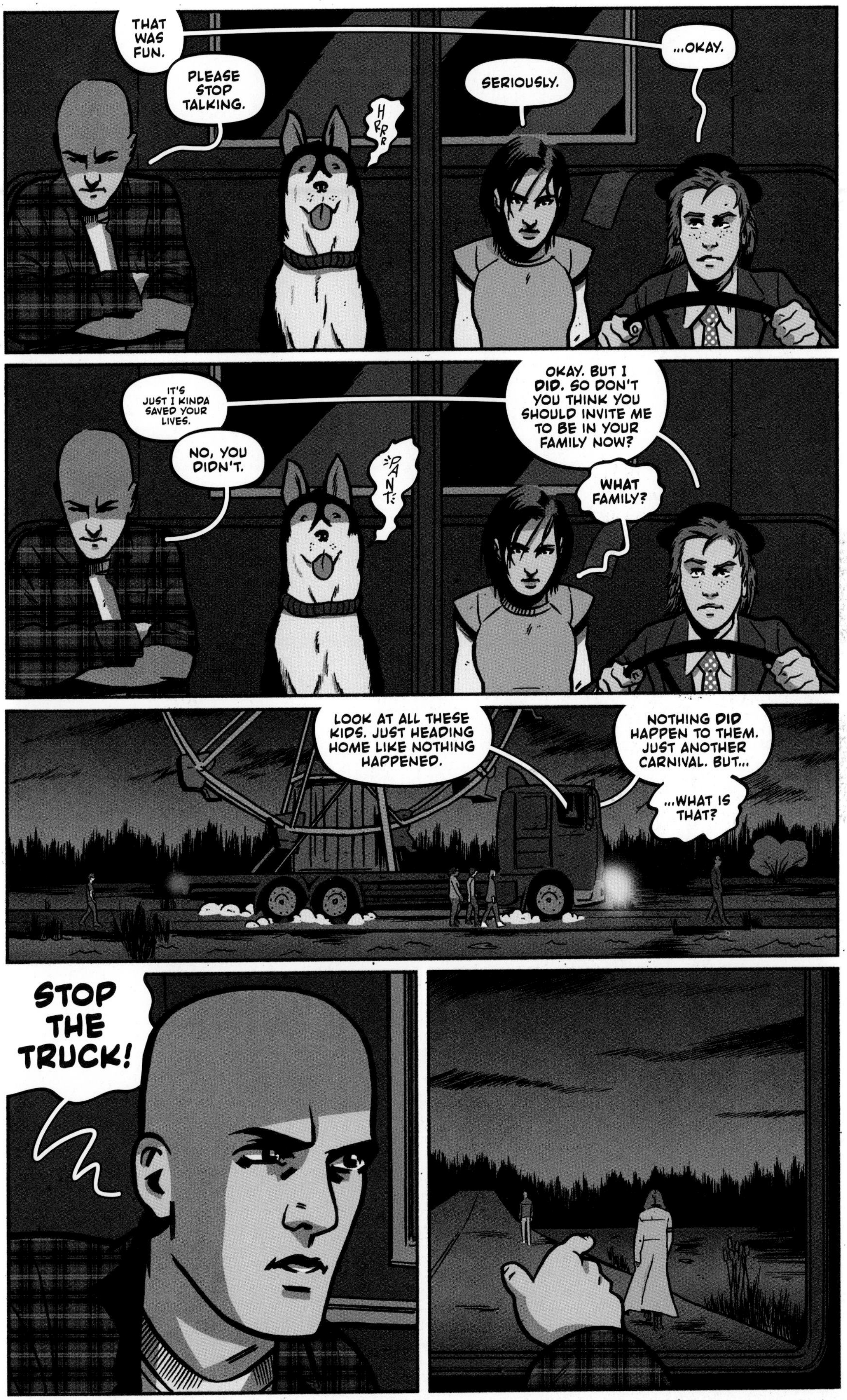
THAT WAS FUN.
PLEASE STOP TALKING.
HRRR
SERIOUSLY.
...OKAY.
IT'S JUST I KINDA SAVED YOUR LIVES.
NO, YOU DIDN'T.
PANT
OKAY. BUT I DID. SO DON'T YOU THINK YOU SHOULD INVITE ME TO BE IN YOUR FAMILY NOW?
WHAT FAMILY?
LOOK AT ALL THESE KIDS. JUST HEADING HOME LIKE NOTHING HAPPENED.
NOTHING DID HAPPEN TO THEM. JUST ANOTHER CARNIVAL. BUT...
...WHAT IS THAT?
STOP THE TRUCK!

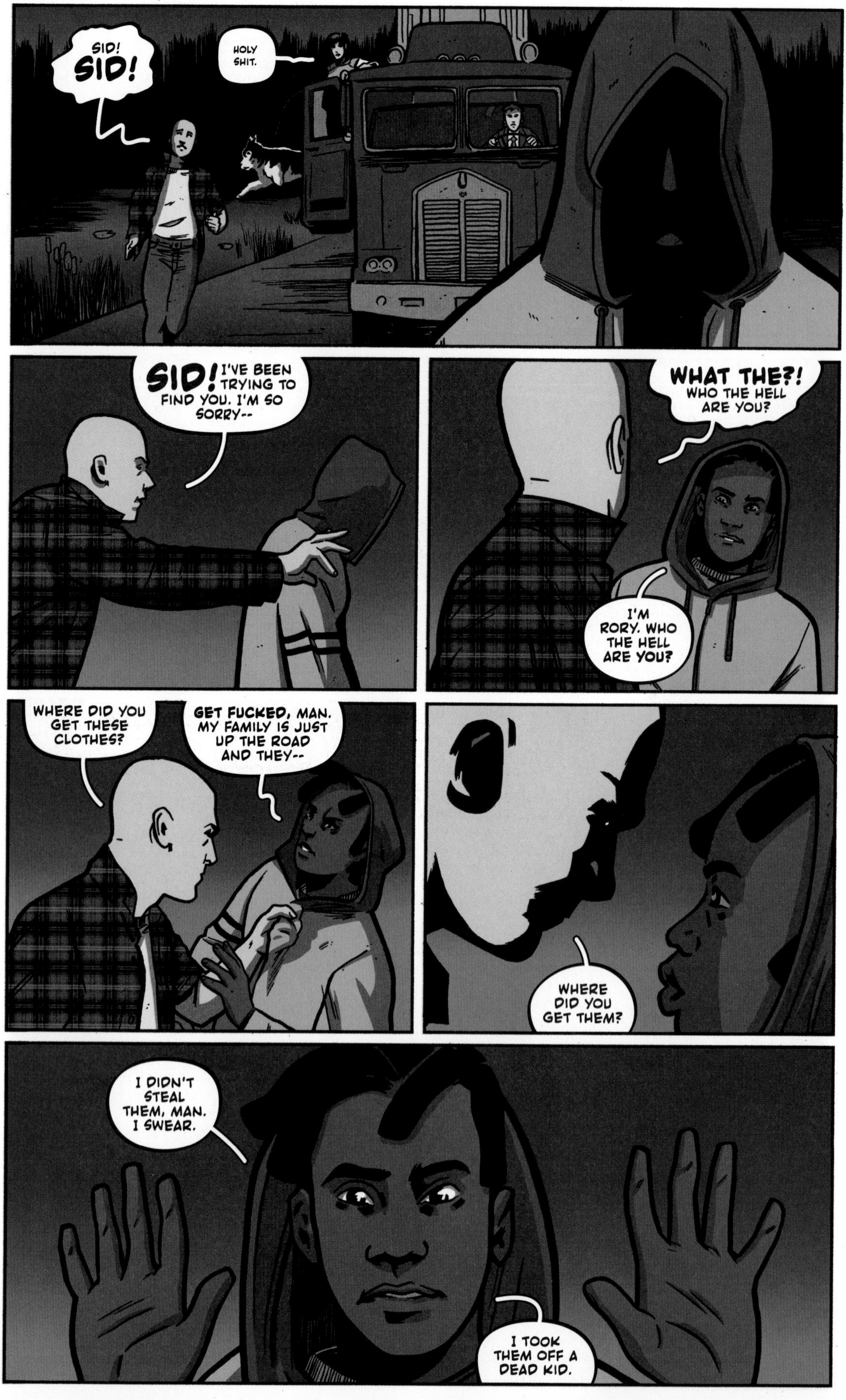
SID! SID!
HOLY SHIT.
SID! I'VE BEEN TRYING TO FIND YOU. I'M SO SORRY--
WHAT THE?! WHO THE HELL ARE YOU?
I'M RORY. WHO THE HELL ARE YOU?
WHERE DID YOU GET THESE CLOTHES?
GET FUCKED, MAN. MY FAMILY IS JUST UP THE ROAD AND THEY--
WHERE DID YOU GET THEM?
I DIDN'T STEAL THEM, MAN. I SWEAR.
I TOOK THEM OFF A DEAD KID.

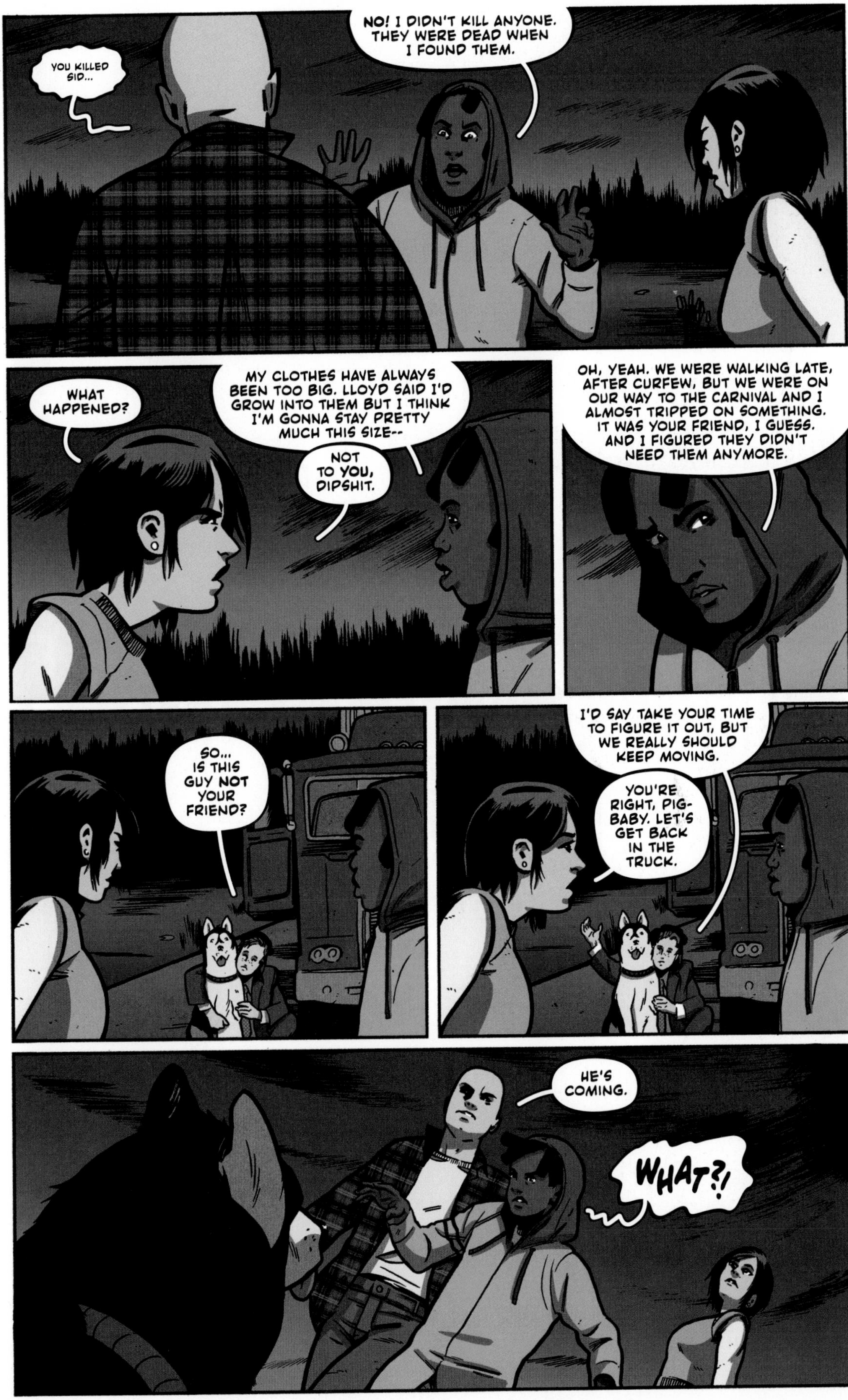
YOU KILLED SID...
NO! I DIDN'T KILL ANYONE. THEY WERE DEAD WHEN I FOUND THEM.
WHAT HAPPENED?
MY CLOTHES HAVE ALWAYS BEEN TOO BIG. LLOYD SAID I'D GROW INTO THEM BUT I THINK I'M GONNA STAY PRETTY MUCH THIS SIZE--
NOT TO YOU, DIPSHIT.
OH, YEAH. WE WERE WALKING LATE, AFTER CURFEW, BUT WE WERE ON OUR WAY TO THE CARNIVAL AND I ALMOST TRIPPED ON SOMETHING. IT WAS YOUR FRIEND, I GUESS. AND I FIGURED THEY DIDN'T NEED THEM ANYMORE.
SO... IS THIS GUY NOT YOUR FRIEND?
I'D SAY TAKE YOUR TIME TO FIGURE IT OUT, BUT WE REALLY SHOULD KEEP MOVING.
YOU'RE RIGHT, PIG-BABY. LET'S GET BACK IN THE TRUCK.
HE'S COMING.
WHAT?!

# CHAPTER FORTY-THREE

## I KNOW YOU'RE OUT THERE.

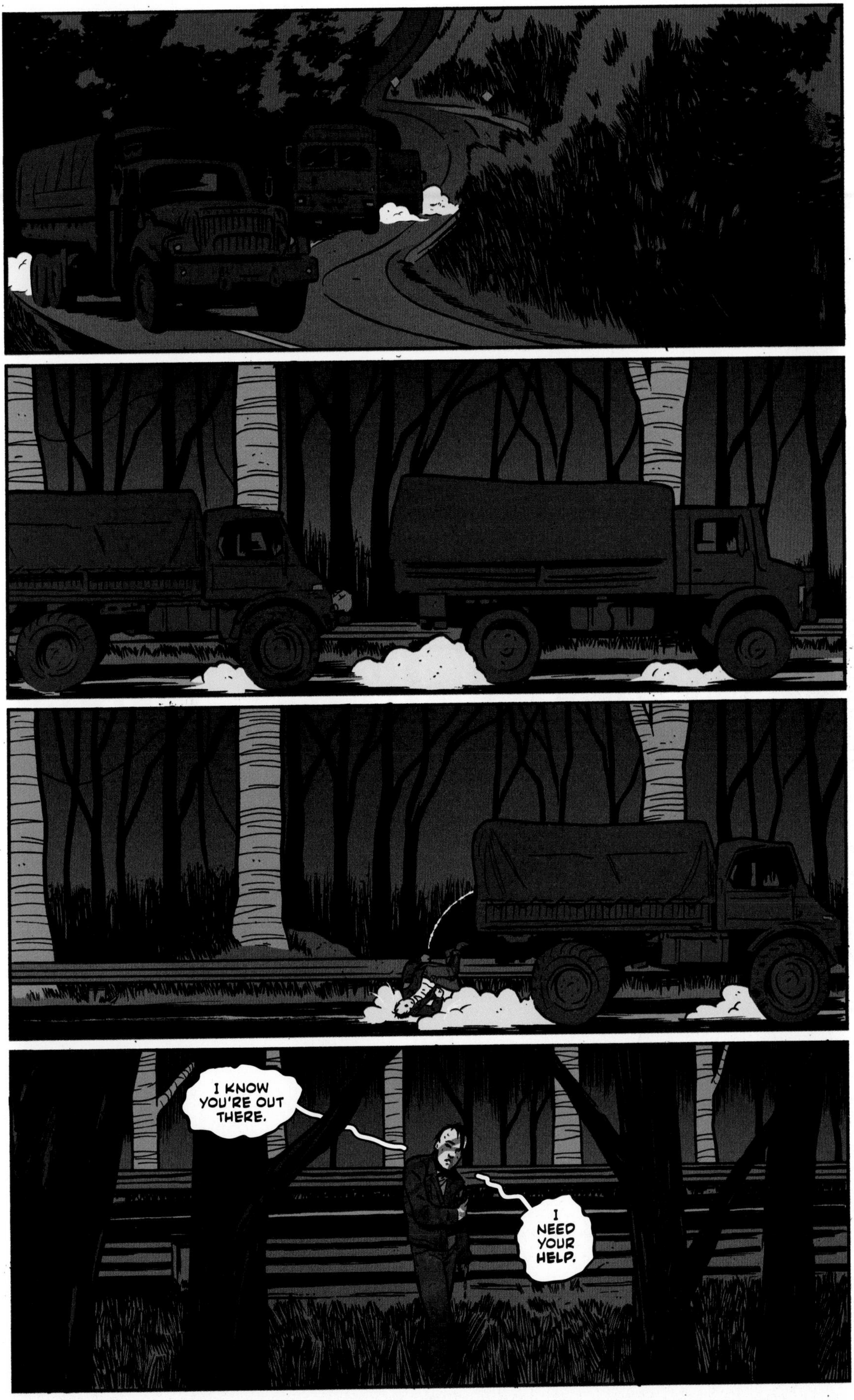
I KNOW YOU'RE OUT THERE.
I NEED YOUR HELP.

# CHAPTER FORTY-FOUR

I'D BE PISSING MYSELF IF I WAS YOU.

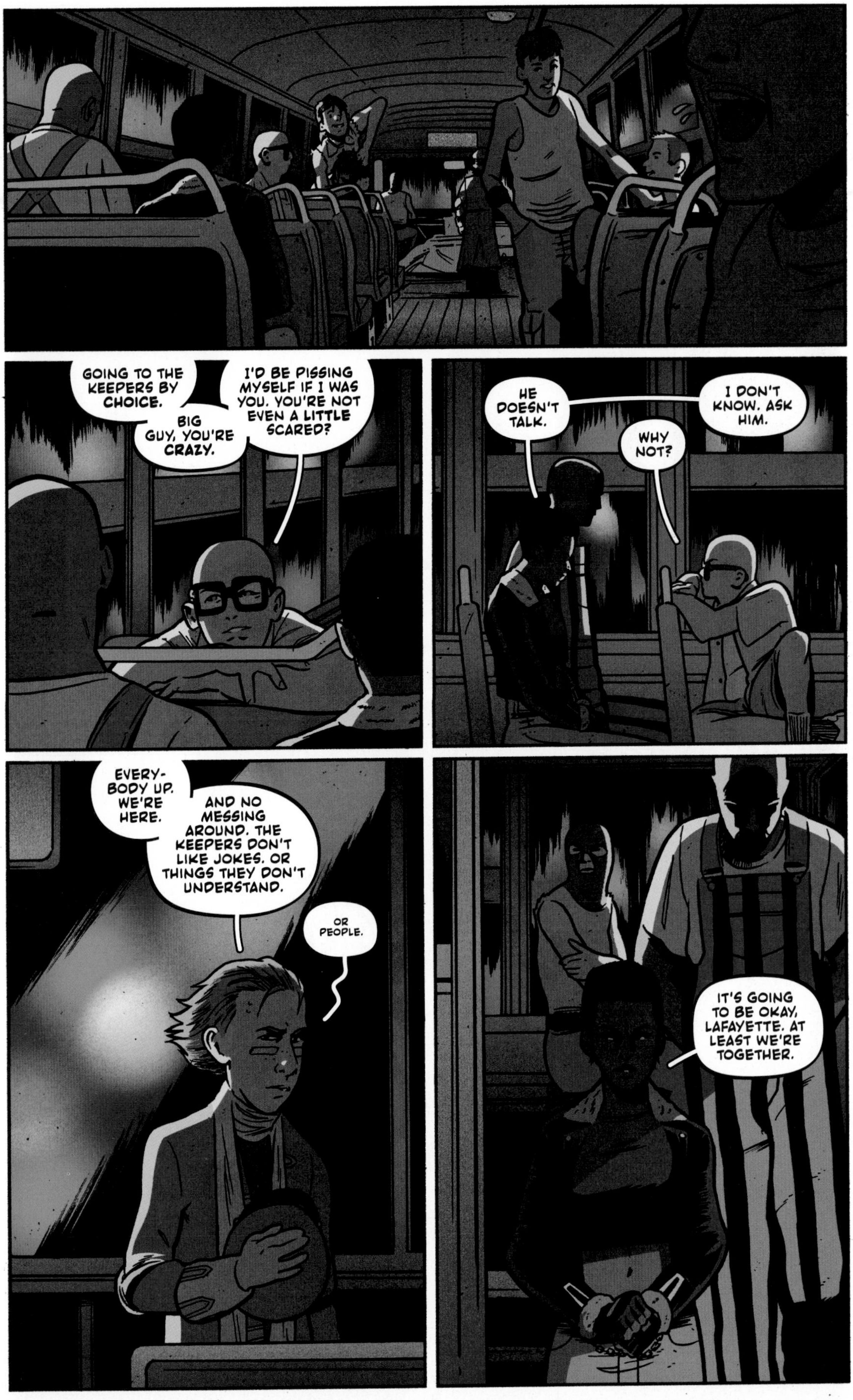
GOING TO THE KEEPERS BY CHOICE.
BIG GUY, YOU'RE CRAZY.
I'D BE PISSING MYSELF IF I WAS YOU. YOU'RE NOT EVEN A LITTLE SCARED?
HE DOESN'T TALK.
WHY NOT?
I DON'T KNOW. ASK HIM.
EVERY-BODY UP. WE'RE HERE.
AND NO MESSING AROUND. THE KEEPERS DON'T LIKE JOKES. OR THINGS THEY DON'T UNDERSTAND.
OR PEOPLE.
IT'S GOING TO BE OKAY, LAFAYETTE. AT LEAST WE'RE TOGETHER.

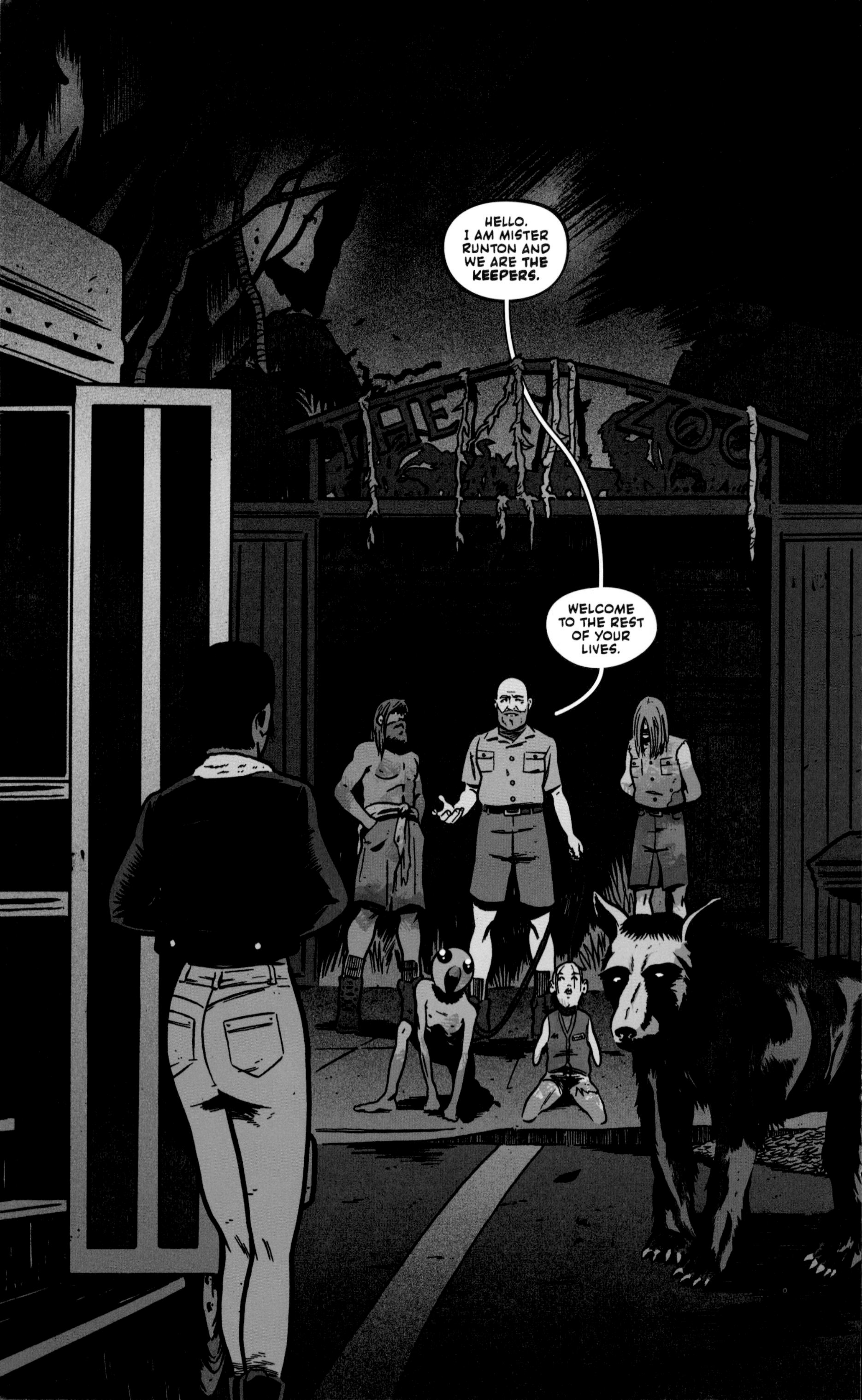
HELLO. I AM MISTER RUNTON AND WE ARE THE KEEPERS.
WELCOME TO THE REST OF YOUR LIVES.

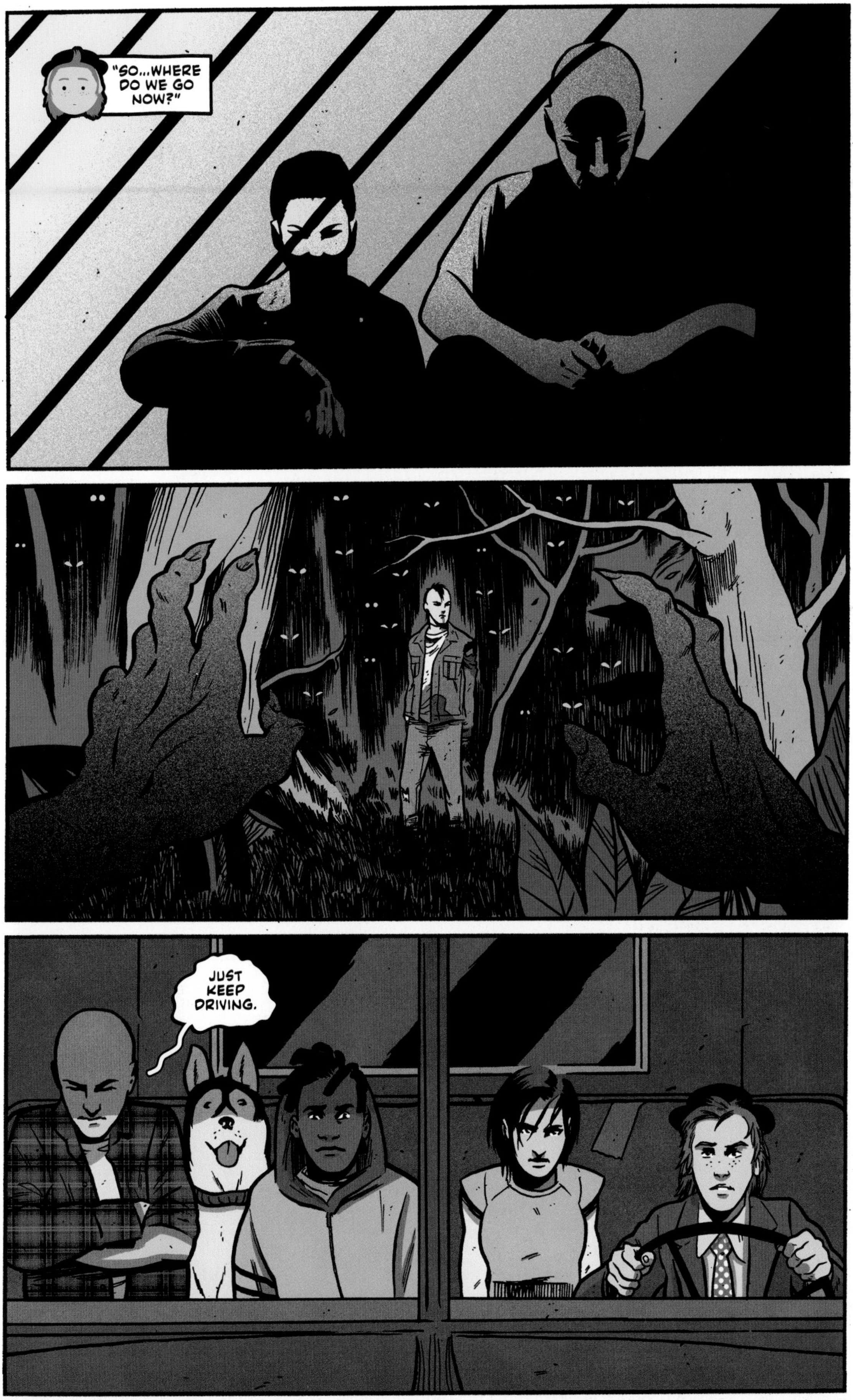
"SO...WHERE DO WE GO NOW?"
JUST KEEP DRIVING.

# CHAPTER FORTY-FIVE

SID.

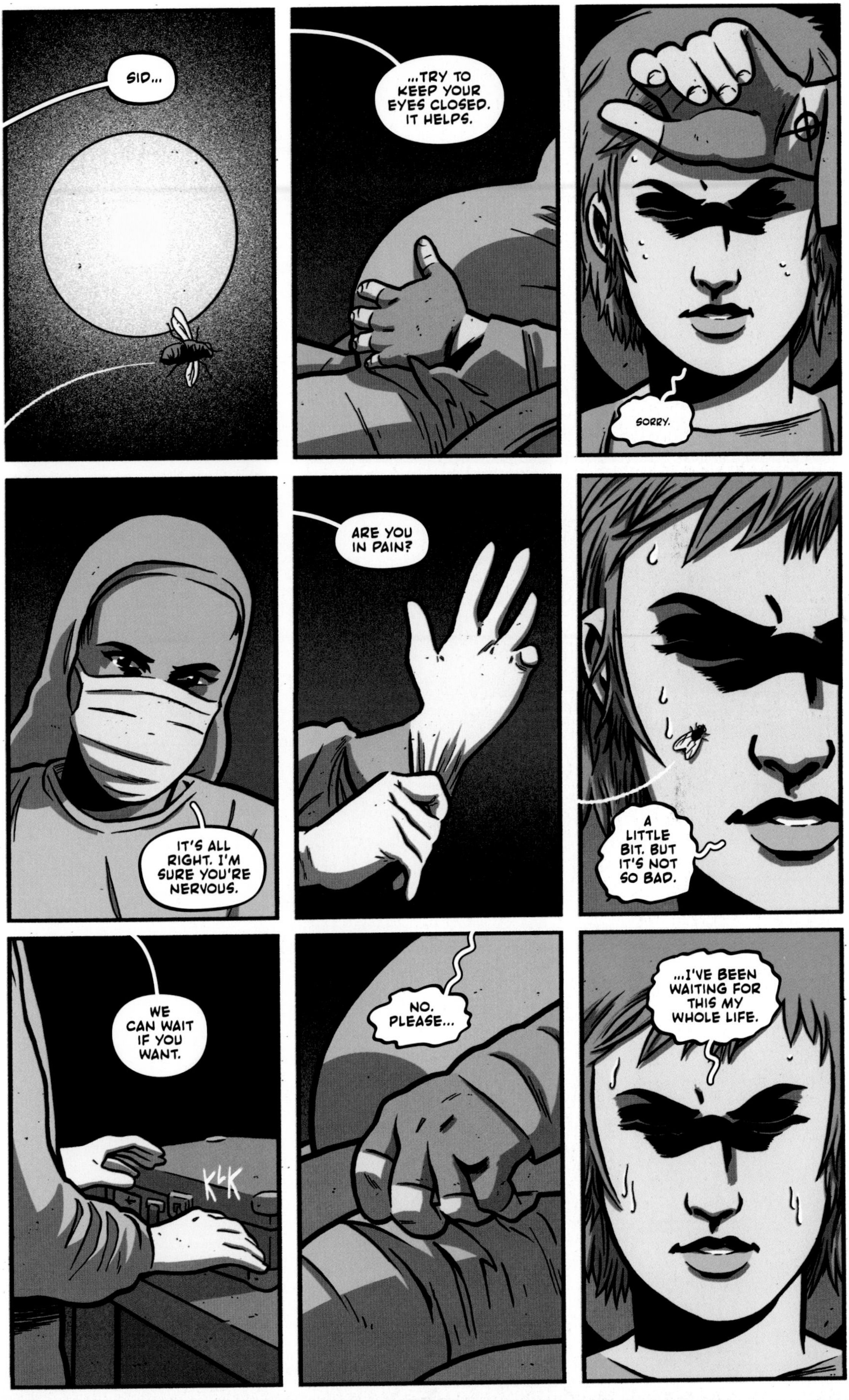
SID...
...TRY TO KEEP YOUR EYES CLOSED. IT HELPS.
SORRY.
IT'S ALL RIGHT. I'M SURE YOU'RE NERVOUS.
ARE YOU IN PAIN?
A LITTLE BIT. BUT IT'S NOT SO BAD.
WE CAN WAIT IF YOU WANT.
KLK
NO. PLEASE...
...I'VE BEEN WAITING FOR THIS MY WHOLE LIFE.

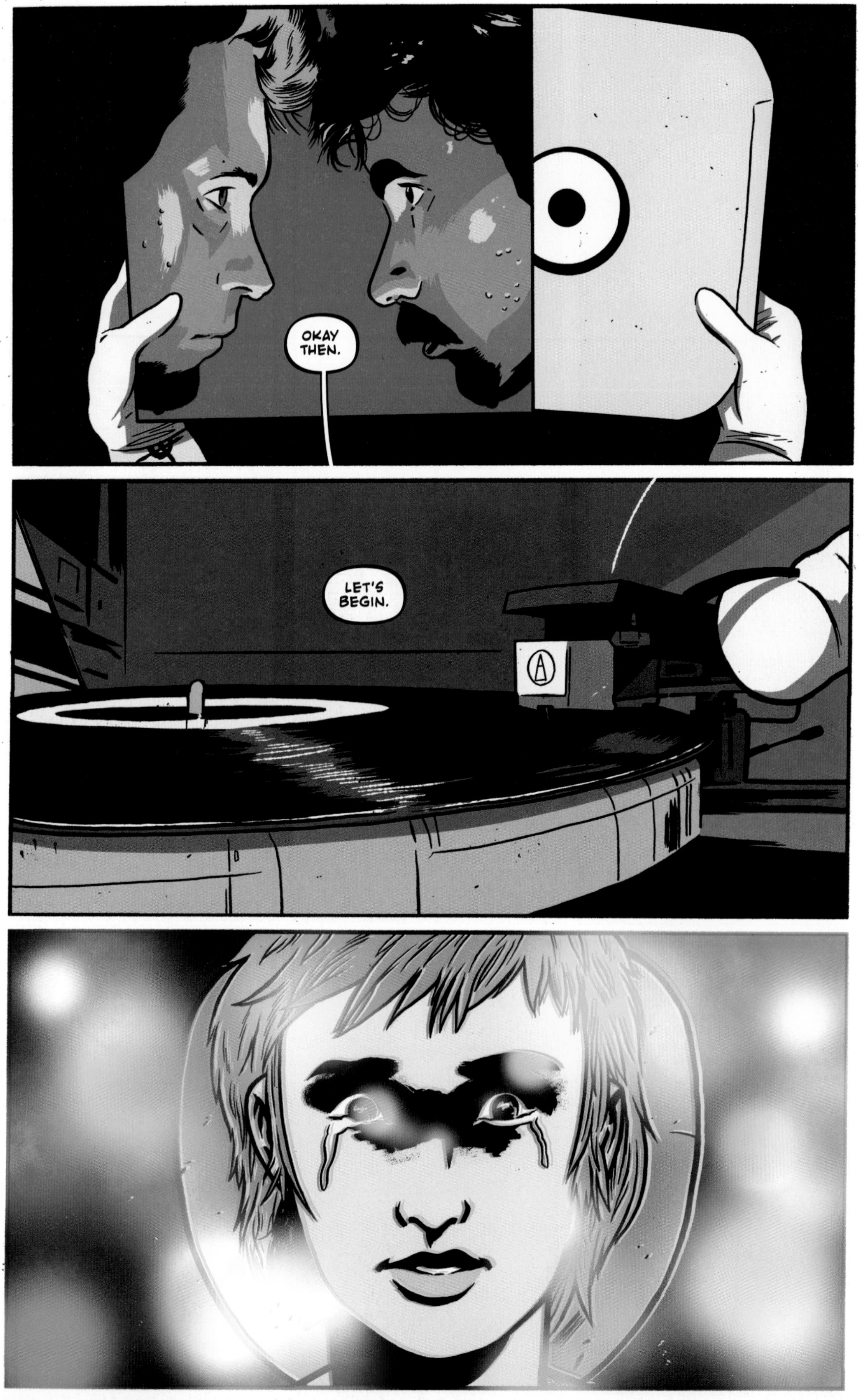

OKAY THEN.
LET'S BEGIN.

TO BE
CONTINUED.

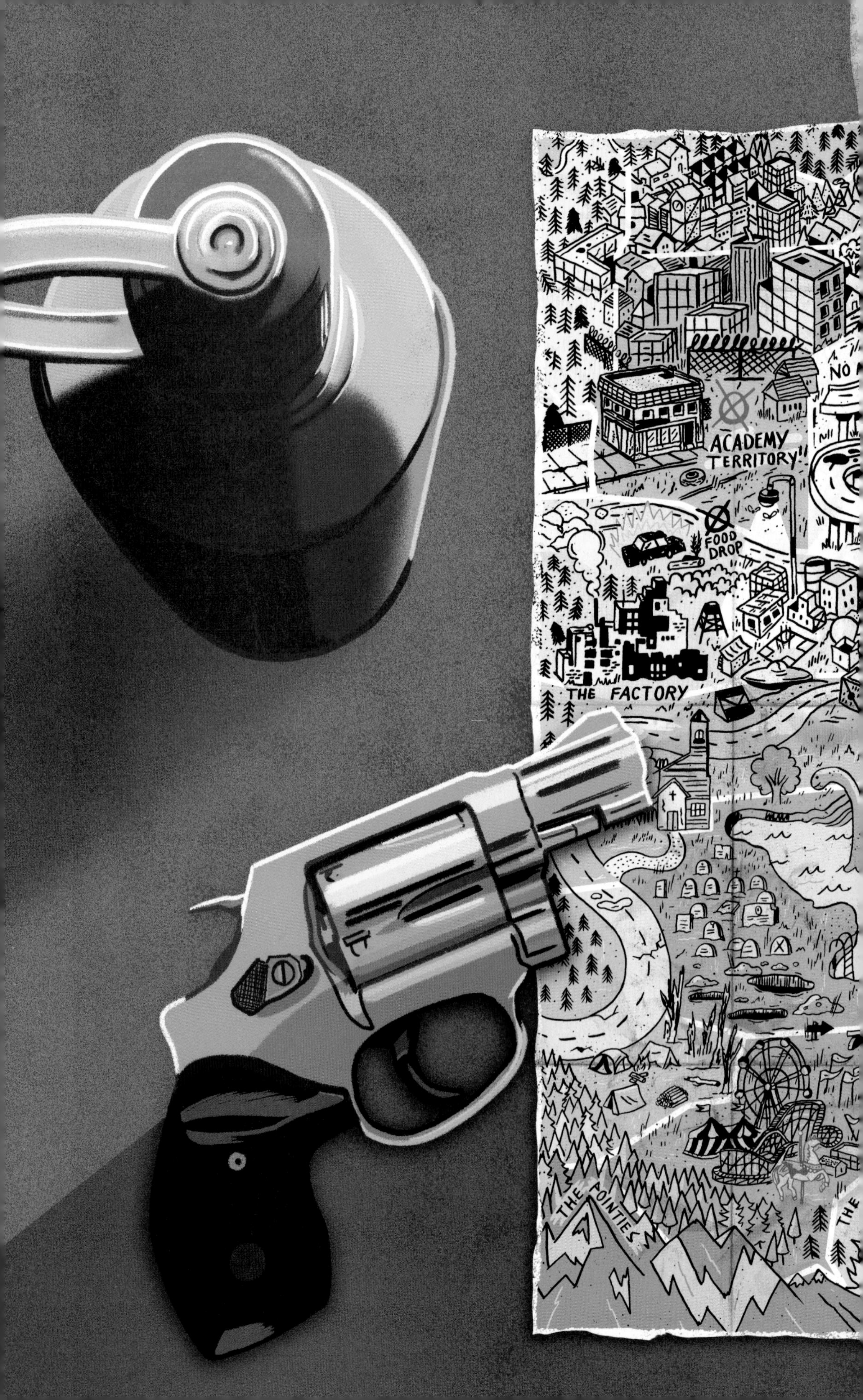
ACADEMY TERRITORY
FOOD DROP
THE FACTORY
THE POINTIES

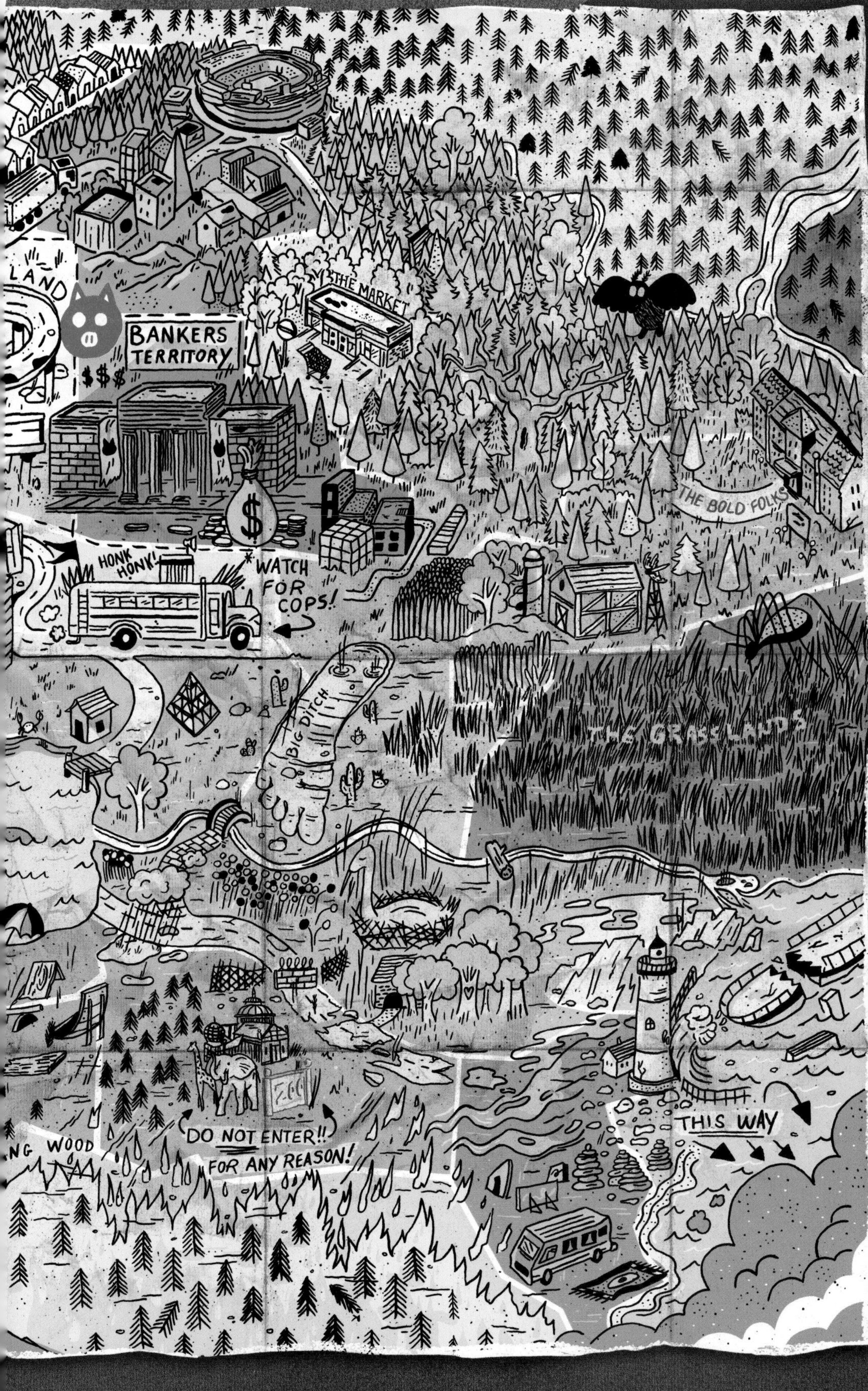
LAND
BANKERS TERRITORY
$$$
THE MARKET
THE BOLD FOLKS
HONK HONK!
WATCH FOR COPS!
BIG DITCH
THE GRASSLANDS
DO NOT ENTER!!
FOR ANY REASON!
NG WOOD
THIS WAY

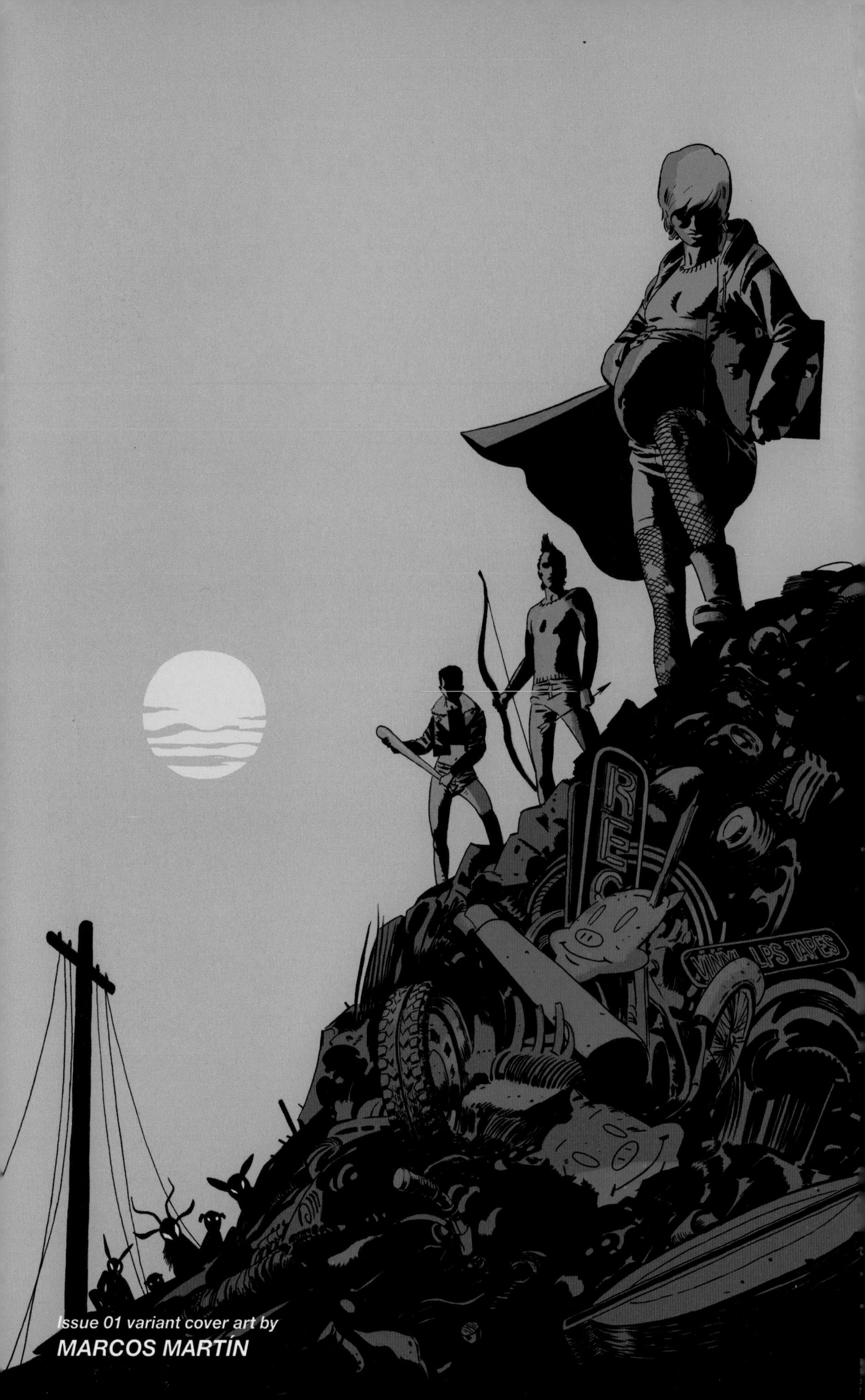
REC
LPS TAPES

*Issue 01 variant cover art by*
***MARCOS MARTÍN***

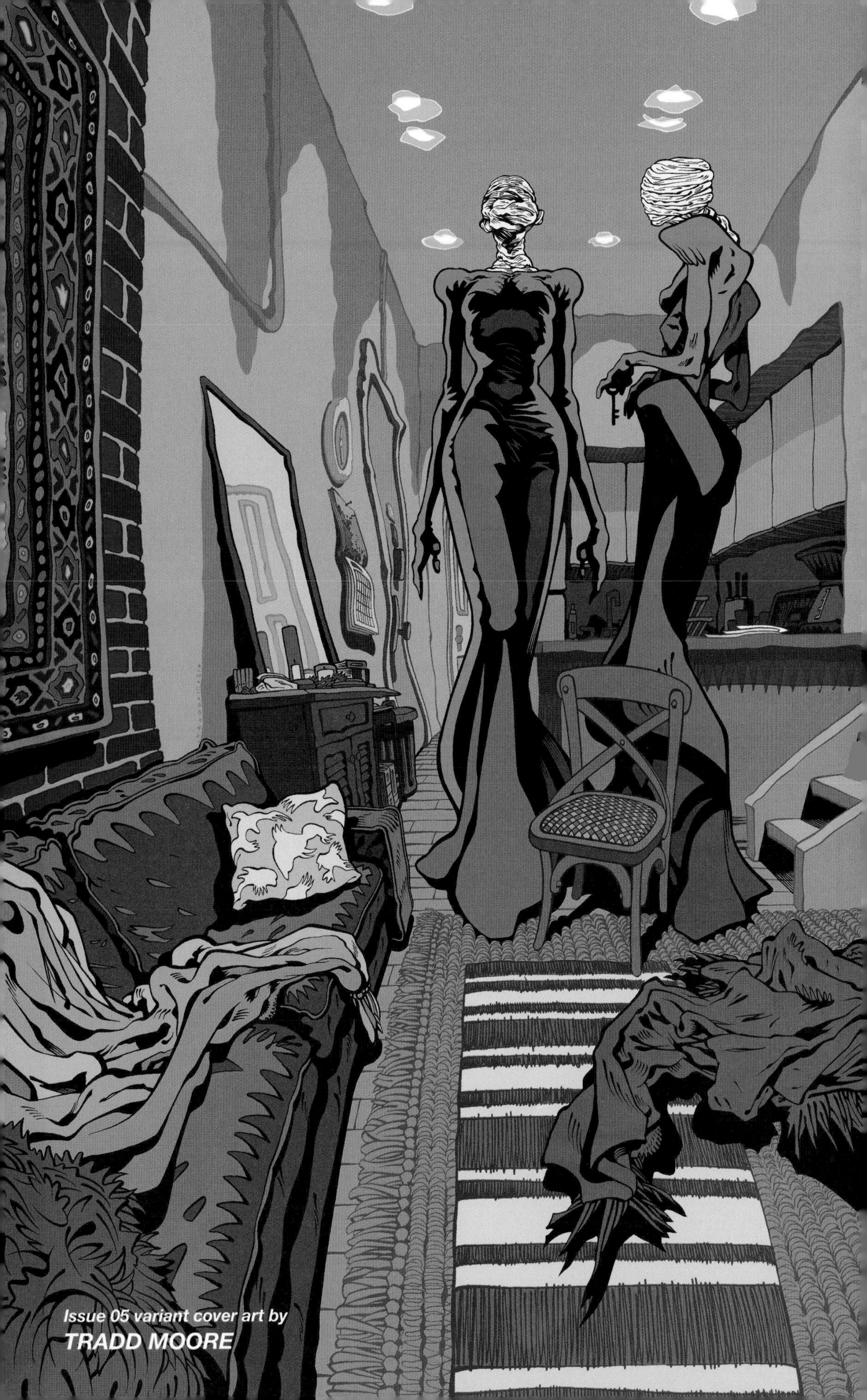

*Issue 05 variant cover art by*
***TRADD MOORE***

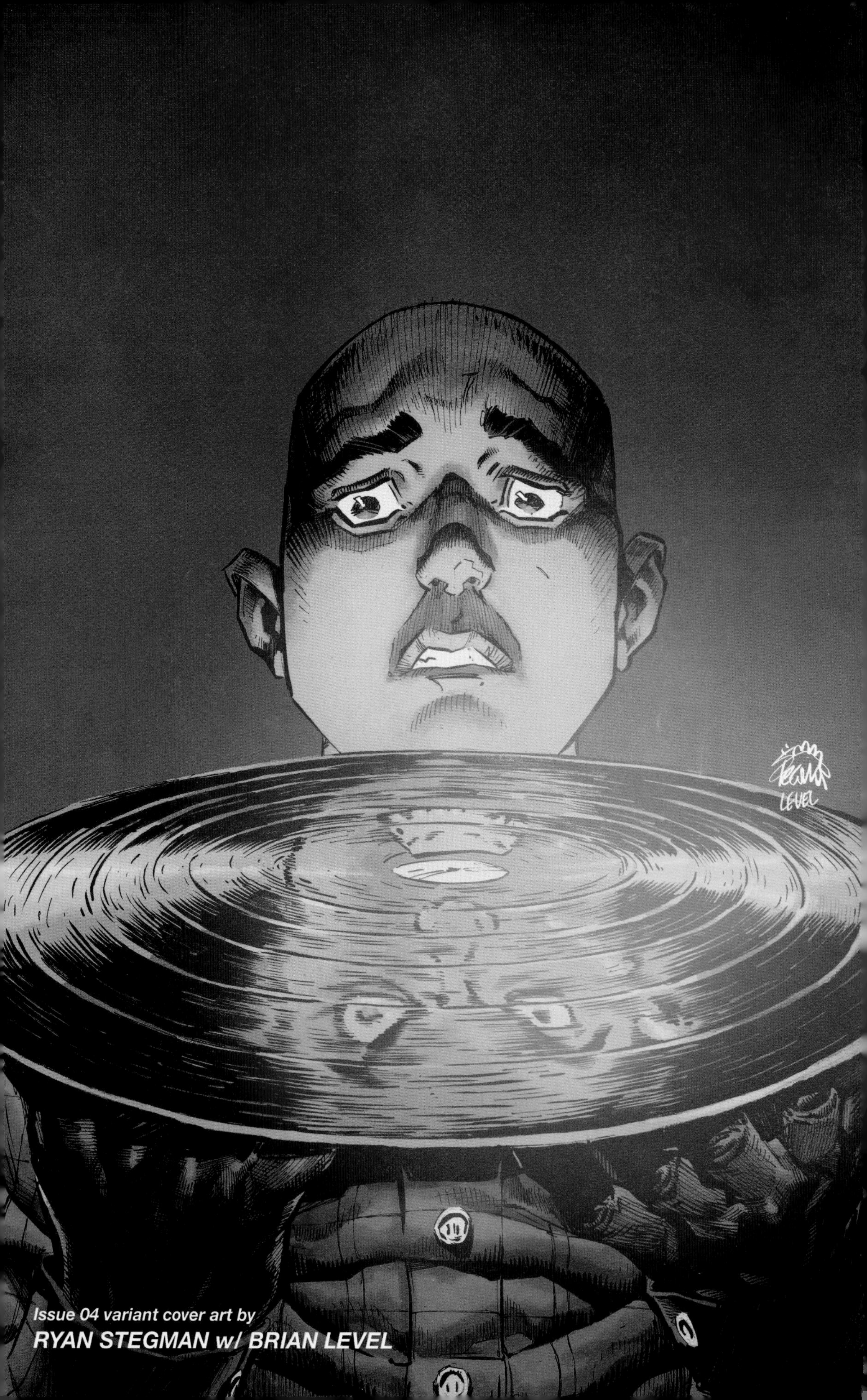
LEVEL

Issue 04 variant cover art by
**RYAN STEGMAN w/ BRIAN LEVEL**

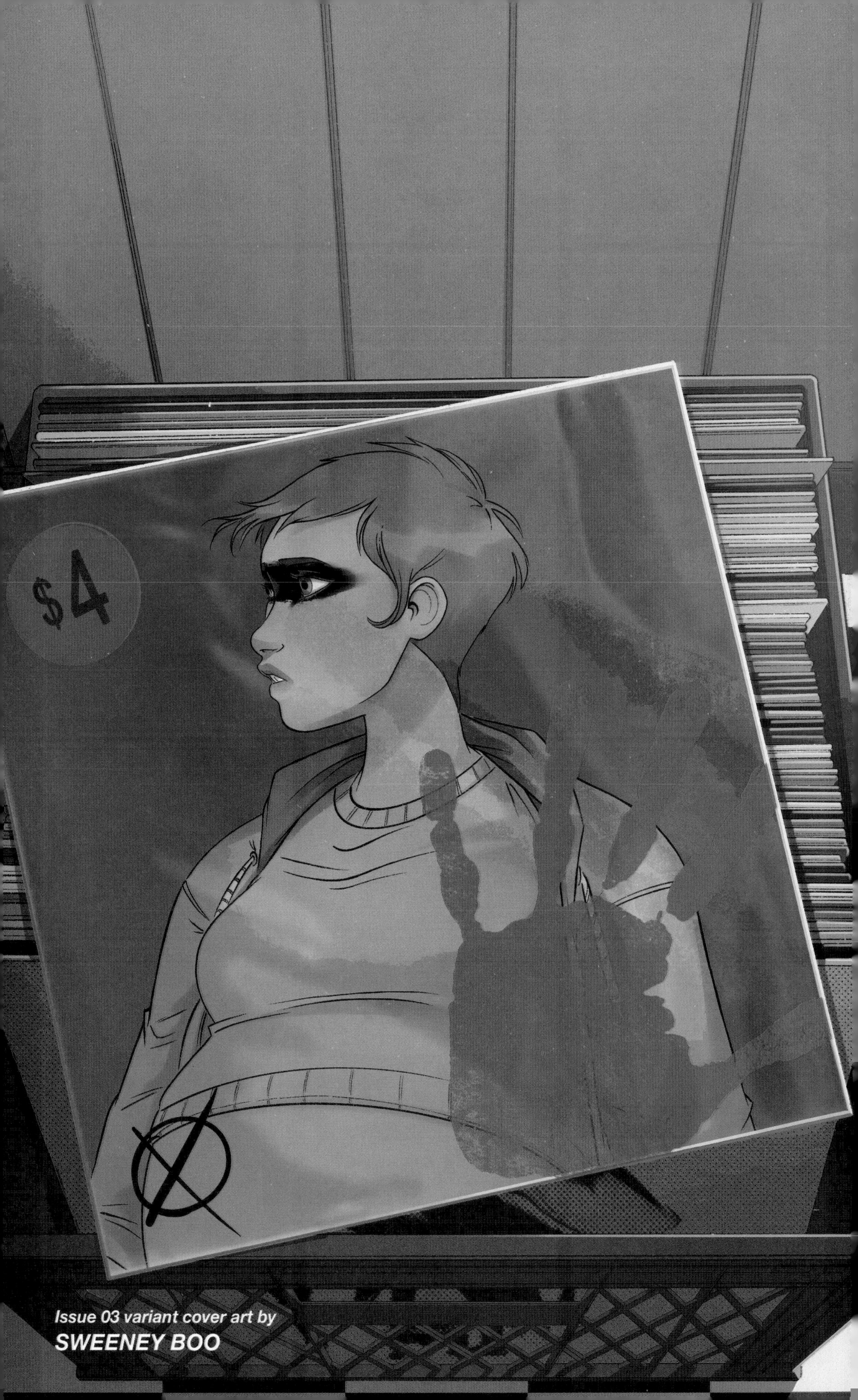
$4

*Issue 03 variant cover art by*
***SWEENEY BOO***

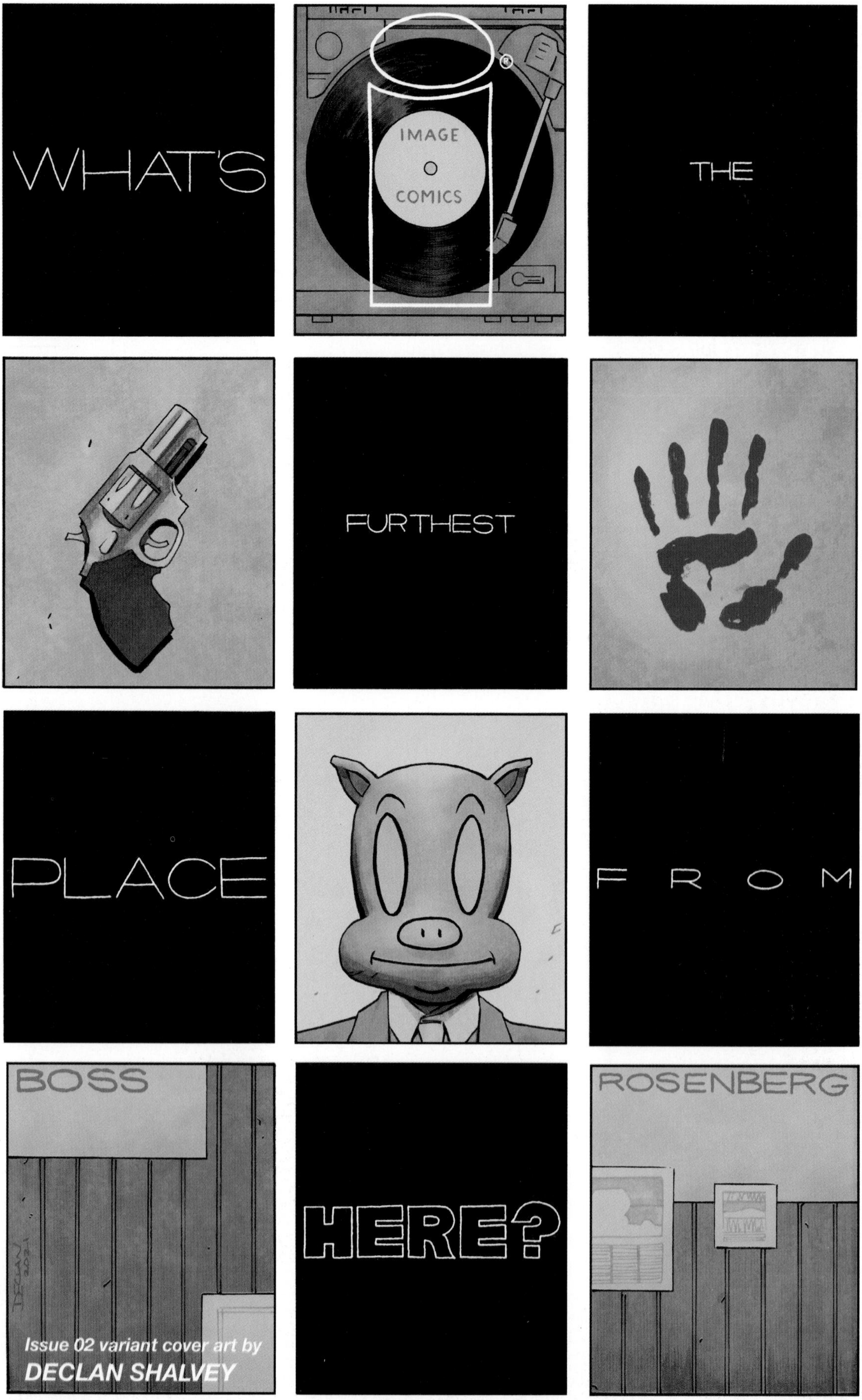
WHAT'S
IMAGE COMICS
THE
FURTHEST
PLACE
FROM
BOSS
HERE?
ROSENBERG
Issue 02 variant cover art by
DECLAN SHALVEY